Sunrise Over the Pumpkin Patch

Sunrise Over the Pumpkin Patch
The Adventures of a Rebellious Girl

Fresh Ink Group
An Imprint of:
The Fresh Ink Group, LLC
1021 Blount Avenue #931
Guntersville, AL 35976
Email: info@FreshInkGroup.com
FreshInkGroup.com

Edition 2.0 2024

Cover art by Anik / FIG
Covers by Stephen Geez / FIG
Book design by Amit Dey / FIG
Associate publisher Beem Weeks / FIG

Cataloging-in-Publication Recommendations:
FIC071000 FICTION / Friendship
FIC008000 FICTION / Sagas
FIC043000 FICTION / Coming of Age

Library of Congress Control Number: 2024915170

ISBN-13: 978-1-964998-05-3 Softcover
ISBN-13: 978-1-964998-06-0 Hardcover
ISBN-13: 978-1-964998-07-7 Ebooks

Sunrise Over the Pumpkin Patch

Karlyle Tomms

DEDICATION

This book is dedicated to Marcia Hayden Young, who taught me to believe in myself, open myself to life's experiences, cherish who I am, and express my creativity. Her unconditional and enduring love and compassion helped convert me from an angry, wounded young man into an emotionally functional adult. She taught me to love myself as I am without believing that I have to live up to anyone's expectations, and she taught me to understand that love still lives beneath the wounded heart. I have no doubt, were she still alive, that she would approve of this book, for she was a conduit of love in expression. Being of the 60s generation, she would have clearly understood and identified with the meaning in these pages. This book is dedicated to those like Marcia who have come to understand that love is the bottom line, for this book is about love.

AUTHOR'S NOTE:

There are words and phrases in this book that would be considered offensive by today's standards. However, the terminology was common during the time frame of the story. These words and phrases are not intended to be offensive toward any person or social group but to portray the time's language accurately. All characters in this book are fictional, and any resemblance to any person or persons other than the author is purely coincidental, as these characters are not drawn from any person known to the author.

Of course, this is a fictional story; the characters are made up in my head. I first encountered Lovella in 2008 when I was joking with a friend about a burned-out hippie woman. That character, Lovella, guided me to completing my first novel, *Confessions from the Pumpkin Patch*, which was published by Tiger Eye Publishing in November 2014. However, Lovella told an entirely different story than I expected when I sat at the keyboard and allowed her to speak through me. That first novel, and every novel since then, was completed the same way by simply allowing the protagonists to tell their own stories. It felt like I was taking dictation of what they had to say rather than making stuff up as I went along, but I know well that it all came out of my mind.

Sunrise over the Pumpkin Patch is a second edition of *Confessions from the Pumpkin Patch* and a revision. I have revised it slightly because I've learned a lot since then. However, the story remains the same. Initially, that novel was endorsed by Marideth Sisco, known for her work on *Winter's Bone* starring Jennifer Lawrence. *Winter's Bone* was based on a novel of the same name by Daniel Woodrell. The film won the Sundance Film Festival Grand Jury Prize and was nominated for four Academy Awards. It was an honor to have Marideth Sisco review my book, especially as it was the first novel I ever completed, and an even greater honor that she had so many positive things to say about it. *Confessions from the Pumpkin Patch* also won a New Apple Awards medal for general fiction in 2016. I hope you enjoy this updated version.

Review of *Confessions from the Pumpkin Patch* by Marideth Sisco:

She is so much in your face that it is at first difficult to scope what this first novel's heroine is up to; she is so brash and self-confident, but no, now she is spiteful, but no, indifferent. Crazed, maybe.

All that, and damaged. Honest. Able. And here to tell you about it. In doing so, the author has handed us a clear and unique view of how one might have experienced directly and viscerally the major issues of the times through her interaction with a small group of individuals with whom she is entangled but from whom she is alienated by her passion and her pain.

Throughout this rollicking romp, she is smart and making do with what she has, which is an overabundance of wit, cunning, guile, and conscience, packed into a dervish of a girl who means to get her way, get outa of town, and figure out what she's doing in this world. What is she good for, and what should she be doing about it? And, by the way, what's all the big to-do about sex, anyway? In some worlds, it's currency; in others, it's a tool. The main thing is to make sure you are the one who says what happens, and when and to whom. Sex is useful in leading the order of play, so long as you make sure you're the one doing the leading and that you're not being led. She's a tough cookie, and she'll need to be as she charges headlong into the changing landscape of the 1960s in small-town middle America.

This chronicle of a young girl's coming of age and into her wisdom is a masterpiece of a character's evolution through experience and insights into an adult, shown through both the people of the time and the circumstances that formed them, led them through war at home and overseas into a maturity they never expected to find. With a skill surpassing what one might expect from a first-book novelist, Tomms guides us through the labyrinthine twists and turns of one person traversing those changing times with a deft appreciation of personalities and a sweet degree of patience for those whom life is tossing about like a large unwieldy dryer load. Never feeling staged, it's a tale that rings true to those of us old enough to have been witness to that ever-changing landscape in those pivotal times. For those younger ones who wonder about the events and circumstances that shaped their parent's and grandparents' worldview, this is an open window. And for the rest of us, it's a darned good read and a remarkable telling.

Marideth Sisco is an author, songwriter, and composer whose credits include the music and an appearance in Sundance winner and 4-time Oscar nominee "*Winter's Bone;*" six years of essays on regional public radio in her broadcast series "These Ozarks Hills;" three recorded albums with her band, Blackberry Winter, and numerous other film and TV credits. More information is available at her website, www.maridethsisco.com/

TABLE OF CONTENTS

LOVELLA'S NOTE:

I've heard it said that any life worth living is worth living well. Perhaps they should have said, "Any life is worth living." At least, I believe that. If you are here, it is because you are meant to be here. Maybe we are all here to live our own story, only that. Maybe the only thing we need to do is watch our story unfold as though we are watching a movie that we have never seen before. It's our movie, and we have the starring role, but we have no idea how it will turn out. It is all total improvisation. I don't know that my story is special in any way, no more special than anyone else's. Despite my plans and intentions to play it differently, it seems to have manifested the way it did.

There is a term in psychology called "scripting." It has to do with how various influences during our upbringing script us into a particular story and path that we subconsciously follow. It could be that, in a way, we are all scripted to become what we become, that our thread in the fabric of humanity is already colored before it is woven. We may have little or no choice over the patterns in our fabric, but we can choose how we weave our thread into the patterns of life. We all have choices, but no matter our decisions, no one controls their destiny. Choice combines with destiny to create each unique story.

I'm fascinated by the idea that billions of people are on the planet, and each of us has our unique story. Some of us write our stories; however, most only live them. We all talk about the little stories that make up the novel of our lives, whether in a cocktail party conversation or a talk given at a lady's luncheon. Our stories intertwine and weave the fabric of humanity. All our stories create a pattern of existence that includes all the stories we each experience and all the stories of those who have gone before us. This is the one tiny thread I have woven into the fabric of humanity. For what it is worth, this is my story.

CHAPTER 1

The Difference Between Mother and Daughter

My name is Lovella Titwallow. Don't laugh. I married into the name. I have to say that it was a significant improvement over my maiden name, Fuchs. Yes, I know how it looks. That's not how it is pronounced. The "u" is long. Fuchs as in "F-you-chs." I learned, over time, to put a line over the "u" when I signed my name, an attempt to tip the reader that the pronunciation is not to be confused with that other four-letter word, which is so popular in English language. It did no good. People still pronounced it the way that it looks. Perhaps it was fated because I enjoyed the other four-letter word so much.

I was born in 1948 and am from Climax, Pennsylvania, a small town on the state's southern end. Now, you are thinking, "*Climax?* What a coincidence!" The town itself, if it can be called that, is merely a bump in the road just a couple of miles from New Bethlehem, which is nothing but a tiny dot on the map.

It's all very funny, isn't it? Life plays little tricks on us, and we have little scripts we seem doomed to play before we realize what is going on. Shakespeare said, "All the world is a stage, and the people merely players." He knew a little something, didn't he? He could not have known what a drama my small-town life would become or that I would develop into my character as a mature woman without even realizing what I was doing.

In elementary school, I dreaded the first day of class when a new teacher or a substitute teacher, who had perhaps never seen my name or failed to be warned beforehand, would call first roll. It would go smoothly until they stumbled into the space between the E and the G. Even then, Foster, Forrest, or Freed fell off the tongue like apples off a tree. Then my name would follow, and there was the inevitable silence as a teacher pondered exactly how to pronounce it. There was the "Fa-chez" pronunciation, the

"Feu-keese," the determination to say anything but "Fucks" even though that pronunciation was obviously the first to pop into the unsuspecting educator's brain. If I possibly could, I would try to get to the teacher before class and give the correct pronunciation of my name. This was my effort to redeem myself after the first-grade teacher mispronounced the name and said it, for some reason, exactly the way it looked. No sooner had the f-word fallen off her lips when Johnny Sigmund shouted, "My Daddy told me that's a dirty word!" The teacher's purple face and rapid stuttering attempt to cover what she had just said led me to realize something was drastically amiss about my name.

From that point on, all was lost. Of course, everyone in class wanted to know why it was a dirty word. Some went home, used the teacher's incorrect pronunciation, and asked parents, "Why is it a dirty word?" They didn't get much, but those who asked older siblings returned to school edified and cruel. After that, any time the name was mispronounced, and often when it wasn't, there followed a room full of cackling children, all gleeful at my embarrassment. The giggles began even when I dared to raise my hand to get the teacher's attention before the tragic mistake was committed. I, therefore, learned to sit in silent indignation and embarrassment.

Outside of class, the taunting began. When I reached puberty, the boys would comment as I walked by, "Hey, I hear Lovella Fuchs." They pronounced the name correctly in their taunt, but the meaning was obvious. Another boy might say, "Yeah, that's right, I fuched her last night."

I would either keep walking silently, attempt to ignore it, or turn to them and shout, "Fuchs you!" Eventually, I decided to embrace my name and all the implications therein. I would honor the word, appreciate it, live up to it, and use it as often as necessary. Who cared whether there was an "h" or a "k" in the name? I would treat it as though there had always been a "k." By the time I was in high school, boys would say, "Hey, I hear Lovella Fuchs." I would turn, smile, and say, "Fucks—Damn right, and good at it!"

My father, John Fuchs, worked in a peanut butter factory and was an alcoholic. He spent his days in the factory, and the family never lacked peanut butter. He held his drinking for the weekends, at least early on. He was a short man, 5' 7", with a round little belly protruding like a basketball. His belly did not flop over his belt, which was good. It was good because he liked to wear the most gaudy and outlandish belt buckles. His hair was mousy and blond, making a horseshoe around his bald head. Thankfully, he opted out of a comb-over. Still, one tiny tuft of hair grew in the middle above his forehead, and he always let it grow too long. Often, I begged him to cut it. Once I caught him passed out drunk, so I shaved it off. The next morning, he cried when he looked into the mirror. I never considered what insecurities that little tuft of hair might have been covering. I felt so guilty that I never touched it or mentioned it to him again, but I was forever at a loss to understand why that little patch meant so much to him.

My Mother was a church lady of sorts. She was more a cross between a church lady, a fashion model want-to-be, and Satan incarnate. Her name was Drucella. The "ella" had been a part of the female names on her side of the family for who knows how many generations. It was a tradition that all female children should have a first name ending in "ella." Who knows why or what nutty ancestor back in Kentucky concocted such an idea? None of the women in the family had ever protested it, so it continued. Hence, my name became Lovella. My grandmother was Claudella. My aunts were Johnella and Cloella, and so on and so on. The "ella" was like some sacred script that must be added to the name of any newborn female if she were to be considered a genuine part of family history. Perhaps it was a kind of finger in the face of patriarchy that determined all children should take their father's last names.

My mother was in church every Sunday, and every other time, the door was open for any church-sponsored activity. I don't think she ever missed a Bible study or a potluck. She wore her hair, nearly jet black when she was young, high above her head. I would say in a beehive style; however, it was more like a hornet's nest. Her temper, like hornets, was swarming with venomous stings. Sometimes, she would sting, and you never knew what hit you until it started to hurt. When she was outraged, the swarm would overwhelm you into either fleeing or submitting. Sometimes, all you could do was duck and cover. Over time, I learned to swat.

As mother began to age and her health diminished into disability, her hair came down in a salt and pepper, mostly salt, rat's nest. A bit before that, she had given up the beehive, yet she kept it stacked above her cranium throughout my childhood. It seemed like a warning that, at any moment, the swarm might be released. However, I have to say that when she finally got rid of that stupid stack above her head, I was shocked and appealed.

I was an adult and married before I saw Mother with her hair down like an average woman. After losing her mind and being placed into a nursing home, we cut it short for easy washing. Yet, she was the utmost example of prim and proper when she was younger. She was slim, two inches taller than Daddy, skinny, and meticulous about her food. Her cheekbones were high enough to provide support for her cat-eye plastic-rimmed glasses. Never a hair was out of place, and she wore a dress and high heels for everything, even when cooking or cleaning the house, and she always smelled like vanilla or cinnamon. She presented an example of the 1950s male fantasy of female perfection, which dominated TV commercials at the time. When *The Stepford Wives* movie came out in 1975, I realized her appearance was the only thing she fit.

I was an only child, pity's sake. I longed to have a brother or sister who might share the torment with me, but it was never to be. I developed a fantasy that, after the consummation that produced me, my mother never allowed coitus again. I could imagine her saying, "Well, that was disgusting. I'll certainly never do that again."

I was both adored and tortured as a child. On the one hand, my father was anything but perfect, and on the other hand, my mother demanded absolute perfection. Daddy's love was always diluted by alcohol, and perfection was the price I paid for Mother's love. Everything was about her and her image, including Daddy and me. I suppose one of the reasons I speak the way I do is because Mother was constantly picking at me, training my words, my diction, and my accent so that I could be her perfect little offspring. The shame of her family's impoverished Kentucky drawl was apparently to be remedied by perfect diction, and by the way, she would never allow me to call her Mom or Mommy. I was required to call her Mother and nothing else.

"Ar-tic-u-late, Lovella!" Her words will forever ring in my ears. It is a wonder I didn't develop a nervous tic from all the harassment. Instead, I developed an exact manner of speaking from a young age. It was the one gift, I suppose, that I could give her. In time, it may have been her gift to me, for rather than having a Kentucky drawl like my grandmother and grandfather Donner, I could communicate at practically any social level and intellectualize with the best of them. Mother, no doubt, had trained herself out of her hillbilly roots.

In the evenings, after a perfect dinner on Mother's perfect dinnerware and after the dishes were washed and put away, we would sit in the living room and watch TV shows like Red Skelton through the static of a black and white TV. Of course, we had one, even though many at the time did not. Mother would see to it that we had the best and the latest regardless of whether we could afford it. She always seemed to find the money for whatever she wanted. As soon as color TV came out, she was on that like a chicken on corn mash. I could have cared less. I would sit in my corner chair reading and occasionally looking up when Mother would cackle with laughter at some joke that, even as a child, I found inane. Daddy would usually fall asleep on one end of the sofa as Mother sat perfectly upright on the other, sipping her iced tea.

In his sleep, Daddy would often snore and fart. This gathered a quick dart of the eyes from Mother and a momentary microsecond of disgust. Then her eyes returned to the television, and she watched every moment of everything that came across the screen. Even if it were a complete failure of broadcast and nothing but static and hiss, she would watch intently, expecting the picture to return at any moment.

At precisely 9:00 p.m., Mother would turn off the television and jab Daddy in the ribs with a long, scarlet-painted fingernail. "John! Get up! It's time for bed!"

He would moan, growl, open his eyes, breathe like a horror film monster, and stretch before staggering off to bed. I often wondered if he had little scars on his rib cage from being poked with that fingernail.

As for myself, Mother would merely give me a stern look, and I would go to bed. However, I often read until late at night, with a flashlight under the covers so Mother wouldn't catch me. Then, I would struggle to wake up the next morning. Nonetheless, I always got up at the first call because I did not want little fingernail scars in my rib cage or the wrath of the hornets.

Breakfast was always ready before Mother called me to get up. The way she cooked, I thought it must be torture for her to stay so skinny because the breakfast table would consist of pork chops, bacon, or sausage, with hash browns, eggs, biscuits, buns, pancakes, or French toast if not almost all the above, and this was every morning. Mother sat and nibbled bits of everything but never what appeared to be a whole serving of anything. At the same time, she consistently admonished Daddy and me to eat.

By age ten, I was allowed coffee, which I looked forward to every morning. What a Godsend! It was liquid alert! I pretended to be more awake than I was as I watched the steaming black miracle fall into my cup. If I had my way, breakfast would have consisted of coffee and a few bites of egg. However, Mother rationed the coffee like a prison camp commodity and insisted I clean my plate. By the time I was a teenager, I was not overweight, but I was a tall, full-figured girl in the days of bone-skinny models like Twiggy.

Mother always drove me to school and Daddy to work. She stated that she had to have our one car during the day because she had meetings to attend and things to do. It was more likely that she had to have control. She got us up early enough that breakfast would be put away and dishes cleaned before we left the house. I never understood why this could not wait until she returned home after dropping us off, but it was part of her perfectionism and routine. She never left the house without everything being perfectly cleaned and in place. Perhaps she thought there could be an inspection by the cleanliness police before she returned.

Most days, I think the car sat in the driveway after she delivered us, but she often went to the church during the week to sit on some lady's committee. How everything looked was very important to Mother, and church was part of her plan to appear in the best possible light. She was a Methodist, a church that I imagined she must have chosen like the story of "Goldilocks and the Three Churches" because it was *just right*: not too ritualized like the Catholics and not too fundamentalist like the Baptists. Unfortunately, she demanded that Daddy and I attend, as well.

On Wednesdays, the battles began over Mother's Friday evening plans. She would inevitably invite some church family, whom she considered among the big wigs, for Friday dinner. Daddy always told her he had arranged a ride home with a friend after work on Friday. Of course, this meant he was going directly to a bar with one or more of his drinking buddies and might be dropped off at home late into the morning on Saturday if he came home over the weekend. Sometimes, we didn't see him until Sunday, and then he would try to sober up enough to return to work on Monday. He would make up some story about having to help someone fix their vehicle or something, but Mother and I both knew what he intended to be doing. Mother would make plans for every Friday night and insist that Daddy had to be there. She had multiple reasons for doing this, but not the least among them was to try to keep Daddy sober. Her announcement about her Friday plans became among the strangest of arguments when she proclaimed what had become her routine ritual at breakfast every Wednesday morning.

"Johnnnnnnnn," she would say, dragging the name out as though it was the last note of a ballad, "I'm having the Millers over for dinner—on Friday. I know that you will want to spend time with Mr. Miller as he owns a burgeoning company, and I'm sure he will be able to help you develop your career." In truth, Daddy had no career, nor was he prepared for one. At best, he had a high school education and had barely earned that.

"Well ... Sissy," Daddy would respond. "You see ... Honey ... I have plans for Friday ... and I just can't be here."

Daddy's nickname for Mother was Sissy. I'm not sure why. Daddy had odd nicknames for almost everyone, including me, and called me Pumpkin Patch. The amazing thing is that Mother tolerated being called Sissy. It would not have surprised me if she had insisted that he call her Mrs. Fuchs.

"Oh, really, dear?" she asked, her lips teetering on being pursed. "What plans would those be?"

"Well, you see, Sissy ... there is this fellow from work who knows this fellow ... who is one of the administrators over at the factory ... and he is sure that this fellow he knows can get me a better-paying position ... ah ... maybe even foreman."

"Ooohhhhh?" Her response extended in a long and slow singsong note. Of course, she knew he was lying. "What would this fellow's name be?"

"Well … uh."

Daddy would stumble, searching his mind for the right words, for he was never quite clever enough to rehearse before Wednesday morning and, therefore, not very good at lying.

"I don't know the name of the other fellow that this fellow at work knows, but the fellow at work … his name is Jim."

"So, you don't know the naaaaaames of the administrators where you work. Hmmmmmmm?"

The angrier Mother became, the more it sounded like she was singing rather than talking, or perhaps it was more like the buzz of hornets.

"This fellow … Jim," she would serenade, "If this person he knows can provide high-powered positions … why isn't he procuring the job for himself?"

"Well, you see," Daddy continued, "there's two jobs open, and Jim likes me and likes to work with me, and he wants both of us to talk to this fellow so we can both move up in management and make more money."

The more intimidated Daddy became, the more his voice would wheeze, and he almost trembled like a mouse in the sight of a stalking cat.

"Wellllll," Mother would sing. "I don't think I can cancel the dinner with the Millers for it has been planned for some time now … and it seems to me that Mr. Miller, as an entre-pre-neurrrrrr, would be in a much better position to further your ca-reerrrrrr."

"But Sissy, now," Daddy would plead, "this is planned too, and Jim is expecting me to be there."

When Mother's song of anger reached a crescendo, the insults began, and rather than singing, the words would pop off her lips like bullets.

"I-would-think … John-Fuchs … if-you-were-the-kind-of-man-who-wanted-to-present-a-good-example-for-his … im-pression-able … daughter … you-would-want-to-have-dinner-with-good-church-going-people … instead-of … rallying-about-the-whims-of-a-factory-worker-who … if-he-could-advance-anyone's-career … including-his-own … ob-vious-ly … would-have-done-so!"

This continued between them until one of them gave in, or there was a stalemate. If one of them gave in, which was rare for either, there would be weeks of subtle resentment to follow that would be expressed in trite passive-aggressive insults on Mother's part and something like farting at the dinner table, with a big meaty grin on Daddy's part. More often than not, there was a stalemate. I hated it either way, but when that happened, the argument continued every moment they were awake together until Friday evening. I watched silently, more like I was watching a live television show than my parents' life.

When there was a stalemate, it went on to the last minute on Friday. First, Mother would pick me up from school. Then, she would drive immediately to the peanut butter factory to stalk and spy on Daddy. My torture was an hour or more sitting in the car with Mother as she repeatedly expressed her displeasure about Daddy. While we waited for him to emerge from the building, Mother pontified how much he had wronged her and all she had done for him. She never could seem to accept that Daddy's drinking was more important to him than any career opportunity, especially more important than listening to the mundane babbling at Mother's Friday night dinners.

"I-don't-know-why-your-father-insists-upon-doing-this ... every-weekend ... week-in-and-week-out."

By this time, her voice's singsong quality had been replaced with a sharp piano tone, like a child pecking out one dissonant note at a time and never being able to create a melody.

"I-do-every-thing-I-can ... to-give-you-and-your-father-a-lovely-home. I-keep-it-spotless. I-make-sure-that-there-is-a-lovely-meal-on-the-table ... on-time ... every-time. The-laundry-is-done. The-cupboards-are-kept-well-stocked. I-have-no-idea-why-he-wants-to-do-this-to-me. Does-he-not-know-that-everything-I-do, I-do-for-my-family ... and—God—of course. I-must-put-God-first ... but ... I-*never*-let-my-church-activities-interfere-with-what-I-do-for-my-family ... and-your-father-doesn't-seem-to-care ... at-all. I-make-a-lovely-nest-for-him ... so-you-would-think-that-he-would-want-to-come-home-to-his-family-every-day ... not-just-weekdays."

One time, Mother was stalking when the factory let out. Daddy came out of the building, unsuspecting, chatting with his drinking buddies. Like a spider in her web, Mother was lying in wait and trotted to him in her perfect high heels as fast as possible. "John! John!" she exclaimed. "We have to go! There's been an emergency at the house! Lovella has been hurt!"

She had insisted that I hunker down in the car seat so Daddy could not see me. The window was down so I could hear their conversation, and I tried to peek up over the door frame without getting caught. I thought it would be a joke, but Mother had a minimal sense of humor.

"What?" Daddy responded, his face filled with shock. No matter what else, it was a fact that Daddy loved me. "What is it? What's the matter?"

"We have to go *now*, John!" Mother went on. "We have to take her to the emergency room!"

"Well, why haven't you already taken her to the emergency room?" he asked, suspicion peaked.

Mother went on with her lie. "She was crying for her daddy, John! She wouldn't go—without you!"

The first time, it worked. By the time Daddy realized I was in the back seat and just fine, his friends had gone on, and Mother was in the car to drive us home while ignoring his protests. However, that would be the last time it worked. Each time Mother tried a ruse, she had to make it more complicated and better thought out than before, but after that, nothing worked. Daddy began sneaking out of the factory a different way. He didn't change his behavior; she didn't change hers, and he delighted in telling her that his co-workers thought he was married to "a real nut case."

This went on for far too long. Mother stalked Daddy at the factory, and I sat silently in the car as Mother complained about Daddy and rehearsed her deception.

As though she didn't know what Daddy did on Friday nights, she complained with her piano-pecking tone, "Your-father-knows-I-love-him. He-has-always-known-that-I-love-him. I-only-want-him-to-be-the-man-he-was-meant-to-be. I-only-want-him-to-succeed-in-life … and-where-is-he-every-Friday-night? After-all-these-years-working-at-a-factory, he-has-never-even-gotten-a-slight-promotion. He-should-have … at-least … gotten-some-kind-of-promotion-by-now. I-don't-know-what-he-is-thinking … going-off … every-Friday-night-when-he-could-be-home-with-his-family-and-with-good-friends … good-people-who-could-help-him-get-some-where-in-life."

I learned to read a book and try to ignore her. She knew exactly what he was thinking and doing, and so did I. She pretended that I didn't know and would make all manner of excuses for him while also criticizing him and trying to force him to make a different choice. One day, when I was about twelve, after a pause in her ranting, I said, "Mother, does it ever occur to you that Daddy likes to get drunk and that he is going to do it regardless of what you or anyone else thinks or does?"

"Lovella Chevon Fuchs!" she exclaimed (yes, my middle name is Chevon). "Whatever would possess you to say such a thing?"

My mother was so overly dramatic. I suppose I got that from her, although my drama is a little different and, I would like to think, a little more sophisticated. But I digress.

"Mother," I said, "he's drunk every weekend. You know it. I know it. Why pretend that we don't know it? Maybe he just likes to get drunk." By the time I had reached that age, I had accepted Daddy's drinking, which had troubled me when I was a little younger. I knew there was nothing I could do about it. Mother, however, could never seem to accept it and kept trying to control him, in one way or another, until the day he died.

For a moment, she was stunned and sat silently, with her breath held until she released it like the air being let out of a tire. After another long moment, she said, "Perhaps you are right, dear."

Nothing else was said. I was stunned that she would ever admit that anyone else could be right, much less let go of her Friday night pursuit of Daddy. She sat there, silent and spent, hand to her forehead, as though exhausted from all those years of trying. For a moment, it seemed as though she would cry, but she didn't. I never saw Mother crying anything but fake, manipulative tears until well into my adult years when she was in a nursing home, mindless and vulnerable. Until then, her stoic facade stood in almost every situation.

After a moment, she started the car, and we drove home. I don't know what kind of reaction Daddy had when he came out of the factory to find that she was not there. Perhaps it had been one of those nights he snuck out a different way and didn't notice, much less care that she wasn't sitting there. Regardless, he didn't come home that night.

Mother and I arrived at an empty house. She had long since stopped inviting anyone for Friday dinner. There was no use. She found that if she could get him home, Daddy would inevitably get drunk anyway and simply embarrass her in front of her church friends. That night, we walked silently into the house. I sat in my chair and continued with my book. Mother sat in her place on the end of the sofa. After a while, she turned to me and said, "Dear, what would you like to have for dinner?"

I looked up from my book, stunned and speechless. For the first time ever, my mother asked me what I wanted.

"Surprise me," I said, sticking my nose back into the book.

CHAPTER 2

Friends and Poison

I met my best friend in the second grade. Her name was Gretta Tannenbaum. At the time, she had stringy brown hair that her mother always braided into neat little pigtails that stood far too high above her ears. She had no front teeth, a pug nose, and black-rimmed glasses with lenses thick enough to be used as submarine windows. Later in life, she got contact lenses, which enhanced her beauty. She was an ugly duckling who became a swan. We met because the bitch stole my swing!

It was recess, and I got a nice swing in the middle of the giant steel swing set on a gravel bed just outside the second-grade classroom. I was swinging along when I noticed what I thought was a quarter lying on the gravel. I stopped the swing and went to investigate. It turned out to be only a bottle cap, and when I turned to reclaim my swing, there was Gretta with her skinny little ass in the very swing that I had claimed. I immediately ran to her, grabbed a pigtail in each hand, and yanked her off the swing. Then it was on. I topped her and slapped her with both hands, screaming, "You stole my swing!" She retaliated by grabbing my hair with her free hand and pulling me to one side. The next thing I knew, she was on top of me, pounding me back.

In those days, my hair was long and black. Mother had insisted that I let it grow and called it my "glory." She would never put it up like hers because she clearly distinguished between adult and children's hairstyles. It was more of a liability than any glory on that particular day. Gretta was able to use it to yank me over, and the next thing I knew, she was on top of me with slobber drooling, unimpeded, through the gap where her baby teeth had once been. Thankfully, the teachers were soon there to pull her off me.

Soon, we were sitting in the principal's office, chairs side by side, facing his desk. He was a bloated man with jowls on either side of his face outlining his thin lips. I sat there imagining him with the nose of a pig, but his nose was more like a small, round protrusion in the middle of his face. His voice occasionally squeaked between a light wheezing and a whisper as he chastised us for our sins. His name was Mr. Buckner. I suppose he was a kind man and always seemed well-intentioned, but at that moment, I was pissed off at even having to be there.

"Now, girls," he proclaimed, "we don't fight in school. It isn't nice. It isn't lady-like, and I am sure your mothers taught you how to be young ladies."

"She stole my swing!" I shouted, ignoring everything Mother had, indeed, taught me about being a proper young lady.

"Did not!" Gretta exclaimed.

"Now, girls," Mr. Buckner continued. "We don't shout either. It isn't nice, and I know you both want to be nice girls, don't you?"

"Well, she did steal my swing," I pleaded again, only slightly more complacent.

"I thought she was done with it," said Gretta.

"Now, girls," responded Mr. Buckner, "we must learn to share. We must take turns with the swings. There aren't enough swings for every child to have one all the time. We must share. Don't you think it is nice to share?"

Gretta and I looked at each other, more confused at his approach than anything else. It would have been quick and straightforward if my mother had handled this. She would have pinched my ear and firmly exclaimed through clenched teeth, "You will *NOT* behave in this manner!" Those were simple, clear instructions. Enough said. I would have gone on about my business until the subsequent infraction. I later learned that Gretta's mother would have turned it over to her father, who would have lectured her incessantly.

Mr. Buckner folded his fat little fingers in front of his pig face. "I am not going to punish you … this time … since it is the first time … but I'm afraid … if you do this again … there will have to be consequences. Now, I want you to hug one another and say you are sorry for being so mean to each other."

We both looked at him with shock and horror. He said he would not punish us, but I could think of no greater punishment than forcing me to hug and apologize to the bitch who stole my swing! We both glared at one another with disgust.

"Now, girls," he continued, "we must make amends and apologize for wrong doing. I want you to hug now and say you are sorry for what you did."

Neither of us moved.

"Go on, girls. Do as I say."

Slowly and silently, like repelling magnets, we rose from our chairs and stood before one another.

"Okay, girls … big hug."

We embraced one another like two porcupines attempting to avoid the other's quills.

"I'm sorry I pulled you off my swing," I said. However, I did not give up the claim that it was *my* swing.

"I'm sorry that I pulled your hair and hit you," she said with no apology for having stolen my damn swing! At this moment, Mr. Buckner applauded, slapping his fat little hands together as he chuckled in his airy, wheezy, squeaky voice.

"Oh, thank you, girls," he said. "That was very sweet. Now, wait in the hall, and I will call the hall monitor to escort you back to your classes."

After we stepped outside Mr. Buckner's office door, Gretta leaned toward me and whispered, "Doody head!"

I responded by leaning toward her and whispering, ever so quietly, "Bitch!"

Without revealing it to Mother until I was older, I had learned to cuss from overhearing Grandmother and Grandfather Donner, who were quite good at it.

Gretta leaned back toward me and said, "I can't believe you called me that. I would call you that, but my mom says I shouldn't use dirty words."

"Oh?" I commented. "And you think *doody head* is not a dirty word?"

Well, it's not dirty like what you said," she defended.

"Doody means shit, doesn't it?" I growled. "Isn't shit a dirty word? You just called me a shithead."

She looked at me, eyes wide like a startled owl. Then, a smirking smile crawled across her face.

"I can't believe you are saying those words," she giggled.

"Why not?" I replied. "They are part of the English language, aren't they? Who made the stupid rule that using some parts of the language is okay but not others?"

Never mind that I would never in a million years, at least not at that point in my life, have allowed Mother to hear me using those words or that argument.

"I never thought of it that way," she said. Then she looked at me, eyes darting to either side to be sure no one else was listening as she giggled the word "Bitch." She quickly covered her mouth with the tips of her fingers as embarrassment hit her.

"Twat!" I said in immediate reply, and she cackled out loud.

From that point on, we were dearest friends. We had found common ground in profanity. After that, we always shared the swing, not because Mr. Buckner had admonished us to do it but because we wanted to. In addition, we became quite skilled at intimidating others on the playground.

By the time we were in the third grade, our mothers occasionally allowed us to sleep over at one another's homes on a weeknight. Daddy would not be drunk throughout the week, so Mother felt comfortable enough to allow Gretta to sleep over. I would later have to beg her into allowing weekend sleepovers, which she seldom granted, for fear that Daddy would embarrass her or that the secret would get out about an alcoholic in our family, as though anyone cared or didn't already know.

When Gretta came to my house, we left Mother and Daddy in the living room and retreated to my room to play. Mother required at least an hour to do homework, so we pretended to do it until she stopped checking on us at about 7:00 p.m. Then we sang songs and played games like patty cake or played with dolls. Sometimes, we would play the "secret game." The game always began with a bit of rhyme, and after the rhyme, the person who sang the rhyme would tell a secret to the other. So, by the time we were teens, there was practically nothing that we did not know about each other.

The first night we played the game after Gretta taught it to me, I sat on the bed and sang. "I have a secret that I must not tell. If I tell it to you, you must not tell, and if you do, you'll fall in a well." Then I said, "My Daddy gets drunk every weekend."

She gave me an inquisitive look and asked, "What's drunk?"

I could not believe that she didn't know this. I said, "Well, do you know what whiskey is?"

"No."

"What about beer?" I asked.

"Oh," she said, "that is the stuff that grown-ups can drink, but kids aren't allowed to drink. My dad likes to have one or two when he watches football."

"Yes," I said, "and beer contains alcohol, and whiskey is a hard liquor, which is really strong alcohol, and when people drink it, they get drunk."

She giggled and said, "When I have a lollypop, I'm a hard licker 'cause I lick a hard lollypop, and I lick it hard!"

I laughed and said, "No, it's not that kind of licker. It's liquor." I spelled it. "L-I-Q-U-O-R."

"I never heard of that," she said.

We went to the dictionary, where we found the definition: *Middle English liquor, from Latin liquor, from Liquere. Date: 13th Century: A: a usually distilled rather than fermented alcoholic beverage. B: a watery solution of a drug.* We learned little more than we knew in the first place, but I knew at the time that liquor, whatever kind he happened to consume, made Daddy drunk, and whatever it was, he would drink it until he got drunk.

"Okay," she said, "but what is drunk?"

We returned to the dictionary, where we found: *'a period of drinking to intoxication or of being intoxicated.'* I hated dictionaries for this very reason—having to look up word upon word because each word used to define something was more complicated than the last. However, that's also how I built my vocabulary. Finally, we looked up intoxication, where we found: *'an abnormal state that is essentially poisoning.'*

This set me to tears. I never understood or realized before that my daddy was poisoning himself every weekend, and I began wondering how soon he would die.

Gretta grabbed me and hugged me. "What's the matter?" she exclaimed.

Mother, having ears like a bat, heard me from the living room. The next thing we knew, she opened my bedroom door. "Is everything all right in here?" she questioned.

I slammed the dictionary closed, sniffled back my tears, and quickly made up a lie. "We were just reading about a bunny who lost his mother," I said.

"Aw, that's so sad," Mother patronized. Then she crookedly smiled, closed the door, and retreated to her television.

I took a deep breath and whispered to Gretta, "My daddy is poisoning himself. What am I going to do?"

"Poisoning?" asked Gretta. "I don't understand how."

"Shush, keep it low so Mother won't hear."

"Okay," she dropped her neck to whisper as though that would quiet her words. "I don't understand."

"He gets drunk every weekend," I said. I waved the dictionary into the air between us. "It says that drunk means intoxicated, and intoxicated is poisoning. We have to stop him."

"But we're just kids," Gretta protested. "How can we do that?"

"Maybe I just need to talk to Daddy," I reasoned. "Maybe if he realizes what he is doing, he will stop."

For the first time, I realized that Mother's stalking every Friday night might be her attempt to stop him. I resolved that, on the following day, I would talk to Daddy about his drinking, but first, I had to make sure that Mother wasn't around. I didn't want her to interfere with my discussion.

Gretta and I talked for another hour and then went to bed early, at least early for me. She slumbered quietly beside me, but I didn't sleep. I had to devise a way to ensure that I could get Daddy alone to talk to him. Finally, I decided to ask Mother for a red velvet cake to have over the weekend. Mother always did her baking from the bottom up without using mixes, and I knew that she would have to shop for ingredients. I would tell her that I had to study for a test, so I could not go to the grocery store with her. The next night was Thursday, and it would be a perfect time, but I had to make sure that I told her after we picked up Daddy, or she would drag me to the store between school and picking him up.

The next afternoon, we sat at the factory waiting to pick Daddy up. This was no problem on any day except Friday.

When Daddy came out of the factory, I got out of the front seat and into the back. Daddy spotted our car in the usual place, and I waited for him to enter the front seat. I knew he would not want to go to the store or wait outside for Mother to shop.

Shortly after Daddy got into the car, I said, "Mother, I have a math test tomorrow. Can I have a red velvet cake for this weekend if I make a good grade?"

"How do I know you will make a good grade?" she questioned.

"Well, a red velvet cake would make me try harder," I replied.

"I don't even have the ingredients to make one," she continued.

"Could you stop and get them?" I questioned. I knew this would get Daddy, and sure enough, it did.

"Hold on there now," he protested. "I've had a long, hard day, and I don't want to be diddling around a grocery store after work. I need to go home and rest."

"But Daddy, please," I pleaded, knowing well that I was deliberately manipulating the situation.

"No, now I told you, I'm tired," he exclaimed gently. Daddy rarely spoke harsh words to me.

Mother knew where this was headed, and more to keep the peace than to please me, she offered, "Why don't I just drop you off at home, John? Then Lovella and I can shop for cake supplies."

"But Mother, I have to study for my test," I pleaded. The test, which I had known was coming, was merely a ten-question weekly exam, but Mother didn't have to know that, at least not until after I got what I needed.

"Okay, then," she submitted, "I will drop the two of you off at home while I shop."

"Thank you, Mother," I said, gloating in my victory. For an eight-year-old, I had quite a conniving mind.

Daddy and I were not long inside the house when he plopped himself on the sofa and was about to turn on the radio to listen to the evening news. Even though we had a television, he still preferred the radio news. I knew I had to catch him quickly before Mother got back. So, I sat on the sofa beside him and said, "Daddy, I have a problem, and I really need to talk to you about it."

He stopped, with his hand halfway to the radio knob, and turned back to me. "What's up, Punkin' Patch?" he said, patting my knee. Daddy always wanted to listen to the news after work, but he also loved me very much and would never hesitate if he thought I was truly in need.

"Daddy," I began, "last night, I was looking in the dictionary and looking up words, and I know you get drunk on weekends, and …"

"Hold on there now," he protested. "We don't need to talk about that. That's not stuff kids should talk about with parents."

"But Daddy," I persisted. "I looked up the word drunk, and it said it's poisoning."

"No, it's not," he comforted. "It is just getting a little off your feet once in a while. It's just a way to relax and blow off a little steam after a hard week."

"But Daddy, why would the dictionary say that it's poisoning? That means it could kill you."

"Honey, it's not going to kill me," he said. "Alcohol has been around for thousands of years. Lots of people drink. It doesn't hurt anybody to drink a little, and lots of people who drink live very long lives."

"Then why can't kids drink it?" I questioned.

He grunted with exasperation. "Because it is not for kids," he said. "Some things you got to be mature enough to handle."

"But if it's not good for kids, it must not be good for you," I continued.

"We don't let you drive yet, do we?" he debated. "There's nothing wrong with driving. You're just not big enough to do it yet. It's like that. You have to be an adult first. Some people drink, and some people don't. It doesn't hurt anyone."

"I know Mother serves sherry to the Millers when they come over, but they each only have one or two little glasses and don't get drunk." I continued to plead with him. "Daddy, sometimes you don't come home all night on Friday, and when your friends drop you off on Saturday, you look sick, all puffy and red, with swollen eyes and stuff."

"Ah, that's more from not getting enough sleep than it is from whiskey," he said. "You stay up late. I've seen you at breakfast, about to fall asleep in your hash browns. Sometimes, we both stay up a little too late, don't we?"

"You're not going to die?" I questioned.

"Well, I hope not," he replied. "I've got a lot of living yet to do. Now you go on and study for your test. Worry about kid stuff, and don't worry about grownups. We will take care of ourselves. Besides, it's our job … your mother and I … to care for you, not the other way around."

"You promise you are not going to die." I pleaded.

"I promise, honey," he went on. "I am not doing anything on Friday night, but trying to blow off some stress from the work week and enjoy some time with my friends. That's good for me."

He hugged me and said, "Now, go study."

I smiled nervously and went to my room, closing the door with trepidation. No matter what Daddy said, I worried about that word: poiso*ning*.

I got an 'A' on my test and got my red velvet cake. When Mother got the graded paper, she shook it at me. "Lovella! This is just a weekly quiz. I thought you had a big exam. How dare you put me to all that trouble for something you do every week and can practically do in your sleep?"

"I'm sorry, Mother," I said. "I was just so worried about this one. It's mostly division."

She sighed, slapped the paper on the kitchen table, and glared at me. "Well, I'm glad you got an 'A.' You did very well." She grabbed her apron from the hook and set about preparing dinner. I took my paper and my books to my room.

We all enjoyed the red velvet cake that Saturday night after dinner. Then, I sat in my chair reading while Daddy snored on one end of the couch and Mother sat upright on the other. My mind, however, was not on the book. Although I loved Daddy and defended him with all my might, and although I wanted so much to believe him when he said that he was fine, some years later, I came to the painful realization that he was wrong about alcohol, and it was poisoning him. However, I also knew that if Mother couldn't control his drinking, no one could. So, I didn't try.

In the meantime, that little worry was occasionally forgotten. I went on as usual and loved him as best I could.

CHAPTER 3

Church and Defiance

Mother always insisted on church every Sunday morning, tedious as it was. When I was small, I obediently complied and enjoyed the separate time for children, coloring outlines of Jesus and such. However, as I matured and was forced to enter the main service, I found it difficult to distinguish it from another school day. Additionally, I felt obliged to disagree with anything I thought Mother wanted. Therefore, going to church was an event that I was doomed to despise, and I didn't develop any real sense of spirituality until well into my adult years.

By the time I was twelve years old, I had begun a regular Sunday morning protest, starting at the breakfast table, where I knew I could employ Daddy's defense. Apparently, through all the years of their marriage, he had also obediently complied with her expectation that the family would dutifully show up at Sunday service and march up the steps in her staged processional. This would have occurred every Sunday if Daddy had not extended his drinking past Saturday night. On those Sundays, he either had not come home until Sunday afternoon, or Mother could not rouse him from sleeping off the alcohol. Although it must have been difficult for him to rise on Sunday morning, he had sometimes managed to sleep off his inevitable hangover in time for her demand that we all attend church together. When she couldn't rouse him, or he didn't come home, she excused his absence as he was too sick to attend. She didn't describe how he was sick, although I'm sure most people knew. Apparently, she didn't consider omitting the truth to be a sin, much less lying outright, which she also tended to do.

Mother dressed Daddy for church and would drag him out of bed unless she couldn't rouse him. She would have nothing of his gaudy belt buckles on Sunday mornings. He should have counted himself lucky that she tolerated them through the rest of the week. Sunday was a time for her to show off her family and display her pretentiousness to the community. Mother was all about the show. No matter what might happen at home, she would display absolute perfection to the community. She scraped enough money together to buy him two well-appointed suits, a few ties, and a couple of white dress shirts. She insisted that he wear them every Sunday morning against his constant protest. However, this did not come until after breakfast.

The Sunday table was displayed with the same opulence as every other morning when we were summoned to the table. The consolation was that it was the only morning of the week she allowed us to eat in our pajamas because she got us up early enough that we would have plenty of time to dress before eleven o'clock services. Mother had perhaps learned her lesson about dressing before Sunday breakfast when Daddy spilled a cup of coffee across the front of one of the expensive suits she had purchased. She would never make that mistake again. From then on, dressing for church occurred after breakfast.

I knew Daddy hated going to church. He hated dressing in those suits. It simply was not him. Rather than find and marry the man she wanted, Mother found it more of a challenge to marry a pig's ear and attempt the miracle of making him into a silk purse. In her mind, if she were to succeed, she would be truly special. Nonetheless, despite all her efforts and Daddy's occasional willingness to act the part, he remained forever who he was, a simple man who wanted little more out of life than to enjoy it.

My first attempts at getting out of church were through faking illness. Of course, this didn't work, for Mother was determined that she would stay home and care for me if I didn't feel well, and then I repeatedly heard the inventory of her resentments about missing church while I pretended to be ill. On the other hand, Daddy was quite pleased to have a day without a suit, and he would either go back to bed or to his work shed near the back of the house, which was his sanctuary from Mother. He had a small heater out there for the winter and a fan for summer heat. He had an old lounge chair pushed to the back corner and was content to sit there for hours. Of course, he also stashed whiskey out there.

For the longest time, it was easier, for me at least, to go to church. After breakfast, I retreated to my room to put on my Sunday dress. I could hear

Daddy complaining from their room. "Drucella! Now, Drucella … Sissy, that tie is too tight. You don't want me to faint in church, do you?"

"John!" she demanded, "the tie is not too tight. It is pulled up to the collar where it is supposed to be, and the collar has been measured to your neck size!"

Daddy protested, "Don't you think we could just leave the top button unbuttoned and kind of pull the tie over it?"

"I will *not* have you looking like a hobo who found a suit coat in a dumpster!" she would shout, and I knew that she was, at that moment, pushing the tie up to his throat in a gesture indicating that he would either comply, or she would choke him with it.

After I dressed, I would find Mother, always in her finest, standing there with a hairbrush and a bow. It was off to the bathroom, where she would sit on the commode lid and have me stand in front of her as she pulled that plastic-toothed demon through my hair.

"Aowaoh! Mother!" I complained, "That hurts!"

"Lovella," she lectured, "if you would occasionally brush your hair and keep the tangles out of it, we wouldn't have to go through such an ordeal to make it look nice for church."

By the end, my hair was smooth as silk, and the top was tied back over the underflow with a bow that perfectly matched the dress. Then, it was off to the living room to gather Daddy, sitting sullenly waiting to follow her instructions.

Her pretentiousness didn't wait for church. It began right there, in the living room. "John, would you please bring the car around?" she commanded more than implored.

This meant that he was to pull it out to the street at the end of our walkway from the one-car garage of our tiny home and wait for our descent down the front porch steps. He was never allowed to pull it onto the street ahead of time because Mother considered it unseemly for him to be sitting in the car waiting for us. Instead, he had his instructions to remain in the living room before going out to pull the car over to the street so that Mother and I, hand in hand, could descend the porch steps and cross the walk, where he would be waiting like a chauffeur to open the passenger doors for us, Mother in the front seat, I in the back. Mother would cross the walk with her chin held up as though she were a movie star navigating the red carpet before her adoring fans. I considered it absurd even as a young child. Yet, this was our ritual every Sunday morning. I would be guided to get in first. Then, Mother would enter the car, seat herself like a Queen, and carefully brush her dress as though the mere act of movement might have soiled it. Since she never allowed pets and meticulously cleaned the house, the chance of imperfection was exceedingly slim.

Daddy would then carefully close the door, as he was not allowed to slam it, and afterward, would come around to the driver's side to enter the car as instructed. Then, it was off to church. Sunday morning was the only time that Daddy was allowed to drive. Mother did all the driving the rest of the time, but if she were to drive on Sunday, it would not fit with the show she wanted to demonstrate to her imaginary fans.

There wasn't much of anything that Mother considered worthy in Climax, so we attended church in New Bethlehem. On the way there, she verbally prepared us.

"John, last week I noticed you nodding a little during the sermon," she scolded. "Please make every effort to stay awake. I wouldn't want you to miss something that might save your soul—and Lovella. Mrs. Dickens said you were giggling in Sunday school last week. Please do try to be appropriate."

Daddy drove in silence. I usually tried to bring a book to read on the way and occasionally pretended to listen. Mother had absolutely forbidden that I bring any book, other than the Bible, into the church, but I could at least read part of a novel on the way.

The Methodist church in New Bethlehem was an ornate brick building with a steeple on either side of the building. The steps spread widely across the front of the building with a rail down the middle and on either side. Atop each steeple, there were matching crosses. I suppose that having two steeples and two crosses somehow made it better than other churches having only one, and I could imagine Mother choosing it for that very reason. Without a church in the area with two steeples, she would probably have selected the one with the tallest steeple, regardless of the denomination.

Two large wooden doors led from the landing at the top of the steps into a single large alcove with marble flooring. This led to an arched double door at the center, which opened onto the sanctuary's center aisle. On either side of the alcove were smaller doors that led to the outside aisles near the windows, as well as some offices and children's classrooms.

The sanctuary was covered with a plush burgundy carpet flanked on either side by tall, arched stained glass windows. Oh, what a glorious setting for a Savior who lived on handouts, admonished the care of the poor, and protested the corruption of the wealthy rabbis in ancient Jerusalem. As a child, I thought it was pretty, but as I aged and read the Bible, I came to think of it as just another example on a long list of Christian hypocrisies. I determined that I would never be a hypocrite. I briefly reneged on that commitment after becoming a young mother.

When I was young, the minister was a tall, handsome man named James Martin. He was at least a couple of inches past six feet. He had dark, straight hair, a square symmetrical jaw, and grey-blue eyes. After service, he stood at the arch leading to the foyer and greeted the parishioners as they left the building. Mother would collect me from Sunday school and insist that Daddy hold my hand as we filed down the center aisle toward the exit. I assumed this was so she could free both hands when greeting Reverend Martin.

Throughout the service, she kept her lace handkerchief to touch her face and show that the sermon moved her. As we approached the Reverend, she would stuff the hanky inside her left hand, lay only three fingers of her right hand across his palm as a "lady-like handshake," and tell him how much she enjoyed the service.

"Reverend Martin, as always," she began, "your sermon was empowering and touching. What an inspiration you are to us all."

Daddy and I smiled and nodded, rarely ever saying anything ourselves. I imagined that Mother wished she had married a man like Reverend Martin rather than Daddy. Perhaps a man like that might have been able to live up to her standards.

By the time I was twelve, the Methodist church, as Methodists are prone to do, had traded Reverend Martin for Reverend Diller, a funny-looking little man who left much to be desired in the looks department. He wasn't much over five feet tall and had buck teeth protruding slightly over his lower lip so that he had the appearance, somewhat, of a chipmunk.

When he spoke his name, he drew out the end of it as though trying to emphasize the last syllable. "How do you do? I am Reverend Dill-eeer." He had an ugly little wife about his height, and they had several children. So, I assumed that, despite my distaste for their looks, they must have found each other attractive and fucked with abandon.

After the change in ministers, my desire to go to church completely faded. At least when Reverend Martin was there, I might have enjoyed looking at that pretty face. When Reverend Diller came around, it was just as I was old enough to stop attending Sunday school and start attending regular services. That clinched it. I was through with church. Reverend Diller's sermons were about as entertaining as watching paint peel. I could find little context to get excited about, and he spoke in a sedative monotone except for drawing out the ends of some words. Daddy and I were both nodding before the end of his sermons, and Mother attempted to keep us attuned to the service with a painful pinch, a big, perfect smile, and a dart of her eyes toward the podium, yet I knew she was just as bored as we were.

A Sunday came in my thirteenth year when I decided I had been pinched enough. I determined I would not go to church anymore and announced this at the breakfast table the following Sunday morning. I could have announced it at any time throughout that week, but I knew that I needed to take her by surprise and that I would need Daddy's support.

Mother had made her usual opulent breakfast that Sunday. I sat at the table, eating my specially prepared omelet and toasted rolls while sipping my coffee. I carried on as though nothing was out of place or different from any other Sunday morning. About a third of the way through the meal, I announced, "Mother, I've decided that I will not go back to church."

She looked up from picking tiny bits of omelet off her plate, smiled as though she had just heard a joke, and said, "You most certainly *are* going to go to church, dear." She continued smiling and took a sip of her coffee.

"No, Mother," I persisted. "I have, indeed, decided that church is not for me, and I will not be returning to Sunday services."

Daddy looked like a deer caught in headlights. His eyes grew wide as he watched the stand-off begin. He must have known there would be no escape from being drawn into it.

"Lovel-la!" Mother spit my name off her tongue with a growl and her piano key tone. "You-*will-not-defy*-me … young-lady! You-*will*-go-to-church … and-there-*will-be*-no-more-arguments!"

I turned to Daddy, who was nervously gouging his omelet. "Daddy, you don't like to go to church either, do you?" I questioned, knowing the answer if he told the truth.

"Well, I … I believe you have to listen to your mother, Punkin' Patch."

"But what's the answer to my question, Daddy?" I persisted.

"Well, I …" He glanced at Mother as she glared at him like a lion stalking prey. "I … ah … can't say it's my favorite thing to do on Sunday morning."

"John Fuchs!" Mother exclaimed, "Don't encourage that child!"

"Well, I was just saying how I feel about it, dear," he receded. "I know it's good for the soul and all, but …"

"Mother," I interjected. "I am thirteen years old. I have reached the church's determined age of accountability, and I have decided not to go back to church."

Mother stood up, leaned over the table, hands flat on the tabletop, and said, "Lovella, how dare you speak to me in this tone!"

"I am simply saying that I have the right to make my own choice about this. The church even says so," I calmly continued.

"No, you do not have the right to choose about this!" she exploded. "You are a child under my jurisdiction and will do as I say!"

As I had hoped, Daddy's need to protect his little girl finally kicked in. "Now … now … Drucella," he pleaded, "There is no need to get all hot under the collar about this. Teenagers get like this. You know, it's all part of growing up."

"WHAT?" Mother twisted toward him. "What-did-you-just-say-to-me?"

I half expected Daddy to back down at this point, but the prey stood up to the lion.

"Kids reach a point where they want to think for themselves," he continued. "It is a normal, natural part of growing up."

"You-have-got-to-be-kidding-me!"

Mother grabbed her plate, paced to the sink, threw it in, food and all, turned, and the zaps began. "She-is-only-thirteen-years-old! She-is-not-old-enough-to-make-that-kind-of-decision, and-besides-her-soul-will-burn-in-hell! Is-that-what-you-want, Johhhhnnnnn? Do-you-want-your-only-child's-soul-to-BURN-IN-HELL?"

"Now, Drucella, you're getting a little extreme there now," said Daddy as he turned in his chair. "You don't know that she won't change her mind in a few weeks and go back. She's just expressing a little normal rebelliousness, that's all."

"I'm not going back," I said. "Neither one of us goes to church because we want to. Neither of us goes because we want to save our souls from damnation. Daddy, you go for the same reason I do because Mother insists on it every Sunday—demands it. This is not about saving our souls. It's about Mother pretending to be hoity-toity for everybody from Kittanning to Hawthorn."

At this point, Mother went into a full-blown tornado rage. The hornets were out. She spun across the kitchen and up to my face as I leaned back in the chair. "WHY-YOU INSOULENT-UNGRATEFUL-LITTLE-BRAT!" she screamed. "I-HAVE-GIVEN-MY-LIFE-TO-THIS-FAMILY! I-HAVE-KEPT-THIS-HOUSE, SENT-YOU-TO-SCHOOL, COOKED-CLEANED-IRONED, SAVED-CUPONS, AND-FOR-WHAT? SO-YOU-COULD-SIT-HERE, DISRESPECT-ME, AND-SAY-HORRIBLE-THINGS-TO-ME?"

Suddenly, she caught herself as though murder had not been far from her thoughts and stood back. Calmly but quite deliberately, she said, "You cannot believe how much effort it is taking for me *not* to strike you right now."

She looked over at Daddy, who sat silently, shocked. "Very well," she said, "the two of you are no longer ... *required* ... to go to church. God forbid you should feel that I am ... *forcing* ... you to go." She pulled herself up as tall as possible and continued her guilt trip. "Therefore ... I will go to church ... on my own ... by myself ... alone ... and when people ask me where my ... lovely family is ... I shall tell them ... that I am widowed and childless."

She turned and marched stoically out of the room, pausing momentarily at the door as though waiting for us to shout, "No, please wait!"

We said nothing, and Mother left the room. Her offer of a guilt trip was met with a refusal to buy tickets. Daddy and I continued to sit at the kitchen table, half in shock, half in glee. We finished our breakfast, and I did the dishes while Daddy sipped more coffee and read the newspaper.

Later, we heard Mother cross through the living room and pause before opening the front door. After an extended silence, she released a long and defeated sigh. Then, the latch clicked, the door closed, and she was gone.

After church, she behaved as though nothing had ever happened.

CHAPTER 4

Like Mother, Like Daughter

You would never know that Mother smoked if you were not a family member. In an age in which it was considered glamorous, the habit of the stars, Mother treated it as her private little sin.

When she smoked, it would be on the back porch in summer and then in the laundry room in winter. When the weather was cold, she locked herself in the laundry room to suck down one or two cigarettes. Then, she tried to destroy the evidence with air freshener spray before coming out. Her ashtray could never be found, nor could her cigarettes, but the wafting smell of tobacco smoke oozed beneath the laundry room door, and of course, we knew.

Sometimes, Daddy liked to taunt her. "Sissy!" he called while banging on the laundry room door as though there had been some emergency. "What are you doing in there? I smell smoke! I'm afraid the house might be on fire! We've got to evacuate and get you to safety!"

Then, Daddy glared at me with a shit-eating grin, and I snickered while he teased her.

"You sure you're not burning the ironing?" Daddy would continue. "It sure does smell like something is burning."

"Oh, for Heaven's sake, John!" she eventually cried out, "Leave me alone and let me have a little peace to myself!"

In summer, if either Daddy or I happened to step onto the back porch, she quickly stuffed her cigarette and ashtray into the back of a ceramic cat that sat by her chair.

Finally, one day, I said, "Mother, why do you do that?"

"Do what, dear?" as though she had completely fooled me.

"Hide your cigarettes like you think, Daddy, and I don't know you smoke," I said.

"Why, for heaven's sake, Lovella," she replied, "I don't know what you are talking about."

As I had gotten older, I became increasingly defiant of Mother and the hypocrisy that regularly dribbled out of her.

"Hmmm," I said, "why don't I come over there and see what you just shoved up the ass of your ceramic cat?"

"Lovella Fuchs!" she exclaimed. "How dare you use language like that in front of me?"

"You prefer I use language like that behind your back?" I questioned. "Come on, let's look in that cat's ass and see what we find."

She stared at me silently, intimidatingly, as though she could stare me away and make me forget about it.

Finally, I said, "You wouldn't lie—would you—Mother? You know the Lord doesn't like liars."

She continued her silent stare, and I stared back until she gave in.

"All right!" she confessed as she straightened her collar like a guilty defendant called to the stand, "I smoke … There you have it. You have heard me say what you already knew. Are you happy now?"

I continued to interrogate. "What I don't understand," I said, sitting in the chair across from her, "is why you think you have to keep it a secret."

She stared at a bundle of tall purple garden phlox blooming by the porch. "It's just not a habit a lady should have," she said.

"But lots of women smoke." I protested. "Betty Davis smokes. Most of the actors and actresses smoke. What's the big deal?"

"I don't care if other women smoke or all of Hollywood smokes," she said. "I just hate that I do."

"But why?" I questioned.

"Because it's nasty," she said, looking at me pleadingly. "I wish I had never started it, and I hope you never will. It makes my mouth taste like a smokestack, creates a nasty mess to clean up, and sometimes makes me cough. I hate it."

"Then, why do you do it?" I continued.

"Because I can't help it," she said. "I started smoking when I was very young, and now, I feel like I have to do it. If I don't do it, I get nervous and grumpy."

"Oh, can we blame all that on being out of cigarettes?" I smirked. "I thought that was just your natural demeanor."

"Don't be crass," she snapped as she went on. "Lovella, you know I like to keep clean. You know I like to keep a certain character and quality about me. Smoking interferes with that, yet I can't seem to quit doing it. It's like I'm hooked on a drug or something."

In those days, there hadn't been much said about cigarettes being addictive or harmful to your health. At the time, cigarettes were advertised everywhere, even on television, until around 1970.

"It would seem to me," I pondered, "that all you would have to do is stop buying them. If you don't buy them, they are not here, and you won't smoke them."

"Lovella, it's not that simple," she said. "I don't know if I can explain it to you, but it's not that simple. Please take my word that it is a nasty, terrible habit that is hard to break, and promise me that you will never do it."

Whoops! She said the wrong thing there. I seemed hell-bent on doing whatever Mother did not want me to do. It might have been different when I was younger, but by the time I was a teen, I had the bug. Maybe I was taking out all those years of frustration for having to comply with her demands. I had to try everything that was displeasing to Mother. For some reason, I had this devilish need to do whatever she didn't want me to do.

"Promise me, Lovella," she said while my mind wandered into a vision of myself leisurely drawing down smoke like one of the Hollywood actresses.

"Why is that so important?" I questioned.

"Because I don't want you to have to fight the battle I am fighting right now." She leaned forward and took my hand. "Promise me that you will never smoke."

I let out a big sigh and lied. "I promise."

She let go of my hand and sat back in her chair. "Why don't you run on now?" she said.

"Why?" I questioned, knowing full well that she wanted me to leave so she could smoke alone.

"Just go on, dear." She looked away, and I could palpate her shame.

"So, you can smoke?" I continued. "I don't see what the big deal is. If you can smoke alone, why can't you smoke in front of me? It's not like I don't know or that I'm going to tell."

"Lovella, please." she pleaded. "I would just rather be alone. You know my secret, okay? Now, please, go read a book or something."

I couldn't see much reason to continue torturing her on that particular day, so I did as she said and went on my way. However, I determined that I was going to find her cigarettes, and I was going to try one. I had to find out what the big deal was about. I knew that I wouldn't be ashamed of it, like her. I knew I wasn't like her, all prim and perfect. I didn't have to be like her. I didn't want to be like her. So, when I smoked, I determined that I would flaunt it. After all, why should anyone make a secret of such a silly thing? My friends whose parents smoked didn't hide it like it was some secret shame. Why should I?

I never did find Mother's cigarettes. Whenever I caught her out of the house, I looked in what I thought was every possible hiding place. I even sneaked into her bedroom one night while she was watching television and went through her purse. Nothing! I found a cigarette lighter behind her jewelry box, but that was it.

This continued for weeks until I finally realized I would never find them. Oddly enough, Daddy didn't smoke. You would think that he would, given that he drank so much and spent so much time in smokey bars, but I guess he never cared for it. However, Gretta's father did smoke, and I finally decided that I would have to enlist her in my quest if I were ever to score that elusive first cigarette. Gretta and I had exchanged overnight visits with one another ever since we were in the third grade. When I was at her house, we spent most of our time in her room, and the same was true when she came to my house. We would have plenty of private time to discuss it, and I was determined to bring it up with her the next time I was over.

So, about two or three weeks after I caught Mother smoking, I got to stay the night at Gretta's house. It was a simple little post-war cottage similar to ours, with three bedrooms. Gretta wasn't an only child like me. She had a pesky little brother named Calvin, and we often had to put a chair under the doorknob in her room to keep him from coming in to harass us. Her father finally put a lock on her door when Gretta kept complaining.

Her dad was so handsome. I tried to restrain myself from the horrible betrayal of lusting for my best friend's father, but by the time I had reached my early teens, I couldn't seem to help it. I had a massive crush on him. Had he not been married and the father of my best friend, I might have thrown myself at him like the shameless hussy I was destined to become.

Mr. Tannenbaum was a tall, rugged man with dark brown hair and piercing hazel eyes. His stiff, firm jaw supported the most kissable mouth I think I have ever seen. His lips were plump and soft, and when he smoked, they caressed the filter of his cigarette as though he were making love to it. He never hesitated to smoke in front of everyone, and I loved watching it. He would pull the cigarette to his lips and draw upon it sensually, or at least, I thought it was sensual. When he blew the smoke from those sexy lips, it was like a sigh after a long, sweet kiss. Years later, I confessed to Gretta that I had a terrible crush on him. She said, "Ewweeewwwweeeeh! That's my dad! Gross!"

"But he's so hot!" I teased. "I couldn't help myself."

By then, we were old enough and close enough to laugh it off.

On the night I stayed over after catching Mother smoking, Gretta and I retired to her room after dinner, and I began my query.

"Gretta," I implored. "I have something so important to tell you."

"What?" she questioned, as though we were acting out the plot of a television teaser.

I looked around the room and whispered softly enough not to be heard outside but loud enough for Gretta to hear on the other side of the bed. "I caught Mother smoking."

"Really?" she said, "You never told me your mother smokes."

"I was pretty sure of it," I said, "but I never confronted her before. She has always hidden it. She smokes in the laundry room or on the porch when she thinks no one is around. I got her to confess that she does it."

"Wow," Gretta reacted, "why doesn't she just smoke in front of people like my dad?"

"Because she is ashamed of it," I replied. "It doesn't fit the proper image she wants to maintain."

"But why?" questioned Gretta. "Lots of people smoke."

"Mother thinks it is some kind of terrible, nasty thing," I replied. "She made me promise I would never do it."

"That's just silly," Gretta countered. "What difference does it make if you smoke? Dad seems to enjoy it."

"I know," I said, rolling my eyes to the ceiling. "I love to watch your dad smoke." Then, I caught my glee and pulled back to the moment lest she realize that watching her father smoke was a turn-on. That confession would have to come later because she could not have handled it then. "I mean," I continued, "why shouldn't anybody just smoke and enjoy it if they want to?"

"I know," said Gretta. "Mom or Dad have never told me I shouldn't smoke."

"Have you ever tried it?" I gleamed.

"No," she said. "I never thought much about it."

"I want to try it," I encouraged. "It is such a pleasure for your dad and such a secret for my mother that I want to find out what it's all about."

"You are not supposed to smoke unless you're an adult," she said, being the obedient daughter.

"Do you always do what you are supposed to?" I taunted.

"Well, no," she replied. "I say bitch, or shit, or damn sometimes. You know, because you're a bad influence."

We giggled, and I said, "Well, listen bitch, we have got to score some cigarettes."

"How are we going to do that?" she questioned. "They won't sell them to kids."

Even though Pennsylvania authorized the sale at sixteen in those days, we were not quite old enough.

"I swear, Gretta," I poked. "Sometimes you are so dense."

"What?" she questioned.

"We don't have to buy them. Your Dad has them lying around. We just borrow some of his."

"Oh, I don't think that would be a good idea," she pleaded. "My dad would not like that. He is very much against stealing."

"Did I say we were going to steal them?" I pushed. "We are just going to borrow them and try them."

I was undoubtedly a bad influence on Gretta, but her parents wouldn't know that until much later, and regardless, we remained close lifelong friends. Still, she turned out all right.

"What's the difference?" she asked. "Besides, why don't you get some of your mother's cigarettes?"

"I tried," I whined. "I've been searching for weeks. She's hidden them somewhere, and apparently, it's a darn good hiding place because I can't find them anywhere."

"My dad doesn't hide his," Gretta said.

"I know," I coaxed. "He wouldn't miss a couple. We could take a couple out of the pack when he is not looking and go somewhere and try them. When we are old enough to buy cigarettes, we'll buy him a whole carton to make up for it."

The forbidden fruit is sweet, indeed! Gretta's eyes lit up, and she said, "Well, it wouldn't really be stealing then, would it? We could go down under the Hetrick Road culvert. No one would ever know. I could get a couple of mom's kitchen matches. When do you think we could do this?"

"How about tomorrow?" I asked.

Over the summer, Gretta and I sometimes spent two or three days together running around each other's neighborhoods before returning home. The Hetrick Road culvert happened to run underneath the street a few blocks from her house at a place where the street curved. It was long and had a wide curve underneath the street level. A little creek ran through it, but there was plenty of room on either side to walk, and it was safe as long as there had not been a lot of rain. Gretta and I had often explored it in the past.

"When do we get the cigarettes?" she probed.

"Where does your dad keep them?" I asked.

"He usually just leaves them lying on the end table by the sofa."

"Okay," I planned. "We wait till your parents have gone to sleep. We sneak into the living room. One of us will watch down the hall by the kitchen, and the other will take a couple of cigarettes out of his pack. Then, we will get a couple of kitchen matches. We bring the cigarettes and the matches back in here and hide them, and then, tomorrow, we have them in our pockets when we go out to ride our bikes. No one will know."

"But what if we get caught taking them?" she considered.

"We won't get caught," I insisted. If anyone comes out, we tell them we were thirsty and came out to get a drink of water. We both have pockets in our nightgowns. We'll put the cigarettes in there, and no one will ever think we are lying. Then, tomorrow, we sneak them out in our pockets."

"Okay," she assessed. "Good plan."

Later, we waited about thirty minutes after we heard her parents go to bed. We tiptoed into the house's darkness, with just the streetlamp's light showing through the living room window. I didn't think about the sounds coming from her parents' bedroom then, but when I got older, I realized they must have been in the middle of lovemaking and quite distracted from anything we were doing. I certainly had never heard those sounds coming from Mother and Daddy's room.

Her dad's cigarette pack was on the end table, where Mr. Tannenbaum always sat. Unfortunately, it only had three cigarettes in it. I watched the hall, and Gretta had gone to get the cigarettes. The next thing I knew, she came tiptoeing back to me and whispered, "There are only three cigarettes in the pack."

"So," I whispered, "we only need two."

"But with so few," she continued, "he'll know someone took them."

"No, he won't," I lectured. "He would probably just think he smoked more than he thought or that your mom borrowed a couple."

"My mom doesn't smoke," she whispered.

"Look!" I muttered, exasperated. "Just get the two cigarettes! If anybody says anything, we'll keep them hidden and flush them down the toilet or something. Then, we'll deny we knew anything about it. Now go on!"

Finally, she went back and took the two cigarettes. Then, we went to the kitchen to get a few matches. Everything went into our pockets, and we tiptoed back to her room, hid them, and went to bed with no one the wiser.

After breakfast the following day, we told Gretta's parents that we were going out to ride our bikes.

"Be back by eleven thirty, girls. I don't want you to miss lunch," her mom said as we left.

In those days, especially in a small town, no one worried about a couple of young teen girls riding bikes around their neighborhoods. It was safe, and we played with a confident, innocent abandon.

We rode straight down to the Hetrick Road culvert, pushed our bikes down the grassy embankment near it, and parked them just inside its entrance.

"What do you think it will be like?" Gretta asked while we carefully walked over the rough concrete edges by the water.

"I don't know," I said, "but it has got to be good if so many people are doing it."

We reached a place near the center, sat down on a couple of blocks of concrete that jutted up from the edge, and took our cigarettes out of our pockets.

"You first," Gretta said and looked to me for inspiration.

"Okay," I replied, cigarette in hand.

I had seen Gretta's father smoke enough that I knew basically what to do. I clutched the cigarette between my fingers, struck the match against the concrete, put it to the cigarette, and pulled smoke into my lungs. Immediately, my throat burned, and I heaved a hoarse and growling cough.

"Are you alright?" pleaded Gretta, touching my arm.

"I'm fine," I lied, still choking. Then, I pulled the cigarette back to my lips as I had seen Mr. Tannenbaum do and attempted to make love to it as he would. I drew the smoke into my mouth, foul-tasting as it was, opened my lips just slightly, and breathed like he did. The smoke curled into my lungs, and I felt slightly dizzy as I coughed it back out.

"Your turn," I coaxed.

"I don't know," she backtracked. "It doesn't look all that enjoyable the way you do it."

"I'm just starting," I said. "I'll learn how. Come on. Try yours."

She hesitantly pulled the remaining cigarette from her pocket but could not light it after two or three tries.

"Here, let me," I said, and I snatched it from her. Within a moment, I lit the cigarette and returned it to her.

"What do I do?" she reviewed as though she had never seen it done before.

"You've seen your dad smoke your whole life," I said. "Just put it in your mouth and suck on it."

She put the cigarette to her lips and sucked it like a straw. The smoke went into her mouth, and she blew it out like she had accomplished something grand.

"I didn't cough," she announced.

"That's because you didn't do it right," I said. "You are supposed to draw it into your lungs."

"Why?" she questioned.

"I don't know why," I said, "but if you watch, everybody does that when they smoke. That's what your dad does. Haven't you watched him? Look," I went on. "Do it like this." Again, I drew the smoke through my lips into my lungs. This time, I only barely coughed when I released the smoke. Gretta did as I instructed, heaved in a gagging cough, and I started to giggle.

"Bitch!" she said, and I laughed even harder.

"Whore!" I exclaimed and put my cigarette back to my lips, drawing it like a pro.

When there was nothing left but cigarette butts, we held the butts between two fingers and pretended to be actresses discussing our upcoming movies. In those days, cigarettes were Hollywood-glamorous, and many big stars smoked on screen and off. It would be many years before the public would understand that cigarettes were more deadly than romantic.

"In my next film," I moaned with my imitation of a deep sultry voice while pulling the butt to my lips, "I'm going to star with Bing Crosby in a little musical dance film called *From There to My Titties.*"

"Oh really," snapped Gretta, not to be outdone in our efforts to be naughty. She put the cigarette butt to her lips, pretended to puff, and snapped it out. "I'm starring with Marlin Brando in an action thriller, *Long Road to Pussy Canyon.*"

We giggled and carried on long after the cigarettes had burned down to the butts. We pretended to be smoking while breaking the rules of decorum with hilarious abandon.

After that, it was all over for both of us. If we were not yet physically hooked on cigarettes, we were hooked on the novelty, the crime, and the intrigue of the cigarettes. Gretta continued to swipe cigarettes from her dad for a while until it seemed we needed them more often. In those days, they didn't keep cigarettes behind the counter as they do now. So, we began stealing them from the local market. Yes, I talked Gretta into stealing. One of us would act as a distraction while the other pocketed the cigarettes. This continued until a young store clerk caught us one day and said, "Look, I'll sell them to you if you want them, but if I catch you stealing them again, I'm going to call the cops." From then on, we picked up bottles beside the road to redeem the return deposit and used that, in addition to our allowances, to buy cigarettes from that particular clerk. Now and then, we would do little odd jobs for elderly neighbors and go knocking on doors to see if we could get paid to help them around their house. Mother just thought I was being responsible and resourceful. She didn't know I was feeding a budding addiction to the most lethal drug of all. None of us knew that at the time.

A little over a year later, when I had just turned fifteen, Mother knocked on the door of my room one night. I was lying in bed studying my history book.

"Lovella, may I come in?" she questioned, tapping lightly on the door.

"Yes, Mother," I replied, and she entered rather sheepishly, a characteristic unlike her.

She came and sat on the edge of my bed and said, "I found this stuffed behind the commode." Then, she held out her hand to reveal a half-smoked pack of cigarettes.

"Did you forget where you hid them?" I taunted, knowing full well that she knew they were not hers.

"Lovella," she explained, "I always know where my cigarettes are hidden, and besides, I haven't smoked in six months."

"Congratulations," I said, "I know that you wanted so much to quit."

"Don't be coy with me," she continued. "I know this means that you are smoking."

"What of it?" I said, glaring at her over my book.

"You know that I don't want you to smoke," she said, long having realized that she had raised a daughter who was at least as stubborn as herself and hell-bent on defying her.

"Yes," I said, leaving the subject open.

"If you are going to quit," she pleaded, "you must do it now while you are young. The longer you wait, the harder it becomes."

"I have no desire to quit, Mother." I folded my book and set it aside. "I enjoy it."

"Lovella, I will not have you do this," she insisted. I'm confiscating this pack, and I will not allow you to bring any more cigarettes into this house."

I smiled. "Mother, I thought you knew me better than that. You can confiscate all you want, but I will get more, and I will smoke them because I want to. There is nothing you can do to stop me."

Surprisingly, she didn't press any further. "Very well," she said, rising and walking to the door. "I will place these back where I found them. Please continue to do this privately."

The next morning, I lit a cigarette at the breakfast table, took a slow drag, and flicked the ash into the saucer under my coffee cup. Daddy shot me a look of surprise, eyes wide, more concerned about the possible conflict between Mother and myself, but he said nothing. I watched Mother nibble at her breakfast as though she hadn't seen a thing. I was disappointed that she didn't scream.

CHAPTER 5

Sex? What's That?

By the time I was sixteen, I had read the Kinsey Reports and the Kama Sutra cover to cover, as well as over and over. I first discovered the Kinsey Report on male sexual behavior published in 1948 at our local library when I was thirteen. I will never know why it was in a small-town library or why our stupid librarian allowed a thirteen-year-old girl to check it out, except I told her it was for a science class report, and she gave no protest. As soon as I stumbled on it and pulled it from the shelf, I knew I was on to something. A year or two later, I found the Kinsey report on female sexual behavior. Then, I discovered that I could order books from catalogs, and Mother never balked if I requested money to purchase a book. I just had to keep her from finding out what I was reading. When the Kama Sutra came in, the cover art was benign, so I told her that it was a novel about an Indian woman's grief after a tiger had killed her husband.

Although she never knew it, in a roundabout way, Mother had gotten me interested in sex. If I had waited for Mother to talk to me about sex, I would still be waiting. It was never going to happen. When I first got my period at the end of my twelfth year, before I found the books, I was terrified. After urinating, I rose from the commode to find it filled with bloody water. I ran to the bathroom door and screamed, "Mother! Mother! Come quick! Please hurry!"

She trotted dutifully into the bathroom and said, in a less-than-excited tone, "Why, dear, what is it?"

Having learned it from Mother, I was always prone to drama. I grabbed the sleeve of her dress and shouted, "I'm bleeding! What if I'm dying?"

Now, seemingly annoyed, she exclaimed, "For Heaven's sake, Lovella! What are you talking about?"

"Come see!" I said, and pulled her to the commode so she could witness the carnage of my urination. "I'm peeing blood!"

She glanced in, flushed the commode, and said, "Wait a moment." She reached into the linen closet behind a stack of towels and pulled out a box of feminine sanitary napkins.

"Here," she said, thrusting the box at me, "the instructions are on the box." Without another word, she made a controlled exit and continued her business. I put the commode lid down, sat on it, and began reading the instructions. There wasn't much to it, no explanation, just instructions on using the product. I applied it as instructed and went to find Mother. She was in her bedroom mending one of Daddy's shirts.

"Mother?" I asked, handing her the box of sanitary napkins. "What is this?"

"They are feminine protection pads, dear. They will keep you from spotting your clothing when you have your period. Now, put the box away and go on. I'm busy." She handed the box back to me and immediately returned to her sewing. "Place it back where it was and retrieve one when you need more," she chirped.

I stood a moment longer while she sewed and acted as if I weren't there. She had never told me about having a period, a topic she discreetly avoided. I had heard about it from girls at school, but my knowledge was minimal, and I had no idea what it would be like. Questioning her would do no good. She had given me as much information as she was willing to.

Well, crap! I thought to myself and turned to leave. *I'm going to have to go to the library!*

Since I enjoyed reading so much, it was lucky that our library was only about ten blocks from our house. When I was little, my mother would take me there on summer afternoons more to occupy me so she didn't have to deal with my boredom than anything else. This early exposure, however, led to an appreciation of the written word and a lifelong joy of reading. When I was a little older, I rode my bike there and sometimes read for hours.

I decided to try to educate myself on what had just happened that afternoon. In the library, I began to explore the medical section. I found some books explaining the female reproductive cycle and was satisfied with the knowledge, although I resented that Mother did not just explain it. I learned about and understood that unpleasant natural phenomenon and accepted it. Still, the messy process of dealing with menstruation was the only thing I disliked about being a woman, even if menopause has long since relieved me of the concern. Yet, menopause was not exactly a walk in the park, either.

I continued to search the library for additional information about the reproductive process. One day, when returning one of the books to the shelf, I glanced at a title that intrigued me: *Sexual Behavior in the Human Male*. It was also known as *The Kinsey Report*. I took it from the shelf and returned to one of the nearby tables to read. Later, with some angst and trepidation, I checked it out, got away with it, and hid the book when I got home.

In one afternoon, I learned more about sex than I had been taught in my previous thirteen years and ended up learning more about it than perhaps most adults of the day. I had never thought of the words heterosexual, bisexual, or homosexual before, but they were defined in the Kinsey Report. Mr. Kinsey had studied a relatively large population of men and concluded that most men engage in various sexual activities, many with both men and women. I thought that was very interesting.

I became intrigued by sex, and even though I found the idea of Mother and Daddy engaging in such activities far-fetched, I considered that I was proof that they must have, at least once. I could never imagine Mother ever consenting to having her body penetrated by Daddy's "dirty part," much less allowing him to ejaculate into her. I also wondered if Daddy had ever engaged in sex with men. Perhaps that was what those Friday nights with "the boys" were all about. Maybe drinking was just a way to hide it. *No, I thought to myself, not Daddy. He enjoys drinking more than anything else, probably more than sex.* Besides, I couldn't imagine that he had much interest in sex.

At first, I thought it was dirty and disgusting, but the more I read, the more I got excited about the idea of sex, and I wanted to learn more. I read as much as I could find, and when I had exhausted the information available, I had to resort back to my more traditional reading pursuits of novels and short stories. I occasionally revisited the medical section of the library to see if any new books had come in, and I perused book catalogs for exciting books about sex. One thing I discovered was romance novels, the soft porn of the day. Then, a couple of years later, the library obtained a copy of *Sexual Behavior in the Human Female,* and my interest was renewed. I learned that twenty-six percent of females engaged in their first intercourse before age fifteen, and I was about to turn sixteen when I came across the information. I learned about female masturbation and decided I would give it a try. When I did and had my first orgasm, I overwhelmingly enjoyed it.

After retiring to bed on a school night, I made the mistake of trying it for the first time. I had read about orgasm, but I had no idea that it would make me feel like my entire body was on a pleasure roller-coaster and that the plummet from the peak would force me to yelp. It was only a few seconds after my breath-halting wail of a first orgasm that Mother came and opened my door without knocking as I was recovering from the aftermath of that first climax. Luckily, I was under the covers.

"Good grief, Lovella!" Mother implored, "Are you alright?"

"I'm fine, Mother," I panted, "I just had a bad dream."

"Oh, you poor dear," she said, sitting on my bed and touching my cheek.

"I'm fine, Mother—really," I said, hoping she would go away.

"Well, go back to sleep, dear, and have a better dream this time." She rose to leave and glanced at me when she closed the door. At that moment, I concluded that Mother must never have had an orgasm. She must have been like some of the women I read about in the report who didn't ever get there. "What a shame," I thought. I turned over in bed and found myself drifting to sleep.

I wondered if there might be any information about the history of sex throughout time, and I began exploring from another perspective. This was when I came across the Kama Sutra in a book catalog. Reading romance novels led to being mailed other interesting catalogs. When I read the Kama Sutra, I was fascinated by all its elaborate drawings of sexual positions. I soon concluded that there must be something even more remarkable about the actual physical contact than mere masturbation and imagination could grant me. When I was sixteen, I began seeking a way to find out.

There was a boy named Tommy Smith who lived up the street. The family had moved to town about a year before my fifteenth birthday. Tommy was about a year older than me and not bad looking, as teen boys go. He didn't have the usual face of a teen boy, pock-marked by acne. There was the occasional zit, but nothing too gross. His hair was blond and curly, his jaw square, and his eyes were hazel. Some days, I would see him mowing the lawn, shirtless and wearing worn jeans. I decided that he would be the object of my planned seduction. I had never paid much attention to him until my sexual interest peaked. Then, a shirtless boy in worn jeans suddenly became enticing.

One sunny weekend afternoon, I heard a lawn mower in the distance and decided to investigate. I told Mother and Daddy I was going out to walk around the neighborhood and then strolled directly toward the Smith house. On the way there, I unbuttoned the top two buttons of my blouse to reveal cleavage, which I had in ample supply. Those parts had matured early and formidably. When I got there, I leaned over their white picket fence and watched while Tommy mowed.

He was intent on his work, and it was a minute before he looked up and saw that I was leaning over, obviously gazing at him. He stopped the mower and came to the fence.

"Hello, Lovella," he said, wiping the sweat from his brow with his handkerchief.

When the Smiths first moved in, Mother dragged me to their house with a cake and a neighborhood welcome. Since then, there had been little more than the occasional passing hello. I was about to change all that.

"What's going on?" he asked, squinting in the summer sun.

"Oh, nothing," I said. "I just heard the mower and thought I would come down … and watch you … mow." As I said this, I deliberately scanned down his body to his crotch and back up to his waiting eyes.

He grinned sheepishly and said, "You must be really bored."

"I'm not so much bored as interested," I said, running my fingers through my hair and pulling it down to the last strand. "I thought you might show me your … technique."

His face went bright red, and I caught his eyes locking, for a moment, on my cleavage. "Well," he said, surely knowing my intentions, "I don't know that there is much technique. I push it back and forth till I'm done."

"I'll bet you do," I said. Then, I shifted my body upward to give him a better look between my breasts and paused before commenting.

"Fascinating … I'm looking forward to seeing you … push it back and forth … until you're … done."

"Uh, okay." He gave a nervous laugh.

"Tommy, come here," I said, curling my finger toward my face. "I have a question I need to ask."

He walked directly to the fence and stopped.

"Closer," I whispered and searched his face with hungry eyes.

When he leaned over the fence, I breathed a whisper into his ear, "Have you ever had sex?"

"Uh, ha?" he leaned back, embarrassed. "Uh, well … uh … yeah."

"Liar," I taunted and curled my finger again, returning his ear to my lips.

He glanced around the yard before leaning over the fence, knowing the increasing bulge in his pants might reveal his thinking. When he leaned in, I whispered, "Do you want to have sex with me?"

"Oh, jeez!" he sighed like his breath had been knocked out of him. "Jeez!" He sighed again and squirmed restlessly where he stood. "Uh … yeah … uh …" He nervously looked around as though the sex police were about to spring from behind a tree and arrest him for having lascivious thoughts. "Uh … well … yeah … uh …" he continued, finally culminating in, "When?"

"When you finish mowing, take a shower. I'll be waiting in the Hetrick Road culvert." I grinned at him, turned, and pranced away, knowing he was watching my swaying ass until I was out of sight.

I had already stashed a blanket and a pillow under the culvert. I sat on a stone, smoking until I heard him call softly and question, "Hello?" from the other end of the culvert.

"Hello," I called back, and he followed my voice to the middle of the culvert.

I mashed the cigarette butt on the concrete wall when he sat beside me and began to speak. He didn't have time to get the words out before I grabbed him and kissed him. I felt him begin to pull back in startled resistance. Then, I felt him relax into the kiss, and his hand moved over my breast.

We had a long and lingering kiss. Then, he pulled back with an anxious whisper, "I … uh … I don't want you to get pregnant."

"I have another week before my period," I said. "I think we're safe."

With that, he began unbuttoning my blouse with nervous hunger as we moved over to the blanket. I had taken the liberty to unfasten my bra before he got there. I didn't want fumbling hands to interfere with the moment. The bra was soon away, and his mouth was on my breast as he pushed his firm erection against my thigh. It seemed too long before we were both disrobed, and then, he pressed his penis down to my vagina and popped it inside me. I winced with a brief moment of pain as I gave my virginity to him, but that was quickly replaced by the pleasure of flesh against flesh as he pushed his hips to my pelvis. There could not have been more than six or eight thrusts of his hips before he suddenly moaned and fell in a lump on top of me. He didn't move. At first, I didn't know what was happening. I kissed his cheek and undulated my hips against him. He rolled over on his back beside me, flaccid and spent. I became quickly aware that that was it. He had climaxed, and it was over—no roller-coaster of pleasure for me, no lying to Mother about having a bad dream. The roller-coaster had barely started to click up the first elevation when the ride ended. My imagination had been infinitely better.

"Wow," he said, lightly panting. "That was wonderful. I never knew being inside a girl would feel so good."

I propped my head on one elbow and said, "I thought you said you had sex before."

"Well, I … uh … I kind of lied," he snickered.

"I'm glad you liked it," I commented, "but it was a bit disappointing for me."

"Disappointing?" he queried.

"Yes," I said. "You had a climax. I never reached mine."

"Wow," he said, in near-total ignorance. "You mean girls cum, too?"

"Well, of course, girls cum," I said and poked a playful finger into his chest. "Why would we want to have sex if it didn't feel good?"

"I don't know," he responded. "I guess I never thought about it. My dad said the main reason a woman has sex is to have kids. You don't need to cum for that."

"Do you think that was the reason I came to your house this morning?" I interrogated him. "Do you think I have acted like someone who wants to have a kid?"

"Yeah, I know," he said, looking around the culvert. "It's a dumb idea, isn't it?"

I lay there in silence and looked at him. He looked back at me, right into my eyes, and said, "So what do I need to do to get you to cum?"

"Are you up for round two?" I smiled as I stroked his face.

"Maybe after a nap," he said, pulling me beside him.

We fell asleep together on that uncomfortable blanket, and then I awoke to his kisses as his hands ran down my body. The sun had begun to set, and the culvert was almost entirely dark, with barely a light streaming in from either end. This time, when we made love, he lasted a bit longer before he climaxed, but he didn't stop pushing after he climaxed, and with my clitoris stimulated, I soon climaxed, too. It wasn't quite the reeling pleasure of my roller-coaster orgasm from masturbation, but it was nice. Afterward, we dressed. I rolled up the blanket, and we walked together to the opening of the culvert. I turned to him and said, "We better walk back separately. Wait here for a while and give me a head start."

"Okay," he said.

I gave him a quick peck on the lips before I turned to climb up the embankment to the street. When I was almost to the top, I heard him call, "Lovella?"

I turned back to him. "Yes."

"This won't be the last time, will it?" He looked up at me with a pleading look on his face.

"No," I said, smiling. "It won't be the last time." Then I climbed the rest of the way up to the street, glanced back at him, and walked home.

CHAPTER 6

The Shocking Truth

The next time I met Tommy in the culvert, I brought a copy of the Kama Sutra.

"Oh my God, Lovella!" he said, thumbing through the illustrations. "Where did you get this?"

"From a catalog," I said.

He turned to me in astonishment.

"From the school?" he asked.

"No, silly," I replied. "I started getting these types of catalogs when I began ordering romance novels from a catalog I found at the city library."

"Still," he gawked, amazed. "This is like … I can't believe you could even order this."

"It's a copy of a book from ancient India, thousands of years old," I said.

"Dang!" he went on, not realizing his oxymoron. "They sure were progressive thousands of years ago."

"What do you think of it?" I queried while I leaned over his shoulder.

He released a long, deep breath. "I mean … is it even possible to get in some of those positions?"

"I am certainly willing to try," I teased and caressed his arm, "but we have got to be a little more careful."

"Careful?" he inquired.

"Yeah," I said, "about not getting me pregnant. Have you ever heard of a condom?"

"A what?" He looked puzzled.

"A rubber," I said.

"Well, yeah," he replied. "My dad told me about them. We had this father and son talk, and he told me that I would probably want to have sex and that I would probably want to use protection and …"

"Could your dad get us some?" I interjected eagerly.

"Well, I … I guess I could ask him," he said, seeming embarrassed to ask his father.

"Great!" I continued. "Ask him, and next time we meet here, bring the condoms."

I started to walk out of the culvert.

"Take that home and read it," I said over my shoulder, "but be sure nobody sees it. We don't need your parents, especially my mother, to find out."

"But wait," he called after me. "Aren't we going to do it?"

"Not today," I called back. "When you get the condoms."

I knew that a brief abstinence period would give him more motivation.

Apparently, Tommy's dad considered it to be a teen boy's rite of passage to have sex, and he had no problem supplying us with condoms, although he did not know just who Tommy was having sex with. As far as he knew, the condoms were just in case Tommy might get laid.

Soon, Tommy and I met in the culvert once or twice a week until the weather started getting cold again. By the time autumn rolled around, he had not only learned several fantastic positions but had learned to hold off until after my orgasm. That summer of my sixteenth year, I discovered I could have more than one orgasm. In fact, on a good day, I might have three or four, and Tommy became an increasingly adept lover.

We met in the culvert on a Sunday afternoon in late September with full intentions of making love all afternoon, but a cold front was moving in. By the time we had barely started, the temperature was falling into the low fifties. I could use some stupid cliché like "we made our own heat," but the fact is, it was too damn cold to have sex. He was intent despite the cold, but I finally stopped him.

"I'm too cold." I pleaded. "We need to go someplace warm."

He began pondering but to no avail. Both our parents were home, and there was no other option. Since Tommy had turned seventeen and had gotten his driver's license over the summer, I got an idea.

"Why don't you borrow your father's car?" I speculated. "And then, we could drive somewhere and make love while we leave the motor running."

"I can't do that," he replied. "What would I tell my dad?"

"Tell him you just want to go for a drive … for practice," I insisted. "He knows you have sex. You don't have to tell him exactly what you need to practice."

"He doesn't like me to drive the car alone in the evening," Tommy resisted, pulling his pants back on.

I had started to dress, as well, no longer being able to tolerate the chill rising across my back. Finally, I looked at him. "You know," I said, shivering as I began, "if we were dating, you would probably be able to take the car on weekends, and we could have it for sex."

He looked at me, startled. "Well, I don't want to take the car just for sex," he said, eyeing me up and down.

"So, I'm just for sex then," I snapped. "I'm not the kind of girl you would want to date, even though you are the boy who took my virginity."

"That's not what I meant," he replied. "But I thought that was what you meant, that all you wanted was sex."

"Sex is wonderful," I said. "But I like you too. I mean, I was using you just because I wanted to try sex, but now I think there is more to us than that."

"You were using me just because you wanted to try sex!" he snarled. "What kind of girl does that?"

"This kind," I snapped back as I poked my finger into my chest. "What's wrong with that? What were you doing it for, and don't tell me it was for love? The bottom line is that you wanted to get laid as much as I did."

"Yeah," he replied, "but it's different. I'm a guy."

"So, does that really make a difference?" I retorted. "What's wrong with a girl wanting sex too? Oh, I forgot, you didn't even think women could have an orgasm till you met me. You didn't know crap about anything. I might never have had sex before, but I taught you more about sex this summer than most guys learn in a lifetime!"

He dropped his head and then looked up at the ceiling of the culvert. "You're right," he said. "I guess it's not fair. I like you, and I think maybe we have become friends. I enjoy having sex with you, but I don't know that I love you. If we hadn't done this, I might even have asked you out sometime. You're pretty, but it feels like we got the cart before the horse, like we did it all backward. That's what I get for being in such a hurry."

I sighed and looked away. "I guess that's what I get, too. I was also in a hurry."

There was a very long and unpleasant silence when he finally spoke.

"So, this dating thing, how do we do that?"

I turned back to him and smiled. "Why don't you come to my house sometime this week and ask me out in front of my parents?"

"Why not just say that I've asked you out, and we can go on a date?" he asked.

"Because my mother will delight with the formality of it and will protest less if she thinks I'm dating a boy from a good family."

"Uh … okay?" he commented.

"Come on," I said. "Let's go."

We walked hand in hand out of the culvert, and I walked home ahead of him.

On the following Tuesday evening at about 6:00 p.m., there was a knock on our front door. Mother was cleaning the kitchen after dinner. I was sitting in my chair in the living room with my nose in a book. Daddy went to the door. When he opened it, Tommy stood on the landing, nervous as a cat in a dog kennel.

"Good evening, Mr. Fuchs. I'm Tommy Smith," he said. "May I come in?"

"Certainly, young man, come on in."

Daddy ushered him in and motioned to one of the chairs for him to sit. Then, Daddy sat back on his end of the sofa. By this time, Mother, hearing the commotion, had come from the kitchen with a dish towel in her hand.

"Oh, hello," she said politely. "You're the Smith boy, aren't you?"

"Yes, Ma'am, Tommy Smith," he replied as he fiddled with his jacket's zipper.

"May I get you some iced tea?" Mother said, darting her eyes back and forth between us.

"No, thank you," replied Tommy. "I don't want to take up your whole evening. I want to ask a question, and then I'll be on my way."

"You've got a question?" Daddy interjected as though he hadn't heard what Tommy had just said.

"Yes, sir," Tommy replied, fixing his gaze on Daddy and trying not to look at me.

"You have a question for me?" Daddy popped. "Is it about peanut butter? I can get you a free case from the factory, you know."

Daddy tried to give everyone peanut butter. We had so much of it in our house when I was growing up that I'm surprised my tongue is not permanently stuck to the roof of my mouth.

"Ah … no … well … ah … yes, but not a question about peanut butter."

Tommy's anxiety was evident. It seemed he thought my parents knew what we had been doing all summer.

"Well, it's a question for you … and Lovella … if you don't mind."

Mother smiled, suddenly realizing that he would probably ask me out.

"What would you like to ask Lovella?" she petitioned.

This kind of *proper* behavior and formality delighted Mother, precisely why I asked him to do it.

"I was wondering," said Tommy, his voice now cracking with anxiety, "if you don't mind," his eyes darted to both parents, "and if Lovella doesn't mind," he said, glancing back at me, "if I might take Lovella out on a date some time?"

I resisted the urge to taunt Mother by shouting, "Date me? When you've already fucked me?" However, my silence was required.

"Lovella is only sixteen," Daddy exclaimed. "Too young to date."

"Most girls date before sixteen, and at least I'm sixteen, Daddy," I protested. "I'm also much more mature than most girls my age."

Daddy snickered. "That you are, Punkin' Patch. Besides, I'm just teasing."

He turned back to Tommy. "How old are you?"

"Sir, I'm seventeen," Tommy said as he adjusted himself upright in the chair.

"So, you're about the same age," Daddy said, turning to Mother. "Drucella, what do you think?"

Mother was leaning against the door frame while she examined Tommy. "You know I don't know much about you, Tommy. I recall that when your family moved into the neighborhood, Lovella and I brought a cake to welcome you, but there hasn't been much contact after that, and I have never had the opportunity to get to know your family."

That was a lie. She knew his father managed the feed store, but she meant they had never socialized at one of her pretentious Friday dinners. She probably also didn't consider that managing a feed store qualified for her delusional status.

"The cake was delicious, Mrs. Fuchs. Thank you." Tommy continued fiddling with his jacket's zipper. "We enjoyed it very much."

"Well," Mother admonished in her air of superiority, "Your mother was very polite, but I didn't get the feeling that she wanted to get to know her neighbors."

"My mother is timid," Tommy replied.

I caught his eye and mouthed, "Don't lie."

He caught himself. "Well, she is shy around some people, like new people. I'm sure she would like you very much if she got the opportunity to know you better."

Mother stared him down. "Do your parents know that you are asking Lovella out?"

It looked like he would tear the zipper loose from the fabric when he tossed it aside and clasped his hands together. "They said it was okay for me to date," he said, "but they don't know that I planned to ask Lovella out—specifically."

"How did the two of you meet?" Mother interrogated.

"We met when you took them the cake," I interjected quickly. "Besides, I go to school with him, and I like to go by their house when I take my walks. Sometimes, I wave at him and say, 'Hi.' Sometimes, I stop, and we chat by the fence."

"Lovella," Mother said firmly. "I presented my question to Mr. Smith, not you."

"Well, she does walk by my house," said Tommy, "and I work in the yard a lot, and we say 'hello' sometimes, not much more than that, and she seems nice, and she's pretty."

"What do you think, John?" Mother said as she looked over at Daddy, with both of us knowing she didn't care about his opinion.

"Oh, it would be fine with me," Daddy replied.

Mother looked directly back at Tommy. "Tell me about your family, Tommy," she said, glaring at him.

"My dad manages the cattle feed mill on the south side of town, and my mom is a stenographer," he replied.

"Oh, your mother is a secretary?" Mother continued. "Where does she work?"

"She works for a business accountant downtown," Tommy replied.

"And you said your father *manages* the feed mill?" Mother interrogated further.

By this time, I was getting boiling mad at her. This had nothing to do with whether it was okay for me to go out with Tommy. This had to do with Mother's socialite-want-to-be hypocrisy and a way of pestering me.

"Yes, my dad manages the feed mill," Tommy said, looking around the room to see if anyone else was interested.

"That's very nice," Mother said, satisfying her social fang. "How about we have your parents over for dinner this Friday night? Then, we will discuss allowing you to date Lovella."

It was all I could do to resist bolting from my chair and strangling her down to the floor. Friday night had nothing to do with me going out with Tommy. It was another one of Mother's attempts to make sure Daddy was home instead of out drinking while she sucked up to anyone she could find who she considered worthy of sucking up to, and it was about being in control.

"Now … now … Drucella," Daddy began chirping. "I have plans for Friday night, and it is too late in the week to change plans."

"Don't you think you could make an exception for Lovella, dear?" she sang sarcastically.

"Well … now … you know I love my daughter, but …"

I chimed in quickly. "Mother, don't you think some other evening of the week would be nice? What about Thursday or maybe even Saturday?"

"Oh, Lovella," she crooned, "you know that Friday is the most optimal time for working people to visit. It leaves the rest of the weekend open and doesn't tax one during the work week."

Tommy must have realized something was happening because he said, "I think Friday is Mom and Dad's bowling night."

"Wonderful!" Mother turned back to him, her demon eyes glaring brightly. "Perhaps we could join them. Wouldn't it be nice to go bowling, John?"

Daddy, cornered, as usual, began his protest. "Oh Lord, I don't even remember the last time I went bowling. I don't even know if I remember how to hold the ball. I … uh …"

By this time, I'd had enough. I stood up and yelled, "STOP IT!" Then, I stormed over to Mother and screamed, "HOW DARE YOU TURN THIS INTO ANOTHER ONE OF YOUR MANIPULATIONS OF DADDY! THIS IS NOT ABOUT YOU! THIS IS NOT ABOUT DADDY! THIS IS ABOUT ME! ME—MOTHER—ME! YOU HAVE NO RIGHT TO HOLD TOMMY'S PARENTS HOSTAGE TO YOUR CONIVING JUST BECAUSE HE WANTS TO GO OUT WITH ME! YOU HAVE NO REAL INTEREST IN MEETING HIS PARENTS! YOU WANT TO USE THIS AS ANOTHER ATTEMPT TO KEEP DADDY FROM GOING OUT FRIDAY NIGHT! HOW DARE YOU EXPLOIT THIS! HOW DARE YOU DO THIS TO ME!" Then, I stormed off to my room and slammed the door.

About ten minutes later, there was a knock at my door.

"Leave me alone!" I yelled.

From the other side of the door, I heard Daddy's voice.

"Punkin' Patch, I don't want to intrude on your time, but I would like to come in for a little while. Is that okay?"

If it had been Mother, and I had suspected that it was, I would have wedged a chair against the door before I would have let her in. She probably knew that, so she sent Daddy.

I got up, unlocked the door, and threw myself back onto the bed. "What is it, Daddy?" I inquired, trying not to glare at him. If nothing else, I always knew that Daddy would rather cut off his hand than hurt me.

"Well, sweetheart," he began. "We sent Tommy home, and then your mother and I talked. You know you hurt her feelings there, don't you?"

"Daddy, I don't care if I hurt her feelings," I huffingly replied. "She doesn't seem to worry about hurting my feelings."

"Now … now … Punkin'," he pleaded. "Your mother loves you. You know that she does. You know she is a bit stern and proper sometimes, but you know she loves you."

"I guess," I said, rolling my eyes and not wanting to have the conversation.

"Well," he continued, "your mother and I talked it over, and we decided it is okay if you want to go out with this boy. We have a few rules to follow, that's all."

I deliberately avoided the bubbly and probably expected response, "Ooh, you mean it, Daddy? Oh, boy!" Instead, I said, "Thank you, Daddy. What are the rules?"

"Well, Punkin' Patch," he continued. "No dating on school nights, be in by 11:00, and no going up to Climax Point."

Climax Point was the local place where lovers went to park and make out, and I'm sure many climaxes had occurred there over the years. The police would cruise through occasionally. I suspected that was more due to their voyeuristic tendencies than catching anyone breaking the law, as though a couple getting off in the dark with a view over the town was some horrible offense. I never understood why sex had been demonized and considered dirty when none of us would exist without it.

"I can live with that, Daddy," I said and hugged him. I knew we could have sex at the drive-in movie theater as easily as Climax Point. That was irrelevant.

The following Saturday night, Tommy picked me up at 6:00 p.m. He took me out for a burger, and we went directly to the drive-in movie. He parked on the far-right side in the back, where we made out for much of the movie. Then, we climbed into the back seat of his father's car to finish it.

The drive-in movie seemed to work perfectly, except that I had to get a summary of each movie from one of my friends before I went home because Mother would inevitably question me about what I had seen when I wasn't, exactly, paying attention.

Somehow, however, our frequency didn't seem to be enough. After all, it was only once a week, and we had initially started having sex two or three times a week. So, we began looking for other ways to get together and became increasingly daring.

Mother had a habit of going grocery shopping every Saturday afternoon. When I could make an excuse not to go with her, I would sneak Tommy into the house while Daddy was out in the shed, and we would make love in my room without either of them knowing about it. This was fine, except we usually went to the movies on Saturday night, so it didn't leave much space between one love-making episode and another. There were times when we simply watched the movie and ate popcorn.

We had sex in his parent's garage a couple of times. Then, over the summer, we returned to the culvert, but that had lost its appeal after we got used to having sex in a nice bed. Sex began to feel a little mundane, so we sought the novel. We did it in a cemetery where he bent me over the headstone of a man who died in 1877. We did it in a changing room at a clothing store. Then, one late afternoon in July, while Daddy was at work and Mother was away at some lady's luncheon, we did it in the laundry room of our house.

Tommy came by right after Mother had left for her luncheon. I stuffed Mother's wringer-washer full and set it to run. When the agitator swished the clothes back and forth in those old washers, it created a lovely vibration. Tommy had me pushed up against the washer in a standing position. I wrapped my legs around him as we combined the vibrations of the washer and his thrust to achieve our excitement. We were moaning and panting furiously when the door to the laundry room suddenly opened, and there stood Mother in her perfect dress. Her face dropped immediately from smiling curiosity to a look of abject horror. She gasped, and one of her white-gloved hands flew over her mouth. She tried to shout my name, but hyperventilation hit her before she could get it out, "Love—el—a!—fa!—ah!—ha!—fa!—fa!—a!—a!—a!—a!"

I watched gleefully as she fell, panting away from the door, collapsing into a chair at the kitchen table just past the laundry room door. Tommy had come to a complete stop and turned to look. Hanging on with one arm around his shoulders, I grabbed his chin with my free hand and twisted it back toward me.

"Finish!" I panted.

"But your mom," he pleaded.

"Finish!" I demanded again. This is the last time she'll let me see you, so finish!"

He began to thrust again, and in only a few more strokes, I reached the most exhilarating climax, right there, in front of Mother. Tommy's nervous whimpering cum briefly followed.

Of course, Mother refused to look and turned pale from hyperventilation. Her eyes squinted, and she turned toward the floor opposite the laundry room door.

After we dressed, Tommy tiptoed past Mother and out the back door. I went and pulled a chair up, knee-to-knee, with Mother. She was still reeling from her panic attack and fanning herself with one glove that she had removed.

"Are you okay?" I said, feigning concern.

When she looked up, horror turned to rage. Abruptly, she stuck a pointed finger in my face and shouted with neck-inflated veins and a jaw-clenching growl. "LOVELLA FUCHS, HOW DARE YOU DESECRATE OUR HOME AND MY REPUTATION LIKE THIS!"

I sat back calmly, watching the havoc, content in my power, smug in the knowledge that I had shaken her to her core. "Desecrate is a strong word, don't you think, Mother?"

"I SWEAR YOU ARE A DEAMON!" she shouted. "I don't know how I even gave birth to you!"

"That's easy, Mother," I said smugly. "You gave birth to me by doing the same thing that Tommy and I just did. You fucked my father."

"STOP YOUR FOUL MOUTH, AND DON'T YOU EVEN COMPARE YOURSELF TO ME!" she screamed. "You cannot compare that ... that ... SIN!"

At seventeen, I found I had little fear of Mother, and I couldn't care less about her approval. I smiled as I said, "Sex is sex whether it is sanctioned by the church or not, Mother. Fucking is fucking, and if sex is dirty, then we're all dirty because we all started with an orgasm."

The veins in her neck swelled to at least twice their normal size. For a moment, I thought she was going to slap me. Then, I thought she might have a stroke, and for a moment, I almost wished she would. By that time, I was fed up with Mother. I had decided that she would never be allowed to control me again. I would do what I wanted, whether she approved or not, and I harbored all the resentment that had accumulated since my early childhood.

"I forbid you EVER to see that boy again! EVER!" she raged. "He will NEVER set foot in this house again, and you will have NOTHING to do with him! DO YOU UNDERSTAND?"

"Yes, Mother," I said calmly and confidently. "I understand."

It didn't matter. I knew I would do as I pleased when I pleased. Only a few obstacles might ever stand in my way, and Mother would never again be one of them.

CHAPTER 7

Prom Queen? Yeah, Right!

To say that I was grounded after the laundry room incident would be an understatement. It was three months before Mother would allow me out the front door without her escort, except for school. Even then, she drove by the school during lunch break to check on me and ensure I wasn't *misbehaving*. I saw Tommy at school and explained how Mother was taking it. I told him I didn't expect him to wait. After all, he was going to graduate that year, anyway, and I think that we both finally had to admit that it was just about the sex. I loved him as a friend, and we had established a pretty solid friendship that didn't require sex to sustain. As well, we had worn out the novelty of learning about sex. So, it was something quickly surrendered.

Gretta had known everything all along. I kept no secrets from her. In a way, she was envious. I didn't realize how envious she was, or exactly why, at the time. I knew she found Tommy attractive, but I didn't realize that she had a crush on him and had secretly wished that she could date him. I had stood in the way of that without realizing it, and she, being the good friend that she was, had never told me that she had a thing for Tommy until after I stopped seeing him for sex. She would never have tried to interfere as long as I was seeing Tommy, but soon after, I caught the two of them stealing glances at one another between classes. It wasn't long before he asked her out. It was no bother to me. If I had known earlier, I would have stepped aside so they could be together. Gretta wanted something much more profound than what I wanted from Tommy, and I think he also wanted that depth of relationship. Anyway, I was done. I had that adventure completed and a whole world left to explore.

I could have marched out or sneaked out of the house at any time, but I abided by Mother's grounding rules if only to give her the illusion that she still maintained some control. Gretta and I saw each other at school, and our friendship easily outlived that little incident.

As soon as Mother would let me go out again, I took Gretta to the public library and introduced her to the Kinsey books. I loaned her my copy of the Kama Sutra; at first, she fanned through the pages with Tommy's same wide-eyed fascination. She pointed at pictures and bit her knuckles. She giggled and blushed, but with me as her guide and Tommy teaching her what we had learned together, she was soon just as hooked on sex as I was, but only with Tommy. He was her man; unlike me, she did not need to explore further. It was love that she wanted, and sex just happened to be the icing on the cake. There was a vast difference between how her relationship with him started and how mine had. There was something much deeper than the physical between them, and it didn't take Einstein to see that they were falling in love.

Gretta wasn't one to get in trouble like I was. She was more reserved, perhaps because she had a good relationship with her parents. She would never get caught fucking any boy in her mother's laundry room, especially the one she loved. Besides, she never needed to piss anyone off. She did not have my obsession to frustrate and anger her mother. She had a good relationship with both her parents and cherished her time with Tommy, whereas I had only cherished sex.

Tommy calmed down quite a bit after the laundry room incident. Maybe that is because I no longer had an evil influence over him. Of course, his parents never found out what happened. Mother was too embarrassed to tell anyone, not even Daddy. She told Daddy I was grounded for stealing a pack of cigarettes from the market. I knew she wouldn't tell. She thought keeping me away from Tommy was a punishment, and I never let her know otherwise. She knew me well enough to know I had been the instigator, not Tommy. Yes, everyone's reputation was safe, even Mother's. However, my reputation was only safe for the time being. I had determined that I would go ahead and become the slut that the boys at school had always accused me of being. They didn't have to taunt me about my name. I would show them just how well I could Fuchs!

By the time Tommy graduated, he and Gretta had dated for several months. That following summer, she dropped out of school and married him. He worked for the feed mill with his father, and Gretta got a job as a waitress at a local truck stop. Tommy's dad bought him a blood-red

Chrysler Imperial convertible for his graduation gift, and when they married, his dad co-signed for them to buy a little house. Before she was eighteen, Gretta was pregnant. I couldn't help but look at it and think, *what a waste.* If that was the life that made them happy, I blessed them for having it, but the older I got, the more I wanted out of Climax, and the less I could see myself settling down into some boring and mundane, small-town life with a blue-collar husband, and a baby on my hip.

They were doing what most kids did in those days. They got married and started a family. I had no such plans. I had dreams. I had exploration to do. I had read books about faraway places and wanted to see them all. Gretta and Tommy could have the small-town life, scraping by and raising kids. I wanted none of it. I would see the world. I would get a college degree, and I might even get a job at the Kinsey Institute, but not necessarily in that order. I planned to go to college as soon as I graduated high school. I assumed that one must have an education to see the world. It certainly wouldn't hurt to be well-versed if I were going to hobnob about the globe. Mother, of course, thought I should do as Gretta: meet a nice boy, get married, and have babies, as long as that nice boy was well-to-do. However, Mother would have wanted to hand-pick the boy and ensure he lived up to her delusional standards of quality and future promise. The mere fact that Mother wanted me to get married was enough to turn me against it. So, despite her nagging me about all the opportunities to *"have a nice, secure home"* in my *"own little hometown,"* I applied to several colleges and took my entrance exams early in my senior year of high school.

My senior year was dull. For one thing, if a boy asked me out, Mother would do everything to sabotage it unless he was from a *"reputable family."* If he met her standards, she would try to shove him so far down my throat I would choke on his shoelaces. After all this time, after knowing that I despised every idea she ever had for me, she still labored under the delusion that I would come around to her way of thinking. She ran off more boys from *"reputable families"* by pushing them at me than she did the *"less acceptable"* boys, whom she deliberately tried to drive away. When she liked a boy, you would have thought she was trying to sell him her prized cow. The boys thought she was weird, and I didn't care. Besides, I would find a way to screw any boy who struck my fancy, and I did. They were lucky to experience my skills, and as time went on and I learned more, my sexual talents expanded.

Of course, I got a bad reputation. Boys talk, don't they? Besides, they had been making fun of my name since elementary school. They had always accused me of being a slut, so why not be one? I even enjoyed having the reputation of a slut. I relished that some little whisper of it would eventually reach Mother's ears, and her torment would linger. However, I wasn't exactly a slut. I wouldn't sleep with just anyone. I just slept with anyone I wanted. There is a difference. By the time I graduated, there was not a single boy in that school that I didn't have—if I wanted him. The others were beggars and wishers. The more they tried to get up my skirt, the more I took pleasure in tossing them to the curb. Some of those were the jocks and the guys that other girls would have thrown themselves at if they thought there was a chance, but I was not going to have sex with some guy I didn't like just because he was cute. Some would stand back and act aloof, pretending that they didn't want me, but let's face it, a girl knows. I was beautiful, and they were horny little high school boys. None of them could pull off acting aloof very well or for long. I always knew who wanted me. If I wanted them, I would pick the time when I was ready. Then, they never knew what hit them.

Ultimately, high school was a bore. I had read every book for every class and more within the semester's first few weeks. By that time, I usually knew more than the teacher. Why bother? I couldn't wait to get my diploma and get out of there. Despite everything else, my grades were excellent, and I got a scholarship to Penn State University, where I planned to major in reproductive biology—of course. I had found my muse, and my muse was between my legs. I was determined to learn everything I could learn about it. I later discovered that reproductive biology wasn't an option, so I had to settle for plain old biology and pre-med. That was fine with me as long as I would have a chance to go into sexual research.

When Mother discovered my intended major, she nearly had a heart attack, but she consoled herself with the illusion that I would have a pre-med degree. She then began telling everyone she knew, those she only half knew and many she had never previously met, that I was going to be a doctor.

I grew sick of hearing her banter over the phone: "Oh yes, yes, our daughter … Lovella is going to Penn State this fall. She is going to be a doctor. Oh yes, we are so proud of her."

One day, I sat in the chair across from the telephone and deliberately wore no panties under my skirt. I watched as she was cooing over my upcoming medical degree and waited for a glance in my direction. As soon as it came, I spread my legs and flashed the muff-dragon full in her face. It roared silently and had the exact frightening result I had hoped it would. She didn't quite scream, but the shrill undertone of her gasp caused a shift in the conversation.

"Oh, nothing," she whimpered, shaking her scornful finger in my direction.

The muff-dragon flared and silently roared again! This time, I even added my sound effects. "*Roar!*" I exclaimed in a whisper. I was barely able to contain my laughter at Mother's revulsion.

She gasped again in disgust, angrily whispering as she clamped her palm over the mouthpiece, "Stop it!" Then, she returned to her call. "Oh, I'm fine, really. It's nothing. I sat on a pin." She held her hand over the phone again and, with an intense whisper, exclaimed, "Lovella! Stop that nonsense this instant!" It wasn't like she could get up and walk away. In those days, the phone was mounted to a specific spot, and one could not continue talking and be able to walk any further than the length of the receiver cord, which was rarely more than three feet.

The muff-dragon could not be contained, and soon, I was laughing hysterically. When she finally made an excuse and hung up the phone, she shouted, "Lovella Fuchs! Do you have one single solitary ounce of decency in you? What if your father had walked in?"

On the one hand, she wanted to throttle me and ground me forever, but on the other hand, I was going to college to be a doctor. That, alone, fed her hunger for prestige to almost overflowing.

"I think that Daddy would have been quite amused, Mother." I smiled gleefully. "Where is your sense of humor?"

"That is not the least bit funny!" she growled.

"Daddy told me he was proud of me," I said. "He told me—just me—not the whole town, not everyone he thought would possibly listen. He said, 'Pumpkin Patch. I'm so proud I could pop,' or did he say 'poop?' Either way, he told me he was proud of me." The grin on my face made the Cheshire Cat look sullen.

"I might be proud of you too," she stammered and shamed, "if you didn't act like such an infidel all the time!"

"Infidel? That's a powerful word, Mother—Mommy," I continued. "Anyway, Daddy said he wished he was as smart as me, and I told him, 'Daddy, you are as smart as me or Mother or anyone else. Just because you didn't go to college doesn't mean that you aren't smart.'"

"Yes," she said, crossing sides, "I've always tried to convince your father that he was meant for something greater."

"There you go again," I said.

"There I go again, what?" She looked puzzled.

I sat up in the chair, crossed my legs, and adjusted my posture to be lady-like. "You really don't get it, do you, Mother? You honestly, in your heart of hearts, don't understand." A revelation had just hit me, and I continued. "All this time, I thought you were just being a bitch, but you actually believe this shit. You honestly have thought, all these years, that you could make Daddy into something he's not. I guess we are from different worlds, aren't we? I love Daddy for who he is. I have no need to make him into anything. You want to turn him into someone you wish you had married."

There was a quick grimace, but the puzzlement on her face expanded as she sat there silently.

Finally, I said, "Go on, Mother. Tell all your friends I'm going to medical school. Take an ad out in the paper if you want to. It's okay. I get it. You think that my success is your success. You think that one day, something will happen to make you finally feel good about yourself, but rather than trying to change yourself, you have tried to change Daddy and me. You have tried to make us into what you want us to be instead of making yourself into someone who could accept imperfection."

She stood and walked out of the room.

Mother kept doing what Mother always did. She was determined that I would meet the right young man, and we would all live happily ever after, or at least she would. She must have put an ad in the paper: "*Wanted, young men between the ages of sixteen and eighteen to annoy my daughter. Must be from a good, "upstanding, worthy family," and it's a plus if you are ugly."*

By the time spring rolled around, all the preparations were going into graduation. I had senior photos taken, and Mother picked her favorite. We bought class rings and ordered caps and gowns. I just went along with it. Whatever she wanted, I accepted. Then, there was senior prom.

At least two months before the prom, Mother asked me if I had a date. The problem was that boys were less likely to ask out the girl who had rocked their world sexually and have the embarrassment of going out with the town slut. Instead, they were looking for *Little Miss Sweet and Pretty*, who would not show them up by being more intelligent and assertive than them. I didn't fit the bill, not that I wasn't pretty enough or could have manners if I wanted to, but I was the girl they fucked. I was the practice model they used to learn the ropes while looking for a virgin, someone they could show off to Mommy and Daddy.

Not only had I matured early sexually, but I had matured early mentally and physically. Before I made it to my senior year, I needed a double-D bra to carry the load I was packing. I still had a nice size waist of 28 inches, but the average prom dress didn't seem to be made for me. I was taller than most girls at 5'11", and my feet, unfortunately, were large enough that I had to start special-ordering shoes. Mother said I must have gotten the height from Uncle Walter on her side of the family. Lord knows I didn't get it from Daddy's side. They were all shrimp. I was a tall, big-busted girl. I didn't think there was a prom dress anywhere for me, nor did I care.

Nonetheless, Mother was determined that I would be the "Belle of the Ball" at senior prom. She dragged me to dress shops and insisted I could go to the prom even if I didn't have a date. On the rare occasion that there was a dress I could wear, it was hideous. Once, she made me put on this baby-pink floral thing with enough lace and ruffles to construct a commercial fishing net. Although very few fit, she still beamed when I came out of the dressing room. "Oh darling, you look—STUNNING!"

"Oh, stop it, Mother!" I exclaimed. "I look like Little Ms. Muffett in her damned kindergarten Easter dress. All we need is a tuffet and a spider!"

"Oh, no-no-no-no-no-no-honey. Don't be like thaaaaat," she cooed as she glanced around to see if anyone had heard me say *damned.* "Why, when we do your hair and make-up, that dress will make you look like the princess that you are."

"Mother!" I snarled, "You are going to make me puke. I am *not* a princess and am *not* wearing this dress!"

"But, honey," she continued to coo, "I hate to say it, but you are a little hard to fit, and we have looked at so many dresses, and this one is very pretty." She grabbed the sleeve of a woman who happened to be passing by. "Excuse me. I was just wondering if I could get your opinion."

The woman turned around, initially startled, and collected herself. "Yes? What?"

Mother pulled her toward me, "Don't you think my daughter looks absolutely stunning in this dress?" she said, lightly pinching the woman's arm.

"Mother!" I snapped. "That's a leading question and totally unfair. Besides, I look like a cartoon whore."

The woman was now nervous, realizing she had just been pulled into a family argument.

Mother completely ignored me and kept her focus on the woman. "Go on," she pleaded. "What is your *honest* opinion? How does my daughter look in this dress?"

The nervous woman darted her eyes, searching for an escape, "Well … I … well …"

"No, please," Mother continued to plead. "*Honestly*—what do you think?"

The woman shored up her courage, "Well, the dress is … well … it's a bit frumpy looking, don't you think?"

I laughed robustly. "You see, Mother!" I proclaimed between giggles, "I'm not going to the prom. Instead, I'm going to meet Shirley Temple for candy-wandy on The Good Ship Lollypop, and we'll pick up lollypop sailors so we can dance a little jig on the pier."

Mother looked at the woman dismissively, "Thank you for your opinion," she said politely but tensely, "I believe you are right."

The woman walked away, and Mother turned to me with one of her glares. I was still laughing while I pranced in the awful thing in front of the mirror. I tried to ignore her, but she walked over, leaned into my face, and whispered crossly, "All right, Lovella. You win. What do you want me to do? We have been to every shop in three towns and found nothing we can agree upon."

I turned to her and smiled. "Mother, I don't have to go to the prom. I don't want to go to the prom. I don't care. Really—I don't. This seems like it is more important to you than it is to me."

"Well, it should be important to you, too," she said, examining her hair in the mirror and straightening her collar. "This is one of the most important events of your life, of any girl's life. Lovella, in just a few months, you will go away to college, and then ... after that ... only the Lord knows where you will end up. You may never see these kids again and have grown up with them. The prom—the prom ..." She searched for words. "The prom is a milestone in life, a memory maker, an unforgettable moment in time."

She took my hand and led me to a chair. Then, she sat across from me and leaned in.

"Here it comes," I thought, "the motherly talk."

I was right.

"Lovella, honey ..." She smiled as she patted my hand. "A prom is so much more important than a dance. It is a rite of passage, just as important as your graduation. It says that you have arrived as an adult. You have made it through, and you will have a party with your classmates and mark the occasion of your transition into adulthood."

I sighed. "So ... If I have a date, I'll only go to the prom with a boy for one night. All I will get out of it is some punch and cake, and then, I'll spend the rest of the evening repeatedly removing his hand from my ass. Why bother? If I don't have a date, which I probably won't, who fucking cares? I would just as soon stay home and read."

"Lovella, please don't use that tone or that language," she pleaded. "Believe me, you will end up regretting it later and wishing you had gone if you don't go to your one-and-only senior prom, dear."

"Mother!" I crackled. "I don't have a date, nor do I want one, and if you think I'm going to go out publicly wearing something like this, you are sorely mistaken."

She leaned back in her chair. "How about we have a dress made for you? Mrs. Newall from the church is an excellent seamstress. I'm sure she could make a dress that would fit you perfectly. All we have to do is find a pattern that she can alter to your measurements. It might cost a little more, but as I said, honey, this is your time to shine."

I despised it when Mother talked to me like a little girl.

"Okay, Mother—fine," I bargained, "but I get to pick the pattern and the material, and there will be no arguments about it."

Mother agreed, and then we went to some sewing stores to look at dress patterns. She wasn't happy that I picked a pattern for a simple strapless gown with clean lines and no frills. Instead of the usual gaudy, colorful prom dress, it looked like something a mature woman would wear to a formal dinner.

"Lovella, your bosom is too big for a strapless gown!" she gasped. "Honey, you will pop right out of that thing."

"Maybe that's just what I want to do," I taunted. "My boobs are kind of like wild horses. They were never meant to be corralled."

"More like planets orbiting the sun," Mother said under her breath, thinking I wouldn't hear. She shot me a quick and pert little smile when I glanced at her and shook them.

Mother finally convinced me to let Mrs. Newall make a neck strap for it, "just in case."

I picked out a black fabric with tiny glints of silver threads, giving it just a hint of sparkle. I thought it was very glamorous, but Mother had to put in her two cents for pink or cream satin. I would have nothing of it. I held her to her bargain and got my black and silver evening gown for the prom. I had not known Mother had ordered a pair of white pumps for my big feet before she took me shopping for a dress. I guess she assumed I would wear what she picked for me. The gown, I thought, would have looked much more fashionable with black stiletto heels, but in the end, the white shoes looked okay. Still, the heels added two inches to my height, so I was stacked to six foot one.

It was many years after those last few months of high school before I realized that Mother was trying to make peace with me. Those shopping trips for my prom dress resulted in a compromise between us that seldom occurred. Too often, we would end up in a stubborn stand-off. But as I look back, I realize that Mother had her moments of insight and understanding. My prom, after all, was going to be a defining moment in my life, but not the way Mother had anticipated.

When Mrs. Newall delivered the dress, it fit perfectly. I put it on in my room and went to the living room to show everyone. I will never forget the look on Daddy's face when I walked in wearing that dress. It was as though he had fallen in love for the first time.

"Oh, Punkin' Patch," he crooned. "Don't you look like a dream walking?"

I smiled, knowing that it pleased him. Mother and Mrs. Newall were both just as pleased and as complimentary.

Mother had taken care of everything. She had thought of everything down to the last little detail, and there was nothing that she hadn't thought of.

At about 3:00 a.m. that night, I bolted straight up in bed. "Oh my God," I groaned. "She's thought of everything! The bitch has picked my date!"

CHAPTER 8

Payback is a Bitch

After preparing me for prom, Mother did not mention boys at all. I found that suspicious. I knew she had to have something up her sleeve. I expected she would bring some boy around to show him off to me, but there was nothing. So, I began to think maybe I was wrong. Maybe she would allow me to go alone, let Daddy drop me off, and pick me up later. When I found out that Daddy had given up a drinking night to do that, I relaxed further. Still, I would ask Mother about prom, and she would say, "Don't you worry about it, honey. I've got it all taken care of."

"Mother," I demanded, "I don't like the sound of that, and I don't want any surprises!"

"Well, your Daddy will be there for you on prom night," she humored me. "Won't you, John?"

"Oh, yeah … yeah!" he acquiesced. "Got it all taken care of."

After all, prom was on a Friday night, and if Daddy had given up his drinking night, maybe it would be taken care of. There was nothing I could do but wait.

I should have trusted my gut. On prom night, after I had dressed, done my hair, put on makeup, and was ready to go, Mother asked me to sit at the kitchen table, and Daddy joined us. She sat in a chair across the corner of the table, took my hand, and lightly patted it. I thought, *Oh Shit! Kill me now! Something's up, and she's already tightening the noose!*

"Lovella," she snickered like a sneaky little kid. "I have a surprise for *you*."

"What, Mother," I glared, "you're secretly a lesbian?"

"Oh, no, no, No," she grinned, offering none of the usual or expected reproaches for my comment. My mind flipped inside my head. *Oh, my God!* I thought. *She didn't even take the bait. She didn't scold me. She didn't grimace. Oh God! This is bad. This is very, very bad.*

I was right. It was very, very bad.

She took a plummeting, deep breath and said, "Guess what? … You have a date for the prom!"

Every superlative in my head was battling for expression. What shall I say, *"Fuck me over a meat saw? Goddamn!"*

It was all too much. My cheeks turned hot, like someone had thrown coffee in my face. I wanted to scream, but I knew it was too late. She had me. I was in her clutches again! I wanted to shriek. I wanted to explode, but I could only sit there and tremble.

"Oh, John," she sang. " Look how nervous the poor thing is. Bless her heart. I know her heart is just a flutter."

As though the sullen look on my face did not communicate it, she did not gather that I was trembling with rage, not twittering with excitement. She ignored my glare that silently communicated; I *want to fucking kill you!*

"Ain't that great?" Daddy chimed. "Sissy got you a date."

Holy Shit! He was in on it! He had betrayed me and collaborated with the bitch from hell. I was furious with both, but my love for Daddy is perhaps the only reason I did not act on my urge to choke the life out of her! It was also the only reason I didn't storm out, refuse to be a part of this charade, and seethe in my room all evening.

You would have thought, from their expressions, that their disabled child had just taken her first steps from the wheelchair. At any moment, I expected Mother to shout, "Praise Jesus! It's a miracle!"

When I could finally squeeze words through the vice grip of my vocal cords, I asked, "And … who would my date be … Mmm—Mother?"

Shades of Hitchcock and images from the bathtub scene in *Psycho* darkened my mind. Perhaps it is good that we choose not to act on some thoughts.

"Well," she replied, "actually … he will be arriving at any moment. I don't think you know him because he is from Grove City. His father is a doctor, and he plans to be a doctor, too. Isn't that wonderful? With your interest in medicine, you'll have so much to talk about."

"Mother," I jeered, "you are expecting me to go to my prom with a boy I've never met, whom I don't even remotely know? Oh, my God … a blind date—for prom?"

"He is a charming boy, Lovella," she continued. "I met his family at a church function. They are wonderful people. It's just a blind date, honey. I'm sure you'll like him."

"Mother!" I emphasized, just trying to get her to shut up. "Have I ever, even once, shown any interest in a boy you liked?"

"No," she said, "but that's just because you like to be a little rebellious and pick boys who don't have good status. If you had ever stopped being so obstinate and just tried to spend a little time with those boys I picked for you, I'm sure there were several of them you would have liked once you got to know them."

"Yeah," Daddy chimed in. "Sissy says this one is a good-looking kid from a nice family."

I had no idea how she had convinced Daddy to participate in her subterfuge, but he was hooked like a trout on a fly rod.

About that time, there was a knock at the door. I felt like an animal in a trap, gathering the courage to chew my leg off rather than be caught, but there I was. I could have thrown one of my usual fits, but if only for Daddy, I decided to go through with the charade.

"John dear, would you get the door, please?" Mother cooed.

She continued to pat my hand, perhaps not knowing that what I really wanted was both my hands around her neck, choking her until her tongue turned blue.

"Well, hello, young man," Daddy exclaimed from the living room, and I knew this farce had to continue.

Mother stopped patting me and gripped my hand. "Come on now, dear, let's go meet him."

Mother stood but never let go of my hand. She must have known that, given half a chance, I would have darted out the back door and run, screaming frantically, into the darkness. She led me to the living room like a little girl led into church. I found myself walking zombie-like under the control of its master. When we rounded the corner, there he stood. A dream? Yes—a nightmare!

He was at least six foot three, gangly and slightly chubby at the same time. He looked like his large, flat ass had been glued on top of a couple of long, old lady legs that narrowed at the ankles. He wore a baby-blue tuxedo with pants so short that the cuff barely covered the top of his mismatched socks. His hair was black, and I counted at least three distinct cowlicks swooping in different directions. He must have had allergies because he kept a handkerchief, which he repeatedly pulled from his pocket, to wipe his snotty red nose. I didn't know whether to puke or faint.

As soon as he saw me, he waddled over, stretched out his hand, and proclaimed in a nasal-clogged tone, "Oh, hi! Hi! I'm Nathan. You must be Lovella. It is so nice to meet you."

I hesitantly extended three fingers, imitating Mother's *lady-like* handshake, hoping to have minimal contact in case the snot was evidence of a cold instead of allergies. "Yes," I said quietly.

"Oh, look at her," Mother proclaimed. "Isn't that sweet? She is usually not this quiet, Nathan. She usually is just talk-talk-talk. Aren't you, dear?"

"Yes, Mother," I hissed through clenched teeth.

He handed me a corsage, and not finding anywhere to put it; Mother finally pinned it between my tits. His little boutonnière was already attached.

"Oh, before you go," Mother reveled in her triumph, "let's get pictures! John, get the camera."

Daddy rushed to the end table, where he had his camera. He had a box of flashbulbs ready to blind us as Mother pushed us together and arranged a pose. I don't know why Daddy insisted on keeping that old camera. Many of the newer models had flash cubes, so you didn't have to change the bulb every time you took a picture. However, he insisted that he had a good camera and there was no use in "changing horses in mid-stream." Suddenly, *pop* went the flash bulb, and the room filled with a flash of blue-white light. Daddy quickly twisted the knob on the camera till the film clicked in place for the next shot. Then, he replaced the bulb and prepared for another as Mother exclaimed, "Oh, here, let me get in this one. I want a picture with my little girl on her special night." Mother quickly posed herself into the picture, and *POP*, we were blinded again. It would be at least ten minutes before I would stop having a navy blue spot in the middle of my vision. The blinding flash was sufficient to cause me to want to run, but when Mother's antics were added to the scene, I began to feel like a hound at a fireworks show. I had to get out of there.

"Come on, let's go," I said, grabbing Nathan's hand and pulling him toward the door.

"But don't you want to get a couple more pictures?" Mother queried.

"No," I exclaimed. "Don't want to be late, do we, Nathan?"

And without too much clamor, I was able to drag Nathan through the door. He wobbled down the sidewalk as Mother and Daddy came out on the front steps to wave goodbye. Oh Lord, help me! It looked like a scene from a Gomer Pile movie!

When we arrived at the car, he stepped to the passenger side door, opened it, bowed, and motioned with his opposite hand for me to enter the vehicle as though he were a valet for the fucking Queen of England.

"Cut the shit," I growled low through clenched teeth. "Just get in the damn car."

I looked back and dutifully smiled at the parents as Nathan did what I told him and moved quickly around to get in on the driver's side. To think that Daddy had given up a drinking night for this horse shit was beyond me. Nathan pulled away from the curb as we waved one more time at the parents. I was more inclined to flip my middle finger but played along.

I must admit that Nathan had a very nice ride—a new, plush, and comfortable Cadillac. As soon as we got in the car, I couldn't take it any longer. I reached into my purse, took out a cigarette, and plugged in the car's cigarette lighter.

"Nice ride," I said, "yours?"

"No," he replied. "It belongs to my dad. I guess your mom told you he's a doctor. He does all right."

The lighter popped out, and as I reached for it to light my cigarette, he said, "You know, some of the new research is beginning to indicate that smoking can be detrimental to your health."

"Really," I replied sarcastically. "Research probably also indicates that a bullet to your head can be detrimental to your health. Wanna try it and see?"

He giggled—actually giggled. "You know, you are hilarious."

"Well, thank you very much," I continued with sarcasm. "That's just what a girl wants to hear from her prom date. Find me a gun, and we'll test my theory."

"Well, you're pretty too," he went on, oblivious. "When your mom told me you were pretty, I thought, oh, she's just pulling my leg to get me to go out with you cause all the pretty girls have dates for the prom, and I thought you must be a troll or something, and that's why your mom was trying to set me up with you. But you're pretty, and I'm glad I let your mom talk me into this."

"Well, she didn't tell me a fucking thing about you," I snarled, "and guess what?"

"What?" he questioned, still oblivious.

"Never mind." I stopped myself from saying, "Because you *are* a troll." I didn't want to be cruel. After all, he was genuinely innocent in all this. Instead, I cooled my heels and took a long drag from my cigarette.

"So," I said, deliberately blowing smoke in his direction, "tell me about yourself."

"Well, like I said," he blabbered, "my dad is a family doctor in Grove City, and I grew up there. I have two sisters, one older, like seven years older, and I have a younger sister about fourteen months younger than me. It's like my parents had Claudia, my oldest sister, and then nothing for seven years, and then, Blam! Blam! Here I came, and then Bernadette, my younger sister. I've been around my dad's clinic my whole life, and I love science and medicine, so I'm going to study medicine. So, I'm starting Carnegie Mellon next fall with a major in pre-med. Oh, by the way, our prom at my high school is next week. Since I came over here to be your date for your prom, do you want to come over to Grove City to be my date for our prom?"

"No, thank you," I said quickly as I popped the lighter in for another cigarette. "I think one prom is more than enough for me."

I had the feeling it was going to be a night of chain-smoking. Mother had picked the boy she wanted me to marry, a wealthy doctor's kid destined to become a doctor, or so she thought. Never mind that he was more annoying than a gang of flies at a picnic and probably asked me to his prom because he couldn't get a date at his school. Luckily, I had a whole pack of cigarettes.

"Anyway," he continued, airheaded, "my sister Claudia is a nurse. She works in Pittsburgh, so this medical thing is all in the family. Say, I don't know how to get to your school."

Great! I thought. *I get to spend the night wandering around Climax, listening to this idiot babble.*

"Well, you missed the street and will have to circle back. Take a right up here," I said, pointing my cigarette between two fingers.

Eventually, we got there, and I was sure to get out of the car before Sir Galahad could run around and chivalrously throw open the door. I straightened my dress, adjusted my purse, and walked ahead, hoping no one would see me with him. There was no such luck. Even though Nathan was three feet behind me, just as we entered the doorway, Jane Murphy, one of the cheerleaders with her date, Mike Fulbright, one of the football players (how very, very, cliché), intercepted us.

"Oh, Lovella!" she exclaimed. "You look stunning in that dress! Mike, doesn't she look stunning?"

Mike grinned and eyed my cleavage, which the dress amply revealed. I had taught him a thing or two that Jane didn't know about, and I could see he was missing it.

She went on. "Oh, is this your date?"

Nathan had caught up with me, and she eyed him up and down like a pig for slaughter. She extended her hand. "Hi, my name is Jane, and this is Mike."

Nathan took her hand and, between sniffles, said, "How do you do? My name is Nathan."

"Well, I'm pleased to meet you, Nathan," she said. As she turned to walk into the building, over her shoulder, she sarcastically chirped, "Lovella, you *really* know how to pick the men, don't you?"

Fucking bitch! I thought. Then, I spouted back at her. "Well, at least you know how to pick your nose, dear." I smiled a snarling smile and walked on. She said nothing, but I know she was thinking, *bitch,* or worse. I avoided the insecure brag of telling her Nathan's father was a doctor. It would have made a difference to her. It didn't, to me, and I did not need to impress her.

Our school had an area that doubled as a theater, meeting hall, and study hall. It was a large expanse with a stage at one end. There were hardwood floors throughout and columns up the middle to support the high ceiling. The band was set up on stage for events like the prom, and the school desks were all moved out to open a dance floor. At the opposite end of the room from the stage was a refreshments area, and chairs had been lined against the walls where people could sit if they chose. The theme for the prom was *Memories of the Beach.* Yet, I'm sure over half the students there had never been to a real beach.

I nearly gagged when I first heard the idea for the prom, and I was not disappointed by the spectacle when I got there. The walls were lined with construction-paper palm trees, and the refreshment table was covered in tacky-looking Tiki masks that doubled as candle holders. Beach towels had been tacked to the wall for additional decoration. I couldn't help thinking it had all been Jane's idea as prom committee president. I snickered as I strolled around the room, eyeing the absurdity with Nathan trotting after me like a puppy.

"You want to dance?" Nathan pleaded as we strolled.

"I think I'll have some punch first," I said, heading for the refreshments table. I hoped someone might have spiked the punch, but teachers were carefully chaperoning the table.

Nathan had to be the gentleman, so he ladled me a cup of punch while I picked at finger foods.

"Thank you, darling," I said semi-politely as I began to sip and look away. The punch tasted more like melted sherbet than anything refreshing and was ten times too sweet, but it was a distraction, momentarily.

Nathan poured himself some punch and then trotted along faithfully behind me. I scanned the room and thought, *what am I doing here? I've gone to school with most of these kids since the first grade and have only cared for the company of very few.* The closest two were Gretta and Tommy, neither of whom were there.

Nathan babbled some inane crap about progress in the medical field, and I gave the occasional gesture or grunt to feign listening, but my mind wandered back in time.

It had been the autumn of my ninth-grade year when JFK was assassinated. The loudspeaker at school announced the event, and the kids collapsed into various reactions, mostly shock. The school was let out early that Friday. I called Mother to pick me up, and when I got in the car, she was stone-faced and silent, something I certainly was not used to seeing in her. When Daddy came home from work that night, he sat and cried as he watched the TV news. Mother never said anything about it, but Daddy fretted for months afterward. The following Monday, students crowded around this room, trying to watch the funeral broadcast, as we huddled to get a view of the one TV in the room. The school had only two or three TVs, so some classes had gone to the gym and others to the cafeteria to watch as America changed forever. For a moment, I felt like we were all friends, no picking on each other, cheap shots, or snide remarks to one another. Not everyone liked President Kennedy, but almost everyone felt the loss, and we grieved together over just one event of the 1960s that shocked the nation.

Over three years later, the assassination seemed almost forgotten except by conspiracy theorists who found it odd that Kennedy's body had illegally been taken out of Texas by the federal government and shipped back to Washington before an autopsy could be conducted. LBJ had completed Kennedy's term and was sworn in as elected president in January. Now, it was May, and graduation was around the corner. There was a feeling of unrest that had begun to filter through the country, especially the younger people, who were becoming frightened about the future.

As I looked around the room, I wondered how many of the boys there would end up dying in Vietnam. I had tried so hard to avoid politics or anything relevant to the future, but there I was, thinking what I was thinking, and I realized that I was changing, too.

More to get my mind off the trepidation than wanting to dance, I turned to Nathan and said, "I'm ready for that dance now."

It was a slow dance that started when he led me to the floor. He pulled me close to him, and I thought, "At least he is tall enough for me." I feared when Mother told me that she had a date for me that he would be just tall enough to bury his face in my tits on the dance floor.

We had not been on the dance floor for a complete minute before Nathan pulled one hand around to cup my breast and, kissing my ear, whispered, "I really want to fuck you."

In total shock at the unexpected, I shoved him backward with so much force that he almost fell over another couple. "WELL, I *REALLY WANT YOU TO GET FUCKED!*" I screamed loud enough for everyone to hear. "FUCK OFF, ASSHOLE!"

The entire room turned to look, and the dancing stopped momentarily. I turned, grabbed my purse off the table by the door, and huffed out of the building. I wondered if my reputation had made it to Grove City. I wondered if the only reason he allowed Mother to set him up with me was that he had heard about the slut from Climax. I didn't realize, at that moment, that most of my anger was displaced.

I went around the building, hiked up my dress, and sat on the steps of the closed side entrance. Except for one light over the doors, it was dark over there, and I hoped that I had gotten around the building fast enough that the creep would not be able to find me. I reached into my purse, pulled out a cigarette, and dug for a light, but there were no matches or a lighter. I had no idea what I had done with them. "Shit!" I said, and I threw the cigarette pack back into my purse. Then, I threw the purse down on the step. I sat there for a while, trying to figure out why that little incident had made me so angry. Most of the time, I would have taken that kind of thing in stride as a joke, made some off-the-cuff remark, put him in his place, and gone on. This time was different.

I didn't have a real boyfriend like most of the other girls. I didn't want to be there and was acting out Mother's fantasy, not mine. Mother was the one who deserved my anger, not some dufus from out of town. I suppose I could have fucked him. Big deal! What difference would it have made? He probably wouldn't have lasted thirty seconds anyway. I just found myself pissed at everybody and everything. I hated that damn school, that damn small town, most of the people in it, and I hated my life. I couldn't wait to get out of Climax, as far away from Mother as possible, and see the real world.

I started imagining what it would be like to attend college in the fall. Unlike Nathan, I couldn't afford a private college. I was going to Penn State, where my scholarship would help me pay for most of the tuition. I recalled photographs on the brochures. I wondered what interesting people I might meet and how an education might change my life. However, the longer I sat there, the more I felt the need for a cigarette.

After a while, I decided that I would walk home. That meant I would have to go back around the building to the front entrance. I didn't want to see or deal with Nathan, so I went sneaking to the corner of the building to peek around. When I did, to my delighted eyes, Tommy's Chrysler

Imperial sat across the parking lot. The top was down, and Tommy stood leaning against the car with Gretta tucked under his arm while they talked to a couple of boys. They were not officially attending the prom and technically should not have been there since they were no longer students. Still, that was a sight for offended eyes.

Gretta wore loose jeans and a baggy T-shirt, but her pregnant belly was still quite visible.

I looked around for any sign of Nathan and then hiked up my dress and went trotting across the parking lot toward Tommy and Gretta. I had no sooner stepped into the light when Nathan, who had apparently been waiting near the door, came running after me.

"Lovella," he called. " There you are. I've been looking all over for you. I'm sorry. I'm so sorry."

I turned on my heels and shouted viciously, "WHAT PART OF FUCK-OFF DON'T YOU GET?"

"I'm sorry," he said. "I was very rude in there, out of line. I don't know what got into me."

"WELL, YOUR DICK IS NOT GETTING INTO ME, ASS-HOLE!" I shouted, "SO, TAKE YOUR TROLL DICK BACK INSIDE, AND SEE IF YOU CAN FIND YOURSELF A BIG UGLY TROLL GIRL TO FUCK!"

"Wooooha, Lovella! Harsh." Tommy shouted, "I've never seen you talk to any guy that way."

"SHUT UP, TOMMY!" I shouted, turning back on Nathan and marching decidedly in his direction. He began to back up as I started my litany. "JUST WHO THE HELL DO YOU THINK YOU ARE? YOU THINK JUST BECAUSE YOU HAVE MONEY, I'M SUP-POSED TO FALL ALL OVER MYSELF, KISS YOUR ASS, SUCK YOUR DICK, OR DO ANYTHING ELSE YOU WANT? YOU THINK BECAUSE MY MOTHER SET US UP, I'M SOME POOR, PATHETIC, DESPERATE LOSER WHO CAN'T GET A DATE? MAYBE YOU THINK THAT MAKES ME EASY. IT DOESN'T MOTHER FUCKER!"

"No, no," he said, waving his hands before him and backing away.

"LISTEN UP, JACK-ASS," I continued. "JUST BECAUSE I DON'T HAVE A DATE FOR THE PROM DOES NOT MEAN THAT I'M DESPERATE! IF I WANTED A FUCKING DATE FOR THIS STUPID BASH, I WOULD HAVE HAD ONE. I CAN HAVE, AS A MATTER OF FACT, HAVE HAD CARNAL KNOWLEDGE WITH ANY BOY I WANTED!"

"Well, I was, I was," Nathan nervously stammered.

"SHUT UP, ASSHOLE!" I screamed. "WATCH THIS!"

I looked around the parking lot, where quite an audience had gathered. As I did, I started calling out names. "John Coonts," I began. "Have I had you?"

John Coonts stood there with some friends while his date went to the powder room. "You sure did, Lovella!" he laughed and shouted back. "You had me in about every position I could get in."

"Whose idea was it, John, yours or mine?" I shouted back.

"You came after me," replied John. "I was too shy to ask a girl out on a date until you came along."

"Terry Dawson!" I went on. "Have I had you?"

"I think you had me a couple of times, Lovella," he responded. "I've been hoping you would have me again."

"Tommy Smith!" I shouted, looking over my shoulder, "Have I had you?"

"Hell, Lovella!" he shouted. "Not only have you had me, but you taught me everything I know."

Then Gretta shouted as she planted a big kiss on his cheek, "And I'm damn glad you did."

"Gene Sutterfield!" I shouted. "Have I had you?"

"Well, I … I," he stammered. His date was standing right beside him.

"Come on!" someone shouted. "Tell it, Gene!" Others egged him on.

Finally, he shouted back, "Yeah, Lovella, you've had me."

His date slapped his arm and pranced away, but he stuck around instead of following her into the building. After that, I turned back to Nathan and sneered. "You see, asshole. I've had all those guys, and they have had me. Not only have they had me, but they are proud of it. But you are not going to have me. You are not going to have any part of me. The only thing you are going to have tonight is your hand! The good news is as long as you have a hand, you have a lover. Enjoy it, mother fucker, because that's probably the only lover you'll ever get!"

I turned on my heels and marched toward Tommy and Gretta. "Get me the fuck out of here!" I exclaimed. I hiked up my dress and climbed into the back seat of Tommy's convertible.

Tommy immediately put Gretta into the passenger's seat and trotted around the car to the driver's side.

One of the guys they had been talking to said, "Hey, do you mind if I go?" The other chimed in, "Yeah, me too."

I had never seen these guys before. They had come just to hang out with Tommy and Gretta in the parking lot. Tommy said, "I don't mind if Lovella doesn't mind."

"You mind if we go, Lovella?" one asked.

"Climb in, boys," I exclaimed. "Why not? Who knows, you might get laid tonight."

They both hopped over the side doors and into the back seat, one on either side.

As Tommy started the engine and began backing the car out of the parking space, he asked, "Where to, Lovella?"

I said, "Anywhere but here, Tommy. I don't care."

Tommy shouted from the front as he drove away, "That was quite a show back there, Lovella. You should take up the theater."

I responded with a quick but cooled down, "Oh fuck off, and drive!"

"By the way," Tommy continued, "These two guys work for my dad at the mill. This is Jason and Rick."

"Pleased to meet you, Lovella. I'm Rick," came a voice from my left.

Jason continued, "I'm Jason. Pleased to meet you, too, and the pleasure is all mine."

At this point, Gretta leaned an elbow over the back seat and said, "I don't think I've seen you that upset since our fight in the second grade. Honey, what did that boy do to you?"

"It wasn't that big a deal," I said, having begun to calm down. "I shouldn't have been so mean to him. I'm not really mad at him, and I shouldn't have taken it out on him. It's just this whole fucking town, especially that fucking conniving witch I have for a mother!"

"Uh, oh," she queried, "what did your mom do, now?"

"What has she done to me my whole fucking life?" I snarled. "What does she do to everybody? She has to control everything. No one else is allowed a choice. If she doesn't outright take control, she manipulates. I had gone along with her about going to the prom. I didn't want to go and wouldn't have if she hadn't lured Daddy into her web of deceit. I don't care. I want out of Climax! So, okay, she had a dress made for me. At least I got to pick the pattern, and it's a nice dress. Although I will likely never wear it again."

"By the way," Tommy interrupted, "you look fucking awesome in that dress."

"Oh yeah!" grinned Rick, eying my cleavage.

Jason echoed, "Mmmmmm … Hmmmmm."

"Shut up. I'm talking to Gretta," I demanded and continued my story.

"Anyway, I dressed for the prom, thinking that Daddy would drive me over and drop me off for a little while. I could visit with a few people and go home, you know? No big deal. But, no! Mother did exactly what I was afraid she would do, except that she didn't even give me the option of trying to back out. She made arrangements with this boy from Grove City. She talked me up and sold the idea to him. He showed up at the house, and it's, 'Oh, by the way, here's your date!' I wanted to fucking choke her right then and there, but there would have been witnesses to the crime!"

"Oh, jeez," Gretta sighed. "Honey, I'm so sorry. I want to say I can't believe she would do something like that, but I know your mom well enough to know that she would." Gretta paused momentarily. "Well, we figured you would be at the prom alone if you came, and thought we would stop by, say hello, and hang out for a while. We had no idea we would end up rescuing you."

"I'm damn glad you did," I said and finally relaxed into the back seat.

"How about Climax Point?" Tommy questioned. "We can go up there now, Lovella, since I have my own car, and I'm over eighteen, so Dad can't tell me not to."

"Yeah, but you aren't going to get laid this time," I teased.

"Don't count on that," Gretta snickered in Tommy's direction while stroking her index finger down his arm.

"It just so happens," said Tommy, "I have a twelve-pack of beer on ice in the trunk."

"Oh, you devil!" I bantered. "I never drank before. Is this my chance?"

"This is your chance," he continued, heading for Climax Point.

"I almost forgot, I wanted a cigarette," I exclaimed while digging in my purse. "Somebody pop the lighter in. I don't have a light."

Gretta obliged, and I fumbled for my cigarette pack. "Where is that damn thing?" I finally found the pack and pulled out a cigarette with it already positioned between my fingers. About that time, the lighter popped out, hot and ready. Gretta handed it to me over the seat. I held the lighter on the tip of my cigarette an pulled the smoke into my mouth. I returned the lighter to Gretta and laid back with an awaited smoke-filled breath of relaxation.

"You boys don't mind if I smoke, do you?" I taunted the men on either side.

"Oh, no," said Jason. "I smoke myself, now and then."

"You do not." Gretta ragged.

"Oh, I do," Jason defended, "but usually only when I drink."

"Yeah, well, that makes sense," Gretta replied. "I've quit, at least for now."

"Oh, when did you quit? And why?" I challenged, puffing away.

Gretta took a deep breath as though she would have to defend her decision. "I quit when I found out I was pregnant. I was reading a magazine in a doctor's office that said there is some research showing that it isn't good for you. So, I figured if it's not good for me, it's not good for the baby."

"Yeah!" I hissed through a clouded exhale. "Dickhead was telling me about that on the way to the prom. I get in the car with him, and the first fucking thing he does is start lecturing me about smoking. I thought, *You're not my fucking daddy, asshole!* Well, anyway, good for you. I'm glad you're taking care of yourself and the baby."

By this time, Tommy was winding up a tree-lined road and then off to the side where there was barely a rut in the grass. He pulled the car almost to the edge of a bluff where the lights of town shimmered in the valley. It was apparent that very few who usually visited Climax Point had taken a drive across those ruts.

"How did you know about this side road?" I asked.

Tommy laughed. "You're not going to believe it. My dad brought me here and showed me after I started getting serious with Gretta. He said some guy at work told him about how he and his wife used to get off the beaten path up here when they were dating, and he thought I might enjoy the view from here. I think he and Mom used to go parking somewhere when they were dating, but that was back in Youngstown before we moved here. Maybe they even came here after the guy told him about it. I don't know, but it's nice to have a place a little bit away from where most folks park."

"Well, good for Dad!" I exclaimed. "Where's the beer?"

Tommy went around and popped the trunk open. He lit a couple of lanterns, hung them on tree branches near the car, and set the cooler under one of the lanterns by the tree. Then, he pulled an ice-cold beer from the cooler. He took the opener to it and handed it to me.

"So," I said, holding the cold can in my hand, eying it like a lab specimen, "my first taste of beer." With that, I took several very long gulps before I removed the can from my lips.

"Whoa, now," Tommy cautioned. "Slow down. You don't want to drink too much too fast."

"Why not?" I questioned. "I'm thirsty."

I had read enough to understand a little about alcohol, and, at that moment, I wanted to get drunk. I wanted to get slobbering, falling down drunk just like Daddy. The way to do that was to drink it fast. I knew enough to understand that beer, unlike hard liquor, probably wouldn't give me alcohol poisoning, even if I drank half of what Tommy had.

"Here's to you, Daddy!" I shouted and downed the rest of the can. I returned the empty can to Tommy and said, "I'll have another, please."

"Only if you promise to take this one slow," Tommy pleaded while he held a fresh beer away from my reach and pulled it back each time I lunged for it.

"Okay!" I said, finally. "I'll take it slow—er."

"That's a promise," said Tommy.

"Okay, that's a promise," I said, already beginning to feel the effects of the first can I had slammed.

He handed me the beer and got beers for everyone else. After everyone had their beer, we all sat in a half-circle facing inward around the rim of the convertible with our drinks.

"So, boys," I said, as my head bobbed between Rick and Jason, "tell me about yourselves."

"Ah," Rick started after glancing at Jason. "We both grew up in Rimersburg. We were friends in high school and just looking for some work after we graduated. Then, we found an ad in the paper that the feed mill in Climax was hiring, so we applied, and that's how we got to know Tommy. Ah … we all work together."

"Fascinating," I said, gulping the beer faster than I had promised. "So, when did you graduate?"

"Well, Rick's a year older than me," chimed Jason, "he graduated three years ago, and I graduated two years ago."

"Oh," I said, lifting my beer can into the air, "so you're not breaking the law by doing this like I am?"

"No. Rick's twenty-one, but I'm twenty," Jason replied. "I guess he is the only one not breaking the law, 'cept, I think he bought the beer for Tommy. So …"

"Oh, so not breaking the law except for contributing to the delinquency of a minor," I responded, swallowing more beer. "I'm cool with that. Anyway, I'm already delinquent."

Gretta quit after one beer. When Tommy returned to the cooler, and she refused the second beer, I exclaimed, "I'll have hers." I thought that was the end of the twelve-pack. Gretta had one, the boys each had two, and I was about to have four by then. I didn't realize that there was one left in the cooler.

I was probably not quite as drunk as I wanted to be, but I had never had alcohol before, and despite my promise, I did drink it pretty fast. So, I was quite a bit drunker than I should have been.

"I need another cigarette," I exclaimed, motioning to Gretta to pop the lighter in again. She handed it back to me shortly. I fumbled to pick the lighter from her fingers without burning either of us since my coordination had become relatively impaired by that time.

While I was lighting up, I began to tempt Rick and Jason. "You know you boys are both kind of cute, and I don't think I've ever been with two boys at once … at least not in the Biblical sense."

Jason was turning red and getting nervous, but I could tell that Rick was enticed. Jason stuttered, "Well, uh, yeah, but don't you think two guys at once is a little queer?"

I slurred through drunk lips, "You know, the Kinsey report on male sexuality says that over a third of all men admit to achieving orgasm with another man, so maybe it's not as queer as you might think."

"Apparently," Rick said, eyeing me up and down, "from what those guys were saying back at the school, you are quite a lover."

"I am … indeed!"

I grinned, kicked off my shoes, and hiked my dress almost to my crotch. "It's hot out here—don't you think? Aren't you a little warm?"

Rick's eyes scanned my body like a road map. Jason was sneaking glances, and when I would catch him, he had a coy grin and averted his gaze.

"No, I'm fine," said Rick. "Not too warm at all."

"So, back to what you were saying," I persisted. "Yes, I am quite a lover. I have been training myself in the arts of love since I was very young, and yes, I have many…" I paused momentarily, stared at the sky, then back at Rick, "carnal talents."

Tommy was laughing at me. "Lovella, I think you are trying to seduce that guy."

"No," I clamored over my words. "I'm just reciting my curriculum vitae of passionate talents, and besides, I'm trying to seduce both of them."

"Oh … So, do you want to tell them about *all* your smoking habits?" Tommy taunted.

"Tommy! Stop it!" Gretta intervened, slapping his shoulder. She knew exactly what he was talking about.

I stared at him momentarily, then said, "Yes, I believe I do want to tell them about my smoking … *talents*." I turned back to Rick and Jason. "You see … I can … smoke a cigarette with my …" I pointed to my crotch. "Well, my favorite term for it is my 'muff-dragon.' It may not breathe fire, but it can blow smoke."

"Oh, hell!" exclaimed Jason. He drew back and almost fell off the edge of the car.

"Well, that sounds like a very interesting talent," said Rick.

"Would you like to see?" I quizzed as I waved my cigarette in the air above my crotch.

"Oh, holy hell!" Jason exclaimed again, darting his head back and forth, torn between his morals and sexual curiosity.

"No! That's enough, Lovella," Tommy pleaded, knowing I would do practically anything, especially if dared, and those odds had increased since having several beers.

"Come on, honey," Gretta joined in, "there's no need to get graphic. We're just having a nice visit and a little fun."

"Well, I think Rick and Jason would like to see," I said, leaning unsteadily toward the front of the car. "You guys may avert your eyes if you want, and I'll just give these boys a little private demonstration."

Tommy sighed deeply. He knew I would do it anyway. I never was much on gaining approval or worrying about being open with my body.

"All right," he surrendered. "Go ahead."

Rick and Jason were gleaming with anticipation when I stood up, staggering slightly, and pulled my hose and panties past my knees. However, Jason remained observably nervous.

Tommy and Gretta had seen it before, so it was no surprise. That's why Tommy brought up my smoking habits in the first place, but he should have known not to dare me or tease me about it, even if I had not been drinking. I sat back down, pulling my dress to my belly button with my left hand, fully exposing my muff-dragon. I ceremoniously took the cigarette to my other lips, used my vaginal muscles to draw in the smoke, removed the cigarette, and released the smoke in one little puff.

"Oh, great God almighty!" Jason exclaimed as he watched in amazement, but the next voice I heard was from neither of the boys.

"All right, what's going on here?" The voice behind me was not familiar. It was deep and authoritarian.

When Rick and Jason heard the voice, they scampered off on opposite sides of the car and ran into the woods. The next thing I knew, a policeman, flashlight in hand, was standing on the passenger side, staring directly at me.

"Hello, officer," I said as the muff-dragon spewed another little puff of smoke from between my legs. The look on the policeman's face was priceless but, unfortunately, unforgiving.

"It looks like a few beer cans are lying around here," he said. Have you kids been having a drink?"

"Why, officer," I said, slurring my drunken words and placing the cigarette between my facial lips to take a long, slow drag, "Whatever gave you that idea?"

I released the sultry smoke from my lungs, extending my lower lip to blow it toward the sky. I leaned over toward the side of the car, cigarette still in hand, with a plan to flash him an enticing grin. However, my hand missed the firm surface, and I fell halfway into the back seat before retrieving myself and pretending that he had not seen it. He walked around to the cooler under the tree and looked up at me as he nudged the half-open lid. Then, he glanced inside to see the last beer wedged into melting ice.

"I think you kids are under arrest," he said when he lifted his eyes from the cooler.

At that moment, I thought, *I got the bitch back. Without an effort, intent, or malice aforethought, I got her back.* I knew Mother would not only be displeased but aghast with embarrassment.

CHAPTER 9

The Shame of it All

We were hauled to the Armstrong County Jail in Kittanning, and since we were all underage, our parents were called. Gretta and I were placed in the women's holding, and I assume Tommy went to the men's holding. I didn't see him again for a while after that.

The jail was an interesting place. The building itself was a plain little, unassuming brick structure. The windows were crossed with metal strands between the glass, and the exterior bars were slightly ornate, covering the windows like a cluster of cast-iron spiders bolted to the brick. But I wasn't there to admire the architecture, and I spent minimal effort thinking about it as I got to experience what it is like to be behind bars.

They stripped us of everything except our clothes, including our shoes, and even took bobby pins out of my hair. Those were the days before they had orange suits for prisoners. They took everything except basic covering, then led us to women's holding. By that time, my elegant prom dress was a very not-so-elegant mess.

After we had gone through booking and were sitting in the *drunk—tank*, Gretta was crying like a baby and shouting, "Oh my God!" over and over until I finally and firmly raised my voice, "For God's sake, Gretta, shut up!"

"But we are marked criminals," she whined.

"No, we are not!" I scolded. "Don't be stupid. You don't think the cops find teenagers doing this silly crap all the time? Besides, I'm the one getting charged with indecent exposure. All you are getting, if anything, is a charge for underage drinking. Whoop-tee-do."

She caught her sniffles and straightened up. "My parents are going to kill me," she continued.

"Your parents are going to kill you?" I pranced around her, making elaborate gestures. "Look at you! You are a married woman! You are pregnant with your first child! You are an adult! Hell, for that matter, we are all adults. So, the stupid state has some archaic law that says adults can't drink or vote till they are twenty-one. That doesn't make any sense. I mean, you are an adult at eighteen, right? Guys are old enough to be drafted into war at eighteen but not old enough to vote or drink? It's a stupid law that needs to be repealed!"

"But it is still against the law," she moaned.

"Well," I taunted, perturbed at her whining, "I guess you should have thought of that before you drank that beer. Hmmm?"

I went over and plopped myself on the bunk beside her. An older woman was lying in the corner, smelling of body odor and rotten booze. She was evidently sleeping off a drunk. Another woman just sat there popping her gum and staring at us, never saying a word. I thought about giving her a shot from the muff-dragon, but I thought better of it.

"I'm sorry," Gretta said, "I guess I'm acting like a big baby. You're right. I need to grow up."

"Well, not too soon," I endorsed. "You will grow up plenty fast when the baby comes. You're going to have to. Me? I'm going to hang on to as much of my life and freedom as I possibly can for as long as I can. I may not ever have kids."

"You were always so adventurous," she smiled. "You remember second grade, standing outside the principal's office after we got in the fight? I couldn't believe you were saying those nasty words out loud. It's like you have never been afraid of anything or anyone, and I don't think I've ever told you how much I admire you for that."

"For what?" I queried. "For being a jackass who doesn't give a shit?"

"That's not what you are, Lovella," she continued. "I don't believe that you don't give a shit. I believe there's a lot you care about. I think, in your family, you had to learn how to be tough early on."

"I'm not so tough," I confessed. "I'm scared, too."

"Really?" she questioned and leaned back, looking at me. "What on earth could you possibly be scared of?"

"Goddamn! I wish I had a cigarette!" I exclaimed as I threw my face into my hands. "Why did they take my fucking cigarettes?" I took a deep breath and turned to her. Then, we were sitting face-to-face on either end of the bunk. "I'm scared of a lot," I said. "As much as I hate Climax, I'm scared of leaving. I'm scared of going to college and meeting people I haven't known all my life. I'm scared of trying to live my life without having my parents there to support me. I'm scared my mother may finally go off the deep end, and my daddy will die from all those years of soaking his liver in alcohol." I fiddled with the fabric of my now quite wrinkled prom dress before looking back at her. "There you have it. I'm fucking scared."

"I think I was too stupid to be scared when I left home," she said. "All I knew was that I had fallen in love with Tommy and wanted to spend the rest of my life with him. My parents didn't want me to drop out of school. They told me that if Tommy loved me, he would wait until I graduated. But I couldn't wait, and now …" she burst into tears, "I'm going to have a baaaaaa-beeeeeeeeeee."

"Oh, honey," I said, gathering her into my arms, "what a beautiful thing. What a beautiful thing that you are going to have a baby with the man you love."

"But I don't know how to be a mother," she sobbed. "I don't know how to do anything."

"You'll learn," I encouraged. "Nobody knows how to be a mother. I think it is something that we pull out of our asses when the time comes. At least some do. It could be worse. At least you are not going to be like my mother."

"Oh, God, Lovella," she returned, wiping tears from her eyes, "your mother is so weird."

"Jeez, that's an understatement," I replied. "Grandmother once told me that, right after I was born, Mother knocked on the doors of people she didn't even know to show them her new baby. Grandmother said she carried me to about thirty houses before a policeman quietly suggested that she go back home and show me off to her own family and friends. Someone must have called in a complaint about some crazy woman wandering around bragging about a newborn." I took a deep breath and sighed, realizing the magnitude of what I had just said. "I think I was never more than a prize to her, something to show off, and more like a pet than a child. It kills her that I won't just play along and be the sweet little doll she expects me to be."

"I could never do that to my baby," Gretta responded. "Don't get me wrong. I know I will be proud and want to show off my baby, but I won't go looking for strangers. She never stopped doing that to you, did she? It's like your whole life was supposed to be for her, and you weren't supposed to have a life of your own."

"I guess that's one of the things that makes me a fighter," I smiled. "I've had to fight to have my own mind and my own choices my whole life. Otherwise, Mother would consume me and turn me into a marionette doll. She does it to Daddy, too, like everyone in the world is there to meet her expectations, and she doesn't get that someone else could have feelings or desires of their own. Daddy deals with it by hiding from her and drinking himself into a stupor whenever she lets him."

"He must really love your mother to stay with her and let her control him like that," she said comfortingly. "I know he loves you, and maybe he stayed because of you because he could never have taken you with him. I mean, they hardly ever give the kid to the father when there is a divorce."

I looked back at her and then hugged her. "You are going to make a wonderful mother, Gretta. I know you are. You care too much not to be a good mother."

About that time, a policewoman walked up to the bars and called, "Lovella Fucks."

"It's Fuuuuchs," I answered, "There's an 'h' at the end, and the 'u' is long."

"That's not what I heard," she snickered. "Come on, Smokey Butt. Your parents are here."

"Are Gretta Smith's parents here?" I questioned.

"No," she said, "they will be a little delayed."

"Then I'm not going," I demanded. "I'll come out when Gretta's parents get here."

"Lovella, go on," Gretta chimed. "Your mom and dad are here. Go on."

"I'm not leaving you here by yourself," I snapped, with one part of me genuinely concerned for her and one part not wanting to face Mother.

"Suit yourself," the officer told me and turned to leave, "but I think if you are married, the state considers you to be emancipated. She may not need her parents to come."

"Wait a minute!" Gretta shouted to the officer and took hold of my arm. "I'm fine, really, Lovella. I'm calmed down now. There is no reason you shouldn't go home. If my parents aren't here soon, Tommy's will be, or Tommy will have things figured out." She turned back to the officer. "Have you heard anything from Tommy Smith's parents?" she asked.

"Oh, *you must be* Mrs. Smith," said the officer sarcastically. "His parents are here. Bail is covered, so he's at the check-out desk."

Gretta's face drained of color as she asked, "So ... do I have to stay in here?"

"Nope," replied the officer. "His parents are bailing you out, too, but I don't think they are very happy about it."

"Why didn't you tell me that before?" snapped Gretta in a much sterner voice.

"You didn't ask," the officer replied as she unlocked the cell door. "Besides, I'm not here for you." She turned to me and said, "Come on Smokey Britches. I'll be back to get your friend in about five minutes."

The officer led me down a corridor into a lobby with a built-in, chest-height desk behind a plexiglass window. Perpendicular to this was a long bench against a dark green wall. Mother sat, wearing sunglasses and an oversized scarf tied over her head like a celebrity going incognito. Her perch on the bench was so stiff she looked like she could fall off if she didn't grip her ass tightly to the boards. Her face was turned opposite, and she stared away from the checkout area. One leg was bouncing up and down furiously. She never turned her head or changed her gaze, even when she knew I had entered the room.

A couple of officers were standing near the same green wall where Mother was sitting. I recognized one of them as the man who had arrested us. He shot me a wicked grin when I walked in. Daddy was standing at the window signing papers, politely saying, "Yes, sir. Uh, huh, yes, sir," as though he was a disobedient schoolboy being scolded by the teacher. The officer behind the window casually explained the process and the rules around setting bail. I heard him say that I would have to return for court on the fourteenth of July and that a warrant would be issued for my arrest if I didn't show up for court.

"Yes sir ... yes sir," Daddy continued politely. "May we go now?"

"Hold on just a minute," the officer replied. "I'll need you to sign for her things." The officer went to the back and brought out a large, thick brown paper bag marked with my personal information. Daddy signed for my things and took the bag. He turned to me and said, "Come on, Punkin' Patch, let's go."

I followed Daddy toward the hall near where Mother was sitting. As we passed the officers, one of them said, "I'd walk a mile for a Camel. You never know when you might see one take a puff." The other officer immediately began trying to stifle a laugh. The advertising slogan for Camel Cigarettes, *I'd walk a mile for a Camel,* implied, I suppose, how far he would go to see my muff-dragon puffing on one.

I kept casually walking behind Daddy, barefoot in my silver prom dress. As we neared the edge of the room, I folded my arm behind me and displayed the length of my middle finger. I have no way of knowing if the officers saw it. Nothing else was said, and I walked on.

When Mother saw Daddy approaching, she stood up in a snit, expressing her obvious displeasure, and marched ahead of us to the door. When we got to the parking lot, she reached into her purse and handed the car keys to Daddy. "You'll have to drive, John," she said. "I feel too faint to drive."

She stared at me and pointed to the front seat, then went to the driver's side back door, motioning for Daddy to open the door for her. When he came around the car to open the door, she sat daintily in the back and motioned him to close the door. It was amazing that she would give up control enough to let Daddy drive, much less take the back seat, but she had to demonstrate how dramatically humiliated she was by my behavior. In the back, she began slinking down as far as possible so that only the top of her scarf-adorned head was showing through the window. I suppose it allowed her to feel a little more hidden from her imaginary critical public, but it was also to show me how wholly ashamed she was. I simply found it amusing.

"Interesting," I said, opening the door and sliding into the front seat.

When Daddy got into the car, he said, "Well, it sure has been an exciting night."

"Shut up, John!" Mother snapped, and he dutifully became quiet.

We all sat silently for a moment. Then, Daddy started the car and pulled onto the street. Over the horizon, the glimmers of morning had risen above the Pennsylvania pines. Finally, Mother could stand it no longer. She took a deep breath and hissed through clenched teeth, "I have never been so humiliated and embarrassed in all my life."

"Congratulations!" I spurted in a cheery voice. "Sorry it took you so long."

"Don't be flippant with me, Lovella!" she shouted, staring straight ahead into the back of the seat.

"Flippant, Mother?" I questioned in feigned confusion. "I merely thought I was stating the obvious."

"How dare you engage in such behavior!" she snarled. "How dare you embarrass this family the way that you have?"

"Exactly what behavior are we talking about, Mother?" I queried. "The drinking underage or smoking cigarettes with my pussy?"

"YOU DID WHAT?" she shouted. "I knew there was a charge for indecent exposure, but OH MY GOD! What did you do? What is that? How could you—you—you—ahh—haaa? She began panting with those familiar strains of an oncoming panic attack.

"I can smoke a cigarette with my vagina, Mother," I said calmly. "It's one of my many talents. It's merely a matter of learning how to control the Kegel muscles. I was demonstrating my talent to my friends and a couple of boys who had ridden with Tommy."

"Ah—ah—ah—ah, MERCIFUL GOD IN HEAVEN!" she huffed. "In—eh—in front of others? The police … caught you … doing that? OH! LORD OF MERCY! This is more hor-hor-hor-horrible than I could have imagined!"

"Now, Sissy," Daddy began his usual attempt to appease.

Mother shouted, "Shut up, John!" At the same time, I shouted, "Shut up, Daddy!" He became quiet, having failed, yet again, to keep us from going at it.

"Personally," I said, after a moment of silence, "I think it is quite a unique talent."

"I DON'T CARE WHAT YOU THINK!" Mother screamed. Her brief, fake panic attack was over, and her hornet's rage flared full throttle. "IT IS HORRIBLE, DISGUSTING AND PERVERTED! … It was bad enough when I thought you had flashed your breasts or something or that maybe you had gotten drunk and didn't quite keep yourself covered, but this is beyond any horrible, disgusting embarrassment that I could have imagined!"

"Really, Mother?" I taunted. "Worse than the time I fucked a dog on the front porch after I had sold tickets to the neighbors for a dog show? Worse than that?"

"HEAVENLY FATHER!" she started, having believed me for just a moment. Then she realized I was saying it to get her reaction. She paused to compose herself. "Lovella," she said momentarily, "we will not discuss this again. We will make no mention of it to anyone. Is that understood?"

Daddy chimed in. "Well, you know they post the arrests in the paper?"

I started laughing. "The secret is out, Mother. Your little girl is a slut, a fallen woman. She is tainted, damaged goods, nothing one would ever want to brag about."

"Do you live just to antagonize me?" she wailed. "Is it your mission in life to TORMENT ME?"

"Do you just live to try to control me?" I returned, "To make me a puppet in your little brag show? Do you think that I live only to make you look good?"

"Lovella, I have done nothing but try to give you a decent, wholesome, and successful life," she whined. "I have done nothing but encourage you and try to give you a happy life."

"You are so fucking dense," I sneered. "You don't even get it. You don't see yourself at all, do you? Everything you have ever done for me was trying to make me look good *for you*. You try to make me into what you want me to be instead of letting me be who I am! You always have! Well, it is my life—Mommy! God gave it to me! It is mine, and I get to do anything I want with it, including fucking it up if I am so inclined!"

"That is exactly what you are doing, Lovella," she droned. "You are—fu—fu—" She gathered her courage, resisting her own rule against using profanity. "You are *fucking* it up!"

I applauded dramatically. "Congratulations, Mother! You said a dirty word! How did that feel? Did it tingle on the tip of your tongue like a tiny oral orgasm? Did it entice you to say more dirty words so you could experience the exhilaration of feeling the word *fuck* shooting from your mouth like a burst of semen?"

"STOP IT! LOVELLA! STOP IT! I'VE HAD ENOUGH!" she angrily pleaded. "If you are not going to try to live a decent life for me, then at least try to live a decent life for yourself! Go on. Live your life any way you want to live it! Fu—" She caught herself, unwilling to use that word again. "Mess it up if that is what you want to do. I am through. I will never monitor your behavior again!"

About this time, Daddy was pulling into the driveway of our house.

"Excellent, Mother," I said as I opened the car door to get out. "I would love to say I believe you, but I don't."

I exited the car and walked up the house's front steps, waiting for Daddy to unlock the door since he still had my purse and keys in the brown bag from the police station. When he unlocked the front door, I marched straight to my room and shut my door. A few moments later, I heard a clamor from the front room. Mother was wailing, "Oh dear Lord! My child! My child! The devil has taken my child!" Daddy was attempting to comfort her fake sobs of remorse.

"Now, Drucella, honey," he said, "It's going to be all right. It is just kids getting out and having a little fun, that's all. Kids make mistakes."

"It's going to be in the newspaper, John!" she snarled. "The paper will print that my daughter was arrested for underage drinking and indecent exposure! I will never be able to show my face in this town again! I'll be jeered out of the church! My life is over!"

"Now, Sissy," he pleaded. "This will all blow over. People are going to forget about it in no time. Other parents have had this kind of thing happen to them."

"John!" she snapped, "she has *publicly humiliated* me!"

Finally, I could stand it no longer. I stormed from my room into the living room and screamed at Mother.

"YOU FUCKING GOD-FORSAKEN, SELFISH BITCH! YOU THINK THIS IS ABOUT YOU? YOU ARE WORRIED ABOUT *YOUR* REPUTATION, *YOUR* APPEARANCE? HELL, YOU DON'T EVEN ACKNOWLEDGE THAT I AM ALSO DADDY'S CHILD! YOU SAY, '*MY CHILD, MY DAUGHTER!* I WILL NEVER

BE ABLE TO SHOW *MY* FACE! *MY LIFE* IS OVER!' … DON'T YOU THINK YOU SHOULD SHARE SOME OF THAT EMBAR-RASSMENT WITH DADDY AND ME?"

"Lovella, go back to your room," she said flatly. "Your father and I are having a discussion."

"NO! YOU ARE NOT!" I screamed. "YOU ARE HAVING A BIG FUCKING PITY PARTY AT MY EXPENSE, AND AS USUAL, DADDY IS TRYING TO TALK YOU OUT OF IT WHILE YOU ARE GLOATING ON THE ATTENTION AND THE SYMPA-THY! YOU HAVE TO MAKE EVERY FUCKING THING THAT HAPPENS ABOUT YOU! WELL, HERE'S A NEWSFLASH—MOMMY! THE WHOLE DAMN FUCKING WORLD DOES NOT REVOLVE AROUND YOU! EVERY PERSON IN THE WORLD IS NOT HERE TO SERVE YOUR NEEDS, AND YOUR FAM-ILY HAS BETTER THINGS TO DO THAN DANCE AROUND LIKE A COUPLE OF MARIONETTES WHILE YOU MANIPU-LATE THE STRINGS! YOU MAY HAVE DADDY FOOLED. MAYBE YOU HAVE HIM TOTALLY HOODWINKED INTO THIS BULLSHIT! MAYBE YOU THINK YOU HAVE THE COM-MUNITY FOOLED, BUT YOU DON'T HAVE ME FOOLED! I KNOW YOUR SHIT! NOW, SHUT UP! QUIT YOUR FUCKING WHINING AND MOVE ON! I'M THE ONE WHO IS GOING TO HAVE TO GO TO COURT—NOT YOU!"

Mother sat momentarily, speechless and dazed. She wadded up the handkerchief she had been pouring her alligator tears into and shoved it into the pocket of her dress. "I think we are all very tired," she said. "Per-haps we should get some rest."

She rose gracefully from her position on the sofa, passed silently by me, went to their bedroom, and closed the door.

Daddy stood there, for a moment, with a blank look. Then, he half smiled, walked past me, kissed me on the cheek, and said, "Have a good nap, Punkin' Patch. We all need a little makeup sleep after being up so late." He then followed her to their room.

I stood there for a while before retreating to my room. Having said what I had wanted to say for so long, I felt a twinge of guilt.

CHAPTER 10

Service, Fear, and Gratitude

Graduation was a bore, a tedious, over-extended orgy of pontification about the future and our place in it. We were all, of course, going to save the world. I would rather have watched stones eroding in the desert. Mother, no surprise, did not attend. She had not spoken to me since my little outburst on the morning after prom. Attending my graduation would have shown she had forgiven me for the "shame and scorn" I had imposed upon her. Daddy made up for it. He took me to graduation and made over me like a mother hen. When I accepted my diploma, Daddy looked like he would fall over with excitement. He stood and applauded so hard that I half expected him to bruise his hands.

To me, the diploma was nothing more than a piece of paper, confirmation that I had jumped through the hoop and could go on to the next hoop. High school meant nothing to me. For years, my attention had been on college, getting a degree, and having something that would get me a permanent ticket out of Climax, a way to escape my crazy family—freedom.

After graduation, life was even more boring, with weeks of sitting around the house and waiting. I had already done my legwork and finished all the Penn State paperwork early. That summer, I did a lot of reading and fantasized about what kind of career I might have after school when I would become a respected yet controversial research specialist in human sexuality.

June was tortuously slow. Everything went along as usual. Daddy continued his Friday night drinking. Mother continued to attempt to manipulate him out of it, but she never said a word to me. We repeated almost the same ritual every evening at dinner time. When I asked her to pass the bread, she handed the basket to Daddy and said, "John, why don't you ask *your* daughter if she wants some bread?"

Daddy dutifully held the basket in my direction and said, "Punkin' Patch, would you like some bread?"

I genteelly replied in a poorly rendered fake Southern Belle voice, "Why, ya-ass, Daaa-deey. I would, indeed, enjoy me some ba-raa-ed. Thank you, ever so much, for then-kin' 'bout' 'Lil 'ole ma-ae." I then dramatically plucked my roll from the basket, held the basket in Mother's direction, and said, "Muuuth-aaa, would you li-ike some ba-raa-ed?"

She said nothing and ignored me while I held the basket across the table, smiling and staring at her. Finally, she said, "John, please tell *your* daughter to place the breadbasket back on the table before her arm becomes fatigued."

I said, "Oh, I aa-am fine, Muuuth-aaa. Would you li-ike some ba-raa-ed?"

Mother stared into the corner as she gingerly chewed her tiny piece of meat. Finally, she asked, "John, would you please take the breadbasket and set it back on the table?"

I quickly smiled at Daddy and chirped, "Oh, that's all right, Daddy, I enjoy holding the breadbasket. I'm just wondering if Mother would like another roll." I switched arms if one got tired, but I continued to hold the basket in Mother's direction.

Daddy, quite in on the joke, said, "Sissy, would you like another roll?"

Mother did not realize that Daddy and I had taken bets before dinner about how long it would take her to lose her patience. "Oh, for heaven's sake, John!" she snapped, "Take—the basket—out of her hand—and set it back—down—on—the—TABLE!"

"Poora, poora Muuth-aaa," I continued with my crude southern accent. "How difficult yah must find it, merely askin' for a ro-all." I held the basket and smiled until Mother finally took a roll and slapped it onto her plate. However, she refused to eat it and later tossed it into the backyard compost. Of course, we didn't have a dog or cat to lap up scraps and leftovers. Mother despised all "nasty little creatures."

When the time finally came for my court date, Mother was committed to attending the event. Far more important than seeing me graduate was her desire and hope to see me punished and, hopefully, humiliated for embarrassing her yet again. She was up early on July fourteenth, dressed in her finest and ready to be at the courthouse in Kittanning. Despite donning her best church dress for the occasion, she still wrapped her head in a scarf and affixed her sunglasses, which she wore in the courtroom until the bailiff instructed her to take them off.

Breakfast had not been prepared that morning; further punishment, I suppose. Daddy and I had a quick fix with peanut butter and jelly on toast. Mother had nothing. Perhaps she expected to dine heavily on my humiliation later that day.

We arrived at the courthouse several minutes before 8:00 a.m. and waited outside until the building was unlocked. We then had the privilege of sitting on hard, wooden benches in the hallway for another three hours before we were finally called into the courtroom. Daddy and I chatted and tried to make small talk or thumbed through magazines while Mother sat in a trance-like state, staring directly ahead, clutching her handbag on her lap.

In the courtroom, the bailiff, of course, did not catch what he was about to say and mispronounced my name. "The State of Pennsylvania versus Lovella Fucks—huh—Lovella, what?" His face reddened with embarrassment when he realized what he had just pronounced to the court, and he returned his attention to the document with an intensified glare.

I shouted, "It's Fuchs! The 'u' is long, and there is an 'h' at the end—not a 'k'."

At this, the judge slammed down the gavel and said, "Young lady, speak only if you are spoken to." He then turned to the bailiff and said, "It's Fuchs. The 'u' is long, and there is an 'h' at the end." The red-faced bailiff replied, "The State of Pennsylvania versus Lovella Fuuuuchs." The judge then looked at the papers before him and stifled a snicker as he read the police report quietly to himself.

I sat quietly, feeling amused by the show. By this time, of course, I no longer had embarrassment about my name and delighted in observing the embarrassment of others when they inevitably got it wrong. Finally, the judge looked at me and said, "Miss. Fuchs, you are charged with underage drinking, a minor in possession of alcohol, and indecent exposure. How do you plead?"

"I am Guilty, Your Honor," I said. "I am ready to accept whatever punishment you wish to provide."

"Oh, you are?" asked the judge.

"Yes, sir," I said. "I was drinking, though I am not yet twenty-one, and I was deliberately exposing myself in front of my friends but in a public park.

I had considered it to be a private matter among friends and that we were technically not in public since no one else was around, and I am assuming that it became *public* when the policeman approached."

"You were in a public park," said the judge.

"Yes, sir. I know it was a public park, and I am therefore guilty of exposing myself in a public area, although no one was there except my friends and me until the policeman arrived. It was, therefore, not a public exposure until the arrival of the police, which made it a public event versus what I previously perceived as a private event with only my friends."

"Are you arguing that you should not be charged with indecent exposure?" asked the judge.

"No, sir," I said. "I am pleading guilty to everything. I did it, and I am prepared for my punishment."

It seemed as if the judge had expected an argument. He paused momentarily, staring at the papers, then said, "Very well, Miss Fuchs. I sentence you to a fine of twenty dollars and eighty hours of public service. For your public service, you will come to the Kittanning courthouse beginning Monday, July 26th, and you will assist in janitorial services forty hours a week for two weeks. You will arrive promptly at 8:00 a.m. and leave at 4:30 p.m. You will have two ten-minute breaks with the county employees, and you will have a thirty-minute break for lunch. I suggest you bring your lunch, as you will not have time to go out to eat. If you are late, arriving for work, returning from breaks, or missing any day, this sentence will be converted to two weeks in county jail. Is that clear?"

"Yes, sir," I responded. "May I opt for the two weeks in county jail instead?" I assumed that I could spend my time reading, and besides, it would be two weeks that I wouldn't have to deal with Mother. In my naiveté, I had not considered what else I might have to deal with in there, whether I might not be allowed to read, or whether it might end up being significantly worse than having to deal with Mother.

"No, you may not," replied the judge. "When you arrive on the twenty-sixth, you will be under the supervision of Mrs. Magus, our janitorial services director. She will meet you in the downstairs hallway that morning." He slapped the gavel against his desk again and said, "Next case."

Mother had still said nothing. We left the courthouse with my papers and returned to the car. As we got into the car, Daddy said, "How about lunch? There's a nice little cafe around the corner."

Mother said tritely, "No, we will go home, and I'll make sandwiches. There is no need for further public display."

I got into the back seat of the car. I knew we would do what Mother wanted—back to her usual control. She got in on the driver's side, and Daddy got in the passenger's seat. As Mother pulled the car away from the curb, Daddy turned to me in the back seat and said, "Don't worry about that fine, Punkin' Patch. I'll pay that for you."

"John Fuchs!" Mother snapped. "You will do no such thing!"

Daddy returned with an unusual vigor, "Well, how is she going to pay it? She doesn't have any money."

"She will earn the money," Mother hissed. "Besides, that's almost a quarter of your weekly salary!"

"How is she going to earn it?" asked Daddy.

"I don't care what she does," Mother continued. "She can get a job. She can pick up bottles by the roadside or sell her body on the street since she is obviously well prepared to engage in the oldest profession! However, regardless of how she earns the money, she will pay that fine—herself! She will also pay us back an additional ten dollars for her bail money, and she will pay for the gas to cart her back and forth to the courthouse!"

"I will be happy to pay for everything myself, Mother," I said quietly but clearly. "I broke the law. I need to take responsibility."

After a long silence, Mother said, "Thank you, Lovella. I appreciate your willingness to be responsible for your actions." Those were the first words she had spoken directly to me since prom night.

"You're welcome, Mother," I said.

Then, she continued to drive in silence.

With July 26th a little more than a week away, I spent time in my room boxing my things, some for college and some for sale. I placed several things in a box to take to the local second-hand store to see if I could sell them. I had books dating back to my early childhood and a sweet sixteen necklace that Daddy gave me for my sixteenth birthday. I didn't want to part with it, but I hoped I could pawn it for enough to pay for at least part of my legal debts. Tommy also gave me a little money, unbeknown to Mother, because he felt guilty about bringing the beer. By the time it was over, I had come up with forty-four dollars and fifty-eight cents. After paying my fine and giving ten dollars back to Mother, I splurged with the remaining amount by inviting Mother to lunch to thank her because she would drive me to Kittanning every day for the following two weeks. I used the remainder to pay for gas. I wasn't sure if she would accept the lunch invitation, but she did. She was talking to me again, although it appeared that our relationship had been permanently damaged, not that it had ever been much, to begin with.

We all got up very early, starting on the 26th. Mother dropped Daddy off at work at 7:15 a.m., where he sat around waiting for his shift to start. She then drove me to the Kittanning courthouse, where we waited on the steps until it was time to go in. She was not about to leave me, even for a minute to myself, for fear of what other trouble I might stir. She picked me up at 4:30, and we drove to Daddy's factory to wait until he got off at 5:00, which was about our arrival time, anyway. It was a tormenting two weeks, more because of the family imposition than my sentence.

Mrs. Magus was an overweight woman in her fifties with a round nose, round chin, and a few short stringy hairs growing from her chin. Her puffy lips stuck out from her face as though attached like the plastic lips on Mrs. Potato Head, and she smelled distinctly of toilet cleaner. Her voice was coarse yet high-pitched. She sounded remarkably like a cartoon character, but she was all business.

When I met her on the first morning, she was waiting for me at the door. As soon as she saw me, she blurted out, "You are Miss Fuchs?" There was no mispronunciation of my name.

"Yes," I said.

She ejected, "Follow me." She turned and pranced military-style down the hall. She never introduced herself. She must have assumed I knew, and I suppose that I did.

She led me to a room on the left side of the main hall. There was an industrial sink, buckets, mops, brooms, and shelves stacked with cleaning supplies. In one corner, a skinny Black man who appeared to be in his fifties or sixties was wearing loose blue coveralls and sat on an inverted bucket smoking a cigarette. He was flicking the ashes into the sink, but he had to extend a long, skinny arm about two feet to reach that sink.

"This is Donny," Mrs. Magus said, pointing at the Black gentleman who nodded in my direction. "His name is Donnelle, but we call him Donny. He will be working upstairs today."

She continued, taking no notice of him.

"You will work the main floor. If you have any questions, find Donny on the second floor, or come to my office at the end of the hall on the second floor. There are two bathrooms on this floor, men's and women's. You will check them every thirty minutes to ensure they are clean, and I *mean* clean. I do not want to find so much as a drop of urine on the edge of the commode or a single hair when I come to check them. Be sure the men's room is clear before entering, and hang this sign on the door when you are cleaning." She handed me a sign that looked like the ones used to hang on hotel doors for *Do Not Disturb*. The only difference was it said *Do not Enter, Cleaning in Progress*. "Beginning at 3:30," she continued, "you will scrub the toilets, sinks, walls, and floors in both bathrooms before you leave. When the courthouse opens at 8:00 am, those bathrooms had better be spotless."

She grabbed a large plastic bottle from the shelf.

"Before leaving shift, place this in all the commodes to sit overnight. Read the instructions for the correct amount to use. During the morning hours, mop the main hall and all the offices on the first floor and mop them again before the end of the shift. Mop them even if they don't look like they need it. Do not leave pooled water on those floors," she emphasized, looking at me sternly. "You can squeeze the mop well enough that the floor will dry quickly. Use this in the mop water." She grabbed another bottle off the shelf and shoved it at me. Then, she pointed to a couple of aluminum *Caution Wet Floor* signs hanging on the wall, "Those fold out for freestanding. Put them on either end of the mopped area until the floor dries completely. Any questions?"

"Yes," I said. "May I smoke?"

"You may smoke only on your breaks and only in this room," she said, "You get one ten-minute break at 10:00 a.m. and one at 2:00 p.m. Do not smoke on the job, and do not stand around the building on your break. Come to this room. This is the janitorial lounge, ain't it, Donny?" She said this without even looking at him.

"Yes, ma'am," he replied, his long, bony fingers pulling a cigarette to his lips for one last puff before he put it out.

"Get to work," she commanded, marching out of the room.

As soon as she left the room, Donny let out a contrived laugh. "Hee! Hee! I'm surprised her butt cheeks don't squeak from all that friction rubbin' back and forth. Makes them polyester pants look like a couple of hippos hoppin' in a bag."

With that comment, I immediately liked him and giggled at his humor. He got up from his bucket and stepped over to the sink. "Them wasn't very good instructions, was they?" he said, smiling at me broadly. "Lookey here. You gonna use this bucket right here for ya moppin'. See this hose here clamps onto the sink faucet. Make sure it is up there good and tight, so it don't leak. Pour a little of that cleanin' stuff in the bucket, then hose ya water on in there. See here; it's got these rollers ya put the mop into and pull back on that leaver to squeeze out the mop. Now, you got these toilet cleanin' sticks up here for the bathrooms. Don't pay no mind to the instructions on that toilet cleanin' bottle. Just pour you a couple of capfuls into the toilet and scrub it out with the cleanin' stick. Now, you can wash the walls and the countertops with that same stuff, too, but don't mix it up with what you put in the mop bucket. Pour a couple of capfuls in one of these buckets with some water, and grab one of these here sponges. You got them dish washin' gloves, laying over there, that you can use so you don't mess up your hands. That stuff'ell kind of make them scaley if you ain't careful."

"Thanks, Donny," I said.

I had the feeling, at least for the next two weeks, that we would probably be buddies. I liked him very much.

He gathered his equipment, and before he stepped out the door, he said, "You need anything, you just come up the stairs and holler." Then, he was gone.

It wasn't as though I had never cleaned anything before. The judge must have thought I was one of those pampered little princesses who had never done a day of dirty work. He was wrong. While I liked to dress up as much as any girl, I didn't mind getting grubby, and Mother had put me to work many times, especially if she thought I needed to be punished.

I had finished everything on the list except for re-checking the bathrooms before the ten o'clock break came. I checked and touched up the bathrooms. Then, I was bored. I meandered around the courthouse, looking for any little speck of dirt that I might clean up. I met office people and asked if they would like their trash removed. Most of them hadn't accumulated enough from the day before to make it worth taking out, but they obliged me anyway, even if there was nothing in the trash basket but a discarded envelope.

At 10:00, I met Donny in the mop room, where we both lit a cigarette. I asked, "Does Mrs. Magus come down here for breaks?"

He chuckled and said, "Hell, she's on break all day up there in that office. You go up there; you'll find her with her feet propped up on that desk while she's eatin' doughnuts and readin' magazines. She ain't got enough to keep her busy. She just makes sure we stay busy while she gets a bigger paycheck."

"Does she just manage the courthouse?" I asked.

"No, not just," Donny continued. "She sees to all the county buildings, includin' the jail. I guess maybe over about five janitorial employees. She don't clean nothin' herself unless somebody don't show up for work, and she can't find somebody else to double up. She used to be down here doin' this, just like the rest of us."

"Must be nice to move up in the world," I said, smiling.

He said, "Say, what kinda' crime did you commit that got you sentenced to do what I do for a livin'?"

"Ahm," I stammered, for some odd reason, feeling a little embarrassed, "I was caught drinking underage, and I was also charged with indecent exposure."

"Oh, now," he said. "Mmmmm. Mmmmm. Pretty young girl like you shouldn't be gettin' in trouble like that. You gonna ruin your reputation."

"What reputation?" I grinned. "The only reputation I have is a bad one."

"Now, that's a shame," Donny said, deliberately not asking the details. "Reputation is important, especially for a woman. Men start talkin' her down. She ain't gonna get nowhere in life, but, you know, everybody makes mistakes."

"I don't think mine were mistakes, Donny," I said, drawing a long drag off my cigarette. "Most of them were, in fact, quite deliberate."

"You mean you set out to get a bad reputation?" he queried.

"No, not exactly," I responded. "I didn't even think about a reputation, but I did set out to explore life, and I didn't care about the rules. I don't mind obeying the rules when I can see a good reason for them and when they make sense, but if I can't see a good reason for a rule, why shouldn't I break it?"

"Well, cause," he pondered, "'cause there must have been a reason for it, sometime."

"But you know, Donny," I said, "the world changes. It always has changed. Society changes. Nothing ever stays the same, and the rule for one generation doesn't have to be the rule for the next. For example, some people would throw a fit if they knew I was in this room with you alone. Some might say it was inappropriate or make accusations."

"Now, now, Miss. Lovella," he twittered nervously and stamped out his cigarette. "Maybe we need to get along back to work now."

"It's okay, Donny." I solaced. "I'm not afraid if you're not. Nobody is doing anything wrong. Magus set us up to be here alone, and we are in the courthouse, for Jesus sake. It's just one more stupid rule that some people have, but others don't. If Magus didn't think anything of us being here for a break together, then I'm certainly not going to worry about it. Obviously, she knows you're a good man."

"Well, we need to be gettin' on back to work," he said, motioning toward the door.

I put my cigarette out and gathered my tools.

That afternoon, I couldn't help thinking about how Mother would take it if she knew I was spending fifty minutes a day, breaks and lunch, in a room, alone, with an old Black man. She would either assume that I was already lost, so why bother, or she would throw a very public and dramatic fit attempting to blame Donny and somehow reclaim my virtue. I would ensure she never found out, not for my sake but for his. Hardly anyone treated Black people even close to right back in those days.

I did my work for those two weeks and had several meaningful conversations with Donny. I never told the family anything more than there was an older man who also worked in janitorial services. I was not about to even hint to Mother that he was Black. By the second week of August, I had paid my fine, completed my public service, and was free to return to life as usual. I never saw Donny again after that, but I always remembered that experience and his kind wisdom.

CHAPTER 11

Many Truths Uncovered

On Sunday, August 15th, at about 2:00 p.m., I got a call from Tommy. He was panting on the phone like he had just run a marathon. "Lovella! Ah, huh, we're at County Hospital. Ah, huh, Gretta's having the baby. Can you come down?"

"Oh, Jesus, Tommy!" I returned. "Mother has gone to one of her church meetings with the car."

"I'll come get you," he panted.

"No, wait. I'll call a cab," I said excitedly. "You stay with Gretta."

"Do you have money for a cab?" he questioned. "I'll pay for it when you get here."

"You don't need to pay for it!" I responded. "You'll have a baby to take care of. Besides, I know where Mother keeps her stash."

"Jeez, Lovella!" he expelled. "She'll eat you alive."

"So, what's new?" I confronted. "Gotta hang up now so I can call a cab. I'll be there as soon as I can."

I hung up and grabbed the phone book to frantically look up the number for cab service. I called and got the cab on the way. Then, I pulled a ten-dollar bill from Mother's stash, much more than I needed, but what the hell? I wrote a quick note to the family, letting them know what happened and telling them not to worry. I included an I.O.U. to Mother for the missing money. I had forgotten entirely that Daddy was in his work shed. It didn't even occur to me to ask him for cab money.

The cab was there in about ten minutes, and I was off to Armstrong County Memorial Hospital.

When I arrived, I paid the cab driver and ran frantically into the lobby. I asked the receptionist for Labor and Delivery and ran in the semi-correct direction, barely getting the instructions as the receptionist shouted after me, "Miss! Miss! Slow down. Don't be running in the hospital." I paid no heed to her and kept going. In short order, I found the little waiting room outside Labor and Delivery, and Tommy was pacing the floor. As soon as he saw me, he ran over and hugged me.

"How is she?" I breathlessly exclaimed.

"I don't know," he said. "They took her in over two hours ago."

"I'm sure everything is fine," I comforted. "These things take time." I ushered him to a chair to sit down. "So," I continued. "Have you decided on a name?"

He nervously glanced toward the door. "Well," he stammered. "That is kind of supposed to be a surprise."

About this time, Tommy's parents walked in, asking the same types of questions, and not five minutes after them, Gretta's parents came in. This would be the first grandchild for both families, so both sets of parents were as nervous as Tommy. I swear it was like watching a hive of bees with the chatter between them. I sat back in the chair beside Tommy and squeezed his hand to let him know I was there if he needed me. Then, I got up and stepped to the side for a while.

Only a few minutes later, the nurse came in and called for "Mr. Smith."

How odd it seemed to hear him referred to as mister.

He turned to the doorway and called, "I'm Mr. Smith."

That sounded even more odd.

The nurse responded. "Mr. Smith, would you like to see your son?"

I saw Tommy's knees almost buckle and his face flush red, just as the grandparents let out a plethora of *ooohs*, *aaahs*, and other gibberish common to such scenes. I thought if I ever had a child, I would prefer to do so in private, without all the family commotion.

"Yes! Yes!" Tommy finally replied after recovering from the shock of becoming a father. "A son!" he stammered excitedly, returning his attention to his family. "I have a son!"

Of course, both families tried to rush the door as the nurse turned and said, "Just Mr. Smith at this time. I'll return shortly to inform you when other visitors might be allowed."

She escorted Tommy through the doors, and the disappointed families settled into the uncomfortable, industrially designed chairs to wait.

After a while, Tommy's father, knowing too much detail about my history with Tommy, said, "So, Lovella, what do you think of all this?"

I smiled politely and responded, "I think that two people I love very much have had a beautiful blessing come into their lives, and I am very happy for them."

"Yeah, yeah, it's a beautiful thing," he bantered, making small talk. "I tell you, I can't wait for the first time I take that boy fishing."

"That will be very nice, Mr. Smith," I said. "I'm sure you will make a wonderful grandfather. After all, I understand that you have been a wonderful father."

"Well, thank you, Lovella. That is very sweet of you to say." He grabbed Mrs. Smith's hand and squeezed it. "Boy, this brings back memories, doesn't it, sweetheart? I remember when you were having Tommy. I was pacing around the hospital lobby, feeling like my heart was going to beat right out of my chest. I was so proud of our first child and the two that followed, but that first one, boy, that's a doozy."

Just then, Daddy and Mother came in. Immediately, I recognized that Daddy was very drunk.

"Well, there you are-P-Punkin'-Pa-Patch," Daddy stuttered and rushed, staggering, over to me. "You had us wo-wo-worried."

He plopped into the chair next to me. Mother said nothing but nodded politely to the other families. Before Daddy's ass hit the chair, I smelled the liquor on his breath. I didn't know what to think. I had smelled that smell before but had never seen Daddy that sloppy drunk. I had seen only the after-effects and had never known him to drink on a Sunday. It had always been Friday night when he had his love affair with alcohol. I then realized that Mother's silence was more her embarrassment than anything else. I had suspected she would be pissed at me for getting into her money, but I saw shame, more than anger, on her face that afternoon.

"WOOOOAH, I TA-TA-TELL YOU WHA-WHAT!" Daddy shouted at the other families far louder than he should have. "THIS IS AN-NA-NA—EH-EVENT! It su-sure issss some-thing wa-watching your k-kids grow up-up, grow up-and st-st-step oa-ut into liii-vaa-es of their OH-OWN AND HAVE BA-BABIEEES AND

ST-STUFF!" His words were slurred and barely understandable, even when he was loud.

Mother snipped quietly, "John, there is no need to shout. I'm sure everyone can hear you."

I could not believe she brought Daddy with her when he was so noticeably intoxicated. I learned later that he had gotten into the car and refused to get out, and she had a time convincing him that he would not drive. Any other time, he would have sheepishly submitted, but excessive alcohol had altered his usual pattern of behavior. When he finally agreed that he was in no shape to drive, he scooted over to the passenger's side and refused to go back in the house. I was surprised they had even come at all. Normally, Mother would never have allowed anyone to see Daddy in such a state if she could possibly help it, but I assumed she thought she needed to pick me up, and she had no convenient way to contact me at the hospital.

"Oh, m-my good-nessssssss, Punkin'-Pa-Patch," Daddy slurred while patting my arm too vigorously. "Little Gret-ta-ta Tan-Tan-Tannenbaum is having a ba-baby. Hell-ya-you have ba-been fa-fa-friends wi-wi-with that girl s-s-s-s-since you wa-were in the fa-fa-first grade. Ya-You na-know that ch-child is al-almost like an-na-other dau-augh-ter to me. H-H-Hell, I wouldn't miss this f-f-for the wo-rld! I-I wa-want ta-to see th-that baby!"

It was then that I realized Mother, in rare behavior, had given in to Daddy's demands to come to the hospital. It wasn't necessary. I could have gotten a ride back with one of the other families or taken a cab. I had this image of Daddy insisting that he had to come to the hospital, that Gretta was like one of his own, and Mother finally giving in after the exhaustion of bickering with a drunk. I could see darting eyes and overheard the faint hint of whispers as the Tannenbaums and Smiths assessed the situation from across the room.

"Daddy," I pleaded, "they will probably not let anyone in today except for family. I only came down to be with Tommy because he called and was nervous while waiting. We could probably go on back home now."

"WH-WHERE'S TA-TOMMY?" Daddy shouted again, scanning the room. Only at that moment did he realize that Tommy wasn't there.

"He has gone back to be with Gretta," I said. "The nurse called him back right after the baby was born."

"Ya-You ma-mean the k-kid is already here? What wa-was it a boy-oh-or-or a girl? HEY! -hey!-ha-ha-HEY! Let's go ba-back and sa-sa-see the baby." He plowed the words out of his mouth, one sentence after another, and didn't give anyone a chance to answer the questions before he was up and headed for the double doors.

"Daddy, NO!" I shouted and grabbed his arm. "We can't go back there yet."

"Wa-Well, why the h-h-hell not?" he exclaimed, pulling on my grip like an eager dog on a leash.

"Because it is a private time for the parents to be with the baby," I said. "We need to wait."

"Oh-a-oh," Daddy softened to a whisper, bringing his finger to his lips as if to shush everyone. "It's a pa-pa-private time, private pa-pa-private time. Ohhhhhh-kay. I s-see. We n-n-need to wu-wu-wait our t-turn."

"Daddy," I implored. "I really need to go home. Can we have Mother take us home?"

"Bu-But d-d-don't you wa-want to sss-see the baby?" he continued to whisper while wobbling on unsteady feet.

"I think I'm going to have to wait until tomorrow to see the baby," I said. "It's just immediate family today, and I really need to go home. Let's go home, Daddy. Okay?"

He looked at me with a brief stare. His love for me was still shining through the haze of intoxication. Then, he said, "Oh-k-kay, my little Puh-Punkin' Pa-Patch, if you wa-want to go home, then we na-need to go home."

I glanced at Mother, and she gave me an acknowledging look. Then, she moved over to Daddy's other side, took his arm, and we began escorting him out.

"I'll be there in a moment," I said briefly, letting go of my grip on Daddy's arm to dash over to the other families.

"Please tell Gretta and Tommy I'm sorry I couldn't be here. I'll try to come back for a visit tomorrow." I stared at them entreatingly, catching sympathetic eyes as I scanned them. In a moment, Gretta's mom said reassuringly, "Sure we will, sweetheart. You go on."

I turned and took Daddy's arm again so Mother and I could escort him safely out the door.

What a waste, I thought to myself as I got into our car. Tommy needed me there for support, but I wasn't there long before the baby was born, and then, this.

Daddy fell asleep on the way home. I sat in the back of the car, thinking, *In only a couple of weeks, I will be going away to college. I will hardly see Gretta and Tommy after that. My life is going in an entirely different direction than theirs. They will be raising a family and settling into the day-to-day mundane life of Climax. Who knows where my life will lead me?*

Mother didn't speak the whole trip back, nor did I. I guess we were both entrenched in thought. When we got home, we woke Daddy, and he had sobered a little from sleep. We helped him stagger into the house. He fell into bed with his clothes on and immediately passed out again.

Mother and I gathered back in the living room and sat down. After a while, she said, "I'm sorry, Lovella. I tried to keep him at home, and when we got there, I told him I would only go in long enough to get you. I told him to wait in the car, but he got out and pushed his way in."

"It's okay, Mother," I replied. "Who can handle a drunk if he doesn't want to be handled?"

Again, we sat silently for another long moment.

Finally, I said, "I've never seen him so drunk before, and I've never known him to drink on a Sunday."

He's been drinking a lot more lately," Mother responded. "He has been pretty good about hiding it from you, at least until today. He hides in the shed and drinks."

"I don't understand why he would hide it from me," I said, reaching into my purse for a cigarette. If Mother continued to care about my smoking, she never let on.

Mother looked down at her hands, which were folded in her lap. She looked up at me with tears welling in her eyes, something I rarely saw. Those tears were never released when she said, "It seems that you are the only person in the world that he can't stand to disappoint."

In that instant, I realized how disappointed she had been, not just with Daddy but with me. I suddenly realized how deeply hurt she had been. I didn't know what to say. I didn't know if I should try to comfort her or if she would even allow it. I had no clue what to do, so I sat dumbfounded in silence, realizing I had been a competition between them. I had been the rope in their interpersonal tug of war.

In a moment, Mother sighed and said, "I think I would like a cup of hot chocolate. How about you?"

"Yes, that would be nice," I replied, following her to the kitchen.

I sat at the table and watched as she prepared the hot chocolate from scratch. While she stood over the stove stirring the milk to warm, I finally asked, "Mother, are you and Daddy going to be alright when I go to school?"

"I'm sure we will be fine, dear," she said, not looking up.

I fiddled with the handle of the cup on the table before me. "This thing today just worries me, I guess."

"I've dealt with your father for a very long time," she said, continuing to stir. "I'm sure we will be okay … but …"

She stopped mid-sentence, eyes gazing into the heating milk.

When her silence felt ominous, I petitioned her, "But what, Mother? Finish the sentence."

She turned the burner off under the hot chocolate, brought the pan to the table, and skillfully poured it into my cup. "But … I'm going to miss you," she said as she finished pouring her cup.

Again, I was dumbfounded. Part of me wanted to reply, "I'm going to miss you too," but I resisted, knowing I didn't think I would mean it. On the one hand, I wanted to slap her for waiting my whole life, even to come close to letting me know I meant more to her than a showpiece. On the other hand, I wanted to affirm my mother. When I finally said, "I'll miss you, too," I felt like I had to pull the words out with pliers. Within me, my empathy competed with the truth. Although I had newfound compassion for her, I also desperately wanted to escape her. That comment, *"I'm going to miss you,"* was the closest thing I had ever heard to *"I love you."*

She put the pan back on the stove and sat at the table, blowing across her hot chocolate, before taking a sip. "I've decided to take a job," she said, not acknowledging my response. "I'm due to start at Martha's Dress Shoppe next Monday."

"That's nice," I said, stirring my chocolate. "Is this something you've wanted to do?"

"Truthfully," she sighed, "I don't know how long your father will be able to keep a job. He has already been reprimanded twice for drinking at work, and it is probably only a matter of time before he gets fired. I have to do something."

I felt guilt rushing over me, as though I were committing some terrible wrong for going to college and leaving them to cope with the misery that was their marriage. Though never spoken, there had always been a thought in my mind that I was supposed to have been the savior of their marriage. I felt the whole burden of their misery had been mine to repair. Somehow, I had failed miserably because I chose rebellion instead of sacrifice.

As I pondered what she had just said, I changed the subject. "Mother," I queried, "why didn't you and Daddy have any more kids after me?"

She snorted, repressing laughter, as though I had just told a gut-busting joke, and when she saw the shock on my face, she said, "I'm sorry, dear." Then, she stammered a bit in her reply. "I just didn't think your father and I could handle more than one." Then, one finger crossed her lips as though telling herself to be quiet, and she said, "No, I'm sorry. That is not true." She sighed and looked away, then looked back at me again. "Your father came home very drunk one night shortly after you were born." She paused for a moment, gathering courage, and continued. "He kept begging for sex, wallowing on me, grabbing me, and refusing to let go. It felt so intrusive, and he stank of liquor. I locked myself in the other room with you. I felt frightened of him. I never wanted to go through anything like that aga—" She caught herself in the middle of the word. "I'm sorry. I'm suturing. I never wanted to deal with that. He pounded on the door for a while and then went to bed. I didn't come out until morning. By that time, I had done a lot of thinking. Your father had sobered up and was apologetic, so I sat with him for a talk. I told him that if he ever tried to force himself on me again, I would leave and that I expected him to control his drinking. Of course, he didn't control his drinking, but he never did that again. I decided that it would be difficult enough to raise one child in a home with a drunk. I wasn't going to do that to any more children. That's why I only had you. I'm sorry I had to put you through growing up with a drunk for a father, but you were already here." She paused as though having to regurgitate her words. "I rewarded him with sex when his behavior was appropriate, but I insisted on protection. After a while, it seemed his drinking was more important than sex, so I resorted to trying to manage him in other ways." I saw tears in her eyes again and watched as she stifled them. "At this point," she continued, sucking back her grief, "there is no managing him anymore."

For the third time that day, I was dumbfounded. I sat staring at her, trying to figure her out, trying to tell if this was acting and she was feeding me a load of bullshit or if she actually believed her reasoning. At last, I said, "Mother, did it ever occur to you that trying to manage others is not the way life works, that maybe the best that most people can hope for is to be able to manage themselves?"

"Well, what was I supposed to do, Lovella?" she snapped. Ah, there were the hornets. "Let my marriage fall apart? Let my child grow up without a father? You adore your father, and he adores you, though, for my life, I cannot fathom what you see in each other!"

Yes, there it was. There was the Mother I had always known. There was the anger and sting, and there had been no honest answer to my questions. I could not confirm whether she had been telling me the truth. My parents' lives were an inaccessible secret. I took the last few sips of my cocoa and said, "Thank you for the cocoa, Mother." Then, I rose and went to my room but didn't read or sleep. I lay on my bed staring at the ceiling, thinking about many things. I tried to dismiss worry about myself and them. However, I was not successful.

The next day, I rode with my parents while Mother took Daddy to work. He was barely able to get up to go, but he managed. Then, she dropped me off at the hospital while she ran errands. Gretta was asleep when I came in—after all, it was early. Tommy had taken the day off and was slumped in a chair near Gretta's hospital bed. When I came into the room, he roused.

"Oh, hi," he yawned and stretched sleep from his arms.

I walked around the bed and leaned over the rail just as Gretta opened her eyes. "Good morning, little momma," I said.

She smiled and reached up to hug me. "Have you seen the baby?" she asked.

"No, honey," I replied. "I wanted to see you first, and besides, seeing the baby would mean peering through a window at a collection of newborns and trying to figure out which one was yours."

"Tommy." She motioned to him. "Go ask the nurse to bring the baby in."

He got up dutifully and walked out of the room.

"How are you feeling?" I queried.

She snickered as she snuggled into the bed, "My coutchie hurts."

"I'm not surprised," I said, grinning. "It got a little bit of badgering, didn't it?"

She nodded in agreement and said, "Oh, Lovella. He is so beautiful. I've never seen a more beautiful baby in my life."

"You think you might be a little biased?" I questioned.

"Just a little, maybe," she said, "but I'll bet you'll think he's beautiful, too."

In short order, Tommy re-entered the room, followed by a nurse holding the baby. She came over and laid the child in Gretta's arms.

When I saw her looking down at that baby with such loving eyes, goose bumps crawled over my arms. For the first time in my life, I realized what true adoration was.

"You're right," I said. "He is beautiful, and you are beautiful with him."

Tommy stood on the opposite side of the bed, staring adoringly at the two of them and stroking Gretta's hair.

"You want to know what we named him?" she asked.

"Yes, what?" I replied without realizing I was about to get the shock of my life.

"We named him Derrick Lovel Smith," she said, looking up at me. "Derrick, after Tommy's grandfather, and Lovel, after you."

"After me?" I exclaimed. "Why in the world would you name your child after me?"

"If it had been a girl," she continued, ignoring my questions, "we would have named it Jeanette Lovella Smith. Jeannette, for my grandmother, and Lovella, after you."

"You guys!" I exclaimed again. "I love you both. You know I do, but I can't understand why you want to name your child after me."

They started to speak at the same time. "Because ..." they glanced at each other, caught themselves, and Gretta continued, "Because, if it hadn't been for you, Tommy and I might never have found each other. You brought us together, Lovella, and together we made Derrick Lovel, and he is both of us together in one body for life."

I couldn't help myself. Happy tears drifted down my cheeks. "You guys are so sweet," I said. "I don't know what to say. I'm just blown away."

"Would you like to hold him?" Gretta asked.

"Oh, hell, yes!" I cried.

Then, she handed the baby to me. I folded him into my arms and stood there cooing to this little person waving his tiny hands randomly and looking at me with the same big, beautiful hazel eyes as his father. I looked up at the two of them, and our eyes exchanged a moment of knowing, of feeling connected in a way that cannot be explained, a soul connection in which you feel you have known each other for eternity. There was a part of me that was envious and a part that was so proud. I had no words, nothing meaningful to say. I said nothing. I kept rocking this beautiful little bundle, cooing to him. At some point, I knew I would have to hand him back, but I didn't have to make that decision because it was only a minute or two before his goo-goos became cries.

"Oh, no-no-no," I cooed, "What's wrong? Don't you like your Aunt Lovella?"

Gretta patiently watched as I tried to calm the baby and finally said, "Maybe I should take him."

I handed him over, and within a few seconds, the crying had stopped, and he settled into her chest.

"I guess he already knows who his real mom is," I said, watching her cuddle the baby. Then, I reached across the bed and set my hand over Tommy's. I put my other hand on Gretta's shoulder and said, "I'm going to miss you guys so much."

"Oh, jeez," Tommy said, "we'll miss you too."

"Oh, God, yeah!" Gretta exclaimed in a whisper to prevent disturbing the baby again.

"You know, I leave for school next week." I wept and pulled back to wipe my eyes.

"But that's going to be so wonderful for you," said Tommy. "Wow! College! That's great!"

"I don't know if it is as great as having Derrick." I sighed.

"But your turn will come," Tommy replied. "You will probably meet some wonderful intellectual guy who will be perfect for you."

"God knows? It's definitely going to be different," I said. "Mother is going to drive me up the Monday after next. I have to meet my advisor and register for classes. I already know which dorm I'll be staying in. My roommate is from Philadelphia. They have already sent our room assignments. I guess I'll meet her when I get there. Her name is Marcy Macintosh. I don't have a clue what she is like."

"So, how often will you be home?" Gretta questioned.

"I don't know," I said hesitantly and paused briefly, "I have mixed emotions. All my life, I've wanted to get out of Climax, and God knows I've wanted to get away from Mother, but now that the time is here, I realize that it means leaving you guys and adjusting to a completely different way of life. It's kind of scary."

"You? Scared?" exclaimed Tommy, "That'll be the day! You might be a girl, Lovella, but you got bigger balls than most men around here, and yours are brass-plated."

I laughed.

"Well, if I did have balls, I would certainly have to apply myself to learning how to use them to my greatest satisfaction."

"So, how often will you be home?" asked Gretta.

"I guess, at least during the holidays," I said. "If Mother has her way, I'll be home every weekend. She wouldn't miss a minute of torturing me or making sure that I don't do something she would consider—unseemly. So, I would prefer not to come home every weekend."

Tommy said, "She still hasn't figured out that you are going to do whatever you damn well please, regardless of what she, or anyone else, thinks."

"No, she hasn't," I replied. "I doubt that she ever will."

About that time, there was a little knock at the door. Mother stuck her head in and said, in a little sing-song voice, "May I come in?"

"Oh sure, Mrs. Fuchs," Tommy said, stepping slightly to the side.

"My, what an adorable child," Mother said, stepping into the room. She glanced briefly over at Gretta and the baby before turning to me.

"I'm done with my errands, dear," she said, all smiles and sweetness. "Are you ready to go home?"

"May I meet you in the lobby, Mother?" I replied. I won't see them again before I go to school and want to say goodbye."

"All right, dear," she said and swished out of the room, nodding to Gretta and Tommy.

Tommy snickered when Mother closed the door, "Do you think she heard us?"

"What the hell difference does it make?" I responded. "I don't think she'll ever hear anything more than her own beliefs rolling around in her head."

"Well, at least she was congenial," Gretta commented.

"Yeah, congeniality is a good place to hide her bullshit," I said, leaning over and kissing her on the cheek. "I hate it, you guys, but I've got to go. I'll miss you so much."

"You have our number," said Tommy as he rounded the bed to hug me.

"You are more likely to get a letter than a phone call," I responded. "Long distance is expensive, but I will most assuredly write."

"We'll write, too," Gretta said. "Be sure to send us all your contact information as soon as you arrive."

"I will, honey," I affirmed, hugging Gretta and crossing around to hug Tommy again before I opened the door to leave. "You'll get the first letter I write." I paused a moment before I passed through the door. "Goodbye for now."

They both said, "Goodbye."

I walked down the hall and took the elevator to the lobby. Once inside, the number for the first floor punched; I leaned my head against the wall and thought anxiously to myself, *Oh my God—life! What am I going to do with life?*

CHAPTER 12

A BOY LIKE NO OTHER

September 13, 1966

Dear Gretta and Tommy,

Jeez, this place is enormous! The first day was hell. I don't have a clue how long I stood in line to register for classes. All Mother could do was bitch about how long it was taking and how much this cost the family. I told her, "I'll get a fucking loan!" My scholarship pays for most of it, but she still had to bitch.

The dorm is okay, except we have to go down the hall and share a bathroom with every other girl on the floor, and Marcy (you remember me telling you about my roommate Marcy?) is a twit! She was a cheerleader in high school, and all she can fucking talk about are boys and ballgames. She is "So looking forward to trying out to be a Penn State Lion cheerleader." I'm hoping she breaks her fucking legs. She says her major is psychology, but I've concluded that her actual major is husband-ology. Her father is an executive for some Philadelphia company, and she has always been used to having money. She spends it like I piss. Pretty girl, all blond and petite. Her head bobbles back and forth as she talks like she's some fucking spring-head doll.

I have this image of her tiny brain rolling around in her head like a marble on a roulette wheel. Now and then, it falls into a slot, and DING! There is a brief moment of clarity. Then it's back to the endless rotation of banter. All I want is for her to shut the fuck up. I'll probably have to do most of my studying at the library.

The campus is beautiful. It's a valley here with mountains on both sides. The buildings are a blend of limestone and brick. I have to walk quite a long way to my first class, Monday, Wednesday and Friday. We only meet three times a week, but the class is two hours. I also have two classes on Tuesday and Thursday. The walk wouldn't be so bad, except that the wind here is a real demon. It whips between the buildings, almost like a storm, every day. I dread it when the weather gets colder. I know the cold wind will claw at my cheeks when I'm walking to class.

Old Main is the administrative building. It is really beautiful. It reeks of antiquity and has a beautiful tower in the center rising high into the sky like a church steeple but somehow more tasteful and understated. The building is white limestone.

I'm looking forward to seeing it after a nice snow. If I can, I'll send you a picture.

They wouldn't let me major in sexual biology, as there is no such major, so I have to major in general biology and pre-med. Maybe I can get a master's or doctorate later that will lead me more toward sexual research, where I know I want to spend my career. Then, again, an M.D. might lend itself well to that, also.

There are a lot of cute boys here and a lot of hippies, too. I'm sorry. I don't get the long-hair, flower-child thing. Why a handsome boy would want to cover his face and head with all that hair is beyond me. The sexiest part of a man is his face, and I want to see it. It doesn't matter how cute the boys are, though. I don't have time for it and don't care right now. I guess I did enough playing around in high school, and it doesn't hold the intrigue for me that it once did. Besides, academics are not as easy as in high school. I need to make the grades so I can stand a good chance of getting accepted into graduate school, and from what I've seen in my classes, the grades are not going to be that easy to come by.

I hope you, Tommy, and little Derrick are doing very well. I love and miss you, and I'll look forward to maybe seeing you at Thanksgiving. So far, to my surprise and gratitude, Mother has not insisted that I come home every weekend. She has been working Saturdays at the dress shop, anyway, and even though she is bringing in a second salary, she likes to remind me how she suffers for my future by supplying me with the money for books and supplies. Maybe I'll get a job and relieve her of the burden.

That's enough for now. If I keep bitching, I'm going to start sounding like Mother. Besides, I have to study. I'm off to the library to do a paper on Edgar Allen Poe for the damned English Literature class that they require - like I haven't had English classes before. I could understand it if I were majoring in English, but I'm not, and I've read enough already that I could probably teach the damn class. Regardless, here we go.

I look forward to hearing from you.

Hugs and Kisses,

Lovella

As soon as I finished my letter to Gretta and Tommy, I headed for the library and dropped it in a post box on the way. Libraries have always been like a second home to me, although English literature has never been a topic of study that I was drawn to. "Nevermore," quoth the raven. Fuck off, Edgar Alan Poe! I would rather study the history of malaria.

Nonetheless, I had to study on that day to see if I could learn a little bit more about Edgar Alan Poe and his motivations. I found a table and collected a stack of books to browse through. I was looking for ideas on how to write a paper about something that was about as interesting as Marcy's banter on sports. While investigating one of the books, I noticed a boy at the next table staring at me. When I first noticed him, he smiled. That might have been intriguing, except that he was a hippie and not a very attractive one. He was skinny and had a bony-looking face with a nose that was too large. His thin, straight, brown hair hung over his chest, and his large ears poked between the strands of thin hair. He had a scraggly beard, a tie-dyed shirt, and beads around his neck. "Jeez!" I thought, burying my nose in my book; *I would rather mate with a praying mantis.*

Even though I kept my gaze on my book and tried to comprehend some of the gibberish I considered poetry to be, I could feel his eyes on me, pulling me to look up again. Although I resisted as long as I could, not wanting to give him even the hint of an invitation, I finally could not help myself. I had no sooner glanced up to catch his unwavering stare when he gave me a gleaming smile and got up, moving in my direction. I could see, then, that he was not only skinny but quite tall. I stuck my nose back into the book as quickly as possible, hoping to give him the idea that I did *not* want to talk to him, but it was a useless gesture. I felt him slide into the chair beside mine and heard him say, "Hi."

"Go away," I said, without looking up.

"You know," he continued. "You are a beautiful, tall girl. I don't see many tall girls."

"And you are a very ugly boy," I replied. "Now, go away."

"I might not be the best-looking dude around," he said, "But I have certain attributes and talents."

"Scaring the farmer's crows?" I said, still not looking up.

"Oh, I've not tried that one," he replied, knowing that he had hooked me into responding to him. "But I'm sure I would be quite good at it. No, you see, I'm a superb lover."

I snickered. I couldn't help myself. The idea of this lanky scarecrow being a superb lover was as laughable as Edgar Allen Poe tap dancing on a variety show.

"You don't believe me?" he questioned. "You know, I could prove it to you."

"You know," I said, with a snarl, as I snapped my book closed and looked at him, "If I wanted to get laid right now, which I don't, I think I could find a much better option than the one I'm looking at."

"Mmmmmm, fire," he said, grinning from ear to ear. "You know that makes the sex even better."

"Why the hell would you think I would be remotely interested in you?" I snapped, trying not to get too loud. I realized that the quick closing of my book had drawn attention. Most girls would have slapped him and walked out, but maybe there was an interest that I didn't acknowledge.

"Well, even though you might deny it, you have responded to my … attention," he said, stretching his long fingers across the top of the table.

"Would you please just go away?" I said.

"Oh, hey, it's all cool," he continued. "I just want to show you one little thing, and if you are not impressed, I'll go away and leave you alone.

I sat there staring at him, wondering what planet this freak had descended from.

"Come on," he said. "Take a look at these long fingers."

"So, you have long fingers," I snapped. "Big deal."

"You know what they say about men with long fingers, right?" He scanned me with an ear-to-ear grin, his white teeth gleaming. At least his teeth were beautiful.

Even though I knew exactly what he was implying, I took the bait. "No, what?" I said sarcastically.

"You know there have been studies," he said, as he wiggled the index finger of his right hand, "that indicate a correlation between the length of a man's index finger and the length of his … flaccid … penis."

"Impressive," I said. "Now, go away."

"I could show you." He continued.

The average girl would have been long gone before then and would have filed a complaint with the librarian or school administration, but I definitely was *not* the average girl. Besides, my curiosity had peaked. After all, I did want to do sexual research. I stared at him and smiled.

Locking eyes with me, he reached for my hand and asked, "Is it okay if I maneuver your hand into place?" I let him take my hand. *What the hell?* I thought. *What have I got to lose? I'll tell him I'm not impressed and be done with him.*

He gently took my hand and moved it ever so tenderly under the table where his penis lay inside his jeans along the side of his leg. "Still okay?" he asked.

I nodded affirmatively.

Then, he placed my hand over his dick and lifted his hand away to let me do what I wanted. It must have been at least seven or eight inches long, completely flaccid. I moved my hand along the length of it and felt it begin to swell with erection. He smiled and said, "I told you I have attributes."

Maybe I should have jerked away and stormed off, but I was not a demure and respectable girl. I was the slut from Climax.

"That's not an attribute," I responded with a glib tone. "That's a tool. Just because the carpenter has a big hammer doesn't mean he knows how to drive a nail. In fact, the bigger the hammer, the harder it is to drive a nail properly. There is such a thing as too big."

I pulled my hand away from his crotch and reopened my book.

"Scare you a little bit?" he asked.

"I'm not afraid of a big hammer," I responded. "I just don't want to use that one."

"You know," he cooed, "I can prove to you that I know how to drive a nail."

I popped back at him. "You undoubtedly think I'm easy."

"I don't know how easy you are," he continued, "but I do know that you are a *damn* sexy and interesting girl, and I would like to get to know you better. How about we continue to talk over a cup of coffee and a cinnamon roll? I know a great little diner that makes the best cinnamon rolls on this side of the Atlantic. No pressure, no expectations, no use of tools, just conversation."

As much as I hated it, I was intrigued by this tall ugly hippie, and it wasn't about the length of his penis. There was something about him, a feeling as though I already knew him, as though I recognized him from some lost and sweet relationship in my past, but there had never been a past that had included him. Still, I tried rejecting him. "How about you let me study," I said, "I've got a paper due tomorrow."

"How about I study with you," he smiled. "I've got a few chapters of my physics book that I need to read because there will probably be a pop test tomorrow."

I looked him dead in the eye. "Are you going to study, or will you sit there and continue pestering me while I try to study?"

"No, I'll study," he confirmed. "I promise I won't say anything else till you are done, and maybe later we could check out that cinnamon roll."

"All right then," I said, "but not a word until then."

"Okay, deal," he smiled. "But one more thing, first. What's your name?"

"Lovella," I replied. "What's yours?"

"Lovella, hmmmmm, that's a beautiful name," he teased. "My name is Earl. What's your last name?"

I hesitated. Years of teasing had led me to believe, especially given what he had just done, that my name would be met with taunts. Finally, I said, "It's Fuchs."

"Spell it," he said.

"What?" I exclaimed.

"Spell it," he said again. "I just want to make sure I've got it right."

"F—u—c—h—s." I spit out each letter with determination. "Spelled with an 'h' not a 'k,'" I explained. F̲u̲u̲u̲chs—not Fucks."

He looked at me, light filling his eyes. He grinned a playful, evil grin. "Great God almighty!" he said, "I've met my soulmate! Wanna know what my last name is?"

"Sure," I said, puzzled.

"Titwallow," he replied. "*Tit*, as in breast, and *wallow*, as in what I like to do with breasts."

I snickered. I couldn't believe there was someone else with a derogatory name like mine. "You know," I said, "That's an amusing name."

"Yeah," he said, "just like Lovella Fuchs. You know, they really should have replaced that 'h' with a 'k.' It would have been a lot more fun."

"It wouldn't have made any difference," I giggled. "People still pronounce it 'Fucks', anyway."

Several people had started shushing us by this time, so we took the hint and began stifling our laughter. He went back to his table and brought his bookcase over to mine. We then sat there, side-by-side, noses in books. But for several minutes, one of us periodically snorted or snickered, triggering the other. We would "*shush*" each other and turn our attention again to our studies.

It was about 7:00 p.m. when I finally put the last line to my handwritten paper. Earl had finished reading much earlier and put his head on the table for a nap. After I finished, I returned the books to the re-shelf bin and returned to the table. He was sound asleep. I thought about just walking out without saying anything, but I found this ugly boy quite interesting, even though I couldn't believe that he put my hand on his dick after talking to me for less than three minutes. His head was lying sideways over his books with his arms wrapped around them. I sat beside him, thinking *I could walk away, and he would likely not wake up or know the difference.* Instead, I touched his arm. His eyes opened. He looked straight at me and said, "Hello, beautiful. Where did you come from?"

"Climax, Pennsylvania," I said, "What about you?"

"Pittsburgh," he said, smiling, and sat up.

"Oh," I teased, "a city boy."

"You still up for that cinnamon roll?" he grinned.

"To tell you the truth, I'm a little hungry," I replied as I gathered my things. "A cinnamon roll might be dessert, but I need a little more. It's probably too late for the cafeteria. You know where we can get a burger?"

"As a matter of fact, I do," he said. He got up, picked up his bookcase, and began to pack his books into it. "It's the same place that makes the cinnamon rolls, and their burgers are even better than the rolls. Wanna go?"

"That sounds good," I replied. Then we walked together toward the door.

"So, are you a Physics major?" I questioned as we walked.

"No, I'm a Business major," he replied. "I just like physics. It's fascinating, you know? It's my minor."

"Well, if you think physics is so fascinating," I pried, "why are you majoring in business?"

"The business major is something I'm doing for the old man," he echoed. "Gotta keep the family happy."

"Don't I know it?" I said. "Have you got a car, or is this place within walking distance?"

"I've got a car," he returned. "Come on."

When we got to the parking lot, he walked up to the strangest car I had ever seen. It looked like a metallic cock and balls with wheels. It had a two-seater cab and a front end that jutted out, rounded and smooth, like a dick. It was teal green, sleek, new, and clean. I had expected something more like a flower-painted hippie van.

"What the hell is this thing?" I asked when he opened the passenger-side door for me.

"It's a Ferrari 250 GT," he said. "It was my high school graduation gift from the family."

"Yeah, but what the hell is it?" I questioned again and slipped into the leather seat.

"It's an Italian sports car," he said while getting in on the driver's side.

"Looks expensive," I said.

"It is," he replied. "Very expensive." Then, he started the motor, and I winced at the sound of it.

"Is your family rich?" I queried.

"A little."

He reached for the gear stick and pulled the car back from the curb. It sounded like a race car and made me feel like I was in a rocket.

"Well, I have to say," I continued, "this is *not* what I expected."

"What did you expect?" he questioned as we drove through the local streets.

"Well, you have on all this hippie garb," I continued. "I expected you to drive some beat-up contraption like an old van painted with flowers or peace signs."

"I wouldn't mind a beat-up old contraption," he said, "but Dad wants me to live the family image, not that he is old money or something. My dad owns a company that makes snacks. You know, potato chips, and crackers, and stuff like that."

"Sounds like you would never run out of snacks," I commented. "Big company?"

"It is kind of regional, actually," he said. "We have distribution over Pennsylvania, and he has spread it over the border in a few neighboring states. You've probably heard of it: 'Chum Snacks.'"

"Yeah," I said, "I like the cheddar cream-filled crackers. Wow! Your family owns that whole company?"

"Well, not the whole company," he replied. "Dad started it about 1947 and retained controlling stock when it went public. He's the C. E. O. It probably brings him about a million a year in personal profit."

"That's great," I said nervously, suddenly feeling intimidated by my lower-middle-class roots, recognizing that a million dollars would have purchased my whole hometown with money left over.

"Yeah, it's great till you have to deal with the bullshit," he said. "Here we are."

When we pulled past the restaurant, he crooked his neck, looking for a parking place. The restaurant looked like a silver train car, and a neon sign over the entry said, *"The Finer Diner."* He soon found a parking spot. I opened the car door, got out, and walked with him toward the diner.

"You're going to love this place," he said as we walked along the sidewalk and entered the building.

The front, inside wall, of the diner was lined with booths. A counter was parallel to and across from the front, where the booths lined up by the windows. The counter was lined with round chrome stools that bellied up to it. Everything was chrome and orange-vinyl, except for the booth tables and countertops, which were a pale blue Formica with green and orange flecks. Behind the counter, a couple of fry cooks were working the grill. We took a seat at one of the booths.

A forty-ish-looking waitress came by momentarily, wearing a ruffled white apron over a robin's egg blue uniform. She had a little ruffled cloth tiara in her hair and a receipt pad in her hand. She handed us each a menu.

"My name's Sally. I'll Be back to get your order in a sec." She then moved on to another customer without giving us a second glance.

I began looking at the menu when Earl said, "I like the *Spice Burger* myself."

I glanced down to see a list of about ten different kinds of burgers. The *Spice Burger* was made with black pepper, melted Swiss cheese, sautéed mushrooms and onions, lettuce, tomato, and mayo.

"That looks interesting," I said. "I don't believe I've ever seen such a selection before. I always thought a burger was a burger—lettuce, pickle, tomato, and onion with a little yellow mustard."

"Hey," he said, "these folks think outside the box, even though they work in a box." He grinned. "I guess that's why I like this place so much."

The waitress returned and gave a quick, little question, "You folks ready to order?"

I looked at Earl, then at the waitress. "I think I'll have the *Spice Burger*," I said.

"*Spice Burger*, right?" she scribbled on the pad. "You want fries, onion rings, bell pepper rings, or batter-fried mushrooms with that?"

"Bell pepper rings?" I asked. "I've never heard of that."

"Yeah," she said, "it's just like onion rings, honey, except it's sliced rings of bell pepper battered and fried."

"Oh, okay," I pondered. "I'll try the bell pepper rings."

"What you want to drink, honey?" she continued questioning.

"Cola, I guess," I responded.

She immediately turned to Earl, "What about you, darlin', what'll you have?"

"I'll have the very same thing," he said.

"Double spice, double green rings," she yelled at the fry cooks and walked away.

Soon, she was back with our drinks.

"So, what about you, Lovella Fuchs," Earl said. "Tell me more about you."

"I'm afraid it's rather boring in comparison," I said, stirring my cola with the straw.

"Who's comparing?" he asked. "Just fill in the blanks."

"Well, I was born and raised in Climax," I began with a sigh. "It's too small to be a real town. New Bethlehem is nearby, but it is not much bigger. My daddy works for a peanut butter factory, and my mother has been a stay-at-home mom until she recently took a job in a lady's dress shop in New Bethlehem. I'm an only child, and that's about it.

"Oh no," he said, leaning toward me over the table. "That's not even the tip, of the tip, of the iceberg. From the moment I first saw you, I could tell that you are a deep and complicated person."

"Really?" I responded. "You could tell all that from a glance across the library?"

"Really," he went on. "For one thing, you are very intellectual. You like to learn. You are very sensual and passionate. You don't like your mother and think your father hung the moon."

I was in shock, not so much from the first part, which could have been concluded from the stack of books on my table at the library, or by the second part, which could have been a continuation of his flirtatious attempts, but the third part, about my parents, threw me back in my seat.

"Why on earth would you conclude that I don't like my mother and adore my father?" I questioned.

"I could feel it," he said. "I feel things. I pick up on the vibe. There was something about the way you said it."

"I haven't even mentioned my parents except for that one sentence just now, and there was nothing in it to intimate your conclusions," I snapped.

"Hey, it's okay," he soothed. "I'm not judging. I just picked up on something in your voice when you were talking about your father working in a peanut butter factory and your mother being a stay-at-home mom. Do you want to try it? See if you can pick up on my vibe."

"Okay," I chirped. "You think your father's an asshole!"

"Bang on! Right you are, Lovella Fuchs," he said, "except for one part. I don't think he's an asshole. I *know* he's an asshole." He laughed. "See, you can read the vibe too."

"I wasn't reading your vibe," I said, "I was just trying to say something mean because I felt put off by your forwardness. Besides, you already said something about having to pick the major your dad wanted instead of what you wanted."

"It doesn't matter," he said. "You're right. My father is an asshole. So why don't you like your mother?"

"I never said I didn't like my mother!" I snapped again. "You did."

"I may have said it," he continued, "but you *did not* deny it."

"Okay! Okay!" I gave in. "My mother's a bitch. Now, are you happy?"

"I was happy before you said it," he replied. "I'm always happy. Happiness is my thing, man. So why is your mother a bitch?"

"I don't know," I went on. "Maybe she doesn't get laid enough. Maybe Grandmother pulled her off the tit too soon. She just is. She tries to control everyone's life—mine, Daddy's, the neighbors, you name it. If she is not manipulating something, she's bored."

"What about your dad?" he asked.

"Daddy loves me with every ounce of his being," I said. "But he's a drunk. I never knew how bad a drunk he was until just before I left for Penn State a few weeks ago. Mother has always contained it, but it became too much for her this summer."

"So, you're a freshman," he said.

"Well, yes, mister-psychic-pick-up-on-the-vibe," I retorted. "You didn't read that in my aura the first moment you set eyes on me?"

He continued to grin. He was always grinning. "Well, as a matter of fact, I did," he covered. "I just wanted to make sure that you knew."

"You are so full of shit!" I laughed.

At that moment, the waitress set our meals on the table.

"Two *Spice Burgers* with green rings," she said, walking away without asking if we needed anything else. The smell of grill-cooked meat wafted from stoneware plates, enticing consumption. We pulled the plates to ourselves and began to eat.

"So, what are you?" I asked.

"I'm an alien from a distant planet on the other side of Andromeda," he replied while piddling with his burger.

"Yes, I know that," I said, "but what is your college class level?"

"Oh? I'm a junior this year," he replied. "Can't wait to get it over with."

"Why?" I questioned. "I love school. I love to learn. Even the bullshit required classes that are a bore still give me knowledge that I didn't have before. I like knowing things."

"Well, for a start," he answered as he nibbled on a bell pepper ring. "I'm not doing it for me. I'm doing it for the old man. That's why I am majoring in business instead of physics, psychology, art, or something else that interests me. He wants me to come back to take over his legacy and run the company when he's gone. Never mind what I fucking want. You know, like, what if I don't want to run a Goddamn potato chip factory and live a bourgeois, fat-cat, fuck everybody else in the world, lifestyle?"

"Sounds like you would be set for life," I said.

"I don't care if I'm set for life," he went on, with a mouth full of burger meat and brown mushroom drizzle sticking to his scraggly beard. "Money isn't everything. I mean, what good is money when people are starving, man? You know, like there are places in this world where people don't have a chance while fat cats like my old man suck up more money than they can ever spend and do nothing of any true value with it."

"Wow," I said. "I never thought about it like that."

"That's the problem, Lovella Fuchs," he went on. "We live in a society that teaches us to consume without any thought of its effect on anyone else, the environment, or even our futures. Americans consume most of the world's resources while people starve around the world and here too, despite all these petty efforts like Peace Corps and shit."

"But your dad is not making money off poor people," I said. "What difference does it make if he has money? It's not like he is taking food out of the mouths of the needy."

"My dad makes money off everyone," he responded. "He makes money off anyone who has a dime to buy a snack. The problem is not that he is taking food directly out of the mouths of the needy, but he is keeping money he doesn't need that could be used to help needy people. He is not doing anything to help people in need unless he writes a check for a photo opportunity to get publicity and make the public think he is altruistic. It's like he is addicted to getting more and more."

"Well, he wants you to take over the company someday," I debated. "You would, then, be in control of all that money, and you could set up foundations for the poor and do all those altruistic things you want to do."

"Yeah, I guess you are right," he said. "I just don't have any interest in the business. Who the hell wants to calculate inventories and overhead versus expenditures? It's boring as hell."

I scrutinized him, watching his expressions. I guess I was trying to pick up on his vibe. "Maybe there's more to it than that. Would you find it as boring if it weren't something your father was pushing you into?"

"I don't know," he replied. "I was never given an opportunity to find out."

"You know, I think you and I are a lot alike." I laid my burger down on the plate to emphasize the point. "Your dad pushes you into things you don't want and tries to control your life, and my mother pushes me into things and tries to control my life. I don't know. It seems like the difference is that I'm not here getting the degree my mother wants me to get. She would prefer I meet a nice boy, according to her standards, and settle down in Climax to raise grandchildren for her. I'm doing what I want, and you are angry with your father for controlling you, but you are still doing what he wants."

"You're right," he replied. "Regardless of how different I am from my old man, I still have this need to please him. I still crave a time when he might slap me on the back and tell me, 'Good job, son.' So … I do what he wants. I work on a business degree, so I'll know how to run the business when he is ready to retire." He looked up and grinned again. "However, he doesn't know that I have a minor in Physics."

"Why Physics?" I asked.

"I just like it," he said. "It's fascinating. I don't have a clue what I would do with a degree. I don't want to teach and can't see myself doing research. It's just that this stuff is cool to know."

"So, tell me something cool about physics?" I asked.

"Okay." He thought for a moment. "Einstein's theory $E = mc$ squared means that the amount of energy contained in any object of mass is equal to the speed of light squared."

"So, what the hell does that mean?" I laughed.

"It means that there is a whole hell of a lot of energy in everything," he replied. "In fact, energy *is* everything. Energy and space. That's all there is. Energy can neither be created nor destroyed. It is eternal, but it constantly changes forms and is literally everything! Hey, you know when they exploded the first atomic bomb in the New Mexico desert, they split the atom, right? Well, what came out of the atom when they split it? A whole fuck-load of energy, man. So, if you split any atom, energy comes out of it. So, ultimately, everything is made of energy and space—you, me, this diner, the air, and the planets. There's space and different manifestations of energy, and that's it. It's like the universe is energy given form by thought; it is all one big dream that we all dream together or something. The fact that we can even be aware of it is a miracle in itself."

"You need to be on medication," I teased. "How much time have you spent in institutions?"

"None so far, Lovella Fuchs," he replied, still grinning. "I'm just living day by day, trying to make sense of all this energy and space around me."

He finished his burger before me, wolfing half of it down like a starving dog and only slowing down on the other half so he could talk. I pointed out that he needed to use his napkin as bits of the meal still clung to the hair around his mouth. I only ate about half of mine, and that was plenty. I was full.

"Didn't you like it?" he asked, looking at the half-eaten burger on my plate.

"I loved it," I replied. "It's pretty big; too much food for me."

The waitress had set the check on the end of the table while we were talking. I hadn't even noticed.

"You ready to go?" he asked, reaching for the check. Then, he reached over and took several bites from the half-eaten burger left on my plate.

"Yes, thank you," I said.

He slapped a tip onto the table, took one last swig of his drink, and took the check to the register to pay. I stepped outside and lit a cigarette. I couldn't believe I had gone so long without smoking. Of course, smoking wasn't allowed in the dorm. For goodness sake, we might start a fire. So, whenever I wanted a cigarette, I had to sneak it, and I usually just went outside somewhere. I stood there, enjoying my first cigarette in several hours, when he stepped out of the diner.

"Oh, you smoke," he said, walking toward me.

"Didn't you pick up on that vibe from the moment you saw me?" I asked, just before taking a long, deliberate drag on my cigarette. "Didn't you even notice my breath smells like a stale ashtray?"

"Nope, I missed that one," he said. "Let me know when you're done. I don't smoke."

I took one more drag, threw the cigarette down, and stamped it out with my shoe on the sidewalk. "I'm ready," I said.

"So, where to?" he asked.

"Back to the dorm," I answered, assuming he also resided on campus.

"Well, I could take you back to your dorm, or we could go to my apartment," he quizzed.

"Your apartment?" I questioned.

"Yeah, I have a flat about ten blocks from campus," he said. "Want to go? You could experience Old Glory in action." He nodded toward his crotch.

"Not tonight," I replied, not believing what I was saying.

The truth was that I curiously found myself wanting to fuck him. I was intrigued by the ugly hippie. I wanted to see if he was as much of a lover as he made himself out to be or if he would be another in a long line of boys I would teach how to screw. Yet, there was more to him than that. He was brilliant, and we had a great conversation.

"Oh, Lovella," he pleaded. "I'm disappointed. I thought you might be the adventurous type."

"My type is, for the time being, none of your business," I said. "Besides, I have an early class tomorrow. I have to turn in my paper and don't function well without sufficient sleep."

"So, you're telling me there's a chance we might get together again some other day?" He grinned. "Come on, I'll drive you back."

We walked to the car with his arm around my shoulder. I looked up at him in the streetlights, and somehow, the filtered darkness softened his looks, making him seem less ugly after all. His long arm felt comforting around my shoulder, and I wanted to lean my head into the side of his chest, but I resisted the temptation.

"Just how tall are you?" I asked when we neared the car.

"Six foot five," he said, walking me to the passenger's side. "Like it?"

"I don't know," I said. "I'll have to think about it." At least he was tall enough for me, not like one of those boys who was just tall enough to stare at my tits.

I slid into his Ferrari's cool leather seats and waited for him to enter the other side. I couldn't help feeling special in that car—elegant and pampered. When we got to my dorm, he walked me to the hall entrance.

"Boys are not allowed beyond this point," I said, turning and gazing up into eyes that now seemed sultry.

He smiled looking down at me, flashing his distinctive grin. His warm eyes caressed me, and I almost felt like he was looking into my soul. "Well, I hope this boy is allowed to see you again," he said.

"Yes, I think so," I replied, not believing the words coming out of my mouth, when before, I had thought him ugly and intrusive. Then, a profound realization hit me. I suddenly realized this was the first actual, real date I had ever been on. I didn't count the fiasco that Mother had arranged for the prom or times with Tommy, which were just for sex. All the other times had been either my decision of who I wanted to fuck, or Mother attempting to impose her control over my life. I couldn't believe I wasn't going to fuck Earl right off the bat, especially after all the invitations he had given me. I don't know why it was different this time, but it was different.

"I'm going to kiss you now," he said, no question, no "May I?" just the identification of his intentions, an announcement of what he was about to do. I felt a smile cross my face and a rush of energy through my chest. I felt like a child about to be bestowed with a birthday gift. I was gleaming with anticipation, not believing what I was observing in myself.

"Yes," I replied as though he had asked, but also saying *yes* to myself. *Yes, he is going to kiss me now. Yes, please kiss me.*

He leaned down and cupped his hand gently behind my head, and then his warm mouth covered mine. Our lips danced together in a slow, sensual chorus. Goose bumps ran down my arms. I felt a tingle of exhilaration, unlike anything I had ever felt. I didn't feel horny but more of a tender passion. When he stopped, our lips parted slowly and sensually. I felt myself sigh. *Jesus Christ! I sighed!* My chest felt light, like my heart had just floated into the air. I had never felt anything like that before.

He reached into his pocket and took out a pen. He lifted my hand and wrote his phone number across my palm. "Here is my number," he said. "Call me anytime." With that, he gave me another slow, sensual, but shorter kiss and walked away.

I stood and watched him gradually fade from the streetlights into the darkness before I turned to enter the dorm.

CHAPTER 13

Consummation

I had images of telling Marcy about Earl and the two of us bouncing our knees up and down on the mattress, screaming, *"Oh, my God! Oh, my God!"*

Yeah—like that was ever going to happen in a million years—not my style. Still, I felt like a giggly little schoolgirl swooning over, of all things, an ugly hippie.

When I got to my room, I copied his number into my address book and went to bed. I fell asleep with fantasies of Earl making love to me.

The following day, I still had a faint trace of Earl's number inked on my hand. The rest came off in the shower as I prepared for my Tuesday morning class. Marcy lay in her bed, still snoring. The lucky bitch didn't have a Tuesday class till 1:00 p.m..

I thought about Earl all day. I couldn't get over the fact that I didn't seem to care that he was ugly, and maybe he wasn't all that ugly. It had only been my initial impression. He was also very sweet and always smiling. I guess you could say that, despite being an ugly hippie, he did have a pretty smile—and that kiss! Oh my God—that kiss! I had never had a boy kiss me that way. I didn't have to teach him how to kiss. He already knew. Maybe he wasn't bullshitting me when he told me he was a fabulous lover.

I finished my last class at 2:00 p.m. and headed for the library. This time, it was to have a quiet place to read the assigned chapters in my Physical and Life Sciences class. At least that class applied to my major. I hoped I might see Earl there, but he didn't show. I kept peeking from my book, looking around the room, but nothing. I had a hard time concentrating on the book. Finally, I finished my chapters and headed to the cafeteria for dinner.

I hate cafeterias, but they are a necessary evil of dorm life. I had not yet made friends. It was too early in the semester, I guess. So, I felt a little lonely. I damn sure was not interested in making friends with Marcy, but there she was in the cafeteria with her bobblehead pals. It sure didn't take her long to find friends. I suppose it is easy to make friends when you have the mentality of a lemur. All you have to do is squeal, hang by your tail, and here come all the other lemurs. I tried to ignore her, but when I got through the line, she was waving and calling out, "Lovella, Lovella, over here. Come sit with us."

I thought, *Oh, Jesus! I don't want to sit at a table full of jock monkeys.* But I was polite and carried my tray to their table.

"Hello, girls," I said as I sat down.

Marcy began immediately. "You guys! You guys! This is my roommate, Lovella. Lovella, this is Staa-see, Nan-see, and Pat-see."

"How do you do," I said politely, thinking, *My, my, a table full of seeeees. How interesting that Mar-seee said each name with a distinct little hiss on the last syllable. It's a good thing there is not a cat around. Someone might have been scratched.*

"Lovella, guess what?" Marcy chirped. "Cheerleading tryouts are this week! We're all going to try out. You should, too."

"That's wonderful for you guys," I commented, "but I have absolutely no interest in cheerleading. Besides, I have about as much bounce as a flat tire, and even if I could bounce, the backlash from my tits would probably knock me out."

This gathered a round of giggles, which I suppose was to be expected. The girls bantered as I picked at my peas.

"Oh, but you look fit, and it will be so much fun!"

"I know, I know!" said Nan-see. "Let's tell her about all the cute guys she'll meet. Football players are so sex—seeee."

"Yes," chimed Pat-see. "There are some very handsome men in sporrrrrrrttts."

I knew my nausea could not have been from the food, so I kept eating. Downing a bite of chicken, I said, "I'm afraid it might be too much of a distraction from my academics."

"Oh, yes, yes, you guys," Marcy twittered. "Lovella is a biology major. She is soooo smart." Then, Marcy turned to me and said, "You're going to be a doctor or a scientist or something, right?"

"I hope to be able to do research," I replied, with no intention of getting into details with those who would spend more energy giggling over it than trying to understand the scientific value of my planned career. After that, thankfully, the conversation went to who was taking what class and how difficult it might be. It was a typical conversation, but I was happy to finish my meal soon and excuse myself. "I have to go now. I need to do a little more studying. You girls have a wonderful time."

"Oh, we will. We will," they chattered together. "You, too."

I was all too glad to excuse myself from the jock monkeys and go back to my room. In the dorm hall, by the elevator, was a bank of phones which dorm residents used. Everything went through the university operator except for local calls. When I got off the elevator, I walked by them, thinking I wanted to call Earl, but I dared not. I had only met him yesterday, and it would be, using Mother's term—*"unseemly"* to call so soon, and I didn't want him to believe that I was desperate. Mind you, I had never had a problem with being forward before, but then, all I wanted was sex and the power of knowing that I could bring a boy to his knees and make him beg for his pleasure. This time was different. I saw more in Earl than sex. I felt something more than sex, but I could not put my finger on precisely what it was. I asked myself if his family's money intrigued me and concluded that I couldn't care less about whether he had money. No, there was something different about this boy. I felt as though I had known him, as though we had had a meeting of souls rather than two people who happened to cross paths. Even though I had tried to reject him, initially, there was some recognition there, like when a toddler encounters another toddler in a room full of adults, and the two are immediately drawn to each other.

Tuesday rolled into Wednesday, and Wednesday rolled into Thursday. For three days, I fought the urge to call him. Finally, on Thursday, I figured that I had waited long enough.

Thursday evening, I went down the hall to the phone bank and dialed the number he had given me. After the phone rang about six times, I was about to hang up, thinking he must not be home, when I heard a click and "Hello."

"Is this Earl?" I asked.

"Is this Lovella?" he asked.

"How did you know it was me?" I questioned.

He reasoned, "I don't exactly have a harem waiting around for my next command, and I recognized your voice. It's good to hear from you. I was afraid you wouldn't call."

"No, I wanted to call," I said. "I've just been too busy."

I had not been too busy to call, but I deliberately avoided it, and the lie seemed sufficient while I waited for his reply.

"How busy will you be tomorrow?" he asked.

"Are you asking me out again?" I teased.

"Could be," he teased back. "Are you interested in going out again?"

"I might be leveraged with the right crowbar," I said.

"You may recall," he teased, "I have a nice, big crowbar that I could use for leverage."

He could not see the smile that crossed my face, but his tool, be it a hammer or crowbar, was not entirely what interested me. I searched my mind for a response.

"That might not leverage me, but dinner might," I replied.

"What time do you finish class tomorrow?" he asked.

"I'll be out by 4:00 p.m.," I replied. "I don't expect to be busy after that."

"So, if I pick you up at the dorm parking lot at 5:30, will that give you enough time to relax after class and freshen up?"

Then, there was a moment of silence as he waited for my response. I gave it a moment purposefully and said, "I think I could be ready by then. What will I be getting ready for?"

"How about dinner and a movie?" he inquired.

"That would be nice," I told him, thinking, *Wow! A real date!*

He continued, "A Chinese place is just around the corner from the Regal Theater. We could grab a quick bite there, and then you have two film choices: *Who's Afraid of Virginia Wolf* with Liz Taylor and Richard Burton or *The Ghost and Mr. Chicken* with Don Knots."

"They both sound good," I replied. "Which one would you prefer?" I was only trying to be polite. I had never been a big fan of comedy, and I had heard a lot of chatter about *Who's Afraid of Virginia Wolf*, including possible Oscar nominations, but I really didn't care. It was just something to do.

"Either one is fine with me," he said. "I want it to be something you would like."

Boom! It hit me! That was it! That separated him from every other boy I had ever known. He wanted to please me. It wasn't me teaching some boy how to have good sex. It wasn't me fighting back some eager twit whose only interest was ejaculation while I tried to get him to hold off long enough that I could get a little something out of it. Granted, I used them, took what I wanted, and did to them what they did to other girls. I fucked them and forgot them, but they all wanted to please themselves and couldn't have cared less about what I got out of it. Earl was the only man I had ever met, except Daddy and maybe Tommy, who wanted me to be happy.

"Still thinking?" he asked, breaking my daze of thought.

"No," I said. "I think I've made up my mind. I love Liz Taylor and Richard Burton, and *Who's Afraid of Virginia Wolf* sounds romantic and exciting."

"Great!" he said. "Do you like Chinese food?"

"I've only had it out of a can," I returned. "There aren't any Chinese restaurants in Climax or New Bethlehem, and Mother would never try to cook anything she considered exotic."

"Then, you've never really had Chinese food," he said. "Are you up for that? There are other options if you don't think you would like it."

"No, Chinese food sounds wonderful!" I exclaimed. "Besides, I like adventure. It will be an adventure, a chance to try something new."

"Okay, then," he said, sounding cheerful. "Five thirty p.m. tomorrow, dorm parking lot. I'll see you then."

"Okay then," I parroted. "Bye."

I don't know why I said "bye," much less in a sing-song little girl voice. I didn't want to hang up. I wanted to keep talking, but "bye" came out of my mouth.

"Bye," he said. "See you tomorrow."

I hung up the phone and walked back to my room. Half of me was disappointed that we didn't talk longer, and the other half was exhilarated that I would see him again. For the life of me, the only thing I could understand about why this ugly hippie intrigued me was the fact that he was so kind and considerate.

The next afternoon, I stood in the parking lot for only a few minutes when he drove up, leaned over, and threw open the passenger door for me. When I got in, the first thing he said was, "I want to kiss you."

I smiled and leaned toward him. He kissed me sensually for about ten seconds. Then, he looked longingly into my eyes and reached for the gear shift. The next thing I knew, the power under his Ferrari's hood surged, and zoom, we were away.

We pulled up in front of a little place called *Happy Dragon*. Earl turned to me and said, "They're open until midnight. Isn't that cool? It's not the finest, most elegant place, but it has delicious food."

We walked up to a glass door in a little shopping center. The wide windows by the door were painted over and decorated with colorful red dragons. Directly inside, there was a little podium with a Chinese lady dressed in a black silk blouse with a tight black skirt around her tiny ass.

"You have take-out?" she asked, with English obviously not having been her first language. From her accent, I realized that she must have immigrated from China or Taiwan.

"No, two for dinner," Earl replied.

"You come," she said, picking up two menus.

We followed her through what appeared to have been a converted, old storefront.

The entire décor was in shades of red and gold. Gold dragons crawled across the burgundy walls, and little silk lanterns with gold tassels were hung around the room. She sat us at a small table, laid the menus before us, and said, "Waiter be with you shortly." She then abruptly walked away. Earl grinned his trademark grin, picked up the menus, and handed one to me.

After briefly perusing the menu, I said, "I don't know what to order. I have no idea what any of this stuff is. All I have ever had is canned *Chicken Chow Mein*, and I didn't exactly like that."

"Well, let me ask you a few questions, and then I'll see if I can direct you to something," he offered. "Do you prefer, or are you in the mood for, spicy, moderately spicy, or mild?"

"Spicy," I said.

"Are there any vegetables you are opposed to?" he inquired.

"Only Brussels sprouts," I replied.

"Do you like a little sweetness in dishes or prefer completely savory?" he continued.

I pondered for a moment and realized that the only time I had anything sweet with a meal was either yams at Thanksgiving or Mother's cornbread, which she made entirely too sweet.

"I'm not very picky," I said.

"Okay," he continued. "Would you prefer beef, chicken, pork or seafood?"

"Seafood," I smiled, loving the attention.

"Okay," he said again. "Shrimp, scallops? What kind of seafood?"

"I love shrimp," I replied.

"All right then," he concluded. "How about *Kung Pow Shrimp?* You can tell the waiter just how spicy you want it. Personally, I like it very spicy."

"Somehow, I knew you would," I replied, smiling broadly.

The Asian waiter brought a teapot and two little porcelain cups to the table. "Would you like anything besides tea?" he asked, with perfect English, and I assumed he had been born and raised in the United States.

Earl looked across at me. "Lovella, this is hot tea," he said. "Would you like something cold to drink, as well?"

"Maybe just some ice water," I replied.

"Are you ready to order?" said the waiter, standing over us like a statue.

"Yes," said Earl. "She will have *Kung Pao Shrimp*, and I will have *Mongolian Pork*."

"How spicy do you want the *Kung Pao?*" asked the waiter.

"Not so spicy that it makes me cry," I said, "but fairly close to that."

The waiter stared at me.

Earl said, "How about a seven on a scale of one to ten?"

The waiter nodded and left.

"So, Lovella Fuchs," Earl said, leaning his elbows on the table and propping his chin onto long fingers. "I've been looking forward to seeing you again all week."

"Me too," I replied.

Then, the conversation fell into nothing, as though neither of us knew anything to say or had any questions to ask. The silence continued until it felt uncomfortable, and then Earl asked. "So, how often do you get home to see your parents?"

"As little as I can," I replied. "I think if I never saw Mother again, it wouldn't bother me that much, and I love Daddy, but …"

"But there's a problem," Earl said.

"Earl, my daddy is an alcoholic," I said. "Remember I told you the other day? As much as I love him, I don't want to be around him when he has been drinking." I sighed. "I feel like I'm confessing my sins and betraying my family's secret."

"Join the club," he commented. "Both my parents drink too much. Well, my mom used to, but she has cut down considerably. My dad still drinks way too much. You would never know it, and they would never admit it for fear of their appearance in the community, but Dad is a lush. Everyone must be protected from this big secret. Yeah, I get it. At one point, they could both drink a sailor under the table."

"Do you worry about them?" I asked. "I worry so about Daddy. I didn't worry for a long time, but just before I left for college, I saw a side of him that I had never seen before. It just seems like his drinking is getting worse and worse."

"My dad has been stopped by the cops a few times," Earl continued. "But all he has to do is wave some cash around, which takes care of that. Besides, several local crooked cops know who he is, and they'll stop him just for some extra cash that nobody talks about. He had a wreck a couple of years ago. He ran off the road. He said he was trying to keep from hitting a cat, but the truth is, he was plastered. Thank God neither he nor Mom got hurt too much. After that, they have done almost all their drinking at home. They will invite people over, sometimes, and let them be the ones who try to navigate their way home after having too much to drink."

"Local cops?" I asked. "I thought you were from Pittsburgh. That's a pretty big town."

"Well, we actually live in Bradford Woods," he replied. "It's a little town just outside Pittsburgh, but people who aren't familiar with the area are rarely familiar with it. It's just easier to say you are from Pittsburgh. Besides, we are so close to the Burgh you can barely tell where one ends and the other begins."

"Oh," I replied, returning to the original subject. "I read about alcohol when I was little. I tried to talk to Daddy about it because the dictionary says it's poison, but he assured me it was okay. I accepted that as a little girl, but it no longer seems okay."

"Maybe poison is determined by dosage," Earl continued. "You know, you take a couple of aspirins, and your headache goes away, but if you take the whole bottle, you get internal bleeding. You have a couple of drinks, and you feel a little relaxed, but if you drink all night, every night, you'll kill your liver."

"Yeah," I said. "That makes a lot of sense. I don't understand why Daddy doesn't have a couple and quit. Mother does. I don't think I've ever seen her have more than two at the absolute most, even at a party. She is so controlled that she wouldn't dare let anything cause her to let her hair down, much less let anyone see her getting the least bit sloppy."

"Yeah, I know," Earl said. "Some people are just uptight that way. You would think there would be some happy medium somewhere."

"Maybe we are the happy medium," I said, sipping my tea. I barely noticed that the waiter had brought my ice water.

"I hope we are," he said, reaching across the table to cover my hand with his. I looked down at his long, gangly fingers, but his hand was not skinny. His full, large, soft palm felt comforting and sensual as it lay across the back of my hand.

The food arrived and was delicious. I couldn't believe how exotic and interesting it tasted. Earl let me taste his pork, which was wonderful, too. We chatted over various things through dinner and almost lost track of the time.

"Goodness!" Earl exclaimed, finally, looking down at his watch. "We better get over to the Regal, or we will be late for the movie. He quickly paid, and we rushed to the theater to see *Who Is Afraid of Virginia Wolf*.

I don't think either of us knew what we were in for. I didn't realize how Earl felt about it until after the film, but it took me through a roller coaster of emotions I had not expected. An alcoholic couple in middle age was entertaining a young couple in their home for the evening. There was a minefield of mind games in the story, almost too many to keep up with. At the movie's end, I didn't know if I wanted to cry, scream, run, or hit someone.

We walked silently back to the car, got in, closed the doors, and sat there. Earl didn't start the engine. He didn't say a word at first. He just stared forward. Finally, he turned to me and said, "Are you okay?"

"I'm not sure," I replied. "I feel like an emotional rag that someone just twisted. Are you okay?"

There was a sigh and almost a snicker with a twinge of grief as he said, "No, I don't think I'm okay. You know, except that my mom and dad were much more private and not that vicious, I feel like someone just took the parents of my childhood and put them into a film."

"Do your parents treat each other like that?" I asked.

"Well, not anymore, and not quite like that, but they certainly have had their moments of mind games and bitterness in the past," he replied. "My mom is much more relaxed now than when I was little. She had a lot more stress on her then, but her drinking is way down now. The wealthier we get, the more she seems to return to normal, and the more my dad goes off the deep end. I guess that's because she initially worked so hard to help him get to where he is now. She relaxes now while he continues to obsess about the business."

Looking down at my purse on my lap, I said, "I don't think I saw my parents on screen because my daddy has a spirit far too sweet to be like that, but except for the subject in the mind games, I think I saw myself and my mother in this story."

"Jesus!" Earl exclaimed after a moment. "Do you think we should have seen *The Ghost and Mr. Chicken?*"

I burst out laughing, and he did, too. Our stress exploded into hilarity.

I said, "It's probably about a drunken ghost who is trying to make it with a chicken, but the chicken's alcoholic rooster husband keeps taunting the ghost that an ethereal cock won't do much for his frigid chicken wife!"

"And–And!" Earl teased. "They invite a younger chicken couple for corn-mash, but it all turns into a complicated, emotional, drunken chicken brawl, and the ghost gets so confused he gives up haunting."

We laughed off our anxiety, and when it faded, Earl said, "You know what I'm in the mood for?" He paused a moment to see if I could guess … "Ice cream."

"You know what I'm in the mood for?" I asked.

"No, what, Lovella Fuchs?" he questioned. "What are you in the mood for?"

"Sex," I said, reaching for his hand.

He immediately kissed me with passionate urgency. We might have consummated in the car but became potently aware that we were in a public parking lot when a young man knocked on the window and shouted, "Wooo, Hooo! Go for it!"

Earl sat back in his seat and asked, "My place?"

"Your place," I replied immediately.

He could barely get to the ignition quick enough.

A few minutes later, we parked on the street in front of a row of brownstone houses. When we got out of the car, he took my hand and led me up the brownstone steps just a few feet from where he parked. Inside was a central hall with stairs on the right side of the hall. Everything was paneled dark wood, and a single light illuminated the entrance. Earl led me up the stairs to a dark wooden door past the landing. He opened it, motioned me inside, and flipped on a light switch.

His apartment was simple. A bank of windows across the front overlooked the street. He had a nice console TV with bookshelves on either side. On the opposite wall was an old leather sofa with a Mexican-style throw over it and a floor lamp beside it. To the right, near the back, was a small kitchen and a little table with two chairs between the kitchen and the living room.

He took my coat and led me to the couch. "Can I get you anything to drink?" he said, neatly hanging my coat in a nearby closet.

"What do you have?" I questioned.

"What would you like?" he returned. "You can have anything from milk to wine."

"I'm a little scared to have anything with alcohol in it after seeing that movie," I said.

"So am I," he commented, "but I also think that if we attend to dosage, a little something might relax us a bit."

"Okay," I said, "I'll have a glass of wine."

"What kind?" he inquired. "Red wine, white wine, dry, sweet, semi-sweet?"

"What the hell?" I exclaimed. "There are that many choices. I don't even know what dry means. How can it be dry when it's a liquid?"

"It means it has more tannin and has more of a savory flavor rather than a sweet flavor," he replied. "You've never had wine, have you?"

"No, I haven't ever had wine," I admitted. "I don't know what I like. I'll have whatever you are having."

"Let's try this," he said, grinning, as he eyed a small wine rack near the kitchen. "You say only one of these words: Red or white?"

I mulled the decision over and finally said, "White. It seems lighter and maybe more refreshing than red."

"White it is!" he proclaimed. Then, he turned from his wine rack and went to his refrigerator while I preoccupied myself with looking around his apartment. In a moment, he returned with three bottles of wine and two glasses.

"You don't expect us to drink all that?" I questioned, a little nervous.

"No," he replied. "We're just going to taste."

He pulled a corkscrew from his pocket and opened one of the bottles. When pouring a little in the bottom of each glass, he said, "First, we will start with a little sweet, but not too sweet. If you were to wish for a really sweet wine, we would have to select a Moscato, but let's keep it light. What we have here is a Riesling from Germany. Now, first, a lesson in wine tasting." He lifted the glass and stuck his large nose over the rim, taking a big whiff. He pulled the glass from his nose and said, "You want to feel the aroma of the wine. Then, you taste." I wanted to ask how you feel a smell, but I just listened and played along. He slurped a portion into his mouth and swished it around like a mouth full of mouthwash. I laughed robustly, and after swallowing, he turned to me, laughing himself, and said, "Now you try."

"You are so full of shit!" I said, giggling.

"No! No! Try it!" he pleaded.

I pulled the glass to my nose and took a big whiff. It was somewhat fruity but not heavy like grape juice, and the cold wine felt cool in my nostrils. Then, I slurped it just as I had seen him do and swished it in my mouth. As I did, the taste seemed to change a bit, and layers of flavors crossed over my tongue, moment by moment. I looked at him, astonished.

"You see! You see!" he smiled. "This is how the hoity-toity do it. By the way, white wines are consumed cold, and red wines are consumed at room temperature, after allowing them to breathe, of course, and if they do not appear to be breathing, you must give them—mouth to mouth."

A gleam filled his face over the pun, and I laughed. "Now, he said, "for the Chardonnay."

I giggled, and he continued to talk while opening the next bottle.

"The Chardonnay, as you might deduce from the name, is from France. It is not quite as sweet as the Riesling and has a hint of dryness. But! But! But! To appreciate it, without contamination, one must have a clean, un-influenced glass." He darted to the kitchen and returned with four more glasses. He poured a bit of the Chardonnay into two of them, and I imitated him this time while he was doing it. He held the glass in the air, swirling the wine around in the bottom. I did the same. Then, we both brought the glass to our noses, whiffed, slurped, and swished. Except, this time, just as he finished swishing, he kicked his head back and gargled!

I laughed so hard I almost choked on the wine in my mouth and almost dropped my glass.

"So, how did you like the Chardonnay?" he queried.

"It had more of a bitter and sour flavor than the Riesling," I said, "but it has a fruity finish that is quite delightful."

"Ooooh, you are getting the hoity-toity rules of wine! And now!" he announced. "Let's bring the Italians to the table! We will have our little European summit here in my living room."

He began opening the third bottle. "This, my dear, is Pinot Grigio. It is a dry Italian wine often served with fish. It has the slightest hint of sourness."

He poured the wine, and we went through the rituals as before, but this time, I smacked my tongue against the roof of my mouth and stuck it out.

Laughing at me, he said, "I take it that Pinot Grigio is not your cup of tea."

"It is not only not my cup of tea but also not my glass of wine," I replied. "I'm not certain that it's not a cup of chilled bull piss."

"Oh, now, now," he comforted. "You must experience it under the right circumstances. Perhaps it is not the best wine to sip and would be better enjoyed with a meal of Lobster Thermidor, but … they say … the more you drink wine, the more you drink it dry."

"Well, you can turn me on to that some other time," I said. "How about a glass of the Riesling?"

He filled my original glass, and we had only taken a few sips before he set his glass on the floor. He leaned in and began to kiss me. He took my glass and fumbled to set it down while he kissed me. When he was not able to reach the coffee table or level it on the floor while he continued to kiss me, he threw it across the room. It hit the bookshelf on the other side of the room, shattered into pieces of glass, and splashed on the floor. Yet, he didn't miss a moment of kissing me.

His kiss was pressured but gentle, passionate, yet sweet and gently sensual. I began to feel the pulsing pressure of his phallus on my thigh as he pressed against me. Then, he stood up, took my hand, and led me to his bedroom, where he slowly and meticulously undressed me, kissing and caressing every part of my body as he revealed it. After removing my blouse one careful button at a time, he reached around and unclasped my bra with surgical precision. His hand moved around my breast, and his mouth covered my nipple. His tongue circled my nipple, and the soft tingle of his long hair fell lightly between my breasts. He gently pushed me back onto the bed, ran his hands around the rim of my panties, and slid them slowly down my legs onto the floor. Then, he stood before me, staring at me as I lay naked and vulnerable on the bed. He began to undress. Slowly and sensually flicking open the buttons of his shirt, he looked at me like an art lover viewing an original Monet. When he pulled off his pants and underwear, his erect cock popped out, and I fought a gasp.

My God! I thought, astonished, *That's the most enormous damn cock I've ever seen.* Then, I felt a little scared that it might be too big. It was not like I was a virgin or that I hadn't had big ones before, but I still found myself wondering if I would be able to handle one that big. I wanted things to go well and feared getting into some fumbling attempt where I would have to make him stop because it hurt. I squelched my fear and surrendered to the moment.

He approached the bed, folded himself over me again, and kissed me gently. He worked his lips tenderly from my mouth over my neck and down my body, his beard assisting in the tingling sensation of pleasure. I felt engorged with anticipation. For once in my life, a man was actually making love to me instead of me having to show him every step or slow him down. For once, I had a man who already knew what to do and was doing it. I didn't have to stop him to redirect or instruct him. He was genuinely making love to me. Yet, he wasn't just doing it. He was enjoying the moment, enjoying the experience of pleasuring me. That, in itself, was exhilarating.

When his mouth finally reached the muff-dragon, I lunged backward with a gasp of electric joy. He continued to thrill me while I alternated between grabbing fists full of the sheets and chirping with pleasure. By the time he laid me back onto the pillow and was about to enter me, I was begging.

"Please ... please," I heard myself whisper.

He reached down and guided himself slowly into me. At first, it was a little painful. Yet, I thought I was going to explode with pleasure. Then, he drew back and pushed again, slowly and tenderly. Unlike other boys who had acted more like rabbits in a mating frenzy, he took his time and lingered with me in the communion of lovemaking.

He was so gentle, so attentive, and yet so passionate that I soon felt the explosion of an orgasm welling within me. Suddenly, the screams and gasps that came out of my mouth were primal, and I pushed my hands across his back in surrender to euphoria! He held me tightly as the energy that was generated by my climax surrounded and infused each of us. Then, he tenderly continued rocking me in lovemaking. Not long after the first wave passed, another followed, and then another. I was having repeated orgasms. I had taught Tommy how to do that, and he became good at it, but Earl's experience was like no other. For the first time, a man pleasured me more than my middle finger.

Shortly, I began to hear Earl's breath quicken. His moans became heavier, his thrusts more rapid, and I knew he was about to finish. This brought me to yet another orgasm. Just knowing that he was about to climax made me climax. Then, we were both engulfed in waves of pleasure, a whirlwind of passion.

After that, he fell silent over me, panting but tenderly kissing my cheek and my ear. Shortly, he rolled over onto his side, pulled me to him, and enfolded me in his arms.

"Oh, my God!" I exclaimed. "You were so gentle, loving, and passionate."

"When you are swinging this much pipe," he grinned, "you have to learn how to be gentle."

"Had sex with a lot of girls, have you?" I teased.

"Well, I don't know what you would call a lot, but a few." He stroked a single finger down between my breasts to the muff dragon and back up. "Some girls," he continued, "are scared of it. One girl even grabbed her clothes and ran out crying as soon as she saw it, but you seemed okay."

"I can't say that I wasn't a little scared, too," I responded, "but I have had some practice, just not with one that big."

"Had sex with a lot of boys, have you?" he teased.

I smiled and stroked his beard. "Well, I don't know what you would call a lot, but a few. Still, I never experienced anything like this. You weren't lying when you said you were good. Where did you learn to be such a great lover?"

"First," he answered, "I read the *Kama Sutra* when I was thirteen, then a couple of other books, and then I experimented. Dad was too busy to tell me about sex, and Mom was too embarrassed. I kept hearing boys talking about sex, but it didn't seem like any of them knew what they were talking about. Some of the ideas they had were ludicrous. So, I knew I had to figure it out for myself."

I started laughing. "Oh, my God! I can't believe this."

"What?" he questioned, suddenly slightly embarrassed. "What? What are you laughing at?"

I gave him a quick peck on the lips, and my face lit up like a candle. "I did the same thing. I read the *Kama Sutra* when I was about thirteen."

"You're kidding, aren't you?" he asked.

"No. I'm not kidding," I replied. "I read the *Kama Sutra* for similar reasons."

His eyes lit up, and a huge smile crossed his face. He pulled me to him and held me as the post-coitus drowsiness of good sex crept in. Then, we fell asleep enfolded in one another's arms, me and the ugly hippie.

CHAPTER 14

Living in Sin

After that first night with Earl, I was hooked. I couldn't get enough of him. Earl Titwallow had become my new obsession. As often as not, I stayed in Earl's flat rather than the dorm. No more Mar-see, Sta-see, Tra-see or, "ooooh goody." At last, I was in the company of an adult. I suddenly felt domestic.

Mother had never taught me to cook. I think she found it frustrating, and besides, she wouldn't take a chance that I might have messed up any of her perfect little concoctions or something in her kitchen. She hoped I would marry into money and forever have servants doing things like cooking and cleaning. Yet even though I was in the company of someone who had grown up to become wealthy enough to have servants, I felt like cooking and cleaning. I don't know what came over me. I just wanted to do it. I wanted to stay with him and take care of him.

When I wasn't studying or finding another excuse to have sex with Earl, not that either of us needed an excuse, I was checking out cookbooks from the library and watching episodes of *The French Chef* with Julia Child. Earl told me that I didn't have to cook, that he could afford to take me out to eat, or that he could have food catered. Nonetheless, when he saw my interest in cooking, he bought me a copy of Julia Child's *Mastering the Art of French Cooking*. I was in heaven. I plowed through the book with fascination. I experimented with the recipes and, unfortunately, destroyed many of them. Yet, even though I put charred and unrecognizable reproductions of Julia's recipes in front of him, Earl cooed over it as though it was a perfect delicacy cooked by Julia herself.

It was all wonderful, a domicile of comfort and happiness. Then, Marcy called Earl's number one night and told me Mother had called the dorm several times, wanting to speak to me. I had given Marcy Earl's number and told her to let me know if Mother had called.

"Oh," she said, "your mom seemed reeeeally worried about you."

"You had Earl's number," I accused. "Why didn't you let me know the first time she called."

"Oh, I'm so busy, I get mixed up," she lied.

"What did you tell Mother?" I asked.

"Wellllll," Marcy dragged out the word, passive-aggressive little bitch that she was. "I told her that you were spending a lot of time at your new boyfriend's apartment. I hope that's o-kaaaaay."

"Marcy," I questioned. "Why would you tell my mother I live with my boyfriend?"

"Oh!" she gasped in feigned concern, "I would never tell her that you were living with him. I only told her that you were spending a lot of time at his apartment."

"How would you like it if I told your mother that you were spending a lot of time at your boyfriend's apartment?" I snapped.

"Oh, that's silly," she snickered. "My boyfriend doesn't have an apartment. Besides, I'm dating two boys on the football team, and they both live on campus. It's hard to decide which one to spend most of my time with."

"How very monogamous of you," I mocked.

"What does that mean?" she asked in apparent shock that I must have just accused her of prostitution or something.

"It means I'm very happy for you," I replied gingerly, hiding my disgust at her ignorance. "What did my mother say?"

"Oh, she said she wants you to call her immediately."

"Thank you for calling, Marcy," I said deliberately. "I will be sure to call her."

"Oh, okay, goodbye now," she spouted with her cheery little tone.

I hung up the phone and stared straight ahead. This was most assuredly going to be a call I would dread. It would be difficult enough trying to explain why I was not to be found in the dorm, but there was a nagging fear that something might be wrong. Perhaps Grandmother had died, or Daddy was ill.

At the time of Marcy's call, Earl had handed me the phone receiver and then sat across the room reading a textbook.

"Earl," I said after a moment of pause. "Do you mind if I call my mother? I will forward the charges."

"Don't worry about it," he replied. "I can afford the phone bill. Call anyone you want."

"No, I have to forward the charges," I continued. "If I don't, Mother will want to know how I'm paying for a long-distance phone call. I could pretend I'm calling her from the dorm, but apparently, she already knows better, and I would have to call collect from there, too."

"Whatever you need to do is fine," he said.

I realized I was merely stalling, not wanting to make the call. Finally, I dialed the zero, and when the operator came on the line, I said, "Yes, I would like to make a collect phone call, please, to Mrs. Drucella Fuchs at …"

After hearing the number, the operator connected me. "I have a collect phone call for Mrs. Drucella Fuchs from Lovella Fuchs. Will you accept the charges?"

"Yes." I heard Mother's terse voice and then, "Hello, Lovella. It is good that you finally decided to call."

"I'm sorry, Mother." I apologized and made an excuse, "I've been busy with my studies."

"Do you have any idea how long I've been trying to get hold of you?" she interrogated and then answered without allowing me to guess. "Three weeks!"

"I'm sorry, Mother," I replied. "Marcy didn't tell me you had been calling until today."

"You know, several girls have answered the phone in the dorm over these past three weeks. A couple of them said they had repeatedly left notes on your door."

"Perhaps they got the wrong door, or Marcy misplaced the notes. She is quite a ditz, you know." I knew there would be no appeasing Mother even as I said that.

"Lovella!" she shouted. "Do you take me for a fool? At first, Marcy said she didn't even know how to reach you. How was I to know you hadn't been abducted or something? Where have you been?"

"It seems you and Marcy have been exchanging information," I replied tersely. "Why don't you tell *me* where I've been?"

"That girl told me you are living with a man!" Mother snapped. "Should I believe her?"

"Mother, I think the question should be, do you believe her?" I responded.

"Unfortunately, Lovella," she continued. "There is nothing that I would not put past you."

"Technically," I countered, "I'm not living with him. My address is still at the University, but I spend most of my nights here."

"Lovella Fuchs!" she screamed. "How dare you!"

"How dare I what, Mother?" I questioned. "How dare I live my own life?"

"Don't be flippant with me!" she bellowed. "How dare you live with a man! Not only is it unseemly and socially inappropriate, but it's also—a sin!"

"Well, so is smoking a cigarette with my pussy in a public park, Mother," I replied. "Sin is my forte. You should have noticed long before now that I do it well."

There was silence on the line, and I thought I had left her speechless. Finally, I said, "So, did you call me to chew me out about living with my boyfriend, or did you have something else on your agenda?"

"So, he is your *boyfriend?* Tell me about this boy," she demanded.

"Oh, now he's a boy," I teased. "I thought I was living with a man."

"Well, whomever you are living with," she raged, "explain yourself!"

"His name is Earl Titwallow," I began. "He is from Bradford Woods, which, if you haven't heard of it, is outside Pittsburgh. He is two years ahead of me in school, and he is studying business."

"Business? Hmm. What kind of character does this boy have?" she continued interrogating, a little calmer after hearing that Earl would get a business degree. "What kind of family is he from?"

There it was, Mother's ultimate question. Regardless that Daddy was a factory worker, and our family was at the bottom end of middle-class straddling the poverty line with ancestors going back to Kentucky coal miners, Mother's aspiration was that we only associate with the most refined. I hesitated to tell her about Earl's background. I would rather have told her that he came from a poor bunch of hillbillies who had used their last pennies to send their toothless red-neck boy to college. She would have squirmed and sputtered. However, despite whatever was going on in my life, I usually told the truth about it, even to Mother. I seldom saw the need for deception. Finally, I said it. Taking a deep breath to compose myself and feeling as though I were confessing, I affirmed just one sentence that would satisfy her, and for that, all else would be overlooked. "His father owns the Chum Snacks Company."

She literally gasped. I imagined her swooning with glee, and then, just as I had anticipated, her tone changed completely.

"Oh, well," she said and then paused.

I could almost hear the gears turning in her head as she began to justify for herself how she might condone her daughter living with someone out of wedlock and the *sin* be forgiven. All in all, it was simply a different form of prostitution that Mother endorsed, and she would now, indeed, find a way to endorse it.

"Well," she said after her pause. "I'm sure he must be a very nice young man."

For all she knew, he could have been a serial killer, but the instant I told her that he was from a wealthy family, all was forgiven. What kind of man he was didn't matter to her; it only mattered that his family was wealthy.

"Yes, Mother," I acknowledged. "I have to say that I am quite fond of him."

"Well, um," she stuttered. "I had originally called to make plans for Thanksgiving. Your Grandmother Claudella would like the family to come to her house, and she said she would like to see you."

I had lost track of how close we were to the nearing holidays. I had not given much thought to Thanksgiving or Christmas. I had been so caught up with Earl and school that I had forgotten to make my regular calls home, much less anything else.

"That's very nice, Mother." I said, "I've been so busy that I haven't thought much about the holidays."

"Yes, I know you must be working very hard, dear. How are your studies?"

She could have cared less about my fucking studies. I had, in her mind, already accomplished what she hoped. Regardless of my major or my desires for a career, she lumped me into the same category as Marcy and her inane little friends. Regardless of what I claimed as my major, Mother secretly hoped I would get a degree in husband-ology.

"As always, I'm doing quite well with my studies," I replied. "However, I have been spending a lot of time with Earl, and I plan to continue doing so as long as he desires it."

Then, she asked something she would never have asked without knowing Earl was wealthy. If Earl had been that poor red-neck kid, the question would never have been asked, and she would have refused the option entirely. "Would you like to spend Thanksgiving with Earl's family this year?"

I stifled the impulse to tear into her about hypocrisy. Instead, I said, "We haven't discussed it, Mother. I don't know." She called to tell me that Grandmother Donner wanted to see me at Thanksgiving, but suddenly, it was okay if I spent it with Earl's family.

"Well, why don't you talk to him about it, dear, and call me back," she happily enticed. "By the way, did you tell me this boy's name?"

"Yes, Mother. I told you his name is Earl Titwallow."

As I said it, I pictured her writing down the name, then gallivanting around the neighborhood, knocking on doors, and telling everyone, "Oh yes, my daughter is dating a wealthy socialite. His name is …" I became embarrassed before she even hung up the phone that she might actually do that. After all, she had allegedly lugged me around from door to door when I was a baby.

"Well, dear," she chirped. "Discuss it with Earl and call me back. If need be, I'll explain to Grandmother. I'm sure she will understand."

I hung up the phone and buried my face in my hands.

"Are you alright?" Earl asked, looking up from his book.

Without removing my face from my hands, I said, "My fucking Mother is a gold-digging cunt!"

"What's up?" he questioned.

"Earl," I said, looking up, "are we officially dating? Are we a couple?"

"Hmmm," he pondered. "We have never really discussed that, have we? I don't know about you, but I assumed we are a couple."

"That's what I assumed, too," I said, "but I've never brought it up, and I probably wouldn't be bringing it up now except for my mother. If it weren't for family, I would be content to let our relationship naturally evolve into whatever form it wishes to take."

"It seems to me," he reflected, "that it has been taking shape, and I don't know that we need to allow family to cause us to worry about that."

"Okay," I finally confessed after building my resolve. "Here is the deal. My Mother was a furious bitch about me living with a man out of wedlock until I told her that your dad owns the Chum Snacks Company. Then, and I know her well enough to know that she would do this, she wanted to know if I would like to spend Thanksgiving with your family. However, she had called to tell me that my grandmother wants me to come spend Thanksgiving with them."

"Jeez," he responded. "Thanksgiving is next week, isn't it? I haven't thought much about that."

"I know," I replied. "Neither have I, but Mother has brought it to the doorstep."

"Well, what would you like to do?" he said.

"I would love to meet your family, Earl," I replied, "but do they even know about me?"

"Well, actually, no, they don't," he answered, "but there is no reason why they shouldn't, and there would be no problem with having you spend the holiday with us."

"See, that's the deal."

I got up, paced the room, and turned back to him. "You don't know my mother. You don't know how she is."

"I've heard you talk about her," he cut in.

"No," I popped back. "It's not the same. You don't understand. She will try to manipulate everything that happens to me and to one end—to see me married into a quote, *respectable family*. She only offered me the option to spend Thanksgiving with your family because she now knows you come from wealth. A moment before I told her who your father is, she was bitching me out for living with someone. I can guarantee you that if I had told her that you were a local grocery clerk, she would have continued to bitch, insist that I must come home for Thanksgiving and that I must move back into the dorm."

"Well, actually, I don't come from wealth," Earl related. "My dad has built this company from the ground up, and it has taken most of my life to do it. We have only been on the opulent end of profits for about the last five or six years. I know what it is like, or at least I think I do, to struggle a little bit."

"No, honey, you are missing the point," I pleaded. "Since I reached puberty, and probably before, Mother has tried to match me up with the kind of boys she thinks are appropriate for me. She set me up on a blind prom date, without my permission, with this doctor's son, who was a jerk. But Mother wanted to push him on me. She has pushed those kinds of boys on me for years, and as hard as she has pushed, I've resisted. By dating you, I'm dating exactly the kind of person she wants me to date. She will even overlook the scruffy hippie exterior if she thinks wealth is behind it."

"Lovella," he pleaded as he rose from his chair to hug me. "I want to be with you. I enjoy being with you. So, what difference will it make if your mother pushes us together?"

"It's the chocolate cake principle," I said. "I love chocolate cake. It is one of my favorite desserts, and given the chance, I will sit and savor it, enjoying every moment, but I don't want it shoved in my face. That completely changes the experience. I don't want Mother shoving me in your face, and I don't want her shoving you in my face, but I know, as sure as I'm breathing, that is probably what she will do."

He paused, cupped his hands on my face, and gently kissed me.

"You know," he said, "I think if someone did shove chocolate cake in my face, it might be fun to lick it from my lips and rake the pieces from my cheeks into my mouth."

I smiled. "You're a freak," I said.

That classic Cheshire grin crossed his face. "You know you like that freaky stuff. So, what do you want to do?"

"I don't know," I whined. "I would love to meet your parents, but I know, at some point, Mother is going to insist on meeting you, and are we at that point? We have only been seeing each other for a few weeks. Are we already at the point where we divide the holidays between in-laws like a married couple?"

"We have been seeing each other since September," he said. "That is longer than a few weeks. We have the option of going, each of us, to our own families over the holidays, or we have the option of trading off. You said your grandmother wanted to see you? I say we go to your family for Thanksgiving if they are willing to have me as a guest. Besides, I would love to meet your family."

"Oh my God, Earl," I pleaded. "My family is a bunch of lower-class lunatics, inbred freaks, and drunks. I think one of the reasons Mother tries to palm herself off as highbrow is because she is ashamed of the whole damned lot. As much as I love Daddy, he is a drunk. His drinking is getting worse, and I have no idea what he might do over Thanksgiving. Mother will give us no peace. Grandmother Donner is a chubby, frumpy little woman who wears strange clothes, has fat lips, smokes cigars, and picks at Mother like an ill-tempered Chihuahua. I don't know who will be there. My Grandfather Fuchs is dead, but Grandmother Fuchs might be there, and she will be quoting the Bible sweetly but persistently at every reference she can find in the conversation. I don't know. I just don't know. I can barely tolerate them, myself."

"Hey, you said I am a freak," he smiled. "I should fit right in."

"If you want to spend Thanksgiving with my family," I said, walking over and plopping myself on the sofa, "then you are a freak."

He came and sat beside me. "Look," he said and put his arm around me. "My family is no piece of cake either. My Dad will give me no peace. There is usually some point when I want to throw him out the window. Now that he has made millions, he thinks that makes him better than others. He may even direct some strategically placed put-downs to you. Long before he made the money, he seemed to think the world should revolve around him, and as far as Mom was concerned, it did. My mom has been a quiet, reserved doormat who has always done whatever he wanted because she thought it was her wifely duty unless she had her fill of him and would scream back. She's grown a little more of a backbone, but when I was small, she worked two part-time jobs and cared for the family so Dad could spend a bajillion hours a day trying to build his company. She drank and resented him for not being there. He drank and resented her for not being more."

He sighed deeply, stared at the floor momentarily, and went on. "When I was very small, I didn't see either of them much. My Grandma Shaw took care of my little sister and me most of the time. My grandma was wonderful, but she was killed in a car wreck when I was fourteen. I would tell you about my Grandpa Shaw, but he is more of a story in the family than anything else. He abandoned my mom's family when she was in her early teens. So, there's no one from Mom's side. On my dad's side, he tries to prove something. He has tried sending a chauffeur to pick up Grandma and Grandpa Titwallow. He does that more to impress my grandpa than anything else. Grandpa could care less if he rides in a limo and refuses to have Dad send a car for them. So, Dad goes to pick them up. It's a battle almost every holiday. Although Dad keeps trying, there will never come a time when he will win Grandpa's approval. Grandma Titwallow gets through it by cracking jokes or ignoring it all."

Earl gave me a quick squeeze around the shoulders and continued to tell his story. "You've heard me talk about my little sister. She's five years younger than me, and she's okay, I guess. I looked after her when we were little kids, but she never endured the hard years when Dad built the company. I went through that alone. She has grown up having things, and she takes it for granted. My dad favors her and gives her everything. Instead of his time, he gives her money and buys her stuff. She only has to think she wants something, and there it is. I don't want to say she is spoiled, but she has always expected to be taken care of and has never been required to put forth any real effort. She says she wants to be a nurse. Yeah, man, I can see that happening. The first time she sees blood or has to empty a bedpan, it's over."

"My family is worse," I said.

"Wanna bet?" he challenged. "I say we tell them all to go fuck themselves while you and I spend Thanksgiving together, just the two of us. Hell, we can drive down to the Keys if you want."

"I can't, Earl," I said. "Either way, if I don't spend Thanksgiving with my family or yours, I'll never hear the end of it. Mother will torture me with it, and if I spend Thanksgiving with your family, she is going to insist that you come for Christmas."

"Whatever," he said. "Want to flip a coin? Heads, we spend Thanksgiving with your family. Tails, we spend it with mine?"

He reached in his pocket for a quarter.

"I suppose it is as good a way to decide as any," I sighed. "Why not?"

He flipped the coin into the air, caught it, and slapped it on his hand. Then, he teased, barely lifting his hand off the results and closing it back.

"Are you sure you want to see?" he grinned.

I punched him playfully in the arm. "Show me the Goddamn quarter!" I insisted.

He gradually lifted his hand, and there it was—heads!

"I guess we go see your folks this first holiday," he smiled.

"You don't know what you are getting yourself into," I cautioned.

"Well," he chided, throwing back his shoulders in a mock display of strength, "Daniel survived the lion's den. Surely Earl can survive Thanksgiving with the Fuchs and the Donners."

CHAPTER 15

My Crazy Family Thanksgiving

November 14, 1966

Dear Gretta and Tommy,

I wanted to let you know that I will be home for Thanksgiving and would love to see you. I have a boyfriend now. His name is Earl Titwallow, and he is from the Pittsburgh area. He is two years ahead of me in school, and although he is not like anyone I ever thought I would be with, he is very nice, and I am quite fond of him. Earl will be coming with me, and I hope for you to meet him. However, I have to say that I am embarrassed over the idea of Earl meeting my family. You know how they are.

Mother will not hear of Earl staying with us. She could not tolerate the community knowing that she let her unmarried daughter and boyfriend sleep in the same house, much less the same bed, even though she knows I am living with him. Earl will, therefore, stay at a hotel and meet us for the family dinner. We will arrive on Wednesday evening, the 23rd, and spend the evening with Mother and Daddy. Thursday belongs to Grandmother Donner, who insisted she wants to see me over the holiday. However, if you guys are not also busy with family on the Friday after Thanksgiving, we hope to spend some time with you before returning to State College. Call me at Mother's next Wednesday evening after 7:00 PM, please.

Much Love,

Lovella.

The whole week after Mother's call, I was a nervous wreck. I usually would have cared less about whether a boy liked my family, but this was different. Earl was different, and he was terrific that whole week. He was constantly reassuring me that everything would be fine, that he didn't mind staying in a hotel, and that he was sure he would love my family.

Mother and Daddy did not have a guest room in our little two-bedroom bungalow. Earl could have stayed with Grandmother Donner, but I could see a complete disaster brewing with that arrangement.

Truthfully, I had little to do with either of my grandmothers when I was growing up. I suspect Mother somehow wanted to shield me from them for fear that I might pick up Grandmother Donner's low-brow ways and penchant for profanity or favor Grandmother Fuchs over her. There were none of the usual sleepovers at grandmother's houses like many other children enjoy. As with so many things Mother insisted on, I accepted it when I was little. It wasn't that important to me anyway. I would rather have my face in a book.

Before the holiday, Earl talked with his parents and told them he was dating me. His mother expressed disappointment that he would not be home for Thanksgiving but enticed him that she would look forward to meeting me at Christmas.

Earl and I arrived in Climax in time for dinner on Wednesday evening. When he pulled the Ferrari up in front of our house, I let out a big sigh. He reached over and took my hand.

"Are you all right?" he asked.

I smiled and looked over at him. "I'm fine," I replied. "I just never want to deal with Mother, especially when she is in one of her little gloat fests, and I know there will be so many questions."

Earl patted my hand, got out of the car to get my bags, and dutifully carried them to the porch.

Rather than walking through the front door, as usual, I knocked on the door like a stranger. Mother came to the door and looked at me, with eyebrow hefting surprise. "Oh, for heaven's sake, Lovella, you have a key. Why didn't you just come in?"

"I suppose I was just feeling formal," I replied, walking across the threshold. I turned, motioned to Earl, and said, "This is my boyfriend, Earl Titwallow."

Mother scanned him like an X-ray machine, I'm sure, trying to pick up every tiny perceived abnormality. She thrust her hand at him, forcing him to put the luggage down and accept the greeting. "How do you do, Earl?" she twittered, her trademark three fingers laid daintily across his palm. "So nice to meet you. I'm Drucella Fuchs, Lovella's mother."

"How nice to meet you, Mrs. Fuchs," Earl said with perfect etiquette.

"What a sweet boy, Lovella. He has very nice manners." She gleamed toward me, overlooking Earl's long hair and hippie clothing. She glanced back and forth between me and the doorway, where she could see the Ferrari parked in front of the house. She didn't care about the scraggly hair or anything else as long as he was rich. She then gleamed back at Earl. "Come in! Come in!" she greeted. "Lovella, would you please show Earl to your room with your luggage?"

"Yes, Mother," I replied and presented my best behavior.

Daddy was nowhere to be found, and I wasn't sure if I wanted to ask.

I led Earl to my room, and he set the luggage beside my bed. After putting the luggage down, he hugged me closely and kissed me. After the kiss, I asked, "Are you ready for this?"

He said, "I'm fine. It's you that I should be worried about. It seems that you are the nervous one."

"I've gotten through eighteen years with this family," I said. "I'm sure I can make it till the weekend. Let's go."

I took him by the hand and led him back into the living room. No one was in the living room or the kitchen, but it soon became evident that

Mother had gone out the back door to the shed to fetch Daddy. As recent years progressed, he spent more of his time in the shed drinking rather than dealing with Mother in the house. I'm sure that situation was not helped when I left for school. I saw Mother through the back window, lecturing him and commanding him into the house with dramatic gestures, and that red, painted fingernail slinging in our direction. When I saw this, I motioned Earl to the living room, where we sat on the sofa. I didn't want him to see any more than I could possibly prevent. I knew, for certain, that he would see enough. Finally, Daddy staggered into the living room with Mother behind him.

"Well, look there!" he shouted in a voice far too loud and far too enthusiastic. "It's my le-little Pa-Punkin' Patch." He made a staggered move to hug me and hit his shin on the coffee table. "Oh, goddamn—ouch!" he exclaimed and then practically fell into me as I was getting up. When he hugged me, the stench of stale alcohol filled my nostrils, and I had a feeling of horror in my heart as I realized that Daddy's drinking was progressing to a point beyond control. "Hi there, ya-ya-young ma-man," he slurred and reached his hand toward Earl.

Earl had stood up when I did. He politely shook Daddy's hand and said, "Pleased to meet you, sir. Earl Titwallow is the name."

"Titwallow," Daddy snickered. "N—N—Now that's a fa-funny name. Not like Fa-Fuchs, eh Pa-Punkin'?" Laughing, he poked me in the shoulder and said, "Sa-Sit down. Make ya-ya-yourself ca-com-forrr-torr-able." He motioned Earl to sit back on the sofa, and then Daddy plopped beside him and pulled on my arm for me to sit. Daddy ended up sitting between us. Across the room, Mother had watched this spectacle with a failed attempt to disguise her disgust.

"I think I will finish dinner," she said irritably, returning to the kitchen. I wished I had tried harder to convince Earl that we should spend the holiday separately or go to his parents' house. However, Grandmother Donner had asked to see me, and we had flipped a coin that directed us to Climax.

"So, ta-tell me, Eh-Eh-Earl," Daddy exclaimed as he slapped Earl on the leg. "What do you-you do for a li—ving?"

"Sir," Earl responded politely. "Right now, I'm a student at Penn State with Lovella. We met in the college library."

"Oh, yeah! Ya—Yeah!" Daddy went on. "My da—daughter's going to co-coll-eh-geh up there. She's go-oh-ing to be a da-doctor. Did ya-you know my da-au-daughter is going to be a da-octor?"

I saw Earl visibly wince from the odor on Daddy's breath when Daddy got much too close during the conversation.

"Earl is studying business," I said, cutting into the conversation and hoping to pull Daddy back in my direction.

"Hey-hey, Punkin' Patch', you-ooo know what?" Daddy turned and slapped me on the knee. The stench of his gullet intruded into my nostrils. "Why da-don't you-ooo go see-see if your mother n-needs some he-help in the kitchen so me an-and Earl can have some ma-an time?"

I had no idea what Daddy meant, and I barely knew what to do because I had never seen him react to a boy that way. I knew his drinking was getting worse, but his entire personality seemed to have changed. I looked at Earl questioningly, and he motioned his eyes toward the kitchen. I did not want to leave Earl alone with Daddy. Still, I got up and left the room with intense hesitation. I had no idea what would ensue if I left them alone, but I also trusted Earl to manage a situation if it were to arise.

Mother was preparing brown and serve rolls for the oven. She looked up briefly as I entered, and I could swear I caught a hint of shame in her eyes.

"Dinner will be ready in a few minutes," she said. "We are having roast beef. After dinner, I will make a pumpkin pie to take with us tomorrow."

"That sounds very nice, Mother," I responded quietly. "Is there anything I can do to help?"

"No, of course not, dear," she smiled faintly. "Sit down. I'll get you some tea."

I sat at the dining table, and briefly, she set a glass of tea in front of me. She saw me glancing back toward the living room and seemed to guess what I was thinking.

"He has been getting worse over the last year, Lovella." She spoke, staring momentarily toward the living room. "I was successful with hiding it from you for most of that time, but you recall how he behaved at the hospital after Gretta had her baby. That was mild compared to the last few months."

"Mother, shouldn't we get him some help?" I asked. "Doesn't he need to see a doctor or something?"

"He won't go to the doctor," she said, slipping the rolls into the oven. "He won't admit that there is anything wrong. Recently, after he created a scene, one of the neighbors told him about Alcoholics Anonymous and offered to go to meetings with him. Still, he keeps saying it's perfectly natural for a man to drink, and he can handle it. Obviously, he can't."

"Maybe we could get Dr. Whitmire to make a house call," I suggested.

Her eyes darted toward the ceiling for a millisecond. "Maybe," she said, seeming to compose herself. "I don't know what else to do. I've tried pouring out his liquor when I can find it, but he finds another place to hide it, or he steals money from my purse to buy more."

"Why would he steal money out of your purse, Mother?" I inquired. "He works. He has money."

"No, he doesn't," she sighed and leaned against the counter. "He got fired the first week of October for coming into work drunk. Coworkers had complained about him being drunk while working machinery and that he was endangering himself and others. Right now, I'm supporting us on my income."

"Oh my God," I exclaimed. "Will that be enough?"

"Well, the house and the car are paid for, thank God," she reasoned. "As long as we have no more than utilities, food, and taxes, I think I can handle it, and I have a little in savings."

"I'm so sorry, Mother," I said with genuine empathy.

"Honey," she said with uncharacteristic concern. "Your father and I will be fine. We will all play the cards that life has dealt us."

I couldn't believe what I was hearing. Where was the control? Where was the manipulation? Was my mother growing a heart?

She checked the oven to see that the rolls were browned. The table had already been set, and she had plucked the roast beef from the oven and set it atop the stove to let the meat rest and cool a bit before putting the rolls in. I might not have realized what she was doing had I never read those cookbooks. I had never really paid much attention before, but Mother's cooking skills were noticeable and making sense now. She had timed the meal perfectly. She opened the roasting pan and lifted the beef onto a serving plate. Then, she surrounded it with the vegetables that had roasted along with it—potatoes, carrots, celery, and onions seasoned with no more than salt, black pepper, and the juices of the roast, but perfectly delicious.

"Go and get the men," she said, placing food on the table for dinner.

Daddy seemed to sober up a bit over dinner. There was no huge fiasco, and nothing was mentioned about his job. I worried about what he and Earl had been discussing in the living room, but I figured that was between them, and I didn't pry. For all I knew, they could have been discussing sports and the weather.

Mother seemed pleased that Earl was so complimentary of her cooking. After dinner, Mother served ice cream and cookies for dessert. We ate it in the living room in front of the TV. This, too, was uncharacteristic of Mother. I was surprised we didn't have dessert and coffee at the table, which she would have considered formally correct. I enjoyed the more relaxed atmosphere and appreciated being able to let go of a bit of stress. I was finishing my ice cream when the phone rang. Mother answered it, and I heard her say, "Yes, dear. She is right here." She motioned me to the phone.

It was Gretta, and as soon as I said, "Hello," she said, "Oh my God, it is so good to hear your voice!"

"It's wonderful to talk to you too, sweetie," I said. "How is everyone?"

"Oh, Derrick is so perfect and precious!" she exclaimed. "Tommy and I are both doing great! I can't wait to see you and meet your new boyfriend!"

"So, is Friday open?" I asked.

"You bet it is!" she bubbled on. "What would you guys like to do? Tommy's mom can keep the baby if you want to go out, or we could have dinner here, whatever?"

"Earl and I were hoping to return late Friday afternoon," I replied. "I have a paper due next week, and I need to get back and research it this weekend."

"Oh, don't you sound like the scholarly type?" she laughed.

"Well, I guess we are growing up," I commented. "So, what does Friday noon-to-afternoon look like for you guys?"

Gretta said, "That would be fine. Would you like to come and hang out at the house?"

"That sounds wonderful," I replied, knowing Earl had already said I could make whatever plans I wanted. "Shall we bring something, box lunches, cookies, or something?"

"Just bring yourselves," she said. "I'll nail the lunch thing. So, about noon on Friday?"

"Yes," I replied. "That sounds wonderful. We will see you then."

I said my goodbyes and looked at Earl as I hung up the phone. "Lunch with Gretta and Tommy on Friday, okay with you?"

"Sounds wonderful," he affirmed. "I'm looking forward to meeting them."

After the call, I couldn't shake the feeling that there was something not quite right underlying Gretta's enthusiasm. I had known her since the first grade, and as far as I was concerned, she was as close to me as a sister. Like a sister, I felt things. I shook it off and went on with my evening, but it continued to nag subtly at the back of my mind.

Not long after that, Earl left for the hotel; Mother went to the kitchen to make a pie, Daddy fell asleep on the sofa, and I went to bed. It was uncharacteristic of me, but I felt tired early.

The next morning, Earl arrived back at the house in time for breakfast, as Mother had insisted. He swore he was not bored staying at the hotel alone because he had brought books to read.

After breakfast, Mother threw together a squash casserole to go with the pumpkin pie she had made the night before. She loaded her goodies into the car and insisted on driving, as always. I had now come to understand that there had been reasons for insisting on driving that I had never considered before. I had suggested that Earl and I could ride separately in his car. I had hoped I might pick his brain about what he and Daddy had discussed the night before, but Mother would not hear it. So, Earl squeezed his long legs into the back seat of Mother's car. I rode in the back with Earl, and Daddy, observably hung over but sober, rode in the front with Mother. The drive was far too long to listen to inane and worthless conversations over nothing. Yet, there we went.

"Oh, look. The Johnsons painted their house," Mother noted as she drove. "I love that color."

Daddy grunted his recognition, and I avoided the urge to say, "Who the fuck cares?"

Earl commented, "Climax seems to be a very nice little town."

Grandmother and Grandfather Donner lived about twenty miles out of town on a few acres they had purchased when they first moved to Pennsylvania. On the trip there, I explained to Earl that they had initially come from southern Kentucky and had settled in Pennsylvania when Mother was a little girl. Mother had been the baby of the family with older sisters. Mother explained that they had gotten a good deal on the land in Pennsylvania, and that's why they moved there. Nonetheless, their move solidified my destiny.

When we finally arrived, Earl carried Mother's casserole to the door. I was about to knock on the front door when it opened as though Grandmother Donner had been peeking and waiting for us to step onto the stoop. There she stood in all her bizarre glory. She had beady little brown eyes and a big nose about as round as her chin. I had never figured out how Mother got her good looks, considering her lineage, but there stood the woman who had born her. I was not at all disappointed in Grandmother's presentation. I knew it would be grand. She had a half-smoked, unlit cigar sticking out one side of her mouth. She was wearing a lemon-yellow-and-white flower print dress that clung to her rolls and massive tits like it had been painted on. On top of her head was a pink, baby blue, and white home-knitted toboggan cap with a little blue knit ball bouncing around the crest. She had no shoes on and had no sooner thrown open the door than exclaimed, "Well, if it ain't my prim and proper daughter, Drucella, and the Fuchs clan come to see me on Thanksgiving! Get your asses in here! I gotta go check my patatas!" Without saying another word, she turned and waddled toward the kitchen.

We stepped through the door and stood there for a moment. Grandfather Donner sat in his recliner beside the door at the front corner of the living room. He was facing the opposite wall where the television played the Macy's Thanksgiving Day Parade. He was wearing nothing but overalls and a white crew-neck T-shirt. His feet were propped up, and he was wearing white tube socks with his big toe poking through the fabric on the right foot.

"Hello, Father," Mother said politely.

He grunted and sang twisted lyrics to the melody of an old children's song: "Hello, Mother. Hello, Father. Here I am at—old Camp Donner. It is very entertaining. It might be fun if Claudella stopped complaining." He bellowed with laughter as though he had just told the funniest joke and waved us further into the room.

Mother was not amused. She said nothing back to Grandfather but turned to Earl and said, "Earl, if you will, please accompany me into the kitchen with the casserole, then you may return to enjoy watching the TV parade with the others."

I had seen her around Grandmother and Grandfather Donner before. She had always been passively defiant of their ways, determined to present herself as something more. She had been ashamed of her family since she was a little girl. There had always been a little bit of anxiety, but I had never seen her as nervous as she was on that day. She carried her pumpkin pie as though it were a presentation for the king, and Earl followed her to the kitchen with the casserole. Daddy and I sat down near Grandfather Donner and stared at the TV. Nothing was said.

In a moment, Earl returned, leaving Mother in the kitchen with Grandmother. He sat beside me and stared at the television. After realizing he would not be introduced, he stood up and offered his hand to Grandfather Donner.

"How do you do, sir," he greeted. "I'm Earl Titwallow, Lovella's boyfriend."

"Oh, Jeez, honey," I exclaimed with embarrassment. "I should have introduced you."

Earl waved at me. "Eh, no big deal."

Grandfather didn't offer to get up and barely offered his handshake back to Earl. "Hell! I know who you are," he said. "Drucella has told me about you. Now sit down and enjoy some TV."

Earl sat back down, and the ominous silence of conversation continued. After a while, he said, "Not a bad day to get together with family, is it?"

To this, Grandfather exclaimed, "Shut the hell up, and watch the damn television!"

When Earl looked startled, Grandfather chuckled, a sinister little chuckle, "Got ya!" he exclaimed, then he turned back toward the TV. "Hey! That's an awful good marchin' band, wouldn't ya say?"

"Come on, Earl," I said, taking his hand. "Let's see what kind of conversation we can get into in the kitchen."

As we left the room, Grandfather and Daddy sat silently, staring at the television. Grandfather didn't want to talk, and Daddy was too hungover to put much effort into it. In the afternoon, they did the same with the football games. Grandfather had long been addicted to television. I think, in some ways, it was his refuge from having to talk because Grandmother scarcely ever shut up. However, she would shut up, for the most part, to watch a television show.

I heard Grandmother shouting when we neared the kitchen. "I don't give a damn what the recipe calls for! This is the way I make it!"

"Very well, Mother." I heard my mother say, tritely. "Make it however you wish."

Insight began to come to me, and I realized that Mother had probably become her perfect stuck-up self in defiance of Grandmother Donner's attitude, just as I had become fiercely independent and liberal-minded in defiance of her. We shared the common trait of bucking our mother's control, albeit a different type of control and a different agenda.

"Anyone else coming today?" I questioned when Earl and I entered the kitchen.

"Oh, hey there!" exclaimed Grandmother, looking up from the counter. "Come here and give your Granny a hug!"

As I neared, I could smell the smoke from her re-lit cigar. I dreaded it but realized that there was no escaping Grandmother's standard greeting. She pulled the cigar out of her mouth, popped it between two fingers, wrapped her arms around me in a vice grip, smashed me into her enormous soft tits, and planted a kiss on my cheek that I dared not wipe off, although it felt like a Great Dane had licked me. If I had given in to the intense temptation to wipe my cheek on my sleeve, the action would have been met, as it had been before, with accusations that I must not truly love her if I had to wipe off her kisses. She had no sooner finished with me than she turned on Earl.

"Now, who is this fellow you have here?" she questioned, as though she hadn't seen him in the kitchen earlier. I supposed he had dropped off the casserole and immediately returned to the living room.

"Grandmother," I said, planning a formal introduction that Mother had always required.

"Granny!" she snapped back. "Call me Granny or Grandma! You don't have to put up with all that prim and proper bullshit et-tee-quite that your momma insists on, not in my house. Now start over."

Between the two of them, I couldn't win. My eyes darted toward Mother, and she looked away. I knew there would never be a time when I could please both simultaneously.

"Grandma," I continued hesitantly. "This is my boyfriend, Earl Titwallow."

Grandmother ambled over to him, held her palm down, fingers pointing toward the floor, and curtsied. "Pleased to meet you, Sir Earl of Titwallow," she gurgled. I couldn't help rolling my eyes. My family was nuts.

Earl softly took her fat little hand and kissed the back of it. "The pleasure is all mine, Madam Donner," he replied.

I heard Mother whisper under her breath, "I think I'm going to vomit."

Grandmother smiled, placed a hand on her hip, and exclaimed, "You know you are probably a damn good-lookin' man, but I don't know if I can tell for sure 'cause I can't see through all that scraggly hair all over your head."

Earl grinned, unphased by this show. "It helps to keep me warm in winter," he responded.

Grandmother glared at him up and down. "You know, I heard you are a rich man, yet you are wearing clothes that look like flea market discards." Her brashness never ceased to amaze me. Perhaps I had inherited part of her tendency to be forward.

"Oh, but I was certain that you would be a fan of interesting clothing," he said, feigning disappointment.

"You're all right!" she laughed, lightly slapping his arm. "Now, sit down and stay out of the way! We got cookin' to do!"

Earl and I sat at the little two-chair side table in Grandmother's kitchen.

"Drucella!" she snapped, "get that boilin' pot off the stove and mash them patatas."

Mother moved the boiled potatoes to the sink and drained the cooking water. She then gathered butter, milk, and salt and quietly did as she had been told.

"Is anyone else coming?" I asked.

"Well, your Aunt Cloella and her bunch are supposed to come," Grandmother explained without looking up. "But if I know them, they will either show up at the last damn minute, in the middle of the meal, or they'll call at-the-last-damn-minute to say they ain't comin'. Johnella and her bunch are goin' over to Frank's parents for Thanksgiving."

"How are Aunt Johnella and Uncle Frank?" I asked, trying to make polite conversation. "I haven't seen them in a long time."

"You ain't missing nothin'," Grandmother forged on. "They're stupid as usual. Frank has gotten them into another one of his stupid, get-rich-quick schemes. Somethin' called Shamway or Claimway or some dumb-ass bullshit like that. It's bad enough they have had to file bankruptcy twice already. They keep askin' his mom & dad for more money. They damn sure ain't gonna get none out of us. I am not gonna front a penny for their stupid crap! He is gonna keep on till they have to live under a damn bridge and skin stray cats for meat."

"Pity," I responded. "So, how are Aunt Cloella and Uncle Joe?"

"Well, I guess you can ask them yourself if they show up."

Mother was totally different from and somewhat estranged from her two sisters, who came closer to being like Grandmother Donner. Mother, the last born, eight years after her next oldest sister, had a completely different upbringing, almost like an only child.

Grandmother Donner waddled across the kitchen and nearly bumped into Mother, who was standing at the counter, mashing potatoes as she was told.

Grandmother exclaimed, "Stay out of the damn way, Drucella!"

Mother said nothing but continued to carry out her orders dutifully, perhaps pressing the potato masher a little more firmly into the bowl.

"I think what I want to know," Grandmother said, "is how the hell are you doin', Dumplin'?" She quickly glanced in my direction with the question, then immediately returned to her work.

"I'm learning a lot," I replied. "College is not exactly what I imagined it would be. I'm enjoying my studies, and, of course, I've met Earl."

"Yeah, what about meetin' Earl?" she interrogated. "What's goin' on with that?"

"I'm not sure what you mean, Grandmother … I mean, Grandma," I queried.

"Are you two gettin' serious?" she questioned as she diddled back and forth between the stove and the sink.

"Well, we have only been dating since September," I replied.

She popped back, "Your Grandpa and I got married after four dates. I knew he was what I wanted, and he knew I was what he wanted. What more do you need to know? If you are going to get with a boy, you are going to get with a boy."

Mother looked up from the mashed potatoes she had been nervously decimating. "Please don't encourage the child into wickedness," she said.

"What the hell!" Grandmother turned in a snap. "Drucella! You better go back to church with all those holier than thou dip shits who think they have got all the damn answers. I'm not encouragin' this child to do nothing but follow her heart. Now shut the hell up!"

Mother said nothing but began furiously pounding the potatoes with the masher, wishing, I suppose, that Grandmother's head had been in that pot.

"Grandma," I said quietly and politely, "Earl and I want to take our time and really get to know each other before we make any big decision."

Mother couldn't help herself at that point. She turned to me and snapped, "So, is that why you waited so long to move in with him? What was it, a week? Two weeks?"

Grandmother burst out laughing. "Holy hell!" she exclaimed. "Are you livin' with this boy; you livin' in sin?"

"Well, not exactly," I stammered. "I am still technically living in the dorm, but I do spend a lot of time at Earl's apartment."

Grandmother snickered. "By spendin' time, you mean spendin' the night, right?"

"Yes," I said sheepishly. "I do spend the night there—some."

Grandmother was laughing again. "Well, ain't that the shits!" she exclaimed. "My perfectly prim and proper daughter has got herself a little sinner child."

Mother had hidden many of my exploits from Grandmother, but it was not as though Grandmother did not already know I was a bit of a sinner.

About that time, the phone rang, and Grandmother yelled, "SID! GET THE DAMN PHONE!"

Grandfather shouted back from the living room, "Get it your DAMN self. Me and John are watchin' the parade."

"Whatever the hell you are doin'," Grandmother shouted, "ain't as important as getting' your damn food on the table! NOW, ANSWER THE DAMN PHONE BEFORE I COME IN THERE AND WHACK YOU IN THE HEAD WITH A SERVIN' SPOON!"

The ringing stopped, and we heard Grandfather say, "Hello."

In those days, there were no special devices for messages, and callers often let the phone ring twenty or more times to see if someone would pick up. If not, they had to call back another time.

Grandmother turned back to me. "You know, little girl, it is just as easy to fall in love with a rich man as it is to fall in love with a jackass like your grandpa. You might as well be gettin' some action with Earl as with anyone else."

"Grandmother," I said, ignoring her demand about what I should call her, "I'm eighteen, and even though you may still see me as a child, I am an adult. I may have a lot to learn about life, but it is—my life, and I will decide how to live it for myself. I am very fond of Earl, but I will not act like a gold-digger or try to push him into anything, much less something as serious as marriage. I will also not be pushed by you, Mother, or anyone else. I appreciate your concern and advice, but I would prefer that from now on, you only offer advice when I have requested it."

I saw a smile come across Mother's face as she realized that I had just given Grandmother the kind of lecture she had always hoped she could have given but never tried.

Grandmother propped both hands on her hips and glared at me. "Well, first of all," she imitated me mockingly, "you are *not* an adult. You may think you are an adult, but it don't really count until you turn twenty-one. However, it is your life, and you are old enough to make your own decisions, so do whatever the hell you want with it."

She then popped her face toward the door between the kitchen and the living room and shouted. "Sid! Who the hell was on the phone?"

"It was Cloella," he shouted back. "Says they can't make it."

"Goddamn it! I knew it!" Grandmother declared. "We got enough damn food to feed a Navy fleet, and they ain't comin'!" She looked around the kitchen, sizing up the efforts, and said, "Well, hell! I say we start getting all this crap on the table and enjoy some Thanksgiving!" She turned to me. "Lovella, you go set the dining table. Drucella, ain't it about damn time you had some mercy on them patatas?"

Grandmother and Grandfather Donner had an actual dining room, unlike the eat-in kitchen at our house. We all stepped to our assignments, and soon, the table was set for a feast. After double-checking the kitchen, Grandmother finally sat down and announced, "Let's all say what we are thankful for. Sid, you start?"

Grandfather snarled back, "Oh, don't start with that stupid *let's be thankful, bull—shit!* Let's eat!"

Grandmother demanded. "This is Thanksgivin'. It is a holiday specifically for being thankful, and we are all gonna talk about what we have to be thankful for. Now you start!"

"Why the hell do I have to start?" Grandfather blurted back.

"'Cause I said so, damn it!" Grandmother commanded. She pointed her fork mincingly toward him and glared. "Now say somethin' you are thankful for, or I'll come across this table and gouge your eyes with this fork!"

Grandfather laughed. Then, he rubbed his chin and said, "Let me see … I'm thankful for my loving wife 'cause she treats me with the *utmost* respect … and damn that bitch can cook!"

Everyone laughed except Mother, who stewed in the embarrassment she must have felt all her life. Daddy sat next to Grandfather, who turned to him as if to say *you're next.*

Daddy began nervously. "I'm also thankful for my loving wife." Tears began to drift from his eyes as he looked at Mother, "Because I don't know if you realize it, Drucella, but you have been my Rock of Gibraltar. You have propped me up and kept me going when I didn't think I could go anymore, and you have been a fine mother to our little girl." He turned to me then. "I'm thankful for you too, my little Punkin' Patch. You have been the light of my life ever since you were born. You have grown up to be such a beautiful and intelligent young woman, and I am so proud of you for going off to college and making something out of your life."

"Stop, Daddy," I said. "You're going to make me cry, too."

"Your turn, Drucella," Grandmother spouted carelessly, completely ignoring the intimacy of that moment.

Mother hesitated and looked down at her plate as though she had something to say but couldn't form the words. As I watched her, I wasn't sure if I would trust anything she had to say. How would I know if she was telling the truth or making something up to placate the situation? Finally, she said, "I, too, am thankful for my child, and like John, I'm thankful that she is in college and has a bright future."

For a moment, she looked as though she wanted to bolt from the table. Instead, she fiddled with her napkin and waited for the ordeal to end.

"You're next, hippie boy." Grandmother said and pointed her fork at Earl.

Earl said, "I am thankful to have the opportunity to be here and meet Lovella's family. I am so glad I met Lovella, such a brilliant, beautiful, and talented girl, and I am thankful for the Penn State library, the setting where I meet her."

"Okay, kid." Grandmother said as she glared at me. "Give it to us. What are you thankful for?"

I looked around the table and caught everyone's eyes, one person at a time. Then I said, "I'm thankful for all of you. I'm thankful for my family and that I met Earl because whether our relationship takes us to a lifetime together or a break-up next week, it has been an experience worth having. I'm thankful for all my experiences and the future adventures of Lovella, wherever they may take me." I then looked back across the table. "Now, your turn, Grandma."

"Hell!" she said. "I'm just thankful we got all this shit done and on the table! Now, let's eat!"

The rest of the day was more of the same. Grandmother would not let Grandfather get away with telling people to shut up when we were all back in the living room watching football on the TV.

"Sid!" she exclaimed. "*You* shut the hell up! We all have as much right to be in this room as you do. We've all got a right to talk, and besides … it wouldn't hurt you to look up from the damn idiot box once in a while and try to have a conversation with your family!"

Grandfather grinned, looked around the room, and said, "Hello family." Then, he immediately returned his gaze to the afternoon football game.

We finally headed home about 5:00 p.m. Grandmother made sure we were loaded with leftovers so there was plenty to snack on for dinner. Daddy and Earl continued their conversations throughout the evening and always seemed to want me to be somewhere else when that was going on. It made me even more curious and a little nervous when I saw Daddy take Earl out to his shed.

Earl returned to the hotel at about 9:00 p.m. and picked me up the next morning to see Gretta, Tommy, and the baby.

The visit with Tommy and Gretta was congenial, and discussions were usual. Little Derrick was growing and healthy at a little over three months old. After lunch and our visit with the baby, Gretta put him down for a nap. Tommy and Gretta professed to still be deeply in love, and I was so happy to see them. I told them stories about college, about Marcy and her inane friends, about meeting Earl, and how he was different from any other boy I had ever met. Gretta and Tommy told stories about the baby and how their parents adored him. Earl went along with the process, answering questions and interjecting periodically, appearing completely comfortable with my family and friends.

Everything seemed perfectly normal with Tommy and Gretta, but I had a nagging feeling that something was wrong. Little tell-tale signs in glances and little momentary expressions ran across their faces for maybe a second. I didn't know if I should ask outright or just let it pass, but the more we visited, the more I felt a knot tightening in my stomach. Gretta had never kept secrets from me, none I ever knew of, and I had no idea why she might be keeping a secret now. I just knew that something wasn't as it appeared on the surface. Finally, I just blurted it out.

"Okay, something is going on here," I exclaimed. "Something is not right. I've known you both for a long time, and whether you like it or not, I can read you both like a first-grade book. What's wrong? Stop pretending and fess up."

Gretta immediately began to tremble, and a tear rolled down her cheek. She glanced over at Tommy and back at me. I could see the struggle in her eyes as she ruminated over what to say.

Finally, Tommy announced. "I've joined the Marines."

"You what?" I exclaimed.

"I didn't want to tell you," he said. "I *knew* how you would react."

"Well, did you not think this might be something I would discover sooner or later?" I questioned. "No wonder she's upset." I pointed back at Gretta and chastised him. "You have a child who is less than six months old, and you are going away and leaving her here to care for that baby by herself?"

"It doesn't necessarily work that way," he said, "I'll only be away for boot camp. After that, we can live on base, and I can be there with them just like any other job."

"Unless they send you on some mission that lasts for months or longer, or you get deployed to Vietnam, for God's sake!" I demanded. "Tommy! Did you stop to think what this would do to your family? It's not like you have to worry about being drafted. They are not drafting married men, especially married men with children."

"But that's exactly it," Tommy responded. "President Johnson changed the law last August. They can draft married men now. So, I have thought about my family. With a military career, I can do more for my family than I ever would be able to do at that damn feed store. They will have benefits that I can't provide now, and if something were to happen to me, she and the baby would be taken care of."

"You have bought into the bullshit, haven't you?" I scolded. "They would not have drafted you when you have a baby."

Earl sat silently, allowing me to have this conversation with my friends. I had a good idea what he thought about it all, but he didn't interfere.

Gretta spoke with tears rolling lightly across her cheeks. She tried unsuccessfully to stifle her emotions. "Yeah ... it will be great," she lied. "The only thing is, we will have to move out of town and live on a base somewhere, maybe." She shot a nervous look at Tommy. "If Tommy can make a career out of the military, we will pretty much be set for life."

"Did you even bother to discuss this with her?" I scolded Tommy again.

"We talked it over," he said. "I didn't just rush into it. We agree it will mean a better life for us in the long run."

"A better life?" I summoned. "That is if you don't get deployed to Vietnam or some other shit hole and leave your beautiful wife and your beautiful baby, and maybe get killed or come back in pieces. How is that that supposed to give you a better life?"

"Well, now," Tommy argued, "Only a small percentage of troops go to Vietnam, and only a small percentage of those go into combat. I know it's a gamble, but I think it's worth taking."

"Too late now. Hugh?" I replied.

Tommy looked down at his feet and then over at Gretta. "Yeah," he said. "I guess so. I've signed the papers. I leave for boot camp in two weeks."

"Oh Jesus, Tommy," I pleaded. "I love you, and I know you think you are doing the right thing. I just pray that everything will be okay."

"It will be fine, Lovella," he assured. "You will see. We will prosper from this. I can retire from the military, probably by the time I'm forty, and maybe even go to officer's training. I know it will be stressful, but we've thought it through. It's gonna work out fine."

I knew I was defeated before I even started the argument. The decision had been made. "Do you have any idea where you are going to be stationed?" I asked.

"Not yet," Tommy said, taking Gretta's hand. "But we're hoping for Germany. Isn't that right, sweetheart?"

Gretta nodded and smiled through her obvious grief. Her head bobbed up and down in affirmation as she pulled the sleeve of her free arm across her tear-soaked cheek. This would mean leaving her family and home, which had always meant much more to her than it had to me.

"You are not really into this, are you?" I questioned her.

"No—yes—no … I'm in," she bantered. "Germany would be great. It will just be a big adjustment and means leaving friends and family. It's not exactly like Grandma will be able to babysit."

"We will hire some sweet old German lady to babysit," Tommy assured as he patted her knee.

"Well," I sighed, "I just hope you both know what you are doing." I looked at Earl with a pleading look, communicating: *Save me.*

He got the message and said, "It's probably about time for us to get on the road."

"Yeah," I tentatively affirmed. "I guess we better get going."

Usually, they would have begged us to stay a little longer, but they were as weary of where the conversation had taken us as I was. They both walked us to the door. Tommy shook Earl's hand and affirmed how glad he was to meet him. Gretta nodded the same affirmation, her attention divided between goodbyes and the baby. She had retrieved him from the crib right after we got up. Before I walked out, I hugged Tommy first and then Gretta. I took Derrick's face and planted a big, wet kiss on his forehead. "I love you, little man," I exclaimed. After goodbyes, I placed my hand firmly on Gretta's shoulder and gazed at her.

"Honey," I admonished. "If you need anything, or if, God forbid, anything should go wrong, I am to be the first person you call after your mom and dad—got that?"

"Got that," she replied with a brief nervous laugh.

We already had our luggage in the trunk but stopped to say goodbye to Mother and Daddy before leaving. We both hugged them and when Earl hugged Daddy, I couldn't help but notice that a bond seemed to have formed between them. Then, we headed to Earl's apartment in College Station. After getting into the car and pulling away, I asked him, "So what was it that I saw going on with you and Daddy these last few days?"

"Well, despite the drunken greeting," he replied, "I think I've developed an appreciation for your father."

"What appreciation?" I questioned.

"I just realize that he is a man who loves very honestly and deeply," he said. "I appreciate that."

"You see something more in Daddy than just an alcoholic factory worker?" I questioned.

He glanced over at me, then back at the road, both hands gripping the steering wheel. "Of course, I see much more than that," he responded firmly. "Despite his flaws, your father is a man who looks out for his family, or at least tries to, and maybe in ways that you and your mother have never fully realized."

I stared at him momentarily, pondering, taking in what he had just said. Then, I settled back comfortably into those leather seats and watched, in the rearview mirror, as the small town that had spawned me flowed gradually out of sight. There was warmth in my heart then. I can't explain how it felt. Until that morning, I was indeed very fond of him, but I think it was then, right there, in that brief passing of time, having watched him with my family and having heard his affirmation of Daddy, that I fell in love with Earl Titwallow.

CHAPTER 16

Students for a Democratic Society

I don't want to sugarcoat it. The 1960s was a tumultuous time. To tell the truth, before I met Earl, I tried not to think that much about it. My family, even Mother, tried to avoid politics. We thought, as long as we were comfortable, why worry about it? However, television brought it straight into our living room. The fact that the Vietnam War was going on all through the '60s, and there were the assassinations of John F. Kennedy, Bobby Kennedy, Malcolm X, and Martin Luther King, not to mention significant riots in multiple cities, made it pretty difficult to ignore. As difficult as it was to avoid the conversation, I always tried to find a way to change the subject or make an excuse to leave. I tried not to listen. Yet, my conversation with Tommy and Gretta indicated that I was not completely oblivious to what was happening.

Earl, on the other hand, was passionate about the fate of people. I'm surprised he didn't want to study social work instead of physics. I don't know how much of his attitude had to do with trying, in many ways, to be the opposite of his father, but his attitude certainly was somewhat socialist. He also could not stand the fact that the Vietnam War seemed to get worse, with no clear objective and no end in sight.

In October 1966, Senator William Fulbright published *The Arrogance of Power*. It happened to be one of the books Earl began to absorb in his hotel room over Thanksgiving. When we got back home, he continued to plow through it. He didn't just read it. He underlined statements and went back over them. He became absorbed with the evening news and managed to bring up criticisms of the war in many of his conversations. I doubted that his ideas would set well with his conservative father or my family, for that matter.

I did my best to ignore it, but that couldn't happen. I was trying to settle into a life of domicile comfort with him, a retreat from the boring dorm room and the inane ranting of Mar-ceeee. Most of the time, when the evening news was on, I was in the kitchen preparing dinner and trying to play housewife. I had a long way to go, considering Mother had taught me little or nothing about cooking. Still, with cooking shows, experiments, and quality cookbooks, I was beginning to get the hang of it. I learned to prepare a few complicated dishes, but as often as not, I cooked fried burgers with a side of something like boxed macaroni and cheese.

Earl didn't seem to mind what I had prepared. When I first started staying with him, we often ate at the tiny two-chair table in his eat-in kitchen with candles and glasses of wine, but as time went on and he became more and more preoccupied with Vietnam, our meals tended to take place in front of the television. I ate quietly as he cursed the TV, spitting out bits of his food and trying to retain it in his mouth between exclamations of "Goddamn it!" and "Those lousy war-mongering bastards!"

I understood that war was terrible. I understood that boys were dying, but I didn't want to know. I would have preferred instead to stick my head in the sand and pretend it wasn't happening. Considering the gruesome scenes of war often shown on the evening news, I certainly didn't want to eat my dinner while watching the news. After the 1960s, the news changed, and gruesome footage of war was not shown anymore. They may talk about it and show some footage, but they don't show the gory details like they did during Vietnam. The 1960s were different.

One evening, as I sat beside Earl on the sofa, I began gagging at the scenes. I slapped my fork back onto my plate and said, "I can't stand this!" I got up and went to the kitchen. I threw my half-eaten plate into the sink and began to cry. The next thing I knew, I felt Earl's gentle hand on my shoulder.

"Honey, what's the matter?" he asked calmly and patiently.

I turned to him and wiped tears from my cheek. "I can't stand this anymore," I said, glancing back toward the living room. "Every night, we sit in front of the TV, watching that horror unfold. I don't want to see it! I don't want to know about it, and I damn sure don't want to be trying to have my dinner while that is going on. I feel like I'm eating the war. I feel like I'm consuming all that anguish and devastation! I mean, how soon till I see some boy I went to high school with on a medic stretcher with his guts falling off the side? I can't help thinking that it could easily be Tommy. Earl, I can't stand it."

He released a long, deep sigh and hugged me. "I'm so sorry," he said. "I guess I got so caught up in my anger that I didn't think about how it might affect you."

"I know it's important to you," I returned without lifting my head from his comforting chest. "I don't want to deter you from it, but maybe we could have dinner later in the evening. I can study while you watch the news."

"No," he responded. "From now on, the rule is TV off during dinner. I'll get whatever I need to know about the war from the newspapers or the radio at some other time."

I said, "I just wish there was something we could do." As soon as I said those words, I wished I had not said them. I hoped we could live in a little cocoon of denial, playing house and loving each other, but life would not allow that.

"Well," he explained softly, "there is something we can do. This week-end, there will be a meeting of a group called *The Students for A Democratic Society*. I learned about the group through a friend, and I think we should go and see what it's about."

If there was anything that I didn't want to do, it was to become involved in anything to do with the war, pro or con. I was torn between wanting to please him and wanting to shut down and hide. I looked up into his eyes and realized they were filled with genuine commitment. He wanted the war to end. He wanted a resolution. I knew he loved me, but I also knew he cared greatly about what was happening in our country. "Sure," I said. "Sure, we can go to that. Maybe there is something we can do."

I had no idea what this *Students for a Democratic Society* was about or what I might be getting myself into. I knew that it was somehow anti-war, but I didn't know anything else.

He held me close and stroked my hair. "I love you," he said quietly.

When Sunday afternoon came, and it was time to attend this meeting, I played a role for him. Never in my life had I ever pretended to be some-thing that I was not. Never in my life had I ever hesitated to say what I was thinking, but for Earl, I was pretending that I wanted to do something about the war, and maybe there was a small part of me that did. However, for the most part, I just wanted it all to go away. I just wanted to live my life in peace, without interruption.

Later that afternoon, we pulled up in front of an old house near downtown. We were met at the front door by the guy Earl had been introduced to, Jimmy. He appeared to be a little older than us. Had it not been for his hippie persona, he would have looked like a very average man in his twenties. However, his brown hair fell down his back like a wavy waterfall. His mustache drifted down to his chin on either side of his lips in a horseshoe shape. His chin was shaved clean like the rest of his face. A pair of miniature orange lens glasses sat low on his nose, and a peace sign necklace lay across the ample hair of his chest, which was exposed by the open collar of a tie-dyed pilgrim's shirt.

"Come in! Come in!" Jimmy motioned, turning around and leaving us standing at the door, expecting us to follow.

To the right, inside, was a living room with a beautiful old Victorian fireplace and ornate walnut mantle. The walls had been hand painted with flowers, peace signs, and slogans like *Make love, not war*. There was no furniture. Instead, there was a circle of floor pillows where several people sat. Some young men sat on the pillows with a girl curled between their legs. All the girls wore blue jeans and assorted tops or some long, loose, frilly, crinkled cotton skirt that went to their ankles. The whole place smelled of patchouli.

I instantly felt out of place. I had dressed like I was going to church, and my outfit was more befitting the traditional middle-class girl of the early 1960s. I wore a tight knee-length baby blue skirt and a white satin blouse. I had placed my hair over my head in a bun with white matching plastic clips, and pearl earrings adorned my ears. I felt like one of those little puzzles that one used to find in the Sunday papers: *One thing does not fit the other. Can you tell me which one?*

A thin, young, barefoot woman glided down a hallway from the back of the house to the front room. Her hair looked almost identical to Jimmy's, but her eyes were a brilliant blue. She wore a reddish-brown, flowing cotton dress, and her smile was magnetic.

"Hey!" Jimmy said as though the woman's presence was a complete surprise. "This is my old lady, Tonya."

"Greetings," she replied, smiling as she extended her hand to each of us. "Welcome. Welcome. Welcome," she continued as though one welcome would not have been sufficient. "May I get you something to drink? Beer? Wine? Soda? Milk?"

"Nothing for me," I said politely.

"I'll have a beer," Earl returned cheerfully.

"All right, okay," Tonya responded in a sing-song tone. "Have a seat. Be right back."

Earl and I found an unclaimed pillow on the floor and descended together. Unfortunately, I had made the mistake of wearing that tight skirt, which made the process somewhat complex even for someone so young. I twisted around uncomfortably for a while, wondering how I was going to manage sitting on the floor without shooting someone a shot of the muff-dragon's outline through my panties. Then, finally, I told myself, *What the hell! Since when have I ever been worried about anyone seeing my pussy, much less my panties?* I stopped trying to hide the inevitable, and sat in whatever position I could find that was somewhat comfortable. Unfortunately, the discomfort of that skirt on the floor required frequent repositioning. At last, I found a reasonably comfortable position where I could lean against Earl. When Tonya returned from the kitchen with Earl's beer, she handed it to him without fanfare or a word spoken, turned on her heel, and left the room.

Sitting beside us, a scraggly boy exclaimed, "Hey, man. Ronnie's the name." He extended his hand.

"I'm Earl, and this is Lovella," Earl said, shaking the boy's hand.

Upon completing the handshake with Earl, Ronnie exclaimed, "Peace!" He then shot two fingers in a *V* toward the ceiling and nodded in my direction.

"Yes," I said, having no real clue what the appropriate response might have been.

A moment later, Jimmy shouted, "Okay, okay, everybody. Let's get this meeting started. Let's get started." He stood by the fireplace mantle with papers in his hand. Tonya had come in from the kitchen and was standing beside him.

Everyone ceased their conversations and twisted their bodies in his direction. Some of them had to turn around to keep from having their backs toward him. I was thankful that Earl and I had gotten a position opposite the fireplace.

"All right. All right," Jimmy began repeating, leaving me to wonder if the couple's last name was Redundancy. Jimmy continued. "You all know this war sucks!"

"Yeah!" shouted the young man next to us.

Jimmy went on, "I don't know if everybody realizes just how serious this shit is, but here is some information you ought to know. First, the number of draftees for the fucking Vietnam War is getting close to a million. Think about it, man. A million or more men are being forced into slavery by the government to fight a war that only serves the fucking military-industrial-complex. Man, it was Eisenhower who said, 'Beware the Military Industrial Complex.'" Why? Because he knew, man. He knew that war had changed. He knew it was about to stop being about a fight for right, but a fight for the rich. He knew that war was about to become an economic decision based on the development of the war industry. These fucking fat cats are making millions off the manufacture of weapons! They don't want to stop the war. They would fucking lose money if they stopped the war. Seventy-five percent of the soldiers in Vietnam are from working-class and poor families. You don't fucking see the rich sending their kids to war. They send their boys to fancy schools like Harvard and Yale where they get a fucking college deferment, or whoops; somebody suddenly has bone spurs."

I wondered if he realized the irony of what he was saying, given that this group was called *The Students for a Democratic Society*. I figured that everyone in the room was likely a student and that each one of the males had been given the college deferment, as well. The irony was not lost on me, but I just continued to listen.

"Man, that is ten percent of our generation, culled out and massacred!" Jimmy continued to preach. "There are ten thousand boys a year, dying in Vietnam, who get drafted out of high school without a chance to choose their future! They can't even fucking vote, man! They can't even fucking vote! At eighteen years old, you are old enough to be drafted to get slaughtered in the jungles of Vietnam, but you can't vote against the mother fucking politicians who put you there! You are old enough to fight in a rich man's war, but you can't buy a fucking beer? What is wrong with this picture, man? What is wrong with this fucking picture?"

I heard myself saying loud, "That's not fair!" I became swayed, not by Jimmy's speech but by the facts he had just stated. I knew that it was true, but I had never taken the time to think about it.

Jimmy went on. "The war is costing the American taxpayer sixty-six million dollars a day! Man! Fucking, imagine that! Sixty-six million dollars a fucking day! Man, Johnson used the Gulf of Tonkin Resolution in 1964 as an excuse to escalate the war and send even more troops, and the bastard hasn't stopped! He is not going to stop. I mean, Kennedy was probably fucking assassinated because he would have tried to stop this damn war! This fucking insanity is not going to stop till the American people start shouting, 'ENOUGH IS ENOUGH!' We need to shout it from the streets, man! We need to shout it from the mountain tops! We need to shout it everywhere! 'ENOUGH IS ENOUGH! No more war! Make love not war!'"

Shouts of "Yeah! Yeah! Peace! No more war! Right on, man!" were scattered throughout the group as Jimmy continued talking.

"We need to take a lesson from David Miller," Jimmy continued, spurred on by the shouts. "He was sentenced to two years in prison last year for burning his draft card. I say we need to get every man in this country to burn his fucking draft card. We need to stand in front of the fucking White House, ten million strong, and burn all of our Goddamn draft cards. They can't send us all to prison!"

The shouts of affirmation continued throughout Jimmy's speech. It could have been a Pentecostal worship service or a Black Baptist church, except for the periodic profanity. I halfway expected someone to stand up and shout, "Praise, Jesus!" but, of course, that never happened.

After Jimmy finished, he and Tonya came down and joined the circle. Then, they began planning how to get protesters together, where they would protest next, and how to get the word out to the whole country. They knew that media coverage would be essential and that the more organized they were, the more likely they would get results. They were taking lessons from the free speech protests at Berkeley in 1964, and there was a commitment to pacifism. The war was violent, so they were going to be the opposite. Passive resistance was the strategy. Most had read about and taken lessons from Mahatma Gandhi's resistance to British rule in India. If the police came to move them, they would go limp, and it would require several police to carry each one away. The idea was to overwhelm the police so they could not stop the protest. I realized why this was important to Earl and wondered why it hadn't been important to me.

We came home with options to participate in a protest called the "Human Be-in" that would take place in San Francisco in January or a protest in April in New York, starting in Central Park and marching to the U.N. The one in New York seemed most plausible for us to attend. A part of me was afraid to be involved in this. What if the government put me on some blacklist so that I would never be able to work except for menial jobs? What if I got arrested or sent to prison? Then, what was I going to do with an arrest record? If I had a felony, I wouldn't be allowed to vote for the rest of my life. I could see my own family shunning me. I could see my career plans being destroyed. I could see most people in Climax thinking of me as a low-life and a criminal. All this was a risk the others seemed to accept, but my heart was not so fully committed. Despite all my years of high school rebelliousness, I had fears greater than Mother. I feared the government and mass conflict.

We had determined, after Thanksgiving, that I would go with Earl to spend Christmas with his parents in Bradford Woods. I wondered if he would tell his father about protesting against the war and suspected that it would likely be at the forefront of his mind as the Christmas gift he most wanted to give his father. Perhaps it was a gift that he wanted to give to himself to see the old man react in disgust that he was not fully applying himself to learning business but was, instead, applying his energies to breaking down the very institution in which his father most believed.

When we returned home that evening, I hung our coats in the closet and went to the kitchen.

"Earl, how does a cold-cut sandwich sound for dinner?" I asked.

"That sounds great," he said, plopping himself on the sofa and picking up a newspaper.

I made the sandwiches and found a few potato chips in the cupboard. After throwing some lettuce and mayo on the bread, I added a couple of slices of bologna, cut the sandwiches in half, and carried a plate to Earl.

"What would you like to drink?" I asked as I headed back toward the kitchen.

"Cola will be fine," he said.

I poured him a cola and then joined him on the sofa with my sandwich and cola.

"So, what did you think?" he quizzed just before biting into his sandwich.

I didn't want to tell him what I thought. I hesitated long enough for him to say, "Well?"

With a few bites out of my sandwich, I laid it back on my plate.

"I'm not sure what I think," I said.

"Jimmy can really stir it up, can't he?" Earl continued, seemingly unaware of what I had just told him.

"Yeah, he got it going there," I replied.

"So, you are unsure what you think?" he questioned again.

I sighed. "I have a mix of feelings, Earl."

"So, what's in the mix?" he asked.

I mustered my courage to tell him my real feelings. "I know the war is bad. I disagree with making boys fight when they can't vote and don't have any say in the matter, but it all scares me. I'm scared of violence, of getting arrested. I'm scared of getting put on a blacklist or something. I'm even scared to meet your family. It's like you and your father are on two opposite ends of the pole concerning the war. You are the rich kid Jimmy was talking about in his speech."

"Yes, I am," he returned.

"Do you think it's fair that you don't get drafted?" I asked.

"Hell no, I don't think it's fair," he flared, "I don't think it's fair for anybody to get drafted, but I don't want to go fight a war I don't believe in, either. Does that make me a hypocrite?"

"No," I responded. "I didn't mean it that way."

"If you want to see a hypocrite, wait till you meet my dad," he reflected. "My dad has some investments in the military complex. He will fucking make money off making weapons to kill innocent people and send other people's kids to war, but he has plans for me."

"Still, your father must be thinking about what he hopes is best for you," I mumbled, taking another bite of my sandwich.

"Yeah, he's just like the government," Earl replied. "He is happy to decide for me but gives me absolutely no say in what I want for my own life. That is exactly what the government is doing to these draftees. I mean, it is one thing if you want to be a soldier, but if you didn't ask for it, it is just another form of slavery. We abolished slavery after the Civil War, didn't we?"

"You're right," I said softly. "I agree. We did abolish slavery, and I think it's wrong to force people into the military, too. It's just …" I hesitated.

"Just what?" he questioned. "Come on—tell me."

I continued to hesitate but finally spoke. "Earl, I've never been afraid of conflict, or at least I never thought I was." I sat my mostly empty plate on the coffee table and sipped my cola.

"When I was growing up," I continued, "I didn't mind letting anyone know what I thought. I've gone toe-to-toe with Mother since I was little, but this is different. I've never gone toe-to-toe with the United States government. It scares me. The government is big and powerful, and I'm not."

"It is a government of the people, for the people, and by the people," he returned. "It is not supposed to be some overlord like a dictatorship. It is not supposed to tell the people what to do. The people are supposed to tell it what to do, and right now, it is not listening."

"Do you think all this will get the government to listen?" I questioned with honest interest.

"I think the government will not listen if we don't organize and make our voices known," he replied. "However, I don't want you to feel obligated to do any of this. It is a freedom movement, and that means your freedom, too. I won't think any less of you if you tell me this is not something you want."

"Can I have time to think about it?" I petitioned.

"Absolutely!" He smiled, sat his plate down, and pulled me to him. "Besides, over the next couple of weeks, I think we need to think about finals."

"Yuck!" I said, laying my head on his chest.

"Yuck indeed," he echoed.

I nuzzled my head into his chest, temporarily comforted by his embrace.

CHAPTER 17

How the Other Half Lives

The time between Thanksgiving and Christmas went fast. Finals and everything else made me feel particularly rushed. Higher education was indeed higher. It was different from high school and a lot more demanding, especially at the end of a semester. However, I was determined to do a few things to prepare for Christmas.

I bought a few gifts for my family, and Earl drove me home the week before Christmas so I could deliver them to Mother. It was only a few hour's drive home and a reasonably easy day trip if one did not plan to stay too long. I bought a cute baby outfit for Derrick and a Christmas ornament for Tommy and Gretta. Mother promised me that she would give them the gifts. I bought Daddy an expensive bottle of Chardonnay. I knew he didn't need it and shouldn't have had it, but maybe—I deluded myself into thinking—if he could learn to drink the finer stuff, he might stay off the rotgut. My reasoning was incredibly flawed, immature, and naive. I bought Mother a new purse and got one of those packaged cheese things for Grandmother and Grandfather Donner. Their greatest pleasure seemed to be eating, anyway. I mailed gifts to Philadelphia for my Grandmother Fuchs and Daddy's little brother, Uncle Raymond.

I had no idea what I might get for Earl's parents, having never met them. They were so rich that I couldn't think of anything they could possibly need or want or anything I could afford, which wouldn't seem tacky and low-brow to them. Earl told me not to worry about it and to enjoy the season, but I felt I had to do something. Finally, I decided to make a *Reine de Saba avec Glaqage au Chocolat cake* from *Mastering the Art of French Cooking*. I figured that even rich people like to eat, especially chocolate with a fancy French name, and if I could make it elegant, they might enjoy it.

I went to a bakery shop and got a cake box. Then, I made the cake just before we left for Bradford Woods. I followed the recipe to the last fraction, and to my surprise, I didn't fuck it up. It was beautiful, so luscious looking that I had difficulty not giving in to the temptation to have a slice. Instead, I put a bow on the box, along with their name.

When we left for Bradford Woods, I carried the cake box on my lap the whole way. I wanted to ensure it would not be jostled around too much. The last thing I wanted was for them to open the box and see it looking like an elephant had sat on it. Since Earl knew this was important to me, he was cautious about his driving.

We arrived in Bradford Woods on Christmas Eve, 1966. I knew college would mean new adventures, but I had no idea! The neighborhood where Earl's family lived was opulent, to say the least, but when we pulled through the rod iron gate to his home, I was almost overwhelmed. Massive brick columns flanked either side of the ornate gate. The paved driveway led to a house like nothing I had ever seen, except perhaps in magazines or movies. It was European stone with towering white Greek columns across the front. The round white columns lined the entire front of the house as though they were standing guard at an ancient temple. A circular drive looped around to the front door, and although it was winter, the lawn was immaculate. Nothing on the lawn was the least bit scraggly or out of place.

As soon as Earl stopped the car at the crest of the drive, a man appeared, seeming to come from nowhere. He pulled open the car's passenger side door, and I was slightly startled. I heard Earl gently say, "It's okay."

I got out of the car with my cake box in hand. The man smiled sweetly and nodded, then went around to Earl's side of the car, where Earl had exited.

"Hello, John," Earl said as he greeted the man with a handshake.

"Welcome home, Sir," the man replied in a fatherly tone. Yet, from descriptions and photos, I knew he certainly was not Earl's father. Besides, there was a distinct air of servitude.

Earl rounded the car and took my arm. "Come on," he said, leading me up the short walk to the house. "John will park the car in the garage and bring in our luggage."

As we stepped onto the veranda, the columns loomed over us. I looked up, almost dizzy from the enormity, and commented, "My God, Earl! This damn place is bigger than my high school!"

He laughed. "It's just stones and mortar," he said, reaching for the door. He opened the door, where a short woman in her forties immediately greeted us. She wore a black and white uniform and a little doily white lace cap on top of her head. Her hair was short and curled perfectly, and her ample bosom hid behind the top ruffle of a white apron. With a cultured British accent, she said, "Earl, so good to see you, Sir!"

"Good to see you too, Nora," he replied.

We stepped into the foyer, and she closed the door behind us. The walls around us were a very dark paneled wood that I assumed to be mahogany. A glistening chandelier three or four feet in diameter lit the space with tiny twinkles of light. White Italian marble floors spread around us like so many blocks of ice. Directly in front of us was a grand staircase with wide fluted rails inviting us to the second floor. To the left was a formal living room with more square footage than the house I had grown up in. I could see the walls were a pale and dusty yellow, and I noticed three people sitting on furniture tufted in a subtle white and gold floral pattern on a cream background. There was an older man, a woman, and a teen girl. They just sat there.

A Christmas tree like nothing I had ever seen was in the far corner. For one thing, it was at least ten feet tall, and it seemed to have been placed there as part of the overall décor. With white and gold ornaments and golden beaded garland, it matched the living room as though the original designer had created it specifically for the room. It was nothing like the little tree that might be found at our home or at Grandmother's house, on which half the decorations were construction paper ornaments that my cousins and I had made when we were small.

To the right of the foyer was a dining room with an ornate chandelier cascading from the high ceiling. It was centered over a sleek, dark, glistening, finely polished cherry wood dining table that would have seated at least a dozen people. The dining room walls were the color of lightly creamed coffee. On the walls, I could see colossal oil paintings lit from above, with individual museum lights protruding from the ceiling and installed specifically to highlight the paintings. The windows, almost floor-to-ceiling, lined the two outside walls. Cream and burgundy striped drapes flowed down the edge of the windows from ornate cornice boxes that crowned the top of the windows. Beyond the side wall, through a large window, was a view of a small lake framed by tall pines. I could see white-painted benches on the edge of the lake. I suddenly felt judged for my poverty simply by being in that environment and didn't realize that I was judging myself. I felt overwhelmed and had never been so uncomfortable.

"May I take your coat, Miss?" Nora said, politely smiling, breaking my daze with the luxury.

"I'm sorry," I said, holding the cake box before me. Suddenly, it seemed insignificant compared to everything else in their lives. "This is for Mr. and Mrs. Titwallow."

"Oh, how sweet," she said. She took the box, trotted it to the dining table, and returned quickly to me.

"Now, your coat, Miss," she said. Earl had already taken his coat off and had it lying across his arm. Nora helped me out of my coat and then took both coats to a closet beneath the side of the stairs.

Earl took my hand and led me to the living room. His whole family sat there, nestled around the large fireplace. They must have known that we had arrived, but they sat patiently waiting instead of getting up and coming to greet us. Mother might have been comfortable with such formality, but there is no way that any such thing would ever have happened in our family. At home, a personal greeting was one of the most essential parts of a visit. Never in a million years would anyone in my family have allowed the door to be opened without standing there to greet their guests unless it might have been Grandfather Donner. Never would Mother or Grandmother have sat waiting when a guest arrived. They would have been at the door to greet them in person. It all seemed rather cold, but I accepted that letting the servants do the greeting must be their custom.

When we entered the living room, Earl's father stood. I immediately knew who he was. He was a giant of a man, not quite as tall as Earl, but almost, and the facial resemblance was uncanny. Soon, after he stood, Earl's mother and sixteen-year-old sister, Anna, rose.

"Hello there, stranger," Earl's father gleefully spoke as he approached Earl and gave him a quick pat on the shoulder. Mr. Titwallow's pot belly was outlined by the suspenders that were visible under his jacket and held up his pin-stripe dress slacks. His suit coat and tie could not have hidden that belly, though they appeared to try. He seemed dressed more appropri-ately for a funeral than a family gathering. Earl's mother stood by. She was tiny but very pretty. She could not have been more than five-and-a-half feet tall and married to such an enormous man. Her dress was an elegant dark, burgundy velvet, and it clung to her figure as though hanging on a manikin in a storefront window. Her blond dyed hair came down from her head in wave flips on either side and around the back. It looked like a machine had molded it atop her head. She waited her turn, and as soon as Earl finished greeting his father, he bent his frame to embrace her. I saw a sweetness there, a reverence for his mother, and he held her gently as though she might break like a fragile porcelain doll.

"I'm so glad you're home, son," she said in a raspy soft voice.

Earl's sister, Anna, stood up more as though it had been expected of her than a courtesy she wished to extend. In some respects, she looked like an average fifteen-year-old girl, but she was at least four inches taller than her mother and wore a formal forest green chiffon dress. I felt as though I wanted to run from the room. I felt entirely out of place. My simple depart-ment store dress suddenly felt like a traitor in a fashion war, and I was humbled and insecure.

After the hugs, Earl said, "Mom, Dad, Anna, this is Lovella."

He placed his hand between my shoulders and pointed me toward them. His mother reached out with both hands, clasped my hand, and said, "Hello, Lovella. It is so good to meet you. My name is Clarisse. This is my husband, Daniel, and our daughter, Anna." She nodded to each of them as she spoke their names.

Earl's father stepped forward and shook my hand. "So glad to have you visit with us, young lady," he grunted, his grip practically breaking the bones in my hand. Even though they were nouveau riche, they seemed to have adopted the formality of old wealth, a trait Earl informed me about his father that was like Mother's need for show. Afterward, the two parted like the gate at the edge of their property, revealing Anna standing coyly behind.

"Hi," she said, reaching her hand out and barely touching mine with the tips of her fingers. *How like Mother's handshake*, I thought, when her cold, little fingers crossed my palm. I realized, as soon as she opened her mouth, that she was wearing braces and that she was embarrassed by it. Even though her upbringing made mine look as though I had been raised in a chimp cage, it was comforting to know she felt a little uncomfortable, too.

"Won't you sit down, dear," Clarisse said, motioning me toward a chair.

"I think Lovella would probably like to sit next to me on the other sofa if you don't mind, Mom," Earl said politely, guiding me to the seat.

"Oh, that's fine, honey," she responded. "Please sit down; be comfortable."

When I sat next to Earl, the others seated themselves. His mother was in a grand chair to the right of the marble-faced fireplace, and his father was in a matching chair to the left.

Nora entered with a silver plate full of hors d'oeuvres. She came straight to me first and held the tray before me. There was a collection of options, none of which I recognized, so I picked one that looked interesting and said, "Thank you."

"So, Lovella, tell us about yourself," Earl's father inquired while picking from the hors d'oeuvres tray.

Nora passed it around the room and then set the tray with the remaining treats on the circular coffee table in the middle.

"Excuse me a moment, Mr. Daniel," Nora said, looking straight at me. "What might I get you to drink, Miss?"

My eyes darted back and forth between her and Earl, hoping he would answer the question for me. He didn't. Then, I asked nervously, "Do you have cola?"

"Yes, ma'am, we do," she smiled sweetly,

"And you, sir?" she queried, switching her gaze to Earl.

"I'll have a glass of Merlot, Nora. Thank you," he said.

She then turned on her heel and walked briskly from the room. I looked around to see that the others had a drink nearby.

When Nora left, I turned my attention back to Mr. Titwallow. I began with much greater formality than I was used to extending and feeling as though I had been asked for a resume. "Sir, to answer your question, I grew up in Climax. My father worked for a peanut butter factory. Mother stayed home until I graduated high school, and she recently took a job at a downtown dress shop in New Bethlehem. I am an only child and entered college …" I hesitated to express my interest in sexual research, "to study medicine and hopefully do medical research."

"Well, that is a grand pursuit, young lady." Earl's father gloated his approval. "That is a fine choice of career indeed. Which peanut company does your father work for?" he interrogated further.

I had never had anyone ask me that question. It was a given that everyone in the area knew. I was momentarily taken aback but answered, "Nutty Boy."

"Oh, yes, yes," he mumbled. "We don't use that brand, but it's a good company. I'm sure Earl has told you about our family's company and his plans to take over after completing a business degree."

I felt Earl's grip on my hand tighten slightly. I didn't know if it was a stifled, angry response to his father's assumption, a subtle message confirming what he had told me about his father, or a simple gesture of reassurance. "Yes," I replied shortly. "He has told me that you started Chum Snacks. I think it's wonderful that you have worked so hard to achieve so much."

"Well, now," his father cleared his throat in false modesty. "It has been quite successful, but we have a long way to go. We now have distribution in five states. I'm looking into building a warehouse in Nashville, and I am certain we can go national in time."

"That would be wonderful, sir," I said, taking a bite of the little cracker I had held since taking it from the tray. I was unsure because I didn't recognize the tiny, algae-colored, gelatinous balls on the cracker. The flavor of decayed brine fish filled my mouth, and my expression was a combination of surprise, horror, and feigned delight as I attempted to cover the initial reactions.

"Beluga!" Mr. Titwallow exclaimed.

I chewed quickly and tried to down the muck as soon as possible.

"I beg your pardon, sir?" I questioned after swallowing.

"Beluga Caviar," he said. "Finest in the world. Delicious, isn't it?"

I was not used to lying. Although I may have kept some secrets, I was never afraid to say what I thought. In a moment of clarity, I realized I could not be so honest in this setting. The rules had changed. If I told the truth,

I would take the chance of insulting Earl's family, and despite my rebellion and independence, I now desperately wanted them to approve of me.

"Oh, yes, sir," I said with a grimace, reaching for my cola, which Nora had placed on a coaster beside me.

Earl's mother must have seen the hint of disgust on my face, for she quickly came to the rescue. "Well, you know," she defended. "I think there is something to be said for good old-fashioned, down-to-earth food instead of all this fancy stuff, don't you, Earl?"

"Yes, Mom, I do," he chimed right in. "I'm not a fan of caviar myself."

Mrs. Titwallow immediately twisted in her chair and called for Nora.

"Yes, Ma'am," Nora said while turning at the edge of the room.

"Nora, I have a craving," Mrs. Titwallow enticed. "Ralph has made wonderful hors d'oeuvres, dear. I don't mean to complain, but I am just a bit peckish for old-fashioned mixed nuts, cheese, and crackers. Do you think you could throw together another snack platter for us?"

"I will get right on it, Ma'am," Nora said, swaying cheerfully from the room. She was gone only briefly before returning with something a bit more palatable. I noticed that Anna didn't hesitate to dig into the new tray.

In the meantime, Mrs. Titwallow changed the subject. She talked about also working in a dress shop when the business started and when the children were young. I began to feel more comfortable and more at home. I also realized that, as Earl had told me, his father was all about the show, a pretense of wealth, the nouveau riche of the twentieth century. In Earl's eyes, and perhaps in truth, he was trying to be something he was not. I couldn't help thinking he and Mother would have made a great pair. Yet, perhaps, they might have been so bent on trying to outshine and outcontrol each other that such a marriage could never have worked.

Earl's mother, however, seemed to have held on to her simple roots. I didn't know if wealth had made her gracious or if she had been that way all along, and the wealth merely complemented it. She seemed to know intuitively how to make me feel more comfortable.

While we chatted around the fire, Nora was busy setting the dining table. When finished, she appeared and announced, "Dinner is served." Then, we all rose and migrated across the foyer to the dining room.

The table was set with fine, gold-rimmed china and crystal stemware. The settings were arranged so that whoever sat at the head of the table had a view across the grounds to the pine-rimmed lake, where uplights accented the pines during the evening darkness. I assumed that was Mr. Titwallow's place.

Earl pulled a chair out for me on the inside wall of the dining room so I could view the opposite window across the front grounds, which were lit abundantly with white lights. He sat beside me while his father pulled the chairs out on the opposite side for his mother and sister.

As we were being seated, Mrs. Titwallow said, "I hope you don't mind salmon, Lovella. We are having braised salmon with fennel for dinner. Tomorrow, we will have a traditional roast goose, English style, for Christmas dinner."

Roast goose, English style, had never been traditional in my home, nor was salmon unless it was out of a can and fried into croquettes. I wondered if Mother and Daddy might be having Christmas Eve dinner with Grandmother Fuchs and Raymond, who sometimes traveled there for the holidays. They were probably having turkey and dressing. Tomorrow, at Grandmother and Grandfather Donner's, they would likely have ham.

"I love salmon," I replied. "Thank you." Little did I know that the salmon I was about to be served was nothing like the salmon croquettes I had only ever eaten.

Over dinner, I discovered that Nora's husband, Ralph, a professional chef, was the cook and that Mr. Titwallow had brought them from England to work for the family. A small two-bedroom house was on the back corner of the property. He had built it for them so they would be nearby and on call but would have comfortable quarters. I assumed that having a maid and cook from Europe was part of the mystique of wealth that he was trying to create.

Nora began to circle the table, first bringing in shallow soup bowls. White wine was poured into the stemware, even for Anna, and water was poured into the other glasses. I learned that the soup was leek and celeriac cream. Whatever it was, the flavor delighted me. I had never tasted anything like it and was hooked from the first spoonful.

I tried to be as gracious and as mannerly as possible, but the truth is, I felt like a cow loose in Macy's. "The soup is wonderful," I muttered after my first taste.

"I'm so glad you like it," Mrs. Titwallow replied. "Ralph has quite a talent in the kitchen."

"I would love to learn how to cook like this," I stammered. "Mother never taught me to cook, so I've been trying to teach myself by watching Julia Child and experimenting with recipes from her cookbook."

"Lovella has developed quite a talent for cooking," Earl said as he smiled gingerly in my direction.

"Cooking is wonderful when it is something you do as a special treat for yourself or others," Mrs. Titwallow commented. "However, I am quite glad to be freed from the drudgery of the kitchen when it comes to daily meals. It is quite another thing when you have to cook for a family. It is not nearly so much fun when it has become a regular chore."

"How long have Ralph and Nora worked for you?" I asked, carefully sipping my soup.

"About three years now," Mr. Titwallow entered. "Best investment I ever made. They have been wonderful, and I think they also enjoy living here. We give them time off and vacations. They have the use of the grounds, and we have part-time staff to work whenever they are away."

"Have you lived here long?" I continued to question.

"We finished building the house when Earl was about fifteen, so we have been here for about six years."

Mr. Titwallow poked his finger into his napkin and touched the corner of his lips. I noticed that Earl wadded his napkin up and smeared it across his lips, drawing a stern look from his father.

When we had just barely started the soup, Mr. Titwallow had already downed his glass of wine and had motioned for Nora to bring another. Earlier, he might have had several mixed drinks before dinner. I sipped the wine gingerly. It was Pino Grigio, not my favorite, but Earl was right. It complemented the salmon.

"So, Lovella," Mr. Titwallow continued, returning his attention to his food. "How long have you known you wanted to go into medicine?"

"Yes … Lovella, tell us about that." Earl looked at me, grinning, taunting me to tell the real story.

I didn't know what to do at that moment, blurt it out, "*Ever since I learned that I like to fuck*", or give the affable answer that was expected. I went with affable.

"I have always been curious," I began, reaching for another spoonful of that delectable soup. "I've always been a bookworm. So, I was curious about my body as I watched myself develop. The curiosity led me to research at the library, where I began to discover medical books." The implication was clear that a developing young girl might want to know more about what was happening to her own body, but it was not overtly stated. I was very proud of my answer.

"So!" Earl snickered. "You needed to figure out why you were growing breasts?"

I quickly darted my eyes toward my soup bowl, knowing I would surely giggle if my eyes met his.

"Earl, don't be rude!" Mr. Titwallow commanded.

"*Yes sir*," Earl replied in mock conformity. "It's just that I am inquisitive about Lovella's breasts, as well. I find them very interesting."

At this point, Anna snorted outright, and I fought hard to keep from laughing.

"Actually, I started to study the books long before that development," I said, trying to quench the brewing conflict. "However, I am interested in gynecology and women's reproductive health. I don't think medicine, in general, pays enough attention to women's bodies."

"Your parents must be very proud of you, Lovella," Mrs. Titwallow interjected, seemingly unphased by the interaction between Earl and his father.

"I know that Daddy worships the ground I walk on," I replied, glad to have a way out of the fray. "And Mother constantly brags that I am becoming a doctor."

"I'm sure when you have set up your practice, one day, they will be extremely proud," Mrs. Titwallow complimented.

"I hope, instead, to go into research rather than have a medical practice," I said, laying my spoon into my empty soup bowl.

By this time, Nora was serving the salmon. I had never seen salmon like this before. There it was, looking more like a pink steak sitting atop a bed of fennel. Sprinkled over the top were bits of fresh dill. I felt as though I was dining in a five-star restaurant. I had never eaten fennel and had never eaten salmon this way. The taste was exquisite. The fish was tender and perfectly seasoned. The fennel, which had some interesting herb blend, seemed to melt in my mouth. I thought quietly; *I could get used to this.*

The conversation continued. Mrs. Titwallow told funny stories about Earl as a small boy who was tall and gangly, towering over the other children in the first grade. We laughed, and I told a few stories myself, including beating the crap out of Gretta for stealing my swing. Nora returned to the room as we finished the entree and posed a question.

Mr. and Mrs. Titwallow," she explained. "Ralph had made blueberry lemon tarts for dessert—however, Miss. Lovella brought a cake for you, which is indeed a beauty. I thought, perhaps, if you would like, we can serve Miss. Lovella's cake for dessert this evening, and Ralph can rework the tarts for something tomorrow."

"Oh?" Mrs. Titwallow questioned gleefully, "What kind of cake is it, Lovella?"

"I'm not sure if I can pronounce it correctly," I answered. "It is called *Reine de Saba avec Glaqage au Chocolat.* I got the recipe from *Mastering the Art of French Cooking* by Julia Child."

"It sounds delightful," Mrs. Titwallow chirped. "Nora, we will have the cake. Thank you."

Nora soon returned with desert dishes, on which my cake was neatly carved and artfully placed. Ralph put some cream glaze around the plates before placing the cake. I was prideful at the dish's beauty and terrified that it would taste horrible.

Mrs. Titwallow was the first to take a bite. "Oh, Lovella, this is mouth-watering delicious," she exclaimed. "You have outdone yourself."

"I wanted to give you something for Christmas," I nervously commented, "But I had no idea what I could give you on a student's allowance." I did not reveal that Earl had paid for the cake's ingredients.

"Well, this is perfect, Lovella," Mrs. Titwallow affirmed. "We would not have expected you to bring anything, but it is lovely of you to think of us. Thank you."

"Yes, indeed," Mr. Titwallow echoed. "Thank you, Lovella, this is a delicious cake."

Earl turned to me and leaned in to give me a little peck on the cheek. "You are so wonderful," he said. "Thank you."

"Thank you all for letting me share Christmas with you," I gleamed. "This will be a treasured memory for me."

After tasting the cake, I realized it was indeed good, and I was proud of myself.

After dinner, we had coffee in the living room and chatted by the fireside. Mr. Titwallow, who had consumed at least eight glasses of wine with dinner, continued to drink by having Nora add some liquor to his coffee. Despite the evident tension between Earl and his father, I soon began to feel very comfortable and welcomed.

At about ten o'clock, Nora came to lead me to my room. She brought me to a six-paneled door with brass fixtures. When the door opened, the room was like a scene from a fairy tale. A cherry wood four-poster bed sat on the room's back wall between two slender windows draped with shimmering cream-colored fabric. The bed was elevated, and the hardwood floors glided under a Turkish-style carpet that surrounded the bed. Beside the bed were matching nightstands, and a beautiful dresser was on the side wall beside another door. The wallpaper was plum and cream with accents of silver.

Nora led me to the side door. "This is your bath, Miss," she said, holding the door open for me.

Shortly after Nora left, there was a light tapping at the door. When I opened the door, there stood Earl with a small box in his hand and a big tooth-filled smile on his face.

"Merry Christmas," he said, handing me the box.

I started to speak but never got the words out before he kissed me. I melted every time he kissed me, and I could never explain why each kiss was like the first kiss, but every time it happened, I felt that same delightful tingle that I had felt standing outside the dorm on that first night. When our lips parted, I said, "Wait, I got you something, too. I didn't know if I should give it to you with the family or if we might exchange gifts privately."

I ran to my suitcase and pulled out a slightly larger box. Mine was wrapped in traditional paper with a tacky little green bow on top that had been crushed in the luggage. His gift was in what appeared to be a black velvet case with no other adornment. I handed my gift to him and said, "You first."

He leaned against the door jam and offered no protest. He carefully unwrapped the package to see the product box under the paper. It was an electric razor. I couldn't think of anything else to give him, and besides, it might entice him to shave some of the fur off his face or get the hint that he might at least trim it.

"Oh, an electric razor." He grinned and kissed me again, this time a little quicker. "That's very sweet, honey. Now, you."

There was no unwrapping. I opened it to see a stunning bracelet. The smooth pink, green, and cream-colored stones lined up around it, each held by tiny gold clips. It took my breath away, and I gasped. "Oh, my God!"

"They're opals," he said.

"Real opals?" I questioned.

"Of course, they're real." he admonished. "Nothing is fake about you, and I would never give you anything fake."

"Oh, Earl, it's too much," I pleaded. "I only got you a crappy little electric razor that was more of a hint than a gift. I didn't expect anything like this."

"Put it on," he pleaded. "It's a beautiful gift for a beautiful girl. It's precious stones for my precious sweetheart."

Tears welled and drifted from my eyes.

"Now, don't cry," he pleaded, pulling me to his chest.

"But it's so beautiful and sweet," I blubbered, "and all I got you was a stupid electric razor, and you don't even shave."

"I will. I will shave," he comforted. "I'm looking forward to using my razor. It's a wonderful gift—really." Then, he held my face back and wiped the tears from my cheeks. He gazed into my eyes and said, "I just wanted you to know how wonderful you are to me. I'm in love with you, Lovella. Right now, I can't see anything but you."

"I love you, too," I pleaded through tears.

He took my hand, led me to the bed, and sat with me on the edge. He then took the box from my hand, lifted the bracelet, and wrapped it around my left wrist.

"This is yours, forever," he whispered. "This is yours no matter what happens. If, for any reason, we might not make it, it is still yours. I want you to have it. I want you to know that no matter what else happens, you are the most wonderful person I have ever known. If our time together lasts only a few months or a lifetime, I will always be grateful."

The tears came again, and I fell into his embrace.

He cupped my face in his hands, and kissed me again. Then, he started for the door.

"Earl," I called after him.

He turned.

"Thank you for loving me," I said.

"Thank you for loving me," he replied, gently closing the door behind him.

After a hot bath, I fell into bed like a zombie.

I didn't realize anything until I heard a faint tapping at the bedroom door the following morning. It didn't even occur to me until then that I had not had a cigarette all evening. The craving hit me shortly after I heard Nora, outside my bedroom door, calling a tender little, "Yoo Hooo—Miss Lovella, time to get up, Miss."

I pulled the covers back and staggered to the door. I opened it, still feeling more asleep than awake, and there stood Nora in her cheerful glory.

"Good morning, Miss," she sang delightfully. "Would you be having breakfast with the family?"

"Yeah, uh, yes, ma'am," I drooled out. "I would love to have breakfast with the family." I had no idea what time it was, but it was still early enough that the sun was barely creeping over the horizon.

"Well then, Miss, we shall meet you in thirty minutes in the kitchen," she explained. "It is down the front stairs and through the dining room to the left. I would give you directions down the back stairs, but it is too confusing for this morning. Will you be having coffee, Miss?"

"Yes, Ma'am," I replied, hoping the door would support me and prevent me from falling into a sleepy lump on the floor.

"Cream? Sugar?" she questioned in her singsong voice.

"Yes, both, please," I replied. I wasn't used to such courtesy.

"We are having Eggs Benedict, Miss," she sang on. "I hope you like it."

"Yes, I love it," I said, familiar with the dish. It was something that Mother used to make as a special breakfast treat when I had pleased her sufficiently.

"Wonderful, Miss, I'll see you downstairs." She then strode down the hall.

I called after her, "Nora."

"Yes, Miss?" She turned.

"I hate to ask, but is there anywhere I could smoke a cigarette?" I asked sheepishly.

"Oh, dear, you have the habit," she said, returning to my door. "I do, too." She looked up and down the hall to be sure no one shared our little secret. "Why don't you smoke in the toilet room with the vent on, Miss? Flick the ashes into the toilet water and flush it. Then, put the cigarette out, wrap the filter in tissue, and bring it to me when you come down for breakfast."

She then cheerfully continued down the hall and tapped on another door. As I closed my door, I heard her sing, "Yoo Hoo, Master Earl. Time to get up, Sir."

I didn't wait to see Earl come to the door but retreated into the bathroom to do as she had instructed. When I got dressed, I didn't know if Earl had been ready before me. So, I went down to the kitchen. Nora met me in the dining room to take care of the little package of my carefully wrapped cigarette butts because I had smoked two. I then entered through the double doors from the dining room to the kitchen to find a large expanse with beige tile floors and a room that was at least half the square footage of my childhood home. Along one wall was a bank of cabinets. There were three built-in ovens and a gas cooktop that had eight burners. It looked to be more like a restaurant than a home kitchen. An average-looking man in his forties, wearing a chef's hat, stood before the stove. I assumed this was Ralph. He didn't look up from his work when I entered and seemed unaware of me.

A round white table with six chairs was in the far corner opposite the dining room door, and Mr. Titwallow sat in his pajamas and robe at the table with a coffee cup before him. His nose was buried in a newspaper.

Mrs. Titwallow sat beside him, also wearing a robe, and she was reading what appeared to be a paperback novel. When she saw me, she called, "Lovella, come sit down."

I crossed the room to sit at the table. "Good morning," I said, pulling myself to the table beside Mrs. Titwallow. A large male hand came from nowhere to set a cup of coffee on the table before me. I didn't even think Ralph had noticed me, but the coffee was there, as if by magic, and then he immediately returned to his work without muttering a word. It was creamed and sugared, just as I had requested.

Mr. Titwallow grunted, "Good morning" from behind his paper without ever peeking out.

Mrs. Titwallow touched my arm gently and asked, "Did you sleep well?"

"Like a rock," I replied, sipping my hot, sweet, caffeinated cup of nectar. I had no sooner answered the question when Earl entered the room from an arch adjacent to the dining table, the back stairs Nora had described.

"Good morning," he chirped cheerfully, taking the chair beside me.

I stared at him in astonishment, but before I could get a word out of my mouth, Mrs. Titwallow said, "My goodness, Earl. You shaved!"

His father instantly popped his paper over to see if his vision would confirm what he had just heard. It seemed as though some miracle had happened. We all gawked at him like spiritual pilgrims at the foot of Fatima. Earl had shaved his entire face clean, pulled his long hair into a ponytail, and wore a white Oxford button-down shirt! I found myself thinking that my ugly hippie wasn't so ugly after all. Behind all that scraggly hair was a chiseled and classic masculine face.

"Son, what in the world prompted you to do that?" his father goaded. "You look good for a change!"

"Ahm, Lovella and I exchanged Christmas gifts last night," Earl explained. "She got me an electric razor. I just felt I … um … I couldn't wait to use it."

"You look very nice," Mrs. Titwallow said softly and sincerely.

At that moment, my right hand went instantly to my left wrist. I had forgotten whether I had put the bracelet back on after my bath, but it was around my wrist.

"Well, Lovella," Mr. Titwallow spouted. "You managed to accomplish, in one night, what I have not been able to accomplish for several years. Congratulations, and thank you."

"I just thought it would be a nice gift," I said after a moment of hesitation. "I had been trying to figure out what I could get him for Christmas. I wasn't sure what to get him."

Seeing that I was fidgeting with my left wrist, Mr. Titwallow commented, "That's a very nice bracelet, Lovella."

"Thank you," I said, embarrassed. "This was my Christmas gift from Earl."

"You're spending quite a lot of money on this young lady, Earl," said Mr. Titwallow. "You must really like her."

"I do more than like her," Earl said, reaching over and taking my hand. "I love her."

"Is that so?" Mr. Titwallow piped. "Well, good luck with that, Lovella. You have your work cut out for you."

"Daniel, please," Mrs. Titwallow scolded under her breath.

A cup of coffee showed up in front of Earl. Nora had entered the room and was beginning to transport food to the table from the island where Ralph had assembled it.

Mr. Titwallow folded his paper and sat it in the empty chair beside him. "I hope you like Eggs Benedict, Lovella. Ralph makes the best I've ever had." He then adjusted himself to the table and began unfolding his napkin.

"Anna won't be joining us," Mrs. Titwallow said sweetly. "She likes to sleep in. She works so hard at school. We usually give her this little indulgence when she is on vacation."

"I can't blame her," I said. "I'm rather fond of sleep myself."

"Oh, I hope we didn't get you up too early," Mrs. Titwallow said apologetically.

"No, this is wonderful!" I replied. "This is something I wouldn't want to have missed by sleeping. I have never had breakfast served like this. Mother usually put the food on the table, and we were on our own."

"Family Style," Mrs. Titwallow commented. "Sometimes, I miss that. Well, I hope you enjoy your breakfast with us."

We began breakfast, and Mr. Titwallow was right. Ralph's Eggs Benedict was the best I ever had. Toward the end of the meal, Mr. Titwallow threw his napkin on the table and pushed his chair back. "If you will excuse me," he said. "I have to go pick up my parents for Christmas dinner. I have offered repeatedly to send a limousine, but my father won't hear of it. So, I have to go pick them up myself."

"Grandpa doesn't enjoy the pomp and circumstance," Earl cast a dig at his father.

"It's good that family can gather," I commented.

Mrs. Titwallow said, "I think I will get dressed and accompany Daniel to pick up his parents."

After Mr. and Mrs. Titwallow ascended the stairs, Earl crooned, "Come on, let's get our coats and go for a walk." He took my hand, and we retrieved our coats from the closet beneath the front stairs. Then, we went out a door behind the kitchen.

It was partly cloudy that day, with an occasional snow flurry. The sun peeked through often but did little to warm my face from the frigid chill. Earl walked with his arm around my shoulder.

A garage with six doors was attached to the house. "You guys have that many cars?" I asked.

"Well, Mom has a car. Dad has a car. I have a car. As soon as she gets her driver's license, Dad will buy Anna a car. There's room for guests to park. Ralph and Nora have a small garage attached to the cottage that Dad built for them, and there is a utility garage on the back of the property for the trucks and equipment that the groundskeepers use."

We walked past the garage to a little knoll in the middle of the property. We stopped there for a moment. I estimated that the property must be at least five or more acres. There were carefully planted trees around the rolling lawn. Around the edge of the property was a bank of mature trees, and through the bare winter limbs, I could see other houses of similar stature, but I could make out only two. I figured that, in the summer, when the trees were fully leafed, the other homes would not be visible at all. To the left, I could see the little cottage that Mr. Titwallow had built for Ralph and Nora.

"It's beautiful," I commented, turning to look at the expanse.

"Yeah, there is a lot that money can buy you," Earl said, eyes scanning the property.

We stood atop the knoll, holding gloved hands and feeling the crisp winter chill on our faces.

"So, your mom doesn't have any family?" I asked. "How does she cope with that?"

"When mom's father abandoned the family, she was still a little girl," he began. "I think she adored her father, and it hit her when he just left one day. He packed some clothes while Grandma and the kids were at church and just left. I don't even think he left a note. They never knew what happened to him, and my mom has never heard from her father since then."

"They don't even know if he is alive or dead, just missing all these years? How old was your mom?" I asked.

"I think she was maybe twelve or thirteen," he replied. "She had two little brothers. One was eight years old, and one was six years old. I think it devastated the whole family. After that, Grandma never remarried and had nothing to do with any man. She worked whatever job she could find to support herself and her kids. She often had to work multiple jobs and left Mom to care for her little brothers. I guess that's where my mom gets her loyalty."

His eyes moved from mine to the sky, and the snow flurries seemed to thicken a bit. Then, he continued his story as the pale gray light of winter filtered across his face. "My Uncle David was killed in World War II before I was born. My Uncle Tim followed my grandfather's footsteps and just left one day. I think I was about six years old when that happened. He was ridiculed, and maybe he was not treated well in the community. I don't know. He just left. At least he went to the trouble of paying his last month's rent before he took off, and he left a note to Mom telling her that he loved her and asked her forgiveness, but not to try to find him."

"Oh, my God," I said, feeling empathy moving through my heart. "Your mother has had a hard life. Was she close to your grandmother?"

I heard a crackle of grief in his voice. "You remember that I told you Grandma died in a car wreck when I was about fourteen?"

"Yes, I remember that you mentioned losing your grandmother." I hugged him. "I've never experienced anything like that. I feel like such a brat for all the complaints that I've had about my mother and growing up in Climax. I've had it so easy and didn't even realize it. So, your mom doesn't have any family but this one. Everyone from her childhood is gone?"

"Except for a couple of aunts and uncles who don't have much to do with her," he said. "Yes, they're gone."

"I am so selfish and spoiled," I whined.

He took my shoulders in his hands and held me away from him so he could look me in the eyes. His eyes scanned mine and then centered on my soul.

"No, you are not selfish," he scolded. "You've done so much for me already. That day in the library, I had no idea what a wonderful person you were. I just wanted to get laid. If I had continued to pursue just that alone, I never would have realized what a treasure I had found in you."

"I'm deeply grateful we met each other, too," I returned.

He put his arm around my shoulders and walked me toward the pine grove surrounding the lake on the south side of their property. The lake had to be more than an acre expanse of water surrounded by beautiful evergreen pines. For much of that morning, we walked without speaking, simply enjoying being with each other.

After a while, I asked, "So, what about your dad's family?" "Your grandfather doesn't like the pomp and circumstance?"

"Just wait till you meet Grandpa Titwallow," he laughed. "I love him. For one thing, he puts Dad in his place. He won't let Dad get away with anything, including nagging me."

"Sounds like it will be a fun evening," I acknowledged.

"Our Christmases can get a bit tense at times," he hesitated, " but they are more likely to behave a bit better with you here."

We walked into the hidden sanctuary of the pines. Pale brown pine needles and fallen pinecones crunched beneath our feet. Earl stopped beneath the canopy, turned to me, and kissed me. There it was again, that feeling I treasured, that tingling in my body down to my toes. Of all the boys I had ever been with, he was the only one who could do that to me. I desired him like no other. I wanted him to make love to me in the cold, lay our coats on the pine needles, and commune passionately, but we both knew it was far too chilly. We kissed, warm lips contrasting cold cheeks, and then he held me for a while. We stood there, a balmy island of embrace within the fridged pines, and he said, "You know what? My nose is a little cold. Want to go back to the house and see what's going on?"

"Sure," I replied, and we walked through the pines, around the lake, and back to the house.

By that time, it was around 11:30 a.m. I asked Earl if I could use the phone to call Mother and Daddy to wish them Merry Christmas. "I'll call collect," I said, not wanting to impose.

"Oh, nonsense," he admonished. "My family can afford thousands of long-distance calls. Just call them and don't worry about it."

He led me to a room adjacent to the formal living room. The décor was entirely different. There were large brown leather sofas and chairs with walls paneled in what appeared to be broad oak boards. Low windows looked over a covered porch, viewing the opposite side of the property. Another fireplace probably backed up to the one in the living room, but this one was stone and had a thick rustic oak mantle. A color console TV sat on one wall. Across from that, near the fireplace, was another Christmas tree. This one looked more like what I had been used to. It had handmade ornaments that Earl and his sister had made while growing up. It had an assortment of ornaments and didn't look like someone had done it as a design project. This Christmas tree also had presents beneath it. It occurred to me that I hadn't even noticed that the tree in the formal living room had no gifts around it and was just for show.

"You have two living rooms?" I questioned.

"No, this is the den," he replied, "the family room, hang-out room. The other room is for formal guests. This is more of a private hang out, just for family."

He led me to a cozy leather sofa with a black phone on the table beside it. I picked it up and dialed our home number directly instead of going through the operator. Daddy answered the phone, and I heard the slur in his voice. As soon as he said, "Hello," I knew he was drunk.

"Daddy, this is Lovella," I said, wondering how Mother was handling this. Normally, she would never have let him answer the phone, much less when he was drunk.

"Oh, hey, my-my li-ittle Pun-kin-Pa-Patch." He was so drunk that speaking seemed to take effort.

I heard Mother shout from the background, "John! I told you never to answer the phone! Let me have it!"

"It's-ss-ss-La-Lo-ve-vell … Lo-vell-ah," he slurred back.

Then, I heard her from close by. "Oh, for goodness sake, John, give me the phone!"

There were sounds in the background, and I could imagine her wrestling the receiver out of his hand. Then, I heard her say, "John! Go sit down." He mumbled something in the background, and she came on the line.

"Hello." She sounded frazzled.

"Hello, Mother," I said. "How are you?"

"I've seen better days," she said. "How are you? Are you enjoying your Christmas?"

"Yes, it's wonderful," I replied. "Earl has a wonderful family and a very nice home."

"That's good, honey," she said, her tone softening. "I'm glad you are having a good time."

I sighed into the phone with some exasperation. "I just called to wish you Merry Christmas. I wanted to catch you before you headed to Grandmother and Grandfather's house."

"We're not going," she said. "I'm not going to expose anyone to your father in this condition, and I can't leave him alone like this, either."

"Yeah," I said quietly. I felt sad for both and wasn't sure what to say. "He sounds like he is really drunk."

"He has been drunk, Lovella," she pleaded with a tone of sadness and grief in her voice that I wasn't used to hearing. "He gets drunk more often and drunker than he ever used to get. I don't know what I'm going to do with him."

What was I going to say? There was nothing I could do. I began to feel sorry for Mother. The inevitable had finally happened after all her years of trying. Despite all the effort that she had put into trying to keep him sober, his drinking was a monster she couldn't defeat. I was no longer the naive little girl who could make herself believe, with his reassurance, that his drinking wasn't a big deal. I knew better, and I was scared for them both.

"How was dinner with Grandmother Fuchs and Uncle Raymond yesterday?" I asked.

"Oh, for Heaven's sake. I called them and told them not to come," she replied. "It is too taxing for your grandmother Fuchs to travel that far and only find her son unable to hold a stable conversation."

"I'm sorry, Mother," I said after a brief silence.

"I'm sorry too, honey," she confessed.

I could imagine that she was not only saying that she was sorry for herself and for what they were going through but that she was saying she was sorry for the way she had raised me, for all the control she had attempted to wage over my life, for my exposure to growing up with an alcoholic. Even though I had deluded myself into believing it hadn't affected me, I began to recognize how much it had.

"Is there anything I can do?" I pleaded, hoping that there might actually be something.

"No, honey, of course not," she comforted. "There appears to be nothing any of us can do. I can't keep him from drinking. God knows I've tried. I can't. He always finds a way. I have poured bottle after bottle of whiskey down the sink, but he finds a way to get another. I try to keep him out of trouble, but I've long since given up the delusion that I could prevent him from embarrassing me. I wish that there was something that someone could do. I pray about it. It seems praying is the only thing I can do, and so far, that doesn't seem to help, either."

I felt a tear roll across my cheek, almost out of nowhere, stealth crying. I rolled my lower lip under my teeth and said, "I will pray, too, Mother."

"Thank you, honey," she soothed. "Now enjoy your Christmas, and don't worry about anything here. I've got it under control for now. He will … hopefully pass out soon. I will cover him up and let him sleep it off."

This was not my mother, not the cold, controlling bitch I thought I had grown up with. That man, who had been on the phone, was not my father. He was not the hard-working family man who adored me. He had deteriorated into some kind of human mush.

I hung up the phone and stared, dazed, into a blur before my eyes. Earl sat beside me, having overheard the conversation. He put his arm around me, pulled me to his chest, and I cried.

I felt so guilty about having gotten Daddy that bottle of Chardonnay. I should have realized that the last thing he needed was more alcohol. Mother had not even mentioned it, which was a kindness unlike her. Perhaps she had hidden it from him or given it to a neighbor. Had it been a year or two earlier, she would not have missed the opportunity to thrust the knife of guilt into my heart and twist. She would have ensured that I realized what a horrible thing I had done. She didn't have to. I realized it myself.

We sat on the sofa for a while, and Earl held me. There were no questions, just comfort. He seemed to have some intuition about when to speak and when not, and if he messed up, he quickly corrected it.

Only a few moments later, we heard a shout from the back of the house, near the garage, a man's voice, clear, yet with an undertone of gravel swirling in an empty glass. "Hey! Hey! What is going on in the big house?"

Earl put a large, comforting hand on the side of my head. "Grandma and Grandpa are here," he said. "Are you ready for this?"

Never having been one to linger too long in the morbid, I sat up straight and said, "I think so. How do I look?"

I know there must have been evidence of sadness on my face. At the very least, mascara must have cut roads across the pits of my eyes. In those days, I seldom wore much makeup, maybe a little lipstick, a thin line of eyeliner, and a touch of rouge at most. However, I tried to prettify myself a little more for his family that day. At that moment, I regretted it.

"You always look beautiful," he said. "But … maybe … you might need a little touch-up." He rose and crossed the room to a tissue box, returned, and wiped the black worm lines from beneath my eyes. When he finished, he smiled and said, "Now, you look stunning."

I snickered at his comment. "It is so good to have adoring fans," I commented.

"Ready?" was his next question.

"Sure," I replied quickly. Then, we rose and ambulated to the formal living room.

When we walked into the formal living room, Nora had already taken the coats, and his grandparents were about to be seated.

His grandfather was a white-haired man of average height, build, and looks. He was moving toward a chair by the fireplace, cane in his right hand, keeping rhythm with his movements. His cane seemed more like an accessory to his persona than a medical necessity. He wore pin-stripe slacks with black suspenders over a white dress shirt but no tie or suit coat.

Earl's grandmother was at least four or five inches taller than his grandfather, and I saw where Earl had probably inherited his height. She had salt and pepper hair in a style reminiscent of the 1930s, with a horseshoe roll circling her head. There was an osteoporosis hump crossing over her shoulders, causing her head to jut out in front of her, arriving at any destination at least a millisecond before the rest of her body. Her hips rocked from side to side when she walked, as if something was trying to pop out of each side. Surprisingly, at least to me, she wore a tan pantsuit with a little waist jacket that fell just at the top of her broad hips. A white blouse with cascading ruffles rippled between the flaps of her jacket.

As soon as we entered the room, Earl's grandfather spotted us, stopped, and waved his left hand.

"Hey, Earl, my boy!" he exclaimed. "Who's that beautiful doll you got hanging on your arm."

Earl led me across the room. "Grandpa, this is Lovella Fuchs, my girlfriend."

"I'm Pleased to meet you, young lady!" he almost shouted. "I hope these folks have been treating you right."

Earl said, "Lovella, this is my grandpa, Frank Titwallow." Then, he motioned to the tall woman behind him, "And this is my grandma, Sarah Titwallow."

"I'm very pleased to meet you both," I said, trying to be as affable as possible, hoping that my mascara was not still smeared around my eyes.

"Good to meet you, too," spewed his grandfather.

With her tick-tock walk, his grandmother crossed around the sofa, held a huge hand out to me, and said, "How do you do? I'm Sarah Titwallow." She acted as though she had not just been introduced.

"I'm very pleased to meet you, Mrs. Titwallow," I said. "I'm Lovella Fuchs."

She waved her hand at me, put a funny little snarl across her lips, and said, "Awah! Call me Sarah. Besides, I wouldn't know if you were talking to me or my daughter-in-law with all that Mrs. Titwallow stuff."

"Yeah, call me Frank," Earl's grandfather echoed as he placed himself in front of the chair and then fell into it as though his ass had suddenly turned into a sack of potatoes.

Sarah crossed back around the sofa, talking as she went. "Come on, sit down, take a load off. Put your feet up."

Earl and I followed her into the seating area. She plopped on the sofa adjacent to Frank's chair, where I had been sitting the night before. She patted her hand on the cushion, looked directly at me, and said, "Right here, sweetie, I wanna talk to you."

I wasn't sure what to think, but I crossed around and sat on the sofa beside her, and Earl sat beside me.

Mr. and Mrs. Titwallow entered through the kitchen and dining room and walked past the foyer.

"Is everyone comfortable?" Mrs. Titwallow asked as she rounded the sofa and stood before us.

"As comfortable as I can be in a fancy house," Frank exclaimed.

Mr. Titwallow followed close behind Earl's mom and asked, "Dad, Mom, would you like a drink?"

"Are you gonna get it?" Frank teased.

"No, I'll have Nora get it," Mr. Titwallow explained. "You know I'm not much of a bartender."

Nora had just entered from the dining room side, almost as if on cue, and asked, "What shall I get everyone?"

"I'll have a gin and tonic," Frank responded, "and I assume Sarah will have her usual."

Nora looked at Earl's grandmother and said, "A Bloody Mary then, Mrs. Sarah."

"Yes, please," Sarah responded.

Nora took the orders for the rest of us and then left for the kitchen.

After seating herself, Mrs. Titwallow asked, "Lovella, did you have a pleasant morning?"

Mr. Titwallow took his chair like a king on a throne surveying his court.

"Yes," I said. "Earl showed me the grounds, and we walked around the lake.

Sarah slapped a large, bejeweled hand on my leg and announced, "Clarisse has been telling us about you, Lovella," she said. "You are studying to be a doctor. How wonderful!"

"I'm actually studying to be a research scientist in the medical field," I replied and quickly changed the subject. "Earl tells me your family has lived in Pittsburgh for several generations." I smiled and crooked my head to the side to glance at her expression.

"Oh, yes, yes," she laughed, "both sides of the family have been in Pennsylvania about as long as there has been a Pennsylvania."

"Really?" I asked. "I don't think I even know that much about my family. I'm afraid I know nothing further than my great-grandparents. My mother's family came from southern Kentucky near the Tennessee border, and my father's family is from southern Pennsylvania."

Before that moment, my family tree and how little I knew about it had never occurred to me.

The conversation ensued, and I learned more about Earl's family than I ever dreamed of knowing about my own. His grandmother's family had been some of the original settlers soon after the Revolutionary War. They were German. I hadn't realized there had been so many German settlers in Pennsylvania, but since my own name was German, Daddy's family must have been among them.

Earl's grandfather's family had been both Dutch and English. This I expected. There was also a brief story about an ancestor who had come from the South shortly after the Civil War and married into the Titwallow clan. It was fascinating that they could sit there and discuss family stories that went back several generations. That sort of thing just never happened in our family. It was not as though Mother wouldn't have loved to be able to account for some historically significant heritage. She always hoped for and dreamed of having a heritage, but I suspected she feared any research might turn up some horrible secret that she would rather not have known. She didn't want to know about it if she couldn't brag about it.

We had drinks and talked for some time, and then Nora came and called us to dinner. A couple of people had been hired to help serve dinner for a larger group. Two young men dressed in black tuxedoes were also assisting with serving. Nora rolled the goose in on a serving cart and carved it beside the table. Ralph had made two. The young men brought each plate to her. She lay the goose meat daintily across each plate with a knife and fork. The meal was huge. There were roast potatoes, Brussels sprouts wrapped in bacon, and a baked medley of root vegetables. The dressing tasted lightly of ginger and an herb I couldn't quite make out. Earl told me it was a chestnut dressing, but I could not discern what herb I was tasting. Several sauces were available, and the bread rolls were so tender and light that it was almost like eating a flavored cloud. Ralph made cranberry sauce from scratch, something I had never tasted before. Although Mother would mash it up and grate orange peel over it, her cranberry sauce always came from a can. The goose meat seemed a little stringy, but it tasted good, nonetheless.

Dinner culminated with a brandy flame over a dessert I learned was a traditional English figgy pudding. Setting it ablaze was all part of the presentation, but the alcohol enhanced the flavor. Like everything else, it was wonderful, and I felt like royalty.

Dinner was amazing, almost overwhelming. I would have felt totally out of my element if I had not known Earl's family had come from earthy roots. I knew his mother had struggled and was where she was, not by marriage but by her commitment and hard work supporting that marriage. I knew Earl's father had not always been wealthy, and he had scraped himself from the lower end of the middle class to become the creator and CEO of his own company.

On the one hand, I felt so proud of them. On the other, I felt out of place. I felt ashamed of my own family. So many thoughts were going through my mind that I could scarcely contain them all. I tried not to do it, but I had difficulty listening to the discussions about family history and accomplishments without judging myself and my family. My father, after all, was a drunkard. As much as I had loved and adored him as a child, I had begun to realize how much he had wasted his life and opportunities. As much as I resented Mother's control of him, I realized that she had a reason for pushing him and that it was not entirely for selfish reasons. She also wanted our family to be more, but it couldn't be.

After dinner, we retired to the den to open Christmas gifts. I sat nervously, watching as gifts were handed out, family member to family member. Earl's parents and his grandparents had both gotten me gifts.

"I'm so embarrassed," I said as the gifts were placed on my lap. "I didn't get anything for any of you."

"Oh, that's not true," Mrs. Titwallow retorted, turning to Earl's grandparents. "Lovella made us a lovely cake. What was that called?" She turned back to me with the question.

"I'm not sure how to pronounce it correctly," I said, feeling the heat of embarrassment flood my face. "But I think it is *de Saba avec Glaqage au Chocolat.*"

Sarah hooted, "It's got a fancy French name and chocolate! That's all I need to know!"

"It was delicious," Mrs. Titwallow said. We had it for dessert last night, and it was wonderful! Lovella is an excellent cook. I think there are leftovers, so I'll have Nora pack some for you, and you can take it home and share Lovella's gift."

Earl put his arm around me and grinned, "Now, Lovella, shut up and open your presents," he teased.

I looked down at the first box in my lap and realized it was probably the most beautiful wrapping I had ever seen. "It's too pretty to unwrap," I said. Nonetheless, I began carefully pulling the paper away. Inside was a white box, and when I opened it and pulled back the tissue, there was a log-shaped leather purse, brown with gold emblems and hand-flaps of softer tan-colored leather. "I've never seen anything like it," I said, pulling it up to examine it.

Earl's mother said, "It's by a French designer, just released this year. Isn't it beautiful? I love the classic and elegant lines."

"Yes," I said, not knowing what I would do with it and feeling like it was too expensive and beautiful to use. My lower-middle-class upbringing had taught me to only use the good stuff for special occasions, a mindset of poverty that would take me years to shake. With an embarrassed smile, I said, "It's wonderful. Thank you so much."

Sarah squawked, "Well, the gift we got you is not quite as fancy as Mr. and Mrs. Moneybags, but we hope you like it."

I nervously smiled as I opened their package to find a cosmetics kit, including tweezers, eyeliner pencils, an eyelash curler, and other items. It was packaged in a nice little box, and I was far more comfortable receiving it.

"Oh, I love this," I smiled. "It was so nice of you to get me something. Next year, I'll be sure to include you on my list."

Following the gift opening, we settled into a comfortable evening of conversation. Having heard Earl talk about his father and grandfather, I was amazed and thankful that there had not been a spat. I thought, perhaps, they were trying to be on their best behavior with me present. I felt more and more cozy and contented with Earl's family. For all his complaints about his father, his family seemed to be the kind of family I would have been grateful to have had. His father might have been controlling, but there was none of the drama I had grown accustomed to with Mother. Even though his father seemed to drink heavily, he never seemed to be drunk, and I never saw him out of control, like Daddy. His grandfather Titwallow occasionally cast a verbal jab at his father but would try to laugh it off as a joke. Nonetheless, his family maintained the appearance of congeniality.

Later, we settled into our rooms. Earl came by my room to wish me goodnight. He stepped through the door, kicked the door closed behind him, lifted me into his arms, and kissed me. I loved it when he did things like that. I loved knowing that he not only loved me but he desired me. When he finished his long, warm kiss, he said, "So, what did you think?"

"I think you are a fortunate person," I replied, stroking his smooth cheek. "I love your family. They are so welcoming and affirming."

"Well, you haven't seen the rough stuff yet," he said.

"Compared to my family, they look like saints." I took his hand and pulled him to sit down on the bed. "So, we leave tomorrow morning?" I questioned.

"Yep," he replied. "About 9:00 a.m. Sound all right to you?"

"Fine," I replied. "I don't know how I can ever thank them—or you," I continued. "This is the best Christmas I've ever had, and just being here without the wonderful gifts still would have been the best Christmas gift I've ever had."

"Just having you with me makes this the best Christmas I've ever had, and it's more than thanks enough for the gifts," he said. "Besides, in time, you'll understand it's just stuff."

"It seems like pretty damn special stuff," I said.

"No," he replied, squeezing my hand. "It's just stuff. There may be more of it. It may be fancier and more expensive than what you are used to, but honestly, it means nothing. No matter what it is, sooner or later, it will end up in a landfill, the same fate as everything else, regardless. Human beings decide the value, and despite the value assigned to it, it all decays and deteriorates, eventually. It's just stuff."

"I'll take your word for it," I said.

He then kissed me, said goodnight, and walked to the door. Just before he opened the door to leave, he turned and said, "Nora will wake you for breakfast, just like today."

"Okay," I replied.

After he left, I got ready for bed and fell asleep quickly, even though my mind was full of the day and all my experiences.

Breakfast the next morning was similar to the first, but this time, it consisted of spinach omelets with melted Swiss cheese and a cream sauce. Along with this, a delicious fruit salad and blueberry scones were served.

Earl and I packed after breakfast. Our bags were taken to the landing, and John brought Earl's car to the front. We said our goodbyes and waved as we drove away. I settled back into the cool leather seats of Earl's Ferrari and couldn't help feeling that something in me had changed, that I would never really be the same again. I couldn't put my finger on it. It was some lingering secret in my subconscious, yet to be revealed, not a bad thing, but a shift in how I thought and viewed the world. I had seen both sides of the coin. After that, life seemed more fulfilled despite the multiple opposing factions of perception and intent. In some way, I felt like I was completing something.

Earl reached over and took my hand. His long, warm fingers lay like a blanket of comfort over mine. I watched the Pennsylvania landscape flow by my window and realized I would go with him whenever and wherever he wanted. Regardless of what I had planned for my life before he found me, from that point on, I would follow him.

CHAPTER 18

Will the Real Hippie Please Stand Up

The winter of 1967 dragged on, frigid and tedious, as Pennsylvania winters are prone to do. I settled back into my routine with Earl while spending enough time in the dorm to keep my status there and stay off the radar of any university official. Most of my time was spent with Earl. He continued his activities with *The Students for a Democratic Society*, and it became evident that if I was going to be with this man, it meant a wardrobe change. A purse designed by a French designer might be a bit too conservative, and getting onto floor pillows in tight knee-length skirts was not the best option.

It was a fact that I didn't own a pair of jeans. Mother considered them to be "un-lady-like," and for all my rebellion against Mother, I didn't rebel much about fashion. I liked looking feminine and chic. I enjoyed feminine hairstyles and pretty dresses, but things had to change if I was going to be a hippie. For Earl, I would be a hippie. If I could have been a chameleon able to morph into anything he wanted, I would have done it. There was no doubt I was in love.

On a mid-January morning, I had gotten ready for class wearing a double-buttoned, long-sleeved, hip-length blouse of thick cotton and a matching knee skirt. Before putting on my coat, I asked Earl, "How do I look in this?"

"You always look beautiful," he said.

"No, I mean honestly, Earl, how do I look?"

He eyed me up and down, confused about what I was trying to determine, and said, "You look like a fashionable, modern woman."

"But you're a hippie," I replied.

"So?" He looked puzzled.

"So," I said, "I don't look like a hippie. Shouldn't I look like a hippie if I'm going to be dating a hippie?"

238

He quickly kissed me on the cheek. "You should look any way you want," he said. "It doesn't matter. Besides, you look like you fit right in with my family."

"Yes," I went on. "But do you remember when we first went to a *Student's for a Democratic Society* meeting?"

"Yes. What?" He said, helping me into my coat before we began our descent down the brownstone's steps.

"You remember my difficulty getting down on the floor in my tight, knee-length skirt?"

"Yeah, so?" A slight grin crossed his face.

"I think I need to have some more comfortable clothes if we are going to participate in the anti-war movement. My wardrobe does not appear conducive to the activities we might encounter with that group."

"Yeah, so we'll get you some more comfortable clothes." He opened the car door for me, and I slipped into the seat like a lady. Then, he stepped off the curb, rounded the car, and entered the driver's side. "We'll go shopping after class this afternoon," he said as soon as he entered the car.

"Do you mind buying me a few new outfits?" I questioned.

"I don't mind buying you anything you want," he replied, pulling away from the curb. "We'll go shopping."

By 1967, several hippie boutiques were appearing in American cities. State College, PA, was no exception, especially as a university town. Earl knew right where they were. In addition, there were second-hand stores where one could buy old sailor's pants with a stripe down the side and bell bottoms. A little tie-dye applied to the pants turned them into an entirely different garment.

I finished my last class at 2:00 p.m., and Earl's class generally ended by noon, but he usually went to the library and studied while he waited for my class to finish. He met me, like always, right outside my classroom, and we walked, holding close to each other, in the cold, crisp winter air. The sun shone without a cloud in the jewel blue sky, and the outlines of winter tree limbs devoid of leaves looked like carved, gray cracks in the brilliant blue overhead.

Later, Earl pulled up in front of an old building, a storefront of years past. The brick had been painted a bright yellow, and the windowpanes were painted with outlines of small blue peace signs around the edges. Manikins stood in the windows, draped in the latest hippie garb. When we walked through the door, jingle bells tinkled, and I realized that they had been tied to the glass door bar inside to announce the arrival of customers. They clinked against the glass as the door closed behind us. There was a smell of incense, and speakers mounted to the ceiling played *The Doors,* *"Come On Baby Light My Fire."*

A man with hair just past his ears came walking toward us. His thin face was strewn with scraggly beard hair, and his brown cotton shirt hung from his shoulders like one of the manikins in the window. The brown shirt was open, and beneath it, a red T-shirt bore the face of Che Guevara.

"Peace, man," he said with a toothy smile. "Get you folks something?"

"My girlfriend is looking for some comfortable clothes," Earl said.

The store attendant then eyed me. "Groovy. Follow me."

He led me to a wall of blouses and t-shirts and pointed out the slacks, jeans, and frilly, colorful cotton dresses behind me. I picked out a couple of paisley blouses with flared sleeves, a t-shirt with a German minicar showing a peace sign in place of the logo hood ornament, a tie-dye shirt, and a shirt depicting the face of Jimi Hendrix. I got a couple of bell-bottom slacks, four pairs of jeans, and several other blouses and T-shirts. I also got a couple of shin-length flowing cotton floral print dresses. Earl paid for it without batting an eye. As we left the store, Earl commented, "There, now you are officially a hippie chick."

The first time I got to wear one of my hippie outfits was at a meeting of *The Students for a Democratic Society.* I had no problem getting down on the floor this time, and I felt more like part of the crowd. I began to feel myself getting into the inspiration of the anti-war movement, and not just because it was important to Earl. I began to realize that it was something important for the whole country, for democracy, and that it had to be done. So, it was becoming important to me, too.

Plans were made to get as many people as possible to go to New York on April 15th, and it looked as though we would have quite a few going to the march. A bus was chartered to carry anyone who didn't have their own transportation, signs were made, and a designated place and time for everyone to meet up was arranged. I was impressed that Martin Luther

King Jr. would be there, leading the march from Central Park to the U.N. This would undoubtedly be an adventure. I had never been to New York. I had never been in a march of any kind, and the possibility of seeing Martin Luther King Jr. was exhilarating.

Winter eventually passed into spring. Tulips and Jonquils began to lift through the ground, spreading color around campus and our building. The march in New York would occur on a Saturday and coincide with spring break so that students could attend without disrupting classes. Earl and I had gotten hotel reservations near Central Park in February, so we were ready to go and be a part of it all. Others would camp out in the park or bunch up in hotel rooms, but we had our own room. Yet, we were open to sharing if anyone needed a place to stay.

We went to New York a few days early. Although the organization had chartered a bus, we decided to travel separately. So, before the others arrived, Earl took me to the Statue of Liberty and the Empire State Building. It was quite a sight for a little girl who had barely been out of Climax, Pennsylvania, her whole life, but it was nothing compared to what I would see on April 15, 1967.

We got up very early that day, and thanks to Earl's planning, we had only a few blocks to walk to Central Park, where we rendezvoused with the others. Even before we arrived, the park's parameters were full of people. There were people of every color, type, and age. I saw Lakota Indians in full Native American regalia. There were hippies, plenty of Black people, and even older people the age of grandparents, although the crowd was primarily young people. There were people with painted faces and people wearing outlandish costumes, but most people were dressed in casual street clothes. I had never seen so many people in one place, at one time, in my life. Afterward, we heard estimates that over a hundred thousand people were there, more than twenty times the population of Climax.

The tone was one of happiness and celebration. Here and there, a joint was passed around. That was the first time I ever smoked pot. I didn't quite know what it was or what to do with it when it was handed to me. I was uncertain about it, but I did what others were doing and assumed it was like a cigarette. Then, I got caught up in the excitement of the moment.

After a joint had passed by me a few times, I noticed the sounds of the crowd becoming crisp. Here and there, bits of music tinkled in my ears, becoming ever so enhanced and beautiful. The colors around me became vibrant, and people's faces seemed more animated. However, I found myself having difficulty thinking clearly, and I felt self-conscious, unsure, and frightened. I was clinging to Earl and suddenly frightened of becoming separated from him. I was having problems following conversations, and there were so many. Although, I found that a conversation with only one person at a time could become enchantingly fascinating.

I met a woman who was perhaps in her seventies, close to or past my grandmother's age. She had a wide-brimmed hat with a giant yellow bow and had stuffed the band with Forsythia blossoms. She had multiple layers of beads around her neck and bright red lipstick. Her gray hair hung off her shoulders like a young girl, filled with life and vitality.

"Hello, darling," she said. "You look—stoned." She then laughed a great cackle. I never dreamed that anyone in my mother's, especially my grandmother's, generation could ever have acted like that. She seemed so free and unencumbered. Grandmother Donner, with all her brashness, would never have flittered around in public like that, and she would have been too busy telling everyone what to do instead of freely enjoying herself.

"I'm not sure what I am," I replied. "I've never felt like this. I don't know what that stuff did to me."

She cackled again. "Isn't it wonderful, darling? I'm stoned, too. Have a good time, sweetie! Enjoy every inch of life while you still can. You only go around once. So, suck the tit of life for all it's worth, baby!"

She disappeared into the crowd as instantly as she had appeared.

Behind me, Earl was having a detailed conversation about the war, the power elite, the military-industrial complex, and I don't know what else. I heard bits and pieces of his conversation with a young man about his age, a tubby boy dressed in a loose-fitting pilgrim shirt and baggy flare-legged jeans. There was so much going on around me that the intensity of the experience was almost overwhelming. There was too much to take in, far too much stimulation, and I found myself becoming increasingly anxious.

Word came around that Martin Luther King Jr. was about to speak. So, we all gathered to hear him. Listening as carefully as possible, I could only make out little bits and pieces of the speech. The one thing I did hear, the one thing that stuck in my mind the most, was, *"There comes a time when silence is betrayal."* I thought deeply about those words. I thought about my avoidance of politics at a time when so much was happening. I thought about how my silence and avoidance had become a betrayal to the men and women of my generation. I had stood silently by while boys my age were slaughtered in the jungles of Vietnam for no worthy reason. I had stood silently by while racism permeated my culture. I heard him say something to the effect that social change comes through non-violent action. He had taken a lesson from Gandhi, who, by non-violent resistance, had been able to overthrow the British rule of India, the only time in history that the British had ever given ruling authority to an occupied country without being driven out by war. I thought about the power of nothing, the act of nothingness, no action, no response to violence or intimidation—but simply being unmoving, resistant, and allowing that to be your response. Sometimes, the opposite of action is the action that is needed, and when applied appropriately, it can be very effective.

There was an action taking place on that day, but it was an action of nothingness. It was an action of non-violent resistance and expression of concern. There were people there who were in opposition to our cause, and they were shouting at us. There were a few very heated arguments, but the action, as a whole, was an action of nothingness, an action of simply being in a place at a particular time and allowing being there to speak for itself. It conveyed that we were against the war, wanted no more violence, and longed for the gentle nothingness of peace, of being allowed to live and let live instead of being forced into unreasonable things against our will. The need for freedom is inherent in the heart of every human being, and any act to suppress it cannot stand without opposition.

Shortly after the speeches were over, we marched. We were marching to the U.N. to ask them to put pressure on the United States to stop the bombing in Vietnam. I had no idea where the U.N. building was. I followed the crowd and walked by Earl's side. Television cameras recorded the event as we marched, and reporters periodically interviewed people. For the most part, we ignored them because our goal was to be present. Still, we passed by some TV cameras, and Earl waved at the reporters.

Somehow, on that day, I was ignorant. I was unaware that I was part of making history and that this would be one of history's most famous war protests. I was ignorant that there could be any personal fallout from the simple experience of listening to speeches and walking from Central Park to the U.N. Yet, it would mean more than I ever dreamed and would ultimately transition my life in a way I never expected.

When we returned to Earl's apartment late Sunday evening, his father's car was parked in front of the building.

"Hmmm," Earl said. " I wonder what the old man is doing here. I hope everything is okay."

His father had a key to Earl's apartment and had let himself in. When we walked in with our luggage, Mr. Titwallow sat on the sofa reading some materials we had picked up at *The Students for a Democratic Society* meeting.

"Hey, Dad," Earl said. "What brought you down here?"

His father tossed the literature back onto the coffee table where he had found it. "I think the more important question is, where the hell have you been?" He glared at Earl.

"We've been to New York," Earl replied, looking confused.

Both of us were wondering what Mr. Titwallow was doing there and why he was acting so strangely and intimidatingly.

"Yes, I know you have been to New York," Mr. Titwallow responded. "I saw your face displayed on the Goddamn national evening news last night."

"Hey, honey," Earl poked me lightly with his elbow. "We made the news."

"WHAT THE HELL DO YOU THINK YOU WERE DOING GOING TO THAT GODDAMN ANTIWAR PROTEST?" His father exploded in anger. The fury on his face frightened me so much that I sunk back toward the door, and I wondered if he was going to become violent.

"Well, sir," Earl replied calmly. "I was exercising my right as a citizen of the United States of America to engage in free speech and peaceful protest."

His father stood up and poked a rigid finger in our direction. "DID YOU EVER STOP TO THINK, FOR ONE GODDAMN MOMENT, WHAT AN EMBARRASSMENT THIS WOULD BE TO YOUR FAMILY?"

Earl set his luggage down, pried mine from my nervous hand, and set it on the floor. "I don't see why it should have embarrassed anyone," he said.

"YOU KNOW GODDAMN WELL THAT YOU HAVE A REPUTATION TO UPHOLD FOR THIS FAMILY!" his father continued shouting. "WHAT THE HELL DO YOU THINK IT IS GOING TO DO TO MY COMPANY'S FINANCES AND BUSINESS IF WORD GETS AROUND THAT MY SON IS A TRAITOR TO THE UNITED STATES GOVERNMENT?"

I remembered Earl telling me that his father had some investments in military manufacturing.

Earl continued to remain calm. "First of all, Dad, I am not a traitor to the government. I am merely protesting the actions of the government with which I disagree. I am well within my constitutional rights to do so. Second," he continued, "it is doubtful that anyone other than close family or friends is even going to recognize my face on TV, much less say to themselves, 'Oh, that's Daniel Titwallow's son. He's acting like a traitor. Let's boycott.'"

"DON'T SMART MOUTH ME!" his father snapped.

For the first time, I realized what Earl was talking about when he said he resented his father's control. It was like Mother's hornet nest of anger when I did anything contrary to her wishes. The difference was that Earl's father had more control over him than Mother ever had over me.

"Dad," Earl said calmly, "don't you think we could sit down and talk about this like civil human beings? There is no need to shout."

"DON'T YOU DARE ACCUSE ME!" his father retorted. "I'VE BEEN AS CIVIL WITH YOU AS I'M EVER GOING TO BE! I'VE RAISED YOU TO BE A MAN AND ACT LIKE A MAN! I SENT YOU TO THIS GODDAMN COLLEGE SO YOU COULD MAKE SOMETHING OF YOURSELF, NOT SO YOU COULD GO BEHIND MY BACK AND ACT LIKE SOME GODDAMN ANARCHIST! YOU WOULD BE FIGHTING IN THAT FUCKING WAR IF IT WEREN'T FOR ME!"

In a reassuring tone, Earl turned to me and said, "Lovella, why don't you go in the kitchen and make us some coffee? I think I would like a cup of coffee. Dad, would you like a cup of coffee?"

His father only glared at him.

I did as instructed, happy to distance myself from the animosity. I busied myself in the kitchen but could still hear the conversation.

Earl sat in the chair adjacent to the sofa. "Why don't you sit down, Dad? It seems this conversation could take a while, too long to be on our feet."

His father did not sit down immediately. "I AM SICK AND TIRED OF YOUR DEFIANCE!" he shouted. "I HAVE WORKED MY ASS OFF TO MAKE A GOOD LIFE FOR YOU AND YOUR SISTER. I HAVE DONE EVERYTHING TO TRY TO GET YOU TO UNDERSTAND THAT THIS COMPANY WILL GIVE YOU, YOUR CHILDREN, AND YOUR GRANDCHILDREN MORE OF A LIFE THAN THEY WILL EVER NEED, MORE THAN I EVER HAD! I AM TRYING TO GIVE YOU A LIFE WHERE YOU DON'T HAVE TO BUST YOUR ASS LIKE I DID, WHERE YOU DON'T HAVE TO SCRAPE FOR PENNIES TO GET BY, AND ALL YOU CAN DO IS FIGHT ME AND DEFY EVERY DAMN STEP I TAKE FOR YOUR FUTURE!"

"Sit down, Dad, please," Earl pleaded.

Finally, his father sat, reluctantly, on the sofa.

From the adjacent chair, Earl continued, "I know you have worked hard. I know you think running the company is best for me. The problem is that you have never asked me what I think or want."

His father continued with bitterness, "I know what you want. You want to run around acting like a jackass, taking no responsibility for yourself, and thinking nothing about how your actions might affect other people."

"Anything that I do," Earl responded, slowly but with bitterness welling in his voice, "which you do not prescribe for me to do, you consider to be acting like a jackass. Yet, everything I do is in consideration of people."

"YOU HAVE A REPUTATION TO UPHOLD FOR THIS FAMILY!" his father yelled.

"And what is a reputation?" Earl queried. "What is it? A reputation is what you try to get other people to think of you. It has nothing to do with your character. It has nothing to do with what you really stand for or self-respect. It is a facade for the world to see, and then others decide what they think of you, no matter what you do. You don't care who I am. You don't care what I believe in or what I want for myself. All you care about is your company and *your* reputation."

"I BUILT THAT COMPANY FOR MY FAMILY!" his father screamed, veins popping in his neck.

"Thank you," Earl said, retreating into his calm tone. "Thank you for building that company for us, Dad. Thank you for a wonderful, beautiful home and all the money we could ever want. Thank you for ensuring we have luxury and opulence available at every whim. Thank you for the servants who do everything for us. Thank you for the European trips, fine cars, and elegant dining. Thank you. But you know, there is one problem, one very big problem. You never asked us if we wanted all that. You never asked any of us if we wanted that much. In my entire life, you have never asked me what I wanted because the truth is, no matter how much you give us, how much money you make, or how much luxury you can afford, it is never enough. It will never be enough. So, if I say, 'That's enough. No, Dad, I'm good. Thanks, I have enough. I don't need any more,' you don't listen because you want me to be just like you. You want me never to be satisfied and never look around and think I'm grateful for what I already have. You want me to take over the company and run it the way you have, like an obsessed madman who is crazy for wealth, who is trying to prove that he is not that impoverished little boy who grew up during The Great Depression. You want me to take the baton and run with it so you can realize your dream of going national and being the world's biggest, best snack company. But you know what? It won't matter. You could be the richest man in the world, and it wouldn't be enough. It's never going to be enough, Dad. I realized that a long time ago. You're addicted to wealth."

"So, you just want to fart around and act like a Goddamn bum? Is that it?" His father spoke as though nothing Earl had said meant anything to him. He didn't get it. He didn't hear. "You don't care about the family business? You don't care about trying to leave something meaningful to your children so they don't have to work as hard as you did?"

Earl leaned in toward his father. "Dad, I'm here because you want me here. I am studying business because you want me to study business. I am doing what you want me to do so I can take over the family business someday and keep your legacy because that is what you want me to do. You are getting your way. I'm suspending my desires to fulfill yours, but I will not stop being who I am because you don't like who I am. I will not stop believing what I believe because you don't like what I believe. I will not stop fighting for what I believe is right because you disagree. I'm holding onto one small morsel of my life, one small part of my true self adrift in the ocean of all you want."

I carried a tray with cups, the coffee percolator, sugar, and cream into the living room and set it on the coffee table. I poured the steaming coffee from the percolator into each cup and let them decide for themselves what additions they might want.

His father turned to me, saying, "So, your influence is dragging my boy down to this."

"GIVE ME A FUCKING BREAK, DAD!" Earl yelled for the first time. "YOU KNOW BETTER! HOW DARE YOU ATTACK LOVELLA OR TRY TO DRAG HER INTO THIS? SHE DIDN'T EVEN DRESS THIS WAY OR KNOW ANYTHING ABOUT THIS STUFF TILL SHE MET ME. IF ANYONE IS INFLUENCING ANYONE. I'M INFLUENCING HER!"

"Mr. Titwallow," I said, grabbing a textbook from the floor at the end of the sofa. "I think I'm going to go to the other room to study while you and Earl work this out."

I retreated quickly to the bedroom. However, I couldn't study. My mind wouldn't take in the words written on the page. I picked the book up briefly but soon threw it on the bed. I lay there worried about what was happening in the living room. I could no longer hear the exact conversation but still heard their yelling. After what seemed like forever, I heard Earl's father scream, "FINE! YOU WANT IT YOUR WAY? YOU CAN HAVE IT YOUR WAY! I'LL CUT YOU OFF SUPPORT, AND YOU CAN SEE WHAT IT'S LIKE TO HAVE TO STRUGGLE TO GET BY!"

After that, I heard the door slam, and there was silence. Earl eventually meandered into the bedroom and lay down beside me.

"Hello, beautiful," he said, rolling over and looking into my eyes.

"Hello, lover," I responded softly. "Is everything okay?"

"Everything is always okay," he said.

"So, your dad is going to cut you off. No more money?"

"We'll see." He smiled and glided his warm hand across my face. "This is not the first time we have had screaming matches like this, but it is the first time I've ever told him what I really think."

"So, what will you do if he cuts you off?" I asked.

"Get a job, maybe. He's not going to cut off school tuition. He wants too much for me to graduate and do what he could never do—get a degree. He'll probably keep paying the tab if he thinks I'm willing to study business."

"So, you are going to keep doing what he wants you to do," I said, as a statement, not a question.

He rolled over on his back and sighed. "You know," he responded, "I've never dared to do what I wanted to do, not really. I've piddled with things I wanted to do while still doing enough to keep the old man happy, but I've never done anything completely my way."

"What would doing it your way mean?" I questioned.

"You know the hell of it is that I don't know for sure." He glanced at me questioningly as though I might know and returned his gaze to the ceiling. "I've lived so much of my life for Dad that I don't know what it would be like to live my life for me."

"How would you find out?" I pondered.

"I don't know," he said. "It might be extreme."

I rolled onto my back beside him, and we stared at the ceiling together. "You know," I said, "I learned something about myself when we visited your family at Christmas."

"Really, what did you learn?" he said without removing his gaze from the ceiling.

"Well, I learned, for one thing, that I like having nice things and great food. I learned I could get used to that easily, but I also learned something much more important."

"What's that?" he wondered, still not wavering his view.

"I learned that I love you, and I'll do anything you want me to do." His eyes left the ceiling and met mine as I continued, "I learned I will follow you wherever you want to go and do whatever you want to do."

"If I asked that of you, how would that be any different from what my dad is doing to me?" He propped himself up on his elbow, inspecting me. "Lovella, I don't want you to live your life for me. I want you to do what makes you happy. You came to Penn State to get a degree in medical science. You need to do that because it is what you want."

"No, it isn't," I said.

"It isn't?" A puzzled look crossed his face.

"No," I responded. "I just went to college to get away from Climax. I didn't know anything about college or what I wanted to do. My interest in sexual research is a product of my lust and an inherent desire to piss Mother off. I don't care if I study anything unless it interests me. Human sexuality interests me, but it's not everything."

"Well, what do you want to do with your life?" he asked.

"I want to love and be with you," I said. "Anything else is just icing on the cake. If I happen to finish my degree and get a job in medical research, that would be wonderful, but I don't care. I don't care if I'm a cleaning lady as long as I'm with you."

He sighed. "Lovella, I don't want you ever to feel like you have given up what you want for what I want."

"Well, since I don't want anything else, it doesn't matter." I stuck my tongue out at him in mock defiance.

He smiled.

"So, Mr. Earl Titwallow," I said after a brief silence. "If you could do anything in the world you wanted and do it just for you, what would you do?"

He lay down on his back, put his arm around me, and pulled my head to his chest. "Other than loving you, I don't know," he said. "I'll have to think about it."

After that, we lay there silently. A short time later, I heard a quiet snore that told me he had fallen asleep. With my eyes closed, my head snuggled in the warm comfort of his chest, I soon followed.

CHAPTER 19

Summer of Love?

The Penn State campus had turned into a green blanket of perfectly manicured lawns in late May. Here and there, mulched flower beds sprouted petunias and geraniums amid the monkey grass. Annual varieties of flowers morphed into a colorful quilt of flora as the season progressed. An entire crew of gardeners kept the campus pristine.

Earl and I had both finished our classes for the semester. Finals were over, and summer vacation was about to begin. Earl's father still was not speaking to him. Before their big fight, he had already paid for the semester's tuition and rent through May on Earl's apartment. Getting through the rest of the semester was, therefore, no problem. His mother tried to mediate between them but to little avail. Earl's father was a stubborn man, and Earl was determined to figure himself out. For once, he decided to do what he wanted, not what his father had insisted he must do. He knew he wanted to finish college and get his degree.

I expected I would probably go home and spend the summer in Climax with Mother and Daddy. I certainly had made no other plans. I had packed my things and made plans for Mother to come pick me up. She would arrive on campus just before Memorial Day weekend. I would go home for the summer, hoping to see Earl as often as possible. The day before Mother was to come get me, Earl popped into the living room with excitement radiating. "Lovella, come look!" he said.

"What?" I questioned.

"No, you know what?" he bubbled. "I want it to be a surprise!" He ran into the bedroom and grabbed one of my scarves. He returned and commanded, "Turn around."

"Okay?"

I turned my back to him with curiosity looming as he tied the scarf over my eyes.

"Now, come on," he insisted, leading me, blindfolded, from the apartment and maneuvering me around the steps and obstacles to the street. He aimed me toward the street, lifted the scarf from my head, and said, "Okay, take a look!"

I found myself staring at a pink van. The sides were painted with huge flowers and peace signs, and I immediately thought, *this looks familiar.*

"So, what do you think?" he asked excitedly.

"I think it's …" I measured, for a moment, what I would say as I wondered what he wanted me to say, "a pink van."

"Isn't it cool?" he queried, with his ongoing excitement.

"It looks familiar," I said.

"Yeah," he responded. "It belonged to Jimmy and Tonya, and now it belongs to us."

"Oooooo!" I dragged the exclamation along, fearing that my acting would not be good enough to convince him of genuine excitement. The truth was, I had no interest in a broken-down, old van. "Where is your Ferrari?" I asked, forming a fake smile.

"I sold it," he replied. "I got enough money to buy the van from Jimmy and Tonya and then have enough left over for us to go on an adventure.

"An adventure?" I questioned. "Where are we going?"

"To San Francisco, man!"

He made a fist of each hand and punched the sky like he was in a boxing match with heaven. "It's going to be awesome!" he declared.

"Okay," I hesitated. "Why are we going to San Francisco?"

"Because that's where it's happening!" He ejected again. "The Haight district. Hippies, Be-ins, Love-ins. We have got to go, Lovella. We have got to be in on this!"

"Okay," I said, with a slight trepidation welling in my voice. "Let's plan a trip."

"No, no, no," he blabbered, his eyes gleaming like a madman. "There's no planning. We just go!"

"Now?" I questioned.

"Right, *fucking*, now!" he exclaimed, grabbing my shoulders and giving me a quick hug. He pulled away from me, gripping my shoulders, and scanned my face for a reaction.

"Earl, Mother is supposed to pick me up tomorrow and take me home for the summer."

"So, call her and tell her you have other plans," he gleamed. "Let's do this, Lovella! You said you would go anywhere with me. Here is your chance: a trial run over the summer to see if that will work for you."

I grinned at him and stepped out of my *responsible young lady* self into my *'don't give a fuck'* self.

"I did say that. Didn't I?" I threw my arms around him and shouted, "Let's do it! Let's go!"

"How soon can you be ready?" he asked.

"I'm already packed to go home," I responded with a sudden ne'er-do-well attitude. "I only need to exchange a few things. Then, as soon as you get yourself packed, I'm ready."

He grabbed my hand, and we ran back into his flat.

I had almost everything packed for the trip home the following morning, but I wouldn't need those neat dresses for this trip. Mother had never seen me in my hippie outfit, so I had not planned to take my hippie clothes home. I quickly hung the traditional things back in the closet. I wasn't sure if Earl would keep the apartment over the summer or if they would even still be hanging there when we returned, and if they weren't, fuck it! I opened my suitcase and began exchanging types of clothing. Earl threw open his suitcase and started shoving in wads of clothing.

"Fold them," I said. "You won't get much to fit in the suitcase if you don't fold them."

"I could fucking care less," he exclaimed, laughing. "I don't fucking care if I go naked."

I looked at him sternly, and he got the message.

"You're right," he said. "I need to fold them." He then pulled them back out of the suitcase, folded them—sort of—and put them back in.

We were both grabbing things like mad. Finally, we looked around and realized there was nothing else we could pack. We ran out of the house, threw the luggage in the van, and headed west out of State College toward Pittsburgh.

We had driven for almost two hours when I exclaimed, "Oh my God! I forgot to call Mother."

It's okay," he said. "When we get to Pittsburgh, we'll stop at a pay phone."

"Since we will be in the area," I questioned, "do you want to stop and see your parents?"

"What for?" he snapped. "The old man is only going to tell me what a fool I am, and Mom will try to figure out how to make us get along."

"Okay."

I understood. I didn't want to call Mother, either, and might not have if she wasn't about to make an unnecessary trip to pick me up.

We arrived in Pittsburgh a little after 7:00 p.m., and Earl pulled into a grocery store parking lot where we had seen a pay phone. I dialed the operator and told her I needed to make a collect call. The phone rang a few times, then Mother answered and accepted the charges.

"Hello, Mother," I began.

"Where are you, Lovella?" she demanded. "I hear traffic in the background."

"I'm at a pay phone in Pittsburgh, Mother," I responded, as though it wouldn't matter to her.

"Lovella Fuchs!" she shouted. "What are you doing in Pittsburgh at this hour of the night? I am supposed to pick you up at State College tomorrow morning."

"I know, Mother," I attempted to soothe. "But we have had a change of plans."

"You what? Is something wrong with someone in Earl's family?" She sounded genuinely concerned for a moment.

"No, Mother, everyone is fine. We have just had a change of plans, that's all." I knew she would not take the news well, but I continued. "Earl and I are going to San Francisco for the summer."

"You absolutely will do no such thing!" she demanded. "Your father and I need you here. Besides, you don't have the money to go to San Francisco."

"No, I don't, Mother, but Earl does."

"Lovella, I took a day off work!" she yelled. "I'm missing a day of pay tomorrow, so I can come pick you up. Now, you better turn your butt around and go back to State College! I'm picking you up tomorrow morning!"

"No," I said, simply and firmly.

"What!" she badgered.

"I said, no, Mother. I won't be there, so you might as well not come. Take the day off and enjoy yourself. I know you need a break. Enjoy it. I'm going to San Francisco with Earl, end of the argument, end of the conversation."

There was silence. She knew there was nothing she could do. She knew there was nothing she could threaten me with, but there was something she could guilt me about. Then, she said mournfully and insincerely, "Lovella, your father is not well. The doctor said that he is dying of cirrhosis and he doesn't have long to live. You know he will want to spend time with you before he goes."

"Oh, that's a good one, Mother," I retorted. "That's one of the best guilt trips you have ever pulled on me."

"I'm telling you the truth, Lovella!" she snarled back at me.

"Even if Daddy was dying," I lectured, "he would never try to guilt me into doing something, and he would never demand anything of me or try to manipulate me like you do."

"Lovella, the doctor has only given him a few months to live," she pleaded.

"Is Daddy there, Mother?"

I would confront her guilt trip with the facts from Daddy. I knew he wouldn't lie to me, but she would. However, if he were drunk, I would have very mixed feelings, and I might have to rethink my decision.

"Yes," she responded hesitantly.

"Well, put him on the phone."

"He's sleeping," she said, and I thought even more that she was using one of her well-known fabrications to trick me into doing what she wanted. I had seen her do it too many times.

"Oh, how convenient," I ridiculed with a snide tone. "Wake him up. I want to talk to him."

She fell silent momentarily and said, "He needs his rest, Lovella. He is not well."

"Get this, Mother!" I shouted. "I think you are lying, and this is just another one of your stupid tricks! If Daddy tells me himself that he is sick, then I will come home, but if I don't hear it from him, fuck you!"

I heard the phone drop and pop as the receiver fell against the table. She went to the sofa where one could almost always find Daddy. I heard her faintly in the background. "John. John, get up. Lovella wants to speak to you."

"What? Huh?" I heard. At least she was telling the truth that he had been sleeping.

Then, in a moment, I heard him come on the phone. He was sober. I could tell from his voice that he hadn't been drinking.

"Hello, Punkin'."

"Hi, Daddy," I said. "How are you?"

"Oh, I'm fine. How are you?"

"I'm good, Daddy. Earl and I are going to San Francisco for the summer."

I heard Mother in the background. "Tell her what Dr. Lewis told you."

He ignored her. "Oh, that's wonderful sweetheart. I hope you have lots of fun."

"Tell her, John!" Mother insisted again.

"Daddy," I cut in. "What's going on? Mother has been telling me about you dying of cirrhosis."

"What?" he declared. "She told you that?"

"Yes, Daddy," I went on. "Is it true?"

"Oh, no, no. I'm fine, Punkin' Patch. Dr. Lewis says my liver enzymes are a little elevated, that's all. He said I needed to quit drinking, so I've been taking his advice and trying to be a good boy. I haven't had a drop in over a month. It was a little rough there for a while. I had the shakes pretty bad, but I think I'm about over it now. No, now that I'm sober, I'm feelin' better every day."

In the background, I heard Mother exclaim, "Oh, for goodness' sake, John!"

At that moment, a part of me wondered which was lying and which was telling the truth, but I had always trusted Daddy and rarely trusted Mother.

"There is nothing wrong that a few months of not drinking won't fix, and I think I might just quit altogether," he said. "You go on with Earl and have a good time. Your mother and I will be fine."

Mother grabbed the phone from his hand. She came on the line and said, "Lovella! Don't believe him! He's lying to you! He's dying! He might not even live till the fall, and he has continued to drink despite the doctor warning him to stop. Don't believe him!"

"Well, that's a problem for you then, isn't it, Mother?" I said coldly. "I do believe him. He's sober now. It's been a long time since he has been sober, and I can't recall a single time that he has ever lied to me."

She was silent. Finally, "All right then." She was silent for another prolonged and dramatic pause. "Call me when you get there and let me know you are safe."

"I will," I said.

A mix of feelings washed over me. I felt guilty and questioned myself over the decision to go. Then, I realized I would be spending a wonderful, exciting summer with the man I loved without distractions from school or family. In my heart, I convinced myself that Daddy was okay. I knew he had a severe problem, but I couldn't remember any time that I had ever caught him in a lie. Besides, he was sober on the phone, and if he had stopped drinking, that was a significant step in the right direction. Still, I didn't know whether to be proud of him or worry about him.

"Bye, now," I said, making a nervous effort to sound reassuring.

She gave a chilly goodbye and hung up the phone.

I jumped back into the van where Earl had patiently waited.

"Let's go!" I exclaimed. "Let's go to San Francisco!"

He sensed something. "Are you okay?"

I quickly hid my trepidation behind a fake laugh.

"I am fucking awesome!" I shouted. "Let's go!"

He steered the van away from the parking lot. We grabbed a burger for dinner at a truck stop and drove until midnight. He found a gravel side road just east of Toledo, Ohio, pulled off the main highway, out of sight, and parked the van by the ditch.

"What are we doing?" I asked, watching him turn onto the gravel road.

"We're spending the night," he said. "Hotel van."

"You're kidding?" I probed.

"Nope, not kidding," he said.

"But I thought we would stay in a hotel?" I pleaded.

"The less we waste on a hotel, the more we have for a good time," he replied. "Remember Dad cut me off when I didn't do what he wanted? All we have is the extra money I got from the Ferrari, which has to last us all summer."

"How much is that?" I asked.

"About five hundred," he said. "Should be plenty."

"Wait a minute," I said. "You sold your Ferrari, which should have brought ten or fifteen thousand dollars, even used. You bought this van, which is used and old and probably should not have cost more than a couple hundred, at the absolute most, but you only have five hundred dollars left?"

"Okay," he said, dropping his head. "Dad and I had another big fight. He took the car to get back at me. I guess he thinks if I have nothing left, I have to turn to him and beg. I had about six fifty left in my bank account, which I got to before he did. I closed it out and took the cash. I paid Jimmy and Tonya a hundred for the van, bought a few things for the trip, and about five hundred is what I have left."

"A hundred is probably more than this is worth," I said. "Earl, why didn't you tell me the truth?"

"I was embarrassed."

He ran his long fingers nervously around the steering wheel.

"What on earth did you have to be embarrassed about?" I asked.

"I don't know," he said. "I'm about to turn twenty-one years old, and my dad can still take the car away from me like I'm a sixteen-year-old who got a speeding ticket. It's pathetic. The car wasn't even in my name. It was my high school graduation gift, but I still didn't have the title. He would not relinquish one inch of power over me unless I broke that chain."

"It doesn't matter," I comforted. "You will make your own way. You are an intelligent and talented man. We will make our own way."

"I'm sorry I lied to you," he said.

"Just don't do it again," I responded. "There is no need to lie to me, Earl. I'm not your dad. I'm not going to come down on you like that. We need to be honest with each other. Trust is the mortar that holds a relationship together. Now, explain something to me."

"Yeah, what?" He stopped running his fingers around the steering wheel and took my hand.

"How are we going to sleep in this van?"

"Sleeping bags," he said. "Camping gear, I bought camping gear before we left."

"Earl, there are seats back there," I reasoned.

"Yeah. They come out," he teased.

He reached behind the front seat, brought out a battery-operated camping lantern, flipped it on, got out of the van, opened the side doors, and fiddled with the back seats until they came off. He lifted them out and set them in front of the van. After he removed the seats, a reasonably smooth surface remained. He rolled out the sleeping bags on the floor of the van.

"So, now what?" I questioned.

"So, now we sleep," he said. "It's late."

I walked around the van smoking a cigarette, and he continued fiddling with the setup for a while before we crawled into the van and snuggled into our individual sleeping bags.

"I would like to brush my teeth," I said, wishing that one bag had been big enough for both of us.

"Sorry," he responded. "It's just for one night, maybe. Maybe we can clean up a little tomorrow morning at a rest stop or a gas station."

The floor of the van was hard, but I was tired. We snuggled our bags close to each other, and in a short time, I was asleep.

I woke the following day with the first glimmering of light coming through the van's windows, and, yes, there was one other thing that woke me. Earl was zipping down the side of my sleeping bag and crawling, already naked, into it. Kissing and caressing me all the way, he moved down and began to open my jeans. He pulled my blouse up over my breasts and began to caress and lick my nipples. The only thing I had taken off the night before was my bra and shoes. It didn't take long for him to wiggle me out of my jeans, and soon, we were making love with the van rocking to his thrusts. Earl was about to climax when we heard a car engine revving as though picking up speed. Earl pulled back and looked out the window. Suddenly he exclaimed, "Goddamn it! Goddamn! NO!"

Earl hurried to get out of the van and ran, naked and barefooted, up the gravel road after an old green truck that had just sped away. I leaned over and looked out the side doors with my sleeping bag pulled around me.

"Earl, what is it? What's the matter?" I called.

"They fucking stole our stuff!" he screamed. "Goddamn it!"

"You mean the van seats?" I inquired.

"The fucking van seats and our luggage, damn it! I fucking left the luggage sitting outside the van last night!"

"Okay," I said, not being overly concerned. "We'll find a flea market or something and buy a few clothes to get us through."

"No, you don't understand!" he ejected. "Damn it! Goddamn it! I was so fucking stupid to leave that stuff out! Lovella, our money was in my suitcase!"

"Oh shit!" I exclaimed.

"Oh, shit is right!" he returned. "Jesus! Now what are we going to fucking do?"

"I guess we could see if our parents will wire us some money," I said.

"No way!" he exclaimed. "No fucking way! I will not beg my dad, have him rub it in my face, and gloat about being right. No fucking way! Besides, he would probably just come, pick us up, and take us back instead of fronting me any money. Then, he would lecture me the whole Goddamn way!"

"Maybe the police could help us get it back," I suggested.

"I don't think we have another option," he responded. "Let's get dressed."

We put on the clothes we had worn the day before. I had kept my shoes in the van, but Earl, unfortunately, had left his outside with the luggage. They had not been stolen but, in the ruckus, were jostled around, and we could only find one. He had to go barefoot. We drove back up the road and found a store where we learned that we were in Seneca County and the county seat was Tiffin. The store clerk gave us directions to Tiffin, and we finally located the sheriff's office.

There was a stark lobby with industrial tile floors. In the back was a plexiglass window with a speak-through. Earl walked up to the window and was greeted by a woman in a tan county deputy uniform.

"We would like to speak to the sheriff," he said through the metallic hole.

"What may I say this is about?" she questioned tersely.

"Our money was stolen," he said. "Well, our bags were stolen, and they had our money in them."

She slapped some papers and a pen underneath the window and said, "You can fill out a report."

Earl took the papers and pen. "Is that it?" he asked. "I fill out some paperwork. Then what?"

"Then, we will examine the paperwork," she responded, "and if you can work on that attitude, I might even allow you to speak to a deputy about it."

Earl sat in a chair that was in a row of hard, plastic chairs shoved up against a concrete block wall painted in an ugly gloss tan. He began to fill out the report. I sat beside him and said nothing.

When he finished filling out the papers, he returned them to the window. She perused them briefly. "Have a seat, Mr. Titwallow. I'll have a deputy speak with you about this."

He sat beside me, leaned his head back into the wall, and took a huge breath. I reached over and took his hand.

In a moment, we heard the lock click on the solid steel door next to the reception window. A very handsome man, who looked to be in his mid-thirties, popped his head through the opening in the door. I couldn't help but notice him and was immediately attracted. His jaw was square, his hair brown, and there was a faint hint of stubble across his face. He had a thick brown mustache and grey-blue eyes. His face was perfect. He spoke to Earl but looked alluringly at me. I had not bothered to put my bra back on in all the fuss and had merely pulled on my blouse. I knew that my natural regalia was easily scrutinized beneath my clothing. My eyes met his, and I felt both guilty and tantalized at the same time.

"Mr. Titwallow, would you please follow me?" he questioned politely.

"Is it okay if my girlfriend comes?" Earl inquired while rising.

"Sure, no problem," he said, reaching out to shake Earl's hand. "I'm Deputy Reynolds."

He then extended his hand to me. I gently shook his hand and felt the huge, soft, warm muscles bulge as he squeezed and slightly lingered. I could almost have had a climax from that handshake. I felt the thrill pulse through me like sensual electricity. I felt such an instant and robust attraction.

When we followed him up the hall, I could see his khaki slacks wrapped tightly around his perfect ass. I tingled in his presence and felt like I was betraying Earl just by looking. I also noticed the wedding band on his left hand and wondered if he thrilled his wife as much as he wished he could thrill me. Part of my attraction was knowing that he wanted me.

Deputy Reynolds led us to a small room with no windows. There was a Formica desk-top bolted to the wall, a seat at the desk, and two more of those plastic chairs with metal legs. He seated us and then went over the report between glances at me.

My large firm tits and erect nipples were outlined beneath my blouse. Officer Reynolds seemed to be having difficulty keeping his eyes off them. On the one hand, he was perfectly professional. On the other hand, I was pretty sure that if we had been in the room alone, he would have been pushing himself into me as I lay back on that desktop with my legs wrapped around him. The fantasies kept me from paying full attention to the process at hand.

"So," Deputy Reynolds started, "You say your bags and the back seats of your van were sitting on the edge of the road, and you saw an older model green truck driving off with your possessions?"

"Yes, sir, that's correct," returned Earl.

"Were you able to get a look at the person driving the truck?"

"Yes, sir. He was an older man, probably in his sixties or maybe seventies. He had gray hair, was skinny, and might have been tall." Earl fidgeted with his long fingers as he answered the questions.

"Did you happen to get a license plate number?" Deputy Reynolds continued.

"No, sir, I didn't," Earl responded. "I don't think there was a license plate."

"Can you tell me what kind of truck it was?" Deputy Reynolds met my eyes right after I caught him staring at my tits. He quickly glanced up at my face to see I noticed, and my smile indicated that I didn't mind.

"It was an older model, maybe fifteen or twenty years old," Earl said, becoming exasperated. "I don't know. I don't know much about truck models and types."

Deputy Reynolds grinned. "I think I might know who took your belongings. Would you like to ride with me to meet this fellow and see if we can get your stuff back?"

"Sure," Earl responded, looking nervously at me.

He caught me staring rather longingly at Deputy Reynolds. Embarrassed, I turned my eyes quickly to meet his and said, "Sure, yeah. We want to find this guy."

Officer Reynolds led us to the back of the station, where his patrol car was parked. "You can either sit in the back together, or one of you can sit up front with me."

"I'll sit in the back," I said, wanting a little distance from the sexual tension that had been amplifying.

"No, I'll sit in the back," Earl said. "Lovella, you sit up front with Officer Reynolds."

Although Earl's response made me nervous, it also enticed me. My feelings were mixed. Of course, I loved Earl, and I would have loved to sit next to him in the back seat, but Deputy Reynolds also enticed me, and I very much wanted to sit in a position where I could catch my eye candy glances at him.

We got into the patrol car, and Deputy Reynolds drove past the edge of town into the county.

"So, what brings you, kids, to Tiffin?" Deputy Reynolds inquired, having seen on the crime report that our address was Pennsylvania.

"We were hoping to spend the summer in San Francisco," Earl replied. "I don't know how we will accomplish that without any money. We sure didn't get very far. This was our first night on the road."

"I'm sure everything will be fine," I interjected between the scans of my eyes up and down Deputy Reynolds's all-too-enticing body.

"So, what's in San Francisco?" Deputy Reynolds continued.

"Well, we just heard there are some cool goings-on out there," Earl replied. "You know, people who are cool, accepting, loving, peaceful folks."

"Shame you should have to go to the other side of the country to find cool and accepting people." Deputy Reynolds said as he darted his eyes up and down my body, making no effort to hide the fact that he was eating my tits with his eyes.

"Yeah, it's a shame, isn't it?" I smiled at him like I would at a piece of cheesecake that I was about to devour.

"You might find that people around here are pretty cool and accepting if you give us a chance," he said.

"Oh, I'm not saying that people around here, or anywhere, aren't cool," said Earl. "We just heard that San Fran has it going on and wanted to check it out. You know, a little summer adventure before we have to go back to classes next fall."

Deputy Reynolds had turned onto the same dirt road where we had parked to sleep the night before. About two or three miles past where we had parked, he turned into a dirt drive that went through the woods and was little more than a couple of tire tracks between the trees. This path curved around between the standing oaks until we came to a clearing in the woods where there were piles of junk everywhere."

"Hey, that's the truck!" Earl exclaimed, leaning forward in his seat and pointing to an old green truck parked next to a dilapidated trailer house. "Hey, and there are the seats to my van!" he exclaimed again, noticing the seats unloaded under a tree and sitting near a pile of junk.

"Hang on," Deputy Reynolds said in a reassuring voice. "Just stay calm. Stay in the car, and let me talk to him."

When the patrol car stopped in front of the trailer, a tall elderly man came out of the front door. He had on a pair of soiled, gray pants and a tank top shirt that looked like it had its share of greasy hands smeared across it. The old guy grinned wide, showing only two or three tobacco-stained teeth inside a nasty mouth. "Hey there, Donny," he proclaimed, jutting out his hand to shake with Deputy Reynolds. "What brings you to these parts?"

"Come on, Fred," Deputy Reynolds said, shaking the old man's hand. "You know why I'm here, don't you? Now, why do I always show up around here?"

"'Cause you are always accusing me of something I didn't do," the old man responded. "I just don't know why you do that. I am a legitimate busi-nessman, just trying to make a living."

Deputy Reynolds cast a look to the side and then back at the old man. "You know I catch you red-handed in almost everything you say you didn't do," he said.

"Well, now, maybe you do, maybe you don't." The old man cackled with laughter. "Just 'cause you say you got proof don't mean nothing, but I try to be fair and give a little, you know. I try to keep the peace. Lord knows I don't want you riled up at me."

"All right," Deputy Reynolds continued, pointing back to the car. "Now, these two young folks over here say that they saw you driving off this morning with their van seats and luggage, and this young man has not only described you and your truck but also already pointed out that those van seats over there belong to him."

"Sheee—eeeeht!" the old man squealed. "I don't know where he would have gotten some idea like that 'cause I didn't even get out of bed till about thirty minutes ago, and I picked up those seats at an auction last week. I was gonna sell 'em for five dollars, but hell, if it makes that young man feel better, he can have 'em—for two fifty."

"Yeah," Deputy Reynolds went on. "It would probably make him feel better to get those back for free since they belong to him. Now, what about the luggage?"

"I don't have any idea what you are talking about," the old man pleaded. "I don't even deal with luggage most of the time. Don't seem to have much of a resale value."

"Come on, Fred," Deputy Reynolds chided. "You know who you are talking to here, and this is not a road we haven't been down before. What happened to these kids' luggage?"

"You know, I don't know what might have happened to it," the old man lied. "I haven't ever seen them kids before. Sure, is a shame they lost their luggage, though."

"How about I have a look inside your trailer?" Deputy Reynolds inquired.

"Oh, now," the old man protested. "I haven't even washed the breakfast dishes or made the bed. I wouldn't want you to see it in that kind of a mess."

Deputy Reynolds laughed. "Come on, Fred. You are not exactly a Suzy Homemaker. Let's have a look."

"Now, now," the old man continued to protest. "I just sprayed for fleas. I was on my way out of the house for a few hours when you folks pulled up."

"You know," Deputy Reynolds negotiated as he rubbed his chin. "If I have to call into town and get Judge Thomas to issue a search warrant, it is probably going to be much more likely that you will spend a few days in county jail, but if you were to cooperate, I think we might be able to keep you from getting in a lot of trouble."

"Oh, hell! All right!" the old man blurted. "But don't blame me if you get sick from flea poison."

"I'll take my chances," Deputy Reynolds said, entering the trailer.

He returned with Earl's empty bag in a few moments, unlocked the back car door for Earl, and motioned us to follow. "Is this your bag?" he asked Earl as we approached the trailer.

"Yeah," Earl replied. "But it wasn't empty when he took it."

"Well, let's go see if we can find what was in it," Deputy Reynolds said, turning to the old man. Fred, you don't mind if these young folks have a look at your beautiful home decor, do you?"

"Oh, hell, no." The old man spit tobacco to the ground. "The more, the fuckin' merrier."

We entered the trailer to find nasty, tattered, old furniture. A 1940s radio stood in one corner, and an early 1950s TV against one wall under a window. Earl's clothes were thrown about the room haphazardly as though they had been dug out of the luggage and thrown in whatever direction was handy. My suitcase sat in one corner, opened a little. At first glance, it seemed essentially undisturbed.

"Are these your clothes?" Deputy Reynolds inquired.

"Yes, they are," Earl replied, "but what about my money? I had five hundred dollars—cash in my luggage."

"I didn't see any money," Deputy Reynolds replied. "Go ahead and pick up your clothes. Here is your suitcase. While you do that, I'll go talk with Fred."

We picked up Earl's things, what we could find, while the deputy went back outside. When we came out with Earl's suitcase re-packed and my unpilfered suitcase in hand, the deputy walked up to Earl and handed him three hundred dollars in cash.

"Look," he said, "this is probably the best I'm going to be able to do. I got him to give up this much, but whether there was any money in that luggage is your word against his."

"I had five hundred fucking dollars in that suitcase!" Earl exclaimed.

"I believe you," Deputy Reynolds responded, "but think about this. Is a judge going to believe you? How will you prove how much money you had in the suitcase, if any at all? How would you prove that you didn't have that money hidden somewhere else and were saying it was in your suitcase? If you press this, it will mean waiting for a court date, going before a judge, and you might still not win about the money. Maybe you could prove he stole your seats and suitcase, but there is no way to prove how much money you may or may not have had in that suitcase. My advice would be to take the three hundred dollars and go on down the road."

"So, I get three hundred back, and he keeps two hundred? Let's search the old bastard!" Earl spouted irritably. "How much fucking money does he have in his pockets. Where did he get it? Doesn't look to me like he is exactly wealthy."

"Well, let's say he has another two hundred in cash on him," the deputy continued calmly. "Can you prove that it is your money? How do you know he didn't sell that much at an auction last night?"

"I could call the bank and see if they could match the serial numbers on the bills," Earl exclaimed.

"How long is that going to take?" Deputy Reynolds continued. "Let's say you can find the money around here and match up the serial numbers on the bills. More than likely, by the time all the legal proceedings are done and the lawyers get their cut, you won't have much left anyway, and it will likely take you all summer to get that. Now you might enjoy spending the summer around here. We have some pretty nice people here in Tiffin, but I heard you say you were looking to meet some nice folks in San Francisco."

"SHIT!" Earl proclaimed. Then, he stood there in silence for a moment. I watched quietly.

"All right, fine," he said, subdued. "But how will we get my van seats back to my van?"

"Fred will load them on his truck and follow us back into town." Deputy Reynolds was sympathetic. "I'm sorry. That's the best I can do."

"Tell him to fucking keep them!" Earl exclaimed as he put the money in his pocket and walked to the car with our bags. Deputy Reynolds walked over to the old man and waved dismissively at the van seats. The old man nodded with a grin. He had won, but we had not completely lost. Then, the deputy came back and opened the back of the car. Earl stacked our suitcases on one side and sat beside them without a word. He was sullen and disappointed. Then, Deputy Reynolds opened the front passenger door for me.

"Thank you," I said and slid into the front seat. "Thank you for everything."

He smiled. Then, he walked around to the driver's side and got in. He backed the car up, turned around, and headed back down the rough, rutted driveway. After a while, Earl asked, "Isn't he even going to jail for this?"

"Not this time," Deputy Reynolds responded. "But he is getting close, and he knows it. He's been there before. He even spent a couple of years in prison, but it didn't do any good. You can't keep him in there forever, and most of the time, his crimes are petty and often fixable."

"This one wasn't exactly fixed," Earl commented, "and I don't think two hundred fucking dollars is petty! Felony larceny is only fifty."

"I'm sorry," Deputy Reynolds returned. "I wish there had been some way to prove that the money was yours, but at least you got some back without too much hassle, and you got your things back."

"Yeah, just a percentage," Earl announced. Then, he caught himself and apologized. "I'm sorry. I'm not ungrateful, just disappointed."

After we returned to the station and got ready to leave, Earl reached out to shake the deputy's hand. "Thank you," he said. "I know you did your best, and I really do appreciate your help."

I shook the deputy's hand again and told him, "Thank you." The sexual arousal seemed to have faded a bit. He was still gorgeous to look at, but my little fantasy was over, and it had become mixed with sadness for Earl's disappointment and concern about how we would spend an entire summer in San Francisco with only three hundred dollars.

I followed Earl to the van, where he put on a spare pair of shoes from his luggage, and we drove away.

"Do you still want to go to San Francisco," I questioned, "or would you rather go back home?"

"Fuck, no I don't want to go back home!" he snapped. "We are going to San Francisco, one Goddamn way or another!"

"Okay," I said quietly. "I'm sorry."

He reached over and took my hand.

"I'm sorry," he said. "I shouldn't have snapped at you. I'm just so pissed off about this."

"I know," I told him. "I understand. I'm a little scared, too."

He sighed. "At least we have enough money to get there and maybe enough to live on for a few weeks, depending on prices."

"We probably have enough to live on for a month, maybe two," I responded.

"I guess," he said softly.

We headed back onto the highway toward the west. After a long silence, Earl said, "You wanted him, didn't you?"

"What?" I questioned as though I didn't know what he was talking about. I had not realized how much he had noticed.

"Deputy Reynolds," he went on. "You wanted to fuck him, didn't you?"

I was quiet momentarily, not knowing what to say or how to say it but knowing I had to be honest. "Yeah," I said, finally. "I thought he was sexy."

"Looked like he wanted you, too," Earl said.

"Yeah, I caught that," I said.

"You want to go back and try him out?" he questioned.

"What do you mean by that?" I responded.

"If you would like to fuck him, we can go back," he said. "I'll give you time with him if you want."

I couldn't believe what I was hearing. I tried to listen for any variance in his voice that would tip me off, whether he was being honest or just testing me. I couldn't tell. Part of me wanted to test him and tell him to turn around and take me back, but instead, I said, "No thanks. I'm already with the man I want. Besides, fantasies are best left as fantasies, and I've already had more men than most women will ever have in a lifetime. I don't need another."

He smiled and drove on. If it was a test, I must have passed it. Some men would have screamed at me or even beaten me just for having thoughts about another man, but not Earl. My fantasies did not threaten him. He might have been threatened if I had chosen to act on those thoughts, but that would not happen this time.

"I love you," he said.

"I love you, too," I replied, and we continued west toward the Summer of Love.

CHAPTER 20

Drugs, sex, Rock, and Roll

Three hundred dollars was a lot less than we started with, but in those days, a little bit would go a long way. If we had the original amount, we likely would not have had any trouble making it through the summer without working and have plenty to go home on, especially if we just slept in the van and paid no rent. However, things had changed. It worried me. We spent the next night parked at a truck stop in Iowa. We ate greasy truck-stop food and loved it, but for every penny we spent, there was a worry that I couldn't shake. That night, Earl was careful to ensure that our luggage was piled in the front seats and that the doors to the van were locked.

The next morning, I gazed down the flat Iowa highway with lines upon lines of unending fields of two-foot-high spring corn and said, "Earl, I think it might be a good idea to stop at a grocery and maybe get a bunch of canned food instead of eating at restaurants. It might make our money stretch a bit further."

"I'm not worried," he said, glancing reassuringly in my direction.

"Don't we have to make it through the entire summer on what we have?"

"We'll be fine," he replied. "We have enough to get us there, and once we get there, we will get jobs or something. If need be, we can sleep in the van all summer. All we have to do is move it from one park to another. We can shower in park facilities. We don't even have to rent a place if we don't want to."

"It is not exactly the lifestyle I'm used to." I fiddled with the fringe of my blouse. "I know it is certainly not the lifestyle that you are used to."

"What is lifestyle?" he questioned, with a hint of irritation. "I mean, what the hell is it anyway, and what do we actually need? My family has millions more than they need or will ever use, while others scrape to get by for a year on less than what we will be spending this summer. What do we need? Food in our bellies? If we have to, we will go to soup kitchens. A roof over our heads? We have the van. Clothes on our backs? We brought that with us."

"I'm sorry," I responded. "I guess I have never had to wonder whether things would be taken care of. As poor as we were, getting by on Daddy's little factory salary, we still had a nice little house, a car, and everything we needed. I never worried about it. If Mother and Daddy ever worried about money, they didn't discuss it, so I guess I grew up in a kind of illusion of protection."

"We're Americans, Lovella," he went on. "Almost all of us grow up in an illusion of protection. Most never realize how protected we are. Compared to most people in the rest of the world, we're rich with what we have right now. Your little house in Climax is a mansion compared to what someone in the slums of Calcutta might be living in. We are also one of the most paranoid countries in the world. You have never been to a foreign country before, have you?"

"No," I replied.

"I have," he continued. "I've been to Mexico and South America. I've been to Africa. Dad could afford it, and he got off on thinking that his kids could do things that others would never have the opportunity to do, so during our summer vacations, when we were old enough, we got to choose a country we wanted to visit. Then, Mom would usually accompany us to those countries while Dad stayed home with his first love, making money. Anna and I would take turns choosing which country we wanted to visit. Sometimes, we would tour several countries over the summer. Anna always picked places like France, England, or Sweden. I picked places like the Belgian Congo. I mean, hell, even visiting a place like Mexico is an experience. Our next-door neighbor is a third-world country. When you drive through villages where people are begging in the street and living in dirt floor huts, you begin to think. Our poor are not poor compared to almost anywhere else in the world, but there should be no such thing as poor as far as I am concerned. Right now, at this moment, you and I are rich. Compared to most people in the world, we are rich. We have almost three hundred dollars left and own our home outright—this van. We are fucking rich!" He reached over and took my hand. "We are going to be fine, Honey. Don't worry about it."

We spent the following evening in Nebraska near the Wyoming border and the next night in Utah. It seemed like no time before we were crossing over Nevada into California and then to San Francisco. We still had about two hundred and sixty dollars left when we arrived. I couldn't believe it. I had imagined that it would take all the money to get there if we didn't run out before we got there. However, the gas prices were cheap, and so was the food. We could buy gas for twenty-five to thirty cents a gallon, and since we slept in the van, we didn't have to pay for a hotel. We found showers in some of the parks, and sometimes, we bathed in little roadside creeks. At a campsite in Utah, Earl taught me the proper way to roast a marshmallow. We cooked hot dogs on sticks held over the fire and had marshmallows for dessert. Then, we made love on the bare ground beside the campfire.

After arriving in San Francisco, we drove through the streets until we finally arrived at the intersection of Haight and Ashbury. It was a sight to see—hippies everywhere. People walked along the street arm-in-arm, throwing peace signs, two fingers jutting in the air like rabbit ears.

Earl found a place to park the van and said, "Let's get out and experience this."

I had thought our painted van would stand out like a sore thumb, but it was a bit tame compared to some of the vehicles I saw there.

We locked the van to walk up and down the streets. Most of the men had long hair, as did the women. I remember coming up behind a person with long, flowing, beautiful blond hair and large, pink hoop earrings visible as her hair wafted in the breeze. She was wearing pink and white striped, hip-hugger, flared jeans and what appeared to be a yellow and pink floral halter top. Tattooed, just above her ass crack, was a heart-shaped garland of flowers, the tip of the heart becoming an arrow pointing down to her ass crack, and in all caps were the words: *FEELS LIKE PUSSY.*

"Well," I thought to myself, approaching from behind her; *she must be into some kinky shit.* Then, I giggled that I had made an unintentional pun on ass-fucking and kinky shit. I had never tried that, but I heard that it was one way for teen girls to keep from getting pregnant. As we passed by this person, I glanced back at her and saw her thick beard, heavy eyebrows, and quite a bulge outlined in the crotch of those pink and white bell bottoms.

Holy crap! I thought to myself. Then I whispered to Earl, "Oh my God! Did you see that guy back there?"

"Which guy?" he questioned.

"The guy that had feels like pussy tattooed over his ass crack, the guy in the pink and white hip-huggers with the big pink hoop earrings."

"Yeah, what about it?" he asked.

"Jesus, it's like a freak show at the circus," I said under my breath.

"No, it's not," he returned. "They are just people expressing themselves. That guy back there is probably a homosexual or might be transexual."

"Well, yeah, I figured that," I told him. "I don't know many girls who would advertise ass fucking."

I had read about homosexuals since I was in my early teens, but I had never actually laid eyes on one, at least not one who admitted it, and definitely not one who flaunted it, but maybe that guy was doing something more. He was messing with gender norms. Part of me wanted to be open and accepting, and another part had small-town sensibilities, shocked by the experience. At least once on every block, something fascinated and surprised me or made me question the ideals I had been taught in small-town America.

"Let's get something to eat," Earl said, putting his arm around my shoulder and pulling me to him.

We walked with his arm on my shoulder and mine around his waist. I realized that we looked pretty much like everyone else. When I adopted the hippie look, I stopped putting my hair up. So, it flowed around my shoulders like almost everyone else. When Earl introduced me to the anti-war movement, I had been letting my hair grow and had not put a perm in it for months. I had stopped wearing skin-tight knee skirts and wore blue jeans and T's as often as not. I hadn't gotten into hippie beads, and maybe I looked a little odd because I retained some of my more traditional jewelry to wear with my casuals. Earl usually used his electric razor, but that summer, he reverted to the scraggly hippie I had met in the library.

Soon, we came upon a little storefront with the smells of food wafting out into the street. The windows were painted with depictions of vegetables and flowers. Wind chimes clinked in the breeze above the door, and the sign over the door said, *"Simone's."* There were about four little, assorted street-side tables with seats for two, and inside, I could hear the music of *Jefferson Airplane* playing rather lightly in the background.

We entered and found a table. A girl with long pigtails brought menus printed on lime green paper, with a watermark of Buddha in the background, and took our orders for drinks. We both ordered iced hibiscus tea. I thought it might be fun to try it.

I scanned the menu. Each dish had odd names like "Peas on Earth" or "Good Vibes Goulash." I hunted for something like a burger or a chicken sandwich, but it was nowhere to be found. There was something called "Tofu You Know, " a fried tofu sandwich. I looked up and asked, "Earl, what is tofu?"

He smiled. "It's soybean curd."

"And what the hell is that?" I returned.

"Well, soybeans are beans, often grown in Asian countries, and many of those Asian countries take the whey, I guess you could say that because I can't think of a better word to describe it, from those beans and press it into blocks that slice kind of like cheese. The 'Temple of Tofu' sounds good, doesn't it?" he questioned. "Sautéed tofu and onions over brown rice with steamed broccoli, kale, and zucchini in a teriyaki sauce."

"I don't see any meat on this menu," I commented without looking up.

"That's because it is a vegetarian restaurant, vegetable-based food only," he said.

"I never knew there was such a thing," I declared with innocent honesty and looked up from the page. As well-read as I was, my brain still contained many pockets of ignorance. There was so much that I had never been exposed to or didn't come across in my reading. Maybe that was because I didn't read much about food or culture, before reading Julia Childe.

"There is probably a lot you haven't known about before now, Honey," he comforted. "It's okay. Just pick something."

"I don't know that I've ever had a meal without meat," I pondered. "I have no clue what any of this will taste like."

"I'm sure it will be good," he encouraged. "Come on, be adventurous."

By this time, the pig-tail waitress had returned to take our order. Earl ordered the "Temple of Tofu," and I ordered something called "Southern Sunshine." At least it contained two things I was familiar with—beans and cornbread. When the meals arrived, there was a lot of food on the plates. The cornbread was a big yellow block with the crust barely toasted. It was a bit dry, but it moistened well with the soup in the beans.

"Try some of my tofu," Earl enticed, handing me a bite of this gelatinous stuff with a brown sauce around the edge. The taste wasn't bad, but the texture in the middle was a little disconcerting. It appeared to have no taste, but the sauce had a nice flavor.

"Yes, it's good," I said after chewing. It was okay, but I figured I would have to develop a taste for it rather than liking it at first bite.

While eating, I noticed a handsome Black man sitting at a table by a window. He was thin but muscular. His hair was about eight inches long in a fully-teased-out Afro. He wore a tie-dyed tank top and blue jeans with cuffs frayed into strings. When he caught my eye, he tossed his chin back in acknowledgment as though I was someone he knew personally.

"Earl," I whispered, leaning forward across the table. "That Black guy at that table over there, is he someone you know?"

Earl glanced over, and the man tilted his head again as though acknowledging recognition.

"No," Earl said, turning back to me. "I've never seen him before."

The next thing we knew, this man had carried his chair and a cup of tea across the room to our table. He turned the chair around backward against the table and straddled it. He set his tea on the table and extended a big muscular hand, first to Earl and then to me. "The name's Screech," he said. "How you folks doing?"

I caught a hint of a Southern accent in his speech.

"We're fine," I said, feeling slightly nervous at his forwardness.

"Cool," he went on. "Well, the name is not really Screech. That's just what they call me. My birth name is Jessie Miller. They call me Screech 'cause that is what I do. I have a band called Blue Horizon. I'm the lead singer. Got that James Brown screech, you know." He then made a noise that sounded like a cross between fingernails down a chalkboard and a musical note followed by a brief little, jazz-style scat.

"Very nice," I said, glancing up at Earl nervously, hoping he would send this strange man on his way.

"Yeah, very nice," Earl said. "My name is Earl, and this is Lovella."

"Sa—weeeet," Screech continued. "Ya'll look like sweet people. I like sweet people. The world needs more sweet people. Peace!" He jutted a peace sign into the air.

"Peace," Earl and I both responded. Earl tossed his peace sign straight up in Screech's direction. I barely lifted mine six inches off the table. I felt as though I must have missed something. There was some social code that I didn't understand, some secret hippie code of conduct that seemed utterly foreign. I wanted this strange man to go away. I didn't want to talk to him or learn the art of hippie socializing.

"You folks been in town long?" Screech questioned.

"No, just rolled in," Earl responded.

"Hey, cool," Screech expressed with an exuberant voice. "Where are you folks from?"

"Pennsylvania," Earl replied. "Lovella just finished her first year at Penn State."

"Oh hey, that's cool! That's cool!" Screech almost sang as he nodded his head in my direction. "I dropped out of school about the tenth grade. I figured what's the use. The Man ain't gonna give the Black Man a chance anyway. I knew I had to get out of Alabama, and besides, I've got this talent, you know. I can screech." His head was bobbing like a spring-loaded doll in the back window of a Buick.

"Wow," Earl said. "We would love to hear your band play sometime."

"Hey, it's your lucky day," Screech announced. "We've got a gig at this club up the street called Aquarius.' My band plays there every Friday and Saturday night. We've been courting a record deal, but we've got to build up the fan base, you know? We have to play mostly covers, but we can throw in some of our own stuff now and then."

"And tomorrow is Friday," Earl responded. "Maybe we can make it up there. What time do you go on?"

"We usually kick it about 10 p.m.," Screech replied. "Say, where you folks staying? You got digs yet?"

"We have a van," Earl explained. "We figured we could sleep in that and catch a shower, wherever."

"Hey, I got a little apartment upstairs, across the street," Screech entreated. "You are welcome to crash, man. Sure beats a van for sleeping comfort, and there is a nice old bathtub." He reached over and patted my arm. I resisted the urge to jerk back from a stranger touching me when I wasn't quite sure that I trusted him. His look lingered too much on me when he said, "Lady might like to have a nice sensual bubble bath and relax."

By this time, I was looking at Earl with 'NO' written all over my face, but to my horror, he said, "Oh, yeah, man, that would be cool. We would love to hang out with you, man."

"Yeah, well, as soon as you finish your meal, I'll take you up to see my pad."

Screech gleamed like a beacon. His head continued to bob, and he glistened a smile full of perfect, white teeth. I had to admit that his smile was beautiful. He was attractive and seemed nice, but I couldn't bring myself to feel comfortable meeting a stranger who had just invited himself to our table and invited us to spend the night with him within a few minutes.

"We're about done," Earl replied. "You about done, Lovella?"

I didn't feel much like eating anymore, anyway. "Yeah, I'm done," I said, dropping my fork on my plate. I was too nervous to eat another bite.

"All riiiiiight," Screech said, head bobbing a perpetual yes.

Earl called the waitress over and paid our check. We followed Screech across the street and up four flights of stairs in a dark stairwell barely lit with old, faded sconces from the 1930s. A few times, I tugged on Earl's shirt tail to indicate that I didn't want to do this, but he either didn't notice, didn't get it, or ignored it.

The old wooden door to Screech's apartment was at the top of the stairs. It had seen too many coats of paint as several shades expressed themselves through scrapes and pealing. When we entered, I noticed there was no other exit door, and a sheet hung over what I assumed to be an entry to a bedroom. A couple of full-sized mattresses were in the middle of the floor, covered with colorful blankets but without sheets. A few odd pillows were scattered around, and at least a couple had pillowcases. Posters of Jimi Hendrix and James Brown were haphazardly tacked to the walls, and there was also a poster of a brightly colored peace sign with a black background. The walls were dingy yellow plaster, likely stained from years of cigarette smoke. There were hints, here and there, that the walls had once been white, such as a pale square spot where a photo might have hung.

Multicolored glass beads hung from what had been the overhead light fixture. They were wired to the rusted metal frame where a large globe had once been part of the fixture. Now, just a single bare bulb caused the beads to gleam with variants of color. I couldn't see any lamps. The only furniture was a rickety old table with a stereo record player on it. Along one wall were shelves made of stacked concrete blocks and what appeared to be salvaged weathered wood. Some clothes were folded on those shelves that ran almost the entire length of the wall, and there was a pile of clothes in the corner. Near the back was a kitchenette with an apartment-sized stove, a small single sink, and a countertop that was about six feet long and covered with a blood-red linoleum with patches torn out of it to expose the plywood below. An old refrigerator stood beneath a couple of mismatched cabinets. Beneath the counter, the cabinet doors were missing, and there were only open shelves where the plumbing was readily visible. There was one small window above the sink, overlooking an alley with only a view of the red brick building on the opposite side. An open door leading off the living room revealed a bathroom with a 1930s pedestal sink near an old, chipped porcelain, claw-foot bathtub. The bathroom walls were lined with aged and cracked black and white subway tile, with a tiny, glazed window over the tub. I learned that the hanging sheet I had seen earlier was a cover for a small closet where at least a few things could hang. That was it: a room with a tiny window over the kitchen sink, a bathroom with a tiny window, and a closet.

"So, what do you think?" Screech asked, a wide grin revealing those perfect teeth. His head was still bobbing, and I began to wonder if he might have Parkinson's, but no, it was only one of his mannerisms.

I bit my tongue. I fought the urge to tell him that the place looked like a badger den with color.

Earl tactfully said, "Yeah … cool." Perhaps he meant it.

"Have a seat … Have a seat," Screech invited, repeating himself. "Yeah, have a seat."

We both plopped onto one of the mattresses.

Although the place had dingy walls and was cluttered, it was clean. Screech busied himself with several albums on the floor, leaning against the wall in the corner opposite the shelves. The next thing I knew, Jimi Hendrix's music was blaring on his record player so loud that we had to shout to be heard over it. Screech returned to the middle of the room where we were sitting and shouted, "You folks toke?"

I looked at him with puzzlement, but Earl said, "Yeah, all right," and gave him a thumbs-up.

I leaned over and shouted in Earl's ear, "What does he mean—toke?"

Earl put his thumb and finger to his lips and sucked in air, imitating smoking marijuana, "You know, pot, weed, marijuana," he shouted back.

"I don't want to smoke marijuana," I shouted over the music. I felt nervous about it, even though I had tried it in New York. There, I didn't actually know what I was doing until the high hit me. I still didn't trust Screech, and who knew what he might give us. It might have some other terrible drug added to it.

"That's cool," Earl replied. "You don't have to. Do you mind if we do?"

I did mind, but I told him *no*. Even though I had smoked it at the peace march in New York back in April, I didn't feel as safe in Screech's apartment as I had felt in the New York crowd.

Screech returned to the middle of the room with a box. He opened it and pulled out a cigarette paper. He then began to sprinkle dark green leaves along the middle of the paper with his large, long fingers. He rolled it, licked one side, pressed it down, and twisted the ends. He popped one end of the joint in his mouth, lit it, puffed, and held his breath momentarily before releasing the smoke. While he was doing this, Jimi Hendrix's music continued to blare in the background, and I realized that the music was not helping my anxiety. It had begun to agitate me.

"Screech!" I shouted, "Can we please turn the music down a little?"

"Oh, yeah, sure, no problem," he said, handing Earl the joint. He returned to the stereo, brought the volume down to a reasonable level, and returned. "I just wanted you to get the full effect of the music, you know, feel the beat, get the vibe. You know, get *Hendrix*, the greatest guitarist who ever lived, man."

"I hope I can get enough of the vibe without having to shout over the music," I said as I watched Earl inhale, hold his breath, and lightly cough.

Earl handed the joint toward me. I looked at him and shook my head, so he returned it to Screech. I found myself sitting there, thinking *Mother would freak out if she knew where I was and what I was doing.* There would be a hornet's rage buzzing around that damn beehive hair of hers while her eyes glared and her tongue was ready to sting. I grinned a little, thinking about it, and then relaxed. I finally got the courage to ask, "So, what does marijuana do for you?"

Screech replied, "Oh, it mellows you out, man. It's smooth."

"Yeah," Earl echoed. "It's a gentle high."

"What about reefer madness?" I questioned with sincerity.

They both began to laugh, not just any laugh but more like uncontrollable giggles.

"Fuck!" I shouted. "I'm just asking. I don't know. I've never seen the damn movie, but I've heard about it, and I've read some things about it."

"Did they show you anti-drug films in high school?" Earl asked.

"Actually, no," I replied. "Daddy told me about it. He told me drugs are terrible, and they can cause you to lose your mind."

"Yet, your dad is a drunk," giggled Earl.

"FUCK YOU! EARL TITWALLOW!" I shouted and stood to my feet, suddenly defensive and enraged.

I don't think Earl had ever seen that side of me. He certainly had never had my anger turned on him. The truth is, I could make Mother's rage look like child's play if I was angry enough, and saying anything amiss about Daddy was enough. I was about to storm out the door had it not been for his reaction.

"Wow, honey, I'm sorry," he pleaded. "That was a crass thing for me to say. Please sit down."

"You don't talk about Daddy like that!" I scolded him and slung a pointed finger at him.

"I know. I know. I'm sorry," he said. "It was very rude. Please sit down."

I sat back down but continued to sulk. Earl reached over and squeezed my hand gently and reassuringly. "I'm just saying that alcohol is a drug, too, and probably a lot more dangerous than pot is. So … no, pot doesn't cause reefer madness. Look at me and Screech. Do we look like we are losing it?"

"No," I said and then continued to sit quietly.

He continued. "Reefer Madness is the name of an old film from the 1920s that was put out as propaganda to squelch the use of marijuana because hemp was becoming a competitor to the American cotton and paper industries. It was a tool for the establishment to maintain its standing, but the fact that people were smoking pot was not causing any problems. There was also racism involved since migrant workers and Black people tended to use it. Your dad had probably seen the film or something and probably really doesn't know anything about marijuana other than the content of that film, and it's purely misleading propaganda. A lot of stuff they put out about pot is propaganda. Besides, didn't you take a few hits when we were at the peace march back in April?"

"Yes," I said sheepishly.

"Well," he said, smiling reassuringly, "marijuana is in the hemp family of plants. Most of them do not cause a high, and the fibers can be used to make everything from paper to clothes. Hemp production was beginning to compete with the cotton industry, among other things. So, they stacked a bunch of negative propaganda on it."

Screech had been silently sitting there all this time, watching with noticeable fascination. He had not taken another toke on the joint. I looked from one to the other and said to Screech, "Hand me that, please."

Screech silently handed the joint to me, and I held it, staring at it while feeling deeply ambivalent. Even though I was going to try it, I continued feeling anxious. I didn't know this Screech guy, and maybe I had bought into racist propaganda more than I had realized. On one hand, I very much believed in the Civil Rights Movement. Still, on the other hand, I was raised as a White kid by White parents in a primarily White town, with White privileges that I had taken for granted. With that came a general ingrained distrust of Black people that I previously would have denied. I felt safe with Donny when doing my public service, but that was a different environment with a totally different person. Thinking back, I realized that the experience had also been an example of White privilege.

I felt safer in New York, but that was a situation of going with the flow and just doing what others were doing.

Finally, I put the joint to my mouth and inhaled deeply but went into a coughing fit. My throat felt like it was on fire. I had not had that problem in New York, but maybe I didn't inhale as much. I was aghast since I had smoked cigarettes for almost half my life. It was like I was starting over, like being that little girl in the culvert with Gretta, smoking cigarettes for the first time. I would have thought my throat would be tolerant of smoke, but it wasn't tolerant of marijuana smoke. I had to squelch my paranoia, yet again, that maybe there was more in it than plain marijuana.

"That shit is harsh!" I exclaimed.

"Yeah, yeah," Earl commented. "You have to get used to it. Hold your mouth open slightly and pull a little air in to cool it when you draw the smoke in. No filters here to mitigate the harshness, like your cigarettes. You want to try it again?"

I put the joint to my mouth again; this time, I could hold the smoke in my lungs a little longer. Then, I passed it on to Earl. Eventually, the three of us smoked it down to the very tip. I figured we would just put it out like a cigarette, but Screech brought out a pair of tweezers from the box and began pulling off the last little portion of a quarter inch left on the joint. I watched this happening as though I was watching the most fascinating film ever created. The fire on the end of the joint and the smoke rising from it seemed as beautiful as any sunset I had ever seen. I watched Screech's lips gently fold over the joint's tip like a child's fingers picking a flower. I just watched with fascination, not realizing yet that I was high. I might have experienced some of that in New York, but not this much. The music now seemed to twinkle in my ears, like some audio fairy dust with magical properties to enhance the experience. Using the tips of the tweezers, Screech snuffed out the roach on a glass jar lid. Then, he leaned back on one arm and began to sing along to the lyrics of *All Along the Watch Tower*. Until that day, I had never paid much attention to Jimi Hendrix, but now the type of music I had dismissed and labeled as too disjointed suddenly seemed ingenious.

"This is nice," I said, seeming to fade into a moment of eternity where time ceased to exist.

Screech replied after what seemed like a near-indefinite pause. "Yeah, man. Hendrix is awesome."

I heard him and searched my mind like a file drawer for what I would say in return. Eventually, I said, "No, I mean the high."

"Oh yeah, yeah," Screech replied, like an echo on a distant island.

Earl seemed to drift into some fantasy. He lay on one side, just smiling. They seemed content to listen to the music. Still, I felt I should talk, not because I wanted to speak or didn't like the music, but because I thought that conversation was socially appropriate when we had only met Screech an hour or two earlier.

"I never realized how much depth Hendrix has," I said while my mind drifted into the music.

"'*When the power of love overcomes the love of power, then the world will know peace,*'" Screech replied. "Jimi Hendrix said that."

"Wow," I commented, as one song became silent between the grooves and another began. Even the silence created a fascinating segue into the next song.

For a very long time, we just sat there, listening and drifting into the time-warping cannabis high. When the Hendrix album finished the first side, the needle drifted to the center of the vinyl and became music itself. *Shhhh, click—Shhhh, click—Shhhh, click—Shhhh, click.* We all sat there listening to it as though it had been a Siren song. Finally, Screech got up to flip the record to the other side.

We must have just laid around the entire afternoon, listening to one album after another. Screech had quite a variety of music, from Jimi Hendrix to The Beatles, New Orleans jazz and Black gospel to Hank Williams and Patsy Cline, and Frank Sinatra to Classical. They all seemed to be infinitely more fascinating when stoned.

Late in the afternoon, a loud knock at the door startled me out of my meditative daze. I jumped and let out a short chirp in my startled response.

"It's all right. It's all right," Screech said, motioning his flat hand toward the floor. He got up and went to the door. When he opened the door, there stood a tall, dark-headed hippie with wavy, shoulder-length hair. He was with a short, skinny girl with thin hair in a stringy ponytail and cheekbones resembling craters.

"Hey, man," Screech proclaimed.

"What's up?" the hippie responded.

"Come in." Screech stood back and motioned them into the room.

"Hey, this is my friend Earl, and ah, ah." He snapped his fingers in my direction.

"Lovella," Earl said.

"Yeah, Lovella," Screech echoed. "This is Dave and his old lady, Lorenda," Screech motioned back to the couple. "Dave is the lead guitarist in our band."

"Hey, Lovella and Lorenda," Dave said. "The names sound so alike; we might have trouble telling them apart."

I thought to myself; if *you can't tell my towering, big tits frame from that mousy-looking, skinny little bitch, you are damn fool blind.* But I smiled and said, "Hello."

Earl repeated my hello. Neither of us got to our feet to shake hands. We were probably too stoned to be motivated toward any social ritual.

"Hey, if you don't mind," Screech said, "we have got rehearsal tonight for our gig tomorrow. You are welcome to hang out here or come to the rehearsal if you want."

"What would you like to do, Lovella?" Earl questioned, turning to me.

"Watching the rehearsal would be fine," I said, "but what about dinner?"

"Oh, we got it," Screech replied. "We potluck and everybody brings something to share. We can get something at Simone's and take that."

I didn't relish the idea of another all-vegetable meal. I said, "I'm sure vegetables are very good for you, but I was hoping to have some kind of meat with dinner, maybe."

"Oh, well, that's cool," said Dave. "Lorenda made a pot roast. You are welcome to join us."

"A pot roast sounds fantastic," I said.

Earl and I got to our feet and followed them out the door. We stopped at Simone's, and Screech ordered a box of potatoes and onions baked with olive oil, black pepper, and some herbs. I could not discern the herbs, although it did have a bit of an Italian food smell. Then, we all walked for what seemed like an eternity before we came upon what appeared to be an abandoned storefront. The windows on the street were boarded up.

Screech and his friends led us down an alley alongside the building. Several extension cords were dangling off the side of the building from an upstairs window going under a side door that opened onto the alley.

We entered to find an ample, dark, open space lit more by portable stage lighting than anything else. The band's instruments were set up on the opposite side of the room. It appeared that everything had been plugged into the extension cords. A couple of lamps were perpendicular to where the band was set up. They were at each end of a sizeable fold-up table lined with food. A couple of women flitted around the table, checking to ensure everything was there. In front of the band area were several different types of chairs; most were metal fold-up. Some people sat in the chairs, eating, and their drinks sat on the floor beside them.

Screech set the potatoes on the table and said, "Go on, help yourselves. I don't eat before I sing."

A muscular young man was already sitting at the drums, popping out noises. There would be a few seconds of rhythm. Then he would stop, bang around on this or that, and start again. I couldn't help noticing that he was the only man in the room who didn't have long hair. His hair was short, well-groomed, and business-like. He wore a white crewneck t-shirt and a pair of gray dress slacks. I saw a suit jacket, shirt, and tie draped near the drums. Somehow, he seemed out of place. Screech caught me staring at him and must have read my mind.

"That's Denny," he said. "He works at the clothing counter at a fancy department store. They won't let him grow his hair. It wouldn't fit their image. He comes straight from work to rehearsal."

"Come on, Hon," Earl tugged at my arm. "Let's go get something to eat. I'm starving."

Earl had pitched in to pay for the potatoes from Simone's. So, I felt better about helping myself than if we had arrived, bringing nothing to contribute. We went to the table, and Screech went to the microphone. He began to warm up vocally while the drummer continued to play drum rifts that clashed with Screech's vocalizations. We got our food, introduced ourselves to several folks around the table, and made complimentary comments about the food. We then sat in the chairs facing the band and ate while we watched the band assemble.

Screech seemed to lead the process. "Let's start with 'Tripped Out'. Dave, we need to tighten up the guitar solo on that, and I've got to work on nailing those higher notes in the bridge." Eventually, he shouted, "One, and a, two, and a …" The band began to play very loud, a song I think I could have gone my entire life without hearing. It was well played but not very appealing.

The band broke down at Dave's guitar solo. Everything came to a halt. There were discussions about what went wrong and where. Then, they picked it back up two or three times before Dave easily flowed through the solo.

There were many stops and starts, and by the time rehearsal was over, about 10:30 p.m., I felt like I had worked all day. I was exhausted and looking forward to sleep. Still, we had to wait until all the instruments were broken down and the equipment was packed before leaving.

I helped the women pack up the remaining food and fold the table to put away. Screech and Earl were talking while I helped with the food. I kept looking over my shoulder, hoping this would all be over soon and we could go somewhere to sleep.

Finally, Earl came and got me. Screech was waiting just outside the door. By that time, it was a quarter to midnight. The nice thing about being a singer is that you don't have to pack up or carry an instrument. So, Screech had nothing to carry back.

As we walked back toward his place, Screech asked, "So what do you think, Lovella? Damn, good music—yeah?"

"Yeah," I said half-heartedly, wondering if I was a good liar. "Very interesting." I didn't have the heart to say that, except for the cover songs; I thought it was all total garbage, and there was no snowball's chance in hell they would ever get a record deal. To say that it was interesting was the closest I could come to the truth. I had not heard a single original song that evening that had made me want to tap my feet, sing along, or had lyrics that touched me in any particular way. I hated all of it.

"Dave has a cousin who works for Columbia Records," Screech continued. "She's a secretary, but I mean, she is around all the producers and executives, you know. Dave says maybe she can get one of them to listen to our demo."

"Yeah, that would be great," I said, again lying and wondering what chance a secretary had to get any executive to listen to anything.

"Hey, what did you think of 'Tripped out'?" he continued.

I hoped he would stop asking about the band. Why me? Why wasn't he asking Earl what he thought? Did he somehow sense that I didn't like the music and was trying to expose my fake enthusiasm?

"Oh, yeah, that's a unique song," I said, still trying to come close to the truth without sounding negative. Then, I took the opportunity to change the subject. "You know, after driving all morning to get here and being out late, I'm pretty tired."

"Hey," Screech affirmed, "like I said, you are welcome to crash at my place. The door is always open. I love to have company."

When Screech said this, he moved next to me, put his arm across my back, looping his thumb over Earl's belt with his fingers on Earl's ass. We walked like this for several more feet. I felt like a piece of meat in a sandwich, mashed by both sides and uncomfortable. I didn't want to offend the person who might be giving us a place to sleep, but something didn't feel right. Finally, I came up with the solution. I pulled out of the triad and took their hands. I took Screech's hand more to keep him at a distance than as an act of affection. We walked holding hands from there. Eventually, we reached Screech's building and drudged up the long flight of stairs to his apartment. He had not locked the door when we left, and he never did. Earl went back downstairs to get our bags from the van while Screech poured me a glass of cold water.

Screech sat across from me on the opposite mattress and said, "You know you are truly a very beautiful woman. You are not what they call a classic beauty. You are maybe taller than most women, but still, there is an essence about you that is … I don't know … enticing."

I thought to myself, *Shit! What the hell! He waits for my boyfriend to leave the room and then makes a pass at me?*

I said, "Thank you," rather smugly, and took a sip from my glass of water.

"No, really," Screech continued. "I could see you in the movies or something. I think you would be like one of those Hollywood beauties with a strange beauty, like Betty Davis. She is beautiful and ordinary at the same time, also really sexy—you know?"

"Well, no, I don't know. I don't think I've ever thought of Betty Davis that way before," I said. "She looks rather ugly to me." I found myself somewhat offended by his left-handed compliment.

"But she's not," Screech went on. "She is anything but ugly. She has a presence that calls to you. You know, you have a presence, Lovella. You don't realize it. I watched you today. People are fascinated with you, and you don't even realize how fascinated they are."

"No, I don't realize that," I responded. "I've never thought of myself as fascinating."

"When you walk into a room, it's like people feel it before they even realize they are feeling it," he said, smiling. "They sense your presence, and they are drawn to it. That's what called me to your table this afternoon." He stood and began unbuttoning his shirt.

Jesus Christ! I thought. *He's stripping! Is he going to try to fuck me while Earl is downstairs getting the luggage?* For a moment, I pondered whether there was any indication that he was thinking of raping me. I confronted myself and tried to be nonchalant. After all, I had seen quite a few naked men before, and Earl would be back soon.

He turned and walked over to the pile of clothes on the floor, digging until he found what appeared to be an extra-long T-shirt. He dropped the shirt that he had been wearing into the pile. Then, he pulled the long t-shirt over his head and took his pants off under it, never revealing anything other than the outline of his dick flopping under the shirt when he walked back across the room. He was a bit of a gentleman, after all. He returned to the mattress, laid down, and pulled the blanket over himself. Then, he propped himself up on an elbow and continued talking. I felt relieved.

"You should develop your senses, Lovella. You should be more aware of your surroundings, recognize what others sense about you, and realize how special you are."

Earl entered with our luggage, and I got up to meet him.

"Thank you, Screech," I said over my shoulder as I walked to the door.

Earl handed my suitcase to me. I took it to the bathroom and changed into a nightgown. It was maybe a little revealing, but not intended to be sexy, just functional. I brushed my teeth, and when I came out, I folded my arms over my tits as though I could actually hide them. I needn't have bothered. Screech was already asleep, and I certainly didn't care if Earl saw me. When I saw that Screech was sleeping, I relaxed.

Earl kissed me when he walked by on his way to the bathroom. I snuggled beneath the blankets on the other mattress, about two feet from Screech's mattress, and Earl soon joined me. I was happy to be on a real mattress, even if it had no sheets, was flat on the floor, and was a bit lumpy. At least it somewhat resembled a real bed instead of a sleeping bag on the hard floor of the van. Earl folded his arms around me. "I love you," he whispered in my ear.

"I love you too," I replied and drifted almost immediately to sleep.

CHAPTER 21

Acid Dreams and Fornication

The following day, I awoke to clinking sounds in the kitchenette area. Screech was busy and humming a familiar song. Beside me, Earl was lightly snoring. When I moved to get up, he also woke and stretched long on the mattress.

"Good morning, beautiful," he said, leaning over and kissing me on the cheek. He examined the room as though he had never seen it before, looking around at every corner. I half expected him to ask, "Where are we?" but he didn't. I kissed him back and got up.

When I stood up and headed for the bathroom, Screech spotted me.

"Oh, hey, good morning!"

"Good morning, Screech," I said as I stumbled toward the bathroom.

Screech had scrambled a few eggs and had made toast and coffee. When I returned from the bathroom, he delivered me a plate and a cup of coffee after I sat on the mattress. Then, he did the same for Earl and joined us, sitting opposite.

"It is nice of you to make breakfast for us," I said. "You didn't have to do that."

"Hey, I make breakfast every morning," he replied. "It don't take nothin' to add a few extra eggs."

"Well, you have been more than gracious," Earl said before biting into his toast.

"So, Screech," I opened a new topic. "You asked us about ourselves and how we got to San Francisco. How about you? How did you get here?"

"I'm from Alabama," he said. "I grew up a few miles outside of Birmingham. My daddy was a sharecropper, and Momma worked the fields beside him. Clevus and Nannette Miller broke their backs for nothin' their whole lives."

"So why did you come out here?" I went on.

"You got any idea what it is like for a Black man in the deep south?" he questioned. "I mean, it's not like we get spit on in the streets every day, but there are still White folks who don't want us to drink from the same water fountain. Most Black folks won't even attempt it, no matter how thirsty they are. There are restaurants we are not allowed to go to because they are all White. I heard that folks out here were free-loving and gentle people, more open-minded. I wanted to see if I could get in on some of that."

"It seems to me," I said, "that a lot of colored … I'm sorry … Black people have been getting involved in the Civil Rights Movement and working with Dr. Martin Luther King."

"Yeah, yeah," he pondered. "I don't know what I think about that. I don't know that the South is ever gonna change. There might be other parts of the country that might be more open to Black folk, but the South?" He stared into space for a moment. "The South ain't ever gonna give colored people a chance."

"Don't you think that Dr. King has been making some progress?" Earl entered. "We were in New York in April for the march on the U.N."

"Yeah, that was more about protesting the war than civil rights," Screech returned.

"I think it was about both," I said. "Did you participate in the protests out here?"

"You know," Screech continued after wolfing down a bite of scrambled eggs, "I figure the best way for me to have peace is not to put myself into a situation where somebody will challenge my peace. You start waving a flag; somebody shoots at it. I don't consider it very conducive to my peace to have some cop beating me over the head with a nightstick. It's best to stay low-key."

"Don't you think we are obligated to our fellow countrymen and women to fight for causes contributing to everyone's freedom?" Earl pressed, staring directly at Screech.

"No, I don't!" Screech returned, obviously upset. He got up, carried his empty plate to the kitchenette, and tossed it in the sink. "I am just trying to live my life as peacefully and as comfortably as I can while staying out of the White man's way."

"That's cool," Earl spoke, gently trying to comfort. "I get it, but we're White, and you came right up to our table yesterday. You seemed to be comfortable with that."

"I'm going to go take a bath," I said, leaving them to talk.

Earl joined Screech in the kitchen when I gathered my things and headed for the bathroom. He put his big, comforting hand between Screech's shoulder blades. Then, the two of them turned around, leaned against the counter, and continued to talk.

After I came out of the bathroom, Screech offered Earl access, but Earl told him to go ahead.

I put my things away, sat beside Earl on the mattress, and brushed my wet hair. It was getting hippie length and took a little longer to dry. I liked my longer hair and began to enjoy t-shirts and jeans that were much easier to deal with and more comfortable.

"It felt so good to have a real bath," I said. "I feel more refreshed than I have in a week."

"Screech has offered to let us live with him if we want," Earl said. "What do you think about that?"

"I guess I'm okay with that," I said, "but I don't think it is fair to him if we don't contribute."

"I know," Earl continued. "I talked with him about that. He said as crappy as this place looks, it is not cheap. He said you can't find cheap in San Francisco unless you are about ready to live on the streets, and that is an option. We do have the van, but we could, maybe, give him about a hundred dollars a month in rent and stay here. That's half the rent."

"That would give us a couple of months with a little left for spending money," I said, "but what about food?"

"I know," Earl continued. "I would probably have to get a job or figure out some way of making a little more money while we are out here. I don't think we'll need much."

"I don't mind getting a job," I said.

"No, I'll do it," Earl replied. "I want you to enjoy your time here as much as possible, and I don't want you to worry about bringing in money."

I grinned at him. "Earl, how much do you think I will enjoy sitting around this apartment day in and day out? Work would give me something to do with my time."

"Okay," he said. "Cool. If you want to try to find a job, that's cool. I might like to hang out with Screech, get to know him better, and help set up the band and stuff."

We, indeed, were not average hippies. Most of the kids who came to Haight-Ashbury did not work that summer. Many of them lived on the streets, and most of them did drugs. The "Summer of Love" turned out to have much less to do with love and much more to do with kids running away from some desperate or horrible situation at home. To most of them, the streets were preferable to living in abusive homes. Some of them engaged in prostitution. Some dealt drugs. Almost all of them were emotionally wounded in some way. On the one hand, it was heartbreaking; on the other hand, I was so glad I wasn't one of those kids. My family had its problems, but I never had a father who raped me or a violent mother. Daddy may have been a drunkard, and Mother may have been angry and manipulative, but neither ever physically abused me. I met kids there who had been through hell, and unfortunately, that hell was in their own homes.

I learned a lot that summer. I learned, eventually, that Screech had run away from a situation in which his father had sexually and physically abused him as far back as grade school and had done the same with a couple of Screech's other siblings. I probably would never have known if we had not gotten drunk one night and started talking about our families. Earl and I both had to admit that Screech won the prize for worst family. He had two sisters, twins Maggie and Molly. They were two years younger than Screech. His oldest brother, Leon, was spending twenty years in prison for armed robbery. Screech had been close to his next oldest brother, Delver, but he drowned when Screech was about twelve years old. He had little to do with his other brother, Simon, who generally avoided everyone. His mother, who was also beaten and abused by his father, was passively compliant with the abuse of her children. What else could she do when there was little recourse for a Black woman in the South in those days, especially with children? I learned that, despite my conflicts with Mother, and

Daddy's alcoholism, compared to many others, my life was a fucking piece of cake. I determined that I would try to be more grateful.

About two weeks after we got there, I was hired as a waitress across the street at Simone's. I learned a great deal about work, vegetarian food, and the restaurant business that summer. I also learned how to cook some pretty good vegetarian dishes. It was technically my first job. We paid rent with Earl's money, but I brought in extra money for spending, plus any food that had not been sold by closing could be taken home by employees. So, there wasn't much we had to spend on food. I bought a few things to fix up the place and give it a feminine touch, including sheets, pillows, and pillowcases. I was sure to ask Screech for permission and careful that his added touches remained in place. I was not about to touch his Jimi Hendrix posters.

Jimi Hendrix played that summer at the Monterey Pop Festival. Even though it was only two hours away and Screech longed to go, he had to fulfill his commitments to play his gigs. He and the band had learned that, although they wanted to front their own songs, they were more likely to land paying gigs when they did covers of known artists.

Earl spent a lot of time with Screech, often hanging out with him at the apartment or accompanying him to band rehearsals, which I had long since decided I could live without. Besides, I often worked evenings at the restaurant.

They came home one evening in late July when I was off work. They were both grinning from ear to ear.

"Well, don't the two of you look like you swallowed the Cheshire cat," I commented.

"We scored some acid," Earl said, giggling. "I've never done acid before. I want to try it."

"I don't think I'm comfortable with that," I cautioned. "I heard that it causes chromosome damage."

"I heard that it doesn't cause any more chromosome damage than taking aspirin," Earl replied.

"Chromosome. Chromosome. Where for art thou, Chromosome?" Screech interjected, and they both began to giggle and snicker as though he had told the funniest joke in the world.

It was evident they had already been smoking pot, maybe quite a bit of it.

"Looks like you guys have already been enjoying a little high," I said.

"Yeah, but we haven't taken the acid yet," Earl replied. "We want to share it with you, Lovella. I want to share it with you. Don't you think it would be so cool to trip out together?"

"Honestly," I went on. "That stuff scares me a lot more than pot. Who knows what it will do?"

"I've done it several times," Screech cut in. "It's not a big deal."

"But I've heard about people having bad trips and stuff," I continued.

"Well, that's usually because they have a bad vibe going in," Screech countered. "As long as you keep your mind positive and feel safe, you'll be fine. I will play some nice comforting music to chill the vibe."

"That's the problem," I pleaded. "I don't feel safe about taking that stuff."

"Hey, it's cool," Screech negotiated. "We're cool. We all get along. We all trust each other, and I can create a nice, relaxing environment. You know I got it all, all kinds of music. How about some classical music to calm the nerves? I even have some Chopin over there in my collection. We'll lock the door. It will just be the three of us."

"Come on, Lovella," Earl begged. "I think this could be a great experience, and I really want to share it with you. I'm so curious to experience tripping."

"Didn't we have some wine in here the other day?" I questioned, getting up and heading for the kitchenette. "If I'm going to do this, I will need a little wine to calm my nerves first."

"All riiiight! Cool!" Screech exclaimed. "That's the spirit. I'll make us a little nest where we can relax on the mattresses and get the music started."

He pushed the two mattresses together and adjusted the blankets over them. So, a big soft mattress island was in the middle of the floor. Then, he spent what seemed like a very long time digging through his albums for Chopin. He placed the gentle piano music on the stereo and returned to the mattresses. Earl joined him, and they lit another joint. I returned from the kitchen with my glass of wine and a lit cigarette. The three of us sat cross-legged on the mattresses, facing each other in a triangle. I gulped more than sipped my wine, and they passed the joint to me. I put out my cigarette in Screech's glass jar lid and took a long, slow drag on the joint. Soon, I began to feel the relaxing effects of the alcohol combined with the mild hallucinatory effects of the cannabis.

Earl removed an envelope from his pocket, opened it, and brought out what appeared to be some elaborately decorated postage stamps. He handed one to Screech and one to me.

"Just place it on your tongue," Screech said, "like this." He stuck out his tongue, laid the stamp across it, and closed his mouth.

Earl followed suit. I sat and stared at mine, lying in the palm of my hand, and hesitated.

"It's okay," Earl said.

I looked up at him, stared for a moment, and placed the LSD on my tongue. Then, I waited.

At first, I didn't notice any difference. I went back to the kitchenette and got myself another glass of wine. When I returned, the mattresses were empty. Screech and Earl had vanished. I stood at the edge of the mattresses, looking down and around the room. I didn't see them anywhere. I thought, *What the fuck! What kind of bullshit is this? They give me a fucking hit of acid and then just leave me to go through this shit by myself!* My anger was about to turn to sadness and fear when I heard Earl say, "What's wrong, honey?" I looked in the direction of his voice, and there they were, both lying on the mattresses, as though they had been there the whole time, but I had seen nothing but an empty space, nothing but the mattresses.

"Come here," he said gently.

I sat beside him, took a sip from my second glass of wine, and set it on the floor. He placed a reassuring hand on my leg and rubbed gently. Surprisingly, it felt like bugs were crawling up and down my leg.

"I need a cigarette," I said.

I reached for my purse lying on the floor nearby, took out a cigarette, and lit it. When I took the first drag, I felt like I was being blown up like a balloon. Warm air filled me, and I felt my body expand. I looked, and it seemed my arms and legs were swelling with air.

"What the fuck!" I exclaimed and snuffed the cigarette out in the jar lid. I pressed to be sure that every ember was extinguished. Still, each little orange glowing ember at the cigarette's tip seemed to sparkle and sparkle and wouldn't go out. Finally, I smashed it very hard into the lid. Then, it turned black and finally stopped glowing.

When I turned back around, Earl said, "I'm hot. I think I'm going to get a little more comfortable." He rose and began to disrobe.

Screech said, "Me too." Then, he also began to take off his clothes. When they were both naked, they sat back down on the mattress.

Earl leaned toward me and placed his hand on my breast, caressing it gently. "Aren't you warm, honey? Do you want to get more comfortable?"

Up to that point, there had been very few times that I had ever felt self-conscious about my nakedness, but this time, I didn't want to take off my clothes. "No," I said, feeling somehow subtly violated.

"Are you sure?" he said, leaning in and kissing me.

His mouth felt wet. His face seemed to trickle with water like rain falling across a window. My emotions surprised me. At the same time, I felt the sexual arousal that I had so much enjoyed, but I also felt like crying. Then, I realized I was crying, and the rain falling was my tears. As Earl pulled back from the kiss, I watched the tears fall from my face and splash, in slow motion, into a pool of water. It was as though the mattresses had become a pool in which we were all floating.

"I can't swim with my clothes on," I said, disrobing. When I pulled off my clothes, I felt as though I was sensually peeling off my skin, emerging from within like a snake pulling free from last year's growth. The skin-like clothes felt lifeless and useless, no longer needed. The sensual touch of the fabric fell softly around me, bringing a sense of freedom and renewal.

By the time I had disrobed, we were no longer in a pool. We were, instead, sitting in soft green grass under a canopy of trees. The sunlight flickered through the leaves overhead. I saw Earl and Screech sitting together, touching one another. Their penises seemed to become two snakes that began to intertwine, encircling each other and rising together toward the canopy. Then, I saw Earl and Screech kissing. I looked in fascination with a blend of emotions, from sexual arousal to jealousy. I asked myself, *Who am I jealous of, Earl or Screech, or maybe both? No one is kissing me.*

It seemed that Chopin's piano music became bird songs in a jungle, and my spirit and body flowed with that music, from the crescendo to the subtle, gentle, tinkling notes.

Then, I noticed across from me that two leopards were mating, a spotted leopard and a black leopard. The spotted leopard was mounting the black leopard, thrusting like animals when they breed. This seemed to go on for a long time while glimmering, florescent eyes peered from the jungle surrounding them, also watching them. After a while, I saw the spotted leopard lift its head and roar. That frightened me. I screamed and slunk back away from it. Then, the spotted leopard rolled off the back of the black leopard and lay down on the grass. As it did, it transitioned into a man, and I saw that the man was Earl. He appeared to be dead.

I shouted, "Earl!"

I was so scared that he had died. He lifted his head from the grass and put a finger to his lips as though to say, *be quiet*. When he went "shuuuuuuush around his finger," I felt a wind sweep by me, blowing my hair back.

Then, the black leopard stood on its hind legs and changed forms. It morphed into a jungle witch doctor with feathers, beads, and native regalia, and I realized I was in an African village. The witch doctor moved with jerky, dance-like movements toward me. He had a rattle in each hand, shaking them, holding them away from his body. He knelt before me when he approached me, and the rattles disappeared. Their sound had been a rhythm of "shhs-shhs-shhs-shhs-shhs," but it had started coming from his lips instead of the rattles. He wrapped his arms around me. Then, I felt warm and safe. He held me close, and I could feel his feathered headdress against my cheek and over my hair. He pulled away and stared at me so I could see directly into his eyes. I noticed that the witch doctor looked like Screech. His eyes were like dark glass, like windows into the universe. Looking into his eyes was like looking into the night sky. In the distance of his eyes, I could see tiny glimmering stars. He kissed me. His lips, like soft pillows, enfolded mine. I felt his tongue on my tongue as he gently laid me down on a mat by a grass hut.

I looked over to see Earl watching and staring as he sat in a meditative position, legs crossed over one another, thumb and forefinger encircled on each knee, like a Buddha. Then, Earl began to fade into the distance. I reached out to him but couldn't reach him.

The witch doctor kissed me again. He held me gently and maneuvered me onto the mat, then stretched himself atop me, along the length of my body. I felt tremendous arousal. I felt his erect penis slide slowly into me, as though it were three or four feet long, like a snake crawling up into the nethermost part of me, slithering around my heart, tugging at my deepest, inner longing. It seemed to slither slowly and deeply into me, sliding, sliding, sliding, and then, it would withdraw just as gradually, tantalizingly, and teasingly. I felt my hands upon his naked back. I caressed his smooth, warm skin and ran my hands down his body. I could feel the silky, warm muscular contour of his back down to his ass, and his ass rolled over me like ocean waves caressing the shore.

It seemed as though he fucked me for days, with the sun setting and the moon rising over his back. I looked up into the sky and watched the days pass, from sunlight to stars, one after another. I felt my body shiver with climax and convulse with ecstasy. I felt myself explode with pleasure that shattered my body and sent pieces of it flying into the sky, and then my body would relax and come back together. This repeated again and again.

Next, Earl was sitting beside us. He loomed above me like a giant looking down from the sky. One hand caressed the witch doctor's back, and the other caressed my face. He gently stroked his hand from my temple to my neck.

Suddenly, the witch doctor began to chant incantations in a language I had never heard before. Slowly and softly, at first, he chanted and then louder and faster until he screamed as though in horrifying pain. He pushed up from me and thrust his hips into me faster and harder. I saw his head tilt back, and as the scream came from his mouth, white doves flew from his lips into the night sky. Then, I began to feel trickles of warm fluid falling out of my vagina, and I realized that the witch doctor was filling me with a magic potion. He poured this potion through his penis, and it filled me so much that I could not contain it. It trickled out of me onto the mat beneath us. I felt a tingle run through my body as the potion began to take effect. I felt the magic implanted into me and realized I had become a shapeshifter.

I felt myself turn into a dove, and the witch doctor had turned into an eagle. I felt us rise and fly over the village. We flew through the sky, looking down on the African land filled with herding animals, rivers, and grasslands. The eagle flew over me, and I flew beneath the protection of its wings. Then, we began to fall, and I became frightened. I started frantically trying to flap my wings so I could stay aloft. I looked up to see that the eagle had folded its wings back, throwing us into a dive. Soon, we hit the ground together with a dull and soundless thud. We were back on the grass mat. We were back in human form, and the witch doctor had fallen over me. He lay atop me and panted with exhaustion. Then, he rolled over to my left side and reached out his muscular hand to caress my cheek. Looking in his direction, I saw Screech looking longingly and lovingly back at me. I saw Earl and Screech lean together above me and sensually kiss.

I had mixed feelings, feelings of having betrayed Earl. Then, Earl lay down beside me and enfolded me lovingly into his arms.

When I awoke late the following afternoon, the three of us were lying naked, side by side, on the mattresses. Screech was between me and Earl. I wasn't sure if I was still tripping, but then everything became familiar with reality. I lay there for a long time, trying to make sense of my memories of what had happened the night before. I rolled over onto my back, stared at the ceiling, and lost myself in thought. Had I seen Earl having sex with Screech, or was it just a hallucination that the drug had created? Did Screech have sex with me, or had it all been part of the acid trip? After all, I more than imagined that I was a dove flying over the African grasslands. I experienced it more vividly than any dream could ever have been. I knew that it couldn't have been real, so the other things that I thought I had experienced might not be real either, but we were all lying there, together, on the mattresses, naked. I felt like I had awakened from an excessively elaborate and intense dream.

After a while, I got up and went to the bathroom. When I returned, the two of them had roused and were sitting on the edge of the mattresses.

I came back across the room, not concerning myself about my nudity. Until then, Earl and I had only made love when Screech was out of the apartment. Screech had never seen me naked before. However, after waking up nude, next to him, I saw no further use in worrying about my clothes. I came and sat down on the mattress next to Earl. When I did, Screech got up and headed for the bathroom without saying a word.

After Screech left the room, Earl and I sat there in silence. Finally, I said, "We need to talk."

"About what?" he asked.

"There is a lot about last night and that whole experience that I need to try to wrap my head around," I began. "Things have changed here. It's not just the acid trip; relationships have changed. We have crossed over into something we didn't start with. I don't know how that happened, and I don't know that we can ever return to where we were."

He buried his face in his hands. "Yes," he said.

"Yes, what?" I questioned.

"Yes, I've been having sex with Screech," he replied. "I'm sorry. I didn't mean to deceive you. It's just that ..."

I sat quietly for a moment, trying to take it all in. I felt hurt and betrayed, but I also felt curious and intrigued, and I knew that, no matter what, I would be okay.

"Earl," I said, "what bothers me about that is not necessarily that you had sex with Screech but that you deceived me again. I thought you understood that I need honesty."

"I'm sorry," he pleaded. "I shouldn't have kept it from you. I don't have an excuse."

"Are you homosexual?" I questioned.

"No," he replied. "I mean, not really. I guess I just like sex. I don't know. It felt good to explore."

"Are you in love with Screech?" I continued.

"No ... well ... not like I'm in love with you ... I don't know," he attempted to explain. "I love Screech, but maybe I just like having sex with him, sometimes. I don't know. It doesn't feel like sex, just for the sake of sex, but like a bonding. This is all so bizarre. I've never felt this way before. I've never had sex with a man before, other than maybe a little curious playing around and kidding around when I was hitting puberty, but that wasn't real sex. I had never climaxed with a man until I began to make love to Screech, and I had never done anything with males since I hit puberty. I thought I was straight. I mean, I've always wanted women. I thought I only wanted women. I thought I wanted only you because I'm in love with you, but I felt something with Screech. I don't know how this happened, Lovella. I feel drawn to him. It's like I have to touch him, and he has to touch me."

He began to cry.

"Is Screech a homosexual?" I asked.

"Actually," he responded. "I don't know how he feels sexually. He has girlfriends, and he sleeps around with quite a few women. I don't know if he sleeps with any other men. I don't know. This is all different. It's different from anything I've ever experienced before, from anything I've ever allowed myself to feel. You should know if he is queer, shouldn't you? I mean, he fucked you last night, didn't he? At least, I think he fucked you. It looked to me like he did. I don't think it was all due to tripping."

I sighed deeply before speaking. "It seems to me that one of the effects of drugs is that they diminish your judgment. You do things that you would not normally do, or you do things that you might have fantasized about doing but wouldn't do otherwise. Either way, they cause you to make choices you maybe shouldn't make."

"Yeah," he said. "I guess we can blame it on the drugs. Still, there must have been something inside of us that made us do it. Regardless, it is still a choice that we made."

"You're right—it was a choice," I said. "Would we have made those choices if we weren't high or drinking? Until you confirmed it just now, I wasn't sure if Screech had fucked me. In my hallucination, it was a witch doctor who fucked me, and I don't know where that came from. Sometimes, the witch doctor looked like Screech. Sometimes he didn't. I had all kinds of other dream-like things that happened too, like flying and the mattresses turning into a pool of water, so I questioned whether it had really happened."

"I think it did," Earl replied, "and before that, I fucked Screech right there on that mattress in front of you." He sobbed. "Lovella, I'm so sorry. I feel so ashamed."

"Shame is not going to fix anything," I said. "Human sexuality is a strange thing. It is amazing to me how it can manifest. I've read about things like this. I've just never experienced anything like it before."

I placed a hand on his shoulder and looked away. I didn't want to see his face when he answered the question I was about to ask. "Is Screech in love with you?"

"I don't know," he responded. "I think it was just something that felt good to both of us, but we're buddies, you know? I love Screech as a friend, and I think he loves me as a friend. We took friendship a little further than usual, but I don't think we want to set up housekeeping together."

I turned back to him. "Then, Earl," I said, "I want to go home."

He lifted his head, tears still streaming down his face. He reached over, took my hand, and squeezed. "Me, too," he said. "I want to go home, too."

The next day, I gave notice at Simone's and resigned. We had a few days before we would leave, and I had a lot more questions, not the least of which had to do with my feelings of betrayal that Earl had not been tripping on acid when he and Screech began having sex and he had hidden that from me all summer. We would go home together, but we could not be the same couple after that.

When we finally told Screech that we were returning to Pennsylvania, he was not at all happy. Maybe he really was in love with Earl. Perhaps he didn't want to lose the steady rental income or money I brought in from working at Simone's. I had done well that summer. I had brought in food, saved money, and had plenty left for us to make the trip home. The three of us lived much better than we could have lived alone, but I brought in most of the income. I learned that men give excellent tips to big-busted, flirty waitresses even at vegetarian restaurants, and I wasn't above dropping some cleavage for a little extra green on the table.

We had waited for a couple of days after our acid trip to tell Screech that we were leaving. We wanted to get everything arranged and ready to go so we wouldn't have to run around trying to tie up loose ends at the last minute. We got up early one morning and packed the van while Screech was still asleep. He had been out late with his band and slept so hard that he didn't notice what we were quietly doing. After loading the van, we returned upstairs and woke Screech to tell him we were going. I realize it was underhanded to do it that way, but Earl suspected that he would be upset, and we didn't want to have to pick through our stuff and move things in the middle of an angry scene. Earl was right.

When we told him, I realized that screeching was not just something he did when he sang. It was something he did when he was angry. The angrier he became, the more the pitch of his voice heightened, and he began to stretch his words like rubber bands and snap them back between quick spurts of syllables.

"SO, YOU ARE GOING TO JUST UP AND FUCKING WALK OUT WITH NO NOTICE, NO TIME FOR ME TO PREPARE FOR SHIT! YOU ARE DOING THE SAME DAMN SHIT TO ME THAT EVERYBODY DOES! JUST LEAVE OLD SCRATCH HANGING. NOBODY FUCKING CARES!"

"Screech, man," Earl responded. "We don't mean to leave you hanging. Lovella will give you a hundred dollars toward next month's rent. That should give you time to find a roommate."

"A HUNDRED DOLLARS?" Screech screamed back. "WELL, BIG FUCKING WHOOPTE DAMN DO! I MIGHT GO OUT AND BUY MYSELF A FUCKING YACHT!"

"Screech, you know we love you," I interjected. "But we have got to get back home."

"Yeah—you love me." He began to lower his tone to be somber but sarcastic. "You really love me. What? You have known me for what—two months? Yeah, that's plenty of time to fall in love, right? Oh, yeah, Lovella, I know you got my back." He turned to Earl and continued. "What is this, Earl? Did the bitch here talk you into going home? Is she a little jealous of us spending time together? You know I ask nothin' of you. I don't fucking pressure you, don't expect anything of you. What is it? She don't want you fucking my ass? I thought we was tight man."

"We are tight," Earl replied. "This doesn't have to mean we will never see each other again. We'll be in touch. We are just tired of the scene out here. We need to go home. We'll start classes again soon, and Lovella's not a bitch. Come on, man. That's not fair. She has worked this summer, fed us, spruced up the place, and has done some pretty nice things for you. She likes you, man. She didn't talk me into anything. We both think it's time to go home. We wouldn't have been able to stay anyway."

A tear rolled from Screech's eye and drifted slowly down his cheek. He began to tremble and turned away. At that point, I realized he was in love with Earl. "Regardless, you're gone," he said. "The two of you are gonna go back and get married, make babies, and have a family. You are going back to live your nine-to-five White man's life. You will go back and work at your daddy's potato chip factory, and the last damn thing you are going to want is to associate with a …" There was a very long pause before he choked out the remaining phrase, "po nigger from the South."

Earl fell silent. His shoulders slumped. The muscle tone drained out of his face. It was then I realized that not only was Screech in love with him, but he obviously had intense feelings for Screech. He looked at me, and I nodded as though understanding. I didn't understand, but I wanted to. He walked over to put a caring arm around Screech's shoulder. Screech threw his arm off and said, "Get the fuck away from me." Earl did not try to touch him again. He stood back away from Screech and said softly, "I thought you knew me better than that. I thought you knew both of us better than that."

"It don't matter," Screech replied without looking up. "It don't fucking matter what kind of good intentions you got, and that's all it fucking is, man, good intentions. You still don't get it. I know how it is. I've been a fool even to let this happen. I should have kept my heart in my chest instead of letting it run around with you."

"I do love you, Screech." Earl pleaded. "Honestly, I do."

"IT DON'T MATTER!" Screech shouted as he turned back. "Cause you know the only fucking thing in the world that is worse than a nigger," he looked up at Earl, his eyes pleading, "is a faggot nigger!"

"Oh, God, man, don't … Please don't." Earl's tears began drifting.

"You know, Screech continued, "I came out here thinking maybe things might be different. Faggots and niggers, neither one ain't too popular around Alabama, especially combined. Sleeping with girls, I can do that, but maybe it's just to cover up the fact that I suck cock. I like girls, but …" His eyes drifted to the other side of the room. "I thought maybe I could get in on the start of the Aquarius Age. You know, peace and love and all that shit. I thought people would see *me* instead of seeing their judgment of me, their imagination of what they think I am, but it don't matter." He walked to the opposite side of the room and turned his back again. "So, you have had your little adventure, rich White boy. You got to go slummin'. You got to have a little taste of this fruit that wasn't as forbidden as you thought. You got to pretend, for a while, that you ain't part of the establishment, but you are. You got no idea how much you are."

"This was not some kind of game!" Earl insisted. "I love you! I love who you are, man! I love you, the real you, not the 'colored' you, not the 'faggot' you. I love you! I love the man who giggles at the silliest jokes, who will take his shirt off and give it to a homeless stranger or hand the homeless kid the leftovers of the potluck, the man who looked at me with eyes of such tenderness and compassion. I love the man beneath all the torment and anguish that you have been through. I love—you!"

"No, you don't," Screech responded. "Cause, in the long run, I'm just another nigger."

At that point, I sat on the mattress and buried my face in my hands. My mind was reeling with so many fears, even though I was trying to keep it all level in my head. I decided to stay out of it, let it go wherever it went, and then try to pick up the pieces. I knew that I wanted to return home more than ever. Whatever happened after that, I didn't know, but at least I would be back in familiar territory.

"Goddamn it!" Earl shouted. "I don't care what fucking color your skin is!"

"Yes, you do," Screech replied. "Even if you don't think you do—you do, man. You might try, but you can't look at me without seeing somebody different from the *supposed to be*, maybe not quite as good as you are. Oh, you tell yourself that you're cool and different from the rest. You tell yourself that you ain't racist, but deep down, nagging at the back of your mind is the truth … and someday it is gonna bite you in the ass. You grew up that way. You can't think no other way. White privilege is instilled in you. It is steeped into your bones like a bubbling broth flavoring your very core, and you are so used to it that you don't even realize when it rewards you."

"I disagree with you, man," Earl replied. "But even if you're right, at least I'm *trying*."

"Well, tell you what," Screech said as he marched up to Earl. "How bout I go back east with you guys and come prancing into your daddy's house? What the hell do you think is gonna happen? Do you think your rich, White, fat-cat daddy is gonna like you any better? You think he is gonna sit me down and have the maid bring me a drink?" Screech lifted both fists and slammed them down in the air as though he were beating them against a table. "FUCK IT, MAN! FUCK IT! FUCK IT! FUCK IT! FUCK IT! I—CAN'T—HAVE—YOU! I CAN'T EVER HAVE YOU … AND YOU CAN'T EVER HAVE ME!" He pointed at me, "EVEN IF YOU DIDN'T HAVE HER, I STILL CAN'T HAVE YOU! We can't be together. It wouldn't make a fucking bit of difference how much we love each other. It's all pretend, man. It can't be real. They won't let it be real. Even if I was White, the world ain't ready for two men to be together. It probably won't ever be. There sits the one you love, man." He pointed back at me as I sat there, helpless, with my arms clenched around my knees.

Screech walked to the back and leaned over the sink, facing the window. "You and your old lady better go," he said without turning around.

Earl started to say his name, still desperately seeking some resolution, but he didn't get the words out of his mouth before Screech screamed, "JUST FUCKING GO!"

Earl turned back toward me, silent and sad, looking very much like a little boy whose puppy had just died. I got up, crossed the room, took his hand, and tilted my head toward the door. There was a brief hesitation when I thought he would tell me he wanted to stay, but he moved with me toward the door. Just before leaving, I quickly walked across the room, behind Screech, and laid a hundred-dollar bill on the countertop. Then, I met Earl back at the door. When we stepped outside the apartment and pulled the door closed, a moment after the click of the latch, we heard Screech fall into wailing sobs. Earl started to turn back but stopped when I touched his arm.

Stepping down those stairs for the last time felt like a sinner's shame descending to hell. Both of us wanted to go back. Both of us wanted to make it okay. We cared enough about Screech to want to make it right, but we couldn't have done that, no matter how much we might have tried. Deep down, we knew Screech was right and that it would take a very long time for the world to truly accept people who were different from certain prescribed norms.

I wanted to be cool about Earl's relationship with Screech, but I couldn't help that my heart was wounded because Earl had not just a homosexual affair but a love affair. If it had just been sex for fun, I might have understood that. After all, I tried to be accepting of all types of human sexuality. Any affair he might have had with anyone would have hurt me, but the fact that he had been in love left doubts in my mind. It made me wonder if he could ever commit himself fully to me, if deep down, he might be homosexual or bisexual or longing for a love he couldn't have. I knew that he loved me. I knew that he had not done this to hurt me. Still, my heart whimpered like a scolded child. He had, after all, betrayed me.

When we returned to the van, Earl sat in the driver's seat, placed both hands firmly on the steering wheel, and said, without moving his gaze from the windshield, "So, which way is home?"

I reached for our maps, even though I had already plotted the course. Gazing intently at the squiggles representing San Francisco, I said, "Head east toward Divisadero Street."

He started the van, pulled onto the street, and turned east.

Except for occasional references to the map, we were silent for a long time.

CHAPTER 22

What You Don't Know Can Hurt You

We stopped at a little roadside cafe in Reno, Nevada. I found a pay phone and called Mother. I knew she would be angry. I hadn't bothered to call her all summer except to tell her that we had arrived safely in San Francisco. The phone rang an inordinate number of times, and I was about to hang up, thinking she wasn't home, when I heard her voice come onto the line.

"Yes, what is it?" she said impatiently. It was entirely out of character for her to answer the phone that way. I wondered what happened to a normal *Hello.*

"Hello, Mother," I said into the staticky line.

"Oh, for goodness' sake, LOVELLA!" she yelled. "It is about time you called! I was frantic with worry! I had no idea how to reach you or what might have happened to you! You have to come home right now! I'm telling you that you absolutely must come home immediately!"

"I'm on my way home, Mother," I replied, calmly ignoring her angst. "What's the rush?"

"I was headed out the door to return to the hospital when the phone rang. John is in intensive care, and they are saying he may only live a few more days."

"Oh, my God!" I exclaimed. "Daddy's in the hospital?"

"I told you, before you left, that he was dying! I told you he had severe cirrhosis!" she grumbled. "I told you, and you wouldn't believe me! You had to go on some childish, selfish adventure instead of spending the last few months of your father's life with him!"

"HE TOLD ME HE WAS FINE!" I shouted back. "He was sober and has never lied to me!"

"Well, he lied!" Mother snapped. "He has lied to you more than you will ever know."

"DON'T YOU SAY THAT!" I screamed. "HE HASN'T LIED A TENTH AS MUCH AS YOU HAVE! If he did lie, he must have been trying to protect my feelings."

"Yes, that's what he does, Lovella," she chirped. "He protects you. You protect him, and meanwhile, the real world is falling apart."

"Oh, my God," I said, contemplating the implications of this. "We are still at least two days away."

"Where are you?" she questioned.

"We are in Reno, Nevada," I said. "We started back this morning, but even if we drove straight through and didn't stop to sleep, it will still be about two days before we can get there. Is Daddy alert? Can he talk? I could call him."

"You missed your chance on that one," she said glibly. "He has been in a coma for several days now."

A massive wave of grief and guilt swept over me. I began to have trouble breathing. I sucked tears back and tried desperately to keep her from knowing my pain. Yet I felt as though I couldn't get my breath, as though I could faint at any moment.

"I'll talk to Earl about it," I said. "We will get there as fast as we can. I'll try to call periodically to check in."

"Fine," she said, sounding very cold. "I will see you when you get here."

"Where is he, Mother? What hospital?" I asked, thinking of it at the last minute.

"He is in Armstrong Memorial," she replied. "If you call, you may want to call directly to the hospital, room 348. I am seldom home anymore. I have to go now."

I didn't get 'goodbye' out of my mouth fast enough. She had already hung up.

Earl had found a booth in the cafe' and ordered coffee while he waited for me. When I walked in, it was apparent that something was wrong. He scooted over and patted the seat for me to sit next to him.

"Baby, you look terrible," he said. "What's wrong? Your mother being mean to you again?"

I sat beside him, buried my face in my hands, leaned over the table, and took a breath before speaking. "When I called her in May to tell her we were headed for California, she told me Daddy was dying. I didn't believe her. I told her to put Daddy on the phone, and he said everything was fine. He was sober, so I believed him. I never felt I ever had a reason not to believe Daddy." I turned to look into Earl's eyes. "But he lied to me, Earl. He's in intensive care. He's dying. They say he may only have a few days to live."

I burst into tears. Earl pulled me to his chest and held me. He didn't say anything. He just let me cry. When I had finally collected myself, I went on.

"Mother says he has severe cirrhosis and that he has been unconscious for several days. He is at Armstrong Memorial."

"Then, we have to get home," he said.

"What am I going to find there?" I asked. "I can't talk to him. I can't tell him that I love him."

"Of course, you can tell him you love him," Earl comforted. "I read, somewhere, that even though people are unconscious, they still know when someone they love is in the room. Even if their body can't move, their mind can still comprehend."

The tears came and went. The waitress avoided us, correctly calculating that this was not the time to take an order.

"We have to go," Earl pleaded. "We have got to get you back so you can be with him. I could put you on a plane in Reno. You could fly, and I'll drive the van back."

"We don't have the money for a plane," I argued, "and it is no guarantee. Reno is not that big. Even if they have commercial flights, there will be layovers—maybe more than one—and I would still have to get to Kittanning from Pittsburg. It could take just as long or longer."

"Maybe you're right," he said. "Even if I called Dad to wire me the money, that could also create a delay."

"It will take us at least two days to get back there," I continued. "What if he dies before we get there?"

"He's not going to die before you get there," Earl consoled. "He will wait for you. You know he will. We'll drive all night. We'll get there."

I nodded my head. Then, Earl called the waitress over and ordered a couple of burgers and fries to go. We returned to the van, and he headed east on Lincoln Highway. He woofed down his burger and the rest of mine after I could only eat a few bites. We had been on the road since about 9:00 a.m., and it was about 2:00 p.m. when we got back on it after lunch.

"Earl, please keep it at the speed limit," I requested. "Getting stopped might be more of a delay than going slower."

"Sure, no problem," he returned and released the gas. Still, he pushed it a little.

Earl drove without rest. We had little bits of small talk here and there, minor bitching about detours and road construction, but that was about it. It was about 10:00 p.m. when we got to Salt Lake City. Earl noticed that I had been nodding in my seat. He reached over, gently touched my arm, and said, "Go in the back and lay down. Get some sleep."

"But, what about you?" I reasoned. "Don't I need to stay up and help keep you awake?"

"I'll be fine," he said. "Go lay down."

I dutifully climbed into the back, pulled a sleeping bag across the floor, and lay on it. I don't know how long I was asleep, but I awoke with a faint, dull, gray light coming through the van's windows. I sat up, looked around, and climbed back into the passenger seat.

"Where are we?" I asked.

"We are about an hour past Cheyenne, Wyoming, headed across Nebraska," he replied.

"My God," I exclaimed. "Haven't you slept?"

"I've been drinking coffee all night," he explained. "I have stopped at a few truck stops and roadside dives to refuel the van and refuel myself on caffeine."

"I'm surprised I didn't wake up," I said. "You must be exhausted. Why don't we pull over so you can sleep, or I'll drive while you sleep?"

"You don't have a driver's license," he responded. "Being pulled over might delay us more than me doing the driving." He tossed my own logic back at me.

I felt a twinge of anger at Mother just then. Never getting my driver's license was another way she controlled everything. She had every excuse under the sun, so I had never learned to drive.

I fumbled in my purse for a cigarette, dug frantically, and finally said, "Shit!"

"What's up?" Earl questioned.

"I don't have any fucking cigarettes," I exclaimed. "I'm a nervous fucking wreck, and I don't have any cigarettes."

"We'll get you some at the next gas station," he said. "I need to get gas pretty soon, anyway."

About twenty minutes later, he stopped to fill the tank. I went in to get a couple of packs of cigarettes and snacks while the tank was filling. After that, he drove while I puffed one cigarette after another and then flipped the butt out the window. We were getting near Lincoln, Nebraska, when I noticed his head beginning to bob.

"EARL!" I shouted, jolting him awake. He had a brief little swerve and then corrected back into the lane.

"What, hum," he said. "I'm alright."

"No, you're not," I pleaded. "Pull over and take a nap, at least."

"No, Honey. We've got to get there," he continued.

"We may never get there if you fall asleep and run us off the road—now pull over!"

"Okay," he said, "when I find a place."

I began pointing out one place after another where he could pull over to nap: a grocery store parking lot, a side road, the underpass of a bridge. He bypassed them all. "Whoops, sorry. Missed that one."

I was getting increasingly frustrated, hearing one excuse after another as to why he couldn't pull over to rest. Finally, I began telling him that I had to pee really badly. I did need to pee a little bit, but I exaggerated it. I just complained about my bladder being about to rupture if we didn't find someplace soon. Eventually, he pulled into a gas station and let me out. I insisted that he park under a nearby tree close to the restrooms. When I returned, he was slumped over the steering wheel, sound asleep. I was torn between letting him sleep like that, knowing that he would probably be sore when he woke up, or going ahead and waking him so he could sleep in the back, where it would be more comfortable. I spent several minutes thinking about it and finally devised a plan. I reached over carefully, took the keys from the ignition, and placed them in my jeans pocket. Then, I nudged him several times before he woke up. He lifted his head and looked at me, his eyes glazed and bloodshot.

"Oh," he mumbled. "You ready to go?"

"No, I'm not," I replied. "I'm ready for you to get in the back of the van, lie down and sleep for a while."

"Honey, I can't," he coaxed. "We have got to get you home to your dad."

"I can handle taking a couple of extra hours, Earl," I responded. "Now, go lie down."

"No, we got to go," he reached for the keys. "Hey, where are the keys?"

"I have them."

"Well, give them to me, and let's go," he begged.

"I'll give them back to you when you have had some time to sleep," I protested.

He knew he needed sleep, so he finally complied and snuggled on top of a sleeping bag in the back of the van. "Wake me in thirty minutes," he commanded.

"Sure," I said. It was only a few seconds after that when I heard him snore.

By that time, it was about 2:00 p.m. Since we had left San Francisco at about 9:00 a.m. the previous morning, as far as I was concerned, we were making good time.

I let Earl sleep until 5:00. I didn't wake him. At various times in the afternoon, I took a magazine and folded it back to fan him in the back of that hot van. With all the windows and doors open and parked in the shade, it was still hot in late summer. At other times, I read the magazine. Most of the time, I just waited, and a time or two, I took little cat naps myself. I contemplated starting the van and heading down the road, but since I had never been trained to drive, I feared that only previous observations of the skill would not be sufficient to allow me to do it smoothly. I could see myself bouncing the van around or choking it out because I didn't have a feel for the clutch. Then, I could see Earl waking up and being mad at me because I was trying to drive when I didn't know how. I decided that I would let him sleep.

When I woke him, he looked around. Then, he looked startled, as though he didn't know where he was.

"Did you have a good nap?" I asked, and this seemed to orient him a bit.

"Where am I?" he responded, not answering my question. Despite my fanning and afternoon breezes, he was drenched in sweat from sleeping in a hot van, and maybe that contributed to some confusion.

"You are in the back of your van, in the parking lot of a gas station, somewhere in Iowa, about an hour and a half east of Lincoln, Nebraska, I think."

"Oh, jeez—Jeez! What time is it?" he questioned.

"It's about 5:00 p.m.," I replied.

"Oh shit!" he exclaimed. "I told you to wake me in thirty minutes! We've got to go!"

He scrambled to the driver's seat and reached for invisible keys. "Where are the keys?" he asked, obviously having forgotten our conversation earlier in the day.

I took the keys from my pocket and handed them to him. He started the van, but before he backed out of the parking space, he reached over, put his hand behind my head, and kissed me. "Don't ever forget that I love you," he said. "No matter what happens, no matter what mistakes I make. Please don't ever forget that I love you." Then, he steered the van clear of the space, and we were on our way again. Before I woke him, I had bought more snacks and drinks. He needed the fluids and slugged back some sodas while driving.

When we got to Davenport, Iowa, it was midnight. Again, I began pleading with him to pull over and take a nap, but he wouldn't do it. At about 2:00 a.m., I went to the back of the van to sleep again. At about 8:00 a.m., I woke again and asked, "Where are we?"

"We are about forty minutes, maybe an hour, from Kittanning," he replied.

He had driven straight through and was not about to stop unless he had to take a piss or gas up the van.

Finally, he pulled up in front of Armstrong Memorial Hospital at about 9:15 a.m. He reached over and took my hand. "Go ahead," he said quietly. "I'll park the van and meet you in there."

My emotions were sizzling, like a broken power line. I pulled the rear-view mirror around to look at my face. "Jesus! I look like shit," I said, trying to straighten my hair.

Earl squeezed my hand. "It doesn't matter," he said, "Go."

I left the van, feeling like a forlorn little girl. I didn't want to face this. I didn't want it to be confirmed. I didn't want to see Daddy lying on a deathbed, and I didn't want to have to deal with Mother's bullshit. I had no idea what I was in for. As Earl pulled the van away, I turned, put on my brave face, and pushed through the double glass doors.

Several chairs were occupied inside the lobby, and a few people were sitting around here and there. I saw a squat little woman seated behind a reception window. I walked over and watched her, and she seemed more interested in a crossword puzzle than in attending to me. Finally, I tapped on the window. She looked up and said, "Yes, may I help you?"

"I am Lovella Fuchs," I replied. "I understand that my father, John Fuchs, is in intensive care."

"Yes," she said, "but his wife is in with him now, and rules only allow one person at a time in the intensive care room."

I fought the urge to ram my fist through that window. "You don't understand," I said abruptly. "I haven't seen my father in two months. I just drove in from San Francisco."

"Oh, well, that is a very long drive. You must be exhausted. Why don't you have a seat and rest for a while until Mrs. Fuchs comes out?" She tilted her head back down to her crossword puzzle.

I slammed my fist on the Formica counter in front of the window. "I HAVE TO SEE MY FATHER NOW!" I screamed.

"Young lady!" she said, aghast. "You will curb that behavior, or I'll call security!"

"I DON'T FUCKING CARE!" I screamed. "I just need to see my daddy."

About that time, a matronly-looking nurse, wearing a dainty little white nurse cap, stepped up behind the receptionist. "Linda," she said sweetly. "Is there a problem?"

"MY DADDY IS DYING! I HAVE TO SEE HIM! WE DROVE STRAIGHT THROUGH FROM SAN FRANCISCO!" I shouted to the nurse without allowing the receptionist to answer her.

"Oh, I'm so sorry," the nurse replied. "Who is your father?"

"My daddy is John Fuchs," I said, angry tears running down my cheeks. "He is in intensive care. I haven't seen him in two months, and now he's dying."

Linda cut in. "I explained to the young lady that Mrs. Fuchs is still in the room, and rules only allow one person at a time."

The nurse, still smiling as though it was permanently painted on her face, said, "I'm sure we could make an exception in this case. Please buzz her through, Linda. I'll meet her in the hall."

She motioned me toward a steel door opposite the main entrance. I walked over and stood for a second in front of it. I heard it buzz and click, so I pushed it open to the hall. The matronly nurse was standing on the other side of the door, still smiling. She put her arm around my shoulder and said, "You must be devastated. Let me walk you up to your father's room."

I felt a mix of anger, relief, revulsion, embarrassment, and tenderness as she placed her arm around my shoulder. We walked together to the elevator. She pushed the call button, and we waited for a few eternal seconds before the door finally opened. She motioned me to get on the gurney-length elevator and followed me. We went up to the third floor. We walked around another hall to yet another steel door, where she pushed a button on the intercom. A voice came back with a, "May I help you?"

"This is Sheila Simpson," the nurse replied to the box, "Please buzz us in."

"Certainly, Mrs. Simpson," the box replied, and then, there was another buzz and click to open the door.

As we walked through together, I said, "Jeez, is this a hospital or Fort Knox?"

Still smiling, she said, "It's kind of both. We do have to keep tight security in some areas. Emotions often run high when loved ones are critically ill, and there are also some standard precautions regarding disease transmission."

Walking around the nurse's station, I noticed employees subtly coming to attention, perking up as though the general had arrived. They all stopped just short of a salute. Later, I learned that Mrs. Simpson was the Director of Nurses. She led me to Daddy's room, opened the door for me, and said, "Here you are. If you should happen to need anything, please let me know. I'll wait for you at the nurse's station."

Mother was sitting in an uncomfortable-looking chair beside the bed. She looked up in acknowledgment but didn't say a word. Daddy already looked like a corpse, gaunt and frail, his skin the color of a carrot. He had tubes in every orifice and an IV dripping into his arm from beside the bed. The stench in the room was like nothing I had ever smelled—sweet, like some spoiled candy, but also salty and rotten.

I barely had time to process it. I burst into tears, threw my purse on the floor, and ran to Daddy's side. "Oh, my God! Oh, my God!" I cried. "Daddy, can you hear me?"

"Of course, he can't hear you, Lovella." Mother spoke as though her words were intended to cut. "He's in a coma."

I gripped Daddy's hand tightly and pulled it to my cheek. "He can, too, hear me!" I shouted back at her. "Daddy, I love you! I love you, and I'm here!"

"Don't be ridiculous," she snarled.

"How long has he been like this … yellow, unresponsive?" I questioned with tears falling off my cheek onto Daddy's hand.

"A little while," Mother replied. "Not that you should care."

"How can you say that?" I snapped back at her, moving Daddy's hand back to his side but continuing to hold it. "You know how much I love Daddy."

"Yes," she replied. "You loved him enough to go gallivanting around California while he was dying. You two have always had such a—*special bond*." Her sarcasm hissed through painted lips like the fork in a snake's tongue.

"Are you jealous?" I asked with contempt.

She didn't reply but sat staring at me.

"You *are* jealous!" I continued, raising my voice. "Because you have never had this kind of a bond with anyone, have you, Mother? You haven't had it with Daddy, your parents or sisters, or me? You have no idea what it is like to really care about someone!"

"Don't start with me, Lovella!" she snapped back. "You have no idea what I've been through!"

I went on. "The one thing you never could stand was that Daddy and I were so close."

"Oh, you *had* such a *special bond* with your father," she hissed, "always taking up for him, protecting him, making excuses for him while he drank himself to death. You see where it got him, Lovella?" She stood up and slung her pointed red fingernail toward Daddy, "You, see?"

"I cannot fucking believe you," I snapped back. "You are *actually* blaming me for Daddy dying. Oh my God! What a pathetic lonely, old bitch you are!"

"I tried to stop him, Lovella! You know I tried. You have watched me, from when you were a little girl, trying to keep him from this. Why do you think I always insisted on having the car? I knew what he would do! If I had given him an inch, he would have been dead in the gutter long before now. He would have been dead ten or fifteen years ago, and you wouldn't have had your precious *Daddy* to moon over. Do you think I did that because it was fun? Do you think I had a good time being married to this man? I had to watch his every move to keep him from killing himself or, God forbid, somebody else! He got arrested for drunk driving when you were not even two years old. He almost ran over a child on a bicycle! I was not about to let that happen again!"

Her face trembled and became even tenser. Her jaw tightened, and she spoke through clenched teeth. "I had to take responsibility because he was not going to, and when you were barely old enough to talk, *you started protecting him!*"

She hurled her hand back and forth in the air as though trying to erase the past, then continued.

"Do I think *you* killed him?" She paused, and that same hand swooped back from the air and rested her fingers over her lips. "I don't think you drove the stake through his heart, but you helped provide the hammer." She trembled and stared at me.

Oh, my God! I thought *She fucking believes this shit!* In astonishment, my jaw dropped as I was shocked and horrified. A part of me recognized she was at least partially correct. I had stood between her and Daddy, and maybe, by doing that, I had kept her from controlling his drinking, but I couldn't bear the thought that I might have been to blame for his dying. I thought I was protecting him because I loved him and wanted her to leave him alone.

"You fucking bitch!" I hissed. "I loved Daddy more than anyone else in the world. I would have done anything for him, and he loved me. He was always warm and comforting to me, and you were nothing but a cold, angry, pathetic block of ice."

"Well, isn't that *sweet?*" she growled. "You two were just two lovely little rotten peas in a pod."

"We *are* two peas in a pod," I taunted. "We love each other like you are incapable of loving."

"Oh, for heaven's sake, Lovella!" she snapped. "He's not even your real father!" She caught herself and snapped her fist over her mouth as though she had uttered words that should never be spoken.

"What? What the hell!" I shot back. "Are you going to stoop that fucking low? You want to hurt me so bad that you would tell that lie while he is lying here, dying?"

"I shouldn't have told you, but it's not a lie, Lovella." She now spoke coldly and deliberately. "I was pregnant by another man when I married John. You can check the marriage license against your date of birth. I can prove it."

"So, you got pregnant before you were married," I announced. "Lots of women get pregnant before they marry. The only thing that proves is that you are not the bastion of perfection that you have always pretended to be."

"I can tell you who your real father is. You can talk to him if you want. He might even own up to it. You can ask your Grandmother Claudella, who I was dating when I got pregnant with you. John Fuchs was just a boy I knew at school. I never had any interest in him."

"Then, why the hell did you marry him?" I chastised. "That doesn't even make sense."

"He had always had a crush on me. Your real father refused to marry me, and since I was pregnant, I needed marriage to protect my reputation," she responded calmly and coldly.

"Stop this nonsense!" I pleaded.

She taunted. "Your real father's name is … Your real father is a doctor. That's all I can tell you."

I feigned laughter. "Some doctor is my biological father? Give me a fucking break, Mother. You couldn't come up with a more pathetic lie than that?"

"Where do you think you got your intelligence?" she asked. "You certainly didn't get it from John Fuchs because he didn't have it to pass on to you and look at him. He is short and small-boned. Compare that to your frame, Lovella. Have you ever considered that you don't look anything like him?"

I interrogated her. "Well, if my biological father is so high on your pretend social scale, why aren't you married to him?"

"It's a long story," she smugly replied. "I'll give you the details someday—maybe."

"You are making this shit up," I snapped back, "just to fucking torture me because you are pissed off that I went to San Francisco with Earl instead of doing what you demanded that I do!"

"Your real father is Carl Whitmire!" she blurted, throwing her fist over her mouth again.

"What?" I snapped back. "Our family doctor? Give me a fucking break, Mother! You couldn't come up with a better bullshit lie than that?"

She was about to come back at me when I felt Daddy's hand move slightly. I hadn't realized that I had held onto it through all that. I looked down at him, and he took a subaqueous breath with a gurgle in his lungs as he exhaled. Then, he stopped breathing. I ignored Mother and began shaking him on the shoulders. "Daddy! Daddy, breathe!" It was at least ten or more seconds before he took another stilted and desperate breath. "Oh, my God, Daddy!" I shouted. "Mother, get a nurse!"

"It won't do any good," Mother said dryly. Then, she stepped to the door and called nonchalantly into the hall, "Nurse."

Shortly, a nurse entered the room and strolled over to the bed on Mother's side. He had stopped breathing after the last breath, and by the time the nurse came in, he had not taken another.

"He can't breathe!" I shouted to her.

She observed him and put a stethoscope on his chest. "I'm sorry," she said. "I think your father has passed away."

Tears filled my eyes, and I began to shiver. I held Daddy's hand, and the nurse stepped back a little. Mother placed one hand on the bed rail but didn't come any closer.

"Oh, God, no!" I pleaded, "Daddy? DADDY!"

His breathing had stopped, and he became still and silent. I waited ten or fifteen seconds, watching for another breath, but it never came.

The nurse leaned over the rail and again placed the stethoscope on his chest. "I am pretty sure he is gone," she said quietly. "We will have his doctor confirm." She smiled sweetly at me and said, "I'm so sorry." Then, she stepped out of the room.

"DADDY!" I broke into heaving wails of grief. I felt like I couldn't breathe, and I couldn't make myself let go of his hand. Mother just stood there quietly, one hand resting on the bed rail. She said nothing. She offered no comfort, and I sobbed until I felt utterly drained and exhausted.

A brief pause after my tears had quieted, Mother said, "Well ... that's that."

I couldn't believe my ears. After nineteen years of marriage to Daddy, she brushed him off like a piece of lint on her shoulder. My grief flipped to rage. I grabbed the bedpan sitting by the nightstand and flung it at her.

"YOU FUCKING BITCH!" I screamed at the top of my lungs as the bedpan, unfortunately empty, passed by her head and clanged with metal force against the wall. "YOU FUCKING, SELF-SERVING, SELFISH, HORRID BITCH!" Then, I fled the room.

Outside the room, more nurses rushed to calm the situation, leaving their posts to investigate the matter.

"GET ME THE FUCK OUT OF HERE!" I screamed at one of them, and she led me quickly to the door. With angry determination, I marched to the elevator and frantically punched the button, not knowing or caring what Mother was saying, thinking, or doing. I only wanted out of that hospital, away from Mother. The elevator was too damn slow. I spotted the stair exit sign nearby and made a beeline for it. On the way down, my tears returned, mixed with my rage, and I found myself hitting the wall as I descended. At the bottom of the stairs, I marched straight for the lobby, threw open the door, and paced angrily through to the outside doors.

Earl was sitting in the lobby, waiting for me. I didn't even see him, but he saw me, as did everyone else sitting there when I flung the hall door open. I was neither quiet about it nor apologetic. Earl stood and followed me, "Lovella ... honey ... oh, my God!"

He followed me outside, where I didn't stop. I stepped with determination around to the side of the building, having no idea where I was going or what I would do.

Following closely on my heels, Earl shouted, "Lovella, please stop, honey."

"LEAVE ME THE FUCK ALONE!" I screamed.

He caught my sleeve. "Baby, please, please, please—please stop."

I swung around and began pounding on him with all my strength. "LET ME GO!" I screeched. "GODDAMN YOU! LET ME GO!"

In all the violence, he managed to put his arms around me and pull me to him, close to his chest, where I couldn't hit him anymore. "Shhhhh, shhhhhh, shhhhh," he whispered, holding me tight to his chest.

Soon, my struggle stopped, and the sobbing started again. I stood whimpering into his chest while he held me. When the crying finally subsided, he led me to a nearby bench, and we sat down. There, he held my hand and was silent.

Finally, I said, "I'm sorry. "I didn't mean to attack you like that. I know you were only trying to help.

"At that moment," he said, "the only thing you knew was hurt … it's okay."

"No, it's not okay," I said. "I shouldn't have hit you."

"Believe me, honey," he replied. "It's okay. I knew this was going to be hard for you."

"It's not just Daddy dying." I looked up at him finally and saw the tenderness in his eyes. "I feel guilty that I wasn't here, and it's her! I fucking hate her with every ounce of my being!"

"I know you and your mom have had a hard time getting along," he pleaded, "but surely you don't hate her."

"Do you know what she said after Daddy passed?" I questioned, without waiting for an answer. "She said, '*Well, that's that,*' like she had thrown out the trash. Jesus Christ! I do fucking hate her!"

"Oh, God," he sighed. "She doesn't have a clue, does she?"

"A clue about what?" I snapped, "That she is a fucking cunt?"

"She doesn't know how to be human," he replied. "She is so caught up in herself and her anguish that she can't seem to understand that other people have feelings."

It was a little comforting to know that he had this insight. I turned and stared across the parking lot, squinting my eyes at sunlight glistening off windshields.

"Or maybe she is just an evil, mean-spirited bitch." I said, finally.

"Now, I understand," he said after a long silence.

"Understand what?" I queried, turning back to him.

After a slow sigh, he replied to my question.

"Do you remember that first time you took me to visit your family over Thanksgiving, and your father and I ended up in so many huddled conversations?"

"Yeah, I figured the two of you must have just hit it off, but it was a little strange."

"Well, there was more to it than that," Earl said. "Your dad must have known that he was going to die because he insisted on telling me your story. He made me promise that I wouldn't tell you till after he had passed. I didn't think you and I had dated long enough for him to assume we would still be together, but he said he thought we were in love and wanted to tell me this. I probably should have told you on the way back before we got here."

"What? What the fuck?" I exclaimed. "Is there some fucking mystery that Daddy kept from me?"

"More a secret that the whole family kept from you," Earl replied.

"So, they kept the Goddamned secret from me but told my *boyfriend?*" I ejected angrily. "Doesn't that just put the fucking cherry on this shit parfait?"

"Well, they didn't tell your boyfriend. Your dad did. He told me he was worried about what might happen between you and your mom when he passed, and he wanted to make sure you knew the truth, not only about you but about your mom. He said he was worried about both of you and wasn't sure you would get the whole truth from your mother."

"So, what's new? I never get the truth from that bitch! Well … so, why the fuck didn't he tell me instead of telling someone who, for all he knew, was going to be an ex-fling in less than a year?"

"He was convinced that you and I would be more than a fling. He said he could read you and knew we were falling in love. He said he had always been under a lot of pressure from your mom and her family not to tell you,"

After a glance away, Earl continued. " He wasn't sure how you would react, and he knew you wouldn't react well if your mother told you. I guess he was a bit of a chicken because he didn't want you to be upset with him."

"Oh, so now that he's dead, I can't yell at him for the big, fucking, family secret!" I rolled my eyes and looked away. "Give me a fucking break!" I turned back to him. "I know Daddy is not my genetic father if that's what you are getting at. Mother made sure that I knew that in the room up there—*while he was dying!* She made sure to torture me with that at the very moment I was losing Daddy—yet another reason, on the long list of reasons, why I fucking hate her! I didn't believe her, but is that what you are talking about?

"Damn! I should have told you before we got here!" he confessed. "Actually, there is more to it than that."

"I also know my biological father is supposed to be Carl Whitmire, assuming Mother was not making that up. Who can tell when the bitch is telling the truth and when she isn't? Carl Whitmire is our family doctor, for Christ's sake! That's so fucking outlandish it can't be true."

I got up and began pacing. "Who the fuck cares?" Then, I started nervously talking to myself. "Where is my Goddamn purse? I need a cigarette. FUCK! I left it up in the room. Damn it!"

Earl stood and reached into his shirt pocket. He pulled out a battered pack of cigarettes that I had smashed in his pocket when I was hitting him. "I thought you might need these," he said and fished in his pants pocket for a lighter. The first couple of cigarettes he pulled out were mutilated beyond any reasonable use, but he finally pulled one out that wasn't too damaged to smoke. He put it to his lips, lit it, and handed it to me. I drew a long drag and let it out slowly.

Earl continued, "I was saying there's more to it than that. Yes, your Daddy told me that he was not your biological father. He told me your mom dated your real father …"

"Don't say, '*real father,*'" I cut in. "The man who just died was my real father!

"Okay, you're right," he continued. "John Fuchs was your real father. He told me your mom was dating the guy who got her pregnant before they married. He didn't say who it was if he knew."

"What the fuck?" I responded with shock. "So, it's true?"

"Yeah, that's really weird," Earl continued. "Your daddy said this guy got your mom pregnant when she was eighteen. She thought she loved him, but he saw her more as a fling. He said that guy's family was well-to-do and didn't want him to marry someone they considered beneath him."

"That's so fucking funny," I said. "She's always had the delusion that she's better than everybody else, but she wasn't good enough for their hoity-toity family."

"Your dad said that your mom had always wanted to move up in the world," Earl informed. "She thought she could do it by marrying into money."

"No shit!" I replied. "She has pushed that shit on me my whole life."

Earl went on, "Maybe she thought that getting pregnant would force your birth father to marry her. It had the opposite effect. He refused to claim you as his child and told your mother that if she tried to make this public, he would accuse her of sleeping around, and there would be no way to prove he was the birth father. His parents backed him up on this and told her the same thing. Your mom's family didn't want to fight it, and it looked like it would be a public embarrassment. So, there she was, a person who considered herself a good Christian girl trapped in a problem she couldn't escape. Your daddy told me he had always had a crush on your mom. He had tried to get her to go out with him many times, and she would have nothing romantic to do with him. Of course, you know their families knew each other, and they grew up together. She had not been opposed to cutting up with him, teasing him a little, but she wouldn't date him. When the pregnancy happened, she told him about it after he questioned her that something seemed different about her. She confessed that she was worried her reputation would be tarnished if she had a baby out of wedlock. That's when he asked her to marry him. He said he had been in love with her for as long as he could remember. He thought she was what he had always wanted and said he would always love her. I don't know if your mom loved him or not. Maybe she just wanted to protect her reputation. He wanted me to ask you to remember that she is your mother, and despite her faults, she has many fine qualities that deserve your respect. He said that he knew you would be upset, and he wanted you to find a way to forgive her."

"Fuck!" I exclaimed and paced a few feet away from him. "Lectured from the grave!"

Earl stood nearby and let me pace. "I know, I know," he said. "I'm just trying to tell you what your dad wanted me to say. I hope I'm remembering it all correctly. He wanted you to know what happened and that he loved you even if he wasn't your genetic father."

"John Fuchs is my *REAL* father!" I exclaimed, "Not some Goddamned fuck 'em and leave 'em prick! Just because some asshole ejaculated doesn't make him a father!"

Earl sighed. "I agree," he said." May I continue?"

I nodded to him and puffed on my cigarette.

"Your dad told me that, when you were born, he could never have loved you more, even if you had been his own flesh, and that he was happy he got to be your Daddy. He said that your mother adored you, as well. She wanted your love terribly but resented that she could not marry your birth father. Something happened to her after you were born. She lost her mind, depression, psychosis, or something. Your dad said she took you around the neighborhood, showing you off, and when people would tell her what a beautiful baby you were, she would tell them they could have you if they wanted. Your daddy said she just lost it and couldn't function. She had a breakdown and spent some time in a mental hospital after someone finally called the police. It happens to some women after childbirth that they get depressed, or crazy, or something. Anyway, while she was away, your dad and grandparents cared for you, mostly your dad. I think he would leave you with your grandparents when he went to work and then pick you up and take you home after work. You were around him much more than your mom when you were little. I guess she was hospitalized several times before you were maybe three or four years old. He said a couple of times, your mom tried to kill herself. You bonded with your dad, and when she came out of the hospital, she was angry and couldn't understand that you would cling to him instead of her. He said he didn't think she would be honest with you about her history of mental problems, but he wanted you to know, and he wanted you to have some sympathy for her."

"Oh, jeez!" I exclaimed. "I do remember when I was maybe four or five years old that it seemed like it was just me and Daddy, and I don't remember Mother being around. I never even thought that was strange till now. She was away a few times after I got a little older, around the first grade. Daddy told me she was visiting relatives in Kentucky, but Christ! She tried to kill herself? That's just fucking bizarre!"

I snuffed out the cigarette and asked him for another one. We sat down together on the bench, and Earl continued the story.

"So, apparently, when you bonded with your dad and didn't have much to do with your mom, she just turned off and wouldn't try. She would care for you but never did the loving things that mothers do with their babies. I guess, maybe a little after you started school, she stopped having to go to the mental hospital, and she was always home after that, but the damage was done. She resented that you were close to a man who wasn't your biological father and not close to her, but then, she distanced herself from you. Your dad thought it was his fault you never got along with your mom."

"It was *her* fucking fault we never got along," I exclaimed. "She's a bitch! Jesus! And I'm supposed to have sympathy for her after she went around the neighborhood trying to give me away? Don't you think we might have had at least a slightly better relationship if she had tried, just a little? So, what is this shit about taking me to Whitmire as my doctor? If she was telling the truth that he got her pregnant, why did she take me to him? So, now, she says he was my fuck father, but she took me to him as my doctor? How fucked up is that? Was she trying to shove me in his face so he might acknowledge me? If it's true, he just went along with it and pretended like I was any other kid to be treated in his clinic. Either he pretended he wasn't my fuck father, or she was just making all this shit up! I mean, it's too fucking bizarre to believe!"

Earl took my hand. "Your dad wanted you to try to have some understanding and compassion for your mom. He said you would understand if you'll give her a chance, maybe understand that she has mental problems."

"Oh, my fucking God!" I snapped, tamping my cigarette out on the edge of the bench. "Give her a chance for what? A chance to be the fucking nut job that she is?"

"I'm just repeating what he told me," Earl replied.

"Is that it? Give her a chance?" I looked at him, puzzled and angry.

"I don't remember anything else right now," he said. "I'll try to remember if there was something else. He told me a lot." Earl placed his large, warm hand over mine. "You want to go see if we can find your mom?"

"Hell, no! I don't," I replied. "Honestly, I don't give a shit if I never see her again. What she did up there, in that hospital room, was cold and heartless to me and Daddy. She didn't care that he was dying, and she didn't care that I was grieving. '*That's that*,' she said—like she had just thrown out the garbage!"

"Maybe she didn't know what to say," Earl empathized. "She's your mother. Doesn't she, at least, deserve a chance to explain herself?"

"You want me to fucking ask her what she meant by that?" I snarled. "I know what she meant by that. I know exactly what she meant. She meant that she wouldn't have to put up with Daddy's drinking anymore. She meant she wouldn't have to try to control him constantly. She meant that her self-proclaimed chore is over. Now, she can devote more energy to trying to control me and make me into the perfect little daughter she thinks she deserves!"

"Lovella, there is going to be a lot going on over the next week or so," he pleaded. "Your family will be grieving. Your Grandmother Fuchs is going to be dealing with having a child preceding her in death. Surely, Grandma and Grandpa Donner will have some grief for the son-in-law they had for nineteen years. Don't you think you could be civil to your mom for at least a little while?"

"You mean overlook her bullshit, pretend like it doesn't matter, that it doesn't hurt?"

"I guess you could put it that way," Earl reasoned. "I just don't think that your father wanted his funeral to be a fight."

Tears welled in my eyes when I saw Mother in the distance, standing in front of the hospital, alone. Earl turned to see what I was looking at. He turned back to me and took my hand. "Come on," he said, "Let's talk to your mom."

Although I wanted to resist, run away, or maybe even attack her, I went with him. We walked around the building to the front, where Mother was standing. As we approached, Mother looked up from nervously fingering at her purse.

"Hello, Earl," she said softly and sternly, without acknowledging me. She handed my purse to him and continued to finger around the straps of her purse.

"Hello, Mrs. Fuchs," he said, "I'm sorry about your loss."

He never turned loose of my hand. He gripped it tightly but gently, holding my purse in his other hand.

"Thank you," Mother responded. "He is being taken to Nash Funeral Home." She dug into her purse, pulled out the car keys, and held them at arm's length toward Earl. "Do you mind driving me there? I don't feel up to driving."

"I would be happy to drive you," Earl said. "Do you mind if Lovella comes along?"

Mother responded with a well-practiced, flat demeanor while looking away from me. "Of course, I don't mind if Lovella comes along. She is my daughter."

Earl released my hand to take the keys and handed my purse to me.

Mother turned and walked across the parking lot toward her car, never looking back, expecting, correctly, that we would follow.

CHAPTER 23

Old Endings and New Beginnings

Sunlight glistened off the clean, polished enamel of the black hearse parked off the curb at the bottom steps of Mother's church. Long ago, Daddy stopped attending church, but on his last day above ground, he finally attended church again with Mother. I suppose it was only fitting that his funeral should be where Mother wanted and how she wanted. He would not have cared, really, and since she had controlled him in life, why not in death? My part in the decisions was to pick the suit and tie that Mother insisted he wear and insisted I pick, even though he hated wearing a suit and tie. I comforted myself that, this time, the tie wouldn't choke him. She could barely ever get him to wear a suit in life, but in death, she would finally dress him the way she always thought he should have been dressed. He was never the man she wanted, but at least in death, she could make him look that way. It would have been more befitting of Daddy's style if he had been buried in a pair of khakis and a flannel shirt with his extra wide cowboy belt buckle, but he would have given in to what she demanded anyway, so why not a suit? I only wanted it over.

To my surprise, Earl's parents had come down for the funeral and booked a hotel room in New Bethlehem. At first, I thought it might have been beneath them to stay at a little ramshackle hotel, but then I recalled that they didn't start rich and had probably stayed in such accommodations before.

Earl and his father were civil to each other despite their conflict back in May. There was no mention of the argument. They treated each other as though it had never happened. I don't know if I could have done that. I would have had to have some words in, some dig to let the opposing party know that I remembered the injustice of being mistreated. I guess in that way, I was way too much like Mother.

All met on a Saturday afternoon for the funeral. Several of Daddy's friends from the factory were there with their wives. I watched them and wondered if their wives had been as displeased with their Friday night drinking as Mother had been with Daddy, but then they might not have taken it as far as Daddy did.

Mother and I stood in the church's foyer, greeting people as they came in and expressed condolences. I would rather have had a hand chopped off than go through that, but Mother insisted on it, like other episodes of pomp and circumstance befitting her illusions of affluence. Earl stood nearby, never letting me out of sight.

I gleamed a bit when I saw Gretta and her parents ascending the steps. Gretta's mom had Derrick, who was almost a year old, straddling one hip. Her parents were more like an aunt and uncle to me. They had known me, practically raised me, since I was seven years old. I went to them, in the middle of the foyer, and held out two hands to Gretta. We touched hands and then hugged. "Oh my God, I've missed you," she said.

I hugged her mom and the baby, then touched Derrick on his little leg and said, "How's my little namesake?"

He buried his head in Mrs. Tannenbaum's shoulder as if to say, "I don't know this strange person, and I'm not going to talk to her."

"Oh, he is wonderful!" exclaimed Gretta. "He is the sweetest, funniest boy."

"How's Tommy?" I questioned with concern. I knew that Gretta had moved home with her parents after Tommy was deployed to Vietnam. She had called me months earlier, before I left for San Francisco, tearfully exclaiming that he had been sent to combat duty.

Her Monalisa smile appeared to be an attempt to hide the worry on her face. "Oh, last we heard, he was, maybe, in someplace called Gia Binh. I don't know. We get bits and pieces, a letter once in a while. I know he is not telling me what's really going on. I know he sugarcoats everything. I just … I pray a lot."

I squeezed her hand and hugged her. What else could I do?

I would have preferred to stay there talking to them, but I heard Mother clear her throat rather loudly and received the message that I was to cut off this conversation and return to her side. I looked over my shoulder to find her staring at me with stern displeasure.

"Maybe I can talk to you later," I said, returning to Mother's side. Gretta gave Mother a brief salutation and went into the sanctuary with her parents.

After having shaken the hand of an obscure stranger who was giving me some rehearsed bullshit about how sorry he was for my loss, I happened to look over and see Grandmother Fuchs and Uncle Raymond coming up the front steps. She had always been thin, but she seemed even thinner. She wore a black dress with black lace around the hem and an overlay around her shoulders. Her thin white hair was pulled back into a French bun, and she wore a little hat that would have looked a bit like a nursing cap except that it was black and covered with black lace. I had not seen Grandmother Fuchs for a long time since she moved to Philadelphia to live with my Uncle Raymond.

Uncle Raymond was a pudgy, short, little man with a round belly that sat over his belt like a sack of beans. Like Daddy, he was bald. He had thick black glasses that saddled his nose, and despite this being a funeral, he wore a tan suit with white shoes. He had never married and had taken care of his mother, off and on, since the middle years of my youth after Grandfather Fuchs passed away. He moved to Philadelphia for a job about three or four years before I graduated high school, and when Grandmother Fuchs couldn't handle living alone anymore, she followed him.

Uncle Raymond held Grandmother Fuchs by one arm while they carefully proceeded up the steps. As I watched them approach, I thought about being her only grandchild. She must have known that I was not her blood kin. Still, like Daddy, she always treated me with the utmost love and kindness.

When they entered the foyer, Grandmother Fuchs saw me and ambled across to greet me. She reached up, placed one hand behind my head, and pulled me forward to kiss me on the forehead. "Oh, my dear!" she said in a trembling little voice. "It is so good to see you. I have missed you very much. I only wish I could have seen you under better circumstances."

She spoke not a word about her own loss but looked me straight in the eye and said, "How are you doing with this?"

I felt the tears well in my eyes, and I thought about how much love she had given me, knowing all along that I must not have been her blood kin and having a son who preceded her into the grave. I knew that I could not be the only one grieving. I sucked in my breath and tried to be strong. "I'm fine, Grandmother Doreen," I replied. "How are you?"

"Well, it's not very easy to lose your child at any age," she said, smiling sweetly with a hint of a tear. "But I keep myself reminded that my John is in God's hands now." Then, as she had always been prone to do, she quoted scripture: "'Weeping may stay for the night, but rejoicing comes in the morning' Psalms 30:5."

I noticed Uncle Raymond standing beside me. He was effeminate and walked with a lift and lightness, as though his girth were filled more with air than weight.

"Hello, Lovella," he complimented through his puckered little mouth. "My—my! You get prettier every day."

Had the timing and generational circumstances been different, I wondered, *Would Uncle Raymond have been strolling down the streets of San Francisco with pink hoop earrings and wearing colorful flared pants?* I caught my drifting mind and brought it back to the moment. "Thank you, Uncle Raymond," I responded. "It is so nice to finally be grown up."

I caught a glimpse of Mother rolling her eyes at that statement. Then, a plastic smile crossed her face as she reached out a black-gloved hand to Grandmother Fuchs and said, "Oh, Doreen ... we've lost our boy."

Emotional nausea filled me like a wave, and I realized that there was no end to her hypocrisy. I wanted to throw another bedpan at her and would have thrown anything within my reach had it not been for my determination that I was going to address Daddy's funeral with dignity.

Grandmother Fuchs seemed to realize the truth. I caught a curious little smirk as she heard Mother speak. She glanced over at me and back at Mother, giving her a stern but gentle look. "And Lovella has lost the one she loved the most," said Grandmother Fuchs. The dig aimed, obviously, at Mother.

"Bless us all," Mother said, turning loose of Grandmother Fuchs's hand with a quick snap.

Raymond escorted Grandmother Doreen into the church's main hall, and they sat at the front in the area that had been cordoned off for family.

Eventually, no more people were coming up the steps. Mother, Earl, and I walked up the center aisle and sat next to Grandmother and Grandfather Donner, who were also seated in the family section. Earl sat on one side of me, and Mother sat between Grandmother Donner and me. I could still smell breakfast bacon reeking off Grandmother Donner and imagined that she had not even bothered to change her clothes, much less shower for the occasion.

Daddy's casket sat at the front center of the sanctuary. The fake copper lining shimmered in the overhead lights, and tufted cream-colored satin lined the top half of the open lid. Looking on, I couldn't help thinking how isolated it seemed from everything and everyone else. We all sat together, and Daddy lay there alone. He had always been alone in many ways, even in his marriage. He lived in the same house as Mother; he loved and adored her but could never be close to her. She would never allow it.

At that time, the church had yet another minister. I didn't pay any attention to him. He seemed to me to be like any average-looking man, although I'm sure Mother thought he was something special. She thought any man with authority, expertise, or prosperity was special, especially the clergy.

The service was conducted as most funeral services are. The congregation sang songs, and Mother had picked a lady from the church who sang a somewhat comical operatic version of "Nearer to Thee."

After all the hoopla and passing by the casket where Daddy lay wholly separated from us and life, we crowded into cars for the processional to the cemetery, where there was even more hoopla by the gravesite. When we arrived, I was escorted to the gravesite by some funeral home employee, as though I would fall on my ass if he didn't have his hand on my elbow. Earl walked behind me. Mother was also escorted and took the opportunity to give the occasion her usual flare of high drama. With her black glove, she pulled a tiny white hanky to her eye, where she pretended to have a tear.

We were seated in a row beneath a tent. Before us was a hole in the ground for Daddy's final rest, and above it, I noticed a double tombstone already carved with Daddy's dates of birth and death on one side and Mother's date of birth with a blank for the date of death on the other. I couldn't believe my eyes. Mother had to have commissioned that tombstone long before the funeral to have it already standing there. There must have been a rush to carve Daddy's date of death into the stone before the funeral. It was evident that Mother was going to play this ruse right up to the point of her own death. She had apparently not considered that she was still young enough to remarry or what she would do if she came across a potential second husband. She had planned to lay down beside Daddy in death with the hope, I suppose, that everyone living would somehow be convinced that she actually did love him. I sat there praying that the soap opera would be over quickly so I could escape. There was no way that it could possibly be quick enough.

Pallbearers carried Daddy's casket to the gravesite and set it on the apparatus designed to lower it into the grave. Then, the minister gave a few more parting words. "Loving Father and husband blah-blah-blah—A good man who would be sorely missed blah-blah-blah—Final resting place in the gentle, loving arms of our Heavenly Father—etc."

I wanted so desperately to scream, "Shut the fuck up!" I wanted to grab Mother's damn beehive and fling her into the grave. I wanted to run screaming somewhere, anywhere. I wanted a cigarette, a drink, some pot, acid—or arsenic, for that matter. The last thing I ever wanted was to be there going through that theatrical production.

As the casket was lowered into the grave, the minister decided there needed to be one last prayer. I couldn't take it anymore. I didn't wait for the prayer to finish. I stood up and marched with rapid determination back toward Earl's flowery pink van, which he had parked on the street at the edge of the cemetery. In the middle of the prayer, I heard Mother call after me with a loud whisper, "Lovella! Sit down!" I wanted to turn around and scream, "Fuck you! You two-faced, hypocritical cunt!" But I said nothing. I kept marching across the cemetery, stopping at one point to pull off those damned high heels and fling them each in different directions.

Earl followed me silently, saying nothing, making no effort to stop me. When I reached the van, I tried to open the side door, and when it wouldn't budge, I pounded the van with my fists and leaned my head against it, sobbing. Then, I felt a big, gentle hand on my shoulder. I turned, and Earl pulled me to him. I cried in his arms, and he held me closely, stroking my hair but saying nothing. He didn't try to quiet me. He only held me and let me cry. When, at last, I had cried enough, I pulled back and looked up at him. "I want to go home," I said.

"Sure, that's fine, Honey." "Your Mother will probably be back there shortly, too."

"No, I don't mean that," I exclaimed. I had been thinking of our apartment back at State College. It had become home to me. It was more of a home to me than anything the bitch had ever provided. However, at that moment, I had forgotten that it was gone. I took a flabbergasted breath. "I'm sorry," I said. "I was talking about the apartment back at State College. I guess I forgot that we don't have it anymore."

"Don't you want to go back to your home and spend some time with your mom and grandparents before we think about what's next?"

"No! I don't want to be around her any more than I absolutely have to, and that's not my home anymore. SHE NEVER GAVE ME A REAL HOME!" After snapping at him, I felt guilty, softened my tone, and gazed up at him. "I guess we don't know what's next, do we?"

I caught a glimpse of Gretta walking up to us. She had followed me from the tent, leaving her parents to care for the baby.

"Honey, are you all right?" she asked, on her approach.

I didn't know if I was all right. When she was close enough, I reached out and took her hand.

"I'm fine," I said, lying about that. "I had just taken all the bullshit I could stand in one day. I just had to get away from it."

"Listen," she said, glancing back at her mother, who had come and stood at a distance with the baby. "Why don't you guys come by our house for a little while, take a load off, get away from family, and just give yourselves some time to chill?"

"Oh, God! That sounds wonderful!" I exclaimed. "Earl, do you mind?" I looked back at him and questioned, even though I knew it would be okay with him.

"Sure, no problem," he said.

"Wonderful," Gretta continued. "You guys can meet us there in twenty or thirty minutes, okay?"

I turned back to Earl and looked up at him longingly. "Thank you." I sighed.

"You want to get your shoes?" he inquired, glancing across the cemetery.

"Fuck the shoes!" I replied. "Let's go."

"I'll go tell my mom and dad that I'll stop by to see them later at the hotel," he said. "I'll be right back."

Earl crossed the lawn to meet his parents. By this time, the ceremonies had been completed, and everyone was crossing back toward the parking area. Earl spoke briefly to his parents, then trotted back across the lawn to me.

"Get in," he said, opening the front door of the van for me.

Soon, we were gone.

Tommy and Gretta had a modest but lovely little house. We passed it on the way to the Tannenbaum home. The house was a small, two-bedroom post-war cracker box painted light blue with white trim. On either side of the steps, the postage stamp lawn had a few flowers left from summer, but most had begun to brown, either from the heat, neglect, or anticipation of winter.

We pulled up to the curb in front of the Tannenbaum house, and in short order, they arrived. Gretta took Derrick while her dad unlocked the front door. The baby's toys were scattered here and there on their living room floor. Having awakened from his nap, Derrick was squirming to be let loose. Gretta sat him on the floor, sat beside him, and began to entertain him with a tiny stuffed giraffe.

"Let me get you some tea," Mrs. Tannenbaum said, departing for the kitchen.

Mr. Tannenbaum motioned to the couch, inviting us to sit. He headed toward a side chair and asked, "Can you believe this heat?"

"Yeah," I replied, "I thought I was going to suffocate before that crap was over."

Mrs. Tannenbaum returned shortly with a serving tray in hand. We each took a glass of tea and began to sip.

"Damn, I'm parched," I said. "Thank you."

"Jesus, honey," Gretta released and then moved to a chair near me. "Are you sure you're all right?" She reached over with a warm smile and touched my hand.

"Oh, you mean besides the fact that I would like to slit my mother's throat and throw her in that grave, as well?" I replied. "Other than that, I guess I'm okay."

I had not had a chance to talk to Gretta and fill her in on all that had happened.

"Well, I know you hate her, but I hope you don't hate her that much," she pleaded.

"Oh, it's fun to imagine," I smirked. "But I don't look good in shackles. There are so many other flattering accessories."

"Your mother told me a few weeks ago that you were spending the summer in San Francisco," Gretta ran her finger around the rim of her glass. "I hope you had a nice time."

I looked at Earl, who gave me a puzzled look, then smiled.

"I guess you could say we had an *interesting* time," I said. "I wish I had known that Daddy was so sick, though. I probably never would have gone. Mother tried to tell me he was sick before I left, but he denied it, and I didn't believe her. Then, I was so pissed at her for insisting that she wouldn't let me go that I didn't call her all summer."

"You got back before your daddy passed, though—right?" There was a hesitation in her voice. I think she understood the guilt that I was feeling.

"Just barely," I continued, feeling the tears welling up a little. "Daddy died only a few minutes after we got there. Earl dropped me off directly at the hospital doors." My voice trembled. "I might as well have not gotten there before he died. There was nothing left of him. He couldn't respond, and I doubt he knew I was there." I wiped a tear from my cheek.

"Oh, honey," she soothed. "You know your daddy knew you were there. The two of you were too close for him not to feel your presence."

"Mother was horrible!" I continued. "She took the opportunity to tell me that Daddy was not my birth father when he hadn't passed yet. How fucked up is that?"

Immediately, I realized that I had just used profanity in front of her parents and looked up, embarrassed. "I'm sorry for my language," I said, glancing back and forth between Mr. & Mrs. Tannenbaum.

"Sweetheart," Mrs. Tannenbaum smiled lovingly. "Profanity is the language of the heart. Sometimes, it is the only way to express what is needed."

My tears began to flow openly.

"Oh my God!" Gretta exclaimed. "She told you that your daddy isn't your real father?" She motioned to her mom, who left the room to return in a moment with a damp washcloth. The cool cloth felt good against my face. Earl wrapped a comforting arm around me, and everyone let me grieve. Thank God the baby was playing with one of his toys and didn't know what was happening.

I vented through my sobs. "Even if it is true, why would she even tell me that, especially as Daddy was lying there, taking his last breaths? And Daddy told Earl instead of telling me! Earl, tell them." I nudged him on the leg.

Earl hesitantly began to tell them what he had said to me outside the hospital. "Ahm, Lovella's dad spoke to me at Thanksgiving and told me about this. Before he told me anything, he made me promise not to tell Lovella till after he was gone. He had to have known he was dying, even then, but I don't think he wanted Lovella to know he was dying. I think I was supposed to have told her before her mother did, but who would have thought her mother would tell her when her dad was dying? He didn't want her mother to tell her this, but he wanted her to know the truth once he was gone. He wanted to make sure she knew he loved her and was happy he got to be her father. I guess I messed up by not telling Lovella first."

"You didn't know," I exclaimed, defending him, "and he made you promise to wait till after he died. He had to have known he was going to die, even back at Thanksgiving." I turned back to Gretta, "And how fucked up is it that Daddy pulls Earl aside to tell him this stuff the first damn time they met, and he never told me?" The anger moved back to grief, and I wailed, "He could have told me himself." Then, the grief switched back to anger. "GODDAMN IT! HE COULD HAVE TOLD ME HIMSELF!" I slammed my fist against my leg.

Immediately, Derrick burst into tears, frightened by my display. My anger switched just as quickly to compassion. "Oh, no, poor baby," I pleaded, getting up and stepping toward him to comfort him. This only made him wail louder, and Gretta rushed to pick him up.

"It's all right ... it's all right, sweetheart," she cooed, gently bouncing him on her hip.

Compassion switched to guilt, and the tears returned. "I'm sorry," I pleaded. "I'm so sorry. I didn't mean to scare him."

Gretta turned to comfort me. "Honey, don't worry. Babies get scared. Things happen. Sit down."

She quickly glanced at Mr. Tannenbaum and said, "Daddy, would you take the baby to the bedroom for a while?"

I felt Earl's warm hand move to rest on my shoulder. Mr. Tannenbaum quietly took the baby from her arms and went toward the back of the house. Earl and I sat back down.

"I'm sorry," I cried.

"Honey, honey … listen." Gretta sat close enough to pat my knee. "Derrick is fine. He just got a little scared. It happens. Don't worry about it."

"Losing Daddy is bad enough," I sobbed. "But then that fucking evil bitch has to lay this shit on me, and then she fucking expects me to come to the funeral and pretend like everything is just peachy! I tried … I tried to hold it together for her stupid pomp and circumstance!"

"Thank God you don't have to hold it together now," Gretta soothed. "You just let it out, honey. I want to hear everything you have to say."

I looked up at her, astounded by her understanding. "You are the best friend anyone could ever have," I sobbed.

She smiled and said, "I'd better be a good friend. You might beat me up. Besides, you taught me how to cuss."

I partially smiled. "Thank you," I said. "Thank you for giving me a place to let go."

"I suspect letting go won't be for a while," she replied. "I'm just giving you a place to rest. Speaking of which, where are you staying?"

I glanced at Earl. "I don't know. Earl's parents got a hotel room and paid for an extra room for him. As much as it killed me to do it, I spent the last few days, since Daddy died, with the bitch from hell so that we could make *funeral plans*." I slurred the last two words. "I can't go back there. I just can't. It took everything I had to tolerate her bullshit for the last couple of nights. I never want to see her again, but I don't have any other place to go. Earl's father stopped paying for the apartment. I haven't even thought about college. I should probably be registered by now if it's not too late.

I hope it's not too late. I guess I could move back into the dorm, but I don't know where that leaves us." I placed a hand on Earl's leg.

"We'll figure something out," Earl said, giving a quick sideways hug.

"Well, you are welcome to stay here for the night," Gretta invited as she glanced back at her mom for reassurance. "We could sleep together just like when we were kids."

"That reminds me," Earl said. "I told the parents I would call them at the hotel. Do you mind if I borrow your phone?"

"No problem," Gretta said. "It's in the kitchen, mounted on the wall by the refrigerator." She pointed, and Earl followed the direction of her finger.

When Earl left the room, Gretta turned back to me and said, "Lovella, I'm more worried about how your heart is than where you are going to stay. I know all this had to have thrown you for a loop."

"What do they say about *that which doesn't kill us?*" I asked.

"It makes us stronger," she answered.

"It leaves scars," I smirked.

"Honey, I have no doubt you will have scars from this," she affirmed. "If anything, that's what I'm apprehensive about."

"I'll be fine," I went on. "Nothing that some alcohol and a few cigarettes won't fix. Jeez, can you believe I haven't smoked through all this? It's like, of all the things that have happened and all the hurt I've felt for the last week, I get upset and think I want a cigarette. Then, I take a few puffs, and I'm disgusted. I think to myself, '*That's not going to help.*' I'm almost as mad at cigarettes as I am at Mother. I get angry when I try to smoke. Then, when I put it out, I'm mad, trying to smash it into the ashtray like it is something I want to hurt."

"Well, that's a reaction I never thought I would ever see," Gretta responded. "Maybe it's a good thing."

Earl returned from the kitchen. "Lovella, my parents also offered you a room. They don't want us in the same room because we aren't married, but they said they would happily get you a room at their hotel. We can probably figure out something else over the next few days. They are returning to Bradford Woods tomorrow but will happily pay for a couple of days for us to stay."

"That's very sweet of them," I said. "Gretta, I hope I won't hurt your feelings if I take Earl's parents up on their offer." I had no sympathy for the fact that Mother would probably be walking back into the house alone. Still, she would have no reason to put on a show if she was alone, and I could see her sitting back, reveling in her freedom, having a glass of sherry and dragging on a cigarette, like Joan Crawford in some film noir.

"Oh, hell no, honey," Gretta exclaimed. "A hotel bed has got to be more comfortable, and we might not fit in my bed like we did when we were kids. I would offer you to stay at our house, but all the utilities are shut off while I stay with Mom and Dad."

Earl continued standing. "Ah, I need to go have a long talk with my parents before they go back tomorrow. Lovella, you can stay here, and I'll come back this evening to pick you up."

"Oh, that would be great!" Gretta interjected.

"That would be wonderful," I parroted. "What time would you be back to pick me up?"

"I don't know how much crow I'm going to have to eat for Dad," Earl commented. "Does nine or nine-thirty sound all right to you?"

Gretta and I glanced at each other and simultaneously said, "That's fine." She laughed at our synchronicity and reached out to pat my arm.

"I'll walk you to the van," I said, rising from my seat.

We walked out the door and down the walk to the curb. Earl turned and hugged me. "Are you going to be okay?" he questioned, continuing the lingering hug.

"I'll be fine," I replied, feeling warm and comfortable against his chest. "It's just that there's a lot to figure out now. I wasted the summer, not paying any attention to going back to school, and now, I don't even know if it is too late to register for fall classes. I don't have much time to waste on that. I mean, I've got to get with it first thing Monday and call the university. If I can't go back to school, I don't know what I will do. I couldn't stand staying here or living with Mother. I might have to see if I can find a job and get an apartment somewhere."

He sighed and said, "We'll see." He held me at arms-length and looked at me. "Right now, you need to go back in there and have a much overdue visit with Gretta. I'm in the same pickle where school is concerned, but I'll bet Dad can pull some strings to get me in, even if they have closed registration. He might be able to pull some strings for you, too. That's why

I'm going to talk to him. I'm going to have to eat crow, but I need to finish college, and if that means kissing the old man's ass, I guess I'll have to go back to kissing ass. We can't roam the country and live in the van forever. Sooner or later, we have to come back down to earth." He nudged me toward the house and said, "Go on. We'll talk more when I return to pick you up tonight."

I nodded in agreement and turned to walk back into the house. I was almost up the front steps when he called, "Lovella."

I turned to see him coming around to the front of the van. He looked down at the pavement and then up at me. After a brief smile, he hesitated and asked, "Do you think we can put this thing with Screech behind us?"

I had been so caught up with Daddy dying that I hadn't paid much attention to anything else. "Do you?" I asked, stalling as I continued searching my soul for how I felt.

"I know I'm damn sure going to try," he said. "I want to try, Lovella. I want us to be us again."

"I'm not very good at predicting the future," I said, leaning against the porch post, "and I don't know if it's possible for us to be us again, but I'll try, too."

He looked around as though searching for something to say, but in the end, he said nothing. Finally, he gave me a brief wave, got in the van, and drove away.

I watched the van disappear up the street, asking myself, *Can I put it behind me? Can I pretend that this hasn't changed everything?*

CHAPTER 24

Love in the Modern World

Earl's father used his influence and got us both enrolled again for the fall semester. However, the deal was that we both had to live in the dorms, and Earl kept the van for his transportation. The Ferrari had been sold, and no such offer would be extended again. Earl had no problem with keeping the van. He had never felt the need for extravagance, anyway.

By early September, we were getting settled in for the next year of classes. The good news was that I didn't have Marcy as a roommate. My new roommate was a chubby, somewhat homely girl named Marlene Crenshaw from Dillsburg, a little town only two or three times bigger than New Bethlehem, which isn't saying much. Marlene was, much to my preference. She was a quiet girl, an English Literature major, who kept her nose in a book even more than I did. Her greatest delight was lying on her bed, nibbling snacks and reading. When she first met Earl and discovered that his family owned the Chum Snacks company, I thought she would fall to the floor and start kissing his feet. Earl took the hint, and every time he went home, he brought back cases of crackers, nuts, and chips for Marlene.

I didn't get to see Earl nearly as often as I wanted. I missed living with him. I missed domestic life, cooking for him, and cuddling on the couch after dinner to watch a sitcom on TV. Earl poured himself into his studies that last year. It suddenly seemed as though he had started wanting to please his father, but the truth was that he wanted that degree so he could prove himself on his own.

On a Friday night in October, a particularly cold day for October, we had made plans to go out for dinner. Earl was picking me up at five o'clock, and we had arrangements for me to wait for him by a tree on the northwest side of the girls' dorm parking lot. I had been out there about five minutes early, and Earl was late. I pulled my coat around my collar because the cold wind chewed at my ears. I was shuffling my feet, trying to keep warm, and watching the parking lot for the van when I was startled from behind.

"Boooh Haaaaa!"

I screamed and jumped as though a bomb had fallen. I lurched to take off running across the parking lot when a hand caught my arm and twirled me around. Earl was standing there, laughing.

"Earl Titwallow! You asshole!" I exclaimed. I swatted him playfully across the arms and chest.

It only took a moment for me to catch myself and realize what I saw. There was no long hair! He was as clean-shaven and well-groomed as any businessman. I stepped back, my mouth wide in amazement.

"What the hell!" I spouted. "Who are you, and what have you done with my hippie?"

He laughed more. "I wanted to surprise you."

"Well, you could have surprised me without giving me a heart attack!" I snapped back.

"Do you like it?" he asked as he smoothed one hand over his barren ear to the back of his head.

"Yeah, you look nice," I complimented. "But I never thought I would ever see you with short hair. What in the world made you want to cut your hair?"

"Come on, let's get warm," he said, taking my arm and leading me toward the van. It was parked behind us and was still running to keep the heater going.

As we walked, he began to explain. "I was just thinking, if I'm going to finish a business degree this year, maybe I need to look a little more business-like. If I want to get a job, I have to be realistic when I get out of school. If my dad and I get into it again, and I don't end up working for the company, I'll have to get a job, and who will hire me if I don't look the part?"

"It would be a shame if someone turned you down just because of how you look," I argued. "That wouldn't be fair. It doesn't have anything to do with your skills and your intellect. Appearance has nothing to do with talent."

"Hey, I agree with you," he responded. "But the truth is we live in a world full of prejudice, and until the time comes that people look beyond the cover of the book to the content, we have to play the role. I have to give them an appealing book cover to get them to consider the content. As Shakespeare said, 'All the world is a stage and the people merely players.'"

"What happened to physics?" I questioned.

He opened the passenger side door, and I got in, glad he left it running to keep the heater going. I felt immediately better to have the wind chill off my face.

"I still like physics," he said, closing the door. He went around to the driver's side and got in the van. "I like physics," he continued, "but ... I don't think I have the talent to land a physics job that could pay my bills. Besides, I would probably have to get a doctorate even to have a chance at a job in physics, and I would probably have to teach. I've got to be realistic, which may mean I do what Dad always wanted me to do."

"Do you think you can be happy doing that?" I pondered.

He put the van in gear and pulled away from the curb. "I think happiness is something I have to decide for myself. I don't think happiness will come from having things or doing things. I think happiness will come from the decision and practice of keeping a positive attitude, regardless of the job."

"Well, yeah. That makes sense, I guess." I fiddled in my purse for a cigarette, having gone back to smoking. "But don't you think that having things and doing things at least contributes to the process?"

"It is much easier to face your problems with money in your pocket than to face them without it, there is no doubt about that," he continued. "But ultimately, happiness comes down to accepting what you can't change and making the best of what you have."

"Damn! How profound," I teased. I pulled the cigarette and lighter from my purse. "Have you been studying the Buddha or something?"

"Well, more than anything, I've just been thinking about it all," he said, ignoring my jab. He looked occasionally, paying attention to traffic and watching for his turns. "I read a lot of philosophy and stuff, and maybe I pick up things here and there."

"You're changing," I said, lighting the cigarette and cracking the window slightly to let the smoke drift outside.

"Maybe I'm changing in some ways, staying the same in others," he acknowledged, turning onto a now very familiar street. "Maybe I'm finding out who I was all along."

"Well, I've heard you say this kind of shit before," I said. "It's just that, now, you seem to be using it to justify pleasing your dad instead of using it to justify why you need to be free from the conservative industrial complex and the war machine. It's interesting. You used to argue so vehemently for standing up against *The Man*."

"I still believe in my principles, Lovella," he rebutted, "but maybe I was incorrectly standing up for my principles. This summer and this whole involvement with Screech kind of scared me, in a way. I need to turn away from that a little. Just because I wear a suit and work for *The Man* doesn't mean I'm giving up who I am. Besides, maybe I can work to change things from the inside instead of trying to knock down the establishment's front door. Maybe I could succeed more at creating change if I sneak in the back door."

I looked at him momentarily, trying to take in what I was hearing. I didn't know how to respond. I finished the last drag of my cigarette as Earl pulled up to the curb in front of *The Finer Diner*. It was where we had our first dinner together, and it continued to be one of our favorite hangouts. We walked, hand in hand, down the sidewalk and into the diner, where we slid into a booth near the door.

"I've come to love this place," I said, taking off my coat and tossing it on the other end of the booth seat. "I think I like it more every time we come here."

"It grows on you," he affirmed, doing the same with his coat. "Good food and service usually will win you and keep you."

It was not long before our bleach-blond, gum-chewing waitress arrived with the menus. She took the drink orders and pranced away in her colorful uniform. We chit-chatted over the food choices for a while, then placed our orders when she returned with the drinks. It was always fun to hear the waitress shout the orders to the grill cook in their unique diner language.

We sat sipping our sodas, waiting for the order to arrive, and I began to muster my courage to tell him what I had been needing to say for several weeks. He was going on about some of the classes he was taking this year and how economics was similar in some ways to physics when I cut in on him.

"Earl," I said, nervously stirring my soda with the straw. "We need to talk."

"Is something wrong?" he questioned. "Something the matter with the family? Is your grandmother Fuchs okay?"

"Would you just shut up and let me talk!" I tersely replied.

"I'm sorry. Okay; what?" He reached his hand across the table and took hold of mine.

I sighed deeply, glanced out the window, and looked back at him. "I'm late."

"Late for what?" he pondered.

"I'm late! You idiot!" I snapped. "Think!"

He looked dumbfounded.

Finally, I spit it out, "I'm late for my period."

His face went pale, and emotions danced across his affect. "Oh," he said. "Okay … well … humph … I don't know what to say." He sat for a moment and pondered. "So, we'll be having a baby. You and I are going to have a baby. Cool! That's cool!" His eyes rolled around while he did the math in his head. "Wow! Ummm—due along about May or June?"

"Try early April," I said.

"April?" Confusion hit him. He thought I must have just missed my period and that I must be, maybe, about six weeks along.

I didn't wait for his comment: "Earl, I haven't had a period for two months. This is the third time I've missed one."

"Third time!" he snapped. "Why the hell didn't you tell me?"

"A lot of reasons," I defended. "I wanted to be sure that it wasn't some fluke that I just happened to miss a period, and maybe my cycle would start up again the next month, but … I was also scared."

"Scared?" he questioned. "Scared of what? You don't have to be scared of anything. You know I would take responsibility. You know I won't leave you hanging with anything like that. You know me better than that, Lovella. I'll take care of you and the baby."

"That's not what I'm scared of," I returned.

The waitress brought our food, and we began preparing ourselves to eat, moving the utensils around and placing our napkins.

"Earl, do the math," I continued after the brief interruption. "You know when I got pregnant. It had to have been the end of July."

"So," he said, dipping his fries into ketchup and eating.

"Think about it," I continued. "What were we doing at the end of July, just before returning to Pennsylvania? What if the baby isn't yours?"

He stopped in mid-chew, frozen in time.

I continued. "What if this is Screech's baby?" I said, staring straight at him.

"Ah … well … jeez," he stammered. "That makes it a bit more complicated. I mean, there are a lot more factors to consider."

"What do you think that would do to us, Earl? You and me?" I pressed him. "What would happen to us if this were Screech's baby?"

"Goddamn!" he spouted with a full mouth and put his burger back on the plate, suddenly seeming surprised. "Oh, shit. I don't know what it does to us." He continued to chew, trying to clear his mouth to talk. Finally, he swallowed. "I don't want it to do anything to us. I want us to be fine. I love you, and I want to be with you, but if this is Screech's baby, there is going to be some shit hitting the fan with my family and yours, and probably also with Screech."

"Exactly," I said, picking at my food, "and also shit hitting the fan with society. That's one of the reasons I've hesitated to talk about it. I've been terrified about what it might mean. I wanted us to think about it. We do have options. I could maybe have an abortion, but it's illegal, it's not safe, and I'm too far along to consider that at this point. One option might be for me to drop out of college, go away, have the baby somewhere, put it up for adoption, and then come back and pretend nothing ever happened. Maybe with your parents' help, we could do that. We could do that and then go on with our lives."

"Oh crap, Lovella!" he popped. "Could you do that to your baby? Could you throw away your child? Could you ever forget about it, knowing you had a child somewhere? Wouldn't you wonder if that child is safe or loved?"

"I wouldn't be throwing away my child, Earl!" I looked down at the table, irritated at his comment. "I would be giving my child a chance!" I whispered, looking up again and suddenly fearing someone might overhear. "I don't know how to give a Black child what it needs. Wouldn't the baby need to be raised by a Black family, someone who understands what it means to be Black, a family that knows how to deal with being Black in a world of prejudice? I don't know how to deal with that."

"Screech's family is out of the question for adoption," he insisted bluntly. I knew he was recalling, as was I, how terribly Screech had been abused as a child. "Hell, for that matter, I'm not sure that Screech is not out of the question."

I hadn't even gone to the subject of Screech's family, or Screech, for that matter. I had never thought about giving the child to one of its biological kin. The stories Screech had told us about them frightened me about ever giving them a chance to raise another child. I knew there had to be loving and supportive Black families out there, and I had figured I would go away, adopt the baby out, and maybe never even tell Screech. However, when I thought about it, I wondered how Screech would feel if he ever happened to find out that he had a child and was never brought into the conversation. I had such conflict inside me and such an incredible mix of emotions.

"Would it be fair for us to judge that?" I returned. "If Screech is the baby's father, would it be fair to shut him out? I admit I have thought about never letting him know, but would that be fair?"

"I just don't know how emotionally stable Screech is," Earl responded. "Lovella, you don't know. He is much more into drugs than you ever realized. I love him. Part of me has to admit, on some level, that I was in love with him, but he was on a collision course with hell and was starting to take me with him. He was even coaxing me to try heroin. I hate to admit it, but I'm glad we got away from him."

Earl reached fingers to his eyes to wipe back brief tears. He paused and collected himself. "I don't think it would be fair to any child for Screech to have anything to do with raising that child. I don't think he could handle it, and I don't think I could handle it if I thought the baby wasn't safe."

"That doesn't mean he doesn't have a right to know about his child, does it?" I questioned.

"And if he knows about his child, then what will he do? Take legal action or something? Tie us up in court? In his current state of mind, he probably doesn't even want to know about it or take responsibility for it." Earl paused. "You know, we are assuming a lot here. I fucked you a lot more than Screech. You had sex with him one time. It is much more likely that you are carrying my baby instead of his."

"I know," I said. "I know the chances are slim, but we don't know for sure, do we? We won't know till the baby is born."

"So, what if you go away to have the kid somewhere, and we have made arrangements to give it up for adoption … What if it's my kid?" he questioned. "I don't want my kid being given up for adoption. If this is my child, I want it. I don't want to think I might have a kid out there somewhere that someone else is raising."

"People do it all the time, Earl," I argued. "At least if a child is adopted, it is going to a home where the parents want it instead of coming into a situation where it messes things up, and it is just going to be a problem. If I have this baby, I will not be able to finish my degree. I'll be stuck being a mother instead of having the career I want."

He sat completely still for a moment and pondered what I had just said. "A problem? A situation where it is just going to be a problem, not a person, a problem?" he repeated my words. "What if this *is* my baby? I don't want my kid or any kid to be thought of as a problem."

"Earl! We can't just sit back and do nothing!" I said, exasperated.

"You're not sure you even want this baby, are you?" he softly asked, his face filled with disappointment.

"I'm not sure of anything, Earl," I pleaded. "If I have a Black child, how will the child be treated? How am I going to be treated? What will it be like for a Black child growing up in a mean and racist White world where nobody tries to understand? I don't understand. I don't have a clue what it is like to be Black or to put up with half the shit Black people put up with." My eyes filled with tears. "What will it be like if I can't understand?"

"And if it is my child, a White child, and you don't have to deal with any of that, then what?" he asked.

"Then, I don't know," I pleaded. "I am so confused and mixed up over this. It is not that I don't want to have *your* baby, Earl. I don't want to have any baby—now. I'm not ready."

"So," he argued back. "When you adopt a child out, where does the baby go? To an orphanage or foster care until it can be adopted? I don't want my kid to go to an orphanage, not when there are parents to raise it. I don't want Screech's kid going to an orphanage, not when there are two perfectly good parents to raise it. I don't like it, Lovella. I don't like this adoption thing."

"So, what other option do we have?" I pleaded.

"We get married," he asserted. "We get married right this week, as soon as we can get the license. We get married and keep the baby, no matter who the father is. If it is my baby, wonderful! If it is Screech's baby, I love the baby's father and will think of his baby as my own. I will love this baby as if it came from my loins."

"And if this is Screech's baby, what do you think that is going to be like?" I pressed. "How is your family going to react? I don't give a shit about how my family will react. They can all go to hell, as far as I'm concerned, but how will your family react? How do you think your ultra-conservative father is going to respond when he comes to the hospital thinking he is going to be passing down what he thinks is his all-important lineage to another generation, only to find out—Whoops!"

"I don't know how he'll react," Earl responded calmly and precisely. "But I do know how I will react. I know that I will finish my degree in May, and whether my father is with me or not, I'll have something I can use to negotiate a job sufficient to raise my family, and I'm willing to do that. I will dig ditches if that's what it takes to put a roof over my family's head. I've decided, Lovella. I've decided, right here, tonight. I want this baby! I want this baby, no matter what. The question is, do you want this baby?"

I realized that I was suddenly feeling melancholy. I found myself pondering his question, confronting myself about racism that I had grown up with, mindsets about boundary and place, and how race fits into all that. I knew the Civil Rights Movement was not occurring because Black people were treated justly and fairly. I wanted to tell myself that I was not racist, but I couldn't. In my heart of hearts, deep down in my soul, I found fear despite all my preaching and determination to see every human being as equal to myself. I found fear that I might think of my child as deserving less because of color. I saw the fear of having people shout at me, judge me, condemn me, and call me names because I had a Black child. More than that, I found fear of how people might judge and condemn my child. I found myself vacillating, back and forth, in my emotions about what a happy and prosperous life I might have if this was indeed Earl's child. In that case, I knew Earl's father would try to hand this baby the world on a silver platter, even if he excluded Earl. I visualized how wonderful that would be, but what if this wasn't Earl's baby? What then? Was I prepared to love a Black child and stand by that child, no matter what, even if society and our own families turned against us because of it? I wasn't sure. I couldn't be sure. I looked everywhere except at Earl, and finally, with pretended enthusiasm, I said, "Yes, I want this baby." Truthfully, I thought I had no choice.

"No matter what?" he confirmed.

"No matter what," I responded hesitantly and felt like I was lying to him, but I wasn't sure. At that time, I couldn't determine the truth in my heart, so I said what I thought he wanted to hear.

Earl got up and came around the table to my side. He kneeled beside the booth, reached out, and took my hand. "Lovella Fuchs …will you take me … Earl Titwallow, as your lawfully wedded husband? Will you marry me?"

His behavior had drawn attention, and we suddenly had an audience. I looked around, feeling sheepish and shy. These were strange and unusual emotions for me. I felt my face flush with embarrassment. I looked at him and gave a hesitant smile.

Yes," I said at last. "I will marry you."

The diner roared with cheers and applause. Earl reached out his hands and motioned for me to stand up. When I did, he swooped me into his arms, twirled me around, and kissed me. Then, he sat my feet back on the floor and looked lovingly into my eyes. I looked back at him with a deep and nagging ambivalence.

I did not sleep that night, not because I was a blushing bride excited about planning my wonderful wedding, but because I didn't think I wanted to get married. This was not because I didn't love Earl or because I didn't want him to be my husband. If the circumstances had been different, if I had not been pregnant, and it had been another year into our relationship, I might have been that blushing bride, but everything had changed.

Not only was there the potential that I was pregnant by a man other than Earl, but it was also the same man that Earl had fallen in love with. He admitted that he was in love with Screech. I was having trouble wrapping my mind around Earl being in love with Screech and me simultaneously. Maybe it was a sensibility from my upbringing, but I had not considered that someone could be fully in love with more than one person at a time. It was obvious that Earl was in love with me, but it seemed he was looking at this baby like it was the love child he conceived through his affair with Screech. I felt like a surrogate giving birth to someone else's child. I was bewildered and mixed up, not only with my feelings but also about what all this meant to Earl.

After lying there too long, staring at the ceiling, and listening to Marlene snore, I dug through my purse for a cigarette. No one was supposed to smoke in the dorm rooms, but I didn't care at that point. I fiddled in my purse, using the faint streetlight through the dorm window. Finally, I pulled out my cigarettes and lit one. I sat on the edge of the bed, smoking, staring at the misty hint of light coming through the window, and thinking. I was trying to understand everything and what it would mean for my life. Earl said he would call me the next day, and we could define how we wanted to approach the marriage. We were supposed to visit his parents and talk about it.

Before I laid back down, I determined there had to be some rules. We couldn't just go on, like mice in a maze, turning this way or that to see where life would lead. We had to have some regulations about how we would relate to each other and our child. Even if Screech had fathered the baby, it would still be our child. There was so much that I didn't want to think about, but there was no way out. I had to think about it. There was no such thing as not facing the problem before us.

Finally, very late into the morning, I felt drowsy and drifted into a light sleep. I awoke not two hours later to the sound of Marlene milling around the room, preparing to take her shower. It was a Saturday, so there was no class, but she had an annoying habit of getting up early, regardless of the day. There was no such thing as sleeping late with Marlene as a roommate. She was a 'seize-the-day' kind of a girl. At that point, I felt more like a *seizure-the-day* kind of girl. I just wanted to be unconscious.

Marlene noticed that I had been roused awake.

"Hey, sleepy head." She smiled much too cheerfully. "The day's a-wasting. Don't you have something wonderful to do today?"

"No, not really," I mumbled through my groggy tongue.

"Well, I am going to go downtown and see what shopping damage I can do with the fifty dollars my parents sent me for my birthday," she beamed. "Want to go? I'll buy lunch."

"No, thank you," I garbled. I rolled away from her and buried my head in the pillow. I didn't hear her leave, and the next thing I knew, someone knocked at the door.

"Lovella," the girl's voice rang out. "You have a phone call."

"Fuck!" I exclaimed, and I threw my face into the pillow.

"Lovella? Are you in there?" the voice chimed.

I mustered the strength to yell back, "Be right there." Then, I dragged my heavy, lead-weight body out of bed and donned a robe and slippers to stagger down the hall to the phone. The phone receiver was dangling against the wall. I picked it up and gave a sleepy, "Hello?"

"Hey, you ready to go?" Earl's voice spoke back from the receiver.

"Go where?" I responded.

"Remember, last night, we said we were going to drive up to Bradford Woods today and talk to my parents about the wedding," he reminded.

"Oh, shit!" I exclaimed. "Yeah, vaguely I remember. I just … I …" My heart said to drop the phone and find somewhere to hide, but after moments of stammering, I finally said, "Yeah, I'm almost ready. Give me another thirty minutes."

I barely heard him say, "Sure, no problem," when I hung up. I staggered back to my room, stuffed a few things into an overnight bag, and ran down the hall for a quick shower. The whole time, I asked myself, "Why am I doing this?" The answer never came.

I tied back my still-too-wet hair, skipped the makeup, and threw on a sweater and jeans. I met Earl in the parking lot by the girl's dorm, where he sat in the van listening to music, patiently waiting. I faintly heard Buffalo Springfield on the radio, *"It's time we stop; hey, what's that sound? Everybody look what's goin' down."*

"I'm sorry," I exclaimed, pulled open the door, and climbed into the passenger seat.

"No problem," he soothed. Then, he took my bag and tossed it over into the back. "We've got time. I called the parents last night and told them I wasn't sure when we would arrive. It's all right. It's just past eleven now. We'll probably be there by two or three, no sweat." He put the van in gear, and we began a journey I never wanted to take and never dreamed I would ever have to.

"Have you eaten?" he asked as we pulled onto the street.

"No," I replied quietly.

"Deli sandwiches, okay?" he questioned.

"Sure," I replied with little emotion.

"Cool," he continued. "Teplitz Deli is on the way."

We stopped at the deli and picked up our sandwiches. Then, we ate in the van on the almost three-hour trip to Bradford Woods.

After finishing our sandwiches and engaging in idle chat, I finally said, "Earl, I have some concerns."

"Oh, the parents will get over it," he quipped. "Yours and mine."

"No, that's not what I'm talking about." I turned sideways in the seat to look at him. "I have some concerns about us."

"I thought we hashed this out last night," he said.

"Well, we hashed a lot of things out last night," I replied. "I agreed to some things, but I had a lot of questions after our talk, and they kept me up most of the night."

"What?" he contemplated, keeping his eyes on the road.

"We have been drifters in our relationship, don't you think?" I went on. "I mean, we have just gone where the wind has blown us, and we haven't really had any direction. If we are going to get married, don't you think we should have some direction?"

"I guess so," he replied. "What direction?"

"For instance," I remarked, "we have never really had any rules in our relationship. We have just gone on trusting that whatever happened, or wherever it took us, would be okay. We have never said what's cool and what's not, what we are comfortable with and not comfortable with."

"Are you uncomfortable about something?" he pondered.

"I … well … I am confused, I guess," I stuttered. "I mean, we never really talked about whether it would be okay if we had sex with someone else or if we wanted to keep it monogamous. I guess, despite all the fucking around that I did before I met you, I just assumed our relationship would be monogamous, and I have been faithful to that. I may have had the occasional fantasy, but I have never been with anyone but you since I met you."

"What the hell are you getting at?" he snapped suddenly.

I stopped, frozen in my tracks, and said nothing. In a moment, I said, "I hoped we could discuss this without getting upset. I mean, I know … I … shit!" I turned away from him and looked out the window.

"I'm sorry," he said. "I shouldn't have snapped at you. Am I right in thinking that we are both frightened?"

"You're right," I said, leaning against the window and watching the roadside spin by. "I have to consider that you are scared, too. I know I am."

"Tell me what you're thinking," he considered. "Ask me what you need to ask me. I love you, and I want to know what you have to say."

"I know you love me," I affirmed, tears streaming silently down my face. "I don't doubt that you love me. What I can't seem to understand is how you could love me and deceive me."

"What are you talking about?" he disputed.

"You told me you are in love with Screech," I sniffled. "You had an affair with him all summer behind my back. It bothers me that you didn't talk to me about it. You never asked me how I felt about it. You just assumed that it wouldn't hurt me."

There was a long silence, and I waited for him to answer.

"I don't know what to say," he said. "I don't—I do love you both. I guess I didn't realize where I was going with that relationship. It just happened. I don't know what I was feeling. I'm straight, Lovella, or at least I thought I was. If you had ever asked me if I would ever have sex with another man, I would have said, 'Hell no,' but I did. I did, and fuck! For my life, I don't know why. It just felt right. We just fell into it. There was always a part of me that knew it would hurt you when you found out, but I told myself that you were open-minded and would be cool with it."

"It was not the sex that bothered me," I commented. "It was the secret, not telling me, and falling in love with someone else that bothered me."

Earl was silent, apparently thinking. Different expressions crossed his face. Then, he began to cry. I watched the tears roll off his cheeks. He made no effort to stop them. "I have to stop," he said, pulling over to the shoulder of the road.

When he had stopped the van and put it in park, he leaned over the steering wheel and sobbed. I watched silently as he cried, and when his tears began to subside, I said, "You fell in love with him. That's what hurts me."

Without looking up, he said, "But I never fell out of love with you, Lovella." He lifted his head, looked at me, and took my hand. "I never, not for a moment, ever stopped loving you, and I am so sorry that I hurt you."

"That's kind of what confuses me," I went on. "There is a part of me that knows you love me, but there is a part of me that asks, 'If you loved me, why would you deceive me? Why would you do this behind my back and never talk with me about it?' Earl … it's not the fact that you fucked Screech that bothers me. I think if it were just sex, you would not have hidden that from me. You hid it because you fell in love with him. Given my attitude about sex, if it were only sex, you might even have asked me to join you. It's not that you had sex that hurts. Betrayal hurts, and knowing you fell in love with someone else hurts. The sex didn't threaten me, but falling in love with him and keeping it secret does."

Halfway in a gasp, he caught his breath as guilt crossed his face. He sat there, frozen momentarily, apparently not knowing what to say. "I love you," he said at last. "I love you with every fiber of my being, and the last thing in the world I would ever want is to hurt you. I have no excuse, only the explanation that I was scared and confused because I came to love Screech, too, and I had never felt anything like that for a man. I don't know why. I just … I love him. Maybe I didn't tell you because I feared it would hurt you. Maybe I was confused about having feelings for a man when I've never felt that way. Maybe I thought … that night that we did the acid … maybe I thought … if Screech and I could bring you into it with us, it would make it okay. Maybe in some delusion, I thought I could have you both."

"We don't live in a world like that," I sighed. "We don't live in a world where egos don't get bruised, and insecurities don't get roused, even for people like me, who pretend to be strong. We live in a world where almost no one is so cool with themselves, so self-assured that they don't see an intimate involvement with someone else as a threat to their relationship. I know I have portrayed myself as cool, Earl, but if you thought I was that cool and secure, you were wrong. No, it's not the sex that bothers me; it's the fear that I might lose you, the fear that you might leave me for him. If we had talked about it and you told me that you just wanted to have sex with Screech, I probably would have said, 'Sure, go ahead,' but it's the fact that you fell in love with him and how that affected you that frightens me."

Earl slumped in the seat. He looked through the van's front window. A car passed by the side window, and he glanced briefly to watch it speed away. "Do you want to call this off?" he asked.

I reached down and placed my hand over my abdomen. "If this is Screech's baby, what will that mean to you?"

He took a disjointed breath, and a single tear drifted from his eye down to his mouth. "It means I will love that baby with all my heart," he said, quivering as he spoke.

"Does it mean this baby will be more important than me?" I asked a very unfair question.

"Can you both be important to me?" he answered. "Can I love you both?"

I knew that he not only meant loving the baby as much as me but also loving Screech as much as me.

"Earl, where I get scared," I said, "where I get really—really scared is not that you will love anyone as much as me, but that you might love someone else more than me. Did you love Screech more than me? Would you ever have left me for Screech if things had been different?"

His eyes looked like terror when I asked that question. He looked terrified, not so much from what I asked as by the answer he contemplated. Tears rolled down his cheeks again, and he gasped. "Probably, the hardest thing I have ever had to do was leave San Francisco and Screech, but I chose you. I knew we had to come home, but I wanted to come home with you. I want you. No matter how much I love Screech, given where he is headed with his life, it could never have worked even if I did love him more than you, but I don't love him more than you. I love you both."

He reached for me, buried his face in my shoulder, and wept. I held him silently, saying nothing. Finally, he stopped crying and gradually pried himself away from me. He sat back in the seat and wiped his eyes on his sleeve.

After a while, I said, "Earl, I have only one rule—honesty. That's it. That's all. Fuck whoever you want to fuck as long as it is just a fuck, but please don't deceive me. Don't go behind my back; if you ever fall in love with someone else and decide to want them more than me, come and tell me. Be clear and open with me. Please don't leave me hanging or guessing. If you ever decide you are not in love with me or think you will be happier somewhere else, please have the balls to let me know. I want you to be happy—with me. I don't want you to be unhappy with me. If you think you could ever be happier somewhere else, then go. I would rather you be happy somewhere else than unhappy with me. Hell, for that matter, I would rather you be unhappy somewhere else than be unhappy with me. I want you to be happy more than anything, but if you can't be happy with me, then at the very least, let me know and move on."

"What do you want to do now?" he asked. "Do you not want to go through with this?"

I eyed him up and down before speaking. "If you, in your heart of hearts, can tell me that you want to go through with this, that you can keep a promise of honesty with me, then I want to go through with this."

He stared at me straight in the eyes, unwavering, and said, "I want you for all my life, Lovella. I want you. If I can spend eternity with you, I will."

The road noise of passing traffic filled my ears, and I suddenly became fully aware of the moment.

"Then drive," I said. "Let's go talk to your parents.

CHAPTER 25

The Big Reveal

To say Earl's father was upset that I was pregnant out of wedlock would be an understatement. His mother was a bit nonplussed, but that's all. On the other hand, his father ranted for quite some time about what a disgrace we had brought upon his family. To my surprise, Earl sat quietly, affirming here and there, "Yes sir" and "No sir." His defiance was either hidden or gone. In the end, his father acquiesced. Mr. Titwallow decided to let us move back together when we were married, but not until after Christmas break. Then, he would foot the bill for a flat, just as he had before.

We were to be married early in November to be sure we didn't let this go any further, lest my showing tipped off the neighborhood. We didn't want even a remotely formal wedding. So, we were to be married at a Justice of the Peace, with only immediate family involved. This was fine with me because I knew Mother would have turned any formal wedding into her pretentious fest. Mother would have loved to rant about me being pregnant out of wedlock, but that was overlooked, given that I was marrying into a wealthy family.

All the arrangements were made, and we met on Wednesday, November 1, 1967, at the Justice of the Peace in Anderson County. We held it there, primarily so Mother could attend, but she used the occasion to do little more than bitch. It had not been my pregnancy that upset her. It was her inability to use the event for one of her pompous presentations, yet again.

Truthfully, after Daddy died, I wanted nothing to do with Mother. I would have been content to shut her out of my life and never speak to her again. Nonetheless, I mentally heard Daddy saying, *Give her a chance.* As much as I hated to do it, I choked back my anger, resumed a relationship with her, and invited her to the wedding.

I wore a white knee-length satin dress and carried a pink and yellow bouquet. Earl wore a gray suit. We stood side by side in the Justice of the Peace office, anxious and confused.

The Justice stood up from behind his desk, with the two of us standing in front of it and our families on either side. He was a blondish man in his fifties with a flat-top haircut. He evidently had a sense of humor. He looked at me first and said, pointing to Earl, "You like him?"

I said, "Yes."

He then spoke to Earl, pointing at me, "You like her?"

Earl said, "Yes."

"Then, by the power vested in me by the great State of Pennsylvania," he exclaimed, "I now pronounce you husband and wife!"

We looked at each other, waiting for him to say the traditional, "You may now kiss the bride," but he said nothing, and finally, after an awkward silence, Earl gave me a nervous little peck on the lips. This brought Mother to clapping her happy little hands furiously together with moans of oohs and aahs. I could only think that she took vicarious pleasure in the fact that I had accomplished, quite by accident, what she could never accomplish despite all her frantic effort. In her mind, I married a well-to-do man from a respectable, wealthy family.

After the ceremony, we had a quick lunch at a small local cafe. Mr. Titwallow bought lunch for everyone. Then, it was back to State College for classes the following day. Earl and I had skipped classes on Wednesday to get married, but we had to return to class by the next morning. I went back to my dorm, and he went back to his. We didn't see any use in a honeymoon or consummating the marriage since we had been consummating vigorously from the beginning of our relationship. I guess San Francisco counted as our honeymoon.

The weeks dragged on to the end of the semester. Earl's parents invited Mother to spend Christmas with them in Bradford Woods. Mother was all too happy to skip out on Grandmother and Grandfather Donner. After all, she now had a wealthy son-in-law and an opportunity to experience the good life she had always thought she deserved. She reveled in having Nora wait on her and fussed over every little detail of etiquette to the point of aggrandizement. Whenever she sipped her tea or coffee, she made sure that her pinky finger was extended, like a tiny hard dick, even though no one in Earl's family did anything similar and couldn't have cared less.

In a conversation over Christmas dinner, she looked at me squarely and questioned, "So, Lovella … dear … what have you decided to name the baby?"

I knew exactly what she was getting at. The *'ella'* had been traditionally placed at the end of every female's name in our family for who knows how many generations. No one seemed to know where it came from, but by God—it was a *"tradition."*

"Mother," I responded, "Earl and I have discussed it, and if it is a boy, we plan on naming it John Gretton after Daddy and my best friend, Gretta, and if it is a girl, we plan to name it Gretta Clarisse after Earl's Mother and after Gretta."

"Oh! What beautiful names," she twittered, "and how sweet you would name the baby after Earl's mother. Of course, Gretta is not a family name. So, I wonder if you might honor our side of the family's tradition by giving the child, if female, a name ending in *ella?* You know, Joyella Clarisse would be a lovely name."

I stared at her with a dead, stern look. I knew she would try to control anything she could for as long as she lived and as long as I would let her.

"Ah-hem … Mother," I responded, "I am not particularly fond of *'ella,'* especially as every female in our family for God knows how many generations has had the damn thing tacked to her name, and since this is my baby, I think Earl and I retain the right to name her or him whatever we please."

Earl's mother chimed in. "I think Joyella is a lovely name, dear."

"You see! You see!" Mother leaped. "It is a wonderful name for a girl child."

"Mother," I replied, trying to maintain my composure, "Gretta has been my dearest and closest friend since I was in the second grade. She named her child after me, and I think it is only fitting that I should also name my child after her.

"Well!" Mother said, in a huff, "If you think some stranger whom you met in grade school is more deserving of a name than a tradition in your blood family, dating back multiple generations, then I suppose the family would simply have to bear that shame."

"What the?" I caught myself before I said, *What the fuck!* and sat silently for a moment, thinking how I would respond to yet another of Mother's infamous guilt trips. I thought about saying, *Wow! You should be a pilot for Guilt Trip Airlines*, but I thought it best not to disturb the hornet nest in front of Earl's family. In time, I said, "Mother, I don't think naming my child after one of the people I love most would bring any kind of shame to my family."

"Only that everyone would know that you were the one who broke the tradition," she jabbed. "You would be the one who brought down a noble and honorable family tradition that, for all we know, could go back hundreds of years."

I wanted to scream, *Give me a fucking break!* But there were things that I might say to Mother, in other situations, that I would not say in front of Earl's parents, and she knew it.

Before I could say anything, Earl's father chimed in with, "You know, I think your mother has a point there. There is something to be said for family and tradition."

I thought, sarcastically, with lips sealed, and wished I could have said aloud, *Yes, that's why Mother is sitting here, at Christmas, having dinner with people she never knew a year ago instead of having Christmas with her own family, who all have the ella tacked behind their names.*

"You see, Lovella," Mother affirmed, "there is something to be said for the old ways, tradition, and family honor."

I sat there fuming, thinking about how much she, behind her stupid façade, was ashamed of her own family. I resisted the urge to climb, screaming, across the table and strangle her. Earl, seeing my anguish, gave me a little reassuring nod.

"All right, Mother," I said, choking back my anger. "If you want 'ella' at the end of the name for a female, I will name her Vanilla … Vanilla Clarisse Titwallow." I initially intended this as a joke but also intended to piss her off. Later, I came to see it as a beautiful name.

Mother twittered, eyes darting, "Oh … oh … as in vanilla extract, a flavoring? You wouldn't! I-I-I-I …" she stuttered, "I don't think that would exactly be a fitting name for a child."

"Take it or leave it, Mother," I said firmly. "It's an 'ella' sound at the end of the name. It, therefore, meets the criteria for the family *tradition*. If the child is a girl … her name will be Vanilla Clarisse Titwallow."

"Oh … well, but it's not a normal-sounding woman's name, such as with the *ella* on the end, and it's spelled differently," she argued, "not like … Joyella."

"So, you think Claudella, Drucella, Cloella, etc., are normal-sounding names?" I spit back. "No, Mother. Take it or leave it. If you insist that there must be an *ella* at the end of the name, then the name is Vanilla, and quoting a phrase you recently used with impunity, '*Well, that's that.*' Now, there's nothing more to say!" I consoled myself that Mother might pass away before my child would give me grandchildren, and I would never pressure the stupid tradition further.

Mother stewed in her thoughts, knowing that I also was not above using guilt trips. After all, I had learned from a master. Then, she asked, "Earl, do you think Vanilla is a fitting name for a child? It would be naming your daughter after a kitchen condiment, for goodness' sake. After all, you have a say in this, as well."

Earl smiled. "I think it's a lovely name; if Lovella likes it, I like it too."

Mother sat for a moment, fiddling with her napkin. She knew I had her and that there was no actual argument. She knew she had better not push it too far. She got her way, but I got mine. She knew if she argued, I would point out that I had been willing to compromise, and she, ultimately, had no say in the matter. She said nothing more.

In January, Earl and I moved back in together. We got an apartment very similar to the one he had when I met him. It was just up the street from his original apartment. By that time, I was practically waddling with pregnancy. I could feel the baby moving, and it was not unusual that in the middle of the night, it would be rumbling around inside of me. I spent many nights falling asleep and waking again every time the baby shifted.

I hated trying to dress, even in maternity clothes. Nothing seemed to fit right. If it fit around my waist, it folded up under my belly and felt like I had a rope tied around me, and of course, nothing would fit around my belly. Something strapping over the belly was totally out of the question. I began to feel like my breasts were twenty-pound bags of water on each side, and any movement made them shift back and forth. Most of the time, I only wore loose-fitting Mumu dresses. Bras were too uncomfortable and also out of the question.

February and March were miserable. I felt like I had to pee every ten minutes. My stomach was as tight as a basketball, and it seemed I couldn't sit down or stand up without the assistance of a forklift. Somehow, with great care, I managed. I had stopped smoking again by the end of October, not because I thought anything about any danger to the baby, but because it triggered morning sickness, and I threw up every time I tried to smoke. It was like the baby was saying, "No, I don't like that, and I'm going to make you puke if you do it."

Earl was wonderful. He fussed over me like a mother hen, propping pillows to my back, bringing me tea, and sitting up with me in the middle of the night when the baby was kicking and I couldn't sleep. Still, he kept up his studies, determined to graduate.

This went on throughout January, February, and March. Then, in the early morning of April 1, 1968, at about 4:30 a.m., I woke with intense pain. I had gone to bed with a dull ache across my lower back and abdomen and had barely gotten to sleep because of it. I finally slept, more from sheer exhaustion than anything else. When I awoke, I noticed a sticky discharge mixed with blood that had come from my vagina, and shortly afterward, I began to have intense cramps.

"Earl! Earl!" I screamed. "Wake up!"

Earl popped up in bed like a jack-in-the-box. "What? Are you all right?"

"Either I'm dying, or the baby is coming!" I snapped.

He looked around, confused. "Oh-Huh-Well!" Then, he leaped out of bed and began dressing furiously. He lifted me to the edge of the bed and wrapped my robe around me.

"Wait! Ha-Ahh—Wait!" he exclaimed, grabbing the suitcase we had packed for the hospital. He ran to the door with the suitcase and turned quickly, raising one hand flat in the air like a traffic cop. "Wait! Wait!" he exclaimed. Then, he was gone.

Earl ran downstairs, threw the suitcase into the van, and returned for me. Then, he walked me in my robe and house shoes, moaning and grimacing, to the van and sped away toward Hershey Medical Center. We arrived at the Penn State facility for Hershey in short order. Parking the van in front of the emergency room, he rushed in to grab a nurse and a wheelchair.

It was not long before I was in Labor and Delivery, panting, pushing, and screaming. It seemed to me like it went on forever. The cramps would come, and there would be waves and waves of them, and then, they would subside for a while, only to come back with a vengeance.

Earl went back and forth between checking on me and pacing the hall. He had called both sides of the family and told them the baby was coming. Then, at around 8:42 a.m., Vanilla Clarisse Titwallow was born. None of the family had arrived at that time. It was at least a two-and-a-half-hour drive for Earl's parents and about a three-hour drive for Mother.

I was taken to a room, exhausted and needing sleep. Vanilla was taken to the nursery. There was about a two-hour gap between her birth and when our families arrived. Earl visited the nursery and then came to sit by my side in the recovery room. The nurse brought me pain medications after delivery and an ice pack to go between my legs. I soon pulled the ice pack away because it felt more uncomfortable than helpful, and then I slept for maybe an hour to an hour and a half. I awoke to Earl sitting by the bed, holding my hand and staring lovingly at me.

"Hey, little mamma," he said when I opened my eyes.

"Hey, big daddy," I responded. "Have you seen the baby?"

"Yep, I saw her," he said, smiling. "She's beautiful."

"As beautiful as me?" I said jokingly.

"Just as beautiful as you," he said.

"How much does she look like me?" I questioned.

"Hard to tell at this stage," he responded. "But I think she has got your eyes and your cheekbones."

"How much does she look like you?" I continued, not knowing how to ask and not wanting to be so blunt as to ask if she was Black.

He reached his free hand over, pushed my hair behind my ears, and stroked my face. He smiled and looked lovingly and reassuringly at me. "She doesn't look like me at all," he said.

My grip tightened on his hand. A wave of emotion flowed over me. I trembled, and a tear ran down my cheek, for I knew exactly what he meant.

"Earl," I said, eyes searching his for whatever reassurance I could find. "What are we going to do?"

"We're going to love her," he said. "We are going to love her with all our might, and we are going to raise her the best way we know how."

"What about our parents?" I questioned.

"They will just have to deal with it," he said. "They might have to challenge themselves to look beyond the limits of their racism, and if they can't, we'll decide how to deal with that."

He gently stroked my hair and the side of my face. Shortly after, the nurse brought the baby in for her first breastfeeding. When I witnessed my child, a wave of love rushed over me, a wave I had not expected, but I received it with gratitude. After she was taken back to the nursery, Earl sat by the bed again, and I fell asleep while he held my hand.

I awoke to a gentle tapping on the door. "May we come in?" Earl's mother said gently and sweetly from outside. I looked around the room, and Earl was nowhere to be found.

"Sure ... please," I responded. Then, Mr. and Mrs. Titwallow glided gently into the room as though they had to walk delicately. Earl followed shortly afterward. He had waited at the hospital entrance to steer them toward the room and away from the nursery.

"I was waiting downstairs for Mom and Dad," he explained. "They can visit with you for a while, and I'll go back down to wait for your mother. I thought it would be nice for all the family to be in the room together when they bring the baby in."

"How are you feeling, dear?" Earl's mom asked as she crossed around the bed. His father sat in a chair and initially said nothing.

I responded. "My ... you-know-what ... hurts like hell, and I am starving."

"Yes, dear," Mrs. Titwallow smiled reassuringly. "That's payment for all the love you will receive later."

Mr. Titwallow grunted at the comment.

"How are you, Mr. Titwallow?" I questioned.

"I'm very well, Lovella," he noted. "Thank you for asking."

We engaged in small talk for about forty-five minutes over various topics, from how I felt about having a girl to the latest news and the weather. I deliberately avoided details about the baby. One of the nurses checked on me and brought me a food tray, which I wolfed down like a starving dog. Later, there was another little knock at the door, and, this time, immediately after the knock, Earl and Mother entered the room without waiting for my invitation.

"Oh, Lovella, honey," Mother began. "You are just glowing." Then, she turned to Mrs. Titwallow. "Doesn't she have that new mother glow?"

"Yes, she is just beaming, isn't she?" Mrs. Titwallow responded.

Earl said, "I asked the nurse if she would bring the baby up in a few minutes."

My heart sank as I contemplated how the family might react when they realized I had given birth to a Black child. I was both exhilarated and terrified. Although it had never been discussed, I knew there was systemic racism in most White people, and our families were no exception.

"Oh, wonderful!" Mother spouted, beaming at Earl. "I'm just dying to see her."

I looked at Earl with both longing and terror. On the one hand, I had no problem with telling Mother to fuck off if she didn't like the way things had turned out, but on the other hand, I wanted to be accepted and reassured, and I was also afraid of how Earl's parents would take it.

In a moment, the nurse entered the room, walked straight over to the bed, and laid Vanilla in my arms.

"Hah!" Mother gasped. "Oh, there must be a mistake. That's not her child!"

"This is Vanilla Clarisse Titwallow," the nurse responded, glancing at Mother.

I took Vanilla into my arms and looked down at her, seeing her so tiny, wrinkled, and helpless. The nurse quickly left the room. Then, I looked up. "This is my baby, Mother," I said.

"What!" Mother exclaimed. "Is this some kind of April Fool's joke?" She scanned the room as though a clown might leap out to shout, "April Fools!"

"What the hell is this?" Mr. Titwallow exclaimed and got to his feet. "Is this some sick joke? If it is, it is not very damn funny."

"It is no joke," Earl stepped in. "This is our baby."

"There is no way you are the father of that child!" Mr. Titwallow demanded. "Now cut the shenanigans. Get that kid out of here and bring in my granddaughter!"

"Yes, Dad," Earl calmly replied. "I am the father of that child. This is the baby that Lovella and I had together. It is not a joke. This is our child, and she is your grandchild."

"Well, maybe there is some nigger blood on her side of the family!" Mr. Titwallow challenged as he pointed an accusing finger at Mother, "but there is damn sure none on our side!"

"Well, there is no such thing on our side!" Mother snapped back.

"First of all," Earl continued, "I demand that you not use that word when referring to my daughter. Never say that word around her, me, or my wife ever again." His lips pursed as he emphasized the seriousness of that demand.

"Your *daughter?*" Mr. Titwallow exclaimed, with Mrs. Titwallow holding and rubbing his arm, trying to calm him. "That is no more your Goddamn daughter than Martin Luther King is my son!"

"Yes," Earl responded. "Yes, she *is* my daughter. She *is* my very own. My name is on the birth certificate, and I am legally her father."

"Over my dead body!" Mr. Titwallow bellowed. "There is a *you-know-what* in the woodpile here! She couldn't have been faithful to you! There is no way you fathered that child!"

"Dad," Earl calmly continued. "First, I will ask you to respect Lovella instead of making wild accusations. Second, this *is* my daughter, my child. I'm sorry if that displeases you, but that's how it is."

"I can cut your ass off from any penny you thought you would ever get out of my estate!" Mr. Titwallow growled.

"Dad, apparently, you haven't learned that I don't care. If you feel you have to do that, we are fine with it," Earl reasoned. "I will have my degree by the end of May, and I'm sure I can find work to support my family without your assistance."

"You are fine with it?" Mr. Titwallow bellowed. "You are fine with knowing that you are going to live like a Goddamn pauper, without a pot to piss in, while you deny your true family, so you can live with this nigger fucking whore, and raise that little nigger bastard baby!"

In a snap, Earl had wadded up his fist and punched his father square in the face, knocking him back into the wall. "DON'T YOU EVER FUCK-ING SAY ANYTHING LIKE THAT TO MY WIFE, MY CHILD OR ME, FUCKING EVER, AGAIN!" he screamed. "YOU WILL RESPECT MY WIFE, AND YOU WILL TREAT MY CHILD WITH THE SAME HONOR YOU WOULD GIVE TO ANY WHITE CHILD, OR YOU CAN STAY THE HELL AWAY FROM ME AND FROM MY FAMILY! DO YOU FUCKING UNDERSTAND ME?"

The baby began to wail at the noise and the anger. I sat rocking her, trying to soothe and comfort her, but I was also terrified. Mr. Titwallow regained his balance and looked at Earl with the utmost contempt. He grabbed Mrs. Titwallow by the arm. "Come on, Clarisse," he said. "We are not welcome here!"

When he began to pull Mrs. Titwallow toward the door, she jerked her hand away from him. "Maybe you are not welcome here," she exclaimed, "but I'm staying here to share this moment with my son, his wife, and *my* granddaughter!"

An astounded shock crossed Mr. Titwallow's face. He looked at her sternly and demanded, "I said … Let's go!"

"No," she said calmly and firmly. "You can go if you want to. I'm sure I can find a way back to Bradford Woods if I need to, but right now, I'm staying here."

Mr. Titwallow's eyes darted around the room at each of us. "YOU CAN ALL GO TO HELL!" he yelled, storming out the door.

After he left, Mrs. Titwallow took a deep breath. "Well," she said, "What family doesn't have a few squabbles here and there?" She smiled sweetly, yet nervously, glanced up at Mother and down at me and the baby. Earl walked over and hugged her. "Thank you, Mom," he said, kissing her forehead.

To my surprise, Mother had kept quiet through all this. I knew she could not be the least bit happy that her first and only grandchild was Black. I knew that racism ran deep in her side of the family, that it went back to the Kentucky hills. I knew she had racist conditioning that had been subtly handed down, generation after generation. I knew the same indoctrination had a lot to do with the struggles I began to find within myself. Yet, unlike Mr. Titwallow, Mother held her tongue. I suspected part of her reason was the situation's intensity and her desire not to get caught up in Earl's wrath, as his father had been.

After Mr. Titwallow rampaged out of the room, Mother strolled over to my bedside, looked down at the baby, and reached out to her. Vanilla was still crying from the uproar. Mother gently stroked her palm down the side of Vanilla's face, and she began to calm.

"So, this is my grandchild?" Mother smiled, watching the baby.

"Yes, Mother," I said. "This is Vanilla Clarisse Titwallow, your granddaughter."

Mother gazed at her with a glowing and unexpected smile. She took Vanilla's tiny hand between her finger and thumb, saying, "But she is not vanilla, dear ... she's mocha."

CHAPTER 26

From Darkness to Awareness

I only had Vanilla home from the hospital for a couple of days when the most horrible thing happened. I had put her down for the evening and was relaxing, watching a little TV, when a special report pre-empted the broadcast. After some introduction, Walter Cronkite announced, *"Good evening. Dr. Martin Luther King, the apostle of nonviolence of the civil rights movement, has been shot in Memphis, Tennessee."*

"Oh, my God!" I cried aloud and held my hand over my mouth.

I watched in horror as awful descriptions of the assassination followed. My eyes filled with tears, and my chest heaved as grief and fear flooded over me. I had seen this man speak at a march in New York only a year before. In many ways, I felt almost as though I knew him personally. I questioned what all this might mean. The fears I had for my child, growing up in a world where racism prevailed, came rushing into my mind with a vengeance. I had images intruding on my mind of the KKK burning crosses on lawns and Black people hanging in trees. I grieved and was afraid, alone. Earl was at the library, and I wondered if he had gotten the news. Surely, if he had, I thought he would come home soon.

I found myself wondering if our child could be shot in cold blood for no more reason than inexplicable hate. I found myself thinking of Jesus and Mahatma Gandhi and how those who strive to bring peace, love, and justice into the world are the ones who are murdered and betrayed for it. I feared that hate was winning the battle over love for ultimate supremacy and that the world would deteriorate into a Nazi-like hell. I worried about a sleeping baby who was only four days old, and I grieved for Dr. King and the entire Black community. I wept for my guilt. Even though I had a Black child, there were traces of prejudice that still found refuge in the recesses of my mind. My own conditioned intolerance troubled me. I wished Earl had been home as I sat on the sofa, watching the broadcast drag on. I was hanging on to every detail. *"Shot in the neck—The bullet exploded in his face—Rushed to a Memphis hospital where he died from a bullet wound in the neck—Mayor Henry Lobe has reinstated the dusk to dawn curfew he imposed on the city last week when a march led by Dr. King erupted in violence."*

"What kind of world have I brought my baby into?" I wailed.

I paced the apartment and watched the news. Then, Vanilla awoke with the classic stilted crying of a newborn. Maybe the TV had awakened her. Maybe it was hearing my anguish. I picked her up from the crib and held her over my shoulder. I rocked her and paced the apartment. I repeatedly went to the window to see if Earl might be coming up the walk. Little did I know that I would spend multiple evenings at home with a child, waiting for him to come home. This was not the life I had planned.

Earl returned late in the evening after finishing his studies. The news went through the campus like wildfire, so he heard about it. He had considered how it might affect me but thought I could handle it while he finished his research. When he came home to find me torn with grief, he was apologetic and affectionate.

"I never dreamed it would affect you this way," he said, putting his arms around me.

That year, I would need a lot of comfort.

Nineteen sixty-eight became the year of hell for me and the nation. The presidential election and political ads on TV and radio were in full swing. Race riots and war protests seemed to headline every newscast. There were no more peaceful protests. There was no more powder keg because the powder keg had blown, and the country was exploding into violence. All this made me even more terrified. I questioned whether there was any future for my baby that would be worth having.

In June, Bobby Kennedy was assassinated in Los Angeles. When the Democratic National Convention was held in Chicago that August, riots broke out again. Every time something happened, I found myself becoming more and more anxious. I refused to take the baby with me if I went out anywhere. I would only go grocery shopping alone if Earl were home with her. I was terrified that someone of either race, White or Black, might see me with a Black child and attack me for it. I stopped talking to friends and stayed in the apartment with Vanilla, day in and day out—isolated and anxious.

Of course, Earl had graduated in May with a degree in business. Before graduation, he had interviews set up in a couple of different cities. Pittsburgh and Philadelphia were on his list for jobs, but neither panned out, so he got a temporary job as a grocery clerk. He spent his days sacking and carrying groceries for old ladies, and when the store closed in the evening, he stocked the shelves and mopped the floors before coming home. He picked up the rent for the apartment after the rift with his father and did his best to care for his family precisely as he said he would.

Earl and his father had not spoken to each other since Vanilla was born, and his mother and sister were the only ones who attended his graduation. I guess his father decided he could not be around us without being rude, so he chose no contact at all. Earl's mom called frequently, and on a couple of occasions, she came to spend the weekend so she could keep the baby and let us go out for a much-needed adult date time together. Even then, I felt uncomfortable leaving the apartment and anxious the whole time.

Mother had even come up a few times to see Vanilla and baby-sit. She had shocked me with her response to the baby. I saw no indication that she acted any differently toward Vanilla than if she had been born a White child. I had expected Mother to throw a gigantic fit like Earl's dad and, at the very least, to shame me about getting pregnant before marriage by a Black man. However, it never came. She never spoke a shameful word to me at all. She was beginning to change. Not long after Daddy died, I confronted her by saying, "Mother, Daddy is gone. You don't have to control everything anymore. Don't you think, for once in your life, you might relax and do what you want?" Maybe she had taken that to heart.

When the grandmothers were there to babysit, Earl would take me to the Finer Diner, but our dating hang-out no longer appealed to me. I couldn't be in public without being constantly terrified that violence or racial tensions might break out at any moment. Earl assured me he would protect me, but I didn't trust that he could, especially during riots. If someone decided to start shooting, how could he protect me from that? The images of violence on TV and the assassinations that had occurred that year constantly plagued my mind. I insisted on sitting where I could see the door and calculated how we could dash out the back if needed. Once delicious and appealing, the food didn't sit well with me. I couldn't finish a meal, rarely eating more than a third of it, and whatever I ate seemed to immediately turn into heartburn.

The election was held in November, and Richard Nixon won. This didn't do anything toward bringing me any peace of mind. Nixon had sworn that he would "crack down on lawlessness," but to what end? I did not see him having any genuine interest in ending the war, and I found myself sure that, when it came down to it, he was a lot like Earl's father, with a deep-seated but usually hidden racism, yet one that was far more insidious, self-serving, and infused with evil. After all, Earl's father had been very cordial with Black people in public, but beneath it all, he was a malignant racist. A few years later, when Nixon had to resign as president due to the Watergate scandal, I felt confirmed that my suspicions about him had been correct.

I did not know Earl's mother had been working on his father to set aside his callous attitude and reunite the family. If I had realized this, I don't know if I would have thought Earl could have been receptive to it at that point. However, I underestimated both men. Mrs. Titwallow had been pushing for reconciliation, hoping to resolve something before the holidays.

Shortly after the November election, Mrs. Titwallow called Earl and asked if he would come to Bradford Woods and speak with his father. When she called, I was nursing the baby on one end of the sofa. Earl sat on the other end, responding over the phone, "Well, if that's the case, why isn't he making this phone call himself instead of you, Mom?"

There was a silence as he listened to whatever argument she was giving. I had the feeling that she had done much pleading with Mr. Titwallow long before she ever called Earl.

"Well, I don't care, Mom," Earl said into the phone. "If he is sorry for what he has done, then he needs to be man enough to call me himself. Well … why can't he come to the phone and tell me that? … Don't give me that crap about how busy he is. I don't care how busy he is. If this is important to him, and he is genuinely sorry, he will tell me himself. … No … no— Mom! I won't come up there unless he asks me himself, not you—him. … Well, you have him call me and tell me that he wants to meet with me, and I'll be far more likely to consider it, but I'll tell you, the person he owes the biggest apology to is Lovella. The baby is too little to know any difference, and I don't want her ever to know that her grandfather thought of her like that or ever treated his family that way. … Well—fine, Mom. Have him call me … I love you too … Okay, bye." When Earl returned the receiver to the black phone on the end table near the sofa, he then turned to me.

"Can you believe that shit?" he exclaimed.

"What's going on?" I questioned while I watched Vanilla pulling on my nipple.

"Mom put him up to this," Earl snarled. "I know the son-of-a-bitch never got the bright idea to apologize on his own. He wants me to drive up to Bradford Woods so he can meet with me and give me an apology, but the asshole coward didn't even have the balls to call me himself! Besides, if he is going to apologize to anyone, he needs to apologize to you."

I continued feeding the baby and said nothing.

About two hours later, the phone rang again. By then, Earl had taken Vanilla into the bedroom and laid her in her crib for a nap. I picked up the phone and said, "Hello." I froze momentarily when I heard the voice on the other end of the line.

"Hello, Lovella," Mr. Titwallow spoke from a distance.

I stood silently and felt myself trembling.

"Hello?" I heard his question.

"Hello, Mr. Titwallow," I said, finally and hesitantly.

"Well, I'm glad you answered," he said. "I need to talk to you."

Again, I stood at the end of the sofa, holding the receiver in my hand and saying nothing, frightened of the screaming and degrading attitude he had displayed when Vanilla was born.

"Lovella," he hesitated momentarily. "I owe you much more than an apology."

In my mind, I imagined Mrs. Titwallow standing beside him, with a pistol to his temple, hissing through clenched teeth, *"Apologize to her, Daniel, or I'll blow your fucking brains out!"* It was not her style, but it was a satisfying fantasy. Still, I knew this was because of her influence. He went on in divided speech segments, "I … ah … I was totally … out of line that day in the hospital … when Vanilla was born. My behavior … was reprehensible … scornful … and wrong. I have no excuse. There is no excuse. I … hope that you will see it in your heart … to forgive me."

Again, I was silent for a moment, offering no forgiveness. The last thing I could bring myself to do was to tell him it was all right. It wasn't all right, and I wondered if I could forgive him. I said, "I suppose you would also like to speak to Earl."

There was a brief pause, and then he said, "Yes … thank you." I heard the misgiving in his voice.

Earl heard the phone ring, got up from his nap, and leaned against the bedroom door frame. I looked at him, knowing that he had overheard at least my end of the conversation. He looked at me momentarily with disdain, then pried himself from the door frame to reach for the phone. I silently handed him the receiver and sat down.

"Hello, Father," he said formally. Then, I watched him roll his eyes and occasionally grimace as he listened to the conversation. Apparently, at some point, his father wondered if Earl was still on the line. I heard Earl say, "Yes, I'm still here. I'm listening." Then, he was silent again for several minutes.

"You understand," Earl said, "that I have doubts about your sincerity."

Earl switched the receiver from one ear to the other and glanced up at me while he listened to his father. I got up and tried to busy myself with picking up magazines tossed about the living room and stacking them neatly on the coffee table.

"Well, that's on your turf," Earl responded a little later. "I think … if you are sincere, and you really want to do this, then you will be the one to make the sacrifice and the effort to get together, not us."

While they were talking, I heard the baby stirring and went into the bedroom to get her. Then, I returned with Vanilla and stood nearby while they continued their conversation.

Earl was silent, listening to his father speak. Then, he let out a deep sigh. "I don't know. I'll have to discuss it with Lovella. I'm not sure she will even be open to the idea. We will have to discuss it. I'll let you know something in a couple of days. All right—fine. I'll let you know—bye."

"What's up?" I asked.

"He wants us to get together for Thanksgiving, but I'm not sure," Earl replied. "If we don't want to come over to Bradford Woods for Thanksgiving, and I don't, he will rent a house at Martha's Vineyard, and we could all have Thanksgiving there."

"Why does he want everyone together like that?" I asked.

"He says he needs to share something with both of us, but he wants it to be face-to-face," Earl explained.

"Can he get a house with such short notice?" I questioned.

"He has connections," Earl said, as he stretched out on the sofa with his hands behind his head, "and besides, there is a house on the shore that he and Mom used to rent for the family when I was a kid, usually in the summer. He can probably get that, and if I know him, he will take Ralph and Nora so they can wait on us. The house has eight bedrooms, so there is plenty of room, and there probably won't be much competition to rent it over Thanksgiving. Summer is the busy time."

"So that means that he is genuinely sorry?" I asked.

"Well, the house, plus taking Ralph and Nora with us and other expenses, will probably set him back about $4,000 or $5,000 or more for the few days we will be there." Earl grinned as he lay back on the sofa. "I'd be willing to bet he is going to fork out more than that so that he can kiss ass and try to make up."

"Well, I'm glad he is willing to try," I commented.

"Mom put him up to this," Earl noted. "I know she has been working on him since he made such a fool of himself when Vanilla was born. I knew Mom would wear him down." Earl got up, moved over next to me, and placed his hand on my arm. "So, what do you think?"

"It's good, I guess, that he wants to apologize," My voice trembled as I continued, "But I'm scared."

"Scared?" he questioned.

"Earl, the last time I saw your father, he was screaming horrible things at me and the baby, and you ended up punching him in the face." My breath shortened to stilted gasps. I felt like a leaf in a heavy wind and could barely get the words out. I struggled to keep holding Vanilla. "With-all-the-violence … out-there … and-the … hatred." Tears streamed from my eyes, and Earl enfolded the baby and me in his arms. "I-don't-know-if-I'm-safe-anywhere-or-that-the-baby-is-sss-safe … especially-around-someone … who-has-been-so … cruel!"

Despite the years of Mother's hornet nest anger, she had never said anything as hurtful and cruel as Mr. Titwallow said that day, and no one in my family had ever been violent.

"Shush … shush … shush," he comforted, pulling my head to his chest and holding me with the baby between us. "We don't have to go if you don't want to, and I understand if you never want to be around my dad again."

"But … I … don't want to break up your family," I pleaded.

"You are not breaking up my family," he reassured. "If anyone has broken up my family, it's my dad."

I collected myself to meet Earl's eyes. "Do you think he still hates me?"

"I don't know what he feels," he said. "Long ago, I stopped trying to figure my father out."

"Is it important to you that we go?" I questioned.

He looked away and thought for a moment. Then, he looked back at me. "It's important to me that you are happy," he said.

I reflected, "But it *is* important to you. I can tell by your response that it's important to you."

"You know …" He led me to the sofa to sit down. "I have wanted, all my life, to have some common ground with my dad, but I've never had it." He placed his hand on my leg and sat close. "I do want peace in my family. I want some reconciliation with my dad, but you and Vanilla are my family now, and I don't want my dad appeased at the expense of your feelings."

"I don't know if I can handle it," I said. "I'm terrified of your dad now, but if it is important to you, I'll go."

"We don't have to go, Lovella," he smiled reassuringly. "Honestly, it will be fine if we don't go."

"I don't want to be alone with your dad," I responded. "I don't think I could take it if he started screaming at me again, and I don't want any violence. I'm afraid you'll get into it with him again."

"Then, we won't go," he concluded.

"No," I continued. "We need to go. You need to go. I need to figure out a way to feel safe."

"You feel safe with my mother, don't you?" he asked. "Who else do you feel safe with? Do you want to ask Gretta to come along? You can invite anyone you want."

"Gretta will be having Thanksgiving with her family," I noted. "It wouldn't be fair to ask them to leave their family holiday for this. Besides, it doesn't concern them."

"Then, ask the whole family or whoever," Earl said. "They can all come up. If there is no room in the house for everyone you want to invite, Dad can start paying for hotels. Invite the whole fucking town of Climax if you want. Believe me, if you invite the whole town, he will pay for it."

"Do you think it would be all right to invite Mother and maybe Grandmother and Grandfather Donner?" I asked.

Earl looked shocked. "I'm surprised," he said, "given your problems with your mother."

"She has been pretty good since the baby was born. Don't you think?" I continued. "She has been different, changed, somehow. Maybe I finally got through to her. She seems more relaxed."

He reached up to stroke my face with the back of his fingers. "Yeah, I do think," he said. "Go ahead and invite them, and Dad will just have to get over it. If you still want to invite Gretta and her family, the whole family, he will have to get over that too."

"I think I'll be fine with just my family," I said. "It will be nice to have an extra babysitter or two, and as crazy as they are, Grandmother and Grandfather Donner can be a fun distraction, and they're good with kids."

The next day, Earl called his father and told him that my family would also be coming and that he expected him to pay for and arrange their transportation. To my surprise, Mr. Titwallow agreed and said to invite whoever I wanted, just as Earl had predicted. When I called Mother, she was initially hesitant since she was also concerned after witnessing Mr. Titwallow's behavior when Vanilla was born. Still, she had grown close to Mrs. Titwallow, and she relaxed when she understood the trip was to hear Mr. Titwallow's apology.

Grandmother and Grandfather Donner jumped at the opportunity when I told them that a limo would be sent to pick them up and that all arrangements would be made. "Hell!" Grandmother Donner exclaimed. "I don't have to cook all day? Damn right, we'll be there!"

On the Tuesday before Thanksgiving, Earl's Dad ensured that a limousine was sent to Climax to gather Mother, Grandmother, and Grandfather Donner for the trip to Martha's Vineyard. It must have been a sight in that tiny town where most people had only seen limousines on TV or in the movies. Since it was more than a ten-hour drive, he also put them in a luxury hotel overnight in New York. They completed the journey, arriving on Wednesday afternoon, before Thanksgiving. He had also sent a limo for Earl, the baby, and me. The limo from Climax could have stopped to get us on the way, but Mr. Titwallow sent a separate limo for us, and we arrived late on Tuesday evening. I had invited Grandmother Fuchs and Raymond, as well, but she was struggling with her health, so she didn't think she would be able to handle the trip, and Raymond, of course, had to be there to care for her.

The house at Martha's Vineyard was a regal home that was both rustic and elegant. A white porch went around three sides with white rocking chairs and other outdoor furniture neatly placed. There were ocean views on all but the backside of the house. I noticed how warm and inviting the house felt as soon as I saw it. The outside was a pale yellow clapboard with white trim. In most rooms, shiplap walls were washed with a light blue, and the wood grain faded through the color. Earl, Vanilla, and I were given a bedroom upstairs with French doors opening onto a balcony over the shoreline. Mr. Titwallow had purchased and delivered a crib for Vanilla to have in the room.

As predicted, Mr. Titwallow had brought Ralph and Nora. There was a separate apartment off the kitchen, at the back of the house, for them. When Earl and I arrived on Tuesday evening, they were already busy preparing for a Thanksgiving feast. Earl's Mom was waiting for us with news that Mr. Titwallow would arrive on Thanksgiving morning. Anna kept herself isolated from the rest of us and spent time talking to her friends on the phone or reading in her bedroom.

On Wednesday afternoon, Earl and I cuddled on the porch under blankets that warmed us in the fifty-degree weather while his mom cared for the baby. The breeze, coming off the ocean, was almost too crisp, and the salt air had a sting, but we were determined that we were going to sit outside and enjoy the full, open view of the water. When we finally decided that nature had overwhelmed us and were about to go back inside, the limousine with the rest of my family arrived. So, we walked around to that side of the porch to greet them.

Grandmother Donner did not wait for the limo driver to come around and open her door. She threw the door open and stepped out onto the driveway, taking in the experience. Seeing that she had beaten him to his job, the driver opened the door on the opposite side for Mother, who had patiently waited, as would be her style.

Grandmother Donner was in her usual bizarre regalia, wearing a bright yellow wide-brimmed hat with a broad red ribbon around the band tied in a grand bow on the side and plastic flowers wired to the bow were drifting off the brim. She wore a blue and pink polka-dotted knee-length dress that wasn't long enough to cover the stocking rolls that clung to her chubby legs. Her green jacket clashed loudly with the rest of her outfit, as did the purple and orange scarf wrapped around her thick neck. One could never accuse her of not being colorful. She stood by the vehicle's door, blocking Grandfather Donner from his exit.

"The Lord of Mercy!" she exclaimed. "Ain't this the fanciest damn place you ever saw in your life?"

"Get the hell out of the way, woman!" Grandfather Donner exclaimed from inside the car and began pushing her hips.

She slapped his hands. "Now, don't you get frisky with me in front of the children," she teased.

"Go on, woman!" he pleaded. "Let me out of this damn car. I gotta piss!"

When she wouldn't move, he scooted over to the other side and came out behind Mother, who had come to the rear of the car and was looking at the house and the view across the ocean. Mother was dressed classically and neatly in a tasteful conservative tan dress. What I noticed immediately, however, was that there was no beehive. I almost gasped in shock, but I was also quietly delighted to see her hair flowing across her shoulders in the afternoon breeze. She, of course, kept those locks dyed jet black.

Grandfather Donner grabbed his crotch like a little boy who was about to wet his pants and trotted up the porch steps where Earl and I were standing.

"Where's the damn bathroom?" he exclaimed.

"Don't I even get a hello?" I giggled.

"Hello! Now where's the damn bathroom?" he demanded again.

"Through that door," I pointed. "Mrs. Titwallow is in the living room. She'll show you from there."

By this time, Mother had come around the car and put her hand behind Grandmother Donner's elbow to walk her to the porch.

"Oh, get your damn hands off me!" Grandmother Donner exclaimed. "I may be old, but I can still walk, and I think I can see the way."

Mother immediately let go and walked ahead of her to the porch.

"Hello, Earl … Lovella," she said formally. "How very nice to be invited for the holiday."

"Mother! What have you done with your hair?" I exclaimed. "What? No beehive?"

"Don't tease, Lovella," she responded. "It isn't seemly."

"I like it," I said with a grin. "I am shocked and appealed. I hope you keep it."

"Thank you," she replied, walking up the steps in her white high heels. Until that moment, I barely realized that Mother was a beautiful woman who, despite her age, had maintained her figure and appearance.

Grandmother Donner was right behind her by this time, farting as she waddled up the steps, almost beating Mother to the top.

"Oh, for goodness sake!" Mother exclaimed as she waved her hand in front of her face. "Try to have some manners!"

"Hee—Yah!" Grandmother Donner chided. "Has your ass got so tight that you don't even pass gas no more?"

Mother looked away and rolled her eyes, and it suddenly occurred to me that I had never, not once, ever heard Mother fart.

Earl and I showed them to the door. Nora came out to instruct the limo driver where to take their luggage. Mrs. Titwallow greeted them sweetly inside. She had never met my grandparents before, and I was a bit worried that she might find them offensive, but if that was the case, there was never any indication. Mrs. Titwallow seemed always to be gracious.

We visited throughout the evening, and the two families shared stories of how Earl, Anna, and I had behaved as small children.

The following day, Earl and I slept late. Mother had tip-toed in during the first pale light of dawn to retrieve Vanilla and take her downstairs. It was so nice to have grandmothers doting over the baby. I could feel some of the freedom that I had before she was born. With a baby, sufficient sleep was a rare event.

Since Ralph was busy preparing dinner for the family, Nora made an omelet for us, which we shared so we wouldn't get too stuffed before the big meal. The rest of the family watched the Macy's parade in the living room. Grandfather Donner had his sock feet propped up on an ottoman, just as he would have at home. He had fallen asleep, and there was an occasional snorting snore. Grandmother Donner was swigging a beer and commenting about the parade. Mother was holding Vanilla, cooing to her, and was so relaxed that I could hardly believe it was her. Earl's mom sat quietly and sweetly watching the TV, and Anna was propped up on floor pillows facing the other direction with her nose in a book.

We sat down with the family and enjoyed the rest of the parade. By early afternoon, Ralph had prepared a sumptuous Thanksgiving feast with tweaks on the traditional, such as roasted pine nuts topping the stuffing. Earl's dad was yet to arrive by almost 1:00 p.m. Then, Mrs. Titwallow decided that we would go ahead and eat.

Grandmother Donner did her usual Thanksgiving announcement and insisted everyone take turns around the table and say what they were thankful for. When it became Mother's turn, she said, "I am thankful that I have a beautiful, intelligent daughter who has given me a sweet and beautiful grandchild."

"Who are you, and what have you done with my mother?" I asked.

She looked up at me sternly.

"Oh, there she is," I teased. "For a minute, I thought we had lost her."

A Mona Lisa smile crossed her face before she broke eye contact with me and turned to the next person in line to give thanks.

After grace, when we began to eat, Mother looked over at Mrs. Titwallow and said, "I do hope that Mr. Titwallow has not come to some harm. Is it like him to miss a holiday gathering?"

"I'm sure he is fine," Earl responded. "There were lots of times when we were growing up that he never made it to a holiday at all. He always had the excuse that he was working and couldn't take time for his family. He is probably sitting in a bar somewhere trying to convince some grocery store owner that it would greatly benefit his business to stock Chum Snacks."

"Earl," Mrs. Titwallow said, handing him a basket of rolls, "why don't you see if Lovella would like some bread?"

The subject changed, as was the intent. Although Nora usually served meals, Mrs. Titwallow had requested that the meal be family-style, with everything on the table or the sideboard for passing around.

After the meal, we retreated to the living room, waiting for the food to settle enough to make room for dessert. The television had been turned off to allow conversation, and Nora had served coffee.

Mother sipped her coffee with the saucer carefully held beneath the cup. She gazed out through the large bank of windows across the front of the living room, which gave a view across the porch to the ocean beyond.

"This view is so amazing," she said. "I just feel so relaxed and at ease here."

To this, Grandmother Donner snickered at Mother and mockingly said, "Oh my, I do declare. Lordy, I believe I am simply overcome. Oh, wait a minute. I feel something coming on. I do hope I don't pass gas again."

Mother said nothing and ignored her. I found myself encountering the rare experience of having compassion for her. I wondered how torturous it must have been growing up while being taunted and ridiculed by her own mother. I was beginning to realize that a lot of the effort she had put into controlling me was to make sure that I did not turn out like her parents. She had tried to control me, but she had never ridiculed me or made fun of me like that.

Mrs. Titwallow was gracious and said, "Drucella, you should come back to visit again. Daniel and I usually come out here once or twice a year. We would be delighted to have you join us."

"Thank you, Clarisse," Mother responded. "I would love to if I ever have the opportunity."

Before Grandmother Donner could make a snide remark, we were startled by the slam of a door in the back of the house near the kitchen. Then, we heard Mr. Titwallow's voice, which was somewhat loud and overbearing. "Nora, see if you can round up enough leftovers for me to make a meal."

"Yes, sir, Mr. Titwallow," she responded.

We had all turned in the direction of the commotion. Shortly, Mr. Titwallow came, somewhat staggeringly, up the hall from the kitchen. It was rather evident that he had been drinking heavily. As soon as I realized that, my muscles tightened, and my breath quickened. I had somewhat trusted that he might be civil to me on this visit, but I began to doubt the possibility when I saw that he was not in complete control of his faculties. It also brought me back to Daddy's drinking and the ache I still carried for losing him.

"Hey! Hey! Hey!" Mr. Titwallow slurred loudly as he entered the room. "I'm so glad you guys could all make it. I'm so sorry I'm late. I had some pressing matters … at the office."

He wobbled over to Grandfather Donner and extended his hand. "I don't believe we have met, sir," he stammered. "I'm Daniel Titwallow, Earl's father, and you must be Lovella's grandfather?"

"Yes, sir," Grandfather Donner replied. Then, to my surprise, he stood and shook his hand, "Sid Donner. Very nice to meet you … and thank you for having us up to your place here."

"Oh, it's not my place," Mr. Titwallow responded. "It's just rented for a few days, but you're welcome."

He then turned to Grandmother Donner. "Now, this beacon of beauty must undoubtedly be Mrs. Donner."

"Flattery will get you my phone number," she giggled without getting up. Reaching her hand with the palm down, as she had done with Earl, I suppose she expected him to bend and kiss it. He shook it briefly between finger and thumb and turned to us.

Lovella! Earl!" he spouted with inebriated charm. His words were so sudden and loud that I was startled, and it seemed he hadn't even noticed. "It is so good to see you two. I have missed you."

"Thank you, Dad," Earl responded.

I glanced up, caught a milli-second of eye contact, and stared at the floor. "Thank you," I said quickly and almost under my breath. I felt terrified. There was a part of me that realized that I was safe and that Earl would protect me, but I was also trying to fight off a full-blown panic attack. I asked myself where the gutsy stand-up-to-anyone Lovella had gone. Perhaps she had been subdued by a cumulative effect. It was not just the fact that Earl's father had screamed at me and called me a "nigger fucking whore," when Vanilla was born. It was the whole year, the death of Dr. Martin Luther King Jr. and Bobby Kennedy, the riots shown constantly on TV, and the isolation in our apartment, where my mind had gone into fear overdrive.

Mr. Titwallow, despite his inebriation, picked up on my discomfort. "Ah … Lovella … I … hmmm … I am going to the kitchen to eat a bite. I … I'm going to try to sober up a bit so I don't make such an ass of myself, and maybe a little later, we could sit down together and have a discussion."

He turned toward the kitchen, and when he was out of the room, Earl turned to me and softly said, "Are you all right?

"I don't know," I said. "I don't know why I'm so scared. It's not like me to be scared like this."

Mrs. Titwallow came to sit on the opposite side from Earl. She reached out and took my hand.

"Lovella," she said so gently. "You know I love you, don't you, and I adore little Vanilla?"

"Yes, I do," I responded.

"Then, believe me when I tell you, it will all be fine." She smiled and looked at me with such gentle eyes. "At this point, honey, Daniel has to face something very difficult. Please understand that he is just as nervous about this as you are, which may account for today's drinking. Earl," she suggested, "why don't you take Lovella and show her the view from the crest?"

"Sure," he responded.

We got our coats and headed out of the house. There was about a fifteen-minute walk to the top of a small hill on the west side of the house. It was steep, but Earl held onto my hand to ensure I had my footing. When we got to the top, the view was magnificent. There was an inlet there, and in the distance, across on the other side, the hills jutted down to the water's edge. Even though it was cold and breezy, the sun shone in a perfect jewel blue and cloudless sky.

"It's beautiful," I said, mesmerized by the sight.

Earl walked behind me, wrapped his arms and coat around me, and held me close to his body.

"I used to love to climb up here when I was a kid," he said. "I didn't have to do anything but just be here, just experience it. There is something so enchanting about it."

"Your mom must have known I would relax if you brought me here," I said.

"We both needed to relax a little bit," he responded.

We stood there a very long time, saying nothing, just watching. The occasional boat could be seen in the distance, even on a cold Thanksgiving Day. Gulls and other water birds sailed low in the open sky. Occasionally, a pelican would skim down just above the water's surface. The waves lapping against the stone shoreline made a soothing rhythm and created a symphony accented by the horn-like cries of the gulls. After a while, Earl asked me if I was ready to go. Then, we navigated our way back down the hillside to the house.

When we returned to the house, it was very toasty and warm. Mr. Titwallow had built and was stoking a fire in the fireplace, and only he and Mrs. Titwallow were in the living room.

"Where is everyone?" I asked, suddenly feeling a little nervous again.

"There is a football game on the television in the den," Mrs. Titwallow replied. "We asked them if they would like to go back there to watch it. Besides, Daniel and I need to have a little time with just the two of you, if you don't mind."

I looked around at Earl for reassurance.

Mrs. Titwallow motioned for us to sit down. We sat side-by-side on the sofa. Mrs. Titwallow sat in a chair just off-center between us and Mr. Titwallow, who had come to sit in a chair opposite the sofa.

"Daniel," Mrs. Titwallow began. "I believe you have some things to say to Earl and his bride."

Mr. Titwallow looked almost as though he was scanning the room for a route to escape. His eyes darted around the room before he spoke.

"Well … you see," he began, finally. "I was far more than out of line when I said those awful things about you, Lovella … and about the baby. I … ah … well, it is wrong for anyone to say things like that, and if anyone should have behaved more respectfully, that should have been me. It was totally inappropriate, and Earl, your mother has helped me to realize that I have no business judging anybody."

"Okay," Earl responded.

"Well … I … I'm sorry for what I said," Mr. Titwallow continued. "I know I can never take it back, but I want you to know." He looked up at me pleadingly. "I want you to know … that I have changed my mind. I've changed … completely changed, and I promise you will never see me act like that again."

"Why the big change, Dad?" Earl chided. "I've never known you to give up on a point. Hell, you demand that you are right when everybody knows you're wrong and even when you know you're wrong. Why would you change your mind about this? Where has the racist gone?"

Mr. Titwallow looked over at Mrs. Titwallow. "You want to tell them, Clarisse," he pleaded.

"No, Daniel," she replied. "I think you need to tell them."

He took a deep breath and let it out in a sigh. "Well, ah … after I had acted like such an ass the day Vanilla was born, Clarisse did her best to convince me that I was wrong and that I should apologize. Of course, I refused because, as you said, Earl, when I think I'm right, I refuse to listen to arguments to the contrary. Finally, she stopped talking to me about it, and I thought we were getting back to normal."

He kept looking at Mrs. Titwallow as though trying to gather some strength from his repeated glances. She kept nodding at him to continue.

He went on. "I felt that you had been out of line to hit me, son, and I kept telling her you owed *me* an apology. I told her I would call you and demand that you apologize. She strongly discouraged me from doing that. I didn't know that your mother had started doing some … research. She even contacted the Mormon church to learn how to do it."

"Research about what?" Earl cut in, glancing back and forth between his parents.

"About … our heritage," Mr. Titwallow responded, "based on when I said that there was no … Black blood … on … on our side of the family, she decided to find out."

"You didn't say 'Black,'" Earl chastened. "You used the N-word slur."

Mr. Titwallow leaned forward, put his hands together, and humbled his words. "Yes, I did, and I'm sorry I ever said that." He stared down at his hands as though some prompt might be written there. Then, he continued. "It seems that one of our ancestors was a plantation owner before and during the Civil War, and he had a habit of raping his slave women, as well as, also their daughters, his own biracial children, and also his grandchildren by those women. It turns out that maybe a generation or two down the line, one of those daughters or granddaughters had become so light-skinned that, if she was careful about it, she could pass as White. Do you remember us talking about a distant relative who came from the South? Apparently, after The Emancipation Proclamation, she found passage to Pennsylvania. She married your great, great Grandfather Simon Titwallow. He knew that she had Black ancestry but helped her hide it. It would have been illegal for him to marry a Black woman in those days. I don't know if he forged papers for her or what. It was easier to do things like that back then. I guess it was never spoken of, even within the family, and after a while, everyone forgot about having a biracial great-grandmother, if they ever knew."

"Holy shit!" Earl burst into laughter after patiently listening. He stood up, pacing back and forth. "Holy fucking shit! This is too damn good for words! Mom! How the hell did you ever find out about this?"

Mrs. Titwallow explained, "When Daniel insisted there was no Negroid blood on our side of the family, I got curious. I first thought, *'What difference does it make?'* and then, I thought, *'How does he know?'* So, I searched both sides of the family, his ancestors and mine. I was able to trace records back and then look at lineages and how the family divided over the years. I got suspicious when I traced back to your great, great Grandpa Simon Titwallow and couldn't find any further information about his wife's family. Her lineage stopped as though she had never had ancestors. I contacted other family members to ask if they knew anything about this. I found a cousin of Daniel's and asked if she might know why the information stopped with Cloretta, Simon's wife, and why there were no records before that. She told me that, after her parents had passed, she found a journal hidden in their attic. It had been kept by Cloretta's daughter regarding stories that her mother had told her. It identified that Cloretta had left the South after the war and had Black ancestry. The journal also revealed things she had been through before leaving. Your cousin was kind enough to send me a copy of one particular telling page of that journal. I then had the evidence to sit down with your father and have a little discussion."

"So, Mom," Earl questioned. "What were you going to do if you had not found this piece of evidence? What if all you found was White, Whiter, and Whitest? Then, what?"

Mrs. Titwallow sighed, "I'm not sure, son. But even as I was searching for the records, I was asking myself if I could continue to remain married to a man who was so rejecting and cruel to his son, daughter-in-law, and granddaughter. It wouldn't matter if she were blood or not. If she had been adopted, she would still be your daughter, his granddaughter. Your father and I have had several heated arguments over the past few months. I just regret that it took proving to him that he has Negroid ancestry for him to finally admit that he was wrong."

"This is so fucking funny!" Earl laughed. "The buzzards have come home to roost. They have found the skeleton in the old man's closet and have picked the last bit of meat off the bone! So, Dad, how does that feel? How does it feel to find out, after all these years of being a bigoted asshole, that you *are* the very thing you were condemning?"

Mr. Titwallow still leaned over his folded hands and said, "It feels very humbling … son. It feels like I should have been more of a man, a caring father and grandfather, even if Clarise had never found out about all that. It feels like I have been a hypocrite, and it is about time I learned to do a little listening instead of so much commanding. I need to free my mind, start considering that there might be another way of looking at things, and realize that any other human being has as much right to be here as I do. You know, your mom brought me a quote by Mark Twain a few months ago before she made this discovery. I should have listened, then. The quote said, '*Loyalty to petrified opinion never yet broke a chain or freed a human soul.*' I can't keep clinging to the idea that I'm somehow better than others. If I had really loved myself in the first place, I never would have tried to condemn or control someone else or act like I was better than them. There would have been nothing to prove if I had truly been confident. I finally realized that I had spent most of my life trying to prove something, trying to overcome the shame of poverty from my childhood. I'm sorry, Son. I'm sorry for everything."

"So, Dad," Earl continued, interrogating, "what would you have done if Mom had never found this evidence of ancestry?"

Mr. Titwallow sighed and looked up at him. "She almost had me broken anyway," he said. "It was only a matter of time before I either had to apologize or lose my whole family. No … not just apologize. I had to come to my senses."

Then, he looked up at me. "I'm sorry, Lovella," he went on. "I'm sorry that I judged you and my granddaughter. I was wrong, and there is no excuse. I shouldn't have been so ignorant and arrogant. I hope you realize I am sincere and truly want and need your forgiveness. I want us to be a family again. I want us to be a better family than ever."

I sat there, looking at him for several seconds, pondering what I would say. At last, I felt more like my old self, but I still wasn't sure. I asked myself if I could forgive him. Finally, I calmly said, "I forgive you, Mr. Titwallow."

A tear drifted down his cheek. "Thank you, Lovella," he said. Looking unsure and glancing at Mrs. Titwallow, he finally asked, "May I have a hug?"

I got up and walked across to him. He stood up and enfolded me in his arms. As we stood there, I felt the warmth of his sincerity. The hug felt real, and I felt like the brash and brave Lovella I used to be. I stepped back from the hug and asked, jokingly, "So, do you think that discovery of this family history might explain why Earl is so—very well endowed?"

Without missing a beat, Earl's Mom said, "No, dear, that probably comes from my side of the family."

CHAPTER 27

Separate but not Equal

The following morning, the skies were a crystal-clear, cold blue again with no clouds to be seen, and sunlight reflected off the chilly earth like a mirror. Earl and I awoke to a tapping on our bedroom door. When I stirred, it woke the baby, who had been sleeping quietly in her crib. Startled, Vanilla wailed against the morning. I picked her up from the crib and began pacing in my gown, rocking her, and trying to quiet her. Earl went to the door. When Earl opened the door, there stood Nora, half bent at the shoulders and being careful not to peek in.

"I am so sorry to disturb you, Master Earl," she said with her classic British accent. "However, John has prepared breakfast, and Mr. Titwallow requests that you join the family in the dining room before preparing for departure."

"Yes, um," Earl said sleepily. "We will be right down."

He closed the door behind him and turned to me. By this time, Vanilla had quieted her crying to a gentle whimper. Earl immediately turned around, threw open the door, and called down the hall. "Nora, Nora." Realizing his nakedness, he grabbed the sheet off the bed and quickly wrapped it around himself.

"Yes, Sir," she said, turning in the hall.

"Could you take Vanilla for a short while so Lovella can dress?" he asked.

"Certainly, Master Earl," she said, walking straight into the room to me. She averted her eyes until I said, "It's okay, Nora." Then she quickly took the baby and exited the room.

"She may need a diaper change," I called after her.

"Will do, Mrs. Titwallow," she called back. "We have a diaper bag downstairs."

As soon as she left, I put on jeans and a ruffled blouse while Earl searched for the pants he had worn the day before. Once dressed, we packed our remaining clothes into our suitcases and met the family.

At the dining table sat the whole family, all fully dressed and sitting about waiting for our arrival. Mrs. Titwallow sat on the side, at one end of the table, holding Vanilla, who was greedily sucking a bottle. Mr. Titwallow sat across the corner from Mrs. Titwallow at the head of the table. The places were set with silverware and napkins but no plates. Most of the family did have bits of coffee sipped down to various levels.

Grandmother Donner spouted immediately, "Hell. It's about time you two got down here. I thought I would plum starve to death before y'all showed up. So, can we eat now?"

"I'm sorry, Grandmother," I said. "You shouldn't have waited on us. Surely you could have started the meal."

"No, this is the last gathering before we all go home," Mr. Titwallow interjected. "I caused myself to miss the Thanksgiving meal yesterday, and I would like us all to share this time together. I'm sure your grandmother has not starved yet. Have you, Mrs. Donner?"

Grandfather Donner chimed in, "She ain't starved yet! Hell, look at her! She could live for two months just on belly fat!"

Grandmother stared at him, then snapped. "Shut up, Sid, before I start gnawing on your belly fat."

Nora had seen us enter. She motioned to John, who had already begun to serve the Eggs Benedict. After serving, Nora took Vanilla to the back so we could all eat without anyone having to fuss with holding the baby.

When we began to eat, Mr. Titwallow announced, "I just want to say how delighted I am that all of you could join us for this holiday, and most of all, I have to say that I am so glad to have my son back, and my family reunited."

Earl leaned over and whispered in my ear. "Shit, here it comes. He's up to something."

I gave only a tiny nod to Earl.

Mr. Titwallow continued. "I say we should make this a family tradition and all meet back here again next year, every year!"

"Here. Here!" Grandmother Donner exclaimed as she raised her coffee cup before bringing it to her lips.

"It has been truly wonderful," Mother said. "Daniel, Clarisse, your gracious hospitality is greatly appreciated." She then stared at me as though I were still a little girl, and manners would insist on an expression of gratitude, as well.

"Thank you, Mr. & Mrs. Titwallow," I said. "It was lovely of you to have us."

"Lovella," Mr. Titwallow replied. "Thank you for allowing me to make amends. I owe you far more than this. I have enjoyed this time as much as anyone here. I … I … hate to see my son go back and work for minimum wage at a grocery store."

"Told you." Earl stifled a sarcastic tone under his breath toward me.

"We are doing fine, Mr. Titwallow," I said, defending Earl. "Honestly, we are quite comfortable."

"Well, I know you are doing okay," Mr. Titwallow replied. "It's okay. I started at the bottom and worked my way into what I have now. In some ways, I think it was sheer luck, as much as hard work, to have built this business." He paused. "I have done some soul-searching over the last few months, and even though I have mixed feelings about it, I do understand that, sometimes, it is important to feel like you have accomplished something on your own, that you have done it yourself, without having it handed to you. I think somewhere along the way, I had forgotten that."

Earl didn't say a word. There were some glances between him and his mother. After a moment, I spoke for him. "Thank you, Mr. Titwallow. It means a lot to us that you have realized our need for independence."

"I hope I understand," Mr. Titwallow responded. "The truth is, I would give you kids everything if I could, but I know I need to back off and let go. I know I haven't been very good at that in the past, and Earl … I also owe you another apology. I apologize for trying to make you into what I wanted you to be instead of letting you be who you are. I have interfered in your life. I have pushed you, and I have tried to make you into me. Instead of loving you for who you are, I have tried to make you into what I expected from a son. I'm sorry I did that to you."

Earl looked up from his plate and across the table at his father. His face was stern. "I am not sure if I believe you," he said.

"I don't blame you for not believing me," Mr. Titwallow replied, his voice trembling. "I just want you to know that I love you, no matter what you want to do with your life. I know, now, that loving you doesn't mean controlling you, but I also want you to know that I have options for you if you ever decide to accept them."

"Oh, here we go," Earl said, not even trying to hide his hostile tone.

Mr. Titwallow leaned forward in his chair. "Son, I know you don't believe me when I say that I am leaving your choices up to you, but I swear to you, this is the commitment I am making to you right here in front of these witnesses. I will *not* continue to interfere in your life. I want to help you if you allow me, but if you want to build a life on your own, then I will bless you in that decision, and if you want to go back to college and get a degree in something else, I'm willing to pay for it."

"What kind of options?" Earl questioned.

Mr. Titwallow sighed again and looked down at his plate. When he looked back up, he said, "Son, I promise you this is an invitation. I have no expectations and will not attempt to interfere in your life whether you accept or reject the invitation. This is an offer, not a demand. If you tell me that you don't want to do this, I will bless you with whatever choice you make."

"What is it?" Earl responded with his voice still hinting at hostility. "You want me to come back to Pittsburgh and follow you around the office so I can learn to imitate you? You want to tell me what I need to do to protect your legacy?"

"No, Son," Mr. Titwallow said with an uncharacteristic softness. "I have already told you I want you to be your own man. I mean that. I'm trying to come to my senses about that. I'm trying to realize where I was wrong. I want you to be who you are, whatever that means to you. Over the last few months, with your mother's help, I have done a lot of soul-searching. I am trying to change. I know that doesn't sound like me, but I have had to rethink a lot of things, including my role as a father. Even if you accept this, I promise I will stay out of your way, allow you to make your own decisions, and only offer advice when you ask."

"What then?" Earl scoffed.

"Like I said," Mr. Titwallow labored on. "This is only if you want to, only if you are willing to try it."

"What? Damn it!" Earl snapped, losing his patience.

Mr. Titwallow did not take the invitation to fight, which he rarely did with Earl. Mrs. Titwallow was showing some anxiety at this point.

Mr. Titwallow reached over to put a calming hand on her arm, and continued. "You know that I have been building a warehouse distribution center in Nashville, Tennessee, over the past two years. I have expanded distribution into the southern states of Georgia, Alabama, Mississippi, and South Carolina. I hope to include Arkansas, Louisiana, and Missouri. The warehouse facility is centrally located in Nashville, allowing us to expand to several other states in the region. The distribution warehouse will be finished in February or March this coming year. I hope to have full distribution out of there by next summer. I would like you to manage it for me if you want."

"Manage it?" Earl questioned, looking obviously confused.

"Well, you have a degree in business management, don't you?" Mr. Titwallow responded. "You should have some idea what it takes to manage a distribution center."

"I have a degree, Dad," Earl pleaded. "That's all. I have a degree. I've never managed anything in my life. I figured that when I finally got a job, I would be working for a few years, probably in lower or middle management, before I tackled anything remotely like a seven-state distribution center. I don't think I know how to do that unless you mean by 'manage' that you want me to be your puppet in Nashville and do what you tell me to do."

"No," Mr. Titwallow proceeded. "I don't want that. I will be available to you if you want or need my advice, and several other managers will also be available. I mean for this to be yours. Yours to run as you see fit. Maybe you have learned something that I don't know. Maybe you might have some creative ideas that I never considered. It will be yours. The company will supply the product. Then, the markets and distribution you create for the product will be up to you and your talent."

"You realize you are taking a huge risk by doing that?" Earl defended. "What if I screw it up? It could mean millions. It is too big for me to fuck it up, too big a loss if I can't handle it."

"I'm putting my faith in you, son," Mr. Titwallow said, looking intently and confidently at Earl. "I know that you can do this. I know you have it in you. If you don't want the job, I understand, but if you do take the job, you have my promise that I will stay out of the way and give only the advice I am asked to give."

"You are taking a risk that could potentially bankrupt Chum Snacks," Earl responded.

"Maybe," said Mr. Titwallow, "but I'm also taking a risk that could potentially triple the company's size. Do you want the job? If you want it, you have it."

"I'll have to think about it," Earl replied, looking over at me. "We will have to think about it."

Mr. Titwallow took a bite of his breakfast and chewed it gingerly. "I am willing to start you out at $150,000 a year and give you a 20% bonus for any profit increases the company makes."

Mother dropped her fork and gasped. That was equivalent to a little over a million a year in today's dollars.

I reached over and took Earl's hand. "Whatever you decide is okay," I said. Inside, my heart was pounding. I would accept if he said no, but my mind was already racing to what my life would be like with that much money. Unlike Earl, I was a transplant hippie. I agreed, to a point, with his causes, but a part of me still reveled in the promise of having the finer things of life.

"How soon do you need to know?" Earl asked.

"A month?" Mr. Titwallow replied. "Does that give you enough time?"

Earl said, "I'll let you know," and changed the subject. He turned to my family and said, "So, are you guys looking forward to going home today?"

Grandmother Donner said, "Hell, if I never go back to that rattrap, shit hole again, it's fine with me. I would just as soon stay here and be waited on. I go back home—I gotta wait on this fat bastard." She slapped Grandfather Donner across the belly, to which he responded, "Goddamn woman! Lighten up!"

I sat there snickering, watching Mother, who was clearly appalled.

"Well," Earl said politely. "I'm glad you enjoyed your stay here."

After breakfast, the limo drivers brought our luggage from the house and stuffed it into the trunks of the cars. Then, they stood dutifully to the side of the open doors, waiting for us to descend the stairs like royalty and enter our gleaming black chariots. There were two limos to take us back, just as there had been two to deliver us.

We said our goodbyes on the porch. That afternoon, Mr. and Mrs. Titwallow returned home in a different car with John and Nora.

Just as we were getting ready to leave, Mother approached me.

"Lovella," she whispered. "Do you mind if I ride back with you and Earl, at least as far as State College? I don't think I can tolerate one more hour with the Donners."

I was shocked at her politeness and keenly aware of how she distanced herself from Grandmother and Grandfather by calling them "The Donners."

"I'm sure it would be fine, Mother," I said. "Besides, maybe you can hold Vanilla while Earl and I talk. We seem to have a lot to talk about after this visit."

"I would be delighted to hold the baby," Mother said. She then shifted her attention behind her to tell Grandmother and Grandfather Donner that she was riding back to State College with us. I heard Grandmother Donner exclaim, "Can't stay away from that grandbaby, huh, Drucella? Hell, I don't blame you. Go ahead."

Mother came to me and took Vanilla from my arms before we descended the steps to the cars. I couldn't help but remember how Mother would always have us procession down the steps at home on Sunday morning as though we were being picked up by a limo. Perhaps all those years of practice had prepared her for this moment.

We had no sooner pulled out of the driveway when Earl leaned his head against the window and exclaimed, "What the hell!"

I reached my hand up to touch his shoulder, and he turned to me, "Can you believe this shit?" he asked.

"I believe what I heard," I replied. "I don't know how you are interpreting all this."

Mother sat quietly holding Vanilla, pretending not to hear. The baby had quickly fallen asleep in her arms.

"That's the problem," Earl replied. "I don't know how I'm interpreting it either. I don't know what to fucking think. I spent my whole life fighting with and resisting the control of my father, trying to give him what he wanted, on the one hand, but rebelling and trying to live my own life without his control on the other. Now, he wants to play nice because he found his humbling roots, but I still don't trust him."

"Sometimes, people change," I said. "Sometimes, we realize things in retrospect that we didn't realize when we were in the moment."

"If it were up to you, Lovella," he stared at me intently. " If it were all up to you, and it wasn't my decision, what would you do? Would you go to Nashville?"

"I don't think that's fair," I moaned. "It is not my decision. It's your decision."

"No," he affirmed. "It is *our* decision. We are a family. You are my wife. Whatever I decide affects you and the baby, so what you think about this is important to me."

I turned and looked at Mother, who remained silent. She glanced at me briefly, then looked away. I could scarcely believe she wasn't butting in with her opinions. It seemed that Earl's dad wasn't the only one who had changed.

I turned back to Earl. "I have mixed feelings, too," I said. "On one hand, I think, '*My God, with that amount of money, I could buy practically anything I want for myself or the baby.*' On the other hand, it might be nice to have all that somewhere besides Nashville, Tennessee—yuck. Still, I want you to be happy, regardless of what I want. I told you I would go wherever you go and live the way you want. So, I am comfortable with what we have now. If you want to start small and work your way up, I'm comfortable supporting you in finding your career. If you don't want a career and want to maintain a job somewhere, I'm comfortable with that, too. I love you no matter what we do."

"You said, 'Yuck, Nashville.' What's wrong with Nashville?" he questioned.

"Oh, jeez!" I pondered. "Minnie Pearl, Earnest Tubb, and the Grand Ole Opry, for starts. I mean, the whole town is about hicks and rednecks. If the TV shows and record stores are any indication, you would think there is not a Black person living within hundreds of miles. What are they going to think about or do to a family with a biracial baby, burn a cross on our lawn?"

"What about Charlie Pride?" he asked.

"Charlie Pride? Honestly, Charlie Pride?" I responded. "They have one token Black country singer, just to prove they aren't racists. That's exactly what racists do."

"Nashville is not like that," he said. "Vanderbilt University is there. It's an Ivy League university, and country music is only one of many different types of music recorded there. The Beatles even recorded there."

"Well, I've never been there," I said. "I only know the stereotype, I guess."

"I'm sorry," Earl responded. "I didn't mean to sound condescending. I have been there. Vanderbilt was one of the universities I applied to. Nashville is much more cosmopolitan and sophisticated than most people imagine. It's even called the "Athens of the South." They have a full-sized replica of the Parthenon there."

"Okay," I said. "I never knew any of that stuff. You make it sound nice. So, they have a little culture, but it is still the South, and I think about the racism in the South. I even worry about bringing up Vanilla in Pennsylvania. I think I would be even more worried about raising her in Tennessee or any other formally Confederate state."

"We don't have to go," he said. "I don't want to make it sound like I want the job. I don't want the job." He paused for a moment. "Well, I don't know if I want the job. Maybe I would like to have it, but I don't know if I have what it takes."

"Do you think you could be happy living in Nashville?" I asked.

He reached over and took my hand. "I could be happy living anywhere with you," he replied.

"Oh, come on, Earl," I pleaded. "There's more to it than that. Cities have a soul just like a person does. Just as you might not like one person's personality but prefer another, you might not like the personality of a city. It needs to draw you to it."

"I suppose," he said.

"Well, did you visit Nashville when you applied to Vanderbilt?" I questioned.

"Yeah," he responded. "I spent a few days there."

"Did you like it?" I continued. "How did it feel to you?"

"It's kind of cool, in a way," he said.

"Is that it?" I pressed.

"Well, I guess there is a mix there," he explained. "It's not just about country music. You can find people from all over the world."

"That's cool," I said. "What do you think it would be like to live there, especially for us to live there?"

He turned to face me. "If we lived there," he said, "we would probably be living in Green Hills or Brentwood. They are sort of the nouveau riche areas of the city. I suppose we might live in Belle Meade, but that's old money, way old money. There are a lot of expensive old mansions there. I think a lot of the country music stars live in Green Hills. Some of them have started living in Hendersonville near the lake. Green Hills and Brentwood are rich but newer, maybe not as rich. I don't know, Lovella. I don't know what I want. Even considering living in those places feels like I'm selling out. It feels like I'm giving in to the establishment."

"Lots of money means having more resources to help others," I said. "If we had that much money, maybe we could contribute a lot to some good causes or maybe even create our own charities."

He turned to stare at the passing landscape that seemed to be flying by the window.

"The truth is," he said, fiddling nervously with a button on his shirt, "the truth is, I feel guilty about having that much money. I've felt guilty about it most of my life. I mean, we didn't always have the best. When I was little, we had it nice, but not great, and when we started having more money when Dad got even bigger dollar signs in his eyes, we moved into bigger and bigger homes with more luxury and servants, but my friends didn't. I had to leave them behind. Dad didn't want me to hang out with the poor kids anymore, but fuck, what was he when he was growing up? He grew up poor just like them, and then, when he got rich, it was like he was better than them, and he expected us to act like we were better than them, but they were my friends, Lovella."

"Your Dad fought so hard to escape poverty," I reasoned. "Maybe he hated poverty so much that he couldn't separate the poor person from the poor condition."

"He thought everybody ought to be able to go out and make millions like he did," Earl snapped. "He thought anyone who didn't go out and make millions must be lazy, but he didn't think about the fact that a lot of those poor people working in our factories had hard times that he didn't face, medical bills or family tragedies that a minimum wage job was not going to cover. He didn't figure that some of them were working harder than he ever worked and were struggling, paycheck to paycheck, to cover their bills and raise a family with no real way to save, much less invest. He didn't think about the fact that not everybody is as smart as he is, or even if they are smart; they might not have the business sense that he has. He just flat-out didn't think. He had the idea that if he could do it, the whole fucking world should be able to do it, but it doesn't work that way. The American dream is not for everyone, or maybe they have different dreams that don't include opulent houses and servants. Some people can never have that, no matter how much they desire it or how hard they are willing to work for it. It takes more than just hard work and know-how. It takes the stars being aligned just right for you. Otherwise, you end up like the next poor schmuck who thought his life was going to be better. If you work your ass off but you can't afford to go to a dentist or see a doctor, then your health deteriorates. If you can't afford the good food that rich people can afford, and you can't afford the healthcare that rich people can afford, your life goes downhill faster. The next thing you know, you are so sick you can't work, and your American dream becomes an American nightmare, and if you're lucky, you can get on disability or some pension plan, maybe health insurance. If you're not lucky, you end up on the streets, in an institution, or having to live with and depend on relatives and friends. It takes more than hard work to be successful, and my dad doesn't seem to get that."

I glanced up at Mother and realized she was paying close attention to his comments.

He looked at me, then back out the window. "I guess the difference between me and my father," he said, "is that I notice things. I watch how things work. I notice people and pay attention to all the factors, and my dad gets a dollar sign in his head and can't see anything else. Like a mule with blinders, he can't see anything but what is right in front of him. If that is a dollar bill, he will follow it like a carrot hung beyond a mule's nose all the way to the end of the road."

I sat there thinking for quite some time before I spoke. "I guess the question is whether you want to grab onto the coattails of your dad's American dream or try to create one of your own and take the chance of ending up like one of those poor schmucks you are talking about?"

"Unless Dad goes bankrupt," he said, "I would never be one of them. He would see to it, one way or another, that I was taken care of. Even if he 'disowned' me, I might not live in the lap of luxury, but he would find a way to ensure my basic needs were met. I've already cashed in just by being his son. The only option I would have if I wanted to build my own dream would be to cut all ties and refuse any assistance from him. Even then, if I didn't disappear where he couldn't find me, he or Mom would find a way to sneak something in, a word to this employer or that to hire me for a job that I'm not even qualified for."

"Are you willing to do that?" I asked. "Disappear?"

A look crossed his face that I had difficulty interpreting. It was a mix of multiple emotions. Then, he glanced around the passenger cabin like a trapped animal trying to find a way out.

"I'm hungry," he said, completely ignoring my question. "Are you hungry, Mrs. Fuchs? You guys want to stop somewhere and have a snack, maybe lunch?"

"I'm fine," Mother replied. "I would perhaps like to have something to drink, however."

Earl reached over and pressed a button on the console intercom, and we heard the chauffeur's voice come through the speaker. "Yes, sir?"

"Driver, please look for a place to stop and have a soft drink or a snack," he said.

"Would a Stubbie's be acceptable, sir?" the driver responded.

"Yes, any place like that would be fine," Earl said.

"Sir," the driver continued, "there is a Stubbie's just over the Connecticut border a few miles ahead."

"Fine," Earl said. "Stop there."

"Should I radio the other car to stop?" the driver asked.

"No!" Mother suddenly exclaimed.

Earl turned and looked at her with a strained curiosity, then told the driver, "No, only this car will be stopping."

Earl settled back into his seat, and we continued the ride while sharing small talk. Nashville was not mentioned again. In about twenty minutes, the limo pulled into the parking lot of the Connecticut Stubbies on I-95. The driver got out and opened the rear doors for us. Then, we all filed into the building. Mother continued to carry Vanilla, who was still quietly sleeping in her arms.

When we strolled to the snack bar in the back, I noticed a middle-aged woman with reddish-brown hair glaring at us. I passed it off as nothing and told Earl to get me a cola and an order of fries. Then, I trotted to the restroom. When I returned, Earl had ordered for everyone. Then, we located a booth and sat down. Mother insisted on keeping Vanilla.

Shortly, we were called to pick up our order. I helped Earl bring it to the booth. Then, as we ate, Mother noticed and kept glancing at a couple in a booth across from us. "What are you doing?" I whispered.

"That couple over there," she said. "They keep looking at us and whispering."

I turned to see the same middle-aged woman who had glared at us sitting in a booth across the aisle, slightly behind me. Also at that booth was a pot-bellied man who appeared to be in his late forties. He wore blue jeans and a flannel shirt with suspenders that caused his extended belly to look even more pronounced. They were indeed whispering and casting disgusted looks in our direction.

"What the hell is their problem?" I asked. Then, I saw Mother struggling to sip her soda while holding the baby. "Let me take her, Mother," I said, reaching for the baby.

"No, dear, I have her," she insisted.

I had no sooner leaned back when Mother stood up and carried Vanilla to the couple staring at us.

"This is my granddaughter," she said, smiling. "Isn't she beautiful? I noticed you kept looking over in our direction, and I can only assume you were thinking what a beautiful baby we have."

"Ah, no, not exactly," the middle-aged woman said with a distinct drawl. "Wasn't thinking that at all."

"Hmmm," Mother sighed. "I wonder, then, what would cause you to be so interested in my family that you were staring and whispering. Perhaps you had mistaken my beautiful daughter for a movie star."

The red-headed woman's skin was aged from tanning and smoking, and the crow's feet streaking across her eye sockets made her look mean and menacing. She snarled at Mother, "Why don't you just take your little eggplant back to your booth, Miss Mammy, and leave us alone."

I heard this and was on my feet. The terrified Lovella was gone, and the pissed-off Lovella was back in full force. I stomped across the aisle and screamed, "WHAT THE FUCK DID YOU JUST SAY TO MY MOTHER? WHAT THE GODDAMN FUCK! YOU SELF-RIGHTEOUS, BIGGOTED, FUCKING, WRINKLED OLD WHORE!"

The woman slid back to the end of the booth, startled by my attack, visibly shaken at the violence of my temper. She had good reason to be shaken because I was on the verge of ripping her throat out.

"YOU APOLOGIZE TO MY MOTHER YOU FUCKING CUNT!" I screamed. "YOU FUCKING APOLOGIZE TO MY MOTHER—AND MY BABY!"

The heads of employees and other customers began turning in our direction with startled looks and grimacing concern.

Earl had gotten to his feet and crossed the aisle to catch my arms and pull me back. "Come on, enough," he said. "Let it go."

I struggled against him, feeling an anger so deep and so vile that I could barely contain it. "I AM GOING TO RIP HER FUCKING FACE OFF!" I screamed.

The man with her got to his feet and pointed an accusing finger at me. "I THINK YOU NEED TO TAKE YOUR NIGGER-LOVING ASS BACK OVER TO YOUR BOOTH AND SIT DOWN, NOW!" he yelled.

Earl turned loose of me and stepped between the man and me. He towered over that pot-bellied old fool by a good foot or more. Grabbing him by the collar, Earl commanded, "I think you need to apologize to my wife and family."

"Fuck you, asshole!" the man spit back.

Earl grabbed both sides of his collar and brought his fists up so tight under the man's chin that it tilted his head back.

"Now, I think you need to apologize to me, my wife, and my family," Earl said through clenched teeth. "Cause, if you don't, I might not let go of this cheap five-and-dime shirt of yours till you stop breathing completely." I noticed the manager frantically dialing the phone and was sure the police were being called. I tugged on Earl's shirt, now realizing the potential consequences of the situation.

"Come on, Honey," I said. "They're calling the cops. We need to go now."

Earl barely noticed.

By this time, the baby had been disturbed and wailed in Mother's arms. Mother bounced her gently and tried to quiet her.

"Apologize!" Earl hissed, grabbing the man's collar even tighter. The man nodded affirmation, and Earl loosened his grip slightly. "Say it!" he demanded.

"I am sorry," he said.

"You are sorry for what?" Earl insisted.

"I am sorry that I called …"

"Don't say that word again!" Earl interrupted, tightening his grip.

The man took a hesitant breath. "I'm sorry for what I said," he squeaked. "I was wrong."

"Thank you," Earl said, loosening his grip slightly, but before he let go, he turned to the woman who had cowered back to the edge of the booth, "You too, bitch," he said.

"I, ah … I'm sorry for what I said," she replied, shivering.

"Now," Earl concluded, "I suggest you try to be a little more civil. After all, this is America, where everyone is created equal. Isn't that right?"

The man didn't answer, and Earl tightened his grip again. "I said—isn't that right?"

"Ah, yes—yes, that's right." The man choked his reply through the cinch around his neck.

Letting go of the man's collar, Earl turned to look at Mother and me. "Come on," he said. "I think we have had our break."

Earl returned to our booth, gathered our coats, and headed for the front door. Mother and I followed dutifully behind him. As Mother passed the booth where the couple sat, she stopped and said, "Hmm … you seem to think you are better than others. Maybe you think the color of your skin makes you superior. That's so interesting since the same brown shit comes out of everybody's ass."

I turned and stared at her in amazement. She looked at me, caught my astonished glare, and cocked her head to one side, then followed me out of the building. We did not hurry but strolled casually across the parking lot to our car. I wanted to hurry. I was as nervous as a feral cat, knowing that the police had probably been called, but Earl kept laying his hand on my shoulder, pulling me back and saying, "Slow down. Calm down."

Upon spotting us, the chauffeur got out of the limo, came around, and opened the door to the passenger compartment. Earl waved at him to close the door. Earl handed the chauffeur a drink he had purchased for him, and the chauffeur waited by the car, sipping his drink, about six feet from where we stood.

"What are we doing?" I asked. "We need to go! Jeez!" I was pacing and felt like I was going to have another panic attack.

"The police will be here any minute," Earl said. "We are going to ensure no surprises or misconceptions."

He handed me my coat. I put it on, then took Vanilla so Mother could put her coat on. Vanilla was well wrapped in blankets, but I still nuzzled her under my coat.

"Jesus! I need a cigarette!" I exclaimed. I had not had a cigarette in a couple of months, and I don't think I had even wanted one till that day.

Mother reached into her purse and pulled out a pack of cigarettes and a lighter. I was filled with mixed emotions when I realized what she had in her hand. I desperately craved a cigarette, but on the other hand, I was angry at cigarettes.

"I thought you quit," I said.

"I did," she responded. "I only started smoking again when John died. I'll give it up again one of these days, hopefully permanently."

Another mix of emotions went over me, and I was transported back to Daddy's deathbed and the cruel things Mother had said to me. There were still too many unanswered questions, and though Mother behaved differently, I still struggled to trust her. She started smoking again after Daddy died, and that was when I began the process of quitting. I realized that I couldn't bring myself to smoke again, at least not then. Besides, it made me throw up when I was pregnant. I had felt abandoned on so many levels when Daddy passed. I guess I even felt abandoned by the cigarettes. Smoking didn't do anything for me anymore. It no longer seemed glamorous or cool. It felt like a stupid thing to do, even though I craved them when upset.

"No, put them away," I said. "I don't want to smoke around the baby anyway." I took some deep breaths and tried to make sense of the avalanche of emotions that had rushed into my body.

As predicted, a State Patrol car soon pulled into the parking lot. We saw the manager meet the officer at the door, point in our direction, and then return to the store. A few minutes later, the officer went inside the building and came out. He strolled across the parking lot in our direction and tipped his hat with his fingers as he approached. He was an older gentleman, probably in his late fifties, yet he still looked dashing in his uniform.

"You folks have been having a little trouble here today?" he questioned.

"No, Sir," Earl responded. "I think we had everything under control."

"The store manager tells me you had a little physical altercation in there a few minutes ago," the officer continued.

"Sir," Earl explained, "we did indeed have to ask a couple of folks to be a little more civil."

"Wasn't the way I heard it," the officer reiterated, nodding in my direction. "Said the young lady here was getting loud and out of hand, and you got a bit physical with those folks."

"Sir," Earl continued, "my wife usually doesn't have much of a temper, but she got a little provoked today. I was doing my best to contain the situation."

"Provoked?" the officer asked, turning his attention to me. "Now, how did you get provoked, young lady?"

I looked at Earl questioningly, and he nodded an affirmation. I pulled back my coat so the officer could see Vanilla's face. I told him, "My Mother was holding the baby, and those people called her a 'Miss Mammy' and my baby an 'eggplant.' They were extremely rude, and I lost my temper. Then, that man yelled that we were …" I hesitated … "'nigger lovers' and Earl … my husband … stepped in when the man threatened me."

"Humph," the officer grunted. Then, he looked at Earl. "You are aware that these folks are within their rights to file charges for assault, and the store manager is within his rights to press charges for disturbing the peace?"

"Yes, sir," Earl quietly responded. "I don't think I could blame them if they did. Unfortunately, no charges could be filed for what they did to start the problem, and I don't think I would be much of a man if I stood by and allowed my family to be bullied."

The officer inspected him for a few seconds. "Unfortunately," he said at last. "You get into these kinds of tussles often?"

"No, sir," Earl responded. "I can't say that I have ever gotten into this kind of tussle, except I punched my dad in the face for saying the same kind of thing the day my baby was born."

The officer glanced at me and sternly back at Earl. "This is your baby?" he questioned.

Earl nodded his affirmation.

"And this is your wife?" the officer continued.

Earl nodded again.

"So, you had the baby before you married this fellow." The officer speculated, returning his gaze to me and operating under the expected assumption.

"No, sir," Earl responded, reaching his arm out to me. "Lovella had the baby after we were married. This is our baby. This is my child."

The officer looked puzzled, but he didn't ask any more questions. He looked down at the ground, pressed his lips tightly over his tongue, and then perused the three of us again.

"You folks wait right here. I will see if I can talk the manager out of filing charges. With the country's current tensions, it's probably best to settle this as amicably as possible. The people in the altercation have already said they don't want to press charges. I think they knew they stirred things up and don't want this to be dragged out in court."

He turned on his heels and walked back to the store.

After a few agonizing minutes, while we stood in the crisp air discussing the situation, the officer casually walked across the parking lot again.

"You folks think you can keep things under control and stay out of trouble?" he asked as he approached.

"Yes, sir," Earl replied.

"Where are you headed," the officer questioned.

"State College, Pennsylvania," Earl responded.

"Well, once you get out of the State of Connecticut, you are not my problem," the officer commanded. "Just make sure I don't hear anything else from you before you cross the state line."

"Yes, sir," Earl said, motioning us to get into the car. "Thank you for your understanding."

Before the driver could reach the door, Earl had already opened it for Mother and me. The driver returned to the wheel, and we left. With nerves still tingling and breath stilted, I sat in the back with Mother and Earl as the car progressed through the remainder of Connecticut, thankfully not that long. Pondering about the situation and having difficulty getting my mind off it, I was well aware that if we had been Black, the whole family would probably be sitting in jail instead of going home. The unfairness of the world began to dawn fully upon me when Vanilla was born and continued to teach me. I could never see the world the same again.

We arrived home late in the day, with nightfall casually engulfing the city. When we arrived, Grandfather and Grandmother Donner's car was waiting on the street by our apartment. When they saw us drive up, Grandmother Donner exited the car and trotted back to meet us.

"Lord have mercy!" she exclaimed. "I thought something terrible must have happened to you. What took you so long?"

"Oh, we stopped to have a bite to eat," Earl responded while we stood in the streetlights and waited for the driver to unload our luggage.

"I guess we could have stopped," Grandmother said, pointing back to their limo, "but I packed up some leftovers for me and fat-butt to eat on the way."

"Where is Grandpa?" I asked.

"He's passed out asleep in the car," Grandmother Donner replied. She then looked at Mother and exclaimed, "Drucella! Let's get a move on!"

Mother ignored her but handed Vanilla to Earl so she could oversee her luggage. The driver delivered Mother's luggage to the other car and our luggage to the apartment. We then had hugs and said goodbye.

When Mother hugged me, I said, "Thank you, Mother."

"For what, Lovella?" she said, standing back.

"For accepting my baby and standing up for her," I said. "You surprise me."

"We surprise each other, dear," she said, then walked toward the other limo. "Take good care of my grandbaby," she called back just before she slipped inside.

The driver closed the door behind her, and our limo left separately as their car departed for Climax. Earl held Vanilla in one arm and put his other arm around me. We walked together back up to our building. Our driver had already placed our luggage in front of our apartment door. Out of habit, I checked the mail when we came in. I realized that I had forgotten to check our box before we left. A letter addressed to both of us had been dated the week before. It must have arrived just before we left. Only the name *Lorenda* was written above the return address from San Francisco. As soon as we got back into the apartment, I sat down and opened the letter. Earl put Vanilla in her crib and returned to sit across from me on the sofa.

November 17, 1968

Dear Earl and Lovella,

We sure hope you guys are loving it back in Pennsylvania. Dave and I have missed you guys. We know you were tight with Screech and all, so we thought we ought to drop you a line and let you know. Super bummer, I know, but about a week ago, me and Dave went to pick Screech up for band practice, and we couldn't find him. We went to his apartment, walked around, and called for him, but he never answered. Man, we didn't even think to look in the bathroom. So, no Screech, and nobody has seen him for the next two days. Finally, we went back up to the apartment and started looking again, and this time, we found him in the bathtub. He had been gone at least three or four days. Man, it was awful. He still had the needle in his arm from shooting up. We knew he had gotten hooked on heroin, but nobody knew how bad. The coroner said he died of a drug overdose. I'm really sorry. I know you guys were close. I thought you ought to know.

Hey, if you ever get back out to San Francisco, look us up. Dave and I would love to see you.

Peace,

Lorenda

As I read the letter, my heart fell. I wondered whether we should have stayed in San Francisco and whether we could have made a difference. Yet, I knew we couldn't have saved him. I wondered what I would tell my daughter about her father when she began to notice her skin was not the same color as ours. I wondered how Earl was going to react, and I hesitated.

Sensing my hesitation, Earl asked, "What's wrong?"

I handed him the letter.

As he read the letter, I saw his face melt into sadness. Tears began drifting down his cheeks. He finished reading the letter and looked up at me with profound anguish. I moved over next to him and put my arm around him. Then, he buried his face in my shoulder and wept.

"I loved him, Lovella," he cried.

"I know," I said softly. "I know."

After weeping, Earl pulled back from my embrace and wiped his eyes with his sleeve. He picked up the letter from the floor where he had dropped it, wadded it into his fist, and said, "I want to go to Nashville. Do you want to go to Nashville?"

"Sure," I said softly. "Wherever you go, that's where I will go. Whatever you want, that's what I want." At that moment, it occurred to me that life often takes us where it wants us, with only the illusion of choice. "I love you," I said softly.

"I love you, too," he said. "I want you to know that I love you, too. I never stopped loving you for Screech. I love you from the depth of my soul, Lovella. I will never stop loving you."

A silence fell over us. We gazed into one another's eyes and shared the recognition of our love for each other as well as the sadness of losing a friend.

CHAPTER 28

Homecoming and Heartache

On a cold morning in January 1969, the phone rang early. I rolled over to look at the clock and realized it was twenty minutes before the alarm was set to go off. Earl stirred, stretched, and took a fluttering breath, "Honey, can you get that?" he asked with a sleepy whine. "Give me just a few more minutes."

My heart sank when I looked at the time, thinking there was no way anyone would call at this hour unless something were wrong, especially when it kept ringing. We didn't have a phone by the bed, so I staggered across the dark bedroom to the phone beside the sofa in the living room. I picked up the receiver with one hand and switched on the sofa lamp with the other. "Hello," I said, almost breathlessly, as I plopped myself on the end of the sofa with my nightgown pulled over my now chilling feet.

"Hello, Lovella?" said the tearful, questioning voice on the other end of the line. I immediately recognized it was Gretta.

"Good morning, sweetie," I said. "What's wrong?"

"Tommy's coming home," she whimpered.

"Oh my God, that's wonderful!" I exclaimed. The moment the words left my mouth, I realized that the tears could be about him coming home in a body bag.

"It is wonderful," she wailed, "but he's coming home wounded. They are sending him to Walter Reed Medical Center in Washington from a military hospital in Japan."

"Oh my God," I gasped, "how bad?"

A nervous barrage of words came flooding out of her. "I don't know. All I know is that he was shot, and thank God he's alive, but he could still die, couldn't he? I don't remember everything they said. They got him stable in Da Nang and sent him to Japan for brief rehab before sending him home for more rehab. I don't understand and don't know what to do.

I want to go to Washington to be with him, but I have the baby to care for, and I don't want to be away from the baby. I know Mom and Dad would care for him, but I don't know. I don't know what I'm supposed to do."

"First," I scolded. "Stop worrying. At least he is coming home alive. Second, there has to be a number at the hospital and some protocol for military families. I'm sure you can go there and probably take Derrick. Wait until 8:00, when the business office opens, call Walter Reed, then call me back. Okay?"

"Okay," she whimpered. I heard the line click—just that—click, and the call was over. I knew she had to be nervous. She didn't even say goodbye.

The day went on from there, and a little before noon, Gretta called me back. When I answered the phone, I could tell there was a distinct difference in her emotional state.

"Lovella, hi, it's Gretta again," she said calmly. "I found out he is there. He is stable, and the wound was not life-threatening, but it is enough for them to give him what they call a medical retirement. So, he is being discharged from service. He was shot in the hip or something. The nurse I spoke with said the bullet chipped his pelvic bone. I don't know how much damage it did, but apparently, it broke off a piece at the edge of his pelvic bone and did something to his hip joint on the left side. He will probably have to have more surgery, and then he will have to go through some rehab before getting released."

"Oh, I am so relieved," I said. "I know you must be, too."

"At least I know he won't die," she said calmly. "There are guest facilities near the hospital. So, I will go to Washington tomorrow. Hopefully, I will get to see Tommy when I get there. I don't suppose there would be a chance you could go with me. You wouldn't have to stay. Maybe overnight. I have no idea how long I'll be staying. Do you think you could go with me?"

"Oh, honey, I don't know," I responded quietly. "Let me talk to Earl when he gets home.

She responded. "So, can you talk to him about it? You know that I get so nervous about big places, traffic, and such things. You have had so much more exposure to the city than I have. If you could go up and help me get settled into the guest quarters, that alone would make me feel a lot more comfortable."

"I'll see what I can do, sweetie," I said. "I'll call you back as soon as I have had a chance to discuss it with Earl. You are planning to go up tomorrow?"

"Yeah, if I can," she replied.

"It is kind of short notice, but I understand it's important," I mused.

"Lovella, I would feel so much safer and more comfortable if you were with me," she begged.

"Okay, so let me call Mother, and then I'll talk to Earl as soon as he gets home."

"Okay, okay," she said nervously. "Call me back."

"You know I will, sweetie," I said. "Love you."

I hung up the phone and immediately began wondering how I would manage everything. I knew it would be okay with Earl. He was so easygoing about everything. Mother had developed an adoration for her grandchild, so I knew Vanilla would be in good hands. She was nine months old by January and a little easier to transport and manage. It was just a matter of planning and packing. The best thing to do was to have everything packed and ready to go by the time Earl got home. The problem would be that we only had one vehicle. Earl had sold the van, and his dad had gotten us a new four-door black Mercedes. He said the sports car was neither good for a family nor was the van. This time, he put the title in Earl's name. With Earl's guidance, I had learned how to drive the previous summer and got my license.

When Earl came home, he told me to take the car and go. He said he could take a taxi for a few days and that I shouldn't worry about it. I never ceased to be amazed at how understanding and supportive he could be. Even though we would soon be moving to Nashville, he had kept his job at the grocery store but was also devoting his time to learning as much as he could before he picked up the Nashville job. Whether he had accepted the job in Nashville or not, more and more, I realized I was married to the right man.

Because I knew he would probably be understanding, I had packed everything for myself and the baby by the time Earl got home, so I was out of the house and on the road by 3:30 that afternoon. I had called Mother that afternoon, and of course, she was okay with keeping Vanilla for a few days. I was in Climax by 6:30 and had plenty of time to spend the rest of the evening with Gretta. We made some phone calls, and she was able to speak with Tommy to let him know that we were coming. He was some-what groggy, as they had done an additional surgery that day, but he was able to ask about Derrick and was clear-minded enough to tell her that he was looking forward to seeing her.

The next morning, Gretta debated about it because she knew Tommy would want to see Derrick, but she finally decided to leave him with her mom and dad. We had a quick breakfast with her parents and left very early for Washington. I drove the entire way. After stopping for lunch, we arrived at Walter Reed Medical Center at about 1:30 that afternoon.

At first, it was chaos, trying to find the right building and the appro-priate person to talk to and get Gretta settled with guest housing. After some fits and starts and a swear word here and there, we could finally navigate to the proper government clerk who could help us. By the time we got through that ordeal and had luggage in the room, it was 3:30. It took another thirty minutes to navigate our way to the medical facili-ties. We finally arrived in an open ward and found Tommy's bed several counts down from the door.

We walked up to the foot of Tommy's bed to see him sleeping in what appeared to be a very awkward position due to an apparatus hooked around him stabilizing his leg.

"Oh, he's asleep," Gretta whined. "Maybe we should go. Maybe we should come back later. Do you think they might have him sedated?"

She turned to walk away. I grabbed her arm. "Stop right where you are," I commanded. "We have just driven five hours and have spent another three hours trying to get our asses settled into this disorganized mess that they call guest housing. You have not seen your husband in a year, and you are just going to give up and walk away? No, I don't think so. You are not going anywhere!"

"But what if they have him sedated?" she questioned.

"Well, we are going to find out," I affirmed. "Wait here."

I left her and went to find an orderly. It only took a minute to discover that Tommy was sleeping and that it would be okay to wake him. I came back and ordered Gretta to wake him.

"But?" she protested.

"Wake him," I demanded. "It's okay."

I walked around the bed to the side behind him, where he couldn't see me. I motioned to Gretta to go around to the other side of the bed. By this time, the orderly had come to stand at the foot of Tommy's bed.

"Go on," I said.

Gretta looked up at me and then back at the orderly as though asking permission.

The orderly nodded to her. "It's all right," he said softly.

Gretta barely touched Tommy's sleeve and looked up at me as though she was still doing something wrong. I reached over from behind and gave his arm a good jostle. Startled, he opened his eyes. Initially, he looked terrified, but as soon as he realized where he was, he looked straight at Gretta and said, "Hi, honey." He still had not seen me.

She burst into tears, and Tommy reached out to her, saying, "Baby … baby … what's the matter? Don't cry."

She sobbed even louder and then began to take air in big gulps. "I-ugh-ah-thought you-ugh-ah-had … died!"

"Oh, sweetheart," Tommy said. "Here I am. I'm okay."

"No-ugh-you're not," Gretta sobbed. "You're hurt-ugh-ah-ah … I never wanted ever to see you hurt!"

"Please … sweetheart … come here," Tommy pleaded. She fell into his chest with waves of tears. He let her cry. Fight as he might, the tears began rolling down his cheeks, quiet tears drifting from his lashes.

I held it together pretty well, allowing Gretta a moment with her husband and letting her have her feelings, but when I saw Tommy's face tear up, I couldn't hold on anymore. I fought to keep silent, but a tiny yelp slipped past my lips, and my tears came.

Hearing this, Tommy cocked his head toward me. When I saw him move, I quickly pulled one finger over my lips to indicate staying silent. Then, I mouthed the words, "I'll be back."

I slipped past the bedside divider curtains and motioned one of the orderlies to ask him where to get a cup of coffee. The orderly directed me to a rather sterile-looking guest lounge. I got my coffee, sat at a table, and watched families visiting with injured soldiers who could ambulate. I sat there, thinking for a long time, and one thought was, *there, but for the grace of God, go I*. If my behavior had been a little different, if circumstances had not been what they were, or if I had gotten pregnant when I was fooling around with Tommy, that could have been me by that bed, letting out all the fears and pent-up worries stuffed over a year of my husband's deployment to Vietnam. It could have been me worried sick that my husband might never be able to work again or, worse yet, that he still might not survive his injuries. I loved them both, and I had worries, too. The awareness came of how much our experience is created not by our choices but by the choices others make that create circumstances beyond our control. I began to realize Tommy's decision to join the military would significantly impact his whole family. Derrick was never going to remember a father who wasn't disabled. Gretta would have to work harder to care for her family than she ever would have had Tommy not made that decision. In some ways, I felt glad that I wasn't Gretta; in others, I felt guilty. After about an hour, I returned to the ward to find Gretta sitting by Tommy's bed, holding his hand and laughing.

"Well, this is a different picture than the one I saw last," I said.

Gretta, still giggling, turned to see me and said, "Hi, sweetie. Tommy was telling me about this guy he met in boot camp who was a really funny kid from Idaho."

"Well, it's good to see you both laughing," I said, searching for a chair.

I finally found a little metal chair and pulled it beside Gretta. We sat talking, laughing, and reminiscing through the serving of Tommy's dinner and for an hour or so beyond.

Finally, the orderly came by. "If you folks would like to have dinner, you might want to head over to the cafeteria. They are gonna stop serving in about thirty minutes," he said, glancing at his watch.

"You go on, Lovella," Gretta said, squeezing Tommy's hand. "I'm not hungry, anyway.

I gave her a stern, motherly look and said, "Honey, you need to eat."

She looked back at Tommy, and he said, "Go on and get something to eat, and then go on back to the guest house and get some rest. We can talk tomorrow."

Gretta hesitantly let go of his hand and said, "Okay then." She leaned over the bed and hugged him. "Good night, honey. I'll see you in the morning."

I walked around her and leaned over to hug him as well. "Take care of yourself, asshole," I said. "You got a family to go home to."

He looked up at me, a bit forlorn, and said, "I know."

I smiled, "I love you. You know that—right?"

"Yeah, I know," he replied. "I love you too."

The following day, we had breakfast at the same cafeteria, and after that, I packed the car to go home. I left and told her to give Tommy my love. Gretta's parents would accompany Tommy's parents the following weekend and bring the baby. I knew she would be fine. She just needed me for support through the initial jitters.

Back home, I went back to our routine. I got update calls from Gretta periodically. Tommy was healing rapidly. His injuries were not so severe that they would be completely debilitating, but they were severe enough for him to be released from the military. He was eligible for service-connected disability based on the damage to his hip and pelvic bone. He would not quite get 100% disability, but it sounded like it might supply enough income to offset the fact that he could not work any strenuous job again. He was also getting a Purple Heart medal, which included multiple benefits, but it would do little toward paying bills. Until Tommy could use those benefits to re-train for a non-strenuous job, Gretta would have to work. I felt terrible for both and felt just as helpless.

March 16, 1969, was a lazy, cold, and dreary Sunday. Clouds hung over the sky and spat out a slow, steady drizzle. Early in the afternoon, I had put Vanilla in her crib for a nap. Then, Earl and I took time to do something that was one of the things I most loved to do with him. We lay down together for an afternoon nap. I loved being cuddled beside him, drifting in and out of sleep, feeling his warm body next to mine, just knowing he was there. Since his father had already started him on salary pending our move to Nashville, he had quit his grocery store job and had more time to spend at home. I was getting up to get the baby when the phone rang. Earl was still lying down but went to get her while I went to the phone.

"Hello," I said, picking up the receiver and sitting beside the phone. I already had a feeling that it was Gretta, and I was right.

"Hi, sweetie," her voice crooned.

"Well, hi back," I responded. "How's your Sunday."

"Still a little too cold for my taste," she said, "but not bad. How's yours?"

"Earl and I just got up from a very nice afternoon nap," I said.

"Perfect day for it," she went on. "Guess what? They are discharging Tommy this week! He said he thinks they will let him come home in a few more days, and I was wondering if I could ask a favor."

"You know that if I got it, honey, it's yours," I said.

"So," she continued, "next weekend, I was thinking about having a homecoming party for Tommy if they release him like they say they will. Maybe you could come pick us up while our parents fix our house for the party, so it will be a surprise when we get there. Just a few people you know, you and Earl, your mom, our parents, and maybe one or two other friends—very small."

"When were you planning to do this?" I questioned.

"I was thinking maybe next Saturday," she whispered as though Tommy might overhear.

"Where are you?" I inquired.

"I'm at a pay phone near the cafeteria," she responded. "Why?"

"Is Tommy there?" I interrogated.

"No, of course not," she said. "He's back on the ward. I wouldn't have him here while I'm planning the party. I wouldn't want him to overhear."

"Then, sweetie, why are you whispering?" I demanded.

"Oh, ah," she giggled. "I didn't realize I was whispering. I guess I'm just excited. So, do you think you could do this for me?"

"Give me a sec," I said, turning to shout to the other room … "Earl!"

"Yeah, Baby," he called back.

"Do we have any plans for next weekend?" I asked.

"Ah … no … I don't think so," he replied. "Give me a second. I'm still pinning on a clean diaper."

I responded to the phone. "Earl says he doesn't think we have plans."

"Oh, wonderful," she exclaimed.

Earl came into the living room about that time, rocking Vanilla. "What's up?" he questioned.

"Tommy is getting out of the hospital this week," I said, holding the receiver slightly from my face. "Gretta wants to know if I can pick them up while her parents set up a surprise party for him."

"Okay, that's cool," he replied. "I'm sure the kid and I will be fine having a weekend to ourselves."

I heard Gretta say on the line, "I want Earl to be there too."

"Gretta wants you at the party," I said. "Either you could go up with us, and we could all ride back together, or Mother could come to pick you and the baby up on Friday while I go pick up Gretta and Tommy."

"Whatever you want to do is fine," he said. "You know I'm pretty cool about stuff."

I turned back to the phone. "You heard that, right?" I asked.

"Every bit of it," she replied. "So, how are we going to do this?"

"Give me some planning time," I answered. "The best thing will probably be to have Mother pick up Earl and the baby unless you want Earl's parents to come and take him down there. Are they invited too?"

"Well, I don't mind if they come," she responded. "But Tommy doesn't know them."

"Then, let me call Mother and make arrangements. I'm sure she will be okay with it. Maybe she has finally forgiven Tommy for our incident in the laundry room."

"Oh my God!" Gretta teased. "I hope she can deal with it."

"Mother has changed, I think," I continued. "I think she will be fine—so listen. Go ahead with your plans. I will come up to stay the night on Friday, and we will take Tommy home on Saturday. Call me on Wednesday to finalize and see if I have run into any snags, but I'm sure it will be fine."

"You're a darling," she said. "Bye now."

"Bye, sweetie," I parroted and hung up the phone.

What I discovered when I arrived the following Friday left me with concerns. Tommy was able to ambulate with a cane, and with a doctor's leave, we were able to go out to dinner. Gretta seemed oblivious because she was so excited just to have him home but I noticed a distinct change in him. It wasn't just his physical injuries. There was a personality change. Often, he appeared more like a scared rabbit in the grass ready to bolt and run at the snap of any twig. After we got Tommy settled back in the hospital and ourselves in guest housing for one more night, I couldn't fight off my mind's nagging that something more than his hip had been wounded.

We got up early on Saturday morning and picked Tommy up at the hospital by 7:00. By timing the trip just right, we would arrive at their house about noon. Gretta had already gotten on the phone to call her mom and ensure everything was going as planned.

The trip was uneventful. We had one stop to fill up on gas and let everyone pee. I was happy to see that when Tommy came around from the bathroom on the side of the gas station, the older man attending the station noticed him. He walked straight up to Tommy, standing by the soda machine, reached out his hand, and said, "Son, thank you for your service."

Tommy smiled, shook the man's hand, and said, "I appreciate your kindness." They nodded, and Tommy limped back to the car with his cane in one hand and a soda in the other.

Nearing home, I noticed that Tommy was quiet in the back seat. I glanced up into the rear-view mirror to see that he was not asleep but had his head leaning against the window, peering out across the landscape. I didn't say anything. I wasn't going to engage in asking if he was all right. I knew that he wasn't. I had witnessed his tendency to startle and his trepidation around people the night before. Gretta chattered about re-claiming the flowerbeds around their little home and said, "This is the perfect time for perennials with the rain we've had this year."

I noticed no cars parked nearby when we got to their little blue house. At first, I wondered if there might have been some mistake and if everyone had forgotten that there was a party. Then, I realized they must have parked around the block so Tommy wouldn't notice, and they could keep the surprise.

Tommy did fine up the sidewalk but struggled up the four steps to their small front landing. Gretta excitedly fumbled to get the key in the front door, and I wondered if her anxiety and giddiness would give away the surprise. Finally, she opened the door and said to Tommy, "You first, sweetheart. Welcome home!"

He no sooner stepped into the living room than eight people waiting inside shouted, "SURPRISE!"

Tommy yelped as though Satan had just landed on cloven hooves. He lunged backward and almost fell had it not been that Gretta and I were behind him. He quickly caught himself and realized he was looking at family and close friends. Then, he laughed a somewhat nervous and insincere laugh, "Boy! Howdy! Ah … ah …" he said. "You guys scared the hell out of me!"

Everyone gathered around him, wanting hugs. I watched him stiffen and barely respond, even when his mom and dad were hugging him. I watched his breath quicken. Then, he said, "Boy, it's a little stuffy in here. Do you guys mind if I step back outside, for just a moment, and get some fresh air?"

He pushed his cane out from his side and limped back toward the front door. In my mind, I saw him rushing down the walk as fast as his cane and bad hip would allow, but he stepped onto the landing and leaned against the house. I saw him through the open door and asked Gretta, "Why don't you go see if your mom needs help in the kitchen?"

She trotted off, still oblivious, and I stepped onto the landing with Tommy. I stood back about four feet from him. Finally, I spoke. "You had it pretty rough over there, didn't you?"

For several seconds, he said nothing. Finally, quietly gazing at the porch ceiling, he said, "I guess so."

I took a deep breath. "Tommy, I have no idea what you have been through or how you feel, but I know you are not the same man who left here two years ago. I can see that you are pushing it to be able to tolerate things you used to revel in."

"It's just too much, Lovella," he clamored, barely glancing at me. "I'm overwhelmed here. I needed some peace and quiet. I needed a little time to get used to things again."

"I know," I said. It's not your hip that's most wounded; it's your heart. I figured that out last night. Gretta still doesn't have a clue. She is so happy to see you and thankful you are home and alive that she isn't noticing some things."

"I love her so much," he said, "but I just don't know if I can take this."

"Well, a couple of things," I went on. "First, you are here with people who love you to the depths of their souls and only want the best for you. You have to get through this afternoon to get your peace and quiet. Second, I don't know if Gretta is going to get it. You are probably going to have to spell it out for her. Make it clear what you need from her, what you can handle, and what you can't."

"That's just the thing," Tommy responded. "I don't know. I don't understand this myself. I feel like every nerve in my body is quivering. I don't know what I can tolerate or can't. This almost feels more tense than Nam."

"Then, you will have to teach Gretta as you learn," I said. "Make sure you communicate with her. At the very least, make sure she knows how you feel, and if possible, let her know what you need."

A crisp Pennsylvania breeze swept through the yard and whisked across our faces. Tommy pushed back from the side of the house and turned around. He looked at me warmly. "You know you're my best friend, don't you?"

"Hell, I am about everybody's best friend," I grinned. "If I'm not their best friend, I'm probably their worst enemy."

The front door creaked, and Tommy's father stuck his head through. He looked at Tommy and then over at me. I was standing on the opposite side of the landing. Tommy didn't see me wink at his dad, who tentatively checked out the situation.

"Son," he said, looking back from me toward Tommy, "Aren't you hungry? These women have enough food in here to feed your whole platoon. I have been resisting the urge to go ahead and tear into it, but it wouldn't be polite if I went to the table before the guest of honor."

"Yeah, you know I am a little hungry now that you mention it," Tommy said, turning his cane and reaching the opposite hand to motion me ahead. As I walked through the door, I felt his warm hand rub between my shoulder blades, and I felt the love that he didn't need to express further.

Inside, positioned between clusters of balloons, was a banner that read, *Welcome Home!* Three tables had been pushed back against the wall in a "u" shape to make more room for food, and they were covered with meats, casseroles, salads, breads, and desserts. Tommy hobbled up to the group of people who were standing around. That included his parents, Gretta's parents, Mother, Earl, and a couple of friends Tommy and Gretta used to hang out with before he joined the military.

Gretta's dad stepped forward from the group and raised his hands to lead everyone in the rehearsed song. As he let his hands drop, they all began to sing, *For He's a Jolly Good Fellow.* When the song ended, they stood silently as though waiting for applause.

"Wow!" Tommy exclaimed. "This is really something. Thank you, guys, so much. I love you." His voice cracked, and he fought tears as he finished. "I love you all."

"Yeah, yeah, yeah! Let's eat!" I exclaimed, coming to his emotional rescue by distracting him. Then, I stepped next to Earl and took his hand.

"Yeah!" Tommy echoed. "I don't know about you guys, but I'm pretty hungry. He ambled toward the table where Gretta intercepted.

"I'll hold your plate, Sweetheart," she said gleefully. "Just tell me what you want as we go around the table."

Gretta grabbed a plate and stood beside him as he moved around the U-shaped formation, selecting food. After that, others joined in line.

We all sat around the living room with food on our laps. Extra chairs had been brought in, and there was barely enough room between them to set our drinks on the floor. Tommy's mom put Derrick down, and he began wabbling around the living room, testing his walking skills.

"Oh my God! Derrick!" Tommy exclaimed and handed his plate to Gretta. He reached his hands out to the baby and enticed him, "Come here, little man. Let Daddy give you a hug."

It became evident that Derrick, even though he had been taken to Walter Reed for visits, still thought of Tommy as a stranger because, as soon as he saw Tommy's reaction, he recoiled into frightened tears. Tommy's face was a combination of horror and sadness as he realized the implication of that moment.

I was about to pick up Derrick when Gretta's mom came to him first. She whisked him into her arms and cooed, "Ooh, now, now. What's the matter, sweetie? You want to see Daddy, don't you? Let's go see Da Da. Can you say Da Da?"

Mrs. Tannenbaum brought him over to Tommy and sat him on the floor before him. Gretta discreetly pinched the side off a cookie and handed it to Tommy.

Tommy held the cookie to his son and said, "Here, little man. Do you want a cookie? Want a goodie?"

I watched from across the room, and my heart broke as I saw the emotions flowing across Tommy's face. He endured, though, and they continued working with Derrick until he took the cookie from Tommy's hand and later allowed Tommy to pull him onto his lap. I wondered if Tommy had really thought it through when he joined the Marines. I know he thought he was planning for his family's future. I know he was dreaming the dreams that some recruiter had fed him, but his reality had become harsh.

Tommy held his son for a fair while and then put him down to go to the restroom. Several of us got up to cart paper plates and empty plastic cups to the trash, and then, we met in the kitchen for clean-up. Earl did his best to pick up things and help clean up while caring for Vanilla. Finally, I said, "Sweetheart, just sit down and enjoy your daughter. We'll take care of this."

In short order, we had it all cleaned up. Family members said their goodbyes and gave their hugs.

Earl and I would spend the night in Tommy and Gretta's spare bedroom and return to State College on Sunday morning, so we stayed behind after everyone else had left.

After all the clamor was over, Tommy sat on the sofa in the living room. Gretta came to his side, grabbed his arm, and hugged him from the side. "I'm so glad my man is home!" she exclaimed.

Tommy reached over and put his arm around her. It was almost as though none of us knew what to do after the party. I knew Tommy would want some time for peace and quiet, but we sat in the living room chatting as the sun drifted into the evening. Derrick tottered around and would occasionally go to Tommy of his own volition.

In the early evening, Gretta announced, "Who wants leftovers?" She rose and headed for the kitchen.

"That sounds good," I said and handed Vanilla to Earl so I could go with her.

"Oh, no, no, no," she exclaimed. "You sit right there. I'll call you if I need you. Besides, I might want to get creative and see what I can create something new out of old leftovers."

Gretta had not been in the kitchen for more than three minutes when we heard her slam a cabinet door. Bam! The sound resonated through the house, and such a sound would have been commonplace in a typical household. Maybe one might have a brief startle but quickly realize that someone was closing a kitchen cabinet and nothing more. However, not this household, not anymore.

As soon as the cabinet door slammed, Tommy was off the sofa and onto the floor. He shoved their coffee table across the room. His arms stretched out in front of him as though he was holding a rifle. He began screaming, "TAYLOR! TAYLOR, GET DOWN, GOD DAMN IT!

GET DOWN! DAWSON, GRAB HIM! GRAB HIS FEET! PULL HIM DOWN! TAYLOR! WHAT THE HELL!"

Tommy covered his head, buried his face in the floor, and a blood-curdling cry came out of him, "OH JESUS FUCKING CHRIST! OH CHRIST! GOD DAMN IT TAYLOR! OH CHRIST!"

Gretta ran back from the kitchen with a horrified look on her face. Derrick and Vanilla both hit a full-throttle cry, and Earl was trying to tend to both of the children. I jumped up and ran across the room to grab Gretta. "Don't touch him!" I yelled. "Let him be."

Gretta was immediately in tears, heaving, "What? What's-ha-ah-happening? What's the matter with him?"

"Just wait," I admonished. "Wait it out."

"What is the matter?" she cried and pleaded.

"I've read about it, honey," I said. "I think he has got what they call shell shock."

"What?" she pleaded and pulled toward him, but I held her back.

Tommy continued to cover his head with both hands, with his face flat on the floor, sobbing as loud and as hard as I had ever heard anyone sob. "JESUS! OH, JESUS CHRIST! TAYLOR!" he continued to wail.

We all stood there watching, waiting, as he cried. Finally, he became still, and the crying stopped.

Once again, Gretta pulled toward him. "Don't touch him," I said. "Just gently call his name."

She moved tentatively toward him as Tommy lay still on the floor, breathing in deep, intermittent gasps.

"Tommy?" she called softly. "Tommy, it's me, Gretta."

"Tommy?" she kept calling gently.

Finally, he said, "Yes."

"Can I come over there?" she said, looking back at me for reassurance.

"Yes," he responded.

She came to her knees beside him. He still had his face on the floor.

"Can I touch you, sweetheart?" she sighed.

"Yes," he said again.

She reached out to put her hand on his back, and he winced at first but then relaxed. She gently rubbed her hand up and down his back. At last, he turned hesitantly over and looked at her.

"I'm sorry," he said, fighting back tears again.

"Oh, baby … baby," she said, leaning over onto the floor to hug him. "It's all right."

"I didn't mean to cause a problem," he whimpered.

"It's no problem, honey," she responded. "What happened?"

"I don't know. For a minute, it felt like I was back in 'Nam," he answered. "I felt like I was dreaming, but it felt like it was really happening again."

"What happened?" she queried.

"Oh Jesus, I can't tell you," he said. "I don't want to put that on you. I don't want to think about it. I need to … I just need to forget about it."

Tommy sat up as well as his hip would allow, and Gretta sat at his knees, facing him.

"Who's Taylor?" she asked.

Tommy heaved, his breathing quickened, and tears pooled in his eyes. Gretta immediately reached out and took his hand. "It's okay," she said. "You don't have to tell me. It's all right."

"Hey," I said. "Why don't we all sit down and play a game of Scrabble after dinner?"

Earl picked up on the distraction and chimed right in. "Yeah, that sounds good. I don't remember the last time I played Scrabble."

"How about that, sweetheart?" Gretta inquired, squeezing Tommy's hand.

"Yeah," Tommy responded, deliberately attempting to move his mind away from the hell he had just experienced. "Scrabble sounds good."

Gretta helped him get up and lay on the sofa. "Damn, that hip and leg hurt!" he groaned. "I must have strained it when I was down there."

"Want me to get you some aspirin?" she asked.

"No, the doctor gave me something for pain when I left Walter Reed," he replied. "Can you check my bag?"

Gretta went to his bag in the back bedroom. We could hear her scrounge, and then she returned with a medicine bottle. "Is this the one?" she asked. "It says it's for pain."

"Yep, that's it," Tommy replied, taking the pill bottle from her hand.

I had already gone to the kitchen for a glass of water while she was in the bedroom.

"I'll get you some water," she exclaimed, turning around to see me standing with the glass.

"Wow! That was easy," she chimed and took the glass to Tommy.

"Come on," I said. "Let's get dinner ready."

Gretta and I retreated to the kitchen. She went to the refrigerator, pulled out a covered dish, and set it on the countertop. Then, she released an excruciating breath and leaned over the sink. I walked up behind her, placed my arm around her shoulder, and said, "I kind of had the feeling it would be hard."

"Damn it, Lovella!" she said. "I am so mad at him for doing this. I am so mad at him for joining the fucking military, and at the same time, my heart breaks for him. I don't know what to do?"

"Honey, right now, what you do is grit your teeth and get through it," I admonished.

"I can't," she whispered.

"Yes, you can, sweetie," I affirmed. "You can. You have to. You both have to be strong because there is a lot more wounded in him than his hip. He is going to need you to be strong."

"Lovella, what do I do?" she asked, turning around and leaning back against the countertop. "I don't know what to do."

"First of all," I commanded, "you go to the library and read everything you can about any diagnosis they give him. You read everything you can about shell shock and then make sure you don't let go till the cows come home. You hold them accountable. Don't be afraid to question every doctor you contact at the VA and find out what he qualifies for. Ask for any assistance or services you can get. If they tell you you can't have it, read their literature and educate yourself about their rules. Then, go back and ask again. Find out if counseling and social work services are available for him or the two of you together or if there are other programs to help vets besides the VA. Persist, sweetie—persist."

She looked at me sternly. "This will go on for the rest of our lives, won't it?"

I sighed and looked back at her with as much compassion and understanding as possible. "Yes, honey," I said. "I'm afraid that it probably will. It may not have to, and it may get better, but it probably will."

Gretta looked to the side, and a tear drifted slowly down her cheek. "I just wanted us to be happy," she whispered. "Is that too much to ask? I just wanted us to be happy."

"It has to get better, sweetie," I said as I reached for her hand.

She sniffled, turned around, pulled herself upright, and exclaimed, "Let's get dinner ready."

The following day, Earl and I drove back to State College. Vanilla lay cooing in her backseat bassinet. I was glad to relax on the passenger's side and occasionally tend to the baby.

"You ever wonder," I asked, "why life seems to turn out so good for some people, without even trying, and it turns out so shitty for others, no matter how hard they try?"

"Yeah, I know," he said, staring down the road. "It's strange. Some of it has to do with the choices we make or don't make, and some of it has to do with the choices others make that affect us. For instance, on the first day we met in the Penn State library, I was teasing and messing with you. You could have told me to fuck off. If you had said an absolute no, that would have been that. Both our lives would have turned out completely different."

"You may recall that I did tell you to fuck off," I smiled. "But that's just it, why didn't I make you fuck off? I mean, you're not really my type." I giggled as I teased him. "But you were the only man I ever met, besides Tommy, and Tommy doesn't count, who was considerate of me and my needs instead of just trying to get off and go home!" I thought about it before continuing. "The way I acted in high school, I am so fucking lucky I didn't get pregnant, and that would have completely changed my life, as well."

"You took precautions, didn't you?" he consoled.

"Usually, but still," I pondered, "the more guys you fuck, the more you increase your chances of getting in trouble, even if you do take precautions."

I reached over and laid my hand on his leg. "I think I am glad to be with just one guy. Just one sweet guy who loves me back and isn't messed up like Tommy will be messed up for the rest of his life."

"I know," he responded. "Poor guy."

"His own choice put him there," I said.

"He gambled and lost," Earl evaluated. "He thought he would have a military career and a better life for his family. He knew there was a risk. He just lost. In the long run, those willing to take risks and work for what they want are more likely to win. He just didn't win."

"I haven't taken any risks," I replied. "Neither have you, really. You inherited the options you have, and I was lucky enough that you fell in love with me. What risk?"

"We all take a risk daily when we get up in the morning," he explained. "We take a risk, when we go to sleep, that our heart will still be beating when the alarm goes off. We take a risk when we have a restaurant meal trusting that the cook washed his hands after he took a poop and we are not going to get e-coli. There are daily risks, and we gamble when we are trying to achieve anything. We are taking a risk by moving to Nashville. I might not be a good manager. The distribution center might fail. My dad's business could go bankrupt. Tommy took a risk to do what he thought was right for his family. It's just a shame that our government would send innocent young guys to their deaths for an obscure, extremely expensive, and unexplainable war. For what? Support the military-industrial complex so some fat cats in the arms industry can get even fatter on the carcasses of the nation's young men? I mean, you know, I think it's a crock of shit, but what can we do? Vote? Protest? Assassinate? But hell, to assassinate another person because they don't think the way you do has to be the ultimate arrogant insanity. Who gives anyone permission or the audacity to think they have the right to impose their will on others or kill somebody for disagreeing? They killed JFK. They killed Bobby Kennedy, Malcolm X, and Martin Luther King. Hell, for that matter, they killed Jesus because he threatened the status quo. They killed him for not thinking the way they thought. Our government commits mass assassination by drafting young men to fight a war that most don't want to fight, that most of the fucking country is against. They got away with it for a long time before people began to catch on, vote, and protest. But hell, the ones who died are the lucky ones. It's the guys like Tommy who are the real victims. He will have to fight their fucking war for the rest of his life unless some genus can come up with a treatment, a way to lead these poor souls out of that hell."

"Do you believe in fate?" I asked.

"Kind of like reincarnation or karma?" he questioned. "Some folks are just destined to have more shit to deal with than others?"

"Yeah, kind of like that," I said.

"I think some people obviously have more shit to deal with than others," he pondered, "and obviously, through no fault of their own. I guess what matters is how skillfully you deal with the shit you have, whether you face it and conquer it or whether you let it drag you down. Maybe it's like lifting weights. When you lift that weight, your muscles feel queasy, and you don't feel strong at the time, but if you keep lifting, you build muscle. The more you lift, the stronger you get, so the strongest people are usually the ones who have dealt with the most shit. They have lifted that weight off themselves, so to speak, but they probably didn't feel very strong when they were pushing life uphill."

"Interesting," I said. "So, in the long run, Gretta and Tommy may end up stronger, emotionally and spiritually, than us because they have to face more challenges and figure them out?"

"If they don't run from the challenges," he continued, "if they face them."

"Maybe that's the genius you were talking about," I said. "The genius to heal is to hit it head-on and keep hitting it till you develop the strength to deal with it. Make sure you don't pull the rug over it and pretend it isn't there. Talk about it, face it, feel it till you heal it." I leaned back into the seat. "Hmmmmmm," I considered. "I need to talk to Gretta and Tommy about that. You are a smart man, Earl Titwallow."

"You are a smart woman, Lovella Titwallow."

"Why do you say that?" I asked.

"You married me, didn't you?" A grin spread broadly across his face. I reached across to take his hand, and we watched the Pennsylvania highway rolling like a black ribbon far in the distance.

CHAPTER 29

Southern Charm Versus Southern Wisdom

In May of 1969, Earl and I moved to Nashville. In so many ways, this was a total change for me. For one thing, I had never lived in such opulent settings. In those days, $150,000 a year went a very long way. We bought a lovely modern ranch home near the Governor's mansion in the Green Hills area of Nashville, off Franklin Road. The driveway curled up the side of the hill to a basement garage on the side of the house. The large windows in the living room overlooked that little hill, and across the road, there was a grove of trees. Faintly through the trees could be seen the white columns of a rather stately mansion, which I learned belonged to the Grand Old Opry star, Minnie Pearl. This was an adjustment for me, as well, because I never expected that she was playing the part of Minnie Pearl for the TV cameras. I thought she was really like that—the backwoods hick. The elegance of her home told a different story. I learned later that the elegance of her personal character was even more impressive.

Earl was gone often, and I wanted to finish my education, so we needed someone to help with Vanilla. We interviewed for a nanny and a maid so I could have time to return to school, hopefully starting in the summer session. I would try to get into Vanderbilt, but I wasn't sure if I could. If not Vanderbilt, then there were a few other options, such as a state school in Murfreesboro, a city not far away.

We hired a middle-aged Black woman named Elmira Shanks as our nanny. I came to love her. She had a rounded face with black eyes that looked at you as though they contained the love of Jesus. Her smile was a perfect heart-warming experience. Her countenance was as sweet as anyone I had ever met. The first time I saw her with Vanilla, I knew she was right for the job. She had not always been a nanny. Yet, when her last daughter left home after finishing a degree at Fisk, a Black college in Nashville,

Elmira decided she needed something to do with her time. She never asked why we had a Black child, but the surprise on her face was evident when I took her to meet Vanilla.

A little over a year old now, our daughter was clamoring around on bowed little legs and frequently getting into things where she didn't belong. One day, when Vanilla got her hand caught between the slats of a heating vent, Elmira freed Vanilla's little hand and rocked her on the hip, wiping her tears when she scolded me. "Miss Lovella, you have got to baby-proof this house. There is too much for this baby to get into."

"Baby-proof?" I questioned, without realizing that a large house might be dangerous for a toddler.

"Lord! Miss Lovella," she responded with shock. "Don't tell me you don't know anything about prepping a home for a baby."

"No, Elmira," I said. "I am afraid I don't. I never had children before and never expected to, so I have a lot to learn."

"You never expected to have children?" she questioned. Still, she didn't ask how it came to be that two rich White kids from Pennsylvania had a Black child. Perhaps she had previously assumed Vanilla was adopted.

"No, ma'am," I responded. "Vanilla was a bit of a surprise. I guess it is different when they are still in the crib than when they start becoming mobile."

"Mmmmm. Hmmmm," Elmira moaned while she rocked the baby. "Well, there's lots of things around here that need some attention. Those cabinets in the kitchen are way too easy to open, and there is stuff under the sink that can hurt a baby. You need to get that stuff up out of the way."

"Well, if you will show me what to do," I pleaded, "I'll see if I can fix it."

"Miss Lovella," Elmira educated. "With the kind of means that you and Mr. Earl have, there is no reason you can't get someone just to come in here and take care of all of it. You might get over there and look through the Yellow Pages. I'm sure there are people in town who will come in and take care of those kinds of things for rich folks. If there ain't, you give me the money, and I will go to the hardware store, get baby locks and whatever I need, and do it myself."

I took the phone book to the dining table, and with Elmira's help, I soon found a handyman to baby-proof the house. I knew Vanilla was in good hands with Elmira and trusted her completely. I was happy that Vanilla had a Black nanny and that she could be exposed to a culture and a way of thinking that I knew was still foreign to me.

Our maid was a pretty little White country girl named Linda Clark. She had come to Nashville to try to break into country music. So, when she wasn't working with us, she was trying to pitch herself as a singer and find gigs to play. But the truth is, she had been in Nashville for five years by the time we hired her, and the chances of achieving stardom appeared increasingly slim. Still, she was young and was twenty-four when we hired her. Her drawl was as thick as a Tennessee fence post, and her naive manner caused others to overlook the fact that she was, actually, a very intelligent person. She was very good at keeping the house clean and presentable. She would come in three times a week and clean the house from top to bottom, most of the time, but adjusted her hours if we had dinner plans for anyone or she had rehearsals or a gig. Earl frequently asked if we could have dinner ready for a potential client or someone he wanted to hire for an executive position. I tried to cook these dinners myself for the longest time, but it soon became evident that I could not pull off preparing the meal and playing the gracious hostess simultaneously, so we hired a part-time cook. I didn't get into Vanderbilt, so more and more, I thought there was nothing for me to do except exist.

All that money was going fast. Earl had bought me a new Mercedes. His was black, and mine was maroon. We had a large house payment and then hired three servants. I was beginning to feel rather worthless and unneeded. I didn't clean the house. I didn't cook. I didn't even take care of my baby. When Earl was there, sometimes he was attentive and affectionate. At other times, he was just as buried in his work at home as in the office. Love-making became a dull routine. Two or three nights a week, he would crawl into bed and start feeling my body and kissing me. Then, with very little foreplay, he would climb on rock until he climaxed, which wasn't long, and then roll over and go to sleep. I stopped feeling like I was making love to him and started feeling like I was servicing him. I barely enjoyed it anymore.

I didn't start college that summer. I didn't even try. After being turned down for admission to Vanderbilt, I didn't care to apply anywhere else and became increasingly bored and depressed. I started smoking again. I didn't have to worry about smoking around the baby because Elmira had her well cared for somewhere else in the house. I often sat by the window in the living room, looking out at the beautiful view, puffing away, feeling drab and useless. In the past, I would have absorbed one book after another, textbook or fiction, but I had stopped reading. I did nothing but stare out the window and smoke. Our sofa sat near the window with a side table on either end. I positioned a chair facing the window where I could set my ashtray on the side table and gaze across the lawn as I smoked. Sometimes, I would look at the white columns through the trees and wonder what kind of life Minnie Pearl might have had, whether she was happy or if her life was better than mine.

Sometimes, I would go shopping and spend some of Earl's money on dresses or jewelry, so much for the hippie chick. I was back dressing like the real Lovella would have dressed, except I picked more classic lines like Mother would have. Occasionally, I would buy a nice gift for Elmira or Linda because I wanted to.

I tried joining some women's clubs but found them inane. Here were grown women talking like Mar-ceeee and Sta-ceeee back in the college dorm, albeit with a southern drawl. Most of the time, they talked about their husbands, and occasionally pictures of children went around. I found myself hesitant to show a picture of my child. I didn't think I felt ashamed of her, but I was ashamed of having had her the way I did, and I knew the kind of response I would likely get. The fear of being judged permeated my emotions, and old anxieties that I thought I had conquered returned.

One day, as children were being discussed, one of the women at our bridge game said, "Lovella, you have a child, don't you? Why don't we ever get to see pictures of your baby?"

I froze, unsure of what to say. I stammered and finally said, "Well, it seems to frighten her when we take a picture, so we haven't taken very many."

"Oh, my goodness," one woman said. "You don't take pictures of your baby? Surely not! How old is your baby now?"

"She is nineteen months," I said shyly.

"Oh, surely you have pictures of your baby," another woman said.

"Well, I …"

The words barely came out of my mouth before someone said, "I'm sure she's adorable. Let's see."

I reluctantly reached into my purse and took out my wallet. I pulled a snapshot of myself with Vanilla from the picture compartment and handed it to the woman beside me. The look on her face was a rapid sequence between scorn and pretended congeniality.

"Why, she is a beautiful baby," she said after the wave of what might be interpreted as nausea crossed her face. "Is she adopted?"

With the most intense ambivalence, I said, "No, she is mine."

"Oh," the woman said as she passed the picture to the next person, casting a look at her that, in my mind, said, *You are not going to believe this.*

The picture went around the table, and the response was essentially the same. I wish it had not been what I had expected, but it was. I felt, at that moment, that the only thing worse than being Black in 1969 was to be a White woman who had a Black baby. The picture was returned to me, and I returned it to my wallet. Afterward, the conversation was trite and stilted, and it didn't take long for someone to suggest that we call it a day. Then, I saw some women whispering to each other as we exited the hostess's home.

When I got home that afternoon, I went immediately to my lone perch in the living room and lit a cigarette. As I sat, staring out the window across the manicured lawn at the white ornate gate of the Minnie Pearl property, tears began to spill from my lashes. I felt terribly alone. My mind went back to high school, to friends in Climax, and how I had pretty much wasted the opportunity to make more friends because I was trying to screw practically every boy. I had grand, though immature, plans for my life, but those plans had all been derailed when Vanilla was born, so much for being a research scientist. I tried desperately not to resent my past, especially my child, but sadness and regret engulfed me. The grandeur of my surroundings meant nothing. I had never felt more alone.

Elmira walked into the room, "Miss Lovella, I have put Vanilla down for her nap, and I was wondering if …"

She stopped cold, seeing the tears streaming down my face, and the mother in her kicked in. She came across the room and sat on the end of the sofa next to my chair. She said nothing for a moment and then said,

"Some folks think a little age gives you wisdom that you don't possess when you are young."

I looked at her and said nothing.

She gave me her sweet, endearing smile and said, "You know I do have the age, and I might have a little wisdom if you want to share your troubles."

I took a last drag off my cigarette and blew the smoke away from her. "I don't know if anything can help," I said, blotting the spent cigarette into the ashtray.

"Well, how about you start by telling me what has upset you?" she smiled.

I retrieved my pack from the end table, reached for another cigarette, and said, "I don't think that *counselor* is in your job description."

"No, it ain't, Miss Lovella," she replied. "I won't go on if you don't want me to, but I have long had mother in my job description. I raised six children, and many times, I've had to come to the rescue of a wounded heart."

I lit the cigarette and looked away from her. "I am ashamed of even having these feelings, Elmira. I would be especially ashamed of discussing them with you."

She leaned toward me.

I heard her move and turned back around. Her eyes met mine, and she said, "One thing I know, Miss Lovella, shame never solved a problem anywhere in the world. There has not been one time that looking back with remorse or self-judgment ever made anything better."

I sat silently, looking at her.

"Tell me what has hurt you, child." Her voice was soft and filled with compassion.

Finally, I gave in. I stared out the window, unable to look at her. "I was at this stupid luncheon bridge game," I said. "They started asking me to see pictures of my daughter." Sadness and shame made my voice tremble. "I was ashamed to show them pictures of my baby. Then, when I showed them the picture, I could see the disgust on their faces. They asked me if she was adopted. There was a part of me that wanted to say—yes. There was a part of me that thought it would be so much easier to deal with if they thought we were this benevolent couple who adopted an orphaned Black child, but I couldn't say it. I couldn't make myself lie. I told them she is my baby, and they were even worse." I wiped tears from my face and continued. "It's like they could maybe have accepted it if I adopted a Black child, but they were disgusted that I gave birth to her. I wanted to tell them she was adopted, but I couldn't make myself do it. I don't know why I didn't stand up to them. I mean, I cussed out this old bitch in Connecticut for making racist remarks about my baby and my family. That was overt, in our faces, somebody I didn't know and could have cared less about, but I couldn't stand up to the disgust behind the smiles at this bridge club gathering. It would have been easier if they had attacked me and called me names instead of pretending to be congenial. At least, then, I would have had something to fight."

Elmira reached a comforting hand to touch my arm. "You are new at this," she said. "Black folks have been dealing with this kind of nonsense for hundreds of years, but it's all brand new to you. One thing I can tell you is what those women think, don't have nothin' to do with you. Judgment tells something about the person doing the judging. It don't say nothin' about the person being judged. Condemnation and gossip are what a lot of Southern women do. Many Southern White women are like coral snakes. The outside might look pretty, but it hides a deadly vinum within."

"I was just trying to make some friends," I sniffled.

"And what you found out was, these people ain't your friends." She patted my arm. "When we face tough times, that teaches us who our real friends are, but it also reveals the enemies we might have thought were friends."

"But Elmira," I countered. "I have to be around these kinds of people. I have to live here and deal with this prejudice. I have to put on a face for Earl's job and the company's reputation."

"Darlin', I have lived here my whole life," she said. "You think I haven't had to deal with uppity White folks who think they are better than you just 'cause their skin is a little lighter? Yes, you have to live with them and deal with their attitude. That's true, but their attitude don't have nothin' to do with you being proud of yourself. You can be proud of who you are, despite what they think, and you can smile right back at them and be as fake as they are when you're around them, knowing that you matter, even if they think you don't. Then, come home, be yourself, and be real with the folks who know you matter."

I smashed another cigarette into the ashtray. "That's just the problem," I said. "I don't have anything to be proud of. I have given up my dreams, and my life has become totally different from what I planned. I haven't finished my education. I don't even care if I get an education anymore. I don't care about anything, and I don't do anything that matters. I don't even take care of my daughter."

"You always have something to be proud of," Elmira responded. "Be proud that you are a child of God."

A quick burst of laughter twisted my face. "I have never been much for God," I said. "Mother forced me to go to church. I always thought it was more of a show and a social event than anything else. I can't say that I ever really got anything out of it or that I ever thought there was any more to religion than control and appeasement."

"Well, now, folks go to church for all kinds of reasons," she replied, "and it ain't always to praise the Lord. When the Bible says, '*Narrow is the way, and few there be that enter therein,*' it means some folks get it, and some don't. It don't matter if they go to church or what church they go to. Some folks get it, and some folks don't."

"I guess I never got it," I said, feeling uncomfortable that the conversation was approaching religion. As far as I was concerned, religion was something to be avoided.

"Well, let me sum it up for you," she said. "God is Love, and God is Holy, and God made you in *His* own divine image. Now, what does that make you?"

"I don't know," I said, nervously trying to determine a way to get out of the conversation. "I'm not even sure I believe in God."

"It means that you are made in the image and likeness of pure and perfect Holy Love itself," she went on. "Honey, God is love. It don't matter who you are. You are made with perfect love. Can't nothin' ever change that. Nothin' that anybody ever said or did can change what God created, and no mistake you ever made can change what God created. You are a child of God. But you see, God made everybody in His likeness. He made us all the same. The Bible says God ain't no respecter of persons. That means He don't favor nobody over somebody else, no matter who they are, the color of their skin, or what mistakes they have made, whether they love

Him back, or whether they think they are good or bad. So, it also means that He loves them uppity, racist White folks as much as He loves you and me. We have to learn to forgive them 'cause they don't know what they do. They don't get it. Now, do you understand?"

"I guess so," I said, relaxing a little and reaching for another cigarette.

"Child, I am telling you that you don't have to do anything to be special."

She leaned forward a little more and patted my arm to draw my attention. When I turned, her eyes met mine with a gaze of pure love. "You are already special," she went on. "You don't have to get an education to be special, but you can get an education if you want to. You don't have to cure cancer to be special, but if you do, the world would be grateful. God don't make nobody who ain't special. It means we are all equal in His love. There is no way around it. If you believe His love is real, then we are all equal in it. You hold your head up high. Don't you worry about what anybody thinks about you. What they think don't have nothin' to do with you. You have a baby with the same worth as any other baby. If somebody else don't think so, then that's their problem. When the Bible says, 'Judge not, lest ye be not judged,' it means the first person hurt by judgment is the one who does it."

"Yes, but they can create problems for us," I countered.

"They might," she said. "Sometimes people do bad things, but you can't spend your life worrying about what bad things they might do, and you don't need to spend your life letting prejudice define you. You define yourself in this world. God defined you before you got here. Nothing would ever get accomplished if everybody sat around worrying about what other people think of them instead of getting on with their lives."

"That's the problem," I replied. "I'm not accomplishing anything. I'm not even raising my child. You are."

"No, I'm not," she popped back. "I am like a grandmother giving you a little help with your baby. You are the one that child bonded with. I have watched you with Vanilla, and I have watched her with you. I see you when you put her down for a nap and when you hold her close to your bosom. Somebody else might feed her once in a while or change her diaper, but that don't mean she ain't yours. I know you love that baby. I see it every day."

"I haven't ever really taken care of her, except for here and there," I pushed back. "Earl's mother has taken care of her, and my mother has. Earl has taken care of her, and you have, but I probably have less to do with her than anyone."

Elmira sat back and smiled. "How much do you want to have to do with her?"

The question caught me off guard. A hot flush of embarrassment filled my face, and I realized I had just passively stood by and let other people have my baby. Maybe it was because there was a hint of shame there, an embarrassment that she wasn't Earl's biological child, embarrassment about that night with Screech. I asked myself if maybe I didn't want her, if maybe I resented her, and realized that there was a part of me that wished she wasn't there, a part of me that saw her as a barrier to what I thought I wanted from life. I knew I had a choice. I could go on with the way things were. I could go ahead and pursue my career, or I could be a mother to my child, or both. No matter what my choice, I realized I had to grow up. I fiddled with the bracelet on my arm as Elmira sat, silently waiting for my answer.

"I want to be a real mother to my baby," I said at last. "Will you show me how?"

Through her beautiful smile, Elmira leaned forward and said, "Honey, I would be proud to teach you everything I know."

CHAPTER 30

Seduction and Commitment

By the time Vanilla was three years old, I was pregnant with my second child. This one, I knew, belonged biologically to Earl. True to her promise, Elmira taught me a great deal about being a mother. I forgot about returning to college because I couldn't see a reason for it anymore. After all, being a sex researcher was more of a teenage fantasy than anything else. The Chum Snacks Company grew, and Earl's income increased to a point where we could have practically anything we wanted any time we wanted it. However, he was busy, and our sex life had bottomed out, but I told myself that I didn't care. I knew I still loved him and extended that love to my child in his absence.

Earl would come home in the evening whenever he could get away early enough and would delight in Vanilla's company. They had a joyful time together, and I realized he meant it when he said he would love her as his own child. I realized that she was somehow a link to the love he had felt for Screech, and in some way, maybe she kept that love alive for him. I wasn't jealous anymore because I knew he loved me just as much as he had ever loved Screech. It had been a moment in his life that caught him off guard, caught both of us off guard. He never expected that he would fall in love with a Black man from Alabama, or any man, for that matter, or that he would meet that man in San Francisco on a whirlwind trip that was more about defying his father than anything else. I certainly never expected to become pregnant by the same man he had fallen in love with. We were young, dumb kids out for an adventure. We did stupid things. The fact that the adventure became a turning point that totally changed life for both of us became more of a comfort than a regret.

I learned to play chit-chat with rich Nashville women while I ignored their gossip and cutting, little digs in the disguise of humor, and I finally found a couple who were genuine friends. On a few occasions, I had attended church with Elmira, and that certainly was an experience worth having. It made Mother's church seem like a piece of stale toast compared to a banquet of soul food. Although I appreciated it and knew I was welcome, it never quite fit with my personality. Besides, Elmira encouraged me to go to any church of my liking, and I had two reasons to attend. The first and foremost reason was to develop my spirituality, to emulate Christ, and to try to live as He lived. However, although I wanted to be a better person, I was not about to hang out with twelve guys and be celibate. The second reason was to attend church, for community, to socialize, meet people, and possibly develop friendships. I kept an open mind that I might also be able to improve myself spiritually.

I attended several churches, trying to see which would best serve the dual purpose recommended to me, and finally settled on a large Evangelical church near Brentwood: Evangelic Temple. The drive was not far from Green Hills, and the church was filled with people who came from money. It was a little bit fun and often enlightening. I certainly didn't mind it. I even convinced Earl that he should go. I could drop Vanilla off at the church daycare on Sunday and pick her up on the way out. After a while, I volunteered to help with weekly church business, such as preparing and printing the bulletins for Sunday morning service. I would generally go in on Wednesday or Thursday to type the bulletin information and get it ready to be printed for Sunday. Unfortunately, it was a challenge to curb the nasty edge of my tongue, which was all too prone to babble profanity. When some little screwup occurred with the typewriter, I repeatedly caught myself on the edge of words that were best not spoken in church. My habitual foul mouth developed in early childhood was a bit of a beast to tame. Later, I returned to believing that my profanity was more of an asset than a liability.

The Evangelic Temple minister was a very nice man named Pastor Wilkes. He was tall, about 6'4", and very healthy and robust for his fifties. In person, he was soft-spoken, gentle, and respectful. At the podium, he was a fireball of energy and enthusiasm. His sermon, which he delivered with a deep, powerful voice, resonated to the back walls of the church.

On a Thursday afternoon in April 1971, he approached me and asked if I had ever heard of Pastor Ronald Dennison.

"Oh," I said, "Isn't he that TV preacher who has the Sunday morning broadcast? He conducts services here occasionally, doesn't he?"

Yes, Pastor Wilkes replied. "Pastor Dennison has a TV show and has been very well known around the country for his work using media to reach the faithful and convert the fallen. He has become a national figure in the evangelical movement."

"Uh-huh," I said, smiling. "I happened to catch his broadcast a couple of months ago when Vanilla was ill, and I stayed home from church that day. He is quite a speaker and a very striking figure of a man, as well."

"So," Pastor Wilkes continued, "Pastor Dennison will broadcast from our church on Sunday, June 20th."

"How wonderful!" I spouted, smiling. "I will look forward to that."

Pastor Wilkes ignored my somewhat less-than-sincere enthusiasm and said, "I was wondering if we might impose upon you to meet with Pastor Dennison regarding his program for that day and work with him to set up the service according to his specifications. Would you be willing to oversee the bulletins for his service?"

I knew a broadcast would require a lot more than bulletins. Camera crews, sound techs, and producers would be in and out of the church for the upcoming weeks preparing for the broadcast. I assumed the bulletins could be a little more complicated for that type of service.

I nodded, "Of course."

"We are always honored to have Pastor Dennison come to our church," Pastor Wilkes continued. "When he speaks here, we want to present ourselves with our best foot forward. Having seen your work, Lovella, I trust you will prepare a very nice program for that service."

"I'm honored," I replied.

"When do you think you might be able to meet with Pastor Dennison?" he questioned.

"I can make myself available at any time," I answered.

"Wonderful. I will contact Pastor Dennison and give you a time that would be convenient for him. You may have to meet with him at his office and studio. Will that be okay with you?"

"Of course," I said.

"It is not uncommon for Pastor Dennison to speak before crowds of two or three thousand," he explained. "We are unsure how many additional parishioners we may have for that day. We may have to have extra bulletins for the day, so be prepared if there are any surprises."

"Just let me know when," I said and returned to my work on the typewriter.

The next day, I received a call at home from Pastor Wilkes informing me that Pastor Dennison wished to meet with me the next afternoon at 2:00. I accepted the appointment. On the following day, I decided to dress in my finest. The hippie days were gone, and I was back to classic lines and makeup. In those days, I tended to wear my hair in a French roll with a clip. I thought it made me look sophisticated and allowed me to show off my earrings since I was accumulating quite a collection. I wore a pale green, sleeveless tube dress with a slight flare around my knees. It had a mock turtleneck-type collar with a little open loop below it, which showed a hint of my cleavage. My earrings were small diamond-studded gold crosses. I was sparing with the eye shadow but liberally applied burgundy-colored lipstick. When finished, I looked at myself in the full-length mirror to see my fourth month of pregnancy protruding slightly beyond the curve of my dress. I thought *I should have worn maternity clothes, but I don't have time to deal with that now.*

It was already 1:45 p.m. when I backed out of the garage. I only had a few minutes to make it to Briley Parkway on the southeast end of town and find the studio. Of course, I was late. I went clamoring up to the receptionist about ten minutes after two o'clock.

"I'm Lovella Titwallow," I said, breathlessly. "I have an appointment with Pastor Dennison. I'm sorry I'm late."

"Oh, yes," she said, with a deep Tennessee drawl and a broad grin. He has been expecting you."

"I'm sure he has," I quipped, "especially since I'm late."

She was a middle-aged woman who looked to be, perhaps, older than Mother. Her hair was short, obviously colored light brown, and permed in large round curls like a hair helmet. Her ample, colorful glasses sat securely over her pointy, little nose. She presented as sweet, but I had the distinct impression she could be quite formidable.

"Oh, you are fine, darlin'," she said sweetly. Then, reaching over to press an intercom button, she said, "Mrs. Titwallow is here to see you, Pastor."

A man's voice returned with, "Send her in."

The receptionist said, "Right this way," and led me to his office.

She led me down a short hall to a large, ornate wooden door. She tapped it lightly and waited to hear, "Come in." Then she opened the door, ushered me through, and closed it behind me.

Pastor Dennison rose from his high-back leather office chair and came around the large mahogany desk near the middle of the room. He was a man in his mid-to-late thirties, of average stature, but he was a strikingly handsome man. He had a full head of thick dark brown hair and swimming pool-blue eyes that topped off the dimples on either side of his square jaw. He wore a black suit, white shirt, and solid pale blue tie. No sooner did he see me than his eyes lit up like he had just seen a long-lost loved one returning home.

"Mrs. Titwallow," he exclaimed exuberantly as he approached me. He took my extended hand between his two large hands. "How good to see you!"

I had intended to shake his hand, but I didn't mind the feel of his full palms on either side of my hand. I looked down at the hairy backs of his thick, full hands to see the wedding band wrapped around his finger. He held my hand and looked at me like his favorite dessert.

"Come. Sit down!" he said with vigor.

He gave a slight tug with both hands still over mine, leading me to the chair without losing physical contact. Although I thought this behavior was odd, I complied with it. Just before I reached the chair, he turned loose and motioned for me to sit.

"Would you like a soda pop or a cup of coffee?" he questioned, returning to his desk. As he passed by, he removed his suit jacket and laid it across his desk chair without turning around. He walked toward the wall behind his desk, where I noticed a small refrigerator and a coffee pot. I couldn't help also noticing that he had a firm, round ass perfectly outlined by his suit pants.

"Yes, please," I said. "Cola if you have it."

"Ice?" he questioned as he bent over and pulled a cola bottle from the fridge.

"Yes, if you have it, thank you," I said.

"I certainly do have it," he responded. He pulled a glass from a nearby shelf and opened a drawer on what appeared to be a small ice maker. He put a scoop of ice in the glass and brought both the glass and the opened bottle of cola back to me. "Don't worry about setting it on the furniture," he said, returning to the fridge, where he poured himself a soda.

I poured the cola and waited patiently for the foam to clear before adding more.

"So, Mrs. Titwallow, what brings you to Nashville?" he questioned, sipping his soda, assuming, I guess, that I was not from the area. Mother's insistence that I articulate probably eliminated any hint of an inherited Kentucky cadence.

I cleared my throat. "My husband is the district manager for the Chum Snacks Company I replied. "His father owns the company, and we moved here about two years ago after they built the distribution center here."

"Well, you must come from fine stock indeed," he flattered. "At least you certainly look like you came from very fine stock."

The little kick of a grin up one side of his mouth and the look in his eyes led me to believe that he was coming on to me with that comment about *fine stock.* I dismissed it, initially, as my imagination.

"My mother's family is from rural Kentucky," I said, "and my father was a factory worker. I just happened to meet the right boy when I went to college."

"Do you love him?" he questioned.

I felt suddenly uncomfortable that his questions became a bit too personal. I avoided snapping that I thought we were here to create bulletins for his service, not pry into my personal life. Instead, I responded, "Yes, I do. I love him very much."

"Well, good! Good!" he sputtered. "A woman ought to love her husband. Are there any children?"

"Yes," I replied quietly. "We have a daughter aged three."

"And one on the way—perhaps," he said, smiling and glancing repeatedly at my belly.

"I'm sorry," I remarked, suddenly embarrassed, covering my belly with my hand. "I should have gotten into maternity clothes."

"Oh, don't be sorry," he pressed. Then, he moved to the front of his desk with his soda, leaned back on it, and crossed his legs at the ankles. He eyed me like a steak dinner. "Pregnancy is when a woman is at her finest and most beautiful. You should be proud that you are with child."

"I am proud," I responded. "Earl and I love our daughter very much, but we have also been looking forward to this baby."

"May I?" he asked and dismounted the desk, coming to kneel on one leg beside my chair. He held his left hand about six inches above my belly and rested his right arm across his knee.

I felt very odd at that moment. This was an incredibly personal and intimate thing for even family to do, much less a man I had never met before. I felt almost violated. Yet, on the other hand, I felt enticed. I looked at him and saw those amazing blue eyes gazing directly at me. His look was both inviting and curious.

I hesitantly nodded, and his hand went smoothly to my belly while he gazed into my eyes. He bowed his head and quickly prayed, "Lord, we ask you to bless this unborn child and the woman who will give birth to it. In Jesus's name, we pray, Amen." I felt the warm, masculine touch of his hand flow over my belly and then quickly around my waist, lightly touching my breast, like a test to check my response. I looked down at his hand, but his gaze returned to my face and never wavered. I looked back at him. Now, I knew he was coming on to me. It felt strange to be seduced. Only Earl had ever seduced me. Pastor Dennison was not exactly subtle, but much more subtle than I ever had to be when seducing boys. Most men are easy, especially if you are pretty.

I watched his hand move around my belly and he made no effort to pull it away. I had a mix of feelings. On the one hand, I had taken on the quest to be a good Christian and do the right thing, and I wanted to be faithful to Earl. On the other hand, Earl had been unfaithful with Screech, and our sex life had become dull and infrequent. The old me was still in there. I felt my groin begin to crave. Yet, I felt guilty that, were I to give in, I would be betraying Earl. The fact that Pastor Dennison was a powerful and beautiful man created an even more enticing temptation. The fact that the fruit was most assuredly forbidden made the craving sweeter.

Then, he whispered, "You are so beautiful. Your lips are like sweet red wine. They make me want to have communion with you. I want to drink the sweet nectar of your lips." He paused while continuing to gaze into my eyes. "May I kiss you, Mrs. Titwallow?"

The whole thing felt bizarre but also strangely enticing. I said nothing but sat looking at him, not knowing what to do. A part of me wanted to get up and leave, and part of me felt motherly toward him, as though he were a little boy to be taken into my arms and comforted. I realized that I did want him to seduce me. I wanted him to make love to me. Yet, a voice in my mind told me it would be very wrong. Although I loved Earl, it had been forever since we had made love instead of having quick and unfulfilling sex. I enjoyed our contact, but it was over briefly and became increasingly mundane as our marriage progressed. Earl had become his father in so many ways. As much as I hated it, and as much as I wanted it to be different, I often felt like my role as a wife was to service him, pleasure him, and keep him going while he did the work that he had to do. Still, I never talked to him about it because I had also become like Clarese, at least in her youth. I played the dutiful wife who gives in to her husband's needs without questioning or thinking of her own. This was a woman's expected role in those days—do whatever it takes for your husband and think little of yourself.

Pastor Dennison leaned in, ever closer to my lips. He did not ask again if he could kiss me, and I never told him he couldn't. Coming slowly closer, at long last, his lips touched mine ever so lightly, and then, he pulled away. A second later, his lips maneuvered skillfully over mine, then pulled away again, but only for the brief second that he gazed into my eyes. Then, he gently covered my mouth with his own. The expertise of his kiss felt as though he could have picked up a single grain of rice with those lips. The sensuality of it was terrific. He kissed me gently, covering my mouth, consuming my mouth with a ravishing hunger. I closed my eyes, melted into his kiss, and allowed it to happen.

His hand moved from my belly to my breast. He caressed it as if he were petting a cat, gently moving his big, hairy hands across to my nipples. I felt them harden beneath my bra as his thumb moved back and forth gently. I felt his other hand move to the back of my neck. Electricity surged throughout my body. I felt sensual tingling from my neck through my lips to my breasts and my groin. I felt myself gasp in pleasure when his lips moved to the nape of my neck. I had fucked boys repeatedly since I was a teen, but this was an entirely different kind of excitement. Before Nashville, Earl had been the most skillful lover I ever had, but the sensuality of the pastor's touch rivaled even the finesse that Earl had in our younger days. I couldn't figure it out. It was almost as though his touch contained some unexplained power.

He gently lifted me with his hand against the back of my neck. I rose with him like the assistant in a magic show, levitated, floating. He moved me across the floor to the back of his desk, kissing me the whole way, his lips moving lightly across my neck while he caressed my body, never losing contact. He stopped, gazed into my eyes, and cupped his mouth over mine again. He pulled a pillow from the desk chair with one hand while his other held firm around my waist. He placed the pillow on the desk to cradle my head and tilted me back onto the desk. Then, he pulled my hips to the edge of the desk and began pulling my panties toward my feet. He dropped his pants, and we proceeded to have the most exhilarating sex I had had in several years.

At last, I heard his breath quicken, felt his rhythm alter, and knew that he was nearing climax. He began to quiver, almost like a baby bird, and exploded into guttural screams as though demons were rushing out of him. I feared that security guards would hear and come rushing in, thinking he was being murdered. In a few seconds, he fell atop me, silent, breathless, unmoving. Then, everything suddenly changed.

He stood up and pleaded immediately, "I'm sorry! I'm sorry! God forgive me! I'm sorry!"

I was taken aback. I had just had one of the most spectacular sessions of sex ever in my life, and this man was telling me he was sorry.

"What for?" I asked.

"I have sinned! I have sinned against God and against you!"

He began to cry, abundant tears rolling over his distorted and overly grieving face.

"I am a worthless no-good sinner!"

He started to turn around, forgetting that his pants were still around his ankles. He tripped over them and fell onto the floor.

"The Lord has struck me down!" he cried, face down on the floor. "I deserve to be struck down. I deserve to be punished! I am a miserable, worthless sinner!"

"Your pants struck you down," I smirked as I got up from his desk and collected myself. I realized that my dress was now wrinkled, and I was a mess. I reached for some tissues from his desk, quickly adjusted myself, and knelt beside him, putting a comforting hand on his shoulder. "Pastor Dennison," I said, "it's okay. It's just sex. Excellent sex, but just sex. I very much enjoyed it. Thank you."

"Don't call me Pastor!" he wailed. "I don't deserve to be called Pastor!"

"Uh … okay … uh … Ronald?" I said after fumbling with what to call him. "You have to pull yourself together now."

"I am a God-forsaken sinner!" he bellowed into the floor.

"Doesn't God forgive?" I questioned.

"Yes, but I keep doing it over and over. I can't stop doing it. I have to seduce women, especially women with beautiful lips with red lipstick. I can't stop myself! I can't! I am a weak and worthless man. I repeatedly betray my wife, my parishioners—and my Lord! I'm a worthless, worthless man!"

"There is no such thing as worthless," I quoted Elmira. "God made everyone equal."

"God punishes the sinful," he wailed. "You have no idea how sinful I am. All I want to do is have sex and seduce women. The devil keeps my mind constantly on women. I have had so many women. I have defiled so many poor, helpless females. I have corrupted the sanctity of the church!"

"It felt like you might have had some practice," I commented, grinning, "but come on. I am not poor or helpless, and I had a choice in this—defiling. I am as responsible as you are."

"YOU *ARE* RESPONSIBLE!" he shouted, finally looking up at me. "YOU ARE A JEZEBEL! A WHORE!"

"Well, I wouldn't take it that far," I joked, not entirely taking him seriously. "I never got paid for it, but I have been a bit of a slut in my day. I like sex, but that doesn't make me a bad person."

"YOU ARE A BAD PERSON!" he bellowed as he buried his face back onto the floor. "You're a seductress! You lured me into sin! But I am worse! I am called by God, and I allowed myself to be lured into sin! I am worthless scum on the shoes of the righteous."

"No, you're not," I argued. "Look, I'll prove it to you. God is love, right?"

"Yes," he quietly responded.

"And God holy?" I went on.

"Yes," he said again.

"And God made you, in His image?"

"Yes."

"Then what does that make you?"

"A miserable, worthless sinner!" he persisted.

"It means you are made in the image and likeness of pure and perfect Holy Love itself!" I argued. "It means there is no such thing as worthless! If God could create worthless, then how could God be perfect?"

"But I have sinned and fallen short," he continued.

"Well, join the fucking club!" I announced, losing patience with him. "Who hasn't?"

"I already have joined the club." He burst into tears again. "The club of eternal hellfire and damnation!"

By that time, I had had enough.

"We have work to do," I commanded. "Get up! We have to prepare you to present at Evangelic Temple in June."

"I should throw myself into a furnace and burn myself, so I know what Hell feels like. I deserve to burn in hell," he cried.

I wondered what happened to the self-assured, determined man I had met when I came in.

"It doesn't matter what you think you should do," I responded. "It only matters what you have to do. Now get up!" He didn't move, so I stood up and commanded firmly, "RONALD! I SAID—GET UP!"

"Yes," he said, responding quietly to the authoritarian tone. "Yes, I need to get up. We have work to do. There are things I need to do." He rolled over but did not get up.

I couldn't help feeling a surge of power as I stood over him, looking down at his now limp dick and his naked body. He looked up at me like a little boy looking at a scolding parent. "GET UP," I commanded again.

He sat up, rolled over to his knees, put one arm on the chair to pull himself up, and into it. Then, he began the task of pulling his pants up. I watched him with curiosity. A few minutes before, a commanding masculine man had given me one of the best fucks of my life, and now he looked sheepish and childlike. He spoke in soft, timid, child-like tones.

"I need to get up. I have work to do," he said. He stood up, pulled his pants the rest of the way up, and fastened them.

I found my panties and hose, slipped back into them, and asked, "Do you have an adjacent restroom?"

"Over there." He pointed quietly to a door near the back corner of his office.

I went in and looked in the mirror at the mess on my face. My burgundy lipstick was now smeared across my face and down my neck because he had fondled my lips during sex. My hair was easy to fix with a few bobby pins, but the makeup took longer. I washed away the excess lipstick with some soap and a hand towel. Finally, I reapplied my makeup, cleaned myself up, and stepped back into the office to find Pastor Dennison fully dressed, back in his suit with the blue tie pulled neatly up to his buttoned collar. He was sitting behind his desk with his hands clasped in front of him. When I initially saw him, he was staring at his hands. However, as soon as he heard me re-enter the room, he looked up and smiled as if nothing had happened. The persona of Pastor Dennison was back, and the little boy who needed to be punished for doing wrong was gone. He stood and came around the desk, just as he had done when I was first ushered into his office. He began to speak with the same masculine commanding voice and reached out to take my hand between his hands, as he had done when we first met. "Mrs. Titwallow," he crooned, "How good of you to come by my office today. I hope this was not inconvenient for you."

I stood there looking at him, thinking, *What the hell?*

"I think we may be out of time this afternoon," he continued as though all we had done was sit there, sipping soda pop, talking about church. "If I write notes for the bulletin format by hand, do you think you might be able to decipher my chicken scratch to put the material together?"

"Uh, yes," I said. Now, I was thinking that the man was totally nuts. To say that his behavior was bizarre would be an understatement. Why did he even want me to come to his office if all he had to do was write notes for me?

"Good," he smiled congenially after I answered his question. "I'll have Miss Smith bring the notes to you tomorrow. Will you be at Evangelic Temple tomorrow afternoon, then?"

"Yes," I replied. He continued to hold my hand, and I looked at him as though I were examining some strange animal on display at the zoo.

"Good. I will have Miss Smith see you out." He finally released my hand and turned to the intercom on his desk.

"That's okay," I said quickly. "No need to involve Miss Smith. I don't think it is so complicated that I can't figure it out."

I walked confidently to the door and opened it. To be a little mean, I turned back to him and, in my best ditzy girl voice, said, "See you later—toots." I gave a dainty little wave and a backward kick of my heel. Then, I left the door open behind me. As I walked past Miss Smith at the reception desk, she looked at me with a curious smirk. *She knows exactly what he does;* I thought to myself as I passed. As I was walking out the door, I saw her get up and walk toward his office.

The following week, after a conversation with the church secretary, I concluded that he had set it up. He had seen me in a picture of church volunteers, must have decided he wanted to fuck me, and asked Pastor Wilkes for my assistance. Putting the bulletins together was a ruse to get me into his office.

Because the sex was so good, I had found myself initially hoping that we might be able to do it again. It certainly would have been nice to make it a habit since I wasn't getting much from Earl anymore, but I was also breaking my own rule about honesty. I realized that I had to have a long overdue talk with Earl. Later, I found myself thinking that the pastor had a mental illness and that I had best keep my distance.

After my tryst with Pastor Dennison, that evening at home was typical. Earl got home from work at about 7:00. We had a quick dinner and played with Vanilla for a while before we put her to bed. He often tucked her into bed, but I went with him this time. After putting her down together, we returned to the living room, where he turned on the TV and sat on the sofa. I went right behind him and turned the TV off. He looked at me curiously but said nothing. I guess he could see the seriousness on my face. I sat down next to him and put my head on his chest. I hugged him, looked up, and said, "I love you. Do you know that?"

"I do know that," he responded. "I love you too."

"Then, why don't we act like we love each other anymore?" I queried. "I miss my husband. He was such a wonderful man."

He sat up and turned toward me. "What do you mean?"

"Earl," I said calmly. "We've become your parents."

A moment of shock went across his face. He sat another moment in thought and then realized what I was saying. "Goddamn!" he exclaimed. "We have! What do you think we should do about it?"

"For starters," I said, "tonight, I want to sit here, cuddle with, and talk to my husband instead of staring at the boob tube and then going off to snore. Maybe we might have a glass of wine. Then later, we could go to bed and make love, the way we used to make love, instead of just having a quick hump. Maybe we could find ourselves again."

He smiled, cupped my face in his hands, and kissed me. "I am so glad you are my girl," he said. Then, he got up from the sofa and headed for the kitchen. Over his shoulder, he asked, "Riesling?"

"Riesling," I affirmed.

CHAPTER 31

And The Truth Shall Piss You Off!

I never told Earl about my tryst with the crazy televangelist. I mulled it over many times. After all, I had said the rule was honesty, but I decided, in the end, that telling him would do nothing to improve our relationship. Besides, Earl was the man I loved, the only man I wanted to spend the rest of my life with, and I was never unfaithful to him again. I should have been honest with him about my feelings before I ran into Pastor Dennison, but I guess it took that for me to have the courage to address what was happening in our marriage. I stopped going to the Evangelical Temple and decided that the Presbyterian church was more to my liking. Earl didn't care where we went to church or even if I went. He thought attending church for show was hypocrisy, and I suppose it was. However, Elmira had taught me to appreciate spirituality and that wisdom could be gained no matter what church I attended. Besides, the Presbyterians seemed like a Goldi Locks denomination, not too focused on judgment and not too far out in space, either. Like Mother, I had found my Goldi Locks church, but for a different reason. Earl went with me for a few years and then decided he preferred to sleep in on Sunday morning. I took the children for as long as they wanted to go, but when they each reached the age of ten, I allowed them to choose whether they wanted to go or whether they wanted to attend a different church. Both of them decided to stay home and sleep in with Daddy. I continued to attend the Presbyterian church.

I heard that the preacher, Ronald Dennison, had done a very controversial broadcast when June 20th rolled around. He had been missing from action through May, and around that time, I decided to stop volunteering at Evangelic Temple. Apparently, he said some very shocking things from the pulpit on the twentieth, which stirred a lot of controversy with his followers. I didn't pay much attention to how that all played out. Honestly, I didn't care. I was over him and the Evangelic Temple experience and ready to move on.

462

On October 24, 1971, our son, Andrew Daniel Titwallow, was born. As had been the case when Vanilla was born, the families gathered. When Earl's father learned that we had named the child after him, tears welled in his eyes, but he looked away, trying to hide that he was touched. We would call the baby Drew for short, but Mr. Titwallow always understood his grandson was his namesake, and they grew close as Drew matured. More than once, Earl commented that his father was more understanding and nurturing with Drew than he ever had been with him.

Over time, I began to understand what family is really about. Sure, there are squabbles, disagreements, mess-ups, and misunderstandings, but ultimately, it is about returning to love and hanging onto it no matter what happens. I wondered if my kids would put me through what I had put Mother through. I wondered if they would misunderstand my intentions or if I would be able to be the kind of mother they would appreciate and respect.

As Vanilla got older, she questioned why she looked different from the rest of the family. We told her we would explain it when she was old enough to understand, and she never asked again until after she started high school. I was thankful that she was close to Elmira and learned from her how to be a proud Black girl, knowing that she was not what others thought of her. She was her own person and began understanding that character is much more important than color. At last, when she was fourteen and began asking questions about sex, we explained a little bit about her biological father and that we had both loved him very much. Earl explained the characteristics that he loved about her father. He emphasized Screech's strength and said nothing about his insecurities or problems. We told her only that he died of mysterious causes. Eventually, when she was an adult, we told her the whole story.

Vanilla had been a little jealous of Drew when we first brought him home, but she soon became a little momma, wanting to hold the baby like the adults. For safety, Earl would hold them both in his lap, Vanilla in his arms and Drew in hers. Earl wrapped his long arms around them and bantered with Vanilla as she looked back and forth between him and Drew, saying, "Baby?"

"Little brother, Bubba, Drew, Drew," Earl would say. He loved both his children more than life, and that only made me love him more. Despite the business, he was determined to be the father that Daniel had failed to be. He was not about to make his career more important than his children, and he always managed to find time for both.

On September 14, 1974, right after Vanilla had entered the first grade, Elmira answered the phone at about 2:00 p.m. Drew was almost speaking complete sentences by that time. He loved Elmira and followed her around the house like a lost puppy, calling her "E-my."

After answering the phone, Elmira asked, "Who's calling, please?" Then, a serious look came across her face. Drew wrapped his little arms around her leg and must have felt her tension when she said, "Miss Lovella, I think you best come to the phone." No sooner had she said the words than Drew burst into tears.

I had finally given up cigarettes and had been reading a book by the window instead of smoking. I had learned that enjoying my window was better with a book than a cigarette. When I turned to look, Elmira's face was stark with apprehension.

"Elmira, what is it?" I said, folding the book and setting it on the side table.

"I think it's best they talk to you," she said, holding the receiver in my direction.

My heart sank. At first, I thought that something must have happened to Earl. When I took the phone from Elmira's hand, she bent over, picked up Drew, and began to console him. She stood with him as I put the receiver to my ear and said, "Hello."

"Is this Lovella Titwallow?" I heard a woman's voice on the other end of the line.

"Yes," I replied.

"Mrs. Titwallow," the voice followed. "My name is Brenda Patterson. I am a nurse with Armstrong Memorial Hospital in Kittanning, Pennsylvania. I regret to inform you that your mother, Drucella Fuchs, has been involved in a serious accident."

"Accident?" I asked. "My mother?" Elmira was nearby, rocking Drew on her hip and watching pensively.

"Yes," the voice responded. "Your mother was involved in a serious automobile accident this morning. We have no idea why she crossed the center line into on-coming traffic. There is some suspicion that she may have passed out or that she might have had a seizure or a stroke."

"Oh, my God!" I winced. "Is she all right?"

"No, Mrs. Titwallow," the voice went on. "I'm afraid your mother has been seriously injured. She crossed over the center line into the path of a semi-truck. No one else was injured seriously, but your mother has had a near-fatal accident and has suffered significant brain trauma."

"Oh, Jesus!" I exclaimed. "Is anyone with her? Where are my grandparents?"

"Your grandparents are at the hospital," Brenda Patterson informed. "However, the accident was potentially fatal, and your mother is in critical condition. Your grandmother felt that she was too distraught to call you herself and asked that we contact you. She said she knew you would want to be here."

"Yes, yes," I said, feeling dazed and confused. "I will get there as soon as I can."

I hung up the phone without thinking while the voice on the other end was still speaking. I must have looked lost when I turned to Elmira.

"Go pack a bag, honey," she said. "I will call Mr. Earl and let him know. Has your momma been hurt bad?"

"Very bad," I said,

"Don't you worry about nothing," Elmira said, placing her comforting hand on my arm. "You know I will take good care of everybody down here. You feel up to driving?"

"I don't know," I whispered.

I was too shocked to cry. In my adult years, my childhood tormentor had become congenial and a wonderful grandmother to my children. She adored both my children, and I considered that she had redeemed herself. Yet, I still had a lingering distrust from my childhood, and now, knowing that she might die, I had a mix of feelings rushing over me, not the least of which was guilt about my past behavior and attitude toward her.

"Go on and start packing," Elmira encouraged. "Pack for Mr. Earl, too. While you do that, I will call him and tell him he needs to come home and drive you to Pennsylvania."

"He has got too much to do," I argued. "I can drive."

"Miss Lovella, that company has got plenty enough money that he can take some time off to drive you over to see your sick momma," she argued. "Chum Snacks is not gonna go out of business because Mr. Earl took a little time away. Now go pack."

I did, dutifully, as she had told me. She called Earl, and of course, he came home immediately. By 4:00 p.m., we were on our way to Kittanning. Elmira would take care of the children while we were gone. I had no worries about that, but it was a long and tedious trip made worse by worry about Mother.

We arrived in Kittanning about 2:00 a.m., exhausted and irritable. Earl pulled his Mercedes into the almost empty parking lot of Armstrong Memorial.

"You know, they are going to have the hospital locked down at this time of night," he said. "Why don't we just get a hotel room and come back in the morning?"

"Take me to the emergency room," I ordered. "I could talk to someone there."

He drove around to the emergency entrance. I got out of the car and walked in alone. There was a reception window in the almost empty lobby beside double doors leading back to the treatment rooms. Behind the window sat a skinny older nurse with mouse-blond hair. When I approached, she looked up. Her cheekbones squared under her gray eyes as she fixed them on me and said, "May I help you?"

"My name is Lovella Titwallow," I replied. "My mother is Drucella Fuchs. She's hospitalized here in intensive care. We just got in from Nashville. I was wondering if I could see her."

"Visiting hours are not in the middle of the night," she affirmed.

"Look," I responded, maintaining my temper, "My mother could die tonight. Are you going to deprive me of possibly my last opportunity to see her alive?"

For a moment, her gaze fixed on me like a raccoon in a flashlight. Then, she said, "I'll call up to that floor and ask."

She closed the sliding glass on the window, and I saw her on the phone briefly. Afterward, she opened the glass again and said, "Your mother is not conscious but stable. Your grandmother is in the room with her. They said they looked in on them about ten minutes ago, and your grandmother was asleep. Why don't you find a place to stay for the night and come back in the morning? There is a nice hotel about a mile from here, on Glade Park East. If you go up Nolte to the east and turn left on Glade Park, you will see it just a few blocks down." She pointed in the general direction.

"Thank you," I said, too exhausted to argue.

"Call us back when you arrive and let us know your room number. We will contact you if your mother's condition changes." She smiled and scribbled a note on a piece of paper. "Here is the hospital number, the name, and the extension of the night nurse on your mother's floor. Call her and let her know how to reach you." She handed the paper to me through the sliding glass window.

"Thank you," I said again and walked out.

I returned to the car and instructed Earl to find the hotel. It was almost 3:00 a.m. when we checked into our room and settled into bed. I called the hospital to give the night nurse our room number and called the hotel front desk for a wake-up call at 7:00 a.m. We were both exhausted, but I couldn't sleep. For most of those four hours, I lay in the dark, staring at the ceiling while Earl slept. I called the front desk and canceled the wake-up call before they could ring the room, showered, dressed, and left Earl a note that I had returned to the hospital. I knew he would want to go with me if I woke him. I thought it best to let him sleep. At least he could.

It was a very short drive back to Armstrong Memorial. I arrived right after they brought a breakfast tray for Grandmother Donner and just before the doctor made rounds. Mother lay unconscious on the bed with a respirator and tubes poked in everywhere. Her head had been shaved, and there were stitches along the side of her head. I thought that she was going to die and assumed this would be the last I would see of Mother.

Grandmother Donner's behavior was significantly more subdued than usual. She quietly ate breakfast while I pulled the doctor aside to ask questions. He explained that Mother had a skull fracture to the front left side and lesions in her left frontal lobe. She had also had the type of injury where the brain is rocked back and forth in the skull, so she had damage to the back part of her brain, as well. He explained that this affected the autonomic nervous system, so the machine had to breathe for her. They had already done surgery to relieve pressure from brain swelling.

"Ultimately," he said, "we don't know, long-term. Right now, we have to stabilize her, and then we will see what happens after that. There are a lot of factors that will determine how well her brain heals. She also has some fractured ribs and narrowly missed a puncture to her lung."

After the discussion with the doctor, I realized that I wouldn't be returning to Nashville for a very long time. I was torn between my mother and my children. They both needed me, and there was no way I could split myself between both places. Earl stayed with me in the hotel room for a few days and then had to go back. He went to a local rental company, rented a car to drive back to Nashville, and left his Mercedes with me. I checked out of the hotel and stayed at Mother's house. The drive to Kittanning was not long, and staying there would be more comfortable in the long run. It felt so strange to be back there, especially alone. Even though I had grown up in that house, and my childhood pictures dotted the walls, I felt like I was intruding into someone else's life.

For the next two months, I went back and forth between there and the hospital and made one short trip back to Nashville, but only for a day. I exchanged Earl's car with him and brought my car back to Pennsylvania. Earl brought the kids up for a weekend a few times, but I still felt torn between them and Mother. During that time, aunts, uncles, and friends from church stopped by or visited. When I wasn't at the hospital with Mother, I busied myself at home. While there, I went through Mother's papers and tried to figure out what she might have had in the way of bills, insurance, burial policies, bank accounts, etc. There was so much to think about and to figure out. It felt like I was locked in a vice with the pressure constantly tightening.

In a little over eight weeks, they moved Mother out of critical care. She was breathing on her own, but just barely. They still had her on oxygen. She appeared coherent at times, and it seemed she could carry on a normal conversation, but within moments, she could not remember the conversation or who had been there.

The holidays were fast approaching, and Thanksgiving was in just a couple of weeks. I had no idea how I would handle that, but it came and went as usual, just another date on the calendar. Earl took the kids to his parents for Thanksgiving Day and brought them to spend the weekend with me. Grandmother and Grandfather Donner came over and brought food, and I baked a pumpkin pie in Mother's kitchen.

A few days after Thanksgiving weekend, Mother spiked a fever, and her condition regressed considerably. I went back to sitting with her in the hospital instead of checking on her a couple of times a day. She became fitfully delirious and had to have restraints. On the following Thursday afternoon, a week past Thanksgiving, I was sitting in her room watching her cycle in and out of sleep and delirium. Then, I heard her saying something that sparked my curiosity. I could scarcely hear what she was saying, but I got up and leaned over her bed when I heard a particular name.

"Carl! Carl!" she moaned fitfully, "Stop! No—no! I don't want to."

I recognized the name. She had told me that Carl Whitmire was my biological father. I had not believed her, but why was she calling out his name? I thought, at the time she told me, that she was making up a cruel story to twist a knife into my pain over losing Daddy. However, there were the things that Daddy had told Earl before he died. I never knew what to believe for certain. My home life and my childhood had become a mystery. What I had thought to be the truth came into question, and I wondered if I would ever really know the truth. Daddy told Earl his side of the story, and who knew if Earl remembered it correctly.

Mother fell silent. Then, after a few minutes, she began thrashing around again. "Carl, I'm a good girl, a good girl—No!"

She was in and out. At one point, it seemed she had quieted down, and I went back to my chair, but it began again: "No, Carl! Stop! Carl, stop! You're hurting me! Stop! Stop! No!"

I rushed back to the bedside and took her hand to comfort her. "It's okay, Mother. You're okay."

I stood there with my mind reeling. Was this a hallucination or a flashback? The way she was reacting made it seem like she was dreaming of being raped.

She went on calling out similar things for a couple of hours. Over that time, I heard my name called. I heard the words 'pregnant' and 'abortion'. I heard the full name—Carl Whitmire.

At about 7:00 that evening, Grandmother Donner came to the room. She was dressed in her usual gaudy garb, but there wasn't much fire or spunk. The humor, spit, and vinegar had gone out of her. Having become a mother, I had some idea what kind of pain she must have experienced watching her daughter suffer.

"Hello, sweetheart," she said. She walked up to me and hugged me quickly, then turned toward Mother and said, "How's she doing today?" She walked over to the hospital bed and looked down at Mother before waiting for my answer.

"She's still delirious," I responded. "She has been saying all kinds of things, but there seems to be a theme."

Grandmother Donner looked down at Mother pitifully and patted her on the shoulder. "Lord have mercy." she lamented. "No momma ever wants to see her baby girl go through something like this. God forbid." Her voice trembled. "I think she is gonna die."

"We don't know that," I encouraged and came to stand beside her. "For all we know, she could have a complete recovery."

Grandmother Donner looked up at me, and I could see floating wells of tears in her eyes that refused to spill across her cheek. "Honey, it sure don't look like it to me," she said mournfully.

I didn't know what to say. I sighed and reached out a hand over her arm.

She patted my hand and smiled. "Anything new?" she asked.

"She has been calling out Carl Whitmire's name," I said.

"Oh, mercy," Grandmother Donner exclaimed, moving quickly to a chair.

"What do you mean, oh mercy?" I asked, following her.

"What has she been saying?" Grandmother Donner questioned back.

"She has been saying things like 'stop, you're hurting me, and I don't want to get pregnant,'" I replied.

Grandmother Donner's face looked stunned, and she turned away from me.

"What do you know that I don't?" I pressed.

She said nothing but kept her face turned away from me.

"Grandmother—what?" I persisted.

Still, she said nothing.

"Grandma!"

"He raped her," she said, finally, without turning around. "Nobody ever wanted you to know that you were a rape baby. As a matter of fact, she had to … Never mind."

I sat silently, taking it in, recalling things said and done when I was a little girl. At last, I said, "Tell me, Grandma. I want to know."

She turned slowly and said, "Baby, Carl Whitmire *is* your blood daddy, but it can't go no farther than you knowing that. You can't tell nobody about it."

"And why the hell can't I tell anybody about it?" I pressed.

"It's complicated," she replied. "Please."

"What the fuck!" I exclaimed. "Mother said he was my blood father, but I just didn't want to believe it. When Mother told me that, I thought she was just making shit up, and I had no idea that he had raped her! If he raped her, why isn't the fucker in jail!"

"She was on a date with him," Grandmother Donner explained. "How are you going to prove it was rape, and she didn't consent to it? Besides, he was a medical student from a wealthy family. They had the money to hire lawyers. We didn't."

My mind burned with rage. No wonder Mother was such a prude. No wonder she tried to make me into a perfect little girl. She tried to control Daddy to protect him from his drinking, but maybe she tried to control me to protect me from what she went through. Her attitude toward men was totally different than mine, maybe because she got raped. She may have loved Daddy, but she was never in love with him, and I doubt they had sex more than three or four times during their entire marriage, if at all. She idolized men for what they could do for her and what she thought they could do for me. Yet, she never let any man get close to her. I could see why she might never want to have sex again after something like that. I could also see her resentment of men and maybe resentment of me, at least mixed feelings about me because I was the product of her rape—no wonder she had lost her mind after I was born. I couldn't imagine all the emotions and internal conflict that she must have been dealing with.

"How did Daddy come into the picture?" I asked.

Grandmother Donner smiled a little. "That man … He had been in love with your momma for as long as he had known her, which went back to the first grade. He would have lassoed a bull elephant for her if he thought that's what she wanted. She wouldn't have anything to do with him, though. He wasn't good enough for Miss Priss over there, who had in mind she was gonna marry herself a rich man. That's why she went out with Whitmire. He was smart, and his family had clout, but your daddy struggled to graduate high school.

"When she got pregnant, she told Whitmire about it, and he told her that he would pay for an abortion, or he could do it himself if she wanted. He didn't care if it was illegal. She told him she could prove it was his baby with a paternity test and demanded that he was gonna marry her. He told her he had plenty of friends who would testify that they had slept with her and would ruin her reputation; he told her he could fake paternity results. He blew her off and told her to get lost.

"Your daddy was always coming around doing things for her, buying stuff for her. He didn't push himself on her too hard, so she tolerated it and pretended she didn't like it, but the truth is she wanted the attention. Your daddy worshiped her. If that girl ever had a teardrop fall, your daddy would have caught it in the palm of his hand before it ever touched the ground. He knew her like a road map in his heart. He saw her getting depressed, and he noticed when she first started to show. He cornered her about it one day, and she told him what had happened, but she wouldn't tell him who. She didn't trust that he wouldn't do something stupid if he knew—probably he would have. The next thing he did was convince her that nobody had to know. They was out of high school by then—grown. They could do what they wanted. He told her if she married him, he would love you like you was his very own, and nobody ever had to know the difference. He did love you, honey, like you was his own blood. He convinced her to go over to Maryland with him and get married. That way, if anybody asked, they could say they got married in Maryland and could lie about when they got married. Everybody knew they had been hangin' around together since grade school.

"When you were born, lord, you were a beautiful baby, but she had the birth blues and went a little bit nuts for a while. We had to intervene when she started hauling you around and showing you off to everybody in town. That was the first time your momma went into a nut hospital. Your daddy cared for you in the meantime, and you bonded more with him than with her. I think that broke her heart. A couple of other times, she went to the hospital, but by the time you was four or five years old, she was stable enough to stay home and take care of you."

I sat there and listened quietly until she stopped talking.

"What about Daddy's drinking?" I asked. "When did that start?"

"Your daddy was an alcoholic, plain and simple," she replied. "He was probably hooked the first time he took a drink. Some people can handle their liquor, and some can't. Your daddy never could handle liquor. One drop, and he was off on a binge. His drinking didn't have anything to do with any of this. It had to do with the fact that he was what he was. It wasn't so bad early on, but the older he got, the worse it got. The worse it got, the more your momma tried to control it. Hell, she was no more in control of it than he was, but she damn sure tried. She wanted him to be what she thought she might have had with Whitmire. You can't make a silk purse out of a pig's ear, but damn, she wanted that silk purse. She never got what she wanted. You got what she wanted without even trying. At first, I think she was a little jealous of that, but then I think she was proud that you got there even if she couldn't. She started to lighten up a little after your daddy died. It took all that pressure off her, trying to control what she couldn't control. Then, when you got settled with Earl, she relaxed even more."

The more I thought about Grandmother Donner's words, the more rage I felt. I left Grandmother to sit with Mother for a while and went home.

I remembered seeing a curious deposit when I went through Mother's bank statements. Every month, like clockwork, there had been a deposit of $300, enough money to live on at the time, but I couldn't find a deposit receipt anywhere. Now, my curiosity had changed to suspicion. I knew Mother kept meticulous records, so I headed straight for the shed. I turned on Daddy's little shed heater and went to work. I pulled out boxes of records and started going through them. I found every bank statement going back to five months before I was born. That's when the deposits started. During the months before that, there had been nothing.

I went to Mother's Bank the following morning and asked about the deposit. Mother had informed them that I could have access to her accounts if anything were ever to happen to her. Mr. Simmons, the bank vice president, sat down with me to talk about it, and I discovered that the deposits came from a fabric company in Kittanning, a check sent directly to the bank every month.

"Mr. Simmons, why would Mother get regular deposits from a fabric company?" I questioned.

"I don't know," he began. "All the deposits are from a trust established through the company. We assumed that your mother must have had some deceased relative who had stock in the company and had set up a trust for her."

"There is no such deceased relative I have ever heard of," I said. "Who owns that company?"

"From what I understand," he replied. "The Whitmire family owns the company."

"Whitmire, as in Dr. Whitmire in New Bethlehem?" I asked.

"Yes, it's the same family," he replied. "That company has been in their family for generations."

I know my face must have turned the color of a tomato as my rage broiled. I then knew what the money had been for. There it was, the payoff, support for the bastard child that Whitmire refused to claim, but more than that, it was hush money that continued long after I was an adult. The deposit was still being made every month. It was, therefore, absolutely not just for child support. It was to keep Mother quiet.

A wildfire of rage ignited inside me. "Thank you, Mr. Simmons," I said politely.

I left the bank, drove home, and dug through more boxes. Then, I found an agreement of Trust to be deposited in mother's account for life with an agreement of non-disclosure regarding Whitmire's paternity legally binding everyone in the family. No wonder no one wanted me to know. Grandmother Donner hadn't even mentioned it when telling me about the rape. I don't know if Daddy ever knew about the non-disclosure agreement or if he ever found out about Whitmire. I continued to try to understand why he didn't want me to know until after he was gone, except he probably suspected that I would take it out on Mother, and she would take it out on him, but I always wished that it could have been something we shared before he was gone.

I wadded the legal papers into my fist, returned to my car, and drove straight to the Whitmire clinic. When I arrived, I walked by the sign on the building that said, 'Carl Whitmire, M.D.,' and spat on it. I burst through the door, marched up to the receptionist, and asked, "Is Dr. Whitmire in?"

She was a new hire, someone I had not seen before. I judged her as a fresh out of high school with nothing more to look forward to than a receptionist job.

"Are you a patient?" she asked.

"Yes, I am," I said, trying not to clench my teeth. "Is he in?"

"Yes," she replied. "May I have your name and date of ..."

She didn't get a chance to say anything else. I pushed through the medical area door before she could get it out of her mouth. A nurse in the hall looked up at me with shock. She had worked in the clinic for as long as I could remember. She knew me, but she had never seen me like that.

"Where is he?" I insisted.

"Lovella," she said, attempting to be calm. "Is there something I can help you with?"

I didn't respond but started throwing open every door as I brushed past her down the hall. By the time I got to the third door, there he was, bent over a pregnant woman with her legs in stirrups. He barely had time to recognize who I was before I crossed the room and slapped him as hard as I could.

"YOU FUCKING LOW-LIFE PIG FROM HELL!" I screamed, shaking the papers in his face. "YOU FUCKING SELFISH IMMORAL DOG FUCKER! YOU RAPED MY MOTHER! THEN, YOU HAD THE FUCKING NERVE TO TREAT ME AS ONE OF YOUR PATIENTS MY WHOLE GODDAMN LIFE, KNOWING I WAS YOUR OWN DAUGHTER! WHAT THE FUCK! HOW COULD YOU? HOW COULD ANY DECENT MAN EVER DO ANY-THING LIKE THAT?"

He put his hands up and backed away from me. "Lovella, I'm sorry. I don't know what you are talking about," he said.

"YOU ARE *INDEED* SORRY!" I screamed. "YOU ARE A SORRY, FUCKING LIAR! YOU ARE A SORRY, LOW-LIFE MOTHER-FUCKING RAPIST, AND YOU ABSOLUTELY—DO KNOW—GODDAMN WELL—EXACTLY WHAT I AM TALKING ABOUT! I KNOW THE TRUTH, MOTHER-FUCKER! GOD-DAMN, IT! I KNOW THE TRUTH! I HAVE PROOF THAT YOU FUCKING SENT HUSH MONEY TO MY MOTHER'S BANK ACCOUNT, STARTING FIVE MONTHS BEFORE I WAS BORN, BECAUSE YOU ARE TOO MUCH OF A FUCKING CHICKEN SHIT TO TAKE RESPONSIBILITY FOR YOUR OWN DAMN CHILD!" Again, I shook the papers at him. "THIS IS A COPY OF YOUR FUICKING NON-DISCLOSURE AGREEMENT TO KEEP HER QUIET! YOU FUCKING KNOW WHAT IT IS!"

The poor woman in the stirrups lay there frightened and helpless while I continued my barrage.

Whitmire was clearly taken aback. "Lovella, how about we step into my office and discuss this privately?" he pleaded.

"SO, YOU CAN KEEP EVERYBODY FROM HEARING IT, FINDING OUT THE TRUTH ABOUT YOU? HOW ABOUT YOU KISS MY ASS, MOTHER FUCKER!" I slapped him again. "I'M GOING TO TELL THE WHOLE FUCKING WORLD AND I DARE YOU TO TRY TO DO ANYTHING ABOUT IT!"

The nurses and other employees had gathered at the door by this time. The older nurse, whom I passed in the hallway, attempted to soothe me. She had known me since I was a little girl and had always been matronly toward me. "Lovella, honey," she said sweetly. "Let's go sit down and talk about what has you so upset." She reached out and touched my arm.

"DON'T FUCKING TOUCH ME!" I screamed at her as I jerked away. Then, I turned back to her. "DO YOU KNOW WHO THIS MAN IS?" I questioned. Then, I went on without giving her a chance to answer. "THIS MAN IS MY FUCKING, RAPIST SPERM DONOR. HE IS MY GODDAMN BIOLOGICAL FATHER. HE RAPED MY MOTHER AND THEN DIDN'T HAVE THE FUCKING BALLS OR DECENCY TO DO THE RIGHT THING WHEN SHE GOT PREGNANT, SO HE AND HIS LOW-LIFE FUCKING FAMILY PAID HER OFF TO KEEP QUIET ABOUT IT FOR THE LAST TWENTY-SIX YEARS OF MY LIFE!"

I turned again on Whitmire.

"AND DON'T FUCKING CALL IT CHILD SUPPORT, MOTHER-FUCKER! IF IT WERE CHILD SUPPORT, IT WOULD HAVE STOPPED WHEN I WAS TWENTY-ONE, AND IT WOULD NOT HAVE STARTED FIVE MONTHS BEFORE I WAS BORN! YOU ARE STILL PAYING YOUR GODDAMNED HUSH MONEY. I KNOW IT CAME FROM YOU. I TRACKED IT DOWN TO YOUR FUCKING FAMILY TRUST! WELL, GUESS WHAT, MOTHER FUCKER, THE HUSH IS OVER! IT'S OUT! MY MOTHER MAY HAVE KEPT HER MOUTH SHUT, BUT I AM NOT GOING TO! I AM GOING TO TELL EVERY-BODY THAT CARL WHITMIRE—*M.D.*—IS A FUCKING RAP-IST, LOW-LIFE PIECE OF SHIT WHO WOULDN'T EVEN ACKNOWLEDGE OR TAKE RESPONSIBILITY FOR HIS OWN GODDAMN CHILD AFTER HE RAPED HER MOTHER!"

I turned to push past the nurses standing in the doorway but turned around and went back for one more rant.

"YOU ARE *NOT* A FATHER!" I screamed, sticking my finger in his face. "YOU ARE A FUCKING RAPE EJACULATION, A SPERM DONER BY FORCE! MY REAL FATHER LOVED ME TILL THE DAY HE TOOK HIS LAST BREATH. HE WAS WHAT A FATHER IS SUPPOSED TO BE. THERE WAS NOT A SINGLE ATOM OF HIS GENETICS IN MY BODY, BUT JOHN FUCHS

WAS MY REAL FATHER. HE MAY HAVE BEEN AN ALCO-
HOLIC FACTORY WORKER, BUT HE WAS MORE OF A MAN
THAN YOU WILL EVER FUCKING DREAM OF BEING! YOU
SHOULD HAVE GONE TO PRISON FOR WHAT YOU DID,
AND YOU DESERVE TO ROT IN HELL!"

I turned to leave again, then whirled back one more time.

"AND, BY THE WAY, MOTHER-FUCKER, MY HUSBAND
CAN BUY AND SELL YOUR WHOLE GODDAMN FAMILY
FIFTY TIMES OVER AND NEVER MISS A FUCKING PENNY!
WE DON'T NEED YOUR GODDAMN MEASLY THREE HUN-
DRED DOLLARS A MONTH!"

Then, I turned on my heels, marched out of the building, got in my car, and left. When I walked through the lobby, the shocked faces and stares of patients made me realize they had heard enough to end the secret. Carl Whitmire's life would never again be the pristine public persona he had always portrayed. The truth was that *"the good doctor"* had an evil secret. Word would get around. He would lose many patients and experience scorn on the streets. I had ripped off his veil of anonymity and deceit. So, he might not have gone to prison for what he did, but I had ensured that he would be punished by small-town sensibilities with little tolerance for such things.

As I was pulling out of the parking lot, a police car pulled in. I kept going. I suppose the asshole could have pressed charges against me, but nothing ever happened.

CHAPTER 32

The Real Treasure

I never heard from the Whitmire family again. I heard Carl Whitmire had considerable public fallout after my little rant, but I did not try to check on him. I didn't care. The fact that I shared his biology meant nothing to me. He was not the kind of man, nor did he have the kind of family I would ever want to be associated with. In short, I had no reason to return to that part of Pennsylvania ever again.

Mother improved over time, but she never recovered. About a year after the accident, we moved her to a nursing home in Nashville so I could visit her regularly and keep an eye on her care. That is where she spent the rest of her life. Within about a year, she got to the point where she could walk a little bit with a walker, but she was never fully coherent again. The damage to her brain created something like dementia. There were times when I would go to see her, and she would recognize me, but there were times when she wouldn't, and there were times when she was lost in her memories or hallucinating. She had recovered her ability to carry on some simple and short conversations but little else.

The years passed. My children grew up, and Mother's hair turned to a lightly peppered white. The days of beehive hairstyles were gone. The abandoned hornet's nest drooped into unruly gray strands, and the hornets had no more sting.

Beyond the point of her accident, she never knew her grandchildren. She never got to see school plays or go to ball games. On Christmas, Earl and I would take the children to the nursing home to visit her. We would take her a present at Christmas, but she seldom even recognized it as a Christmas gift. She accepted the package one year and politely said, "Thank you." Then, she sat with the box on her lap and did nothing with it.

After a while, Earl said, "Here, Drucella. Let me open that for you." But she held tightly to the box and would not let it go. We left that day with Mother still sitting there, holding the box in her lap. A week later, when I returned to see her, the gift sat on her bedside table, still unopened. From that point on, we didn't bring gifts. We only tried to give her what she needed.

My kids grew tired of going to visit. No Grandmother Fuchs was left for them to relate to, and they had been too young when she was injured to remember how much she had doted over them before. Mother was gone, and a lost and confused spirit was in her place. I didn't blame the kids and never tried to force them. There were times when I found it challenging to go, as well. I often wondered what kind of grandmother Drucella Fuchs might have become as the children grew older. She loved and bonded with Vanilla like she had never been able to bond with me. The accident robbed her of the opportunity to be a doting grandmother, and my kids missed the chance to be thrilled about a visit to Grandmother's house. However, the kids were close to Earl's parents, and Drew, especially, loved his great-grandma Donner, so it wasn't like they didn't have grandparents, but they could never have Mother. We regularly traveled to Pennsylvania, and Earl's parents frequently visited Nashville. Making a business trip that included seeing the grandkids was very convenient. While Earl and his father had their noses in the company, Clarisse and I would take the kids to the park or a museum.

Grandmother and Grandfather Donner became increasingly feeble as they aged. So, we took the kids to see them at least two or three times a year, often only on holidays. In 1982, Grandfather Donner died of a sudden heart attack. After that, Grandmother Donner seemed lost. As much as she bitched about him, all those years, she needed him and loved him. When he was gone, she didn't know what to do with herself. She came to live with us for a while and then decided that it was time for her to move into the nursing home. She moved into the same room as Mother and watched over her until her own health began to deteriorate, and she could no longer help the nurses. She passed away within a year after that.

The world has changed so much, and yes, it has stayed so much the same. We went from the assassinations of the 1960s to planes flying into the

World Trade Center, from Vietnam to Iraq and Afghanistan. Technology has changed, but prejudice and hatred still abound, if not toward Black people, then toward Hispanics, lgbtqia people, Native Americans, Asians, Muslims, Christians, Buddhists, or whatever. Ignorance abounds with the new bully pulpit of social media. Hate and division continue to be rampant, but the only reason people need hate is to define that someone is less worthy than themselves, and that comes from an already profoundly wounded self-esteem. I know that all hate is ultimately based on fear, and most fear is based on ignorance. If we took a little time to listen to each other instead of judging and making assumptions about each other, the world could be much better. Sometimes, I wonder if we will ever truly be free, and I know in my heart that as long as any human being seeks to control another, we will not be free. None of us are free as long as any one of us is in chains to another person's prejudiced ideology.

Sometimes, I think of all the billions of people in the world, how each one has their own unique story, and how those stories seem to unfold, only partly because of our intent. We are all like boats on an open sea with no sails and limited maneuverability. The slightest bump can often completely change our course. When those bumps are significant, the course change is often impossible to avoid. I sometimes wonder how many people have lives that have turned out the way they wanted or planned and how many people get to live, or even continue to want, the dreams they dreamed of in their youth. The world is ever-changing, and our perceptions of it are also ever-changing. When we seek more to understand the truth than to defend what we believe, we will come closer to truth and the dawn of true freedom. When we recognize the difference between perceptions and facts, emotions and facts, we come close to understanding one another. When we respect one another's beliefs and differences, we come closer to peace with one another. I look back on history and realize there has always been a veil of illusion over the truth. I doubt that anyone ever sees reality as it actually is. Judgment and perception, beliefs and emotions, ego and doubt cloud everything.

One day, as I sat looking out that picture window where I had found comfort after we first moved to Nashville, I looked across the way to what had been Minnie Pearl's house, but it was no longer her house because she had long since passed away. I wondered if the people living there now had the same vision as Minnie Pearl or if decorators and designers had come in and changed everything. I thought about how we each have our own vision of things and our idea of what is beautiful and what is not. Then, I thought to myself, *No one else in the world sees what I am seeing at this moment. No one else in the world has this experience, only me, and my experience is determined more by my perceptions, beliefs, judgment, and personality than by what I determine to be reality. Even if someone were to come and sit exactly where I am sitting, even if some scientist could calibrate their head into precisely the same position as mine, they would see something different, if for no other reason than the passage of time. Some bird on a limb would have flown away. Some car would have passed.* I realized two things at that moment: first, no one can ever see the world the way I see it, and second, no matter what I look upon, it has changed in the very next millisecond. The current moment is the only moment that exists. Now is the only reality, for the future can only come in the next moment, and the past is already gone.

I have learned that my perception is not the truth, and I have learned that, even though I can have empathy, I can never truly walk in another person's shoes. I can never know what it feels like to be inside that person. I think one of the most horrible things someone can say to another person, especially if they are grieving, is, "I know how you feel." The truth is, only I know how I feel, which is colored more by my judgment than by any event that ever happens. I now know I had no idea what it felt like to be my mother. I learned her life story, but I never really knew her. I try to imagine why she made her choices, but I will never fully understand. I know she had a hidden anguish that I never comprehended while growing up. There was a real person there who I never truly came to know. The walls around her heart were too high, the ramparts too wide.

They say that any life worth living is worth living well. With all my heart, I know that every life is worth living. Every life has a reason. We may not know the reason, but maybe we don't have to know. We must understand that if we are here, it is because we are meant to be here, and anyone else here is also meant to be here. Maybe all we need to do is be here and live on life's terms as it unfolds.

When I was a little girl, I saw my mother as a tyrant, bent on controlling everyone around her. I realize now that all control is born of fear. Now,

I understand how terrified she must have been and that she saw control as her path to redemption. We do not need to control when we trust. Mother did not trust that life would be safe, that I would be safe, or that Daddy could continue to support us. I don't know if she ever came to love him, but Daddy devoted himself to the one woman he thought he loved most. He allowed her to control him to a point, and I rebelled against her control due to my fear of not being given a choice. Now, I find myself speculating. Did Daddy drink because he knew he could never truly have the woman he loved, even though he was married to her? Was I his emotional substitute?

It isn't very clear, but that is the one thing that can be said of everyone's life. Nothing is very clear. It's all confusing. No one ever has all the answers. No one lives without mistakes or regrets. If anyone says they have no regrets, they are either a saint, a liar, or insane. We are all where we are by destiny and by choice. Destiny is everything we can't control, and our choice is the only thing we can. We choose based on what we are thinking when we have a choice. We choose based on our beliefs about ourselves, about the world, about others, and about all that is around us. Belief has more to do with how we think and choose than any circumstance we could ever experience. We are handed what we are handed, and then we are left to choose based on the dominant beliefs in our minds. The good news is that beliefs can change. This story would have been different if I, as that rebellious child, could have seen the world differently. If Mother could only have made sense of what happened to her instead of letting fear control her thinking, maybe we could have been close. I suppose that is a story in some distant parallel universe, but not here. The truth is, Mother made the best choices she knew how to make with the destiny she had been given. I made the best choices I knew how to make with mine. Unfortunately, our destiny is often determined by the choices that others make.

For as long as she lived, I went to see Mother at the nursing home every Wednesday and Sunday afternoon. Much of the time was spent just sitting there. Sometimes, we talked, meaning I would respond to whatever gibberish she was babbling on that particular day. Most days, I sat and held her hand with no communication. About a week before she died, I walked into her room to find her sitting in the wheelchair and smiling. She looked up at me, gleaming, as I approached, and said, "Oh my, aren't you a beautiful girl."

"Thank you," I replied. I walked over and patted her hand. "How are you doing today?"

She did not respond but said, "I had a beautiful daughter like you. Her name was Lovella, and I don't know what ever happened to her."

I watched as grief spread across her wrinkled face. I patted her arm again and knelt in front of her, face to face.

"Mother—It's me. I'm Lovella."

Her eyes never met mine, but she continued. "My daughter was a little rambunctious. Sometimes, she was defiant, but that's because she had spirit and grit, and oh my goodness, she was so smart!"

"Mother," I said again, "It's me—Lovella."

Her head turned to one side. She stared as though gazing into a great distance as a single tear drifted across her cheek, and said only one last thing.

"I loved her with all of my heart."

THERE IS NO SUCH THING AS THE END

Follow-up Author's Note:

This has been a fictional story. The characters are fictional. However, the experiences that these characters went through are not entirely fictional. They are not drawn from this author's observation but from the author's awareness of these experiences. Alcoholism and drug addiction, for instance, are not fiction. Millions of people struggle with those issues every day. Co-dependency and families desperately attempting to control the behavior of addicts and alcoholics are not fiction. School bullying is not fiction. Mental illness, depression, psychosis, and suicidal ideation are not fiction. PTSD is not fiction, and many people struggle with it, both resulting from combat experiences and other traumas such as physical abuse, domestic violence, sexual abuse, and rape. Of course, racism and homophobia are absolutely not fiction, and it is shown in this book that they can manifest either overtly or subtly. They can arise from ignorance or malice, but it is essential to discern whether the perpetrator is ignorant or malicious, for if it is only ignorance, we need to take responsibility to educate them as best we can. This is a story about the types of struggles the people of America went through in the 1960s, but it also reflects upon the struggles in America today.

Amid everything else occurring in the book, this is a story about Lovella's relationship with her mother and her discovery at long last that she was loved far more than she ever thought. In a fictional way, this story is about real life, growing up, and learning to see the world from a different perspective. As in real life, there are moments of humor as well as moments of tragedy. I hope I have shown that people struggling with these issues are everyday people. Although the extremes are out there, most are not monsters, just people struggling with life like all the rest of us. I hope that I have also shown that love can live through tragedy, addiction, mental illness, racism, and homophobia. To say "Love Wins" is not an understatement. In truth, love never dies, no matter how much it is battered by the events of the world and our fears of each other.

"When I despair, I remember that all through history, the way of truth and love has always won. There have been tyrants and murderers, and for a time, they seem invincible, but in the end, they always fall - think of it, always. An eye for an eye makes the whole world blind."

Mahatma Gandhi

Crisis Lines:
National Suicide Hotline is to call or text **988**
Suicide Prevention Lifeline: 800-273-7386
National Sexual Assault Hotline, operated by RAINN, for free, confidential counseling, 24 hours a day: 1-800-656-HOPE(4673)
Trevor Project (LGBTQIA Crisis): 866-488-7386
National Domestic Violence Hotline: 800-799-SAFE (7233)

Resources:
Anyone can contact their state department of mental health. Often, Addiction Recovery Services are within the same department. Also, looking up your state department of mental health can help you with guidance to licensed professionals in your area and other resources in your home state. Mental health providers with specific specialties may also be located through the online search option provided by Psychology Today. Many other resources and organizations are available for contact by searching any of these topics.

Recommended Self-Help Books:
These are only a few of the possible options for self-help books available. However, these are my favorites.

Codependent No More – Melody Beatty
Healing The Child Within – Charles L Whitfield
Love is Letting Go of Fear - Jerald Jampaulski
Say Goodbye to Guilt - Jerald Jampaulski
Teach Only Love - Jerald Jampaulski
A Woman's Worth - Marianne Williamson

<u>A Return to Love</u> - Marianne Williamson
<u>Your Sacred Self -</u> Wayne Dyer
<u>Adult Children of Alcoholics -</u> Janet Woititz
<u>On the Family</u> - John Bradshaw
<u>Healing the Shame that Binds You</u> - John Bradshaw
<u>Getting the Love You Want</u> - Harville Hendrix

Other Books of Interest:
<u>Caste </u> – Isabel Wilkerson
<u>The Warmth of Other Suns</u> – Isabel Wilkerson
<u>White Fragility</u> – Robin Diangelo
<u>Nice Racism</u> – Robin Diangelo
<u>Lies My Teacher Told Me</u> – James W. Lowen
<u>Stranger At the Gate</u> – Mel White
<u>The Velvet Rage</u> – Alan Downs PhD
<u>A New Earth</u> – Ekart Tolle

About Karlyle Tomms

Karlyle Tomms grew up in rural Ozarks poverty. He completed his master's degree in 1981. He has written for regional magazines and newspapers, and is often invited to speak at both professional and non-professional events, as well as radio talk shows. However, he had never published fiction until completing his first novel in 2014. His general method for fiction has been to define a character and allow that character to tell his or her own story from first person perspective as though the character is presenting an autobiography. Through his characters he explores the psychology of the human condition as well as the various elements and entanglements of personalities. Incorporating the social and historical influences surrounding his characters, Karlyle's stories explore overcoming social, emotional, and spiritual challenges.

In 1945, ten-year-old Ronald Dennison, the son of a back-woods Arkansas preacher, began having profound dreams about religion and a strange red-haired woman. The dreams follow him for decades with the woman sometimes seducing him, other times calling him to become a televangelist, but eventually berating him for his sins of lust. She holds a secret so dark that he dares never admit it, even to himself. The more famous and wealthier he becomes, the more he struggles with his adultery, his fetish, and his shame until his torment can no longer be contained. Staggering revelations challenge everything he ever believed. Will truth bring him the peace he always craved, or will the woman's demands prove more than he can bear?

Jacketed Hardcover
Softcover
All Ebooks Editions

In the Pruitt Igoe slums of St. Louis in the 1960s, a heroin-addict mother breaks her son's dolls and screams, "You are not a girl!" However, no one can convince Stephanie to live as Stephen. Her mother pimps her out to a man who rapes her and takes pictures of her as others rape her. After finding her mother brutally murdered, she is placed in Christian foster care, where they also try to convince her to accept being male. Her mother's lover is sentenced to life in prison for the murder. Famed Televangelist Pastor Ronald Dennison sets up a trust that allows a compassionate old neighbor to adopt her out of foster care. Still, she is violently bullied at school for identifying as female. The trust pays for transition surgery at eighteen, and she begins to live fully as a woman. Frightened by men, she remains a virgin until she falls in love with Jordan, but she runs into the man who abused her and remembers her childhood pledge to kill him. Will her lust for murdering the man who brutalized her as a child cause her to lose the man she loves, or will she come to her senses before it's too late?

Jacketed Hardcover
Softcover
All Ebooks Editions